Indaba, My Children

Philip D Shenefelt
10/29/2019 F/6.33

Indaba, My Children

VUSAMAZULU CREDO MUTWA

GROVE PRESS
New York

Originally published by The Viking Press

Printed in the United States of America
Published simultaneously in Canada

Library of Congress Cataloging-in-Publication Data
Hannah, Barry.
Geronimo Rex / Barry Hannah.
p. cm.
ISBN 978-0-8021-3569-8
eISBN 978-1-55584-643-5
1. Young men—Southern States—Fiction. I. Title.
PS3558.A476G47 1998
813'.54—dc21 97-51147

Grove Press
an imprint of Grove Atlantic
154 West 14th Street
New York, NY 10011

Distributed by Publishers Group West
groveatlantic.com

I DEDICATE THIS BOOK TO

ALBERT S WATKINSON
known to us as *'Beka-pansi'*
(the observant one who looks on the ground)
and his wife
ELLEN WATKINSON
known to us as *'Londiningi'*
(the one who shelters and protects many people)
for their help, faith and encouragement
in making this book possible.

CONTENTS

CHARACTER CAST

uNkulunkulu	The Great Spirit
Ninavanhu-Ma	The Great Mother, Goddess of Creation
Tree of Life	Personified male counterpart of the Goddess of Creation
Kei-Lei-Si (Nelesi)	Mother of Za-Ha-Rrellel
Za-Ha-Rrellel (Sareleli)	Wicked Emperor of the Empire of the First People – Father of all *tokoloshes*
The *Kaa-U-La* birds	Legendary talking birds
Amarava (Mamiravi)	Last survivor of the First People, the Amarire, Mother of the Second People
Odu	Last survivor of the Bjaa-Uni – artificially produced flesh-and-blood slaves – Father of the Second People, the Bantu
Gorogo	Chief of the Frog People – Father of all Bushmen and Pygmies
Marimba	Mother of all Tribal Singers, Goddess of Music, Goddess of Happiness
Zumangwe	The Hunter, Marimba's first husband
Watamaraka	The Goddess of Evil, Mother of all Demons
The Monster	Dragon commissioned to exercise control over Wata-Maraka
Kahawa	Son of Marimba and Zumangwe
Mpushu	Ka-Hawa's closest friend
Somojo / *Kiambo*	Witchdoctor and his friend in the First Village of the Wakambi Tribe
Namuwiza	The Priestess, a Witch in the same village
Nangai	– of the Mountains, Outcast God of the Masai, subsequently Chief of the Wakambi
Mulungu	The Father of Light
Koma-Tembo	The Masai captive, third husband of Marimba
Dzumangwe	The God of Hunting
Lozana / *Lukiko*	Ka-Hawa's two wives
Rarati	Nubian girl who introduced cattle to the Bantu

Malinge	Youth executed for wantonly killing an animal
Ngungu *Katimbe* *Lembe*	His father, grandfather and great-grandfather
The High Accuser	Legal Prosecutor
The Mercy of Heaven	Legal Defendant
Mandingwe	A cook
Kamago	A woodcarver
Nonikwe	A blind, hunchback 'clairvoyant'
Mutengu	Her uncle, Headman of a village
Lusu	Her real father
Luchiza	Mutengu's son
Mbomongo	A one-eyed scoundrel, a fellow conspirator
Kalembe	The Wizard-Lord of the Wakambi
Lumbedu	The Witchdoctor – usurped Chieftainship
Ojoyo *Vunakwe* *Taundi* *Lulinda*	High wives of Lumbedu
Mulumbi *Gumbu*	Sons of Lumbedu and Ojoyo
Temana	Gumbu's Batswana wife
Songozo	Headman of a neighbouring village
Mbimba	Boy from Songozo's village
Chikongo	Lover of Lulinda, youngest wife of Lumbedu
Timburu	His grandfather
Mburu	His father
Manjanja	His mother
Chwenyana	Another of his father's wives
Chungwe	High Chief of the tribe
The Strange Ones	Ma-Iti – Phoenicians, probably from the town of Gatti
Their 'King'	
His Son	
The Red-haired Giant	
The Odd Man	Arab slave to the Strange Ones
Another Odd Man	
The Tribal Avengers	The men who enforce tribal law
Mulaba	Chief of the Batswana
A Headman of a neighbouring village	
Zozo	Hunchback brother of Vunakwe, wife of Lumbedu
Kadimo	Son of Dimo
Dimo	His father, King of the Cannibals

Sodimo	His grandfather
Karesu	Emperor of the Phoenicians' Empire in Africa
Kadesi	Successor to Karesu, but murdered by him
Makira-Kadesi	Half-caste Empress, successor to her murdered husband
The Boy Emperor	Last Ruler in the Phoenicians' Empire
A Nobleman in the Phoenicians' Empire.	
Lumukanda *Lubo* *Obu* *Luluma*	Slaves in his household
The Mother of *Lumukanda*	
Her Mistress	
Two Concubines	
Three Priestesses	
Slaves	
Makira-Luluma	Makira-Kadesi's spirit in the body of Luluma
Watamaraka-Kadesi	The Spirit of Evil in the body of the Empress Kadesi
The Wild Huntress	Albino daughter of Marika-Kadesi
Battle Leaders	
Two Concubines	
Munumutaba I – V	Successive Emperors of the Empire of Munumu-Taba
Malandela	High Chief – Mighty Lion of the Nguni
Muxakaza *Zuzeni* *Celiwe* *Katazile* *Nolizwa* *Lulamani* *Notemba*	High Wives of Malandela, and the rest of his 850 seraglio
Vivimpi *Bekizwe* *Zwangezwi*	His last three sons
Nomikonto	His sister
Vamba Nyaloti	Witchdoctor to Malandela
Nyaloti	His father
Mulinda	His sister
Luojoyo	His mother
His Three Wives	
Mukingo	His cousin, sire to his three wives
Luva	His witchdoctor colleague, a spy
Dombozo *Mutumbi*	His two homosexual followers
Lumukanda	The 'Lost Immortal' – a cannibal

Luanaledi *Mvurayakucha* *Mbaliyamswira*	His three daughters, the 'Spirit Virgins'
Mukombe	Last survivor of a murdered family – adopted by Lumukanda
Madondo	Relative who plotted the murder of Mukombe's family
Muti	His father
Nomeva *Mamana* *Muwaniwani* *Lozana*	Madondo's wives, turned into zombies by Lumukanda
Three Sons of *Nomeva*	
Tribal Avengers, especially the Leader and ten principals	
Bafana *Madoda-Doda*	Two personal boy servants to Malandela
Dambisa-Luwewe	A spy from a neighbouring tribe, the Ba-Luba
Ngovolo *Malangabi* *Mapepela* *Ziko* *Majozi* *Solozi* *Jeleza*	Some of Malandela's Rainbow *Indunas* (Councillors in peace and Generals in war)
Mitiyonka	Malandela's father
Munengu	Dambisa-Luwewe's father
Muvedu	Luva's real name
Luao	A spy passing under the name of *Dahodi*
Mbobo *Lusu* *Mabewe*	Later friends of Vamba Nyaloti
The *Lufiti-Ogo*	The Star Mother – the Perfect Goddess – created by the Children of the Star, a race of human beings which had evolved to perfection and became extinct as a result
The Spirit of Nature	
The son of the Spirit of Nature	
Namulembu	A Vamangwe woman in Malandela's seraglio
Lulama-Maneruana	Lulamani's new name
Burumutara	A legendary half-bull, half-crocodile monster in the Underworld
Bekizwe	Malandela's brother, High Chief of the Mambo
Tandani	His deceased First Wife
Zulu *Qwabe*	Their two sons, adopted by Malandela

Kanyisile	Bekizwe's Second Wife
Pindisa	Her daughter
Tembani	Pindisa's foster mother
Nunu	Bekizwe's new First Wife
Shondo	High Witchdoctor of the Mambo
Nsongololo *Ntombela* *Mavimbela* *Mavusu* *Dudula* *Shungu*	Some of the Mambo *Indunas*
Mpungozo	Master of Ceremonies at the Peace Ceremony
Luti	Son of *Vezi*, Mambo volunteer buried alive
Mdelwa	Nguni volunteer buried alive
Nozipo	Girlfriend of Mdelwa
Nonsizi	Mdelwa's mother
Nonudu	Mambo woman playing opposite Celiwe of the Nguni at the Peace Ceremony
Mboza	Principal Cook.
Govu	Another cook
Celiwe	Chieftainess of the Nguni
Mabovu	One of her consorts
Xhosa	Founder of a new tribe, the Ama-Xhosa
Noliyanda	Daughter of Xhosa, immortalised by Lumukanda and proclaimed Queen of the Mambo
Vumani	Young boy accosted by Noliyanda
Ngozo	Old man left behind in Vamba's kraal
Valindlu	Messenger of Fate
Tandi	His young bride
Gojela	The coward
Mlomo	His father
Malevu	Gojela's Battle Leader
Kokovula	The Great Witchdoctor
Mandatane *Silwane*	Two assistant witchdoctors
Hlabati *Madolo*	Two other witchdoctors
Munumutaba V	Last male ruler of the Kingdom of Munumu-Taba
Munengo *Shabasha* *Shumba*	Three of the Munumu-Taba's twelve sons
Mpolo	One of the Munumu-Taba's Councillors
Muwende-Lutanana	The Munumu-Taba's orphaned granddaughter
Muxakaza	One time First Wife of Malandela, successor to the throne of the Kingdom of Munumu-Taba
Lumbewe	A Prophet in the camp of Munumu-Taba

Tondo	The gravedigger
Demane *Demazana*	Two of the triplets that Muwende-Lutanana presented to Lumukanda
Vura-Muinda	The Black Goddess, Patron Saint of all the tribes
Sozozo	Self appointed leader of a breakaway group of Mambo tribesmen
Mpongo	One of his newly-appointed councillors
Luzwi-Muundi	A 'Saviour of the Bantu Race' still to be born in the distant future
Zodwa (Ntombi-Zodwa) *Ntutana* *Duduzile* *Nonsizi* *Tandiwe*	Five daughters of a Headman
Gawula *Mvezi* *Fanyana*	Boy friends of three of the above girls
Tambo	Gawula's witchdoctor grandfather
Liva	A Drummer of Honour
Mbewu	The Mighty Hunter
Tetiwe	His First Wife
Kikiza	A rival in marriage
Ndawo	A cattle thief
Dedani *Baningi*	A brother and sister, strange victims of the Famine
Ma-Ouzarauena	One female body inhabited by the three separate souls of Noliyanda, Vuramuinda and Ninavanhu-Ma
Lishati-Shumba	New name for the rejuvenated Lumukanda
Gandaya	A legendary elephant, guardian of the sacred Kariba Gorge
Luamerava	The Illusion of Kariba
Lokota	An agitator
Vundla *Dondolo*	Two assistant witchdoctors
Mabashana *Nontombi*	Two handmaidens of Nomikonto
Jovu *Audi*	Two eunuch attendants to Muxakaza in the temple of Zima-Mbje
Lukuma	A half-caste slave
Wadaswa	A Hottentot handmaiden
Bengu	An old man
Dolo	His son

A Portuguese 'Kapitanoh' and his crew

PROLOGUE

These are the stories that old men and old women tell to boys and girls seated with open mouths around the spark-wreathed fires in the centres of the villages in the dark forests and on the aloe-scented plains of Africa.

Under the gaze of the laughing stars the Old One sits, his *kaross* wrapped around his age-blasted shoulders, staring with rheumy eyes at the semi-circle of eager expectant faces before him – faces of those who have taken but a few steps along the dark and uncertain footpath called Life – faces of the ones as yet oblivious to the pain of life's bitter scourges – faces as yet unmarked by furrows of bitterness, ill-health and anger – the fresh, pure, open faces of . . . children.

The fire dances in the middle of the round clay fireplace like a virgin revelling in the simple joy of being alive. It devours the dry twigs and logs that a little girl is constantly feeding it, leaving nothing but glowing ashes. It mocks the silent sky with a redly luminous column of smoke against its starry face and by sending up short-lived stars of its own.

Suddenly the Old One feels a great burden on his shoulders – a heavy responsibility towards the young ones sitting so expectantly around him. Suddenly there is a visible sag to his thin, aged shoulders. He sighs – a harsh, rasping sound – and clears his throat, spitting and blowing his nose into the fire, as his father and his father's father did before him. And he begins the story – the old, old story which he knows he must repeat exactly as he heard it so long ago, without changing, adding or subtracting a single word: '*Indaba*, My Children, . . .'

It is through these stories that we are able to reconstruct the past of the Bantu of Africa. It is through these stories that intertribal friendship or hatred was kept alive and burning; that the young were told who their ancestors were, who their enemies were and who their friends were. In short, it is these stories that shaped Africa as we know it – years and years ago . . .

True, the Black man of Africa had no mighty scrolls on which to write the history of his land. True, the Black tribes of Africa had no pyramids on which to carve the history of each and every crowned thief and tyrant who ruled them – on which to carve the history of every battle lost and won. *But this they did, and still do!*

There are men and women, preferably with black birth-marks on either of the palms of their hands, with good memories and a great capacity to remember words and to repeat them exactly as they had heard them spoken. These people were told the history of the Tribes, under oath never to alter, add or subtract any word. Anyone who so much as thought of changing any of the stories of his tribe that he had been told fell immediately under a High Curse which covered him, his children and his children's children. These tribal story-tellers were called Guardians of the *Umlando* or Tribal History.

And I, Vusamazulu the Outcast, am proud to be one of these, and here I shall tell these stories to you in the very words of the Guardians who told them to me.

'*Indaba*, My Children . . .'

INTRODUCTION

Many strange things have happened in Africa; things that have puzzled, disgusted and shocked the world, especially in recent years; things for which the world has had little or no explanation and things that can best be explained by first laying bare – to the rest of humanity – the strange working of the mind of the African.

Many will find it hard to believe much of what I have revealed in this book, but I am not in the least concerned, because whether I am believed or not, everything I write here is *true.*

Much of what I shall reveal here will shock and anger many people – most of all my fellow Bantu, who resent having their doings and secrets exposed to foreigners. By writing many of these things, I am becoming, in terms of our tribal laws, a traitor to my own race. And this is going to make me hold back much of what I should also reveal. Terrible as the stigma of *traitor* is, I shall risk bearing it in the belief that what I am doing here will help my people in the end. Only time will tell whether I am right or wrong. There has been much suffering and bloodshed in Africa in recent years – bloodshed that has led to hatred and still more suffering. And the most pathetic thing about it is that much of this could have been prevented had the White rulers of Africa had a better knowledge and a better understanding of the way a Black man's mind works than they do, even now.

Kenya's Mau Mau uprising, Angola's rebellion, the massacres in the Congo, riots and killings in South Africa – all soon to be written in blood permanently on the highway of human history, all soon to be written in bleached bones on the desert of time – all were started by one thing – the total lack of understanding between Black and White; the utter failure of one race of human beings to understand what goes on in the minds of the other race.

The saddest thing is that the misunderstanding is mostly on one side – the more powerful side – the White man's side. If any Black man with a little knowledge of English, French or Portuguese wants to study the White man – as I have done – all he has to do is to go into the nearest town and become a regular customer of one of the second-hand bookshops there. He must buy and read at least twenty different kinds of books and magazines a month for a period of no less than ten years. He must read classics, philosophical works and even cheap murder mysteries and science fiction. He must read Homer, Virgil, Aristotle, and the rest. He must turn the pages of Walter Scott, Voltaire or Peter Cheyney. He must read the newspapers with great care.

Gradually, as the years pass, he will gain more or less a clear understanding of the White man, his way of life, his hopes and ambitions. But few White people have ever bothered to study the African people carefully – and by this I do not mean driving round the African villages taking photographs of dancing tribesmen and women and asking a few questions, and then going back and writing a book – a useless book full of errors, wrong impressions and just plain nonsense. Many of the books written by Europeans about Africans should be relegated to the dustbin.

There are doctors, missionaries and scientists who have spent years and years among Africans – many of them can even speak the local language better than the indigenous people – but what they know about them as human beings amounts to nothing. Many have studied the African only to compare him with the White man – intellectually for instance. Many more have studied the African in order to find justification for the policies of the ruling group they work for and support.

I once heard a well-known and respected White intellectual state that when Zulus perform a war dance before going into battle they are dancing themselves into a frenzy of rage and showing what they are going to do to their enemies on the battlefield. This statement, logical though it may sound, is as far from the truth as the Day Star is from the worm crawling on a rotten pumpkin.

Another fallacy dear to many people, both overseas and in South Africa, is that Africans practise polygamy as a sign of wealth and prestige. And if that is so then I, Vusamazulu Mutwa, am the favourite 'wife' of the first High Chief of Ashanti! Ask any anthropologist in South Africa who was the greatest Zulu King and he will reply instantly: 'Tshaka, of course'. That is not so; Tshaka (or Shaka) was not the great Chief White historians make him out to be.

Thus you see what I am trying to achieve with this book: simply to lay the foundation for better understanding between two different types of human beings, by destroying wrong notions and false 'facts', and exposing much of what *must* be known at the risk of censure by both Black and White people.

There is a saying dear to lawyers that justice cannot be founded on lies, and I think the same is true with human association and mutual trust and understanding. A marriage of persons who fear and distrust each other cannot long survive, nor can one where the partners hold false ideas about each other.

The same is true between races in any country. There can be no real understanding between them so long as neither has a clear picture of the other: what it really thinks, believes in, hopes for, and why. You cannot found friendship on faulty guesswork because guessing breeds suspicion, hate and bloodshed. And there is much that is guesswork between Black and White. Many of the so-called problems facing Africa today can be traced back to foolish acts on the part of one or other of the two races in the past: acts that were the result of lack of understanding. Only by being presented with a full, clear and unvarnished picture of the African – seen from his worst as well as his best side – can the White man hope to avoid repeating the incredible mistakes he made in the past, blunders that have cost Africa a lot of suffering and close to three million human lives in the short space of ten years.

Why, so great is the lack of understanding between White and Black that there are Africans – hundreds of them – who still believe, in this jet and sputnik age, that White people never mate as common human beings do; that White women do not bear their children in the painful way Black *mamanas* bear their piccanins . . . *but that they lay shining glass eggs that hatch out little Bwanas a day after being laid*! Surprising? Maybe, but it is true!

Thousands of Black people in Rhodesia and Portuguese East Africa attribute godlike and terrible powers to Whites. They believe that White people are the sons of some great living flower that grows somewhere under the 'restless, cold, passionless seas' and that blond Europeans are half-human and half-plant (because, they argue, who ever saw yellow hair on a human head, yellow hair like that which one sees on the 'head' of a mealie cob?).

So great is the lack of understanding between Black and White in Africa that there are White men who refuse to accept the fact that a Black man is a human being like the Indian, the Coloured, the Chinese and the European himself. They would rather die than accept the fact that there are Black artists, sculptors, builders, teachers and the like. These people believe nothing else about Africans but that they are lazy, stupid, stubborn creatures, something between an ape and a human being. In my travels through South Africa and beyond, I have met hundreds of such White men and women.

Hence this book . . .

'You cannot fight an evil disease with sweet medicine,' is the saying popular amongst us witchdoctors. And one cannot hope to cure a putrid malady like inter-racial hatred and misunderstanding by mincing words. So I warn readers that they are in for a nasty shock. This is not a book for people who prefer hypocrisy to fact. In this book the love life of many African tribes will be openly and frankly discussed, as will their religious beliefs, their crafts, and so forth. In later chapters you will read about the African peoples of the present time, their strange and varied reactions to civilisation and also what they think about events in Africa today.

You will read about many things that have been deliberately withheld from the world – things that are common knowledge to all African people within the shores of this continent.

In offering this information to the world, I do not claim it to be the last word – the book to end all books. I intend this book to be the forerunner of many more to come, and one to pave the way for other African writers, some of whom may have amassed much more knowledge of our fatherlands in the course of their lives than I have done. As I also said at the outset, the second most important purpose of this book is to shatter many fallacies that have become accepted as facts through the years for the simple reason that nobody has ever questioned their accuracy or dared give the other side of the story, as, for instance, the facts in the case of the killing of the White Voortrekker, Piet Retief, by the Zulu King, Dingana (which I shall disclose in a subsequent chapter).

In order to best understand this book, the reader should be given a glimpse into the life of the author.

I am a Native of South Africa, a Zulu from the province of Natal. My father is a former Catholic catechist from the turbulent district of Embo in the south of Natal.

My mother Nomabunu is the daughter of Ziko Shezi, an *Induna* and veteran of the battle of Ulundi, which ended the Zulu War. He was also a confirmed High Witchdoctor and a custodian of the relics of our tribe and Guardian of our Tribe's History.

Because my mother, a 'heathen', refused to be converted to Christianity, my parents parted just after I was born. I grew up under the protection of my grandfather, and was initiated as his attendant who carried his medicine bags for him, thus sharing some of his forbidden secrets.

In 1928 my father came and asked permission of my grandfather to take me away and because of my being an illegitimate child and therefore a disgrace to Ziko's family, my grandfather (Ziko himself) agreed, despite my mother's protests.

My father and stepmother, their three children and I came to the Transvaal in the middle of the same year. We lived on a farm beyond Potchefstroom, my father being a labourer there, and it was here in 1932 that my stepbrother Emmanuel died after being whipped by the farmer, my father's employer, under circumstances which are best left undisclosed.

For the next 20 years we lived on different farms and then lastly at the mine where my father still works today as a carpenter. This mine is in the southern suburbs of Johannesburg.

In 1954 I found myself employment in one of Johannesburg's leading curio shops, a shop specialising in African art. Except for six months when I was working in a pottery firm, I have been employed there ever since.

Being an amateur artist of sorts, I have travelled quite widely in the country of my birth, first with Catholic priests in 1946 and 1948 and then with my present employer in 1958.

On returning from Rhodesia that year I visited my mother and grandfather in Zululand after more than 30 years and, at their command, I renounced Christianity and underwent the 'Ceremony of Purification' in order to begin training as a witchdoctor and also in preparation for assuming the post of Custodian of our sacred Tribal Relics, in the event of my grandfather's death.

I have now completed my training as a medicine man, and have gained a lot of knowledge that I shall lay out in this book.

In March 1960, a young Basuto woman whom I loved, and hoped to wed in place of my present faithless spouse, was among those who died when police fired on the crowd at Sharpeville, near Vereeniging.

On the night before she was to be buried her parents, her brother and two sisters, and three of their children, cut off tufts of their hair and threw them into her still open coffin, swearing to avenge her if it took them a million years, even if they should die in doing so. I took what is called a 'Chief's Great Blood Oath', cutting a vein in my hand (the left one) and letting ten drops of blood flow into one of the gaping bullet wounds that defiled her dark brown slender body, swearing to tell the world the *truth* about the Bantu people and so save many of my countrymen the agony of the bereavement we felt. I swore to do this, come imprisonment, torture or death, and even if the very fires of Hell or the cold of Eternal Darkness stood in my way.

This book is only the beginning of the fulfilment of my oath, an oath whose keeping has become the only purpose of my intolerable life, and which will still be binding on my children and their children's children. So, even if this manuscript is destroyed, I shall write other works like it until one of them does get published – be it after my death.

Book One

The Bud Slowly Opens

THIS I CHOOSE

Oh, give me not the strident, Demon wail
Of penny whistle and tea-chest guitar;
Nor give me tales of those who rode the trail
Deep in the West of far America!

Oh, not for me the songs and nonsense tales
That thrill the modern rabble rout
Who, leaving far behind their tribal vales
With traitor zest, ape 'culture' from without!

Rather than the modern crooner's foreign voice,
Or the loud howls of modern township jive,
I shall leave far behind that mad'ning noise
And hurry home where Tribal Elders live.

There, 'neath baobabs or flat-topped *munga* trees,
Where nestling birds with many tongues argue,
And flaming aloes bless the smiling breeze
With heady scent; and where the distant view
Of scowling mountains 'gainst the silver sky
With dread and reverence fill the misted eye!

Where, on the gentle slopes of ancient hills there browse
The bearded goats, the sheep, the shambling cows;
And loud above his lowing wives the bull
With awful bellow, dares the distant foe!

There I shall sit before *Ubabamkulu*
Who shall relate to me the Tales of Yore.
There I shall kneel before the old *Gegulu*
And hear legends of Those-that-lived-Before.

* * *

There I shall live, in spirit, once again
In those great days now gone forever more;
And see again upon the timeless plain
The massed *impi* of so long ago!

The words of men long dead shall reach my soul
From the dark depths of all-consuming Time
Which, like a *muti*, shall inflame my whole—
And guide my life's canoe to shores sublime!

Clear with the soul's time-penetrating eye
I shall see great empires rise, flourish and die.
I shall see deeds of courage or of shame
Now carved forever on the Drum of Fame.

With *Shaka's* legions I shall march again—
A puppet knowing neither joy nor fear;
Which, trained to kill, heeds neither wound nor pain
And knows no other love save for its spear.

I shall feel once again the searing heat
Of love in hearts that have long ceased to pulse
And with *Mukanda* shall captain the fleet
Of war canoes; and storm *Zima-Mbje's* walls.

Here, in these stories still told by the old,
I feel the soul and heartbeat of my race,
Which I cannot, in tales by strangers told—
For these, within my heart I have no place!

The tree grows well and strong, Oh children mine,
That hath its roots deep in the native earth;
So honour always thy ancestral line
And traditions of thy land of birth!

THE SACRED STORY OF THE TREE OF LIFE

THE SELF-CREATED

No stars were there – no sun,
Neither moon nor earth—
Nothing existed but darkness itself—
A darkness everywhere.
Nothing existed but nothingness,
A Nothingness neither hot nor cold,
Dead nor alive—
A Nothingness far worse than nothing
And frightening in its utter nothingness.

For how long this Nothingness lasted,
No one will ever know;
And why there was nothing but Nothing is something
We must never try to learn.

Nothingness had been floating
For no one knows how long,
Upon the invisible waters of Time—
That mighty River with
Neither source nor mouth,
Which was—
Which is
And ever shall be.

Then one day—
Or is it right to say 'one day'?—
The River Time desired Nothingness
Like a flesh-and-blood male beast
Desires his female partner.
And as a result of this strangest mating

Of Time and Nothingness,
A most tiny nigh invisible spark
Of living Fire was born.

This tiny, so tiny spark of Fire could think
And grew conscious of its lonely state;
No one nor nothing could hear its cries
In the lonely depths of Utter Nothingness—
Like forlorn a babe,
Lost and in despair,
In a cold dark forest.

'I exist – I am what I am!'
Was the living thought that pulsed through the 'mind'
Of the tiny spark as it wildly flew through the dark
Trying to flee from where there was no escape—
Trying to evade the lifeless,
Empty, dark and Utter Nothingness.
It was like a tiny firefly lost
In a dark cave 'neath a berg
From where it could never escape.

'I must either grow or end my life,'
Thought the spark at long, long last;
'If Nothingness wishes to engulf me
In my present size and state,
Then I must increase my size
Till I equal that of Nothingness!'

There was nothing for the spark to feed upon and grow,
So it fed upon itself
And grew in size until at last its mother Nothingness
Became aware of its unwelcome presence
And decided to destroy it.

Nothingness at first had tried
To smother it in Darkness which is
The enemy of Light,
But the spark resisted brighter – and became yet brighter.
Then Nothingness cast a spell of cold upon the spark;
Cold – a deadly foe of heat,
But this induced the spark to grow
Only hotter and yet more hot.

* * *

The Living Spark did grow, and grew until
At last it equalled Nothingness in size,
And to sustain itself – proceed with growth,
It devour'd its mother, Nothingness—
And digested her
With the most awful flash of light
That anyone or anything had ever chanced to see.
'I am what I am,' it boasted.

But River Time was very cross with what the spark had done
And quickly sent the Spirit Cold to fight the spark outright.
A mighty battle soon ensued, in which the spark,
Now a universal roaring Flame
Which filled the sky with many soaring tongues,
Tried to melt Cold's Spirit, and devour it complete,
While Cold its icy Spirit blew,
Its cold wet breath into the Flame;
But it only turned a portion of the Flame
Into cold white ash.

And this ferocious battle, which started so long ago,
Today still rages unabating, and shall yet proceed
Till Time shall cease to flow.
And the Wise Men of the tribes relate
That if the Flame one day shall win,
All that exist shall perish
In one consuming Fire,
While if victory goes to the Spirit of Cold
All living things shall freeze to death!

May the Great Spirit who is Lord Almighty
And Paramount Chief of all
Grant that neither Flame nor Cold
Shall ever win the War,
Because whosoever beats the other—
The sun, the moon, the earth and stars
And all that live shall cease to be!
May both antagonists fight forth for everlasting Time,
Because on their unceasing conflict
All Life depends.

From the still warm ashes – wounds in Flame's existence,
Inflicted in Battle by the Spirit of Cold,
There arose the Great Mother *Ma*,

The very first Goddess of human shape.
The All-knowing Omniscient Most-merciful Goddess *Ma*
Had created herself by the Great Spirit's wish
Who, displeased with the wasteful and senseless War
Between the Flame and the Cold
Had come from far beyond
The Ten Gates of Eternity
To bring order to the Universe.

Now *Ma* the Great Mother began to execute
Commands of *uNkulunkulu*, the Great Spirit:—
From the sparks that Flame shot out
She created the stars, the sun,
And the body on which we stand.
(We shall relate anon, from whence the moon)

Although Immortal, the Great Mother was cursed
With strange desires and feelings
Which afterwards she passed to man and beast alike.
These are feelings, strange to Immortals,
Like anger, hunger, jealousy and misery
Or love and lust and craving for luscious food.
With such desires the Great Mother *Ma* was cursed
And they were like diseases within her being;
And because of this the Storytellers,
The Wise Men of the Tribes,
Depict her as the Imperfect Undying One.
That is why woodcarvers
Throughout this continent
Always make their carvings of her
Imperfect.

Either a leg is shown deformed
Or one breast much bigger than the other;
Hands of unequal size.
It is from the Great Mother *Ma*
That we mortal souls and our brothers the beasts
Inherited all our faults—
Imperfect seed bring forth imperfect plants.

When the Great Mother *Ma* had finished creating the stars,
The sun and the earth,
She seated herself on the Mountain of Iron, Taba-Zimbi,
To rest and await the Great Spirit's further instructions.

It was while she thus was sitting
That a strange feeling came over her—
A feeling she could not interpret
But loneliness now we know it had been,
And she wept most bitterly.
So long and so loud did the Goddess cry
That the very stars trembled and fell from the sky
While the tears that the Goddess shed
Flowed in a great lake at her feet—
Flowed across the land in all directions
Forming murmuring streams and the mighty rivers we see today.

At last the Great Spirit commanded the Goddess
To end her queer emotional display
And to repair the damage done to earth
By falling stars and floods of tears,
And then continue with creating
A perfect Universe from Chaos.

'No!' cried *Ma* through her flood of tears
Far greater than that of *Musi-Wa-Tunya*
The falls that tumble in the river Zambesi—
'No! Never! I shall not move from where I am
Until I have a companion to work with!
Is it not clear that I'm utterly lonely?
Who can I talk to in my lonely hours?
These barren plains – these silent craggy mountains?
Those stupid stars that twinkle foolishly at me?
Aieeee! Where, oh where is the sense in ord'ring me to create
These useless things anyway?
Those stars, the sun, and this miserable bowl called earth?
Who am I,
And how long will I work here, creating all this?
This utterly senseless rubbish!'

From far beyond Eternity's borders
Where no God, or Goddess, or Demon can e'er go,
Came the Great Spirit's cold and hollow, and unemotional voice:
It howled like a tempest through the star-spangled skies
Like thunder upon the plains—
Re-echoing through the valleys and gorges
And shaking the great barren crags
Like trees in a gale.
Bolt after bolt of crashing lightning

Tore across the shrieking skies;
Howling cyclones swept the rocky plains
While mighty earthquakes sent the mountains roaring
To level with the ground,
While plains were upwards heaved to form new mountain ranges.

The shattered world—
Not yet defiled by human beings,
By grass and trees, and beasts,
Was cringing and shudd'ring before this awe-inspiring Voice
Of the Highest of the Very High.

'Being most imperfect – listen to the voice
Of thy Lord and Master.
I beseeched thee to create and my commands
Are not for thee to question.
Thy duty it is to *do* and not to doubt—
Thy duty it is to *obey* without a murmur.
Thou shalt do what I commanded thee to do
Whether thou seest the reason or not.
The purpose behind the creation of all the Universe
Is known to ME alone
And with me it shall rest a secret
Till the end of Time.
Proceed to create as I commanded,
Without delay!'

The Goddess rose and stood on the summit of Mount Taba-Zimbi—
The eternal Iron Mountain.
She stood erect, a pillar of incredible beauty
Such as no mortal has ever or will ever see.
Her golden glittering eyes pierced the dark of the starry sky
And peered into the remotest reaches of Infinity
Where, far, oh so far away
She could vaguely discern the blaze of Light,
The formless, ageless, immortal *uNkulunkulu*,
The Highest of the High.

Slowly *Ma* raised her luminous hands to the heavens;
The sorrow and pity she felt o'er her great loneliness
Evaporating to the seven winds—
And op'ning her silvery lips she spoke:
'Thou hast spoken, oh Great Spirit, and I have heard;

As a tool and a toy in thy Hand I shall obey forthwith
The ev'ry command for better or worse.'

A dreadful silence fell upon the earth
And the troubled heavens were stilled,
While the sea which had been devouring
With its waves vast areas of land,
Retreated to the coast, shamefully like a boy
Caught in an act of naughtiness.

For the first time in its existence the Universe
Had heard the voice of the Great, the Supremely High.
As the great red sun went to rest beyond the jagged mountains
And the drifting clouds caught his fiery light on their bellies,
The first Goddess heard His voice once again:

'Oh, imperfect being, your wish for a partner
Shall soon be granted.'

The silvery Goddess's golden luminous eyes
Lit with a glow of joy so intense
That only a Goddess can feel – and still live—
While the roaring liquid fire flowing through her crystal veins
Grew hotter and roared through her quivering body
With greater, far greater, fury than that
Of the waters that thunder o'er *Kebura-Ba-Sa* rapids.
Her chest so heavily laden with four immense breasts,
Each with a sharp pointed nipple of emerald green,
Heaved as she let out a gusty sigh o'er her heartfelt relief.
The heat of her breath which could vaporise elephants
Left her dilated nostrils and wide open mouth
In three shimm'ring jets and which merged in a cloud
Of red-hot searing luminescence.
'Great Master,' asked she,
'What manner of companion wilt thou send me?'

'You are what in future shall be known as a female
And your opposite shall be your companion – a Male!'

'A male?' asked the Goddess, bathing in pools of intense invisible joy,
'What shall this, Oh my Master, this Male be like in appearance?
Will it share my beauty with me?'

* * *

'Verily' – thundered the Almighty Spirit
Across the boundless reaches of Infinity—
'In my presence nothing is ugly – nothing beautiful.'

'Great One,' insisted *Ma*,
Her curiosity smoth'ring her being complete—
'Surely your child has the right to know more
About the companion you hold as a prospect for her!
Of what use will he be to me?'

'He shall bring contentment to you
And both you and he will bring forth
Life upon the earth.'

'But what will he look like?' the over-curious Goddess insisted,
'Will he be something as lovely as I?'
To which the Great Spirit made no reply.
'What will he look like,' insisted *Ma*,
'How shall I recognise him?'

'He will be conscious, though unlike yourself,
More I refuse to disclose.'

The Goddess retired forthwith
To her sanctuary under the hill
To rest awhile, but not sleep—
For Gods and Goddesses never sleep.
Her mind was full of lovely dreams
Of her future companion male,
And curiosity burnt through her soul
As she wondered at what he can be
And what contentment he will bring to her.
But above all she wished that he'd be
A being as beautiful as herself
In spite of the diff'rence foretold.

She patiently waited with burning flames of desire
And as the night wore on the Goddess, who ate
Particular kinds of a metal for food,
Felt hungry indeed and leaving her cave
Searched through the plains for her favourite dish.
The first thing she found was howe'er a piece
Of tasteless, unpalatable granite which she spat
In a donga disgruntedly.

She continued to search and her appetite finally stilled
She returned to impatiently await the dawn.

Then when the first rays of light
Burst over the many-fanged range to the east
And the mountains cast sharp shadows over the plains,
The Goddess heard an awful voice
Calling out hoarsely at her:

'Come, oh my mate, I await thee here,'
And the shimmering silvery Goddess arose
With a cry of immeasurable joy
And, not heeding the regular exit,
She burst through the side of the hill;
And midst roaring boulders, thund'ring clouds of blinding dust
She held her arms outstretched . . .
'My Mate! My Mate! You have . . .'

Her voice faded out into gasping silence
As hungry limbs reached out with might
From the billowing dust for her lithe silv'ry form
And – Oh Great Spirit – how horrible they were!

They were not arms like her own
But those of great creeping vines
Whose very bark was studded
With jagged pieces of granite
And diamonds and iron ore
A horrible mineral display!

These branches, as they'll henceforth be called,
Sprang with a host of others
From the top of a monstrous trunk,
Resembling the biggest baobab tree
That ever grew on earth.
From the middle of the monstrous trunk
Bulged dozens of bloodshot eyes
Which burnt with a lecherous hunger,
While beneath them grinned a wicked mouth
With a thousand pointed fangs.
Now and then a long green tongue
Like the hide of a crocodile
Would lick the granite lips.

* * *

From some of the tree's branches grew
Great udders which oozed a golden honey-like fluid.
Unlike the ordinary tree, this one had roots which it used
Like a crab or a spider to move from one place to another;
And the sight alone
Of those crawling living roots
Scrabbling o'er the rock-hard plain as they moved
Was enough for the mountains to shudder!

'Come, my beloved, come to me!'
Roared the tree and drew the Goddess close
And with its rock-studded mouth bruised her silvery lips
With a savage kiss!
'I am the Tree of Life, thy mate, and I desire thee!'
'*Aieeee*,' shrieked *Ma* – 'It cannot be!
My mate you are not – my companion – NO!
Release me, you ugly, most monstrous thing!'

'Release you, while I've only just caught you!
You, my heart's desire!
I did not catch you only to release you!'

'What . . . ?' gasped the Goddess.
As more and more branches
Held her fast beyond all hope . . .
And here, my dear reader, I shall, as the saying goes,
Cut the fowl's beak,
Leaving the rest to your most respected imagination!
Suffice it to say that in agonised moments that followed
The Goddess had very good cause to regret
Her folly of requesting the Almighty Spirit
To grant her a wish of her own.

When the Tree of Life released her at last,
The thoroughly frightened *Ma*
Fled madly across the plains with loud shrieks
To the Great Spirit with entreaties to rid her
Of a most unpleasant mate,
But the reply that the First Goddess got
Was – 'You have had your wish—
What more do you want?'
You may wonder, dear reader,
How the Goddess managed her escape.
Well the tree had pursued her relentlessly

With all its tremendous bulk.
Like any young man he had no wish to see
Even his metaphysical bride escape
And return to his mother-in-law!
Do not the Wise Ones say
That 'They who have for the first time tasted
The nectar-filled cup of Love
Never let it drop undrained?'

So, over plain and valley, and over the hills
And down many a cruel mountainside
Fled the terrified Goddess, and racing forth,
Now on the ground on her silvery feet—
Now through the air like a bird of prey,
But no matter how far and how fast she fled
The Tree of Life kept close on her heels
Until at last both pursuer and pursued
Reached the bleak barren wastelands which in future years
Became known to mortals as Ka-Lahari.

By now the great Tree was on fire with love,
But tired ne'ertheless while his quarry,
Urged by the cold breath of fear,
Was still as fresh as ever.
At long last, after many years of flight and pursuit
Both Goddess and tree plunged headlong
In the waters of lake Makarikari
And it was here that *Ma* streaked through the water
Like some silvery luminous fish,
And then soared like an owl through the night sky
While below, her mate, the Tree of Life,
Waddled in the mud of the lake.

Here it was that the Imperfect Immortal
Very nearly made good her escape,
But here too a flash of pure inspiration
Tore through the sluggish brain of the Tree.
Acting fast on a chance idea, it scooped
A mighty mound of rock and clay and sand
From the bottom of the lake
And he rolled it into a mighty ball,
Greater in size than Killima-Njaro itself.
Then in one lightning movement
Of all his branches combined,

He hurled this formidable missile
Skyward at the object of his love,
Now almost one with the stars.

Straight and true went the soaring ball
And the next thing the fugitive Goddess felt
Was a great blow on the back of her silvery head;
And as she plunged through the air,
Limp and unconscious, but still of unearthly beauty—
The great ugly tree spread its manifold arms
To save her in her headlong fall—
'My dearest beloved,' he gurgled.

The great ball rebounded from the Goddess's head
And went into orbit as the moon of today,
And the Great Spirit in his Almighty wisdom
With radiance declared it the Guardian of Love,
To regulate the Love of Gods,
And of Men and beasts and birds and fishes yet to come.
Today all the Tribes of this Dark Continent
Respect the power of the Holy Missile
And its influence upon all our lives and love.
Drums still beat and most secret rituals are performed
In dark forests in honour of that missile
Which helped to restore the very first marriage
Between our Goddess *Ma* and our Most Sacred Tree,
The Tree of Life.

Even today, as in all ages past,
The moon makes lovers seek each other's arms
And wives the company
Of their children's fathers.

Aieeee! Great is the power of the moon—
And who dares to doubt it?
Lo! thus sing the Holy Singers of Kariba
Whenever the full moon rises
And turns the timeless Zambesi into a dazzling serpent
Of shimmering liquid silver and gold:—

'Oh missile which through the starry sky
At fleeting *Ma* the Tree of Life let fly,
Shed still on earth thy heatless silver light
And let all things feel Love's consuming might.

Shoot burning darts into the lion's soul
Make him forget to stalk the zebra foal.

And turn him back to where, beneath the trees
His mate awaits, and there to find release
From unpleasant anguish. Bid the warring king
Forget awhile his bloody lance and cling
To his beloved of the pointed breast.
Command the North, the South, the East and the West
To pause from war and thieving, and to LOVE!'

BEHOLD THE FIRST IS BORN!

After her capture
The Tree of Life held the Goddess fast
Never to let her escape again;
And it came about one day
That movements occurred within her,
Movements which increased with the passage of time,
Much to her fear and distress.
At long last, after a thousand years,
The Goddess felt a sudden tearing pain
That prompted her to cry out suddenly
And writhe in anguish in her mineral husband's tentacles.
The first cruel pains were followed by others—
A third and fourth and the glittering voice of the Goddess
Rang loudly across the plains
To rebound against the stunned distant mountains.
The foolish Tree of Life not understanding,
Thought his bride was trying another escape,
So he held her more tightly in his manifold arms,
Greatly increasing her pain.

As time went on the intensity of her suffering
Increased twofold, and after fifty agonising years
Turned so utterly unbearable that she freed herself
From the Tree of Life's endearing embrace,
And wriggled and rolled on the barren earth
In efforts to ease her inexplicable agony.
Such was her suff'ring, and desp'rate her efforts,
That with self-hypnosis she counted the stars.
E'en today many Tribes have the saying:
'To count the very stars in pain.'

The first father, the Tree of Life, kept watch,
With typical helplessness

As his mate writhed and wailed through her birth pains.
But at long, long last the Great Goddess
Was relieved from her hideous pain,
And the first mighty nation of flesh and blood,
A countless number of human beings, was born.
And in their multitudes they spread
To populate the barren Ka-Lahari.

Meanwhile, however, the strangest change came over the Tree of Life;
Green buds burst from its writhing limbs
And clouds of seeds emerged and fell upon the rocky plains.
Wherever they struck the ground they shot out roots
Into the stubborn rock and barren sand,
Breaking through to reach some moisture
And soon all manner of plants grew forth—
A creeping carpet of lush living green.
Soon mighty forests covered the earth,
Contending with the mountains themselves.
Howling winds and sheets of rain
And roots of forest trees
Worked hand in hand to mould the craggy mountains
Into undulating plains.

Soon after all this effort the Tree of Life
Bore living, snarling, howling animal fruit.
From its widespread branches they fell with a thud
On the grassy ground below,
And scampered off into the forests
In their countless millions.
From great cracks in the trunk of the tree
Birds of all kinds came flying and waddling forth,
Filling the air with all their love calls;
Ostriches and ibises,
Eagles, hawks and flamingoes,
The kinds we know and those we've never seen,
Like the two-headed talking Kaa-U-La birds.
These we know from legend alone
And I'll relate about them anon.

The earth which had hitherto been lifeless and dead,
Began to live, and sounds of all kinds
Resounded from the forests and valleys
As beast fought beast—

Beast called beast—
And birds sang their happiness loudly
Towards the smiling sun.
Many, many kinds of beasts
That the Tree of Life brought forth
Since vanished for ever from the face of the earth,
Because *Efa* the Spirit of Total Extinction
Has long since consumed them all—
And the kinds of animals we see today,
However many they are,
Are but the pitiful scraps that survived.
(Legends tell of three kinds of lion
Of which only one survived)

From the roots of the Tree of Life
Came reptiles of all kinds and shapes,
And cloud after cloud of all sorts of insects
Hummed upwards in continuous streams.
The Song of Life had begun on earth—
The Song which is still being sung,
But which one day may trail off into oblivion—
Leaving at most the faintest echo.
History's sun had risen, and still shines today,
But it will no doubt set one day – fore'er!

THE RACE THAT DIED

The Holy Ones of Kariba Gorge tell us
That the first men to walk the earth
Were all of a similar kind.
They looked exactly alike, and were all of similar height,
And their colour was red like Africa's plains.
In those days there were no black-skinned or dark-brown men;
No Pygmies and Bushmen, nor Hottentots either.

The Wise Ones of the Ba-Kongo agree
With the Holy Ones of Kariba Gorge,
And they even go as far as to say
That the First People had no hair on their bodies at all;
All had the golden eyes of *Ma*—
The Goddess who launched them on earth with such pain.
All the Wise Ones and Holy Ones of this Dark Continent
Agree that the splitting of all Humanity into races;
The tall Wa-Tu-Tutsi, the Pygmies, or the Ba-Twa,
The short yellow Bushmen of Ka-Lahari,
Even those long-bearded A-Rabi
Who raided our villages mercilessly for slaves—
Resulted from one great accident which occurred
Through the sinfulness of these First Men.

Inspire me, oh Spirit of my Fathers!
Give me courage to proceed and tell the world
What say the Holy Ones of these First Men!
Let me break, oh Demon of Disobedience—
Let me break the stout stockade but once
Of Tribal Secrecy.
Let me relate to the world outside
The Forbidden Story that all Wise Ones—
All witchdoctors know but keep firmly shut
In the darkest tunnels of their souls!

What is this Forbidden Legend about these First Men—
Tales of the Nguni, the Mambo, the Lunda and the Ba-Kongo?
When the muted beat
Of the Drum of Sworn Secrecy has sounded
And the Holy Ones gather to re-tell once again
The most secret tales to the young generation;
'Tales-that-must-never-be-told-to-strangers-
And-to-the-low-born-peasant-dogs'
What say the Holy Ones of this First Nation?

Lo! I shall open my mouth
The mouth of a traitor most foul
Who, for what he believes to be good for his people,
Here betrays the secrets of his land—
I shall open my mouth and tell you,
So gather around me – '*Indaba*, my children . . .'

It is said that more than a thousand times ten years went by
In which there was peace on this virgin earth;
Peace in the sky—
Peace on the forest-veiled plains—
On the scented valleys and timeless hills.
Only certain beasts were permitted to kill,
By the Laws of the Great Spirit,
In accordance with their victual needs.
There was none of this savage
And wanton destruction of Life
Such as men today indulge in
To gratify their warped and evil souls.
Man against man forged no evil spear
With secret and murd'rous intent.
There were no such things as anger and hate
And nothing of 'this is mine and that is yours',
No contention and rivalry.

Man breathed peace on the cheek of his brother men.
Man walked in peace without fear of wild beasts
Which in turn had no reason to fear him.
Men in those days did not suffer
From our emotional curses.
They knew no worry like our sin-laden selves.
Death they welcomed with open arms
And a smile on the face, because,

Unlike our degenerate selves,
They knew Death for what it was—
Life's ultimate Friend!

But the evil star of self-righteousness,
Was emerging from yonder horizon
And man's undoing was nigh.

Once in a shady recess of a vine-screened cave
A beautiful woman whom some call *Nelesi*,
But whom many more call *Kei-Lei-Si*,
Gave birth to the first deformed child;
Deformed not in flesh alone, but also in his soul.
His shrunken body supported a big flat head
Containing one short-sighted cyclopian eye.
His arms and his legs were shrunken stiff
And were twisted like a sun-dried impala,
While his mouth was completely displaced to one side
In a perpetual obscene leer.
His scrawny neck was wrinkled,
Like a starved old vulture two days dead,
And his round little paunch protruded 'neath his chest
In a most revolting way.
Strings of crystallised saliva drooled
Continuously from his sagging lips;
He breathed through only one nostril
With a sickening hissing sound.

The name of this very unpleasant monstrosity—
Tribal Narrators tell today—
Was *Zaralleli* or *Zah-Ha-Rrellel*, The Wicked!
This was the man – no, rather the Thing
That introduced all evil to this earth.

Whenever a child was born to these First Men
The mother would take it straight for a blessing
To the two-headed talking Kaa-U-La birds,
And also to ask them to give it a name.
Thus it came about that when *Nelesi*
(Let us rather abide by *Kei-Lei-Si*, for this is
Her proper and uncorrupted name)
Took her terrible offspring to the big old Kaa-U-La bird,
Which nested not far from her cave,
It gave one glance at her
And shuddered at what she carried!

In the half-dead deformed thing that the girl held aloft
The Kaa-U-La bird could see Evil so great
And so utterly monstrous that if unchecked
There and then it would def'nitely overrun
The Universe outright with its bad influence.
And what it saw beyond the veil of tomorrow
Made it screech with unrestrained horror and pain:
'*Kaaaaaauk!* Oh woman, what have you there!
Destroy it, kill it, without delay!'
'What, but this is my baby, my child!'
Cried the mother in utter despair.
But the bird's voice rang like metal
And echoed o'er valleys and mountains;
'Female of the human race – I appeal to thee,
Destroy thy offspring before it's too late!'
'But where have you ever seen mothers kill babies?'
The poor mother pleaded, now on her knees.

'For the sake of Mankind, and that of the stars,
And for all those as yet unborn,
I command thee oh female of thy race,
Destroy that thing in your arms!
No baby is that which you're holding there,
But Naked Evil, devouring and pure—
A Bloody Future it spells for the Human Race!'

'My baby evil? He is the dearest baby on earth!
My loveliest baby – destroy it? Not on your life!'

'I command thee . . .' But *Kei-Lei-Si* screamed;
She turned and ran like a buck through the bush
Her baby clutching her heaving breasts.
The Kaa-U-La immediately took off in pursuit
By telepathy calling all others to join
In the hunt for the fugitive girl.

Only once she paused for a gasp of breath
On the grassy slope of a hill,
And on looking around she saw a black flock—
Hordes of the two-headed, six-winged rainbow birds.
It struck her that these birds rarely flew,
And did so only when the need was great.
'*Aieeee!* My baby, they seek you—

But they will not get you as long as I live!'
And with this she turned and sped up the hill;
But as she descended the other side
The great birds were on her and diving at her
Ripping with talons deep furrows on her back.

She reached the dark depths of the forest anon
And the birds in their tireless pursuit
Uprooted trees and moved the rocks
And dived with a roar of air.
Again and again they appealed to her
To surrender her child for Humanity's sake.

'No, a thousand times no!' she panted and onwards fled,
Tripping and falling and bruising her legs,
Only to rise and speed forth faster than e'er.

At long, long last she found a deep hole
In which she sprang with no second thought.
They fell for what seemed like a thousand years
And struck the floor with a bone-jarring thud.
For a long time they lay there completely stunned
On the bank of an underground stream—
A river which roared and crashed with great noise
Through miles of underground caverns.

The evil spawn of the foolish girl
Did not die, as he fell on his mother,
And was thus due to rise soon to menace the world
With the fumes of his evil soul.
Soon the stars would weep in shame
While cursing the woman *Kei-Lei-Si*
And the wicked *Za-Ha-Rrellel.*

The otherwise beautiful woman and her monstrous son,
Lived for years in the bowls of the earth.
Fish, and crabs from the muddy banks,
Were abundant enough to keep them alive,
While above ground the Kaa-U-La birds were searching
The forests and plains in vain.

On returning from a crab-hunt one day

Kei-Lei-Si saw her son sitting near the fire
Humming a happy tune to himself.
This greatly surprised her, for never before
Had he spoken a word – leave humming a tune!
'My son!' she breathed, her soul overflowing with joy,
'You can talk . . . you are singing . . .'
'Shhhhhh . . .' he said, and *Kei-Lei-Si* saw
Him fixedly stare at some iron ore,
The very piece she had brought to the cave herself,
Which she used on the flints in the cavern walls
When she wished to kindle a fire.

A cold terror struck the poor woman
As her gaze came to rest on the ore;
Her whole body froze with horror and fear
As the penetrating stare of her son
Caused the ore to grow in size!
Still hypnotised she watched and saw
The ore turn soft and starting to flow.
A few heartbeats later two bright stalks grew
At the tips of which glowed small bloodred eyes,
And a hungry-looking mouth took shape
Snarling viciously at *Kei-Lei-Si*
With a display of razor-sharp teeth!

The woman shrieked with horror and undiluted fear
When she realised her son was in fact creating—
That the tune he was humming was an incantation—
Commanding the hitherto lifeless iron
To assume a shape and Life!

She watched spellbound as the living thing grew
And legs like those of a grasshopper took shape—
Then came pairs of dragonfly wings
And a rat-like shining metal tail, with a sting,
A crystal sting with dark green poison!

'My son!' cried she, 'What . . . and how . . . and why . . . ?'
'This,' he said, without emotion,
'Is one of my weapons of conquest!'
'Conquest? Conquest of what, my son?'
'Of everything – the earth, the sun and the moon!'

Then turning to the fast-growing metal beast

And indicating his mother with a deformed limb
Snapped, 'Seize her, and drink your fill!'
At which command the horror leapt
And pounced upon the startled woman,
Seizing her with his insect-like legs.

'My son, my son, what have I done—
Why do you do this to me?
I am the woman who bore you, and brought you up!'
'I know very well who and what you are—
But nobody asked you to bear me and rear me
And least of all did I.'
'I saved you from the big birds my son;
They desperately wanted to kill you!'
'All that I know,' said *Za-Ha-Rrellel* calmly,
'It was only the instinct of a female beast
And you were obeying a natural law.'
'Have mercy, my son,' cried *Kei-Lei-Si.*
'What is this thing called mercy?
You are of no use to me any more.
I have now grown to full independence
And I no longer need your protection.
All I need now is nourishment for my new servant
To grow and reproduce its kind.'

From the mouth of the metallic *Tokoloshe*
Protruded a long needle structure
With which it pierced her chest and heart
And as it sucked it grew.

Through the mists of her last agony
The mother of the wicked *Za-Ha-Rrellel*
Saw her son's outrageous future;
She saw his great evil swallow the earth
And the Universe itself.

Too late she appreciated her error—
That after all the birds were right,
But now she could not destroy her child
To save all mankind from its atrocious influence.

Through eyes that were slowly glazing in death
She saw the object withdraw its cruel probe.
She saw it lay some hundreds of silvery eggs

At her son's express command;
And they all exploded into hundreds
Of fast-growing winged things like itself.
The last thing she saw was how a litter of four
Bore her son aloft in triumph.
'Farewell, mother,' he said as he glanced back at her,
With a last contemptuous look in his eyes.

They carried him forth from the lighted cave
Into the darker parts of the caverns
And slowly the glow from all the luminous eyes
Faded in darkness in the echoing distance;
While with a last soft sigh *Kei-Lei-Si* died
Alone and utterly forgotten for all time to come
In that maze of underground tunnels.

The fantastic reign of the First Chief on earth,
That of *Za-Ha-Rrellel* was about to begin.
Today known as *Tsareleli* or *Sareleli*
He was the deformed incarnation of naked evil
And was about to burst upon the world
Like a glittering poisonous flower.
Woe, oh woe, to all mankind—
Woe to all those, as yet unborn!

Za-Ha-Rrellel, the Wicked, emerged from the tunnels,
Borne aloft by a litter of four of these metal things,
While all the rest of the metal *Tokoloshes*
Came swarming behind in a vast and glittering cloud
Awaiting his word to enslave and to kill.
The first that this airborne metallic army engaged
In a battle of complete extermination,
Was the Holy two-headed Kaa-U-La birds.
From miles away came the sacred birds
In hundreds upon thousands to stem the tide
Of evil in a final most desp'rate endeavour.
A mighty aerial battle took place
That lasted more than a hundred days without pause,
Watched in amazement by all men and all beasts.

The birds inflicted a great deal of damage
Tearing and ripping with talons and beaks,
But the poisonous stings of these metal things
Caused havoc among the attackers.

In their hundreds they fell down to earth,
Followed to be sucked of their blood
And as fast as these metal things nourished themselves
They produced more and more of their metal kind.
For each one destroyed by the Holy Birds
A thousand took its place
And thus the birds were soon heavily defeated
And the remnant fled to the ends of the earth.
'All is lost!' cried one as it flew away in the sunset,
'Woe to mankind – woe to the world.'
But the millions of red-skinned First People
Who heard this last agonising cry
Did not understand its meaning.
They did not interpret it this way
Till many centuries later
When together with *Za-Ha-Rrellel*, the Wicked,
They died in agony;
They who were later to be known
As the Race That Died.

THY DOOM, OH AMARIRE!

After his victory over the Kaa-U-La birds,
The deformed offspring of *Kei-Lei-Si*,
Descended with his victorious hordes of insects
And promised the millions of hiding First People
A new life of plenty of luxury and peace
And pleasure in limitless measure.
At first he told them he was sent by a god
To vanquish the evil Kaa-U-La birds
Which had thus far been keeping all mankind
In savagery and ignorance;
That in fact the Great Spirit had sent him
To deliver them all from poverty and disease;
That if they followed him humbly
They need dwell in shelters and caves no more.
They must render the world safe for mankind
By exterminating all dangerous beasts;
And till the land no longer, nor harvest,
While metal slaves could serve their human masters.
He promised them all these
And a life of luxury and ease,
Which the gullible First People believed
And they blindly followed the advice they received.

Two generations later and now *Za-Ha-Rrellel*,
Who had meantime discovered the Immortal Secret,
Was ruling supreme at the head of an empire—
The most fantastic the world has ever seen.
This was the empire which legends tell—
The Empire of Amarire, or Murire—
In which men lived in shining golden huts
With a life and a conscience of their own.
They could move from place to place
In accordance with their occupants' wish;

While metal *Tokoloshes* served in every way
From tilling the land to storing grain.
There was no need for lighting a fire
When all one had to do was fill the pot
With whatever one wished to eat,
And then command the pot to boil.
No longer was it necess'ry to walk long distances,
When all they had to do
Was stand outside their huts
And wish themselves to wherever they wanted to go.

No bother to use one's hands to lift
A drinking pot to one's lips,
When all one did was to command the pot
To pour its contents down one's throat.

But as time went on a decay descended
Upon these very lazy men
And they began to think that the simplest things
Like chewing food was far too strenuous indeed!
The High Chief *Za-Ha-Rrellel* then gave them powers
To wish their food right into their stomachs—
No straining the jaws with mastication
Or bruising the gullet with swallowing too hard!

The result of all this was that men lost the use
Of their arms and their legs and their gullets and jaws,
And on top of all this both women and men
Felt that begetting was too much of a strain!
Thus all men and all women began to lose
Their powers of reproduction;
Sterile they all turned, except the Singer
The beautiful *Amarava* – about whom, anon.

There was little more that the wicked tyrant
Could do to exploit his powers—
So he turned to knowledge and Forbidden Things
Which the Great Spirit asked us never to seek.
First he passed to his subjects the secret
Of Immortality and Eternal Youth,
To save his Empire – now completely sterile
Save *Amarava* who remained fertile.

He secondly sent out his metal beasts

To capture wild beasts and then crush them to pulp,
And from this pulp he created new creatures
Resembling the human being.
These queer creatures he earmarked as slaves;
Entertainers and workers in his expanding empire—
These creatures, produced like kaffircorn cakes,
Were Bjaauni, the Lowest of the Low.

Legends tell us that these Bjaauni
Looked something like giant gorillas;
Completely hairless and of dead flesh and blood—
They constantly had a putrid odour.
They were greenish-darkbrown in colour
Like rotten animal flesh,
And also unlike their red-skinned masters,
Could reproduce their kind.

Za-Ha-Rrellel's mis'rable products,
Unlike the Great Mother's creations,
Had no power of speech
And could not think for themselves.
They dumbly and blindly obeyed their masters
However mad the instruction;
If asked to drink a river dry
They would drink till they burst and died.

While these Amarire were indulging in all this fun
The Tree of Life said to the First Goddess *Ma*;
'What kind of beings did we bring forth?
Look, they're depriving all Life of its purpose!
They live selfish and useless lives
And no longer beget their kind;
We must now destroy our first effort
And begin all over again.'

'No, let us send them a warning first
In the hope that they'll mend their ways;
It is only that evil tyrant
Who has gone and led them astray.'

'Yes, that most foul being dared to create
Creatures of metal and flesh—
Now he thinks he's a god – a creator
But I shall teach him a lesson or two.'

And with this the Tree of Life ordered clouds
To gather and cover the earth,
Obstruct the sun, and ravage all
With lightning and torrents and hailstones.
In no time the empire's lands were covered
In waters many feet deep
And half the Amarire nation drowned
In their mighty glittering towns.
But this did by no means deter the tyrant—
It fired his warped and inventive spirit;
With all his metal and subhuman slaves
They built many vast and oblong rafts.
Each was a hundred miles long – with a breadth about half—
And on these rafts he had them build new cities of solid gold;
And artificial sun was made to float below the clouds
Which shone with a brilliance that put the real one to shame!

And then one day in the glittering splendour
Of his own domestic retreat,
Za-Ha-Rrellel played his final trump—
A last, most terrible decision!

THE LAST SIN OF ZA-HA-RRELLEL

The inside of his golden sanctuary
Was a blaze of dazzling light
From millions of precious stones reflecting,
Which encrusted the golden walls.
On a gold and ivory couch on the far side
Reclined the misconstrued form of the hideous tyrant—
Draped with a golden kaross,
Studded with sunstones and sea beads.
A great golden bowl of beer floated in
On the wings of the air at arm's length away—
Stopped short of the bald cyclopian head of the ruler
And emptied itself in the twisted, leering mouth.
(Legends say that this queer bowl
Needed no refilling—
No sooner was it drained
Than it created new beer again).

Hundreds of nobles sat in a semi-circle
Facing the Immortal Emperor,
All resplendent in golden necklaces and ear-rings
And loin cloths of woven silver.
On a living grass mat that floated above ground
They sat in the order of their rank.

In the centre a great cage of silver
Was enclosing a dozen of Bjaauni slaves
And these were beheading and disembowling each other
To amuse their Amarire creators!
This had been going on for some time
And now only one Bjaauni was left.
This hulking great brute named *Odu* now stepped to the bars
And stood waiting for the next command.

'Sleep!' snapped the Emperor and *Odu* dropped
Like a log on the bodies of his slain comrades;
'He is my favourite,' chuckled the tyrant—
'The strongest I've ever created.'
'Too true, oh Giver of Eternal Youth,'
Laughed one noble as the cage slowly sank through the floor—
'A splendid fighter and a pity to waste him.'

'Would you like to have him, *Zarabaza*?—
I shall gladly make you a present of him.'
'O Highest Emperor, be ever powerful—
I thank you so much indeed!'
Za-Ha-Rrellel then wickedly smiled as he noticed
His nobles' looks of jealousy and envy;
He always kept the spirit of rivalry burning,
For he believed in the principle: 'divide and rule.'
(Other tyrants were to follow this example
In many an empire in later years—
Wise Men say that tyrannies flourish best
When subjects are disunited).

Bjaauni females were then ordered in
And they danced and danced until all but one
Fell to the floor in fatal exhaustion.
The survivor he presented to another noble
And called upon silence as the hour was late:
'My people, I summoned you here because
I made a discovery fantastic'ly great—
One that might lead me to become the Master—
Not of the Universe, but Eternity itself.
I have discovered that all of us were—
Or rather – I should say – our ancestors were—
Brought into this world by a great Female
Whom legends call the First Mother *Ma*.
I'm intent upon sending an army most vast
To beyond the River Time itself
To capture this Female, or First Goddess,
Consid'ring that legends are speaking the truth.

He paused while a shuddering gasp of astonishment
Rose from every throat in the circle—
'Come, I will show you . . .' and with these very words
A huge silver bowl filled with magic fluid

Emerged as from nowhere and hovered near him.
'Come around . . . come closer, all of you . . .'
At which command they gathered closer
While the Emperor instructed the bowl to rotate
And to stir up the magic fluid.
After the fluid had settled again
All of them saw a fantastic scene,
A scene of a mighty, most terrible tree
Embracing a frightfully beautiful girl.

The woman had eyes of gold,
A silvery form and a chest
Laden with four heavy breasts,
Each with an emerald nipple.

'Lo and behold . . .' cried the Great Emperor,
'By force of Arms I shall wrest her from that Tree
And become the Master of All Creation!'
And thus, not many days later,
The dwellers in the great floating city,
Called Amak-Habaret, the Empire's capital,
Saw a most incredible scene:
Vast armies of giant insects of metal,
Each bristling with savage stings,
Serrated mandibles and razor-sharp claws,
Poured from the 'Palace of Creation'.

They first assembled in the great Royal Square,
Received one sharp order, then completely vanished—
Vanished to emerge in the Spirit World—
A sacrilegious war had begun!

By gazing into the magic bowl's fluid,
They saw the vast hordes converge
Upon the Tree of Life
On the plains of the Spirit World.
They saw ravening bolts of sheet lightning
Lash from the eyes of the Tree,
Obliterating thousands and thousands
Of the metal monstrosities.
But they came in their metal hordes
To be slashed by the branches of the Tree.
It vanquished more than half its attackers
And that was as much as the Tree could achieve.

On they came in their countless numbers
And completely overpowered the Tree—
Eternity wept in shame!

Za-Ha-Rrellel shrieked with abandoned delight
As four of his metal slaves
Tore the Goddess from the Great Tree's hold
And bore her away in triumph.
The rest of the metal monstrosities—
Having achieved their atrocious objective—
Momentarily had their attention diverted
And were entirely annihilated
By the wounded though undaunted Tree.

With great expectation the Emperor watched through the bowl
The four and their prey cross the plains of the Spirit World,
Till they vanished and emerged with their silvery burden
In the square in front of his Royal Abode.

The dwellers of the floating city came in their thousands
To gaze at the Mother of Men
With her fantastic, most radiant beauty,
Lying on the shining, golden square.
They stared with the wide-eyed stares of the curious
But they had no reverence in their hearts,
For long since had they lost their appreciation
And reverence for Holy Things.
To them the silvery form on the ground
Was an animate object from another world—
Another Plane of Existence that only tickled
Their vulgar curiosity.

But even as they stared
They were dying,
And dying they were—
Utterly foully!

The radiant heat of the sacred Goddess
Was blistering the skins off their bodies.
One by one dropped, and those that could, stampeded
Leaving a trail of death in their wake.
The Goddess rose slowly and clasped her hands:
'My children! My children – you whom I bore with such pain,
Doomed are you, my children . . .' And with these words
A mighty earthquake shook the world . . .

The scowling clouds
Lashed the heaving earth
With rain and hail
And sheet lightning,
While underworld fires
Burst from cracks in the Earth—
Turning the flooding waters
Into boiling cauldrons
Of molten mud
And roaring steam.

Whole continents vanished under steaming waters
And new ones appeared from below;
Great plains tilted on their sides
And capsized like wooden boats,
Forever entombing countless millions
Of animals and men.
Howling hurricanes ravaged the steaming earth
From north to south, from east to west.
Great mountain ranges split asunder
And collapsed with nauseating sounds.

The shining cities of the Amarire
Were swamped with boiling water
And steam so superheated . . .
It melted metal and rock.
But most dreadful of all was the ultimate fate
Of the greatest city of Amak-Harabeti,
The Empire's glittering capital.
When they witnessed their masters in flight
The Bjaauni felt the blissful kiss
Of the Spirit of Rebellion within their hearts!

They rose in their countless thousands,
Led by *Odu* the Killer;
They fell upon their panic-ridden overlords
And killed them with a great delight.
They sacked the city from end to end,
Disembowelling and cruelly beheading
Both masters and mistresses.
This display set a fine example
To all the robot insects
And they proceeded to slaughter outright

Both Bjaauni and Amarire.
All were now struggling for mastery
In a tortured world already half sacked,
When suddenly the man-made sun exploded
With a hideous and dazzling peal of thunder.
Za-Ha-Rrellel witnessed all this but remained unmoved,
Being insolently confident of his own ability
To remain immortal and rebuild from scratch
A new world with his creative power.
Thus from the safety of his indestructible shelter
He watched most unconcernedly as his subjects
Died in their thousands and millions.

The Great Goddess *Ma* stood ankle-deep in blood
Among the countless dead bodies,
Pleading for mercy on behalf of the human race,
But the Great Spirit was totally unmoved.

Suddenly a huge green giant with a bloody axe,
And a disembowelled woman across the shoulder,
Announced his presence to the Emperor himself;
Odu the Killer was the last Bjaauni alive.
'I . . . kill!' bellowed the giant,
Suddenly acquiring the gift of speech.
'Die! Kill yourself!' commanded the Emperor—
'I am your god – your creator!'

No longer subservient, the subhuman roared—
Plucked out the Emperor's windpipe with lungs and all.
Flung in a corner he had time to nurse
Second thoughts on his Immortality!

Za-Ha-Rrellel died, the miserable beast that he was—
After two hundred years he was dying at last—
A most miserable death it was that he died—
But in body alone . . . Yea! Not in spirit!

Somehow he knew that Mankind would survive
And flourish again in future years—
And future Humanity he intended to infest
With ambition and cruelty and love of bloodshed!
This evil spirit is still alive today
In the hearts of all mankind,

Where ambitiously it is working towards one goal—
Complete destruction of our present race!

With a last lungless gasp *Za-Ha-Rrellel* observed
His indestructable shelter crash
And over the towering ruin-like walls
Smiled the hideous mouth of the Tree of Life.
'You failed to destroy me, *Za-Ha-Rrellel!*'

The Goddess threw herself into her beloved lord's many arms;
'Those two . . . those two must live . . .
Spare them as the parents of the Second People;
Mercy on all creatures still alive!'
'The world, and what little is left on it,
Has my mercy, oh beloved one;
Calm down – earthquakes, fires and storms,
Trouble my earth no more!'

The great city tilted and sank
Forever below the seas;
The real sun broke through the dissolving clouds
And the sea turned a blazing copper-red.
Two figures, one male and one female,
Joyfully rode on the back of a fish;
They were riding towards the rising sun—
Blessed by our Goddess and the Tree of Life!

POSTSCRIPT

Indaba . . . Let us pause here, oh my children, and reflect most seriously upon the rather lengthy legends we have heard.

It is said, briefly, that the Great Spirit had created the Universe for reasons that nobody must endeavour to fathom. The Great Spirit used a being called the First Goddess, who worked as a tool under His directions. In answer to a request she was granted as a companion a weird kind of 'being', half plant and half animal, the Tree of Life. This Tree of Life is the most revered deity throughout Bantu Africa, even today. Numerous representative designs are engraved on clay pots, burnt on wooden spoons, trays and other vessels. It is also frequently depicted in all kinds of ornamental carvings, in ebony, ivory and mahogany. Some of these designs are illustrated in the accompanying figures.

The Ndebele tribes of the Transvaal are the most fanatical worshippers of the Tree of Life, south of the Zambesi. The Zulus, too, are strong believers in this deity, but some interpret it as a huge hollow reed, rather than a tree. They call it *Uhlanga Lwe Zizwe*, which means 'Reed of all Nations.'

We then came to *Za-Ha-Rrellel* (Tsarelleli or Sarelleli to most tribes today), who was said to have been responsible for the infection of all mankind with mental diseases like ambition and a love for all the wicked things that mostly ensue from it, including bloodshed.

The main reason why the Africans used to destroy crippled and otherwise deformed children was to prevent this fabled tyrant from ever being reborn or reincarnated, to spread his evil and dangerous knowledge amongst men once more.

Many of the mighty cliffs in Zululand and the Transkei stand today as dumb witnesses of many sacrifices of deformed children that have been made in the course of time.

SYMBOL OF TREE OF LIFE
OFTEN FOUND IN PREHISTORIC
BANTU CAVE PAINTINGS

SYMBOL OF TREE OF LIFE
AS FEATURED IN NDEBELE
POTTERY AND BEADWORK

CARVED EBONY BOWL — EARLY CONGO,
SYMBOLISING THE TREE OF LIFE
NOURISHING AND SPAWNING ANIMALS.
TOP SHAPED LIKE A FLOWER, HOLLOW,
CHARRED FROM MANY OFFERINGS.
WATKINSON'S COLLECTION OF ANTIQUE BANTU CARVINGS

THE COMING OF THE SECOND PEOPLE

OR

'THY ORDEAL, OH AMARAVA'

BEHOLD THE SURVIVORS!

Like the rest of the First Amarire People,
The beautiful *Amarava* was immortal and could live forever
Unless deliberately stabbed with a spear
Or devoured by a ferocious beast.
But unlike the rest of the Amarire People,
She had not become sterile, nor had she lost
The power of walking and running
In that world of floating mats and sleds;
Except, of course, those sub-human beings
Which *Za-Ha-Rrellel*, the Emperor, had created.
In that glittering fantastic world of the obese
Where even yawning had become a strenuous thing,
Amarava stood alone, like a full-hipped
Heavy-breasted narrow-waisted goddess
Amongst so many bloated, sterile
And depraved swine.
People laughed at her and called her a barbarian,
A crude and uncivilised atavism,
Who should have been cast off the floating golden city
To live in a cave like the savage she was.

But *Amarava*, whose name was later corrupted
By the Bantu to *Mamiravi* or *Mamerafe*
The so-called 'Mother of Nations,'
Heeded none of all this ridicule.
She contented herself with composing—

Singing songs in which she bitterly derided
Her people with their hollow, meaningless,
Depraved and selfish civilization.

When the Emperor *Za-Ha-Rrellel*
Massed his metal beasts for his most disastrous attack
On the Tree of Life,
Amarava stood alone in the doorway
Of her humble silver hut
And watched with horror and deep fascination
As the clanking hordes of iron grass-hoppers
And huge bronze poisonous scorpions
Thundered by on their way to the Great Square.

Like the rest of the Amarire she already knew
The purpose of those myriads of robot insects
And just what they were intending to attack.
As she stood there a cloud of horrible apprehension
Darkened the pure blue skies of her virgin soul.
'Oh no!' she whispered, 'Oh Great *Za-Ha-Rrellel*,
Now with this you are going too far!'

Then, sick at heart she turned
And commanding the door to close,
She dropped on her silver floating mat
And soon fell fast asleep.

She was awakened by a torrent
Of the most dreadful sounds she had ever heard
In her very many years of life.
Wild shrieks of incredible agony
Were mingled with growls and ululations of savage triumph;
And it felt as though the entire city was pitching
On waves of fantastic proportions.

Amarava leapt off her floating mat, at the same time calling
To her short green skirt of a second-class citizen,
To wrap itself around her hips.
The apparently living cloth obeyed
And the red girl leapt through the door of her hut,
Only to leap back with greater speed
As a heavy spear from a snarling Bjaauni female
Hummed past her head and rebounded with a clash
From the polished silver wall of her hut.

A mob of ferocious Bjaauni came running towards her hut,
Brandishing bloody axes and swords,
And the prostrate girl with horror noticed
That each one was messing around with an Amarire head.
These they threw like stones at those
Who were trying to escape on their flying mats;
None of the missiles was missing its target
And with screams they plunged back to earth.
Even before they reached the ground
They were impaled on awaiting spears.

A huge Bjaauni, whose body was criss-crossed with many scars
From countless death duels in *Za-Ha-Rrellel's* arenas,
And who seemed to be the leader of the mob
Reached the crouching, terrified *Amarava* first.
He seized her by one leg and lifted her up
Like a small boy would lift a mouse by its tail,
And was about to plunge his sword through her body
When a blinding flash of unearthly silver light
And a shattering, glittering voice rang out from nowhere:
'No, not her! Put that female down!'

Slowly the hulking savage
Laid *Amarava* down on the floor
And fell on his horny knees before
The awful silvery apparition
Dominantly towering over him.
The rest of the Bjaauni mob
Fled to the centre of the city
To seek more victims to butcher.

When her vision returned *Amarava* saw
The most terrifying sight of her life;
Towering above her prostrate form was a luminous silvery giantess,
Standing higher than the highest towers of the city—
The doomed city of Amak-Harabeti.
This giantess looked down at her,
And also the prostrate Bjaauni male,
With flashing golden eyes from which
A strange pity seemed to radiate.
Four heavy emerald-tipped breasts quivered
As she opened her mouth and spoke:
'All, all are doomed to die, oh *Amarava*—

But I shall see to it that you are spared!'
'Who – who are you?' gasped the breathless *Amarava.*
'I am *Ninavanhu-Ma*, the First Goddess
The wife of the Tree of Life.'

Amarava sprang to her feet and leapt
Over the grovelling Bjaauni who was moaning with fear—
With his ugly face buried in his hands;
'*Ma!* Mother of Men! Great Goddess—
So the legends are right – all along they've been right!'
Shrieked the Amarire girl with tears in her eyes,
'Forgive, oh forgive our sacrilege, Great One,
Forgive, oh forgive and spare thy misled children,
Spare the misguided Amarire! Spare us, oh Goddess!'

Crystal tears welled from the golden eyes of the Great Mother *Ma*
And fell like raindrops on the bloodstained street of the dying city.
A sob shook her tall silver form, and slowly,
As if struck by some deadly unseen missile,
The Goddess sagged to the ground.
Above her lightning ripped like flaming assegais
Through the growling rain-pregnant clouds,
And a howling wind roared through the golden streets
On which lay scattered dead bodies – in heaps,
Like fish in a fisherman's boat.

The Great Goddess knelt before the startled girl—
A shimmering form of living silver that reflected the golden domes
Of the doomed city like in a mirror of bronze
Or a pool in the bowls of some deep forest.
Her radiant hands clasped the puny *Amarava*
And she writhed and cried out in agony;
Then with the tip of a silvery finger
She touched both the nipples of *Amarava's* breasts.
She caressed her hips, and then lifting her up,
Kissed her in the centre of her abdomen.
'Mother of Men!' murmured *Ma*—
'You shall bear the new races of men
Who shall in due course roam this earth.
You are the only Amarire I'll spare,
You and you alone shall survive this holocaust.
I wish I could have spared
A great deal more of my children;
But I cannot, as a Power greater than myself

Bids me to save only you from all the Red People.
A Power greater than myself bids me also to save *Odu*—
The sub-human here, for he shall be your mate
And the Father of Future Races.'

Amarava stared horrified down at the sub-man
And a flood of unimaginable contempt,
Hatred and naked revulsion
Swept and overwhelmed her completely.
Surely the Goddess was not giving her,
The beautiful *Amarava*,
To this smelly, hideous thing for a mate!
Surely she, *Amarava*,
Daughter of the First Red People,
Was not being mated to this—
This odorous revolting, soulless beast—
This beast-of-burden the Emperor created
From putrid animal flesh!

A scream left the girl's mouth in repulsive horror—
She cried and begged to be killed outright
Rather than be wedded to so contemptuous a thing
As *Odu* the Bjaauni – the Lowest of the Low!

'My child,' said the Goddess above the howling storm,
'Forget your childish feelings and obey my commands;
Now place your hand on my thigh and swear
That you shall do as I tell you now—
Lo! There is little time left and I must needs leave
This evil world at the earliest moment!'

Suddenly the girl's eyes were opened
In a strange and mysterious way—
She peered into the depths of Eternity itself;
She saw a cloud of swirling, dazzling living vapour
That shone brighter than the brightest star,
Brighter than the summer noonday sun,
And faintly across the immeasurable distance
Came a voice: 'I Command – All Obey!'

The voice, faint as it was, seemed to tear
Into the very fibres of *Amarava's* being,
Until each of her pulsing veins
Strained and tensed in agony.

'What . . . what was that?' queried *Amarava.*
'That, my child, is the All-powerful—
Who is, who was, and ever will be—
That is the Great Spirit, my child, Whom we must Obey!'

'Goddess, First Mother, I promise to obey,' she sighed,
Placing her hand on the deity's blazing thigh,
Taking the Oath – 'I swear to obey!'

'Swear again, my child, this time
With your hand on my lower left breast'
This she did and found her hand scorched
By the radiance of the Goddess's being.

'I shall now create a robot shark
To transport you across the seas
And there you shall find new land
Which the earthquakes have left in peace.
There you, and *Odu* here, shall love each other
And once again re-populate the earth with men.
But since I can fathom your stubbornness
I am forced to take measures to see you obey—
You have touched me with your right hand
Which has been badly burnt as a result—
And I have burnt both your nipples with my finger,
While leaving a burn mark on your abdomen.
Now, whenever you think of breaking your oath,
Those parts I have touched shall give you such pain
As you have never felt before.
If you try to escape your mate and go into hiding,
I'll give you three days of grace in agony—
Agony that will build up progressively.
After the three days in which to return,
Your flesh shall rot and fall off your body
But death will never come to your rescue
To release you from your eternal suffering.

I shall now take you to the robot shark—
That I have specially created for your transport,
And the mate I have chosen for you;
And child, may your breasts be ever full—
And your hips be ever fertile—'

* * *

These were the last words that *Amarava* heard
From the radiant lips of *Ninavanhu-Ma*;
For at that very instant she fell unconscious to the ground
As the strain of the experience was too great for her.

Then the Goddess diverted her attention to *Odu*
Who cringed in animal fear at her feet;
This creature forlorn – neither man nor beast—
Greatly moved the compassionate Goddess to pity.
But as she extended her hand to this man-made soulless thing
He uttered a hoarse scream of undiluted terror,
And shrank back gibbering like a hypnotised ape
Which in features he so closely resembled.

'*Odu!*' spoke the Goddess sharply,
'Look up and listen to me – I command!'
And *Odu* raised his revolting apology for a face,
Groping sightlessly with deepest bloodshot eyes.
'Do you see this female here *Odu* – do you see her?'
'Yes . . . *Odu* sees . . . Female of hateful masters.'
'I give her to you – take good care of her;
With her you shall once again populate the world.'

Odu's animal mind could not grasp all this,
But he humbly indicated agreement, faithful slave that he was;
For once in his artificial life he tried to think for himself,
But became much more confused than he ever was before.
His bulky body was quaking with pure terror
And he felt the urge to escape as fast and as far
As his massive legs could carry him.
He knew he had killed *Za-Ha-Rrellel*,
The Big One of the hated masters,
And very many other Amarire,
But he was only completely puzzled
At not being punished for all he did.
On the contrary, now he is lovingly asked
To take good care of the last survivor!

The Goddess suddenly conjured a massive net
Into which she bundled both terrified creatures;
On regaining their senses they were clinging to each other
As they plunged through the waves on a robot fish.

The giant city capsized and sank behind them,

But onward dashed the artificial fish
Through restless waves – ploughing a foaming path
To safety beyond the horizon.
The sea was still filthy, having just devoured
Whole continents and millions of beasts and men;
Cruel and restless, and still scalding hot
While above, the clouds continued to grumble—
Vomiting forth bolt after bolt of thunderous lightning.

Amarava cried out aloud as the realisation struck her
That well and truly she was the last living human being;
For three whole days she cried without ceasing
While forward they sped through seas, now slowly calming.

Night fell and the moon smiled weakly
Upon a destructed earth;
Dancing waves turned to liquid silver
And still the great fish went on—
Eastward and eastward, without a pause.

The sun rose in all its torrid splendour—
The Song of Day whispered a wordless melody
Over guilty waters and naked mountains—
Swept clean of animal and human life.
Now and again *Amarava* saw
Rocks rearing above the foaming waters—
All that were left of a continent she knew,
Now drowned beneath the passionless seas.
Amarava lost count of the number of days
That floated by like migrating birds
And was conscious only of a weakness she felt
In both her body and soul.
She felt like a plant which had lost its roots—
Like driftwood on the waters of time;
Naked and helpless in a mad Universe—
She wept till she could weep no more.
Loud within the vaults of her mind
Was the thought that the world she had known
And loved, for she knew no better,
Was dead forever – and Future loomed as an ugly ghost.

The poem of Amarire had been chanted
Through to its very last verse
And now the drums of Fate are sounding

The beginning of yet another poem.
The parent plant had withered and died
But from its mould it cast forth a seed,
Soon to arise as a fresh new plant,
For such is the law of Nature.

BETWEEN GOROGO AND ODU

The mighty fish had nosed up
The mouth of a mighty river,
Which future generations were to call
The river of the Bu-Kongo.
It paused long enough to permit the weary wanderers
To alight on its grassy banks with a splash.

Now it was evening of the second day
Since they had stood on solid ground
And *Amarava* was lying in the cool interior
Of a hut which *Odu* had built.
This hut stood on tall strong poles,
Sunk into the mud of the river,
And she had a magnificent view
Of the dull silver streak with approaching dusk.
She could see across the vast stretch of water
The frowning forests on the opposite bank,
And a canoe, with *Odu* returning home from a hunt.
The forest was alive with all kinds of sound
From that of water birds among the reeds
To the distant roaring of lions—
Boldly challenging the approaching night.

The fact that she was in a part of the world
Which miraculously had survived destruction—
Ruled by beasts and undefiled by man,
Did not interest *Amarava* at all.
She was still dazed and could not care less
Whether the sun rose in the West
And set in the North, as the Wise Ones often say.

She was fighting a fierce battle with herself

And her soul was a reeking cauldron of emotions;
Her greatest problem was whether she should
Yield her beautiful self to the monstrous *Odu.*
Great was her hatred of this sub-human ape,
But equally great was her fear of incurring
The Goddess's displeasure on breaking her oath
On which future humanity depended.

But human instincts are often much stronger
Than a thousand commands from heaven;
And not for the sake of a thousand worlds
Could she submit to sharing a love-mat with *Odu.*
Then suddenly a bright idea struck her
Which made new strength course like fire through her veins:
What if . . . supposing . . . *Odu* should fall a victim . . .
A fatal accident while out on a hunt!
The Goddess could never blame her—
Amarava – for the accidental death
Of her uncomely and revolting mate!

Supposing a hole were drilled in the side of *Odu's* canoe
And temporarily sealed with a soluble gum . . .
Her eyes were lit up by the strangest fire
When she recalled that *Odu* was unable to swim.
But then another, much better idea
Struck the already excited girl—
An idea so patently simple
It took her breath completely away . . .

Odu came crawling into the hut
With an impala slung over his back;
This he humbly presented his mistress
Whom he could not regard as a mate as yet.
Amarava sang with delight as she skinned
And cut up the meat for supper—
Her hands were trembling so slightly
With barely suppressed excitement.
Soon, soon she would be free, she thought,
Well rid of this clumsy and ugly monster
Who was completely unaware of the fact
That he was a living creature.

When at last they had eaten enough
She curtly commanded *Odu* to sleep

And this he promptly did, being completely unable
To do anything unless instructed.

For a time she sat with her knees drawn up,
Staring fixedly into the fire
Which was burning on a slab in the centre of the hut—
Then she rose to add some more wood
And did not care much about slipping a piece
From the stone slab on to the floor.

As the grass floor took fire and quickly spread,
She leapt to her feet and dived through the door;
Once on dry ground she dashed like a pursued impala
Through the forest with a pounding heart.
Once she paused and looked behind her
At the blazing red glare in the night sky—
'He is dead . . . most assuredly he's dead by now,'
She breathed, 'that revolting brute – I'm free!'
Through the forest she sped as fast as she could go—
Rapidly increasing the distance between herself and her crime;
Soon she burst into a treeless clearing,
Face to face with dozens of luminous eyes.

In the moonlight she recognised lions
Twice the size of their recent descendants—
Paralysed she stood and could only watch
As the biggest maned lion came crouching towards her.
It sniffed her belly and licked her buttocks
And for a few terrifying moments both woman and beast
Stared deep into each other's eyes.
With a low growl of deep puzzlement it slowly turned tail
And made off promptly with the rest of the pride!
It dawned upon *Amarava* after some considerable time,
That these lions had not been molested by humans before
And that the old one's behaviour was prompted by curiosity alone.

After this rather interesting experience
Amarava spent the night up a *mopani* tree;
She did not relish another encounter
With four-footed tribes such as these.
Dawn found her wide awake, but exhausted
And only sheer hunger could force her
To descend and start searching for food.
It was as she was eating some wild figs,

That sudden pains like scorpion stings
Erupted on her nipples, right hand and stomach.
She squirmed in agony on the ground,
But the pain mounted to intolerable intensity
With every passing moment.
Through the purple haze of hideous aching
The words of the Great Mother came to her
And she remembered . . . she remembered!
She also realised quite plainly now
That her deed of the night before was no accident,
But plain and straightforward murder!
Maddened by pain she now dashed through the forest,
Hoping to reach the burnt-out hut again,
But having lost all sense of direction
She lost herself in the primaeval wilderness.

Eventually she begged the Goddess for mercy,
But the blue skies kept a stony silence;
Forward she dashed again in blind agony
Until she reached a lake which she mistook
For the river where the hut had stood.
Repeatedly she called out *Odu's* name
And with another forward lunge she leapt
The vertical face of a precipice.
At the bottom of the cliff she struck a tree
And that was all she could remember . . .

There were three of them . . .
And the one was more hideous than the other;
Like nightmares torturing a fevered man . . .
They stood on their hind legs with front legs crossed
Over pale-green protruding bellies.
They were taller than a man
And their girth was incredible;
For all the world they looked like
Crosses between frogs and crocodiles,
And they were watching the woman *Amarava*
Slowly recovering her consciousness.
She cried out weakly in terror when she saw herself surrounded
By such gigantic monsters
Inside a humid smelly cave;
She tried to rise but was gently pushed back
On her bed of damp rotting reeds
By one of her three weird captors.

The biggest opened his terrible mouth
And uttered sounds unbelievably ugly,
To which the second one asked an obvious question
And the first answered 'Gwarr *Gorogo*!'
Upon which he left the cave,
Leaving two to guard the female.

On returning he introduced to his friends
A fourth one double their size;
He wore a belt of threaded reeds
And a headdress of crocodile skin.
'Their Chief', thought *Amarava*,
'Quite an intelligent race of frogs—
They even have a Chief!'

High Chief *Gorogo* of a dying race
Of gigantic intelligent frog-men,
Looked down upon their very strange foundling
And wondered just what to do.

They classed her as animal, and obviously female,
But *Gorogo* could not understand
Why the Great Mother had saved her
While the rest of her kind were destroyed.
It slowly entered his mind
That perhaps the Great Mother had sent her
To save a dying race;
That through her the world could be repopulated
With a kind that could rule again.

Then fear filled *Gorogo's* soul
As he caught a glimpse of the future
Through the misty veil of time.
He saw this species before him
Ruling the world supreme,
Exterminating all animal life
From the jungles and seas—
He saw this species contaminate the very stars . . .
And turn upon each other,
Killing their own kind like ravaging beasts
Across the astonished face of the earth.

With a hoarse croak the Chief quickly summoned his Elders

And they went into council till deep in the night,
Discussing what exactly they should do
With the female of this queer species.
Many suggestions were made,
All aiming at her outright destruction,
But in the end it dawned on them
That through her they might save their own race!
Their own females had recently gone sterile
And their Chief should have the honour . . .
The vote in favour was unanimous
With *Gorogo's* vote in the lead!

But under the earnest discussion,
Amarava made good her escape
And by the time they took their decision
She had put a great distance between them and herself.
But her freedom was actually of short duration;
Towards sunset they recaptured her
And frogmarched her back to *Gorogo's* cave
Where a rather forcible marriage took place.

Indaba, my children, now you know
What we mean by 'a Frog's Bride'—
Throughout this Dark Land
From the Xhoza to the land of the Baganda
'A Frog's Bride' means a forced marriage—
A girl thrashed into marrying
A man she does not love.

The Holy Legends tell us that *Amarava*
Became the Queen of the Frogmen
And in due course fulfilled her purpose
By laying numerous eggs.
From these eggs there soon hatched
A yellow frog-like people
Cunning little rascals these—
The Bushmen and the Pygmies.

In the third year the Frogmen were struck by disaster;
In those days all men reached maturity
In only a year or three,
And *Amarava's* offspring was adult and fighting fit.
As usual she could not sleep
As a result of the pain she suffered;

The Frogmen had prescribed a special root powder,
But this was not fully effective.

She was lying in her cave overlooking the lake
And the half-submerged village of these queer people,
When loud yells, mingled with dying croaks, reached her ears
And she realised a battle was in progress.
Her offspring were now armed with bows and arrows,
Tipped with a deadly paralysing poison;
And in no time the Frogmen ceased to exist—
The last to fall was *Gorogo*, their Chief.

Thus died a near perfect race,
Nearly as perfect as the Kaa-U-La birds;
Imperfect man had made his return—
Foul, destructive, homicidal man.

My children, our tribal Wise Men solemnly curse
The day that Man set his foot upon this earth,
And they insist most seriously that the Universe
Shall never know peace as long as Man
Infests the earth like a vile leprosy.

Amarava had grown to like the intelligent non-human Frogmen
And her grief knew no bounds as she saw them wantonly murdered;
She raised her voice and called on the murderous bands,
Now skulking amongst the mud huts of their victims.
'Come out of there, you creatures most foul!
Come and hear what I have to say.'
They came out and stood some distance away—
A wild and brazen-eyed naked rabble—
Far worse in appearance and general behaviour
Than a hunger-ravaged troop of thieving baboons.

Amarava felt hatred boiling within her—
Anger and grief deprived her of speech;
When she found her voice she harshly shouted
A blistering curse on her sons and daughters.
'Be gone – hence you vile little bastards . . .
Henceforth you and your miserable descendants
Shall be nothing but vagabonds and thieves!
By thieving and cunning you shall live to the end of time,
And never progress or rise above
What you are today.'

They fled wildly into the forest
And *Amarava* left the valley of Frogmen—
Soon to sink in the haze of legend;
She did not know just where she was going
And could not care less, for her pains
Became more acute and she longed for death,
But a Greater Power always thwarted
Her attempts at suicide.
For days and months she wandered aimlessly,
Sucking at the magic pain-killing root powder;
Then one day as she stood on a point of vantage
A gigantic hand gripped her smooth round shoulder!

She spun around and stood face to face
With the creature she thought she had murdered;
Her surprise had no bounds, of course,
When she recognised *Odu*, the man-made man.

Odu explained that while out on his hunt
He encountered the Great Mother who gave him a warning;
Having read *Amarava's* mind and fathomed her shrewd plan,
She advised that *Odu* should feign a deep slumber.

Even as they spoke *Amarava* felt a deep gratitude
To be back with a sincere friend she knew;
She felt her pains vanish in the Seven Winds
And suddenly felt young and free again.

Odu snatched her up like a baby
And took off through the forest with her—
A terrible smile was fixed on his hideous face,
But much less hideous than *Gorogo's*, thought she.
He did not stop until they reached the stockade
He had built around his new kraal;
In the biggest hut he laid her down
On a pile of lion skins and fed her tenderly.

Afterwards they went through the forest
Past a huge Idol of the Great Mother,
Which *Odu* had carved from sandstone,
And finally reached his canoes on the bank of the river.
She saw some poles protruding from the water
And recognised the site of the hut she had burnt;
Odu dived in and swam to these poles

And from one of them recovered a mysterious article.
This was a delicately carved piece of ebony,
Shaped like a paddle for steering a canoe;
The patterns and figures intrigued her much
And she wished to know their meaning.

Odu gave her no explanation
As he knew she would soon find out—
Back at the Idol he suddenly did
What he had never done before!
He slipped his arm about her
And dragged her across the altar—
With the specially carved paddle
He gave her a healthy spanking.

The spanking was interrupted by the silvery voice of *Ma*,
Who suddenly appeared on the scene;
She suggested that *Odu* had given her enough
And should save some of her for the love-mat.
'So you are back at long, long last, I see,
And I hope you have now thoroughly learnt, my child,
That no one should try to circumvent
The express commands of the gods;
And now I shall expect you to carry out
My instructions as already given;
And you, *Odu*, must never hesitate to use that handy object
When she starts with her tricks again.'

With this the Goddess slowly vanished
While the two of them stooped in prayer;
Together they returned through the forest
And two butterflies settled on the altar.

THE BUD SLOWLY OPENS

The legends tell us that after her return
Amarava the Immortal, most beautiful,
Lived happily with *Odu*, her lord,
For a hundred thousand years;
And during this period she presented him
With five thousand sturdy sons and daughters.

The Wise Men of the Tribes also relate
That *Amarava* did not give birth to her young,
But that like the earliest Amarire people,
She laid crystal eggs that hatched in a month
And adulthood was reached in the space of two years.
On reaching puberty their parents turned them out,
In carefully chosen pairs to fend for themselves;
Soon they were grandparents to the ultimate power
Of no less than twice times ten million souls.

What did these new people—
These so-called Second People look like?
We have it from legend that they resembled exactly
The present-day Bantu – my children.
Some were as black as a much-used pot;
Some were brown and even yellow-brown;
Some were tall as a stockade gatepost
And some were as short as our favourite thornbush.
There were types as thin as bullrush reeds
And others as fat as the proverbial thief's bundle.
Some were idiots—
From dimwits they ranged
Down to utter nitwits;
Very few were truly wise!
In short, my children, they exactly resembled

The puzzling muddle of present day humanity!
Gone forever was the uniform appearance
Of the First People who could have achieved perfection
If they had been properly governed.
Not in appearance alone they differed,
But also in mind and heart and soul;
Where there had been perfect equality,
We now encounter diversity.

For thousands of years our *Odu* and *Amarava*
(Now called *Mameravi* or Mother of Nations)
Watched the bud of humanity slowly open
And burst into brilliant flower.
They worked, like the good parents they were,
Towards welding their countless descendants
Into one harmonious whole.
Advice they gave – they taught, and meted out justice
When disputes arose amongst their diverse progeny.

Finally *Odu* grew tired of life
And developed an inferiority complex;
Odu the Mighty – increasingly aware of his humble past
Now turned his mind to suicide.
He knew this demanded most careful planning
As an immortal cannot die,
Unless he destroys himself
Utterly beyond recovery.
So one night when all had gone to bed
He crept out into the sullen darkness
And embarked on a lengthy journey eastwards—
A journey that lasted a hundred days.

Finally he reached the active volcano—
Now the silent snow-capped Killima-Njaro—
And with anxious strides he scaled the grey slopes
Of the feature he had chosen for a grave.
The billowing smoke from multiple craters
Burnt his eyes and choked his lungs—
And dust-like molten ashes blistered his skin,
But he relentlessly pursued his aim.
When he reached the summit he paused
In the heavy clouds of choking smoke
And with a last prayer to *Ma* and the Tree of Life
He gracefully dived into one of the red-hot craters.

Odu, the soulless being, died
Without a world of his own;
He who had survived one world
To become the Father of the second.

In her lonely hut far away in the west
Amarava sensed her husband's fiery death
And with a loud cry she snatched a copper dagger
And drove it savagely into her chest.
But the soft copper blade buckled
Against her breastbone and in her frustration
She tried to run herself through with a spear,
Though in this effort she was also defeated.

Zumangwe the Hunter
And *Marimba* the Singer,
Two of her youngest descendants,
Rushed in and overpowered her.
'No!' cried *Marimba*, with quivering ebony-black breasts,
'No, you must not take your own life!
We shall not allow the star that lights our way
To fall thus from the skies—
If you are no longer burning,
Oh beautiful torch of our race—
Who shall guide our failing steps
Along all the thorny footpaths
Through the uncertain valley of Life?'

Thus spoke the dark and beautiful *Marimba*,
From whom our Tribal Singers claim descent;
So spoke the first Bantu poetess
Whose voice was the Voice of Spring
And whose singing it was said, could make
Even mountains cry cold tears.
Many, oh many are the tales about her
As many as the lice on an old skin blanket;
Many and countless as the hair on a dog's back—
And one day – the gods willing – I might be able
To tell you the story of *Marimba*, my children.

Zumangwe and *Marimba* seized
The badly wounded *Amarava*
And tied her hand and foot

To prevent her from trying again.
But the grief-maddened immortal
Snapped the bonds
With one sharp look
And shrieked into the forest
In search of her beloved *Odu*!

Zumangwe and *Marimba* raised the alarm
And soon an army of men and women
Clamoured in hot pursuit
After their greatest great-grandmother.
'Come, all my brothers and sisters,'
Sounded *Marimba's* melodious voice—
'Come let us cling to her trail like hunting dogs—
If she dies we shall all be lost
Like leaves in a storm – like a young impala
Whose mother was devoured by a lion—
Great shall be our misfortune
If we fail to capture her alive.'

Legends say that the number in pursuit
Counted eighty times a thousand souls;
Along the Bu-Kongo river they followed a trail
Of blood from the wound in her chest.
The valiant hunter *Zumangwe*
And his very young bride *Marimba*,
Ruthlessly led their followers
In a futile attempt at overtaking *Amarava*
Who was now stumbling, falling and rising
A day's journey ahead of them.

After two months one of the trackers
Made a rather startling discovery
Which sent cold bolts of fear through the spines of all;
Something else was tracking *Amarava*—
Something so utterly big and monstrous,
As they could tell from the footprints it left—
Footprints like that of a vulture
Of incredible size and weight.

A new strategic approach was now called for;
The search party stopped to build a fortified kraal
While the two leading figures and some others
Formed a small, more flexible patrol.

Three days later they found *Amarava*
Lying exhausted on a mudbank
In the middle of a very vast river,
A river in boisterous foaming flood!
There was no way of reaching her
And *Marimba* sang out in utter despair;
'Oh beautiful star of the human race!
Oh mother of countless men—
Is there nothing we can do to help?
Lo! here we stand as helpless as
A dove in the mouth of a civet cat!
Our only wish is to be by your side—
What is there you can advise us to do?'

'You can do nothing, my loyal children,'
Her voice carried faintly across the flood;
'My only wish is to be left alone,
As I wish to die in peace.'
'Mother of Nations,' cried *Marimba*,
'Is it thus that you sacrifice your life?
Is it thus that the beloved *Amarava*
Turns her back on her destitute children?'

Instead of hearing *Amarava's* reply,
They all heard a frightening splash—
Some distance upstream a mighty Monster
Had entered the water in a cloud of spray.
Marimba immediately plunged in as well
And tried to reach the mudbank first,
But the current was much stronger than her courage
And swept her helplessly downstream.
Twice she tried and twice she failed,
And in an alternative desperate attempt
At frightening the monster away
Zumangwe ordered his men to launch
A hail of sling-stones across the water.

All their efforts, with spears and arrows included
And another brave and nearly successful attempt
On the part of *Marimba* to reach her through the flood—
Were futile and they could only helplessly witness
The most horrible scene they had ever experienced.

* * *

Amarava had noticed the Monster
And in blind terror she summoned all her strength;
With a shriek she plunged into the water,
But was equally promptly snatched up by the Monster.
'Release her, you vilest reincarnation of Evil,'
Marimba now shouted in utter despair—
And then to everyone's breathless surprise
The scaly Monster calmly turned and spoke:

'Poor ignorant, foolish human creatures—
How terribly sentimental you are!
It is for your own good and safety that I remove
This Thing which you knew as *Amarava*!'
The Monster spoke with infinite tenderness;
'You are blindly loyal to the outward form—
To superficial appearance alone;
When will your clouded brains appreciate
That things are not what they appear to be!
That there is more to anything than meets the eye!'

'*Aieeee!*' cried Marimba, the only one
Who still had power of speech,
'Do you mean to tell us that *Amarava*
Is not what she appears to be!'

'*Yebo*,' replied the Monster that Walks,
To which *Marimba* lost control of herself;
'*Haiee!* not only are you a monster
As foul as the cesspools of hell
But the father of all lies as well!'

'Human female – I speak only the truth—
This creature you know as *Amarava*
Is a reincarnation at the same time
Of the Fire Bride, or Rebel Goddess,
Who has been evading the Great Spirit
For many millions of years!'

Even as *Marimba* listened and looked,
The limp and naked from of *Amarava*
Was slowly changing in the Monster's clutches;
Her red skin turned to the colour of gold
With the polished brightness of that metal.
Now she had an udder of five breasts—

Ruby tipped and standing out—
Like anthills on a desolate plain;
And her eyes, once so soft and clear,
Had the greeny hardness of emeralds.
Her hands had acquired a sixth finger,
And all her fingers flourished
Razor-sharp diamond claws.
A lion's tail sprang from her backside
Which curled and uncurled
Like a whip of living gold!
A flaming forked tongue protruded
And licked her pig-iron lips.

'Behold her! Look well upon her,'
Cried the Monster, holding her up,
'Behold the foul creature who not only deceived you,
But *Ma*, the First Goddess as well.
Look upon the thing you knew as *Amarava*
And for which you were prepared to sacrifice your lives!
See the one you adored as *Amarava*,
In whom is now reincarnated
Watamaraka, the Spirit of Evil!'

Before the Monster and its captive
Vanished in a flash of unearthly flame,
Marimba saw the sneer of contempt
On the once beloved *Amarava's* face;
'I shall return one day and avenge myself
On all living things – I shall . . .'

Night had fallen by the time *Zumangwe*
And his followers reached the gate of their new village—
The first village in the country which in future years
Acquired the name of Tanga-Nyika.
He had ordered all those who had witnessed events
Never to repeat what they had seen—
They all agreed to abide by the make-belief
That the search for *Amarava* had failed.

The secret of *Amarava's* identity
Went with these men to their grave.
Zumangwe wished that the name of *Amarava*
Should remain one which future generations
Must honour and respect.

Now all of you my dear children
Have to some small extent inherited
Amarava's split personality.
Within each of you there are two different beings,
One good and one evil – in constant conflict.

THE SPAWN OF THE DRAGON

Simba the lion was old. Simba the lion was weak – mad with hunger and frustration. There is nothing more terrible for a beast once strong than to find itself slowly succumbing to the ravages of old age. And, in the hostile forest, age is the greatest and most final calamity that can befall a living creature, be it lion or antelope.

Antelopes that feel the onset of old age in the weakness it brings to their swift limbs, know that the stream of their lives has at last run dry. They know that for them the hour of Kalunga, the God of Death, has come and, when the herd madly flees from the smell of lions, they will be forced to lag behind – an easy prey even to the most inexperienced young lion.

The lion who feels the icy claws of old age slowly paralysing his mighty leaping muscles, and who feels the dizziness of old woman Time clouding his mind and dimming his eyes, comes inevitably to realise that he has already hunted his last impala, and that for him the sun of life is setting in a blaze of gold, scarlet and purple.

So, Simba the lion was lying under the young *musharagi* tree not far from a sluggish river bordered by rustling reeds, and in whose cool bosom a herd of water beasts bathed lazily, their enormous bodies protruding like so many smooth glistening rocks in the rippling waters.

One of the water beasts raised its ugly head and yawned hugely, exposing blunt tusks insultingly in the direction of the slowly weakening lion with the golden light of the setting sun full on his face. The lazy breeze of sunset was softly playing with his ancient mane, and the tall grass through which his head was barely visible.

Among the reeds bordering the river something moved and a sacred flamingo rose into the forest-scented air, slowly beating its graceful pinkish-white wings as it crossed the river to join three of its females on the other side. But Simba the lion had no eyes for all this; the forest had lost its magic. The silvery river with its water beasts, its nesting flamingoes and playful otters had lost its enchantment. The only voice for which he had ears was the voice of hunger growing savagely in his famished, shrunken belly. The only music for which he had ears was the song of starvation roaring like a wild tempest through the caverns and tunnels of his dulled mind.

Aieeee! Simba the lion would have given his eyes, yea, his very life for just a mouthful of meat from the side of a wildebeest three days dead! Surely anything, no matter how putrid and vile, any worm-crawling carrion, was better than a slow death of starvation. In vain the old lion wished that just one thin, spavined antelope should pass within reach of his age-numbed claws. He had not eaten for three whole days.

It was cruelly strange to see that the older one grew the faster the impalas and zebras seemed to be. Why were these wretched creatures so incredible? Did they not know that they were created by the Great Ones for the sole benefit of lions? A vision of a herd of zebras floated briefly across the troubled skies of his disordered mind. A million curses on the striped over-fat wretched brutes! Why did the Great Spirit have to give them such swift feet?

The old lion's thoughts were cleaved abruptly by an interruption. They faded out like morning mist before the rising sun and old Simba lifted his battered head with a start! Something was coming . . . and it was coming his way!

With a cautiousness born of years of bitter experience Simba lowered his scarred head until he was looking through the long elephant grass, rather than over it. He breathed a deep breath of living air. *Eyah!* there was no doubt about it – the strange scent was there and it was getting stronger. Whatever was coming was taking its time. But of one thing the old lion was now sure – it was some kind of food that was coming his way! Fresh and vibrant strength poured like liquid fire along his spine. His excited tail slowly stiffened and a low growl of satisfaction involuntarily pushed itself forth from the depths of his ancient chest, to be promptly stilled by the voice of experience. Nothing must give the approaching prey a hint of his presence. Silence now . . . absolute silence . . .

It seemed as if the very stream of Time had come to a standstill as the lion waited; the forest, the river and everything about his environment suddenly assumed an odd unreality. Then they casually emerged into view . . . strolling slowly through the long grass . . . Human Beings!

There were two of the creatures – male and female. And old Simba narrowed his yellow eyes as he contemplated their approach. They were walking for all the world as if they owned the forest – as if all the trees and the mighty ageless river belonged to them or their fathers. They were walking as if they were the chief and chieftainess of Creation. Simba the lion watched them coldly and in his animal mind took in each detail of their features and attire, as they drew nearer and nearer . . . and their scent grew stronger in his anxious nostrils!

The female was the Spirit of Beauty personified. She was Perfection in a most perfect form. She was not only beautiful, but she radiated beauty as a hot stone radiates heat. The waiting Simba could sense the great beauty of the human female and he could sense also the great goodness in her soul. He beheld the sensitive beauty of her face, the oval face with its round prominent forehead, its clear eyes that scanned the world with an expression of deep wonder. He noticed the small flat nose and the tiny nostrils, well placed above a smiling mouth. A mischievous goddess had placed that mouth there as a trap with which to catch the lips of men.

She was the essence of purest perfection. Some Goddess of Skill must have spent days of precious time moulding each bulge and curve of that heavenly physique. This woman was living beauty carved in dark brown *musharagi* – a statue of perfection carved in living ebony.

Her attire was simple indeed: she wore a short skirt of tanned cheetah skin heavily trimmed with cowrie shells around the hems. Bracelets of copper and ivory flourished on her arms and around her neck blazed a necklace of bright copper oblongs engraved with signs of secret wisdom. Her hair was combed up into two lobes, a hairstyle known as the 'ears of the caracal' – the oldest hairstyle in the Land of the Tribes. Sacred cowrie shells decorated her soft hair and a beautifully carved comb of ivory showed in the back of her head.

The old lion did not know it, of course, but he was looking at the most famous and most beautiful woman that ever lived – *Marimba*, the daughter of *Odu* and the incomparable *Amarava*, Mother of Nations. He was looking at the woman who gave the tribes some of the oldest and most beautiful songs on earth and who invented countless musical instruments, each destined to carry her name in some form or other – *Marimba*, the Mother of Music.

The man was tall and slender, but strongly built. His face was not handsome, but it was determined and manly, like the rest of his body. And whereas the woman beside him was beauty incarnate, he was the personification of strength and invincible loyalty. He wore a crude loinskin around his manly hips and a band of python skin around his head. A necklace of the teeth of hyaenas was around his muscle-corded neck, while a solitary bracelet of copper shone on his right forearm. In his left hand he held a crude shield of buffalo skin while in his right he carried a weighty harpoon of wood, tipped with a flake from the shin-bone of a giraffe. He carried this strange weapon because at this time the tribes had not yet learned the secret of extracting the hard iron from the ironstone. That knowledge was brought to this continent by the Strange Ones very many generations after the events here mentioned occurred. Only copper was known to our ancestors at this stage and this metal was too soft for use in weapons. It was good only for ornaments.

The old lion waited quietly while the two human beings drew closer. The forest and the river seemed to vanish and in the lion's eyes only the two humans had any substance – only them he now saw, to the exclusion of all else.

He saw how the man's eyes never left the bewitching face of the woman by his side – how he looked for all the world like an impala helplessly caught in the hypnotic spell of a glittering python. He could see how the man smiled at her gently, reassuringly, and spoke softly to her as if trying to banish the great sadness that clouded her gentle eyes – a sadness that the old lion could sense was clouding the soul of the beautiful human female, like a foul storm-cloud clinging and obstructing from view the snowy top of a beautiful peak.

Then it dawned on the old lion that the human female was trying to urge her man to go back with her to where both came from and not to penetrate the forest any deeper. The unusually beautiful woman had a premonition of danger. But just then something happened which left both humans paralysed with fear and which gave old Simba the golden opportunity he had been waiting for! A bird of thunder – an eagle – had been circling high in the heavens for some time and now this rider of the storm suddenly dived from the red, blue and gold expanse of the sunset sky. He dived with wings partly spread and cruel talons fully at the ready to grab what his keen eyes had spotted. He passed directly over the heads of the startled humans, fanning them with the wind of his fearful passage. He dived into the tall grass to their left and shot up again into the glowing heavens – a young steenbuck struggling in terror in the grip of those pitiless claws.

While the shocked humans stood rooted to the ground, numbed by this awful and rare omen of violent death, old Simba gathered every ounce of his fast-ebbing strength, and launched himself in an all but feeble charge!

Marimba felt the heavy blow that struck her on the side of her head, sending her reeling to the ground, straight into the dark valleys of unconsciousness. She did not see her fearless husband hurl himself upon the lion that had brought her down. She did not see how his bone harpoon glanced aside harmlessly from the shaggy flank of the hunger-demented beast. Neither did she see how he, with a strength above the strength of an ordinary man, threw himself barehanded upon the snarling lion and dragged it off her. She did not see her husband locked in mortal battle with the lion whose claws all but tore his strong body to shreds. And she did not see the shaggy maned savage beast drag the limp form of her lord and husband away through the tall grass.

Simba the lion had found a meal at last.

And the Princess *Marimba*, Chieftainess of the Wakambi Tribe, had lost yet another husband, the second husband she had lost since the cruel Goddess of Evil, the night-walking *Watamaraka*, had laid a curse upon her. The Mother of Demons had one day approached her and commanded the shocked daughter of *Odu* and *Amarava* to become one of her handmaidens in the Land of Darkness, and this *Marimba* had flatly refused to do. *Watamaraka* then placed a curse upon *Marimba* saying that any man she would love and marry would die violently, and in her presence, within three moons of their marriage. Exactly three moons after the curse was pronounced, *Marimba's* husband, the hunter *Zumangwe* whom she had married sixteen years earlier and who was the father of her young son, had been trampled to death by a rogue elephant.

Marimba and the boy *Kahawa* had managed to escape by climbing a tall tree and had watched in horror as the head of their home met his untimely death almost immediately below them. Two years later *Marimba* had married again, and in order to prevent the curse of *Watamaraka* from being fulfilled, the Princess *Marimba* had kept her new husband a virtual prisoner for two whole moons, confined to the village of the Wakambi and never allowed him to go out with the other men on a hunt.

But the man had tired of being protected like an overgrown child by a woman. He wanted to face the perils of the forest and risk his life as all brave men should. *Marimba* had pleaded again and again, resorting to all her womanly subterfuges to keep her lord and husband at home. Finally *Marimba* had to give in to her valiant consort; she allowed him to go into the forest, but provided she could accompany him, hoping he would then exercise greater care.

They had spent the whole day in the forest and as the time passed she felt the voice of presentiment growing in her heart. She began to beg her husband to return home with her. But he, the stubborn, stupid and stone-headed fool, had laughed at her fears and had assured her that nothing would happen. It had been in the course of their tenth argument that afternoon that Simba the lion pounced upon them.

Now, the sun slowly set beyond the mountains to the west, and as the skies swept their blazing farewell to the departing Lord of Day, the Princess *Marimba* lay unconscious in all her beauty in the long grass while the water beasts began to leave the gurgling mud to commence their greedy nightly grazing. The sacred flamingoes gracefully retired to their mud and reed nests. And in the silent distance there came the faint sound of a hunter's horn. It sounded once, twice, thrice, and then it was silent again.

A search party of Wakambi warriors was on its way to find out what had happened to their beloved princess and her consort – why they had not returned to the crude settlement of caves and huts which the Wakambi, the Tribe of Wanderers, knew as their home. In the long elephant grass the breezes of sunset fanned the soul of the beautiful *Marimba* back from the land of Nothingness and she stirred. She sat up with a blinding headache that dimmed her vision.

The first thing she saw was blood – slowly drying blood all over the patch of trampled down grass, the unmistakable signs of a violent struggle. 'My husband!' was the first thought that came to her mind. Struggling against the mists of shock and apprehension *Marimba* tried to stand up. But she fell back and could only lie flat on her back, quite helpless.

Then out of the empty air above her a bright bronze-coloured apparition took shape. *Watamaraka*, the Mother of all Demons, presented herself in visible form, with a cruel smile on her dark lips.

'You will look around for your husband in vain, Oh *Marimba*: he is in a land far from here, beyond the seventh gateway of creation – the land of Forever-Night.'

'My husband . . . dead! How can he be dead? I tried to tell him!'

'You poor babbling fool,' murmured *Watamaraka*. 'I told you that every man you marry would die violently within three moons of your marriage, did I not?'

Fires of hate and fierce anger flamed in the gentle breast of the beautiful *Marimba* and words of wanton harshness spilled like a fierce torrent from her lovely mouth: 'You pitiless blackhearted sexless monster! You foul witch from the lowest pits of hell! So you would place a curse on my head, would you? But I can yet defeat your vile schemes. I have already made up my mind that I shall never love another man again.'

'You stupid human beings! You are all the same, whether mortal or immortal,' purred *Watamaraka* nastily. 'You make a lot of wonderful resolutions, you swear a lot of oaths to do this and not to do that. You bind yourselves with promises without first studying your secret natures – without knowing yourselves first.

You never size up your ability to keep your oaths. And you say you will never marry again, my little ugly cockroach!'

'*Ayieeee!*' flared *Marimba*, 'I shall never marry again, I swear by my mother's sacred breasts.' Her voice rose to a mad shriek.

'Look down there,' smiled *Watamaraka*, pointing down to *Marimba's* jutting breasts, 'What is the purpose of those, do you think?'

'What have my breasts to do with my oath?'

The harsh voice of the evil goddess turned soft and gentle as she said to the angry and frightened widow: '*Marimba*, you are a very beautiful and desirable woman. And you, the youngest of the few immortals left upon this earth, have one very delightful weakness which you inherited from your mother, *Amarava*, long before she came under my spell. You know well enough what I am referring to. That weakness will force you to marry again in exactly twelve moons from now. And once again you will suffer the pain of my curse; within three moons of your marriage your husband will die violently and evilly in your presence, and I shall stand nearby and laugh! Until then, farewell, *namirika*!'

'*Namirika!*'* – the unfriendly epithet was more than adequate to describe the great weakness that the Wakambi princess had. But she was shocked at hearing this accusation hurled at her for the first time in her life – and by her arch enemy of all creatures. The Queen of Falsehoods had spoken the truth for once and this truth had brought *Marimba* face to face with the realities of her character. She now saw herself exactly for what she was, not the wise and tender-hearted ruler of the first tribe ever organised in the land – the first tribe ruled not by force but by wisdom and love. She saw herself not as the loving mother of a boy wiser than his fifteen tender years and braver than a thousand lions, but as a very ordinary, frail woman tormented by the unceasing demands of her own exotic body. The silent forest suddenly seemed to possess voices. The distant tree trunks seemed to have grown faces and eyes that leered at her and mouths that laughed hideously. 'Oh no!' gasped *Marimba*. And just as she lapsed once again into the valleys of unconsciousness she heard the harsh brazen laughter of the Mother of Demons rippling through the forest as the triumphant goddess took her departure to the Land of Forever-Night.

Oko! For the beautiful one this was not only the day of soul-searing

* *An old Wakambi word which has no exact equivalent in English. In that language it would have a very vulgar meaning, but not in its Bantu sense. Literally, it combines the two words 'itch' and 'hips'. It is used to describe a woman who has an insatiable thirst for a man.*

sadness and cruel bereavement; it was the day of self-revelation too. And this day which comes to all of us sooner or later in the course of our lives on this earth is the most painful in a human being's existence. Many of us go through the swamplands and deserts of life swathed in a glossy *kaross* of self-delusion. We deceive ourselves into believing that we are wise, strong and invincible, and that in all the world there is no one like oneself. We believe this until the day when we have to stand and look down upon the false images of ourselves lying shattered at our feet. And on that day we discover that we are the exact opposite of what we thought we were.

Thus it was with the Princess *Marimba* on the day her lord and husband died – that day when Time itself was still in its infancy, so many hundreds of generations ago.

She had been firm in her belief that she was wise and strong enough to withstand the savage onslaughts of cruel fate. But she never realised that every human being born of a woman carries in him, or her, the seeds of his or her undoing. Even as she lapsed into unconsciousness *Marimba* knew with a sick feeling in the valleys of her mind that she would marry again and that she would suffer bereavement once again.

Kahawa, the son of *Marimba*, was very angry; his young eyes were red from weeping and he could not sleep. He was angry with his dead stepfather for having exposed his dear mother to the dangers of the forest in spite of her warnings and protests. He was also angry with his stepfather for having been foolish enough to let a lion, and an old lame one at that, eat him. The tall, stone-headed, stupid son of a club-footed hyaena should have known better than to let himself get killed and so make the incomparable *Marimba* and the whole of the Wakambi tribe unhappy. Serve the stupid wretch right! Did he not know that his wife was an immortal and that her words and her warnings had to be obeyed and heeded? 'Good riddance!' thought the boy coldly. 'Now my mother can concentrate on ruling the tribe instead of spending the greater part of the day in that silly fool's arms!'

It was well known that *Kahawa* had intensely disliked his stepfather while he lived, and he disliked him even more now that he was dead. He could not understand his mother's grief. Why, that idle good-for-nothing was much better off dead, so why waste tears over him?

Kahawa let out a snort of anger and turned over on his left side on his bed of skins and dry grass in the cave. He stared angrily at the pale silver moon through the mouth of the cave. He heard the distant low wailing of the women of the settlement who were gathered in the Great Hut to mourn with their Chieftainess the death of her husband. He also heard the low groans of the two thousand warriors who were gathered, fully armed with clubs and bone-tipped harpoons, outside the Great Hut to pay tribute to the dead Royal Consort.

All these sounds disgusted *Kahawa*, and he was still snorting his anger at the moon like a young buffalo bull when the open entrance of the cave was briefly darkened by a fat silhouette. His best friend, *Mpushu* the Cunning, entered and sat down near the entrance, regarding the son of his beloved Chieftainess with the usual expression of admiration on his fat, sweaty and fish-like face.

'I see you, Oh *Mpushu*,' said *Kahawa*.

Mpushu's ivory-white teeth gleamed in the moonlight against the ebony of his oily face. 'and I see you too, Oh Eagle of *Marimba*.'

'You are well known for an early sleeper, Oh *Mpushu*, so pray tell me, what brings you out at this time of the night?'

Mpushu's face seemed to grow oilier. His big round eyes seemed about to fly out of their sockets and he swallowed noisily once or twice. And then he just sat staring at *Kahawa* – his big mouth opening and shutting. He was obviously lost in the forests of fear.

'Has the Hyaena of Darkness eaten your tongue, Oh *Mpushu?* asked *Kahawa*. 'Why is it that you do not talk, Oh my friend?'

'This unworthy one is afraid to arouse the anger of the Royal One,' said *Mpushu* softly. 'This lowly *Mpushu* is afraid to be burned by the sun that is the wrath of *Kahawa*.'

'*Mpushu*,' *Kahawa* said gently, 'to me you are like a brother and I have always found reason to be thankful for your advice. Speak your mind and tell me what troubles you so.'

'Eagle of *Marimba*,' said *Mpushu* after a short silence, '*Mpushu* never worries about himself but for the prince who honours him with his friendship. And while this unworthy lay on his side in his hut early this night he heard men whispering outside.'

'The ears of *Mpushu* are sharper than the bone needles the women use for sewing skin blankets together and his brain is more cunning than that of the jackal in the forest. Tell me, Oh *Mpushu*, what were the men whispering about?'

'The miserable sons of tree-dwelling monkeys were speaking ill of my prince *Kahawa*,' growled *Mpushu*. 'It was that night-walking charlatan *Somojo* and that fat fool *Kiambo*. They were saying it was a thing of deep disgrace that the Eagle of *Marimba* was not showing his sorrow for his dead stepfather by standing outside the Great Hut in armed vigil as the rest of the Wakambi men are doing. *Kiambo* even went as far as to say that *Kahawa* seems pleased that his royal stepfather has gone to the land of Forever-Night.'

'The miserable fat hyaena is quite right!' cried *Kahawa* savagely. 'I am glad that my stepfather is dead, and tomorrow I intend to go into the council hut and tell these back-biting jackals so to their faces! I loathed the man while he lived and I hate him still though he is dead.'

Mpushu wiped his sweaty face with the back of his hand and the expression on his cunning face became even more fish-like as he said: 'Eagle of *Marimba*, there are times when a man must swallow his pride and push his personal likes and dislikes into the depths of the darkest forests of his mind and do things which he would never have dreamt of doing. And for you, my prince, such a time has come.'

'If you think that I must pretend – and like a hypocrite mourn a man I hated, Oh *Mpushu*, then you can go back to sleep, because that I shall never do. I have never pretended in all my life and I shall not start now.'

'Eagle of *Marimba*,' insisted *Mpushu* calmly, 'when you are a chief, or the son of one, there are things you have to do simply for appearance's sake, simply for the benefit of the stupid fools you rule, even if such things go against your feelings and your pride and conscience. A chieftain must hold the love and respect and the esteem of his subjects, always, otherwise he is lost. A chief or a prince must avoid being the laughing stock of his people, or evoke their scorn, because once that happens he is a chief no more. And your obvious pleasure at the death of your stepfather is fast making you the laughing stock of the Wakambi, Oh Royal *Kahawa*.'

'What are they laughing at me for?' demanded *Kahawa* hotly.

'As they went away I heard *Kiambo* and *Somojo* agreeing that you are a petty-minded fool who carries hatred to ridiculous levels, to beyond the grave . . .'

'What!' cried *Kahawa* furiously, leaping to his feet and reaching for his spear. 'The foul beasts dare insult me, the son of *Marimba*! Their muddy sour apology for blood shall redden my spear!'

'Killing those two will only make matters worse, Oh my prince,' said *Mpushu* calmly. 'Violence and force are sure signs of failure on the part of the ruler, Eagle of *Marimba*. Killing his own people can only increase a ruler's unpopularity.'

'Well?' cried *Kahawa* fiercely, 'what do you then suggest I should do? Do you want me to go out there and kiss the buttocks of the men who have insulted me?'

'No, my Lord, I would never dream of suggesting that you do something so easy. But I *do* suggest that early tomorrow morning you and I go out into the forest, hunt the lion that ate your stepfather, kill it and bring its head here for the rest of the people to see. That would greatly impress our tribe and make you very popular.'

'And it would also please my poor mother!' cried *Kahawa*, becoming quite excited about this brilliant suggestion. 'Oh *Mpushu*, you are the very fountain of wisdom!'

'I believe so . . . yes,' said *Mpushu* modestly.

Kahawa was so excited by the prospect of the coming lion hunt that he could not sleep that night. It was months since he had killed a lion and if there was one kind of beast that the son of *Marimba* wanted to wipe out of existence it was lion. *Kahawa* hated this kind of animal only a shade less than he hated his stepfather, and deep in his rebellious and turbulent soul this youth nursed a profound contempt for the custom of his tribe of first asking the gods for permission to kill lions.

When dawn stained the eastern skies a pink-red, *Kahawa* deliberately omitted to perform the lion-hunter's ceremony and to request Heaven's permission. He was content with washing his face, gargling with water mixed with powdered *mbaba* root, and combing his hair with a four-toothed ivory comb. Seizing his bone-tipped spears and elephant-skin shield, he rushed out to wait for his friend *Mpushu* at the gate of the vast Wakambi settlement.

At the gate the young prince waited with fuming impatience and he watched as the slowly rising sun sent its first rays to bathe the huts of the settlement where his mother ruled the first organised tribe in the land. It was a tribe of nomads and pioneers, the first Bantu to penetrate the land which in later years was to be known as Tanga-Nyika. Still later, the northern division would be known as Lu-Kenya. This great settlement was built near the top of a steep hill, and it circled this hill as a 'headband of honour' around a bald chief's head. A heavy palisade of thick logs with a solitary gate went round the outside of the settlement like some formidable diadem. Behind this stockade were five thousand huts. These huts were crude and rather ugly compared with those built many generations later. The upper reaches of the hill were honey-combed with caves and natural shelters, where lived those of the Wakambi who disliked the too modern idea of huts.

The Wakambi had fortified their settlement, not against attack by men because, as far as they knew, they were the only representatives of the human race in the fantastic and frightening land, but against the terrible beasts which no story-teller must ever describe – beasts known simply as the *Dija-Nwana*, or 'Night Howlers'. These terrible demons loved to raid human villages during their mating season in the first moon of summer, and they would carry away men, women and children and devour these in their dark dens on the shores of the mighty lake of the Falling Star – known today as Nyanza.

Those were terrible days – those days when the Dawn of Time was still red in the horizon of Eternity. Those were the days when Outcast Gods, Dimo Giants, Viper Maidens, Life Eaters and Fire Leopards and many other monsters, vicious and horrible beyond description, still roamed a frightened earth.

But let us not delude ourselves into thinking that these horrible creatures no longer exist; they do. They take human shapes and cause evil in the lands of men. They disguise themselves as human beings and cause mighty wars in the lands of the tribes before vanishing once more into the 'Land-that-is-and-is-not'. They leave thousands of foolish human beings to kill each other. They can take over the bodies of people whom we know and commit vile crimes as them. These Evil Ones are with us yet.

Kahawa waited with growing impatience for the coming of his friend, his feet itching to take off into the mysterious forest. He longed to see the red blood of a hateful lion splatter the earth.

At last *Mpushu* appeared, unarmed and very scared-looking indeed. His thick-lipped fish-like mouth opened and closed like that of one just speared by a fisherman. *Kahawa* was amazed. He was disgusted and annoyed when his fat friend suddenly gasped: 'My lord, we must not go and hunt this lion today.'

For a few moments *Kahawa* was too angry to speak. His one great wish was to send *Mpushu* flying to the ground with a blow from his fist. But with great effort he controlled himself, fighting down the savage rage – the fumes of which clouded his brain and dimmed his vision with a red haze. When he found his voice at last he said, coldly and in measured tones: 'I have always suspected you are a coward, Oh *Mpushu*, and now I am sure!'

Mpushu's eyes bulged and his ebony black face grew blacker. He swallowed noisily once and then said hoarsely: 'You know that I am no coward, Oh *Kahawa* . . . you know it!'

'If you are not a coward then go and get your weapons and let us proceed,' said *Kahawa*, still in the same cold voice.

A few moments later the two friends made their silent way down the hillside towards the brooding forest. *Kahawa* was thirsting for the blood of the old lion. His brain was already alive with pictures of himself standing triumphant over the old beast slowly dying at his feet.

But *Mpushu* was quaking with fear – fear from no earthly cause.

It was well past midday when the two friends, who had not spoken a single word to each other since leaving the settlement, came at last upon the trail of the lame old lion *Kahawa* had sworn to kill. They followed the trail from where the lion had eaten *Kahawa's* stepfather to where he had lain for the night. They followed the trail thence to where he had brought down a young impala which he had only partly eaten. They followed the trail from the carcass to where the old beast himself lay peacefully under an overhanging rock not far from the northern shore of the great 'Lake of the star that fell'.

It was *Mpushu* who first saw the lion lying there, the many battle scars on his tawny hide plainly visible. His eyes were still shining with that fire of greatness and unconquerable courage that one finds in all these noble beasts. Lonely, mateless and weak with age, this lion was still as regal as he had been in his younger days. A chief dethroned in some savage woodland battle, yea, but a chieftain nevertheless.

'Your lion, my lord,' whispered *Mpushu*.

A gleam of demon-like delight burst upon the cold eyes of *Kahawa*. He raised his long spear with the needle-sharp point of bone and covered himself with his knee-length shield of elephant hide. Slowly he approached the lion with *Mpushu* close behind him.

He was about ten paces away from it when the beast turned his head and swept both his would-be attackers with his burning golden stare. He watched them as they came through the long grass, quietly, almost contemptuously, and he did not even move a muscle. His teeth bared and his eyes narrowed as *Kahawa* ventured another step or two. But for the rest he just lay there, calmly watching the hunters.

Suddenly *Kahawa* felt his fierce courage deserting him. Suddenly he was not a warrior thirsting for blood but a puzzled young boy facing a situation he could not understand. Lowering his spear he turned and looked at his friend – just in time to see *Mpushu* also lowering his spear, which he had held poised a thumb's length above *Kahawa's* kidneys.

'You treacherous jackal! You were trying to stab me from behind! Are you mad?'

'No, my prince. I had made it my unpleasant duty to kill you in order to stop you from killing this lion.'

'What are you talking about, *Mpushu*?' asked Kahawa in blank amazement. 'You ... my friend ... would have killed me ... and you yourself suggested it.'

'I would not have allowed you to take another step closer to the lion, my lord. You see, that lion is set there as a trap by the gods. If you kill that beast the Wakambi will be exposed to total annihilation.'

Kahawa's face was a mask of sheer astonishment and open-mouthed surprise. He stared at his friend for a few moments as if doubting his sanity. Then he said: 'You are talking gibberish like a drunken monkey, Oh *Mpushu*; I beg you to make yourself clear.'

'After I left you last night, Oh Eagle of *Marimba*,' said *Mpushu* in his customary respectful tone of voice, 'I went straight into the soft valleys of slumber. Then I had a dream such as I have never had before in all my life. I dreamt that you and I went into the forest to hunt this lion you see lying there. The dream was so clear that even now I am still amazed at its clarity and accuracy. In my dream we came upon the lion exactly as you see him here, and that clump of herbs between his paws was there, in clear detail. I saw you stab the lion, and just as you withdrew your spear the lion changed into the princess *Marimba*, your mother, and she screamed at you while lying there, blood pouring from her mouth.

'I woke up with a start, but a few moments later I must have drifted off to sleep again. I dreamt the same dream over again – exactly the same, in every detail. Early this morning I went to see that toothless crone *Namuwiza*, the priestess, who told me that she too had a dream similar to mine, only longer and more detailed. She said I must prevent you at all costs from killing the lion, because if you did the whole Wakambi settlement would be wiped out this very night by a race of men who never smile, a race of men from the north. Both you and I would be slain and your immortal mother would be carried away.'

For a long time after *Mpushu* had finished talking, Kahawa still stared at him like a man in a deep trance. Then, dropping his weapons, the son of *Marimba* approached the old lion and stood looking down at him. The old lion stared indifferently up at the human youth. There were tears in *Kahawa's* eyes as he turned to his friend and said, almost harshly: 'Come, let us go.'

Simba the lion watched the two humans turn and go, watched them until the forest swallowed them and they vanished forever from his sight. Disinterestedly, he wondered just what they had come to do to him and why they left without doing it.

Simba the lion was overcome by a great weakness; he wanted to stay just where he was, come what may. He was aware of a deep sense of contentment and peace, and a pleasant weakness was slowly creeping through the valleys of his brain like heavy, soothing mist. He slowly lowered his shaggy head between his great front paws as the gathering mists in his mind made his head feel very heavy.

Softly he closed his eyes. He never opened them again.

Mpushu and his subdued, strangely silent friend *Kahawa* were still some distance from the hilltop settlement that was their home when the son of *Marimba* said to the older youth quietly: '*Mpushu*, do not look behind you now. Neither must you show any signs of fear or excitement – but we are being followed by a strange man and he is not far behind.'

'Is ... is he one of the Evil Ones ... a Life Eater maybe?' stammered *Mpushu*, his teeth chattering with fear.

'I know not, *Mpushu*, but this much I am sure of – he is following us to find out where we stay, and at all costs we must not let him discover the settlement!'

'What ... what are we going to do?'

'We must ambush him, kill or capture him,' said *Kahawa* coldly. 'I saw his face through the corner of my eye as he looked over a bush some time back, Oh *Mpushu*, and I know he is not one of our people. His hair, for one thing, is of a strange hair-style, with a bundle above his forehead.'

'Where can he have come from?'

'I do not know, but I think we have been wrong in thinking that we, the Wakambi, are the only human beings in this land. There is another race of men we have not realised existed, and that man following us is a member of this race.'

'And this means that ...' gasped *Mpushu*.

'This means that our first duty now is to reach the settlement and alert the people. But first we must dispose of that man behind us. Now this is what we must do ...'

The stranger was tall and lean, and there was an inbred viciousness about him that made *Marimba* sick with fear. Although he was now unarmed and bound securely hand and foot with strong thongs of kudu skin, he still looked dangerous and the Wakambi warriors standing around him seemed to worry him not in the least. In fact, he looked up at them as if they were just so much useless vermin.

Mpushu and *Kahawa* had carried the tall stranger between them for a long distnace after knocking him unconscious with a stone when he blundered upon their ambush. They had brought him to the base of the hill of the settlement and shouted to the guards to help them with their captive. They had tied him securely and brought him to *Marimba*, who was trying her best to interrogate him, without any response.

'We mean you no harm,' she was saying; 'we only want to know who you are ... and from where you come.'

'Humph,' grunted the stranger.

'I know you are not a Life Eater or a Night Howler,' pleaded *Marimba*. 'You are a new race of man we never knew existed. Tell me, to what race do you belong and where are the rest of your people?'

'Huh,' growled the stranger.

'This creature will not answer your questions, Oh *Marimba*,' cackled the toothless witch *Namuwiza*. 'But I know why he was following the two young men. He is a scout for a large force of other creatures like him which is even now a quarter of a day's journey from here . . . and coming fast.'

'How do you know this, Oh honourable wise woman *Namuwiza*?' asked the princess, turning her beautiful, troubled face to look at the scrawny hag.

The old woman cackled a weird witch-laugh: 'Little *Namuwiza* dreamt it all last night, all by her sweet self . . .'

'To me, all warriors!' cried *Kahawa* fiercely. 'All available spear-men to me! They must not catch us unprepared . . . whoever they are. All warriors to my side – recall all hunting parties from the forest. Bring out every spear, every axe in the village . . .'

The people hurried into action, inspired by their fierce leader *Kahawa*. Great bundles of bone-tipped spears and harpoons were brought out while blasts from horn bugles recalled the hunting parties from the forest. Men ran hither and thither spreading the word throughout the great settlement.

Oblivious to the burst of activity around her, the princess *Marimba* was kneeling down beside the trussed-up stranger, study-ing him with great interest and curiosity, not unmixed with fear and admiration. The stranger was a man such as she had never seen before – handsome and yet very evil looking: one who could, she imagined, kill thousands of fellow men without the slightest pang of pity or remorse. She saw his long nar-row face with its high forehead and square jaw. She saw his thin-lipped cruel mouth with its hard wrinkles at the corners. She saw his strange-looking long nose and deepset hard eyes, from whose depths gleamed the fire of resentment. She saw the strange hair-style – the thick bundle of plaited hair gathered above the forehead and tied firmly with a fine skin cord that went around the head to another bigger bundle jutting out like a woman's breast at the back of his head. She saw how his ears were pierced above and below, with heavy copper ear-rings that weighed them down. She saw ten necklaces made from the bones of human fingers and claws of lions and leopards adorning his neck. Lastly she saw his long spear lying some distance away where *Mpushu* had thrown it, with the other strange weapons the stranger carried.

This spear was not bone-tipped like those of the Wakambi. It was tipped with a heavy shard of *ligwadla* rock, and the princess noted with great relief that the spear, though formidable looking and heavy, was inferior to the bone-tipped Wakambi lances, because the latter could be sharpened, while when the more fragile stone point became broken the whole head had to be replaced.

But the other weapon filled *Marimba* with fear. It seemed that the stranger relied mostly on this weapon. It was a great bow with a well greased string and a heavy quiver full of stone-tipped arrows.

The bow was unknown to the Wakambi and many warriors were standing around and looking down at it in obvious puzzlement and dismay. It was clearly a deadly weapon and the Wakambi had no answer to it.

It was *Mpushu* who found the secret of opening the stranger's tight-lipped mouth after all else had failed. He merely strode up to the prisoner and said in cold disgust: 'Whatever race spawned a miserable coward like this one is indeed very unlucky. Just look at him lying there; he is almost wetting his loinskin with fear and yet he tries to look brave!'

The stranger's eyes narrowed with anger and his gleaming teeth were bared in savage rage. His voice, heavy with a foreign accent, was barely a whisper as he said in clear though halting Si-Wakambi: 'What did you call me?'

Mpushu whistled jubilantly. 'So the beast can talk, can it? It is not dumb after all! I called you a coward, Oh vermin, and that you most certainly are.'

'Untie my hands and feet, then we can talk further . . .'

'Untie your limbs?' exclaimed *Mpushu* in mock surprise, to drag out more conversation. 'But we have only just caught you.'

'You miserable fat idiot!' bellowed the stranger. 'I'll tear you limb from limb as soon as I am free of these bonds.'

'No loinskin-wetting foreign coward is ever going to tear me apart,' said *Mpushu* happily. 'And especially not a starveling like you.'

'I am no starveling,' roared the stranger. 'You are speaking to a Masai, you bloated dog!'

'You are what?' asked *Mpushu*, highly amused, 'a Makai? What is a Makai? From what slime-pit does a Makai crawl? It sounds like some kind of carrion worm.'

'I said I am a Masai!' bellowed the captive. 'And soon you will be cracking your stupid jokes in the land of the dead. The armies of my father, *Fesi* the Wolf, are very close at hand. You will all be dead by midnight.'

'But what have we done that you wish to make war on us?' asked *Marimba* softly, now that the prisoner's tongue was thoroughly loosened.

'The Masai need no reason for making war,' sneered the captive. 'They fight whom they please, whenever and wherever they feel like it.'

'But you are human like us, and you cannot kill people for no reason,' protested the beautiful woman.

'The Masai are more than human. They are invincible and their might in war is beyond all human might,' boasted the prisoner. 'The Masai are gods and 'tis you who are low-down human vermin.'

'Oh!' breathed *Marimba*. Her breasts heaved and a rare flash of anger brightened her large eyes briefly.

'The Masai are the "Great People", the true lords of Creation. To us, war and killing are the very breath of life, more pleasant than a woman's kiss, and more heady than *marula* beer.'

'For a captive in enemy hands you have far too big a mouth,' said *Kahawa* coldly. 'I am strongly tempted to take a deep breath of your life, if you find such an experience so recommendable.'

'A Masai welcomes death at any time it chooses to come, and in whatever guise it comes. So your childish threat is wasted on me.'

'You persistently praise your race,' said *Mpushu* brutally. 'But we are far from impressed. To us you sound like a zombie repeating words that some wizard has taught you. You are a poor example of the human race.'

'My soul, my body, my life, my whole being belongs to *Nangai* of the Mountains,' said the man in a terribly inhuman tone. '*Nangai* commands, I obey. *Nangai* is everything, I am nothing.'

'Who is *Nangai*?' asked Marimba.

'*Nangai* is the One who Is. *Nangai* is the One who commands and is heard.'

The little witch *Namuwiza* cackled weirdly. 'These poor Masai are a race under the cruel spell of an outcast god who lives in the forests of Killima-Njaro. Little *Namuwiza* knows it all . . . Te-he-he-he . . .'

The hunting parties had all returned safely and the great gate was securely shut. The Wakambi were in tense readiness as they scanned the forests below for the first sign of the oncoming enemy. Night was falling fast and the land was once more shrouded in mystery.

On the high palisades warriors stood to arms – hard-eyed and tense in every muscle – waiting for the Masai to come storming up the slopes of the ancient hill on which the First Village stood. As the night crept across the land with its sombre mantle, people became touchy and easily irritated, but they remained hard of eye and grim of face. The First Village ever built in the land was under the shadow of suspense and was firmly gripped in the cruel claws of the vulture of fear. Then the people heard a strange sound: a sound that was not of this world, that flowed through the silent dusk like a silver river through dark forests.

It was a sound such as no human ears have ever heard before. It penetrated the very depths of the soul like cool water down a thirsty throat – like oil, soothing oil killing a cruel pain. Men stared at each other with incredulous wonder. Others groaned, and wept, blatantly and without shame.

It was a sound of unearthly beauty, and to the surprise of everybody it came from the throat of *Marimba!*

She had taken the deadly bow of the captive Masai and had fitted a gourd to the middle of the bow itself, transforming the deadly weapon of war thus into the first *makweyana* bow-harp the world had ever seen. Not only had *Marimba* invented the first musical instrument, but she was singing the world's first song as well:

> Oh, little star so far above—
> Oh, smiling moon up yonder;
> You who on these fruitful vales
> Shed, aye, your heatless light.
>
> Carry my song on the wings of your light—
> Bear my refrains to the ends of the world;
> Carry my voice to the Land of the Gods
> Beyond the plains of Tura-ya-Moya.
>
> Tell the Great Ones that live there forever—
> Tell those that rule all the stars up above—
> Tell the mother of all the seas and the earth
> Beyond the plains of Tura-ya-Moya:
>
> Tell them that though the hyaenas of death
> Prowl without my kraal tonight—
> Tell them that all these perils I'll face
> And that I'll never cringe nor cower.
>
> Tell them that I, their humble servant maid,
> Shrink not from the scowl of a foe—
> For they who have the Great God as ally
> Are twice the victors in war!
>
> Tell them their servant implores them
> For strength and their guidance true;
> Mad is he who through Life's swamplands goes
> Without the guides from Tura-ya-Moya!

The Wakambi gathered in awe around their princess, their eyes wide open like so many astonished children. They had never heard a human being sing before. Never before had they heard sounds like those that streamed forth from the bow-harp as the princess gracefully struck the string with a short length of cane. They joined her as the magic of the song overwhelmed them, and soon the whole settlement was singing.

Their voices, most discordant from lack of experience, rang out across the startled heavens and the sleeping forests echoed and re-echoed to the heavenly strains of Tura-ya-Moya.

And the vast Masai armies advancing through the forests upon the Wakambi settlement paused in bewildered confusion as that unearthly melody reached their ears faintly across the dark distance.

'*Nangai* of the Mountains, save us!'

Like a deadly flower growing in a meadow of green grass, another strange idea was born in the brain of the princess *Marimba* as she sang. This idea had nothing to do with music; it had a lot to do with death – soon to be meted out to the advancing Masai!

She promptly ordered her warriors to cut broad, long strips of strong kudu hide while she organised the women into gathering piles of round stones in strategic positions behind the palisades. This done, the princess called her commanders together and explained to them the use of the slings of hide with the stone shot. The men listened in blank amazement as the incredible woman explained the use of this simple and yet deadly weapon that she had just invented.

The night was as dark as the face of death. A mighty storm was building up its wrath in the east and into the ears of *Kahawa* came muted peals of savage thunder and he also saw the distant flickers of searing lightning. *Kahawa* was alone; he was one of the many guards posted all along the narrow walk inside the great stockade to give the alarm should the Masai risk a night attack. He was excited and his pounding heart beat faster than usual. This was war. This was no stupid conflict between mere clans over a mere trifle. This was the real thing: war in its deadliest form, a war between two different races of men!

Never since the very dawn of time had the land seen anything like it – two different races locked in a battle to death.

Kahawa was impatient; he wanted the Masai to come quickly so that the battle might begin sooner. He wanted to see the effectiveness of the weapons used by either tribe and especially the effectiveness of his mother's latest invention. Its effect should be devastating indeed!

A soft footfall induced him to whirl around, his heavy war club firmly gripped in his hand. But he gave a sigh of relief when a well-known and beloved voice said softly through the darkness: '*Kahawa*?'

'Mother!' whispered *Kahawa* fiercely, 'what are you doing here?'

'I, too, am a warrior, *Kahawa*,' came the rich voice from the darkness. 'My son must not think that he is the only one who knows no fear. His mother is fearless too.'

The dark shape that was *Marimba* moved closer to her son and a far-off flash of lightning was reflected briefly from the copper ornaments she wore. *Kahawa* felt a strong urge to tell his beloved parent to stop being foolish and to retire to her hut. *Kahawa* loved no one on earth more than he loved his mother and it did not matter if the whole Wakambi nation were wiped out, as long as his mother was safe. It was understandable therefore that his mother's next words filled him with an insane rage and an unquenchable hatred of the Masai.

'Kahawa, I wonder whether it would not be wise for me to surrender myself to the Masai when they come. It might stop them from attacking the village, and stop a needless war.'

'Mother! What in the name . . .'

'Listen child, that Masai you captured has been talking to us again. He told us the Masai have known for a long time that we were here. They have known about us for many generations but have simply chosen to leave us alone and continue fighting amongst themselves as they had always done. But some while ago their evil outcast god *Nangai*, who has enslaved the very souls of the Masai, ordered them to attack us and, after wiping our tribe out, bring me back to him alive.'

'Bring you to him!' cried *Kahawa* furiously. 'And what does he want to do with you?'

It seems that when *Nangai* was driven out of the land of the gods he was wounded grievously by an arrow of *Mulungu*, the Father of Light, and he has been bleeding slowly out of existence ever since. His left arm has been almost completely eaten away by the poison from *Mulungu's* arrow and he is dying the slow death of an immortal god. In order to survive he needs the living flesh of another immortal, a human immortal, to consume raw. He must also drink a little of that immortal's blood every day. And I happen to be the only immortal within reach.'

'*Ayieeee!*' cried *Kahawa* in utter disgust. 'You must not think of surrendering yourself to that foul monster, Oh my mother. I cannot bear to think of you being mutilated by that ogre!'

'My son, there is no other way. *Nangai* is dying fast and he is getting desperate. If he cannot get me one way he will the other, even if it means annihilating the entire Wakambi tribe. I cannot let this happen. I love the Wakambi people too much to be the cause of their destruction.'

With that she turned to go and *Kahawa* felt like a man who had been stabbed to the heart. His mother was his very life and she was the only person for whom he had any love. He did not relish the prospect of losing his only surviving parent. Come what may, he was not going to allow his mother to surrender herself to *Nangai.*

He leapt after the departing silhouette and struck her a stunning blow on the back of her head with his war club. Using two of the five battle slings he had with him, he tied the heavenly form of his unconscious parent securely hand and foot. He then carried her to a small cave near the summit of the hill and gently laid her down within, rolling a great boulder over the mouth of the cave.

As he turned away from the cave the Masai launched the long-awaited attack. It was as sudden as it was ferocious. One moment the settlement had been wrapped in silence, with the distant growls of the oncoming storm the only sounds heard; the next moment alarm horns were sounding all along the stockade as keen-eyed night guardsmen saw shadowy figures creeping up the boulder-strewn slopes towards the village.

Wakambi warriors burst out of their huts and raced for the stockades as a withering storm of Masai arrows fell upon the village. Men and women caught in the open screamed hideously as falling arrows tore into their bodies. But the palisades were manned by then and the Wakambi were fighting back fiercely. About five thousand battle slings snapped and a hail of humming stones decimated the first wave of attacking Masai warriors. The survivors dived back into cover, from where they directed a hurricane of arrows at the settlement.

Covered by the fire from the survivors of the first wave, a second Masai attack-wave erupted from the darkness, rushing against the palisades. Though another humming tornado of slingstones mowed into this wave, too. Men died horribly in the battle-torn night; they died as slingstones crashed through their skulls or thudded into their bodies. They fell screaming as stones, as large as fists and larger, shattered their arm bones and shins.

A group of Masai reached the stockade in one place and tried to climb it. A fierce hand-to-hand battle ensued. Spears of all descriptions were flourished – bone-tipped and stone-headed; heavy wooden clubs and maces with heads of stone or copper; axes with heads of bone or common granite – all these hacked, smashed and thrust pitilessly. Quite a few Wakambi found the massive jaws of hippopotami most useful, and amongst these was *Mpushu* the Cunning.

The battle raged till well past midnight while the storm crept nearer and nearer, adding its own senseless fury to the clamour of the fighting below.

Twice on that horrible night the son of *Marimba* hurled back single-handed groups of Masai climbing the stockade; he was wounded thrice in the fierce fighting.

The angry storm put an end to the battle. The wildly furious thunder crashed and boomed its anger at the struggling human creatures down below. Men were deafened and shocked by the loud peals of unearthly thunder. The ground shook and vibrated as the voice of the Thunder Demon tore through the very fibre of the earth and the rain-pregnant clouds seemed to burst into hideous flame as sheets of purplish-white lightning ripped them to shreds of billowing, whirling wool. Bolt after bolt of forked lightning split the heavens apart as an axe splits the head of a man. And then, with a flare of flame as bright as the midday sun and a crack that sent even the bravest of the brave cowering down like whimpering children, a bolt of lightning split a tall *mopani* tree from the crown to the very roots.

Rain had not yet started to fall, but the Masai broke away and fled. The Wakambi, too, ran like so many rabbits for the safety of their huts and caves. A roaring fire was started in the forest by the lightning that had struck the *mopani* tree and hungry flames leaped high with joy, like a Sunfish Maiden leaping and writhing at a kiss from her lover. Shrill screams were heard above the shattering anger of the storm as Masai, frightened out of their wits, ran through the burning forest to escape the deadly embrace of the flames. Many were caught by the grumbling wind-fanned fire and burnt to death, shrieking like insane women for their traitor god to save them.

Then hail came, as big as babies' fists, in a howling curtain to scourge the dazed earth with insane mercilessness.

The storm thundered for the best part of the midnight hour and the Wakambi cringed and cowered in the darkness of their huts and caves. But gradually the storm spent its passion and the midnight winds of heaven carried the angry clouds away. A silence deeper than the deepest wells fell upon the dazed land. It was an eerie silence that was as ugly as it was frightening; it was the silence of Death.

'Listen, Oh *Kahawa*,' whispered the grizzled old witchdoctor *Somojo*. 'Listen!'

'I hear nothing, Oh *Somojo*,' whispered *Kahawa*.

'Yes, my prince, that is what I mean – the silence is unusual. And yet it is terribly familiar!'

'It is like the silence that precedes an attack by the Night Howlers,' said *Mpushu* soberly.

'The Night Howlers only attack in early summer,' argued *Kahawa*, 'and now it is well into late summer.'

The frightened men lapsed once more into silence and the Great Silence seemed to deepen. *Kahawa* found his thoughts drifting towards his mother. He found himself wondering how she was faring in the dark cave in which he had imprisoned her. Heedless of his cruel throbbing wounds, he rose and made for the door of the hut. He never passed through it.

The hut was torn apart as though it were a ball of cobwebs, showering the petrified men inside with grass and broken twigs. *Kahawa* looked up and found himself staring into the great redly luminous eyes of a creature of unbelievable proportions whose dark silhouette obstructed the stars now peering through the clouds – a nightmare creature which had grasped the big hut in its vulture-like talons and was slowly and gloatingly tearing it apart to get at the men inside.

For a few moments the brave son of *Marimba* was paralysed with fear. He stared with hypnotic fascination deep into the huge eyes of the Night Howler – eyes that blazed like glowing embers, lined with veins that glowed like red-hot copper. The burning split pupils were the size of warriors' shields.

Then *Kahawa* instinctively hurled his war club, landing it straight in one of the Night Howler's eyes. The eye shattered and the glowing fluid poured down to the ground while the huge monstrosity let out a howl that split the night in two. Other Night Howlers descended upon their wounded comrade and quickly devoured him.

Others were still raising havoc amongst the huts. Most people managed to flee in wild terror into the caves, but quite a number were caught in the open and these were being driven into one area. Stray ones were promptly gobbled down. Many a warrior who had fought like a thousand lions, defending his wife and children against the alien Masai only a while earlier, ran like a rabbit, wetting his loinskin all the way and screaming like a mad girl, while a bloody-jawed Night Howler played havoc with those same wives and children.

Only *Mpushu* and his badly wounded friend *Kahawa* had the courage to fight, urged by their initial stroke of success. Already between them they could account for six of the hideous hell-monsters. They had accidentally discovered that the Night-Howlers' eyes were most vulnerable and easy targets in the dark. And each time they succeeded in hitting the target the creature would cringe and fall and many others would settle upon it, giving the tribe a brief respite.

The newly invented slings turned out to be most formidable weapons and practice was making *Kahawa* and *Mpushu* quite expert in their aim.

The great settlement was already razed to the ground and all the people who could not reach the safety of the caves were concentrated by the Night Howlers into one panic-striken madly screaming mob, ready for an orgy of devouring. But they were waiting as though to commence on a particular command.

Mpushu and *Kahawa* knew they were fighting their last battle. Their arms were numb through handling the slings without pause and they knew it was now simply a matter of time before they too were overwhelmed. Finally, they decided they could do nothing about those already herded together and they made off to reach the safety of a cave. As *Mpushu* turned to flee, a strange manly voice halted him in blank astonishment:

'My friends, I am with you.'

Kahawa, too, turned to look at their newly found friend and got the shock of his life. Running with them was the tall Masai whom they had captured earlier – *Koma-Tembo.*

This totally unexpected ally put new strength into the two young men and, standing together, the three of them took a heavy toll of the Night Howlers. They fought until a voice of no earthly origin rang out as though from the empty air above their heads:

'Lay down your weapons, oh mortals, and yield yourselves into my mercy. I am *Nangai* and when I command I am obeyed.'

The three men dropped their slings to the blood-stained ground in paralysed amazement. They could vaguely discern a queer apparition in midair above them. They knew very well what *Nangai* wanted even before he spoke.

'Where is the immortal female *Marimba*?'

No one answered. *Mpushu* noticed that silence had once more claimed the village – or what was left of it. The Night Howlers were silently awaiting further instructions.

'I asked you a question, young mortal dog!'

'*Marimba* is my mother, Oh Nangai, and I have taken her to a place of safety. You, and even the Most Ultimate God will reach her only over my dead body!'

'*Nangai* is not here to bandy words with immature mortals and he does not appreciate childish sentiments. Bring forth the female *Marimba*!'

'The mighty god *Nangai* can go and relieve himself in a rat hole!'

'Wretched mortal, you obey my command this instant, or I shall pass further instructions to my beasts that howl in the night.'

Kahawa knew the meaning of naked fear for the first time in his life. He knew that *Nangai* was serious and that gods, high or low, active or outcast, never make idle threats. They are not burdened with a conscience like human beings, nor are they loaded with emotion. A god does not know the meaning of love or loyalty; these are human weaknesses. Only the Goddess *Ma* suffers from these weaknesses and we have inherited ours from her.

'You keep me waiting, miserable mortal. I give you ten more heartbeats!'

Mpushu began to weep. He tried to implore *Nangai*, but the god ignored him and addressed himself only to *Kahawa*. The Night Howlers looked appealingly at *Nangai*, waiting for the order to commence their delicious meal. *Nangai* ignored them just as he ignored *Mpushu*.

'Well, mortal, your time is up.'

There was no reply from *Kahawa*. Through further moments of silence *Kahawa's* hand closed firmly around the hilt of his bone dagger and *Mpushu* saw a gleam of unearthly light in the eyes of his young friend. Then very calmly *Kahawa* measured his words: 'My answer is still No, Oh *Nangai*!'

The young prince *Kahawa* half-drew his bone dagger from its sheath. Into his eyes there came a look that *Mpushu* could not at first explain. It was the look that comes into the eyes of one who has just had a shattering inspiration, one who has suddenly found the answer to a problem that had been gnawing at the back of his mind with the persistence of a rat. *Mpushu* saw his friend direct a stare of unspeakable contempt at the god *Nangai* floating on his throne in empty air. Then the young *Kahawa* sneered right into the god's face, sneered as one sneers at a human enemy whom one holds beneath contempt.

Suddenly the eyes of the god blazed with cold, murderous fury. He realised that a dead *Kahawa* was more unlikely to speak than a live *Kahawa*. He made a snap signal to the nearest Night Howler, who promptly snatched up *Kahawa* and held him aloft in one vulture-like claw.

'Now, mortal, speak or you shall die!'

Kahawa began to laugh, a harsh, contemptuous and insulting laugh. The Night Howlers stared first at him and then at *Nangai* in great puzzlement and even the human beings huddled together looked at the son of *Marimba* in blank amazement.

'Under the sun that shines in the skies above,' *Kahawa* said at last, 'there is nothing more tragic, more pathetic, than a creature once great and powerful, still clinging with stubborn tenacity to the tattered shreds of his vanished power. There is nothing more tragic than the sight of this creature trying to deceive itself and others into thinking that it still holds the power it held in the past. You are such, *Nangai*, you are no longer a god. You are nothing but a slightly higher form of common demon. When *Mulungu* drove you from the golden valleys of Tura-ya-Moya like a wounded and beaten cur he also stripped you of your immortal powers. You use force, *Nangai*, you torture like a common human thug. You used to have powers with which, if you had retained them, you could have learnt the whereabouts of my mother by simply reading my mind. Using force is an admission of failure. You are a failure, a pathetic fetish that-once-was and the Masai are your dupes. You send them in force to attack the whole settlement when all you could have done was to render yourself invisible, enter our village unseen and carry my mother away. You had to have help – on a large scale at that – you wretched fallen fetish . . .'

'Silence, mortal dog! When I wish to hear your raving and idiotic prattling I'll ask for it! Where is your mother?'

'Find her yourself . . . use your godly powers . . .'

Nangai gave a brisk command to the Night Howler, who slowly started sinking his talons into the flesh of *Kahawa*.

It was just then that a miracle happened – a miracle in the form of a song that came floating through the night air like a ghost of pure mercy and deliverance. This song had a magic spell about it. It stunned the fiendish Night Howlers. There was a musical instrument in the singer's hands which in future years became known as the *karimba* or *kalimba*. This unearthly music sent a haunting melody through the night and wove a mighty spell around the squatting Night Howlers. It paralysed them – destroyed them.

They let out a mighty roar in unison and, as though they had all become victims of an alien virulent leprosy, their scaly flesh began to slough off their skeletons and to flow sluggishly down the slope of the clearing in the ruined village. Wisps of reeking steam erupted from their distended slime-green bellies as their foul bowels burst with sounds terrible to hear, and from these wisps floated the ghosts of the people they had already devoured.

These ghosts were happy – happy to escape and float away to the land of Forever-Night, there to await their reincarnation.

But first they joined in the song sung by the woman with the *kalimba*. They soared and dived and soared again. They danced and weaved and leaped in the dark night air, and a regiment of them capsized the evil *Nangai's* throne and he fell like a lump of cow dung into the reeking, oozing slime that had been the flesh of the Night Howlers. All the people who had been herded together became caught in the webs of the Song of the *Kalimba.* They tore off their soiled loinskins, skirts and ornaments, flung them aside, and raised their arms in thanksgiving to the High Gods for their deliverance, after which they too joined in the sacred Song of the *Kalimba.*

Dead and living joined in and the very stars rejoiced. The gods wept crystal tears and bowed their heads in tribute and acclaim. *Marimba* led the hosts of dead and living with her song until the eastern sky greyed with the first promise of coming dawn.

Eventually she dropped her *kalimba* and ran to where her son was lying. She threw her arms around him and wept. She kissed his forehead and both his ears and, drawing him close to her soft breasts, she wept long and loud, tears not of sorrow but of pride and pure joy and unfathomable happiness. When she released him *Kahawa* did something which shocked his gentle parent and the rest of the Wakambi but which was to become a firm Law of the Tribes in generations to come. With an abandoned axe of sharpened stone he deliberately chopped off his own right hand.

With the bleeding stump raised high, he addressed the shocked Wakambi: 'People of the Wakambi, with this gesture I am laying down a new law that you must accept with your hearts and souls, and make it part of your lives until the rending of the knot of Time. In order to prevent my parent from delivering herself to the evil *Nangai,* I had to strike her unconscious with a club before I could hide her. But the ends do not justify the means; I broke the very Law of the Stars by striking the sacred vessel that carried me for more than nine agonising moons. Let this be your law, your very *siko,* that anyone, male or female, who strikes his or her mother for any reason, shall forfeit his or her right hand – voluntarily or otherwise. By this *siko* I beg my ancestors to cleanse me, and my children's children, of the foul taint of my sin, and I also beg the forgiveness of both *Ma* the Great Mother, and of the beautiful *Marimba,* who is my mother.'

'My son, my dear child, did you have to do it?' *Marimba* caught her son as he sagged to the ground and everybody crowded around to assist with easing the agony of the brave prince. *Kahawa* smiled up at his mother and whispered: 'Tell me mother, how did you manage to escape from the cave?'

'I did not, son; I was rescued by the witchwoman *Namuwiza* and her two sons just before the Night Howlers devoured them, and I spent some time making this instrument to help you . . .'

Kahawa heard no more as unconsciousness claimed him.

* * *

A great happiness settled over the land and the Wakambi prospered and multiplied, so they could afford to wrinkle their noses at the Masai in contempt and defiance. The Masai were forever freed of the evil spell of the traitor god *Nangai*, though they never lost their stiff-necked pride and their arrogance, which was like a disease.

Marimba invented many more songs: love songs, hunting songs and even songs to sing when a beloved one was interred. She invented the xylophone, which is still called the *marimba* to this day.

People sang and whistled and their souls were uplifted by the melodies and tunes their immortal queen had given them. For the first time since the escape of *Odu* and *Amarava* from the destroyed land of the First People, human beings held feasts and dances and came to know again the soothing joy that beautiful tunes bring to depressed and life-weary souls.

For a full ten years *Marimba* refused marriage. She sturdily resisted the powerful demands of her own bothersome body and endured the searing agony of lonely nights of weeping herself to sleep. She saw her son happily married to two Wakambi girls and prospering in general happiness. She saw more villages of Wakambi clans built to accommodate the spreading population. Soon the original settlement became the High Village of a small empire which she ruled with wisdom that only an immortal can possess.

As the years wore on she found it more and more difficult to resist the ardent wooing of her greatest suitor, *Koma-Tembo*, the lion-hearted Masai whom *Kahawa* had captured and who had stood side by side with him against the evil god and the Night Howlers, so many years earlier.

Then one night that which was written in the stars and destined to happen, did happen! *Lo*, not even immortals are immune to fate.

The hut was dark. The hut was lonely. And in its dark interior on a pile of lion and leopard skin blankets reclined, in queenly solitude, one of the most beautiful women that ever trod this earth – *Marimba* the peerless, *Marimba* the Goddess of Music, the Goddess of Happiness.

There was a deep sadness in her long-lashed eyes and a crystal-clear tear stole unbidden down the side of her flat little nose. The battle is hardest when one has oneself for an enemy, and *Marimba* was her own enemy in many ways. Outside the hut there was merriment. Hundreds of Wakambi were feasting and dancing round a great fire in the village clearing. The happy night rang with their laughter and lusty singing. The appetising smell of boiling and roasting meat was heavy in the night air. But she who had brought the happiness to her people was no partaker of it that night.

A dark shadow crawled into the hut through the low arched entrance and the immortal heart of *Marimba* stopped beating for a few misty moments. Well she knew who it was who had just slipped into the hut. It was the man whom she loved with all her immortality – a man she desired with every vein and artery in her hungry body. But she dared not accept him for fear of sealing his doom.

The reddish-yellow light of the distant feast fires played on one side of his manly face. It accentuated the deepset smouldering eyes and it made the hard lines about his imperious mouth and strong nose appear more harsh.

Koma-Tembo the Masai was, even though seated and at peace, a man born and bred to love, to command and to fight. *Marimba* watched him through misted eyes as he sat there near the door of the hut and longed for him as an impala longs for the cool waters of a woodland stream. Yet she was praying to the One Thousand Gods that the man should keep his distance and not come any nearer than he was. Well did the deathless woman know that should the great Masai come any closer her fiery emotions would betray her – and him!

'I see you, Oh *Koma-Tembo*,' she said with a great effort.

'And *Koma-Tembo* sees the bright sun of his life,' was his measured reply.

'*Koma-Tembo* basks in the sun that scorches,' she said, forcing a smile. 'There are suns in whose light it is not wise to sit.'

'I mind not being scorched by the sun that is the incomparable *Marimba*,' he said with a smile. 'Neither do I mind being drowned by the pure river that is she.'

'*Marimba* has told the woodheaded Masai many times why she cannot accept him as a husband,' said *Marimba*. 'And yet *Koma-Tembo* is as stubborn as a frog that refuses to be driven out of the hut with a broom.'

'From the incomparable *Marimba, Koma-Tembo* will never take No for an answer.'

Suddenly the princess lost her temper and even as the angry words poured from her mouth, her desire for this son of the Dragon of the Waters grew until it seemed like a mighty wave of burning lava from the fiery belly of Killima-Njaro. 'You are a fool, *Koma-Tembo!* You men are all stupid, stubborn fools! Your lust pulls you by the nose right into the valleys of undoing. You will never leave things well alone. I have told you a hundred times that I cannot accept you as my man, because you would be dead within three moons of our marriage. I am trying to save your life, you porridge-brained fool! You must now leave this hut immediately.'

'Before I leave your presence, Oh sun of my life, I must first hear you say you love me.'

This was too much for the tormented woman. Tears welled out of her eyes, wetting her face, and deep sobs shook her beautiful form. She turned and shrieked at the Masai: 'You know that I love you – you have known for two years. You only keep on asking because you like to torture me. Now get out of this hut quickly . . . *hamba! simbira!* You . . . you *mulila-busiko* . . . Night Howler!'

Koma-Tembo was astonished. His mouth hung open in a most un-Masai fashion. He had not known that his queen had been in love with him for two years already, and that she was held back from marrying him only by the curse on her head. Like all Masai, *Koma-Tembo* had little use for life – be it his own or anyone else's – and it was more pleasant for him to spend three moons with *Marimba* in love and happiness than a whole lifetime of suffering and loneliness. And as he advanced those few paces that separated him from the object of his love, *Koma-Tembo* knew very well that he had exactly three moons to live – but he also knew that each day of it would be worth more than a thousand lifetimes.

As he took his beloved gently into his battle-scarred arms, he told her so.

Marimba was shocked to feel the hands of the Masai on her. She shuddered and let out a small gasp of fear. Feebly she tried to push him away. But her arms, instead of thrusting, tightened about his neck and drew him closer, while her body strained savagely against him. Her willpower shattered against the rocks of desire and went flying into a million shards of rainbow-coloured crystal. What deadlier betrayer is there than one's own body? What fouler enemy had the human being than the desire that flows in the blood of his own veins? *Marimba* was lost.

Later – much later that night *Marimba* went out into the village clearing to join in the all-night feasting and dancing round the great fires. Never before had her people seen her more lively, more active and vivacious. She was the very fount of song and hilarity, and she danced like an uninhibited tempest ravaging a country.

But *Kahawa* was not deceived by his mother's cheerfulness. He saw through it clearly as through a crystal-clear drop of water. He had seen the tall Masai enter his mother's hut and he guessed the decision she had made even before she announced it to the cheering people.

Marimba had decided to marry again after more than ten years

– and she was going to suffer the agony of bereavement once again. All her cheerfulness, all her vivacity, was an attempt at shutting out of her mind this unpleasant fact.

It was a year-and-a-half later and the beautiful queen of the Wakambi was alone in the dark forest. She sat on the bank of the same river which, so many years ago, had seen her second husband attacked and devoured by an old lion. That same river had seen the death of *Koma-Tembo*, the valiant Masai, whom she had loved as she had never loved any other man before.

Koma-Tembo had gone out with about fifty hunters and snare diggers to trap a rhinoceros that had taken up residence near the river and had developed the habit of charging groups of women who came from the village to fetch water. As usual, *Koma-Tembo* had volunteered to take the most risky duty of all; this time he had chosen to be the decoy man. In this capacity he had to lure the beast towards the circle of great pits cleverly covered with poles and grass. Once inside the circle, the animal was provoked to blind fury by a shower of stones and sticks hurled by the other hunters who were hiding in the undergrowth. As decoy, *Koma-Tembo* had to expose himself at this stage and invite the beast to charge him. He would then lead the beast to one of the pits whose cover was strong enough to carry the weight of a human being, but not that of a heavy beast.

Koma-Tembo had successfully decoyed the furious rhinoceros right into one of the great snare-pits, but he had tripped and fallen into it himself. The Masai and the rhinoceros had met the same fate at the points of the deadly stakes planted in the bottom of the pit.

Marimba was disconsolate. She had taken to the habit of going alone into the forest merely to sit in a secluded spot and meditate – with her songs as her only company. But the people she ruled noticed that the more their queen suffered at the hands of the gods the more beautiful became the songs she composed and sang, and the more fantastic the musical instruments she invented.

She invented six different kinds of reed flutes, and pipes.

She was sitting alone near the river when *Kahawa*, now known as 'The Left-handed', came along the river bank at a run and in obvious excitement – a rare thing with him indeed!

'I am here, Oh *Kahawa*. I am over here.'

Kahawa came striding through the undergrowth. He was fully armed and he wore the usual hard expression on his face. But his brow was, in addition, clouded by a great puzzlement which surprised *Marimba* very much.

'What is the matter, Oh *Kahawa*?' she asked as she rose to her feet. 'What has happened, my child?'

'Come with me, Oh mother,' said *Kahawa* with barely concealed excitement. 'Come with me, for I have to show you yet the strangest sight of your life.'

Marimba followed her son through the dark scowling forest. She followed him through glades where the breeze whispered in the tall grass and through swamps where otters played amongst the reeds, and swamp birds nested in the tall *lubaqa*.

They went eastward towards the distant mountains and soon *Marimba* found herself paving a way up the boulder-strewn slopes while the ground fell gradually behind her. A cruel shrub armed with vicious dry thorns scratched her smooth immortal thigh, drawing blood of heavenly purity. She let out a small cry of pain and *Kahawa* whirled, his stone-headed mace gripped tightly and at the ready. Then he saw the scratch and the blood and a strange intense feeling he could not identify swept through the valleys of his soul.

'*Maie agwe!*' he cried; 'you are hurt, mother!'

'It is nothing, Oh my son. It is nothing but a scratch from a thorn-bush.'

'Sit down and rest, mother.'

'I am not tired, my child; we can still go on.'

'Mother, sit down,' commanded *Kahawa* fiercely.

'You are a true son of your father,' said the surprised woman with a weak smile as she sat down on a boulder. 'But you must not use force all the time, son; force destroys him who uses it.'

'Mother, force is good when used to defend or protect things that one holds dear, and to defend you I am prepared to use all the force in the world.'

'My son, you must never concentrate all your love on one thing or one person. You must learn to extend your love to the world in general, because you are part of it and the world is part of you.'

'I hear you, Oh mother,' said *Kahawa* softly.

'And above all, you must try and be a good husband to the two girls I gave you for wives, my son. They are always complaining that you come home with a terrible temper – you refuse to touch them and criticise the food they cook for you.'

'But mother,' protested *Kahawa*, 'I did not want to get married in the first place. I have no time for women. Besides, those two you gave me are the worst you could find. The first one, *Lozana*, is a frightened bore who chatters like a jungle monkey from dawn to dusk without pause, and the second, *Lukiko*, is a fat stupid idiot who not only reminds one of a lost buffalo stuck in the mud, but smells like one too, and has the brains of one . . .'

'My son!' cried the mother. 'What words are these? What horrible things are these that you are talking? It is your duty to beget children to carry your father's name on to generations to come and your personal feelings must never interfere with that duty. Whether you love your wives or not is beside the point. Now, *Kahawa*, I want to see either or both your wives pregnant in two months' time . . . and I shall tolerate no further back-talk from you!'

'Oh mother, I have far better things to do in life than begetting noisy bawling babies.'

Marimba was about to make a heated reply when she was interrupted by the sudden appearance from behind a boulder of *Kahawa's* friend, *Mpushu* the Cunning. *Mpushu* was sweating profusely from his hard climb up the hill. He threw himself on his knees and crossed his arms in front of his fat face in salutation to *Marimba*. Then he lifted his fish-like face and said to *Kahawa*: 'I have been down to the strange beasts, Oh Eagle of *Marimba*, and I have found out something that is a great surprise. The beasts are not only harmless but they are so docile that you can actually pull the ears of some of the females and they will follow you.'

'What strange beasts are you talking about, Oh *Mpushu*?' asked the puzzled *Marimba*.

'Come with me, Oh Mother; come and see,' *Kahawa* urged.

Puzzled, *Marimba* followed her son and his friend farther into the rocky hills of the north-east. They climbed over a hill and halfway down the other side they stopped. 'Look, mother, look down there in the valley.'

Marimba followed her son's pointing arm and her eyes met the strangest sight she had ever seen. The valley below was full of the strangest animals. These animals were like buffalo but a shade smaller and, unlike the buffaloes which are all the same colour, these animals ranged in colour from black to dark brown, from red to white. Many of them were either brown-and-white, black-and-white, or had brown bodies and white bellies. All had horns that were totally unlike anything *Marimba* had seen before.

'What are they, my son?'

'I do not know for sure, mother, but from what I gathered from the survivors of the people who brought them here, they are known as tame animals, mother.'

'Tame animals? They look dangerous enough to me.'

'They are quite docile, mother, and there is something about them one does not find amongst wild beasts.'

'How did you find them, my son?'

'*Mpushu* and I had been out on a hunt, mother. We saw these strange animals from where we are standing now. At first we thought they were a kind of antelope and we decided to hunt them. But, strangely, they did not run when they saw us, neither did they charge us as buffaloes would. Then *Mpushu* noticed that there were people with the strange creatures and we went down to investigate. We found that all but one of these people were lying in the tall grass and dying of some sort of epidemic. We saw that there were ten men and three women, and all the men were either dead or dying fast, and that of the women, one was still alive. And she does not seem to be suffering from the malady at all.'

'Whence come these people, my son?'

'I do not know, mother. The surviving woman is too frightened of us to talk clearly. But when she does talk, it is a pleasure to listen.'

The surviving woman was hardly more than a girl, a pretty little thing with rather prominent front teeth, and with a skin that was as black as pure ebony. She wore her hair plaited into numerous tiny plaits that hung down her forehead and down her back. She wore an ankle-length skirt of leopard skin and a necklace of strange shining beads and sea shells. Broad bracelets of bronze blazed upon her arms and forearms. She looked up as *Marimba* came and stood facing her. Under the curious gaze of the immortal woman the strange girl lowered her eyes selfconsciously.

'Tell me, child,' said *Marimba* at last, 'where do you come from?'

It took some time for the strange girl to answer. 'From Nuba . . . we come . . .'

'Where is Nuba?'

'Away – far, far, far.'

'What are those animals you have brought with you?'

'Meat animals – we eat. Also milk – we drink.'

'You eat the meat of those animals, and drink their milk?'

'So – so we do.'

Then *Kahawa* asked the girl what had killed those people with whom she had been. In her strange halting way she explained that her father and his servants, and her mother, had eaten mushrooms cooked and served by the other female servant, who had also eaten some. The girl had been saved by the fact that at the time of the eating she had been suffering from a bad headache and had no appetite at all.

Marimba asked the girl what her father had been doing so far away from his native land. Her answer shocked *Kahawa* and brought tears into the eyes of *Marimba*. The girl said it was a belief among their people that if one travelled southward long enough one will eventually reach the Land of Peace. Her father had been a priest in their native land and a firm believer in this myth. He had taken all his wealth and wife, daughter and servants and had set out southwards in search of the Land of Peace.

Abruptly the little stranger girl threw herself into the arms of *Marimba* and begged for protection, as she now had no parents. It was customary in their land for orphans to be adopted, even by complete strangers, and would *Marimba* please adopt her and protect her? As for the cattle, would *Marimba* please take them?

As *Kahawa* and *Mpushu* rounded up the two thousand beasts and drove them towards the High Village of the Wakambi, *Marimba* asked the girl what her name was and the girl answered: '*Rarati* . . . it is this one . . . my name . . . respected *Ma-Rimba*.'

'*Rarati*,' said the princess *Marimba*, 'your name shall never be forgotten. Future generations shall hail you as the one who brought the secret of cattle-keeping into the Land of the Tribes. I greet you, Oh *Rarati*, my daughter.'

The beautiful queen of the Wakambi, the peerless *Marimba*, was walking through the forest with her handmaidens on her way to the riverside to bathe her body in the cool waters. Birds sang in the trees overhead and the forest was heavy with the scent of thousands of flowering shrubs. Myriads of butterflies and colourful insects were fluttering in clouds of white, blue and brown among the wild flowers and the buzzing song of *nyoshi*, the bee, was clearly heard in the blinding sunlight. Timid hares galloped through the long grass and the cooing voice of *le-iba*, the turtle dove, added yet more enchantment to an already enchanting day.

The sky was the purest of blue. Only a few clouds were to be seen in the eternal expanse of the heavens and these were as soft as wool and as delicate as the body of a Sun-maiden.

As the queen went through the forest, her great eyes were as alive as moon crystal. From the enchanting woodland scene she drank in inspiration as the grateful grass drinks the morning dew. Where the ordinary man sees only the trees, she saw them in their dignity and superb beauty; and where the ordinary man hears only the rustling of the breeze through the branches of the trees, and the senseless twittering of the numerous birds, she heard the soul-stirring verses of the Song of Creation.

She was not very far from the river when she saw a number of young boys gathered together above something that lay in the tall grass. The boys were talking and gesticulating excitedly and were all patting one amongst them on the back in obvious congratulation. Their voices floated through the scented air into the keen ears of *Marimba* and, as one might expect from this great woman, she left her retinue and went to investigate. What she saw there filled her with anger and disgust, and tears sprang unbidden into her eyes. One of these boys had invented a particularly vicious and cowardly kind of snare with which to catch young antelopes. He had tried it out and it had worked all too well. Lying on the ground with a cruel noose around her lifeless neck was a young steenbuck ewe which had fallen a victim of this fiendish trap, and the poor animal had only a few days to go before it produced young.

'Which of you sons of night-howling, splay-footed, green-bellied hyaenas invented this thing?' demanded *Marimba* hotly.

The boys made no reply. They just stared at their dusty feet in very frightened silence. Two of them wetted their loinskins at the same time, much to the amusement of the royal handmaidens.

'I asked you a question, you mud-wallowing tadpoles!' cried *Marimba.*

At last one of them said in a voice that was hardly a whisper: 'I . . . I did, Oh Great One.'

'You did, did you?' cried *Marimba* in a burst of ecstatic fury. 'Now indeed, you are going to suffer for your deed!'

'Mercy please, Oh Great One,' whispered the boy.

'*Marimba* has no mercy for bloodthirsty little idiots of your kind,' said the angry queen coldly. 'Breathe into the nostrils of that animal and bring it back to life.'

The astonished followers of *Marimba* saw the boy lift the head of the dead buck and actually try to breathe life back into it. There was a gale of feminine laughter which the angry chieftainess quelled with a look of cold fury in her glittering eyes. A deep respectful silence settled upon the group of watching maidservants while the boy, with sweating face and inflated cheeks, and a heart that was almost stopping with cold fear, huffed and puffed in vain to revive the dead animal.

'That animal had better come back to life, Oh little vermin,' said the princess cruelly. 'If it does not you will soon wish that you had never been born.'

The badly frightened boy tried his best. He tried everything he could while the queen watched him coldly and impassively, and the handmaidens watched with broad smiles on their faces.

'Why,' said *Marimba* at long last, 'it seems to me as if you find it easier to kill an animal than to bring it back to life!'

'I cannot make it live again, Oh Great Queen,' stammered the boy. 'It still wants to remain dead.'

'Then you must surrender yourself to punishment,' said the queen ominously.

'Please do not kill me!' screamed the boy in utter terror. 'I am still too young to die . . . I do not want to die!'

'The animal that you killed with the fruits of your evil brain did not want to die either,' observed *Marimba.*

'Please . . .'

'Seize him!' cried the princess to her attendants. 'Seize and hold fast the pestilential horror!'

The giggling girls fell upon the boy and held him fast. He struggled and kicked and bawled in vain. He yelled to his friends to save him. But those loyal friends had proved their loyalty by vanishing into the sheltering bush, leaving him to face the music alone. 'Bring him to the village – I want to deal with him properly in the presence of all the people.'

The gathered Wakambi were sitting in a great semicircle in the High Place of Justice at the very summit of the hill which was now known as the Hill of the Wakambi. The princess *Marimba* sat on her throne at the foot of an upright slab of rock that was known as the Rock of Justice. She was flanked on either side by two old men.

The old man on her left was known as the High Accuser and the one on her right was known as the Mercy of Heaven, and it was his duty to plead for mercy on the prisoner's behalf – but not to defend him from the accusation.

Marimba was the one empowered to execute the prisoner after he had been found guilty. The power to execute was granted to all those people who had seen the prisoner actually commit the offence for which he was charged.

Trials were held only at the 'rising of the moon' among the Wakambi and everybody was waiting in silence, where even a whisper was strictly forbidden, for the rising of the heavenly orb. Night had fallen and the land was swathed in the dark mantle of obscurity, and in the scowling forests below the Great Village lions were roaring their fury at the glittering stars, while leopards coughed defiance to all and sundry.

The boy, *Malinge,* who had been caught by *Marimba* in the act of wantonly destroying living things, knew that the coming of the moon would also mean the coming of his own death, and he was numb with fear. He turned round and looked in the direction of his parents seated with the other villagers near one of the great Fires of Justice that had been lit in a semicircle to illuminate the High Place of Justice. There were seven such fires, each representing the Seven Gates of Creation that separate this material world from the bright bronze plains and crystal forests of Tura-ya-Moya, where the gods have birth and where *Lizuli,* the whore of eternity, dances nightly before the thousand eyes of the Most Ultimate.

These fires were not kindled with wood, but with the leaves of the *mpepo* plant and were fed with the bones of that kind of animal against which the accused had committed the offence. When a man was charged with murder, human bones were fed into the fires. On this occasion the bones of antelope were fed into the fires.

Malinge cast a pleading glance at the face of the grim and bearded warrior that was his father and found no mercy and no recognition there. Nor did his own mother and other brothers seem to know him at all. He knew he was alone – and lost. Then, with that breath-taking majesty that fills the eyes with tears, the moon rose above the distant mountains.

As it rose, a wild scream of naked terror was torn from the lips of the wretched *Malinge* and he tried to bolt out of the Place of Justice. But *Mpushu* and *Kahawa* seized him and held him fast.

'Stand still and take your punishment like a man, Oh *Malinge*,' said *Mpushu*. 'Do not try to cheat the lion of justice of his juicy prey. Nothing very serious is going to happen to you. You will only be deprived of your nose and ears and then thrown to very, very hungry crocodiles. Something worth looking forward to, eh?'

'*Aiyeeee!*' shrieked Malinge in appreciation.

'*Malinge*, the son of *Katimbe*, the son of *Ngungu*, the son of *Lembe*, here stands accused of having wantonly and wilfully destroyed a living thing for no other reason than to see the effect of the new kind of snare that he had invented.' The voice of the High Accuser was harsh, a rasping croak. 'He destroyed a little steenbuck ewe with young in its belly, and here you can see for yourself the sorry remains of his victim on the Tray of Accusation. This boy was not hungry when he committed this deed, neither had he the intention of taking the animal to his father to prepare for food. It was a clear case of wanton useless destruction of life, in direct defiance of the Laws of *Odu*. *Malinge* must die. He must die so that the Great Mother's displeasure at this demon-like act should be disarmed, so that the wrath of the High Gods be not showered upon us like evil hail. *Malinge* must die – not to deter others from committing the same offence, but that by dying he can take his heinous sin with him to the land of Forever-Night, away from the huts and villages of the Wakambi.'

With this the High Accuser sat down, fiercely scowling at the villagers assembled before him. An even deeper silence settled heavily upon the High Place of Justice.

The other Old One, the Mercy of Heaven, then rose totteringly to his ancient, withered feet. 'People of the Wakambi: to you this unworthy one addresses this message. We all know that the young boy *Malinge* is guilty and we all know that he must suffer the most ultimate form of punishment, because if we let irresponsible young people kill the animals of the forest wastefully, it will not be long before the High Gods will deprive us of all living things on which we depend for food. It will not be long before the forests become only the haunts of starving jackals and hyaenas with no other animals in sight, and we would all die the shameful death of hunger. So I, too, agree that this young man must be punished. But I plead that we give the boy the opportunity to explain to us in his own words just why he did this thing and why he felt prompted to break one of the oldest and most sacred laws of our people, and above all, why he dared to improve on our standard methods – why he rendered these more cruel as the very design of this trap shows.'

His voice faltered and he sat down, wiping the sweat from his wrinkled brow with the back of his hand. There were tears on his wrinkled cheeks and his gentle tired eyes were inflamed and bloodshot.

'Stand up, prisoner,' bellowed the High Accuser. 'Stand up and tell us why you broke the laws of the gods, why you dared to improve upon the things that our ancestors invented. Do you consider yourself wiser than your forefathers?'

'N-No,' stammered the boy, 'I only thought . . .'

'Listen, oh vermin,' rasped the High Accuser, 'this is not a world that belongs to you. If you want a world which you can improve then you can go and create one for yourself. In this world you will take your place as the insignificant speck that you are and you must conform to the rules as laid down by our forefathers. You must not try to improve on anything that they found good enough. You seem to have forgotten that it was the love for inventing new things that caused the destruction of the First People. Don't tell me that you have never heard the Seven High Laws of Living, because I know that you have.'

There is something known as hope, and that something has the habit of shining brightest when a man gets most hopelessly lost in the forest of fear and despair. Hope is a false star shining brightest on the darkest night of one's life. In the words of the High Accuser, the doomed boy *Malinge* saw a glimmering thread of hope and he seized it and held fast to it. A man about to die loses all fear. He throws all respect and dignity to the Seven Winds and says and does exactly as he pleases, and *Malinge* did exactly that.

'You doddering old hypocrites!' he screamed at the top of his squeaky voice. 'You are not fit to sit in judgment over a lame and half-dead fly. You say I broke a law by inventing something new.

Why then is our Queen *Marimba* not being accused of inventing all those new instruments with which she makes music?'

Malinge's hope of revenge on the woman who had brought him to trial was drowned in a flood of laughter that followed immediately on his impudent outburst. The assembly laughed long and loud till the High Accuser had to stand up and roar for silence.

'You utter fool!' he bellowed. 'You miserable, impudent rat! *Marimba* is an immortal, an appointed servant of the gods on this earth, and what she does is done at the command of the most High Gods. Royal *Marimba*, pronounce sentence upon this mud-wallowing dog.'

Marimba stood up and her great eyes were bright in the moonlight. There was also a great sadness in those eyes that was beyond human understanding. Her voice was soft and gentle as she said: '*Malinge*, I am not your executioner and I find myself unable to order your death. But I am not going to let you escape lightly. The High Gods tell me that you are an habitual and stubborn law-breaker, who acts thus for the sheer pleasure it gives you. It also gives you pleasure to see innocent animals die in agony. I now order that you be taken away from here and your legs broken with clubs so that you may never walk again, and your hands destroyed by paralysing your fingers.'

Marimba looked down at the ugly snare that *Malinge* had invented and shuddered. There was no mistaking it – the thing was deadly and only a madman, a monster of cruelty, could have invented this sort of thing. No wonder the old men had overruled her and had thrown *Malinge* to the crocodiles just before daybreak.

Then *Marimba* got down on her knees and began to work. She dismantled the long trapdoor consisting of oblong flat pieces of wood tied together with buckskin thongs and gut. She made small alterations to the pieces of wood so that they were no longer of the same length and thickness. She ordered her handmaidens to bring her a number of *cusana* gourds of different sizes and to open each end, making a big hole in one end and a small one in the side. Her next order was equally peculiar: the gourds were to be put in a large clay bowl at the gate of the village and word spread that all the old women of the village were to pass their morning water into the big bowl for three successive days. This, explained the great princess, was not only to place a permanent blessing upon the instrument; it would also make the gourds resilient and durable.

Afterwards the gourds were boiled in animal fat to make them more resilient and waterproof. With her own delicate hands *Marimba* assembled the instrument while vast crowds of Wakambi men and women watched in awe and astonishment. She first assembled the hardwood frame with four carved legs, and along a flat piece of wood that connected the two ends of the oblong frame she stuck the gourds by their mouths firmly with tree resin.

She then covered each of the holes in the sides of the gourds with silky laminae which she obtained from the nests of the *munyovu* wasp, also stuck firmly with tree resin. The gourds were arranged under the central plank in gradually diminishing size. Then came the pieces of wood that formed the trapdoor, also arranged in the same order according to size, each piece directly across a corresponding gourd resonator. The strips of wood were suspended above their resonators by two lengths of thong.

Thus the xylophone – the *marimba* – was born. Soon this melodious companion of the feast and the dance was sending its notes through the festive air, each note as gentle as a maiden's promise. The xylophone is a living instrument which can bend its notes to fit the blood-warming melody of a wedding song or harshen its voice and convey to the human mind the clamour and dark horrors of war – or the thrilling excitement and suspense of the hunt. Even without the accompaniment of a human voice one can tell a whole story with the xylophone alone. One can use the voice of this holy instrument to create various moods in one's audience. While other instruments speak to the ears, the xylophone speaks to the heart and the soul. Indeed it is an instrument worthy of bearing the name of the Goddess of Music.

In building xylophones only hard and well seasoned woods must be used. Great care must be exercised in selecting the wood for the various notes. There must be no pores, or the slightest crack.

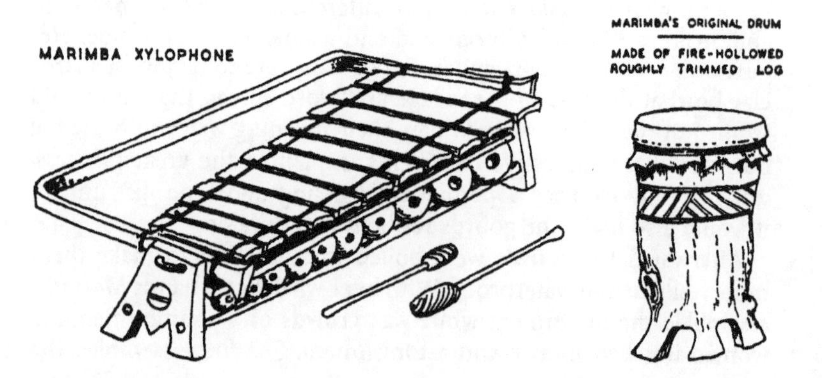

Timber from a hardwood tree once struck by lightning is excellent. These sacred instruments must never be built in times of war and famine; neither must they be made by people who are sterile or spiritually perverted, or physically deformed in any way.

'Great *Marimba*,' – the voice of the tremendous woman, a cook, was low and full of great love and respect – 'it is with great regret that your servants failed to cook your favourite dish of stamped peanuts today, for *lo*, the old mortar has finally worn through its bottom and is now nothing but a useless hollow log. It is only good for firewood now and we must ask the woodcarvers to fashion us a new one.'

'Do not burn the old mortar, Oh *Mandingwe*,' said the princess with a mysterious smile. 'The truth is that I have been waiting for something like this to happen for quite some time. I shall transform it into something which will add yet more pleasure to the lives of the people whom the gods have entrusted to me to rule and guide along the paths of peace and wisdom.'

'*Marimba* is indeed the mother of wisdom,' whispered the fat cook.

'Nobody is the parent of wisdom in this world, *Mandingwe*. I am nothing but a puppet serving the will of Those-we-do-not-see, and I try to serve as best I can. Now bring me the skin of a newly killed wildebeest, and also send *Kamago* the woodcarver to me.'

'As you say, Oh *Marimba*,' said the cook respectfully, falling on her face in obeisance and then crawling backwards out of the Royal Hut.

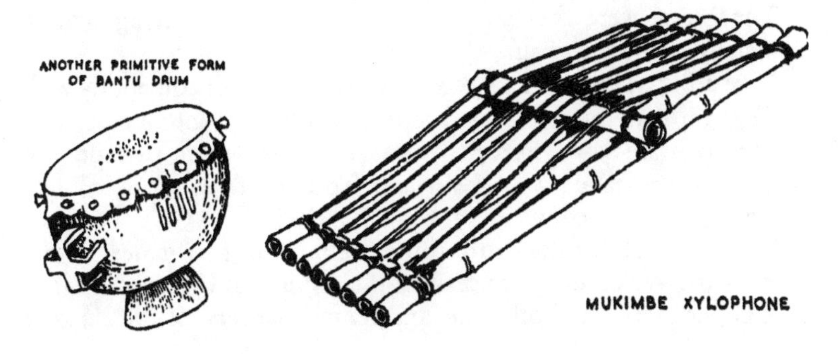

Marimba turned the old nut-grinding mortar into the first drum the world had ever seen and for the first time since the dawn of creation the forests shook to the pulsing beat of a drum. This instrument became so popular with the Wakambi that almost everybody wanted to have a drum in his own hut. The woodcarvers were very busy indeed. The princess *Marimba* made them of different sizes, each with a different quality of sound, from the loud hollow boom to the gentle pow-pow. The big ones were known as the 'male drums'; smaller ones were 'female drums', and the very small ones that children could carry around were known as 'sparrow drums'.

The largest drums she ordered to be reserved for purposes of worship only and these had the symbol of the River of Eternity carved into them in a continuous pattern all round, and on many of these drums were also carved symbols representing passages from the great poems of creation and sacred symbols of Spiritual Secret Knowledge. This she did to preserve the knowledge of the Wakambi for all time. Men were elected to look after these drums and this became their sole duty in life. These 'Drummers of High Honour' had to daub the instruments periodically with animal fat to preserve both the wood and the skin. When a drum was attacked by a wood-boring pest they had to wrap it in wet animal skins and then leave it to steam in a hollow anthill which had been heated by a fire till it was red hot.

When a drum deteriorated beyond repair it was the duty of the oldest woodcarver to carve a new one – an exact replica in every detail, and the old one was buried with the full burial honours with which a chief is buried.

Marimba's drums became so popular that even the Masai copied them, but not for peaceful purposes. One day when *Mpushu* was carrying a number of drums to a village of the Wakambi he was set upon by three Masai who knocked him flying into a muddy stream and stole off with the drums, but only after requesting him to fetch some more as they would like to steal those too.

The Masai were the first to use the drum for relaying signals, especially military signals.

Give a Masai a stone and he will hit something or somebody with it. Give him any piece of wood and he will turn it into a club with which to brain you. 'Peace' or 'peaceful' are words that do not occur in the vocabulary of the Masai. To them these are absolutely meaningless abstractions.

With the birth of the drum came the birth of new dances in the land of the Wakambi – dances like the *bupiro-mukiti*, or the dance of life, performed by both male and female dancers, or the *chukuza ya sandanda*, the dance of the baboon, which is performed by male dancers only. This is the most muscle-punishing dance that can ever be performed. All these dances were invented for one reason only – expression of tribal religion and the release of that beneficial life-force dormant in every human being, but which, when released, makes one feel closer in the 'arms of Eternity'.

Also some of the dances performed by young people, like the famous 'love dance' of the Kavirondo, and the *gqashiya* of the Nguni, were invented so that the young people might find an opportunity to use up their excess energy.

Little *Nonikwe* was waiting. She was waiting with great impatience for something big and exciting to happen and she could hardly conceal the wild excitement she felt; it lighted her face like a midnight beacon. This was all because *Nonikwe* knew something the other girls in her village did not know as yet. She knew that the Great One, *Marimba*, was on her way to spend the night in the village – the very village in which *Nonikwe's* uncle, *Mutengu*, was headman.

Little *Nonikwe* was a pathetic creature. She was not only a hunchback, but she was also totally blind. But all this was amply compensated by the great and rare gift the gods gave her of seeing things clearly long before they happened.

This gift had saved the little hunchback child from being destroyed at the age of eight as all crippled and deformed children were normally destroyed according to the laws of the Wakambi. A child born with any defect was, however, allowed to live till the age of eight to see if it had any special gifts like seeing into the future or the past, reading minds or communicating thoughts to animals.

Little *Nonikwe* was allowed to live and she lived like a chieftainess in her uncle's village. She was the most well-hidden and well-guarded piece of property in the village, and this was because *Mutengu* had a bitter rival and enemy in another new village just beyond the river. This enemy was *Lusu*, the father of *Nonikwe* herself. When *Nonikwe* had been born, *Lusu* had been so disgusted with the child with which his wife had presented him that he had publicly declared that his wife had slept with a night-walking demon.

Nonikwe's mother had been disgracefully driven from *Lusu's* village and had sought refuge in the village of her brother *Mutengu*, where she died of a broken heart two moons later. Years had passed, the little girl had grown, and soon word had got around that she was a Blessed One, gifted with powers beyond human concept. When he heard this, *Lusu* the rascal tried to move the very stars and the mountains to get *Nonikwe* back. *Mutengu* had not only refused; he had seized *Lusu* and beaten him within a thumb's length of his fat and rascally life.

Mutengu and *Lusu* had since been deadly enemies and to get his own back, *Lusu* developed the habit of reporting directly to *Marimba* with all kinds of accusations against *Mutengu* – acts of corruption and many breaches of the laws of the Wakambi. These accusations were, of course, utterly false and unfounded.

Eventually *Marimba* decided to pay *Mutengu* a secret visit in order to find out for herself if he was really as corrupt and evil as *Lusu* had made him out to be.

But *Marimba* had forgotten about *Nonikwe.* The little hunchback had actually dreamt what the great princess intended to do and woke up early that morning to warn her uncle to expect a secret visit from his queen some time in the afternoon. *Mutengu,* though startled by this warning, had acted quickly upon it because the blind little hunchback had never before been wrong with her predictions. He had ordered scouts to be posted to give him early warning of the approach of the great queen and her retinue. He had made his wives prepare all manner of food to give the peerless *Marimba* a welcome feast fit for one of her high and queenly position.

Mutengu had nothing to fear from a visit by his chieftainess because he had no secrets to hide. And not only was he as loyal as the southern wind but he was also as honest as a worker bee. But he did not want to be caught unprepared in anything and he was a strong believer in giving each and every visitor to his village a welcome in accordance with his or her stature.

Mutengu was a very popular headman. Every man and woman in the village could vouch for his great kindness, courage and honesty, and they were all prepared to defend him with their lives against any scandal-mongering back-biter.

The huge clay pots were full of delicious buffalo meat. There were great basins full of well cooked yams and corn cakes. There were also wooden trays full of roast wild fowl, partridge and guinea fowl. There were baskets full of wild figs and stewed *marulas,* and large cakes of fresh honey from his own beehives. *Mutengu* was the first man in the land of the tribes to keep bees. He kept them in hollow anthills, and handled them after drugging them with *dagga* smoke. He had also discovered that bees were inclined to leave him in peace when he dressed himself in a hyaena skin *kaross.*

Thus the great feast was prepared and brought in readiness for the unannounced arrival of the great queen *Marimba.* All the villagers settled down to await the arrival of someone who did not know she was already expected, whose surprise visit was a sursprise no more. Visitors from surrounding kraals and villages came as usual to have a free meal in this generous headman's village, and as usual they told him a lot of tales-that-are-not-true and departed with full bellies and oily smiles. It was also customary for angry men to bring their disputes to *Mutengu's* kraal and long arguments and trials took place under the Tree of Justice in the centre of the village. Fines were paid in ivory, ebony, and copper ore, and malefactors were taken outside and executed.

Life was taking its normal course in *Mutengu's* village. An old and very tired-looking man came into the teeming village at midday accompanied by his remarkably beautiful daughter and begged a guardsman at the gate to let him spend the night in their spare hut, as he was very tired and had come a long way. This was not unusual and the guards were all too happy to admit the old doddering traveller and his daughter. The shy, beautiful girl greatly interested the burly guards and many were the ravenous glances cast in her direction.

The old man was given the whole haunch of a buffalo and asked to eat his fill; what was left he could take with him on his journey the following day.

The rest of the afternoon was taken up by ordinary activities, such as hauling yelling prisoners to the council tree for trial.

The sun was already setting beyond the western mountains and lengthy shadows were creeping eastwards when headman *Mutengu* completed his duties in administering tribal law. And still the queen of the Wakambi had not arrived. A small doubt began to gnaw at the back of the mind of the great *Induna*; he began to wonder for the first time whether his little deformed niece was wrong in her prophecy. Eventually he strode into her hut and knelt down beside the blind child, holding her hand gently, reassuringly.

'Little one, for once the little spirits have played a trick upon my niece, for *lo*, the queen Marimba has not come yet.'

'But she has, Oh honourable uncle, the queen of the Wakambi is here. I can feel the pulse of her thoughts.'

Mutengu was aghast: 'Child! What words are these? My scouts have brought no news of the coming of the queen. They have seen no warrior escort. And yet you say that the royal *Marimba* is already within this village!'

'She is, Oh uncle. I receive her thoughts quite clearly. At this moment she is pleased with the joke she has played on you, and she is convinced that my real father *Lusu* has accused you falsely.'

'Where is she?' *Mutengu* demanded. 'Has she made herself invisible?'

'No, uncle. Tell me, how many visitors are spending the night with us?'

'Well over a hundred, child, men and women, young and old.'

'The Great One has come into the village as a common visitor, my uncle. You must command all visitors to report to your Great Hut and there I shall pick her out for you.'

The one hundred and ten visitors were gathered at the Great Hut and a sumptuous supper was in progress. Already the *induna* knew that one of these many women was *Marimba* and one thing remained – the identification parade!

Mutengu led his little blind niece, gently holding her hand, past all the guests. He noticed how most of the visitors shrank slightly with revulsion as the deformed child approached. He saw this and he smiled; if only these fools knew that the little deformed child was the equivalent of ten so-called normal human beings. Led by powers beyond human comprehension, the young girl made her way towards the old man and his daughter. The child knelt down beside the girl and gently removed the *kaross* of respect with which she had covered her head. *Mutengu* immediately recognised his chieftainess – in spite of her shaven head and the false scar she had improvised with a piece of fish bladder. *Mutengu* gently pulled off the scar and the great, mischievous eyes of *Marimba* smiled softly at him.

'My queen ... living goddess of the Wakambi ... what is the meaning of this cruel joke?'

'I heard that you were a corrupt and vicious man who broke every tribal law laid down. I wanted to see for myself, Oh *Induna*, and I am glad to say that I found all accusations against you false and groundless.'

The assembled visitors fell on their faces in the presence of their great queen and a deep silence fell upon the gathering like a thick skin blanket. Then came *Marimba's* clear voice: 'Arise, my people, and let us enjoy our meal. Then we shall perform a little dance to thank our host for his great kindness and generosity.' And turning to *Mutengu* she spoke softly: 'Tell me, Oh *Mutengu*, how did you know about my secret arrival?'

'This child, with her god-given sight, indicated you to me, your humble servant, Oh *Marimba*.'

'I shall give the little one a gift to remember me by. And when we have unseated her evil father in the village across the river we shall appoint your niece as headwoman of that village for the rest of her life.'

A roar of applause greeted the announcement. Men stood up and raised their right hands in salute to the little *Nonikwe*, Headwoman-for-life of a village and district. And then, into the hands of the little girl *Marimba* pressed the newest instrument of music that she had invented. It was a 'hand xylophone' – a *mukimbe* – made entirely of reeds.

A *mukimbe* is an instrument particularly suited for use by blind people or those left weak and convalescing after an attack of one of the numerous tropical diseases. Many a convalescent owed his recovery to the sweet, birdlike, soothing notes of the *mukimbe.* Thus this instrument soon acquired the nickname of 'the sick one's comforter'.

A good *mukimbe* is constructed as follows: The bulrush reeds must be cut in the middle of summer when fully grown but not yet hard or dry. They must be of equal thickness (a man's little finger) and of equal length (from the wrist to the elbow). Eight of these are cut and woven together with lengths of reed bark till the whole thing looks like a miniature raft. More strips of green reed are then attached to the raft, fixed both ends, and a strip of wood is then inserted to lift these strips away from the raft in the middle. The whole contraption is then left to dry in the sun for ten days. The woven knots tighten and the strips become taut while the spirit of music enters into them. The strips must all be of unequal breadth and arranged in order of thickness. For an additional rattle effect tiny pebbles can be inserted in the hollow reeds and the openings sealed with tree resin.

The blind child was overjoyed. Tears of pure gratitude welled from her sightless eyes and she clutched the instrument to her heart. She wept as if her soul would melt. 'Thank you, Oh my queen. I honour you with all my heart, and may you grow as tall as the tallest of tall trees.'

'Now, now, little *Nonikwe,* do not cry so. I am going to see to it that you are happy for the rest of your life and that you will never want for anything. Now come, all my people, let us dance before we go to sleep. I have a new dance for you, my lazy ones – the "Three-Fire Dance".'

The women had become wands of living fire; they were leaping and swaying, twisting and shaking, like things gone completely mad. *Marimba* was leading the group of dancers in the centre, symbolising the 'flame of life' while the other groups of dancers represented the forces that try to snuff out the flame. It was a wild, uninhibited, savage dance that sent the flood of desire surging through the bodies of the men and brought tears into the eyes of the old ones. Every woman of the village was now taking part in the strangest dance of all time, while all the men watched intensely, deeply moved.

But elsewhere in the village three men were conferring – three whose hearts were full of evil and whose souls were caught in the dark webs of evil being hatched against the peerless *Marimba.* One, called *Luchiza,* was nothing but a stripling boy, the first-born son of the headman *Mutengu.* The second was a one-eyed scoundrel named *Mbomongo* and the third was *Kalembi,* the old man who had posed as *Marimba's* father when they entered the village earlier that day. *Kalembi* had found an opportunity to slip away unnoticed during the earlier part of the dancing and he now addressed the two others in a bitter and cracked voice: 'We cannot allow this thing to go on! If we do not put a stop to this woman's antics soon we shall all be turned into a mob of brainless, capering fools who will do nothing but dance ourselves from the childbirth-hut to the very grave, and on to the land of Forever-Night. I tell you, we have to do something about this.'

'*Tsaaaiieee!*' spat the young man *Luchiza,* the son of *Mutengu,* 'I am a firm believer that the woman is mad. Who ever heard of a nation of dancers? That is what we are already – a mad nation of capering idiots!'

'Well, my lords,' said *Mbomongo* with an obscene leer, 'if you want to get rid of *Marimba* I am the man to do it for you. I would enjoy nothing better.'

'What do you propose we do, *Kalembi*?' asked the young man *Luchiza,* 'you are the wisest one of the three of us and all the deciding must come from you.'

'In two years' time,' said the old man slowly, 'we are going to celebrate the escape of *Odu* and *Amarava* from the lost land of the First People, and that will give us the opportunity to get rid not only of this loathsome female, but of her impish son *Kahawa* as well.'

'I would never relish an open fight with that left-handed madman,' said young *Luchiza.* 'It is easier to fight an angry rhinoceros than engage *Kahawa* in battle. The man is a monster and to him fear is an unknown thing.'

'But an ordinary drug can vanquish the fiercest beast, Oh *Luchiza,*' said the old man *Kalembi.* 'And during that festival there will be many an opportunity to slip a drug into whatever mother or son would care to eat or drink.'

'But *Marimba* is an immortal!' said *Luchiza* soberly. 'You cannot kill an immortal, although you can seriously wound one.'

'I just want to get *Marimba* into my hands for a few moments,' said *Kalembi.* 'And I want her drugged and helpless. Then I would not only make sure that she never again invented any new musical contraptions but also that she forever forgot who she was. I want to turn her into a zombie on that day, my sons. You forsaken fools seem to have forgotten that I am the wizard-lord of the Wakambi!'

'You mean to say you intend tampering with that immortal's brain?' cried the young man. 'But even you will never dare to go that far, *Kalembi*!'

'Somewhere in the forest is a slowly dying god, and this god is willing to reward with immortality anyone who can deliver *Marimba* into his hands,' said the wizard-lord. 'I would like to be the one to do so.'

'You mean *Nangai*, the Evil, the monster who nearly destroyed the Wakambi!' cried *Luchiza*. 'I would watch my step with that heavenly renegade if I were you, Oh Wizard-Lord.'

'I am willing to take any risk to attain immortality, my boy,' the old man replied.

Meanwhile at the Great Hut the 'Three Fire Dance' had reached a shattering climax as *Marimba*, now symbolising the human soul that cannot die, leapt high into the air with arms spread out appealingly to the gods on high, leapt into the air to fall back into a forest of hands raised by the circle of women below her. The women bore their beloved queen in triumph to her sleeping hut. The assembled men let out a thunderous cheer and raised their war weapons high in salute.

In the darkness, beyond the light of the flickering torches, an old man's cold narrow eyes blazed with unspeakable hatred and bitter contempt, and a one-eyed man of great ugliness sneered, while a young man whispered: 'In two years, you putrid slut – in just two years' time!'

A dark cloud had formed in the peaceful skies of *Marimba's* life – a dark cloud that was to explode into a ravening storm of incredible fury.

Lusu was scared, and he had a very good reason to be. When one has slandered an innocent man for many days with intent to destroy him one becomes scared when one learns that all one's lies have been exposed and the victim's name cleared of all the slime one hurled at it. But *Lusu* had reason to be more scared; his victim had challenged him to mortal combat in the presence of the people of the two villages. And now he stood in the middle of the village clearing, his cowardly eyes so misty with fear that the hundreds of people sitting around watching him seemed strangely unreal – like ghosts in a distant spirit land. The only thing that felt real to him was his drenched loinskin.

There was a thunderous cheer as *Mutengu* crawled out of his hut and made straight for *Lusu*, and everybody saw with great surprise that he was completely unarmed. The watching villagers were even more surprised when his voice rang out harshly: 'I intend to make this a battle without weapons. It is my intention to give that lying dog a beating such as no-one has ever seen before. Drop that club, *Lusu*, and use your bare hands – I dare you!'

Lusu felt his shaky courage evaporating fast. He had depended on this club because he was quite skilled with it. He wept openly with fear and the villagers howled with laughter. Cries of 'shame' and 'coward' assailed his ears and his nerve collapsed altogether. He turned and tried to run, but one of his own advisors kicked him in the buttocks, cuffed him soundly and pushed him back into the clearing. *Mutengu* tore into him with the violence of a thunderstorm.

Violent clouds of dust were stirred up by the feet of the fighting men and for a long time the only sounds were those of blows well and truly landed. Then finally a loud scream was torn from the throat of the coward *Lusu* and he turned and ran like a madman. He bowled men over in his great hurry to escape the wrath of *Mutengu*. He leapt a high fence and thudded to the ground beyond like a hippopotamus. He got to his feet again and sped blindly into the forest with *Mutengu* and all the villagers, *Marimba* included, in hot pursuit. When he noticed the pursuit was gaining on him he urged his short fat legs to increase their effort.

Lusu ran on and on – like the wind through the forest. Loud sobbing gasps left his labouring lungs through a dry mouth. He ran on heedless of the thorns that tore his feet and heedless of the fact that his loinskin had fallen off and that his great shiny black buttocks were exposed to the glare of the sun.

Then the voice of *Mutengu* was heard above the excited shouts and shrieks of the villagers – a voice raised in fear and great urgency: 'Do not go there, *Lusu* . . . watch out!'

The pursuing villagers fell back, but *Lusu* saw in this an opportunity to run all the faster and he ran straight into *Mutengu's* apiary. Like a cloud of dark midnight vengeance, vast swarms of bees set on him. *Lusu* screamed horribly as the bees all but smothered him; he screamed as they stung him on every part of his swarthy sweating stark-naked body.

He ran screeching to the riverside and leapt blindly into the murky waters. As they closed over his head he suddenly felt incredible pain as the mighty jaws of a giant crocodile closed around his fat thighs.

He thought he saw a gleam of great pleasure in the eyes of the crocodile. That was the last he saw. But there was time for another thought: Had he recognised in those eyes, the eyes of his long-dead wife – mother of *Nonikwe*? Had she been reincarnated . . . ?

* * *

The silver moon was high in the midnight heavens and the great lake Nyanza was like a plain of shimmering silver in the land of Tura-ya-Moya; the waters of the great lake were so still that one could count the stars reflected from the surface. The night was oppressively hot and humid. In the scowling forests bordering the lake there lay a deep and inscrutable silence.

Very surprising indeed was the total absence of animals; no lions roared and no leopards coughed their opinions about. There was no place on earth like the dark forests that bordered the lake in those days. They were forests of abandon, of desolation, of Hell itself. They did not crawl with life, but with death – in its most hideous form.

It was because the lake Nyanza was not an ordinary lake in those days. It was the Heart of the very Earth and the gateway to lands strange and utterly terrible. These lands were once on the surface of the earth but had sunk to its core as a result of the evil that inhabited them. The gods wanted to bury this evil land forever to save the race of Man. The forests around this lake were the haunts of hideous things emerging periodically from the bowels of the earth: Life Eaters, Night Howlers, Fire Brides and Viper Maidens, who hunted each other the whole night long. Woe betide any venturesome human creature stupid enough to be lost in those forests!

In the great silence under the light of the moon a grim and deadly hunt was in progress this night. The Viper Maidens were stalking the Night Howlers whose blood they drank. Here and there one could catch a glimpse of a naked female form with a long tail and eyes like those of cats, darting from bush to bush in a desperate search for the huge monsters that were the source of their food and sport. Evil was hunting itself for lack of human victims and such hunts by Lower World creatures are well known for their utter pitilessness. *Lo!* is it not said in our Words of Wisdom that 'evil hunts and destroys itself'?

While this great, silent hunt was in progress in the moon-bathed forests, the slowly dying outcast god *Nangai* was lying on his soft bed of silver cloud in the dark depths of a cave that he knew as his home. For once the god experienced a flicker of hope: at long last the woman he needed in order to survive was about to be delivered into his hands and into his mercy. The beautiful immortal woman who had done so much to bring happiness into the land of ungrateful men had been betrayed by one of her son's wives, *Lozana*, who poured an evil drug into her food. This was on the occasion of the Festival of *Odu* and the drug had caused

Marimba to fall into a deep coma – and into the arms of her ruthless enemy.

The old wizard-lord of the Wakambi had vowed to hand over the princess to *Nangai* in exchange for immortality. The fierce *Kahawa* was far away when this happened, having been lured away by the scheming group with a false report that a great lion was terrorising one of the new outpost villages on the border of the land of the Wakambi. *Kahawa*, who hated lions and loved to hunt them, had set out with *Mpushu* to the distant village to direct the hunt.

And this night, three days after the wizard-lord of the Wakambi had terrorised the shocked people into making him Chief, a long canoe was gliding its silent way to the island home of *Nangai*, the Outcast God. There were five people in the canoe: *Marimba* who was still unconscious, *Mbomongo* the one-eyed, *Luchiza* the son of *Mutengu*, the old wizard-lord himself, and *Kahawa's* treacherous second wife *Lozana*. All these people hoped to gain immortality from *Nangai* as a prize for delivering *Marimba*, to whom they had done the most cowardly thing one human being can do to another. The very stars knew already that *Marimba* would never sing again . . .

Nangai had, on receiving a dream message from the triumphant wizard-lord, promised to use his waning powers of godhood to protect the passengers of the midnight canoe from attack by any of the many kinds of unearthly monsters haunting the lake and its environs. Now he was lying on his fantastic bed of shimmering cloud awaiting their arrival with great impatience; watching with expressionless eyes as the poison in his body attacked the remaining stump of his upper arm; watching without feeling as great blisters erupted down his left side and burst into purulent oozing sores. A god knows no fear and *Nangai* was not afraid, nor did he feel any pain. He was only interested in containing his existence for reasons he could not bother to find out.

Footsteps sounded somewhere in the darkness beyond the light shed by his own radiance, and he sat up as the wizard-lord of the Wakambi stepped into his presence, leading *Marimba* by the arm and closely followed by his evil friends.

Nangai did not bother to waste a glance on the nervous humans before him. He was only interested in *Marimba* – his one chance of survival – and it was she that he caught by the wrist and drew close to him. *Marimba* knelt down with downcast eyes like the soulless puppet she had become; the god sank his hollow claws into her upper arm and siphoned some of her blood through them into his own system. In front of the astonished mortals a strange thing happened to the outcast god; the blisters covering his body from head to foot gradually healed and a new left arm began to grow. His hard cold eyes lighted with a brilliance of new-born stars and his powerful body started vibrating with an extraordinary quality and power.

Eventually he released the woman's arm and stood regarding her in great bewilderment. With a voice of strange hardness he addressed the wizard-lord for the first time: 'What did you do to this immortal female?'

'I made her into a zombie, Oh great *Nangai*,' the man replied in gloating tones. 'She is now completely at your mercy, and not only does she fail to remember who she is and what she was – she is totally incapable of independent thought of any kind. She shall remain like this forever – a beautiful, soulless, immortal zombie.'

'Wretch of a mortal!' cried *Nangai*. 'You dare to gloat over what you have done? Does not this blind little brain of yours realise the enormity of your crime? You have committed a crime so great that the very stars are weeping at the sight of it.'

Fear and naked terror seized the old wizard-lord at the strange turn of events and with a hoarse scream he turned to flee. But the rejuvenated god seized him and held him fast while his evil followers fainted one by one. 'No, mortal, you do not so easily escape the consequences of your vile sacrilege. Both you and I stand here ready for judgment by one much higher than I.'

'But my lord . . .,' begged the old wizard.

'Be silent, you sinful wretch! As a result of your deed I must now surrender myself to punishment by the other gods. I only hope that I am tried by one who is just and impartial.

At that precise moment there came a flash of incredibly brilliant light and a clap of blood-freezing thunder. In the whirling mist of many-coloured light that filled the cavern a dark form took shape and soon, as the flaming mist dispersed, the whimpering wizard-lord found himself staring into the great eyes of a silvery giantess whose very presence seemed to shrivel his dirty soul.

'Merciful *Ma*, mother of the stars,' said *Nangai*, throwing himself flat on his face, 'this unworthy creature, unfit to bear the name of god, yields himself into your mercy and justice. And he also yields into your mercy the mortals who committed this evil crime upon the person of *Marimba*, your loyal servant who has done so much for mankind.'

'That does not sound at all like you, Oh *Nangai*,' said *Ma* coldly. 'When one hears you speak in this way one is tempted to wonder just what has become of your usual insolent bluster – and why you speak as though you have at last discovered how to distinguish good from evil.'

'Great *Ma*, I began repenting my evil ways immediately I saw what this wretched mortal has done to your servant, and it occurred to me that for a god to stoop so low as to tolerate the committing of crimes of this sort in his name is, in fact, the deepest form of evil. It occurred to me that gods should fight against evil and neither countenance nor encourage it.'

'That is indeed so, Oh *Nangai*; a god who works for evil principles is a traitor to his kind, because while the good principles which we support stand for Existence and Life, the former characterise Non-existence and Death. And now I am going to pass sentence on you, *Nangai*. You have reformed, that is true; but the taint of your sins still clings to you, and therefore you are not allowed to return to Tura-ya-Moya, but you are demoted from god to ordinary High Immortal and you are to be exiled into the land of mortals until the end of time.'

Nangai bowed his head and said at length: 'Your sentence is milder than my crimes, Oh Great Mother of All, and I praise you for your leniency. But what about this poor woman, this beautiful victim of the ingratitude of mortal men?'

'It is my will that you be the husband and guardian of *Marimba* until the very world ceases to be. *Marimba* had a great love for turning evil things into good, and it is strange indeed to find that as a result of her terrible suffering she has helped in reforming an evil god.'

'Please restore her brain to her, Great Goddess; please heal the brain of the one I love!'

'No!' said *Ma* firmly. 'You must take this beautiful woman back to her son and her people as she is, and you must rule and guide the Wakambi for more than a hundred years with this beautiful zombie always by your side – an immortal monument to the evil-heartedness and ingratitude of the creatures known as Man – wanton creatures who destroy ruthlessly those things they should love and revere; unnatural beasts that destroy the trees whose shelter they seek, and defile with excrement the cool streams from which they heal their thirst.

'She imparted happiness to the spawn of Man; she gave the race of Man music, but what reward has Man given her? Take her, *Nangai*, and carry her back to the village of the Wakambi. Love and cherish her, soulless though she be, because physically she will yet bear you a hundred sons and fifty daughters and these shall be the rulers of the Wakambi and many other future tribes. Rule with wisdom and strength for a hundred summers, and after that you can retire with your beloved *Marimba* to a golden sanctuary I shall prepare for you at the bottom of Lake Nyanza.

'And as for these evil mortals here who sought fame in delivering out a friend of theirs, I now deliver them out to the mercy of the Viper Maidens.'

With these words the goddess slowly vanished, while a host of Viper Maidens appeared on the scene. Dreadful were the shrieks of the wizard-lord when one Viper Maiden sank her fangs into the scruff of his neck and terrible were his struggles and contortions as her venom coursed through his scrawny body. *Lozana*, the treacherous wife of Kahawa, died shrieking for her husband while the fangs of another Viper Maiden were still buried in one of her ripe buttocks.

Dreadful was the hissing of the happy Viper Maidens as they feasted under the silent moon.

In the dark cave of *Nangai* the re-born god turned his eyes upon the woman he desired with every vein in his body. She was still kneeling where he had left her, like a soulless toy a child had forgotten. He came towards her and she raised her head and looked up at him with great empty eyes. Tears sprang to the eyes of *Nangai* and he stooped and raised the beautiful thing that once was *Marimba* to its feet – drew it close to him and wept his heart out. Then he laid it gently on his cloudy couch.

'Tomorrow we are going home, my beloved. You shall see *Kahawa* and *Rarati* and the rest of your people again. *Kahawa* has come back after finding that the story of the lion was false. Already he and *Mpushu* and *Rarati* have rallied all the people and they are searching for you. Do you hear?'

He might as well have spoken to a carved idol. She merely stared at him, her lips parted . . .

Nangai took his unresisting wife into his arms and kissed her lips for the first time. Her body trembled with a feeling she no longer recognised and her eyes closed in sudden fear and shyness. Outside the cavern the moon seemed brighter and a pleased smile seemed to linger on its round face.

Book Two

Stand Forever, Oh Zima-Mbje

(Compiled from numerous old Mashona, Venda, Bechuana and Varozwi songs and stories)

This is the story of the Lost Phoenician empire in Southern Africa, a story which is still sung and told around village fires in South and Central Africa today, a true story – it has thousands of relics in the hands of witchdoctors to support it.

Badly rusted and crumbling swords of ancient Greek manufacture, old gold coins and parts of bronze shields and helmets, bronze spears and Egyptian battle axes, all of which are in the secret possession of witchdoctors throughout Southern Africa, confirm the truth of the story of *Zima-Mbje*.

THE COMING OF THE STRANGE ONES

Lumbedu, the witchdoctor, had not slept well at all the previous night; in fact, for him the night had been one long hideous, screaming nightmare in which he had been alternately chased, strangled, mauled and torn apart by no fewer than ten different kinds of monsters, from giant crocodiles to bright red monkeys with ten eyes apiece.

The cause of all these unpleasant nocturnal visitations from the Demon World was not far to seek at all: it was nothing more than the fact that the rather overweight *Lumbedu* had stuffed his capacious belly well-nigh to bursting during the feast held in his honour on the previous day. This feast had been held by one of his patients he had cured of a bad fever by forcing down claypots-full, one after the other, of a strong purgative into the luckless man's stomach, with the result that although the poor fellow had been quickly cured of his fever, his stomach and intestines had been almost purged out of existence.

During the feast *Lumbedu* had brought forth loud shouts of amazement and admiration from the rest of the guests by excelling himself in his elephantine appetite. He had eaten the large half of a goat – haunch, ribs, shoulder, neck and head – pushing the smaller portion across to a starveling who had been staring at him with bright astonished eyes and a wet, drooling mouth. Then he had attacked a great bowl of boiled ox intestines and a pile of hot corn cakes, flavoured with kaffirbeer, with the ferocity of an invading conquerer. He had concluded this most royal repast with an almighty draught of two full claypots of bubbling cornbeer.

The midsummer sun was going down and the distant forests were now veiled by a smoky, mistlike haze, which made them look farther away than they really were. Wisps of smoke rose into the windless pale blue sky from great kraals and villages, while loud in the ears were the lowing of cows and the hollow bellowing of bulls as large herds of cattle were driven homewards from the forest-fringed pastures.

The rays of the slowly departing God of Light shone on the sweat-drenched face of the panting boy who was running through the forest as if *Watamaraka*, the Queen of Evil herself, was after his blood. He was a very frightened boy indeed – anyone could tell from his eyes. What had he seen?

Follow the boy, my children – dark-brown, thin, naked, swift as a wild eagle of the hills. Follow the boy to whom the breath of fear has given the strength of a thousand men and the endurance of a wild buffalo. His toes and feet are bleeding – his left thigh is red with blood where a cruel thorn from a *meva* bush is deeply buried in his flesh. But he runs on heedless of pain and tiredness.

What has he seen? Guess, my children, guess!

Lo, he bursts through the forest and before him rears the stockade of a big kraal, a kraal consisting of sixteen huts surrounded by a stockade of pointed poles interwoven with thorny creepers. It is the kraal of his father, *Lumbedu* the witchdoctor, and the boy runs into the kraal as if he were the Seventh Wind itself.

'Father, father,' he cries shrilly.

Ojoyo, his mother, sees him and comes waddling fatly to investigate the reason for her son's fright.

'My son, what is the matter?' Her fat greasy arms encircle the frightened boy and he collapses. She carries him away like a baby to her hut and there, after removing the thorn from his thigh and washing his many wounds, she makes him drink a bowl of sleep-causing *luika* water, and he falls fast asleep.

'I think he must have seen an animal in the forest,' says *Vunakwe*, the third wife, to *Ojoyo* later.

'My son is no coward,' snaps *Ojoyo*. 'I still insist he must have been frightened by an evil spirit in the forest, Oh *Vunakwe*; he saw one of the demons which afflicted his father only this morning. Dare you try to contradict me?'

'I do not wish to argue with you *Ojoyo*,' says the peace-loving *Vunakwe*. 'It is best that we ask the child himself if he awakes . . .'

'If he awakes?' *Ojoyo* explodes. 'If he awakes? Do you wish my son *not* to wake up then *Vunakwe*? Do you want him to die?'

'No, no!' cries *Vunakwe*, cringing from the advancing *Ojoyo*. 'My tongue slipped; I meant to say *when* he awakes, believe me.'

'You witch, you know very well that you meant what you said. I am going to . . .'

But she gets no further as her attention is claimed by another of the wives of *Lumbedu.*

The sun was high in the silver skies when the boy *Mulumbi,* who had come running into the kraal on the previous evening, crawled painfully into *Lumbedu's* hut and knelt near the low entrance, facing his many parents who regarded him with bloodshot eyes and blank expressions on their haggard faces.

'Father,' said *Mulumbi* at last, 'I have something to tell you and I only ask you, please, to believe me.'

'What is it?' snapped *Lumbedu,* who was as bad a parent as he was cowardly and selfish. 'Speak up and then get out!'

'Father,' said the boy, 'we were out hunting wild cats with the other boys from *Songozo's* village yesterday afternoon; we went farther and farther into the forest until we reached the Zambezi and then started to follow the river eastwards. We did not find any wild cats but we did find a young buck which we speared and roasted and shared. We were still eating when *Mbimba* stood up and gave a loud shout of great fear. We all threw down our meat and grabbed our spears and bows thinking that some animal was about to attack us. "Look over there – what is it?" cried *Mbimba.* We all looked and saw something terrible coming up the Zambezi. Believe me, my parents, it was something terrible!'

'What was it?' chorused *Lumbedu* and *Ojoyo* together.

'It was a canoe, a very big canoe, father. It looked like a terrible serpent of the waters. Along its side ran two rows of long paddles and a great sheet of what looked like a skin was stretched on a long stick that hung on many ropes across a tall pole that stood in the centre of the giant canoe. There were three great knives attached to the front end and a carving shaped like a man, with hair as shaggy as a lion's mane. The other boys fled, my father, but I decided to hide in the grass to see what the canoe would do next. It came nearer and nearer . . .'

'My brave little son,' murmured *Ojoyo.* 'Go on, what happened next?'

'To my surprise, the canoe came closer and closer to the river bank and then it stopped. I saw men running on its top and the long rows of paddles being drawn up. Great metal vessels were lowered to scoop up water – lowered on ropes down the side of the great canoe. So near was it that I could see the many men on it quite clearly and they were the strangest looking men you ever saw. They had pink skins – they were pink all over; they had hair like the mane of lions – hair that fell to their shoulders. Some had hair as black and shiny as that of a panther, some red as fire. But one had hair the colour of corn in autumn. It was terrible – I was so afraid I just lay in the grass, all strength gone from me. I saw some of the men leap over the sides of the great canoe; they leapt naked and with their long hair flowing behind their heads. They leapt into the water and started swimming and splashing in the Zambezi like so many pink fish. Some were wrestling and laughing and some just swam about, leisurely, enjoying the cool water.

'Then a group of them ran out of the water on to the bank and started coming to where I lay in the long grass, too terrified to move. I closed my eyes and lay quite still. I heard their footsteps coming nearer and their voices grew louder. Then I heard a shout as the foremost of them had seen me. I felt a wet hand seize me roughly by the wrist and haul me to my feet in one movement. I found myself looking deep into the green eyes of one of the strange ones, my parents . . .'

'*Iaia-eeee*! – no human being can ever have green eyes,' said *Lumbedu*. 'No human being can ever have long hair like that of a lion, and a pink skin. This brat is lying!'

'Be quiet *Lumbedu*,' screamed *Ojoyo*. 'I know my children more than anybody else does and I know when they tell lies and when they tell the truth. *Mulumbi* is not lying.'

By this time the boy *Mulumbi* was bathed in sweat, his hands

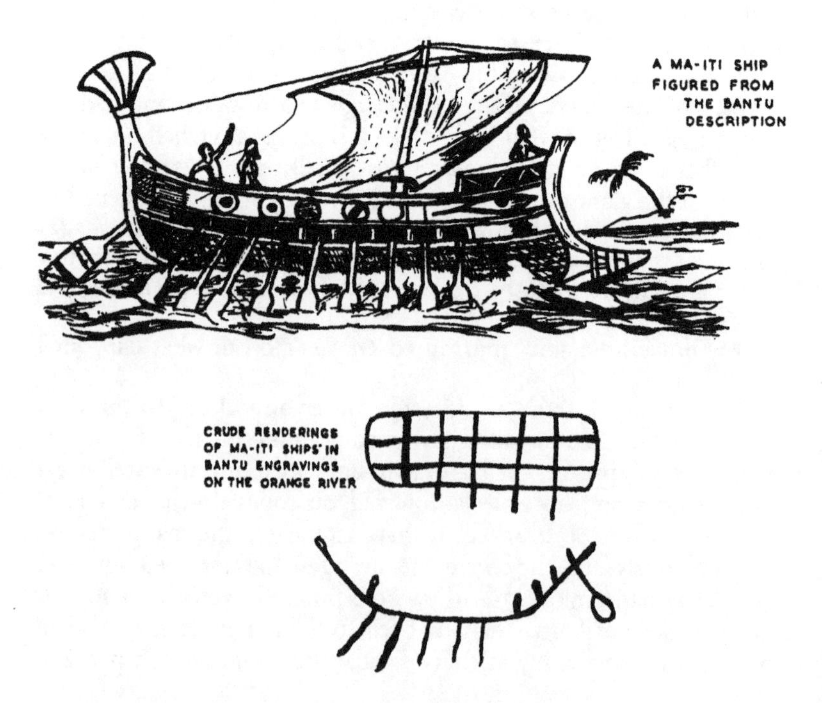

shook like leaves in the wind and a look of wild fear distorted his young boyish features. It was *Lulinda* who first noticed this. Worry clouded her beautiful face and she whispered to *Lumbedu*: 'Be careful, husband, please be careful; he has had a great shock; he is a very frightened child.'

'I have never seen this boy like this,' spoke *Vunakwe*. 'He is not a child who is easy to frighten and I know he tells the truth.'

'Continue son, tell us the rest, then you can go and lie down in your hut,' said *Taundi*. 'You are not looking well.'

'The strange ones have strange eyes, Oh my parents,' continued *Mulumbi*, very slowly and weakly now. 'Some have blue eyes, some brown, and the one who was holding me had green eyes. But those eyes seem to see through and through you; they make you feel naked and unhuman. I cried and struggled in the strange one's grasp, and he laughed and put me down. Then he gave me something small and shiny and round, something that was metal. But I must have dropped it as I turned and ran and ran with the alien laughter of the strange ones loud in my ears. I ran on and on without even looking behind me.'

Suddenly he fell heavily to one side and lay still. His audience leapt to their feet, but it was *Lulinda* who reached him first and threw her arms about him. 'He . . . he is dead . . . dead,' she choked.

A heavy silence fell inside the hut, a silence as heavy as the veil of time that conceals the future from our eyes. Then *Ojoyo* began to sob softly.

The story spread like wildfire through the land and within a few days nearly everybody knew about the strange pink human beings in a great canoe that had come splashing up the timeless Zambezi. The boys from *Songozo's* village who had watched *Mulumbi's* adventure with the Strange Ones from a distant hill, swore he had told the truth.

The barbed claws of the vulture of fear slowly closed their grip on the frightened land and soon people began to be so scared about what they had heard that they no longer ventured outside the stockades of their villages and kraals except in groups of tens and twenties.

Warriors armed with long bone-tipped war spears and stone axes escorted women whenever they went to the stream to get water or to the cornfields to reap corn. Drums beat out long warnings that were relayed to the farthest villages, telling people to look out for strangers with pink skins and long hair. Soon all the villages along the banks of the Zambezi were empty of life, having been evacuated by the inhabitants.

Everyone began to live in fear, everybody that is, except two people who were carrying on a secret and adulterous love affair.

Night had fallen upon the earth like a panther-skin *kaross*, powdered with silver shining stars, and an ugly brooding silence lay heavily upon the fear-haunted land. Deep shadows, black and forbidding, lay like crouching demons under the trees – shadows that concealed prowling night-hunting animals such as leopards, hyaenas and jackals. Only a madman dared walk into the forest in the middle of the night; only a madman – or a man on fire with passion and desire for another man's woman and who was willing to risk his life by keeping an adulterous appointment in an abandoned village on the bank of the Zambezi.

Chikongo, the son of *Mburu,* was the name of this man. He was actually risking his young life to keep an appointment with another man's wife – and that wife was *Lulinda,* the youngest wife of *Lumbedu,* the most feared witchdoctor in the land.

The heart of *Chikongo* pounded like a mad thing within him. He reached the abandoned village deep in the forest, the village which he and *Lulinda* had been using as a 'place of secret appointment' for one month now. He stood waiting just outside the fallen gate, his stone axe firmly gripped in his right hand, ready to deal with any animal that might emerge from the village to attack him. He stood thus for a long time until just as the moon rose above the trees in the east a low call sounded from the bushes close at hand. *Lulinda!* His stolen *Lulinda* had come . . . she had come!

Chikongo threw down his axe and jumped into the bushes with his hungry arms outstretched before him. *Lulinda* met him with a ferocity only a shade greater than his own and the love-demented pair went sprawling into the prickly embrace of a thornbush.

Chikongo picked himself up ruefully and helped *Lulinda* to her feet. Once more the lovers sought each other's arms, though in a more dignified and less violent way. *Lulinda* pressed herself fiercely against her lover's muscular frame, her nails digging deep and painfully into *Chikongo's* broad back, drawing blood. She kissed his pulsing neck, his ears, his forehead and his chest. Then she rubbed her nose fiercely against his. Then she broke free from his iron clutches and danced away with a low husky and musical laugh. The moonlight danced in her great big eyes like a silver ghost over a stream.

'Oh, my stolen one,' sighed *Chikongo,* 'I thought you were not coming.'

'I very nearly did not come. I think that bloated female crocodile *Ojoyo* is getting suspicious. She kept on peeping into my hut to see if I was there, but I tricked her. I do think that this should be our last appointment.'

His arm about her slender waist, they walked into the deserted village, unaware that many eyes were now watching them. Cautiously *Lulinda* and *Chikongo* entered the largest of the huts which happened to have a big hole in its grass roof, through which moonlight streamed, making a big splash of silver light on the pitted mud floor of the hut. It was here that the young man did an incredibly foolish thing – he did not explore the great hut first to see if it was really as empty as it seemed . . .

* * *

Lulinda woke very slowly and found to her surprise and horror that she had slept so long that dawn was breaking. The sky was red in the east, and soon the sun would rise in all its glory, bringing with it a new day. Her heart beating faster than usual, *Lulinda* tried to sit up, but found to her great astonishment that she was securely bound hand and foot – and so was *Chikongo*, who was still fast asleep beside her. Nor was that all . . .

Standing around them in a semicircle were six of the fantastic pink men whom the dead boy *Mulumbi* had seen and now they were in full battle dress. Tall and handsome in an unimaginably alien and fantastic way, the terrible Strange Ones towered above the frightened girl and her sleeping partner like colossal statues of pink flesh and shining bronze armour.

Each of them now wore a cuirass of heavy bronze scales and a helmet with one or three crests and what was obviously the hair of some animal. Two of them wore shining bronze leggings, and all of them carried shields either of leather studded with iron or bronze, or of iron with bronze bosses. All carried heavy iron-headed spears and all wore at their sides what were obviously deadly swords.

'Now I am dead,' thought *Lulinda*. 'Now we are both as good as dead.'

It was just then that *Chikongo* woke up and an expression of great surprise spread across his face. His mouth dropped open and his eyes widened. He looked as surprised as a fish that had just discovered its parents were a frog and a lizard!

The Strange Ones roared with laughter at this and *Lulinda* was astonished to discover just how human their laughter was, and how warm and genuine it sounded. This was not the hollow laughter of Evil Spirits, but that of very amused men, differing in colour, features, hair and form of dress from *Chikongo's* and *Lulinda's* race – yes, but human beings none the less. Then the one who seemed to be the leader of the Strange Ones put a question to *Chikongo* in a strange language that reminded *Lulinda* of a clear stream murmuring in the cool depths of a forest.

But they could not understand one another and eventually the voices of the red-headed Strange One and *Chikongo* became aggressive in tone.

It was the youngest of the Strange Ones who saved the situation. He came forward and looked down at *Lulinda* and beckoned her to look at him, which she at last managed to do. He pointed to himself, then to his companions – and then he pointed to his own mouth and stomach. Then, from his leather pouch he took out a piece of meat and glared at it in a most menacing way, bit off a piece and then spat it out in great disgust. Again he pointed to himself and the rest of his companions, then eastward once more. He then counted his fingers and toes and raised his hands with all fingers extended to indicate 'ten times twenty'.

A smile budded and burst into flower on *Lulinda's* lovely face and she nodded vigorously to show she understood. Then the brown-haired, blue-eyed Strange One counted fifty times on his fingers. He indicated on his bronze-scaled chest the breasts of a female and he counted twenty-three on his fingers and made a gesture showing 'little person'. Again *Lulinda* smiled and nodded rapidly.

'What are you both here grinning about?' *Chikongo* demanded. 'You seem to be getting quite friendly with this dangerous beast, *Lulinda.*'

'I understand what they want; he says there are two hundred of them in the east down the river and fifty of them are females and twenty-three of them are children. He says they are tired of eating meat and are hungry for other food. I think they are human beings of a sort – I am quite sure they are human.'

'Listen, *Lulinda,*' growled *Chikongo*, 'these things here are no more human than I am the son of a web-footed rhinoceros with seven tails. I am positive they are some form of evil spirit come to destroy our people. Do not let them get you under their spell.'

'Do not bother your great and all-knowing brain on my account, beloved one,' smiled *Lulinda.* 'The only spell I have fallen under is the spell of understanding. I think we should take these people to our Chief *Chungwe.*'

'You mean *you* should take these people to him, Oh pleasure of my veins,' smiled *Chikongo.* 'You forget that if I go with you, people will start asking a lot of embarrassing questions, my love. They will want to know just what we were doing in the forest at night to begin with and, as you know, our tribe has a very unpleasant way of dealing with boys and girls who commit adultery and I have no wish to be shorn of my manhood and flung to the nearest crocodile, you know.'

'I know,' said *Lulinda.* 'I do not need you to remind me of that.'

Meanwhile the Strange Ones were also engaged in animated conversation amongst themselves, a conversation in which the giant red-bearded leader and the brown-haired youth talked loudest. Once or twice the tall red giant took a step forward and half-drew his sword, snarling threateningly at the younger man, who only threw up his arms and laughed impudently at the infuriated giant.

At last the red-bearded one seemed to yield to whatever the young man had suggested and it was not long before the bonds on *Lulinda's* and *Chikongo's* wrists and ankles were cut. Then the brown-haired blue-eyed one cocked his curly head to one side and looked questioningly at her. She and *Chikongo* led the way through the forest towards the village of *Lumbedu* the witchdoctor.

It was one of the strangest and most fantastic processions of all time that wound its way through the great forest that morning. First came *Lulinda*, walking proudly in front. Then came *Chikongo*, whose nerves seemed to grow more and more taut with each step. Beads of perspiration stood out on his forehead like morning dew on a leaf, and he was as tense and as agitated as a kudu bull which has just caught the faint scent of a marauding lion.

Behind him came the shining company of the Strange Ones – twenty in all, some of whom had been in the other huts of the village during the long discussion between the Strange Ones and *Lulinda*. Their tall crested helmets hid half of their finely carved features, except their eyes, noses, firm thin-lipped mouths and square chins. Only three of them wore beards, besides the heavily armoured full-bearded giant who was their leader. They moved through the forest like a serpent of living, shimmering bronze, each as alert as an angry lion, cold deep-set eyes scanning the forest with the lofty contemptuousness of gods – as if they were ready for anything that might try to attack them, and all too happy to strike it down.

There was one man in whom *Lulinda* and *Chikongo* had become very interested indeed; this was the one at the very end of the glittering line of armed men. He obviously belonged to a race totally different from the Strange Ones, whom he resembled only very slightly. His skin was much darker and even his dress was totally different from that of his companions.

While the Strange Ones wore under their armour short tunics of what looked like cloth, this man wore nothing save a green and black striped loin-cloth. While the Strange Ones had long flowing hair, this man's head was clean-shaven and he wore a tight-fitting green leather cap on his head. He was totally unarmed; the only item he carried was a big leather bag containing rolls of what seemed like calfskin, small clay jars of medicine of different colours, ranging from white to deep blue. He also carried many pointed reeds and strange sticks with tiny tufts of animal hair at one end. This odd man walked with a slow step and an expression of unfathomable bitterness on his face and *Lulinda* wondered about him greatly; was he one of the Strange Ones or was he a captive, or slave? But she was to find out very soon.

Lulinda saw the village of *Lumbedu* in the distance, sitting like a circular scar on the domed forehead of an ancient hill. *Chikongo*, who had also seen the kraal at the same time, drew *Lulinda* to him, swiftly kissed her forehead and nose, and vanished in the forest. But the two young culprits knew nothing of the fact that a pair of eyes had seen them from the bush, the eyes of the last person on earth whom *Lulinda* would have wanted to discover her secret love affair. They were the eyes of *Ojoyo*, the First Wife of *Lumbedu* no less, and that boded ill for the lovers.

Lumbedu, the witchdoctor, was lying on a pile of leopard skins in his hut, pretending as usual to be very sick. He groaned and whined and writhed whenever one of his many wives entered his hut, but laughed and chortled and patted his greasy stomach when he was alone. It was while his Third Wife, *Vunakwe*, was holding a bowl of milk to his spatulate and blubbery lips that *Ojoyo's* strident voice crashed through the hut, edged with great fear and urgency.

'Hide the children; take them out of the kraal into the forest. *Lulinda* is coming – she is bringing the Strange Ones with her,' she cried. 'The Strange Ones are coming!'

Tumult, and confusion twice confused, burst like a violet poisonous flower through the kraal; screams, bawls, shrieks and the yapping of dogs tore the astonished skies apart. Women and howling children ran hither and thither like frightened goats among the huts. The fat ebony-black Second Wife, *Taundi*, grew so wild with fear that she threw her youngest child into a great bowl of ground corn and ran squealing fatly out of the kraal. She ran like a woman gone mad, down the hill and straight into *Lulinda* and her glittering companions.

The astonished Strange Ones saw a black mountain of a woman come tearing down the footpath and then leap high into the air with an unearthly, smothered shriek, and fall like a great female hippopotamus into a very prickly thornbush, as unconscious as the dreams of yester-year.

Lulinda paused and placed her small hand on her unconscious rival's fat chest. On finding her alive, she beckoned to her foreign companions to follow her. As they passed into the distance, *Taundi* slowly recovered consciousness and staggered to her feet, to start running again, faster than before, farther away from her husband's kraal, deeper and deeper into the dark forest.

Midday found her still running, sobbing hoarsely and bathed in sweat – but still running. She ran until she burst through into a clearing in the centre of which stood a village whose gate and stockade were lavishly decorated with human skulls, ribs and thigh-bones. *Taundi* recognised the village as that of *Dimo*, the Dreaded One, King of the Cannibals. With a loud scream she turned and stumbled back into the forest, but it was too late.

A crowd of slim and very beautiful female cannibals came running out of the village with *Dimo* himself bringing up the rear.

With loud squeaks and giggles of unspeakable joy they chased the panic-stricken *Taundi* through the forest until she dropped from sheer exhaustion. They seized her and frog-marched her back into the village with loud shrieks of laughter. They took her to a roofless hut where three great pots were already filled with water at the boil. The last thing *Taundi* saw on this earth was an incredibly beautiful young cannibal woman with filed teeth and heavy copper ornaments that blazed in the sun. A wicked-looking copper knife was clutched in the young cannibal's small hand.

'We see you, oh breakfast,' said the cannibal girl quite sweetly. 'We see you and are thankful for your having come to feed us.'

Lulinda entered *Lumbedu's* silent kraal with the Strange Ones close behind her. She raised her voice and called out, but nobody came. Then she began a systematic search through the kraal, finding nothing but broken pots and calabashes, spilt sourmilk and a sick dog lying behind a hut. She was about to give up her search when a muffled sneeze exploded within one of the great round *sisulu* granaries. She looked into the basket and there, crouching fat and monstrous and terribly afraid, was the great witchdoctor himself, bathed in sweat and quaking like a bowlful of sour porridge. 'Don't tell them,' he whispered. 'Please don't tell them I'm here!'

Like the disloyal and disobedient wife she was, *Lulinda* went to the gate of the kraal and beckoned to the Strange Ones to follow her. She calmly indicated the basket in which her fat lord was hiding. *Lumbedu* let out a loud scream of fear as he saw three bronze helmeted and pink-faced heads looking down into his basket. He uttered a loud scream as the basket was hacked to pieces by the giant leader of the Strange Ones, who then sheathed his big sword and hauled *Lumbedu* out by one arm.

Lumbedu wetted his loinskin and the Strange Ones roared with laughter. While the red-bearded giant and the brown-haired young man held the quaking witchdoctor forcibly erect, *Lulinda* explained the situation to him and when she had finished the young Strange One turned and snapped a few words to the odd man with the green striped loincloth and skull cap and concluded by kicking him soundly in the buttocks.

The odd man picked himself up out of the dust and sat down on one of *Ojoyo's* grindstones. He then opened his bag and, spreading its contents on the ground before him, he selected one of the rolled sheets of what looked like calf-skin and one of his pointed reeds. This reed he dipped into a small jar containing a black fluid and began tracing patterns and what looked like human figures on the roll of skin. Before the astonished eyes of *Lumbedu* and *Lulinda*, the odd man was making a long series of drawings on the calfskin roll – he was telling the story of the Strange Ones. He was telling in clear, unmistakable and beautiful pictures why the Strange Ones left their country and came to the Country of the Black Men.

First he showed a savage battle between the Strange Ones and another race with long flowing beards and hair. Then he showed the Strange Ones being routed in a charge by foot soldiers and warriors riding on fantastic vehicles drawn by strange beasts with long flowing tails and manes, like zebras without stripes. After this he showed a number of canoes with long poles in the middle and he drew figures representing the Strange Ones fleeing towards these canoes in wild panic.

He showed the males of the Strange Ones fighting a brave rear-guard battle while figures, obviously female and young, clambered aboard the canoes. The canoes were then represented in full sail over what was obviously water with fish and crabs swimming below the surface. He drew a circle representing the sun and made a hundred strokes under it.

'A hundred days,' breathed *Lulinda.*

Silently, ignoring the interruption, the odd man showed battles between Strange Ones and wild beasts, lions and elephants and leopards, battles that the Strange Ones, with their superior metal weapons always won. He dropped the now full calfskin and took out a second one.

Lulinda screamed when the odd man finished the first picture on the second sheet. The picture showed two black figures, male and female, embracing under a full moon near an old and dilapidated cluster of huts, and those two figures represented *Chikongo* and herself.

Unknowingly, unwittingly, the odd man was betraying *Lulinda* to *Lumbedu,* her husband. And soon, on the silent sheet of calfskin, the whole nocturnal adventure was exposed, up to the time when *Chikongo* kissed *Lulinda* for the last time and fled into the forest. There, on the silent parchment, the trembling *Lumbedu* not only read the story of the Strange Ones, but also that of *Lulinda* and her secret partner. All was set out in clear lines and many colours as plain as daylight. The adulterous love affair of his youngest and favourite wife stood out for all to see.

The odd man then started to explain in pictures that the Strange Ones were more than willing to trade some of their weapons for any foodstuffs, except meat. Then, after that, the red-bearded leader and the younger brown-haired man dropped *Lumbedu* contemptuously on the ground and started, together with the other Strange Ones, carrying off some of *Lumbedu's* full corn baskets. But for every basket they took they left a spear, an axe, or a knife behind – all superb weapons of gleaming steel or bronze.

While this was going on, *Lulinda* saw the odd man with the green striped loincloth leap over *Lumbedu's* kraal stockade with two stolen swords in his hand and vanish into the forest.

The Strange Ones left after drinking every drop of milk in the kraal and after the ever-smiling young man with the brown hair had stood over the prostrate and still badly scared *Lumbedu* taunting him cruelly in sign language for his great cowardice. It became plain to *Lulinda* that the Strange Ones had not yet noticed the odd man's escape.

Ojoyo and the rest of *Lumbedu's* wives and children did not return to the kraal until well after sunset. They found *Lumbedu* staring in blank fascination at the pile of weapons the Strange Ones had left in exchange for the corn. The first thing *Ojoyo* did on coming into the kraal was to root out *Lulinda* and call her an adultress to her face, describing in vivid language how she had seen her being kissed by *Chikongo* in the forest.

Lumbedu was still suffering from the after-effects of his great fright and could not think or talk straight, so his wives took the law into their own hands and bound *Lulinda* securely hand and foot in preparation for her ceremonial execution on the day to follow. They beat the helpless woman with their skin skirts, burned her thighs with hot stones, spat on her and blew their noses at her. They seized her breasts and pulled them until she shrieked with pain and, before they left her, they forced her to drink the entire contents from *Lumbedu's* clay urinal.

They were not being cruel; they were only doing exactly what the law and the customs of the tribes of the Dark Land say should be done to adultresses before they are executed. Then on the following morning, *Ojoyo* sent her eldest son *Gumbu* to the kraal of the Tribal Avengers with the request for the arrest of *Chikongo* as an adulterer.

Now, the Tribal Avengers were a group of men over whom no chief had any power and who had no tribal loyalty. They were men dedicated to the destruction of all those who broke tribal customs and, being members of no particular tribe, their assistance could be enlisted by anybody from any tribe. Even the chiefs lived in fear of the fanatically dedicated Avengers and many, in our land's strange history, are the chiefs who fell victims to the spears of this secret group of men who had chosen to be shorn of their powers of fatherhood and who could kill a woman with the same pitilessness with which they killed a man.

They led loveless, joyless lives, these strange men, living only for the enforcement of the centuries-old customs of the Black Race. Very often nobody knew just who they were because they always wore heavy woven bark masks whenever they emerged from their isolated kraal during daytime.

Thus it was that by midday on that cloudy day, a strange figure was seen coming up the hill on which *Mburu's* tiny kraal was perched like a lost bird on a rock. *Mburu* was the father of *Chikongo*, who was an only son amongst many daughters.

'Look, what is that coming up the path?' said one of the girls to *Manjanja*, the First Wife.

Manjanja's eyes were fast losing their sight although she was only four-and-forty years old, and they groped blindly in an effort to see what the girl was pointing at. 'I see nothing, child,' she said. 'Tell me what you see.'

'It is a man, but he is wearing a *chinyau* mask on his head and he is clothed from ankle to neck in leopard skin. He is carrying in one hand a big club shaped like a man, a carved club with a big head and ugly face. He has an axe that looks terrible.'

The half-blind woman leapt to her feet with a choking cry; she knew very well who and what the masked man was. She called urgently for her husband and to *Chwenyana*, the Second Wife.

'Oh my fathers,' cried *Mburu*, 'an Avenger!' The Tribal Avenger paused outside *Mburu's* kraal and called out harshly: 'You in there ... you, *Mburu*, the son of *Timburu*, the son of *Chumba*, son of *Kondo* ... come out and stand outside the gate of your kraal, which I will not defile my feet by entering. Come on out and hear what I have to say.'

Mburu came out, a proud, brave man who had once been a leopard hunter until a leopard mauled his right arm, paralysing it forever. He stood facing the dreaded Avenger without fear and without expression on his strong, bearded face.

'Speak, Avenger, I listen.'

'Your miserable son, whom I shall not defile my mouth by mentioning by name,' said the Avenger, 'has slept more than once with one *Lulinda*, who is the youngest of the females of one *Lumbedu* who pretends to be a witchdoctor. Your wretched son knew very well what he was doing and he knew that stealing another man's love-mat from under him is a breach of custom, punishable by any kind of slow death that the insulted man may choose for the offender. And since *Lumbedu* has sent a complaint to us, we are positive that your son is guilty and we have already sentenced him to death. So your son is now bound by law to go to *Lumbedu's* kraal and receive the death he so richly deserves. Do you have any questions to ask?'

'No, Avenger, we have none,' *Mburu* replied, choking back a sob. 'If you say my son is guilty then he is guilty.'

'Now I shall make a trail of cowrie shells from here to *Lumbedu's* kraal,' said the Avenger, 'and your son must come out naked and follow that trail – he must be at *Lumbedu's* kraal before sunset, and he must be dead by evening.'

As *Chikongo* dropped his loinskin and took leave of his parents, his mother *Manjanja* clung desperately to him, her only son, crying bitterly and saying: 'Oh, Oh light of my fading eyes, my child, why . . . why did you do it?'

'I do not know, mother,' whispered *Chikongo.* 'Goodbye now, mother.'

'My son,' said his father, 'do not be afraid. Just show that fat bloated dog of a *Lumbedu* how *Timburu's* grandson can die. Die like a warrior, my son; die with a smile on your lips as your warrior grandfather died.'

As *Chikongo* took the last cowrie-strewn journey of his young life, *Mburu* drew his weeping wives into his hut and took an Oath of Vengeance in which he swore to kill the witchdoctor *Lumbedu* one day, even if it took him years of waiting.

It was in the afternoon when *Chikongo* came through the gate of *Lumbedu's* kraal and to his own great surprise he felt utterly unafraid; in fact, he felt very angry and actually wanted to die. As he entered the kraal he saw *Ojoyo* and the rest of *Lumbedu's* wives standing in a scowling semicircle, leering, with bone or copper knives in their hands. Beyond them he saw the tall Avenger standing with folded arms next to *Lumbedu* and his son *Gumbu,* who was now armed with one of the metal spears the Strange Ones had left.

'Come on, you foul bitches,' cried *Chikongo.* 'Come on and get it over with?'

'No, my boy,' said *Ojoyo,* with a nasty smile, 'we shall come on, but we shall not get it over with in a hurry. You shall suffer a lot before you die. I would like to hear you scream for mercy before we despatch you.'

'You shall never make me whine, you dirty slut,' snarled *Chikongo.* 'I am not your husband who squeals like a pig when you so much as point a finger at him. Come on, do your worst.'

And do their worst they did. But never once did the brave young man cry out, even when his entire lower abdomen had become one bloody mess of spurting blood and tattered flesh. They held him down, but he never so much as attempted to struggle and at long last he opened his mouth and gave one long shuddering gasp.

'Now you are going to squeal, my bush-pig. Come on, let us hear you squeal,' *Ojoyo* cried.

'No, you foul she-hyaena,' gasped *Chikongo.* 'I shall not cry out. But I am feeling very sorry for you all. Today you kill me, but tomorrow, or a few moons from now, you . . . you too shall be dying. You have fallen like trapped flies into the web of Death and soon he shall come and consume you all.'

With that, the son of *Mburu,* son of *Timburu,* died. He died as his valiant father had told him to die; he died as his grandfather *Timburu* had died so long ago – bravely, without a murmur.

'He cursed us . . . he cursed us with his last breath,' sobbed *Vunakwe,* who had taken no part in the ghastly execution. 'We are all cursed.'

'Be silent, you weak-bellied bitch,' snarled *Ojoyo.* 'Some of you bring out *Lulinda* quickly.'

Lulinda was dragged out of her hut and flung brutally upon her dead lover's body and all eyes turned towards the tall masked form of the Tribal Avenger for further instructions.

'Did you make the raft?' snapped the Tribal Avenger to *Gumbu,* the son of *Lumbedu.*

'Yes, Mighty One, we did.'

'Then drag this adultress and this dead dog out of here to the riverside and tie them together face to face. Roll them on to the raft and tie them firmly to it. Then push the raft into the river – the scaly crocodiles shall deal with both dead and living. I have spoken.'

How long *Lulinda* drifted down the Zambezi she did not know; it seemed like aeons and aeons. Her body was numb and her brain was fast approaching the valley of madness. She kept her eyes tightly shut all the time because whenever she opened them she stared into the wide-open eyes of her dead *Chikongo.* The cruel leather thongs that tied her to the raft were biting into her flesh like red-hot copper knives, and the wake of blood – *Chikongo's* blood – that the raft was leaving behind, was attracting whole tribes of ravaging crocodiles. Something huge, scaly and long-snouted clambered on to the raft and fastened its teeth on the dead man's leg, towing the raft nearer to the south bank of the river. But just when *Lulinda* had given herself up for dead, she saw a canoe creep into her limited field of vision, a canoe that turned its prow and bore down upon her raft and the swarming crocodiles clustering about it. *Lulinda* saw that there was only one man in the canoe – she could see him clearly silhouetted against the last glow of the dying sun.

The darting canoe rammed the raft and tore it out of the crowd of crocodiles swimming around it. Then *Lulinda* felt a weapon of unbelievable sharpness cutting her bonds to pieces. She felt strong hands snatch her out of the very jaws of a crocodile. She had a glimpse of a smiling thin-lipped mouth, a straight nose and a pair of bright black eyes. She saw a face handsome in a strange alien way – a face she had seen before. It was the face of the odd man who had escaped from the Strange Ones at *Lumbedu's* kraal. *Lulinda* passed into the vale of unconsciousness in the arms of the light brown-skinned foreigner.

The legends say the odd man took *Lulinda* away to the safety of the great forests in the south of what was in later years to be known as the land of the Varozwi people. There the odd man gathered all the small tribes and clans and welded them into one mighty tribe to which he tried to impart some of the arts and the knowledge of his faraway native land. Even today the tribe this tawny-skinned foreigner founded is known throughout the land of the Black Tribes as the only one that practises the strange art of fortune-telling by gazing at the stars. The Varozwi is the only tribe practising mummification of its chiefs. Before a young Varozwi prince can assume the headdress and *kaross* of chief, he is forced to spend four nights in a cave in which are the mummified bodies of his father and ancestors. He must pray to each of these desiccated corpses for strength and wisdom and demand from each a blessing and a spiritual light to show him the road of life.

But, apart from the fact that the odd man founded the Varozwi Tribe, no clear details of his adventures and eventual death have reached us from across the gulf of time and his is one of the few stories in the land of the tribes where the story-teller must speak but a few words and be silent, because there is no more left to tell, for Time, that devouring monster, has devoured the rest.

Gumbu, the rascally son of a rascally father, knelt before his fat parents *Lumbedu* and *Ojoyo* and gave them advice – advice that was to affect thousands of lives and change the history of the whole southern part of the land of the tribes; advice that was to lead *Lumbedu* along the downward path to the valley of undoing and a miserable death.

Gumbu told his parents that since they were the only people who knew what the Strange Ones wanted, they should be the only people to trade big baskets full of corn, yams and pots full of milk for the superior iron and bronze weapons of the Strange Ones. With these weapons, *Lumbedu* could easily seize power and rule the whole land as a High Chief. *Gumbu* pointed out with jackal-like cunning that a few men armed with these metal weapons could easily rout a whole army armed with bone-tipped spears and stone axes, as was the case with all the armies of the tribal chiefs at this time. It must be remembered that at this time the only metal that Black people knew was copper, with which they made ornaments and knives for stabbing only.

The selfish, ambitious old charlatan *Lumbedu* fell down on his hands and knees and actually kissed his son's feet like a beggarly slave for the suggestion he had made and the next few days saw a brisk trade between *Lumbedu* and the ships of the Strange Ones, which came crawling like many-legged sea serpents up the Zambezi river. *Lumbedu's* wives and daughters would put full baskets of corn or yams in a particular place on the bank of the Zambezi and then beat a tattoo on a big drum before retiring into the forest. The ship of the Strange Ones would then edge nearer to the bank and its occupants would pick up the baskets, leaving a pile of spears in exchange. Within five days, the witchdoctor had enough weapons to arm close to two hundred men and it was then that *Gumbu* gathered together a small army of ruffianly cut-throats and armed them with the deadly metal spears and swords. In one short, savage battle he overthrew the High Chief of the land, *Chungwe*, and slew him on the doorstep of his own Royal Hut.

Lumbedu became a High Chief in one day. The gross, whining and utterly selfish wretch suddenly found himself waddling like an overfed vulture at the head of twenty thousand subjects and the heady fumes of the mead of power and ambition made him drunk as yesterday's nightmare. He wanted to conquer until he ruled the whole world and traded and pleaded with the Strange Ones for more weapons and still more.

His wild, undisciplined armies tore like wildfire across the shocked land and chief after chief fell before the new weapons of metal, and tribe after tribe was enslaved. *Gumbu's* savage hordes swept southward into the land of the ancient people known as the Ba-Tswana who, blessed by the Great Spirit itself centuries earlier, had been living in peace for generations. Here, in this land, *Gumbu* demanded that the defeated tribal chief, *Mulaba*, should give him his daughter *Temana* as a wife and as a hostage, and he took this lovely maiden back home with him to *Lumbedu's* kraal after leaving governors to hold the land in his father's name.

On the way back, however, *Gumbu* was stricken by the eye disease called *karkatchi* and became totally blind in less than six weeks. Then one night *Temana* led the blind *Gumbu* to the very edge of a great cliff and pushed him over before leaping to her own death. The legends say that where *Temana* fell at the base of the cliff a cluster of tiny sweet-smelling red wild flowers soon grew, the origin of the *letemana* flowers which still grow there among the rocks to this day.

Meanwhile *Lumbedu* had become the undisputed chief of the biggest empire the tribes had ever seen – an empire that sprawled from the Inyangani mountains to the shores of the western ocean. What is so amusing about *Lumbedu's* empire and reign is that it lasted only one full year and eight moons.

While *Lumbedu* bathed in the sunshine of power and drank deep from his beer-pot; while his woman *Ojoyo* bedecked herself with hundreds of gleaming ornaments and had numerous slaves to obey her every wish and the land trembled at the mention of *Lumbedu's* name, a strange conference was taking place in the great grass village the Strange Ones had built for themselves at the mouth of the Zambezi river.

Four men sat around a wooden table inside a great four-cornered grass hut. One of these men was a tall bearded red-haired giant with the scars of many battles on his massive body and the other was an old man with long hair and a flowing beard that was as white as mountain snow. This old man wore broad circlets of gold, studded with precious stones, around his head and he wore a long tunic of purple cloth, over which he had thrown a flaming red cloak. The third man was of the same race as the odd man who had saved *Lulinda* and he had a white loincloth painted with strange and mysterious signs in red and black. On his head he wore a headdress of blue and red striped cloth and a yellow cobra reared menacingly above his forehead from the golden band around his head.

The fourth member of the council was a happy-looking brown-haired young man with blue eyes who entered the council hut long after the first three had been sitting. He had entered the hut with mischief dancing in his bright eyes and had then proceeded to make faces at the red-bearded giant before giving his big broken nose a playful tweak.

'You are late, my son,' said the old Strange One.

'That I am, my father, is your fault. You gave me a wife at my tender age and now half my nights are without sleep. You see . . .'

'Be quiet, the King awaits your report and not details of what you do at night with your wife,' roared the red-haired giant.

'My son,' said the white-haired King gravely, 'we are here to discuss a serious matter and not to jest. All we want to know is whether our plan is working properly – the plan of supplying the fat *Lumbedu* with weapons under the pretence of trade and then letting him conquer his own fellow people for us. We would like to know whether he is still unaware of our intent to come in once he has finished and to take over from him.'

'Our plan is working well, beyond our wildest dreams, my father,' said the young man. 'Even now our bloated greasy friend has added yet another tribe to his empire and it will not be long before a great empire, with thousands of slaves, falls into our hands like ripe fruit.'

'We cannot afford to wait much longer – we must strike now. Where we had a hundred separate tribes to conquer, we now have only one fat son of a vile hippopotamus to strike down and all his empire shall be in our hands,' said the man with the loincloth.

'I agree,' said the King. 'We have waited far too long. Tonight we must attack that dog's village.'

Lumbedu was feeling on top of the very stars, let alone on top of the world, and he was as happy as a starveling beggar's stomach which has just digested a stolen fowl. He was as happy as a lion with a million teeth and a thousand mouths.

Now if *Lumbedu* was as proud of his being a chief as a lion with many mouths, his First Wife *Ojoyo* was as proud of her suddenly finding herself a queen, as a vulture with many gizzards. Every morning she was carried in an elaborately carved litter to the riverside by a veritable bevy of beauties from her husband's harem and there she was bathed, smeared with crushed *tambuti* leaves all over until she smelt like a big fat sweet-scented flower. Then she was bedecked with copper necklaces and bracelets. She feasted all day long on wild honey, corn cakes, very fatty meat, and greasy yam stew.

She was shrill and cruel to the rest of the wives of *Lumbedu* and she could kill any one of them on the slightest provocation. She was, however, a woman with two guilty secrets lying heavy on her rotten soul and both these secrets would have earned her a slow and miserable death at the hands of the Tribal Avengers, had they become known. Firstly, she had poisoned the kind-hearted *Vunakwe* who had been *Lumbedu's* Second Wife and had buried her secretly in the hut where she, *Ojoyo*, always slept. And she had lied to *Lumbedu* by saying that *Vunakwe* had fallen into the Zambezi.

Secondly, *Ojoyo* had a secret lover whom she kept imprisoned in a cave in the forest and whom she always visited whenever the flame of desire burnt within her. This secret lover was a young boy of eighteen years and *Ojoyo* knew that seducing a person of that age who had not been initiated into adulthood according to custom was an offence punishable by death. No persons under twenty-five are allowed to so much as kiss, or be kissed by, members of the opposite sex.

Ojoyo had never asked her prisoner lover who his parents were and all she knew about the youth was that his name was *Kadimo. Kadimo* had been captured by *Lumbedu's* warriors while wandering aimlessly in the forest and, being a member of an unknown tribe, he had been brought into *Lumbedu's* kraal for questioning and execution. *Kadimo*, however, could not speak the language of *Lumbedu's* tribe and his only answer to the harsh questioning by the warriors as to the name and whereabouts of his tribe, had been nothing but a series of pathetic head-shakings. *Ojoyo* had suddenly felt herself drawn to the godlike youth *Kadimo* and had asked *Lumbedu* to give her the captive ostensibly for torture and killing, but in reality to imprison him in a cave and use him as a secret source of pleasure.

On the fateful day when the Strange Ones had finally decided to attack *Lumbedu's* village during the coming night, *Lumbedu* and *Ojoyo* had been feasting in their great hut from early morning to late afternoon. They had been celebrating twenty-five years of marriage according to tribal custom; they had eaten together a whole raw flamingo and then drunk a bowl of milk mixed with honey. They continued their gigantic feast with fowls and roasted meat washed down with pots full of cornbeer – till they passed into the valley of unconsciousness together. Now nobody else in *Lumbedu's* kraal had been invited to this private feast, because only the man and his wife should be present during the ceremony of the 'Eating of the Flamingo'. The result of this was that, although *Lumbedu* and *Ojoyo* were lying drunk and insensible in their hut, everyone else in the Great Kraal was as sober as the morning breeze.

A man came running into the kraal at about midnight – he had been running through the forest for he knew not how long – and he had come to warn *Lumbedu* that the Strange Ones were advancing up the southern bank of the Zambezi in full force and that their intentions were definitely not friendly, as the now dead villagers whose headman this man had been, had found out. The man found sentries at the gate of *Lumbedu's* kraal and to them he whispered his story before he collapsed at their feet.

'I am the headman of the village of *Lumoja* – quickly, warn the High Chief that the Strange Ones are coming. They mean war – they have killed all the people in my village and will soon be here.'

While two of the guards ran to warn everybody in the kraal, one stopped to help the fallen man to his feet. But he discovered that the man's back was covered in blood and that there was a long deep wound under his left shoulder-blade. Only sheer willpower and great courage had kept this brave man running for so long, while badly wounded.

Panic reigned supreme in *Lumbedu's* kraal that dark and star-spangled night. People fled naked out of the threatened kraal into the doubtful safety of the forests. Screams tore the night as some were pounced upon by leopards and night-hunting lions. Instead of standing and preparing to fight to the death in the kraal of their High Chief, the undisciplined and disloyal warriors of *Lumbedu* launched their fleet of battle canoes and escaped into the night carrying off *Lumbedu's* many wives and concubines with them to safety across the Zambezi.

Meanwhile *Lumbedu* and *Ojoyo* still lay in drunken stupor inside their hut where they had defied the best efforts of their subjects and children to wake them up. An hour before dawn something must have warned *Ojoyo* because she stirred uneasily and woke up. A few moments later she crawled out of the hut, urged by a strange sense of uneasiness that suddenly burst into flower in her soul. She called out to the night guards at the gate, but no one answered. The whole kraal was mysteriously deserted.

This stunning fact penetrated deep into *Ojoyo's* drunken brain and a terrible fear tore through her, leaving her as sober as the morning dew.

Then somewhere in the forest she heard the steady sounds of marching feet and the clash of metal on metal coming nearer and nearer. She sensed the murderous purpose behind those sounds and the dead man at the gate confirmed her worst suspicions. *Ojoyo* screamed in terror.

She ran back to the Royal Hut and tried to waken *Lumbedu* by shaking him violently and calling his name repeatedly. But he only turned over on his back and snored louder than ever.

An alien war-cry shattered the starry night like a blow from a knobkierie as the Strange Ones burst into the kraal like a horde of mad bronze-clad demons from hell itself. *Ojoyo* crawled out of the Great Hut like a scalded snake and made her escape through one of the small emergency gates in the stockade, leaving the drunken *Lumbedu* to his fate.

First one and then the other of the two guard-huts flanking the gate burst into flame as the attackers set them on fire. Soon the whole lower portion of the kraal near the main gate was a mass of flames and redly glowing clouds of billowing smoke. The Strange Ones began to ransack the empty huts and to remove hundreds of sourmilk calabashes and dozens of baskets full of corn and yams. These they placed in the centre of the vast clearing before they set the huts on fire.

It was then that *Lumbedu* awoke and crawled drunkenly out of his hut and stood swaying on the raised clay doorstep.

'You . . . why are you burning my kraal?' he cried thickly.

A group of Strange Ones came running towards him, brandishing swords and gleaming bronze spears, but *Lumbedu* was far too intoxicated to be scared and stared blearily at them, standing his ground.

One of the Strange Ones aimed a sword blow at *Lumbedu's* head, a blow that was not intended to kill or to injure, but which passed harmlessly over his shiny bald pate. *Lumbedu* balled his fists and stood his ground, not even blinking.

One of the Strange Ones said to the King's brown-haired son: 'Behold, how brave this fat barbarian is; he has chosen to remain behind while the rest of his people escape. I did not know these black pigs could be so brave.'

Suddenly *Lumbedu* began to dance, urged by nothing less than the fumes of the strong beer he had drunk in such quantities. He stamped and capered like a mad gorilla up and down the firelit clearing in the centre of his burning kraal. He puffed and stamped and grunted and shook until his fat feet stirred up clouds of dust around them. Then, for a reason which even he could not understand, he snatched a spear from the hands of one of the astonished Strange Ones and ran himself through with it.

The young prince of the Strange Ones stood over the body of the dead *Lumbedu* and for once he was not smiling. He shook his helmeted head and said: 'He was a very brave man. He chose death instead of slavery – just as we would do.'

'Let us take what we can and leave here,' said the prince a while later. 'I'm sure that my father will be pleased to hear that he is now the Emperor of a great land full of thousands of black, thieving dirty-skinned barbarians!'

The traitor *Lumbedu* who had played into the hands of the Strange Ones and had betrayed hundreds of thousands of his people into slavery, was dead, but of his woman, *Ojoyo*, a story remains to be told.

Ojoyo paused once in her wild flight through the forest and, looking behind her, saw the two huts near the main gate in flames. That blood-chilling sight caused yet another spurt of speed and she ran even faster than before. In the course of her flight she heard the sounds of a wild animal in the forest and stopped dead in her tracks with her heart in her mouth, until the beast had gone past. At last she came to a familiar stream which she knew flowed past the cave where she was keeping the youth *Kadimo* a prisoner. As the grey light of dawn touched the sky, *Ojoyo* found the well-worn path that led up to *Kadimo's* cave and followed it slowly and wearily as it twisted and turned past great rocks and boulders. As she approached the cave, a squat ugly figure detached itself from the rock behind which it had been hiding and barred her way.

'Ho! Who you?' growled the ugly one. 'You go back or you die.'

'It is I, *Ojoyo*, my trustworthy *Zozo*,' said she with a smile at the hunch-backed and unbelievably ugly idiot whom she had placed to guard the youth *Kadimo* day and night.

'*Zozo* see you, Queen,' said the idiot, dropping on his knee.

'Open the cave for me, *Zozo*, and then you can go into your own cave and sleep,' *Ojoyo* commanded.

The powerful hunchback rolled aside the boulder that stood in the entrance of the cave and then fled into his own cave. *Ojoyo* entered the prison cave and felt around in the darkness for her youthful captive.

'Wake up, *Kadimo*,' said she, 'wake up, my love.'

For a long time after that *Ojoyo* and *Kadimo* sat side by side in a dark recess of the cave conversing in low voices. *Ojoyo* told the youth about what had happened in *Lumbedu's* kraal that night and concluded by saying she feared *Lumbedu* had been killed.

'Now you . . . belong . . . *Kadimo*, . . . all his,' said the youth who could by then speak a few words of the language of *Ojoyo's* tribe.

'Yes, *Kadimo*.'

'When dawn comes, we . . . go away . . . back to my village. You come . . . back with me.'

'And *Zozo* too?' asked *Ojoyo*.

'No, *Kadimo* hates *Zozo* . . . *Kadimo* wants *Ojoyo* . . . alone.'

'As you say, *Kadimo*.'

By midday of the day that followed *Ojoyo* and *Kadimo* were far away from the burnt-out kraal which *Ojoyo* had ruled with cruelty and insolence only the day before.

Ojoyo was beginning to become very afraid of *Kadimo* as his attitude rapidly changed from one of respect to insolence. He had now stopped calling her Queen and addressed her as 'you'. He even threatened to beat her up if she tried to sit down and rest. But the greatest surprise was yet to come.

'I'm tired, I want you to carry me on your back, you fat cow,' he indicated in a broken tongue.

'Fat . . . fat cow!' gasped *Ojoyo*. 'Did I hear you call me a fat cow?'

'Yes . . . you fat cow,' said the youth. 'Now bend down . . . and carry me.'

'Never!'

Kadimo's great knobkierie thudded solidly against *Ojoyo's* royal ribs many times. She screamed and writhed and rolled on the ground as *Kadimo* gave her the greatest beating of her life. At long last the pain became such that *Ojoyo* began to whimper like a child and to beg *Kadimo* not to hit her again.

'Why are you so cruel to me?' she sobbed. 'I am your Queen.'

'You are my supper . . . you are my edible queen!'

'What, you mean that you are a cannibal!'

'I am *Kadimo* . . . son of *Dimo* . . . son of *Sodimo* . . . my father . . . King of the Cannibals.'

'But you can't eat me, beloved one,' pleaded *Ojoyo.* 'I love you and I am still beautiful . . .'

'You . . . more beautiful . . . in stewpot. Tonight . . . we come to father's village. Come . . . carry me!'

How long *Ojoyo* carried the youth she did not know – it seemed like hundreds of years. When she stumbled and fell, throwing *Kadimo,* he always got up to beat her cruelly before getting on her back again. On and on she stumbled until the skies became as black as midnight and bolts of bluish lightning began to scourge the tortured heavens, while peal after peal of thunder shook the very roots of the earth. *Kadimo* prodded his human steed to the shelter of the forest where they found a small cave and in this cave *Ojoyo* found a chance to rest.

'Not far from . . . father's village. When arrive . . . *Kadimo* shall have . . . nice slice . . . for supper.'

'*Kadimo* . . . I beg you . . .'

But she got no further as a squat, hunchbacked and incredibly ugly shape burst into the cave and seized *Kadimo* by the ankle, dragging him outside into the howling rains. There was a short savage struggle, a loud gurgling scream and silence. Then the bowlegged and hunchbacked monstrosity called *Zozo,* who had trailed them relentlessly across the plains and through the forests, entered the cave.

'*Zozo*!' cried *Ojoyo.* 'You saved me – he was going to eat me!'

'Yes, I saved you, but not for long. You knew *Vunakwe*?' asked the hunchback.

'Yes, I knew her very well; she fell into the Zambezi and . . .'

'You lie shamefully . . . you killed *Vunakwe,* and *Zozo* is *Vunakwe's* brother.'

'*Vunakwe* had no brothers, I knew her father, her whole family.'

'Father of *Vunakwe* . . . never owned that *Zozo* was his son, because *Zozo* a deformed thing. *Zozo* always lived alone. Now you die.'

'No *Zozo*! You saved me . . .'

'Die *Ojoyo*!'

A copper knife stabbed down fiercely . . . once . . . twice . . .

* * *

After *Lumbedu's* death the Strange Ones came out into the open and took over the astonished land. Soon hundreds of people began to feel the sting of the slave-driver's whip within the borders of their own native land. Dozens, scores of kraals and villages stood empty, their inhabitants having been forced into the Strange Ones' ships and taken away across the seas, never to be seen again.

The shocked land saw sights it had never seen before – long lines of men, women and children tied together with chains like living beads on a string, hauling sleds of stones the Strange Ones used to build great forts all over the land as far south as beyond the Herero. The shocked land also saw thousands of its black sons made to dig into the bowels of the earth like so many ants, to bring up iron ore, copper, and the yellow 'sun metal'. The Sacred Iron Mountain of Taba-Tsipi, or Taba-Zimbi, became a mass of tunnels in which tens of thousands of chained slaves worked and died.

Long trains of oxen and even tamed zebras began to wind their way eastward over mountains and across plains, heavily laden with gold, iron ore and ivory, to be loaded on to ships of the Strange Ones and taken across the sea.

Elephants and hippos – the animals hitherto regarded as sacred by nearly all the tribes – were butchered by the Strange Ones from one corner of the agonised land to the other, the elephants for their ivory and the hippos for their bones and blubber.

Many tribes fled from the wanton destruction and oppression of the Strange Ones and some of these tribes even reached that country which is now Swaziland.

Contrary to those who claim to know about the Black people, the Swazi people did *not* branch from the Nguni tribes that migrated into the lands south of the Limpopoma about eight hundred years ago. The Swazi and the Bomvana tribes came south of the Limpopoma much earlier than did the Nguni. When the Nguni came, they found the Swazi had degenerated to such an extent that they no longer built villages, but lived in trees like monkeys; hence the popular insult of 'Tree Dwellers' the Nguni (from whom the Zulus sprang) applied to the Swazis.

The Swazis adopted the culture and even the language of the Nguni, which they speak with a hissing accent. They even adopted the weapons and the battle tactics of the Nguni. The Swazi are well known for their habit of wearing their hair very long and even dyeing it red with clay and wild root juices. They still imitate the long hair of those long-dead White men who invaded the Black land more than two thousand years ago.

The Strange Ones established great plantations near the Inyangani Mountains and here thousands of slaves also toiled, planting, hoeing and reaping corn and other crops which the Strange Ones had brought from their native lands. Even today, traces of these fantastic plantations that legends say were fertilised with hacked bits of bodies of dead slaves during winter, still survive for all to see and marvel at. These are known today as the terraced plantations of Inyanga. No Black people ever farmed in the terraced style.

In the course of time, more of the Strange Ones came to settle in the land, together with members of that hated race called the Arabi, which was to wreak so much havoc in our land in years that followed. Many of the Strange Ones took wives from the Lawu (Hottentots) and from the Batwa (Bushmen) races and many became the sons and daughters of Strange Ones and Yellow Ones.

Fifty years after *Lumbedu's* death the Strange Ones began to build many cities and villages in the land. But the biggest and most important city was on the shores of lake Makarikari – today a vast shallow salt pan.

This city was big enough to contain more than a thousand people, the legends say, and it was surrounded by a strong stockade of wood with stone towers at regular intervals. A deep ditch, filled with water, went completely around the city, rendering it utterly impregnable to attack, and the only entry into the city was over a short wooden bridge across the ditch into a gateway. A great settlement sprang up around the city in the course of time as hundreds of traders, slave-raiders and ordinary settlers built their homes outside the city walls, and there raised their families.

The Strange Ones began to multiply in the land, although fever and all-too-frequent epidemics killed many of them. As a result of their trade with lands beyond the great waters, the Strange Ones amassed fantastic wealth in their homes and cities and they lived their lives in great luxury. Today, one still finds in the possession of Bantu witchdoctors incredibly old and rusted swords with bronze hilts, swords so old that their blades crumble at a light blow with a stone. There are unbelievably old ornaments of gold and silver and bronze – ornaments that are neither Bantu nor Arabi; worn, pitted and even distorted by age – ornaments that are today very jealously guarded by Tribal Historians and High Witchdoctors as the Secret Charms of the tribe. These ornaments are still used today in secret rituals and they still keep the memory of the Strange Ones fresh in Tribal Story-Tellers' minds.

As time went on, the empire of the Strange Ones, like all things based on murder, oppression and theft, began to take the downward path of decay. The number of ships that crawled up the mouth of the Zambezi began to lessen gradually and many of the sites where gold, iron and copper had been mined were abandoned and forgotten.

Gradually the empire of the Strange Ones was isolated from the world outside and the Strange Ones turned more and more of their attention to making their lives as full of luxury and pleasure as possible. Soon the lives of each and every one of them became one long orgy of song, dance, food and drink. They invented new and fantastic ways of entertainment. They had idols before which they performed orgies both revolting and utterly fantastic. The legends say that some of their queens and empresses began mating with beasts in attempts at finding new sources of carnal pleasure. Some even tried to mate their daughters to lions in an attempt at producing a new race of men who were supposed to combine the courage, endurance and ferocity of lions with the intelligence of human beings.

The legends also say that one of the Emperors of the Strange Ones had a young man for a Queen and he used to kill women, both of his own race and of the Bantu race, with great cruelty, as entertainment.

It is said that the Emperors of the Strange Ones called themselves the 'Children of the Star', because they claimed to have descended from a star that fell on earth, which took a young woman of the Strange Ones and had sons by her.

The next part of this strange story of the Strange Ones begins with the birth of a man called *Mukanda*, or *Lumukanda*, the Destroyer, who was destined to play a major role in the history of the Strange Ones. *Lumukanda* was born of slave parents in one of the filthy underground stalls where the slaves were kept in the great city on the shores of lake Makarikari.

He grew up a slave who knew no other kind of life except that of

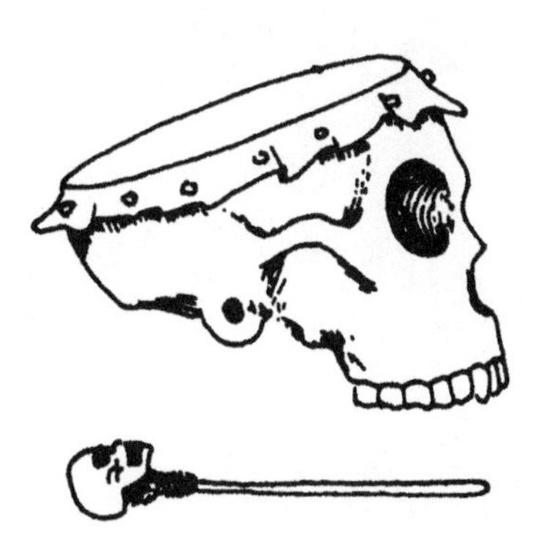

SKULL DRUM USED IN
MACABRE MA-ITI RITES

a slave. To him, as to all others born in slavery, the word freedom meant absolutely nothing and he lived only to be commanded and to obey. He was nothing but a puppet, dancing and capering at the commands of cruel masters.

By this time, the Black race between the Zambezi and Limpopoma rivers had been all but totally annihilated and the only free people there were the dead ones. At the time when the mighty hero *Lumakanda* was a youth of sixteen the empire of the Strange Ones was suddenly split violently into two as the result of a war between the White Emperors whose names have come down to us as *Kadesi* and *Karesu.* (These are not their true names; the Tribal Chroniclers have corrupted them in the course of time.)

When the story (which custom commands us to tell in *Lumakanda's* own words) commences, this war between the quarrelling foreign rulers had just ended in defeat and flight for *Kadesi,* and victory for the unnatural *Karesu* who had a male and not a female consort.

And so, my children, now begins the strangest story of all – the second sequel of our great Zima-Mbje Story, the grand epic that is still sung and chanted by many tribes even today, the undying story of the undying man who loved a goddess and who changed the destiny of an empire.

THE STORY OF LUMUKANDA

THE WHISPERING NIGHT

Night had fallen, but the feasting in the house of the man who owned me went on without pause. The great hall was one blaze of light from the many torches burning steadily inside. The sounds of merriment were loud in my ears as I stood guard at the gate with my friend *Lubo.*

Many were the masters who came into the gate, but few were those who went out – and they left only because they were so full of good food and so drunk they could eat and drink no more.

Some left our owner's house on gilded stretchers carried by slaves because they had passed into the dark valleys of unconsciousness as a result of the vast quantities of beer and wine they had consumed. One of them came out in the most un-masterly fashion, being dragged out by the hair by no less a person than our owner's son, and flung head over heels down the clay steps of the great house into the dust. We learnt later that this worthy had been treated in such a fashion because he had heatedly told the owner of the house that rather than see the mad and unnatural *Karesu* ruling the Empire, he would have *Kadesi* on the throne. That was treasonable talk and *Lubo* and I agreed that the offending master had got off very lightly indeed.

The moon rose and its eerie light gave the white-painted houses of the great city a delicate, ghostly quality that had to be seen to be believed. Beyond the brooding stockades that guarded the city like a crocodile's jaws, the huge expanse of water that was Makarikari became one fantastic sheet of living silver. A few stars sparkled faintly in the heavens, fighting a losing battle against the grey soft light of the sacred orb of the night and the song of thousands of crickets was loud.

There were no thoughts of what the future held for me; I had no speculations over what was in store for me. I, and the rest of my shackled race, led our lives like the beasts of burden we were; it was of no use for us to speculate or to dream, because daydreams make a slave's life more intolerable than the chains around his ankles and neck.

A rasping voice rang out from the top of the steps behind us: '*Lumukanda*, the second slave, the master calls for you.'

It was the old man, *Obu*, the first slave, who was in charge of all of us younger slaves in the master's house and grainfields. I turned and ran up the short flight of steps and then stood with bowed head just inside the door of the great hall. The masters and their females lay, or reclined, on gilded wooden couches along the three walls of the great high-roofed hall. Along the fourth wall, on either side of the door, stood cup-bearer slaves. Female slaves were carrying big baskets loaded with fruit, meat and corncakes, all ready to replenish the cup or the plate of any of the masters who might so wish.

There were small ivory-legged tables near each couch. On one stood the shining beer-cups while on the other stood the cake trays and meat plates. I could not help noticing that most of the masters now paid more attention to the beer cups than to the meat trays. The masters wore nothing save golden necklaces and bracelets, and white cloaks which they had only thrown around their waists because of the humidity. The females wore only light skirts and many golden bracelets and necklaces. A few even had broad golden bands around their heads. Their hair, ranging in colour from red to brown and to jet black, cascaded about their smooth shoulders like living smoke. Through the ringing of loud laughter and buzz of talking came my owner's voice from the far corner of the hall:

'You there, at the door, come to the middle of the hall.'

'As you command, Master,' I called out, drawing myself erect and stepping into the open space in the centre of the great hall.

'Look at him,' roared my owner to the rest of the masters. 'Look at that tall black brute – only sixteen and yet as tall as an adult and just as heavily muscled. I am willing to wager two big elephant tusks full of gold dust that none of your slaves can beat him in a sword fight.'

'Taken,' shrieked one of the others – a White woman. 'I have a female slave who can tear that brute of yours to pieces!'

'What do you wager?' demanded a chorus of excited voices.

'Four cups of gold and two golden plates,' snapped the black-haired female.

'Taken!' cried my owner. 'Go and fetch your bitch and let us have a good fight tonight.'

The woman snapped a command to one of her slave boys and he flew out of the hall into the night. Then my owner ordered a bronze helmet and a sword brought and given to me to arm myself with. The helmet was shaped like a human head and had a nose and two holes shaped like eyes; it covered my face completely. The sword was of iron with a bronze hilt and was both sharp and very heavy, with a needle-sharp point. It was the same sword I had used in six previous fights – fights between me and fellow slaves in which I always had the doubtful honour of being the winner.

'Fight well and win, second slave,' roared my owner. 'Fight well and win or, by the demons of hell, I shall cut your dirty black throat and fling your smelly carcass to the dogs!'

I drew myself up with pride and raised my sword high in salute. 'I shall fight and win, Oh Master, I shall win as I have always won before.'

'Insolent pig,' hissed the White female whose slave I was due to fight. 'We shall see about that.'

Putting women fighters against men was one of the new ways of entertainment the Strange Ones had invented. But I had never had to fight a woman before and also, as I stood there waiting, a strange feeling of uneasiness began to grow within me – so much so that at one time I almost felt like dropping my sword and running out of the hall.

A few moments later, my tall female opponent came striding through the door wearing, like myself, a helmet and carrying a long sharp sword. Like me, too, she was naked save for a green loincloth around her broad womanly hips. She went to where her mistress lay on the couch like a glittering snake and prostrated herself in salute. Then she saluted everybody else in the hall by raising her sword.

'Fight,' snapped her mistress. 'Kill him, quick!'

Like a striking mamba, the fighting woman whirled upon me, her sword thrusting viciously at my stomach. But I sidestepped and the flashing sword only gave me a slight, though painful, cut in the side. Then I closed with her and our blades flashed and whirled in the torchlight, both of us fighting like the trained killers we were. Twice she wounded me with the darting point of her blade and twice I returned the compliment. For a while neither of us gained any advantage, then at last I forced her to give way by wounding her deeply in the thigh and above the left breast.

By this time the hall was in uproar, and none of the masters and their females was sitting any more; all were on their feet like so many bloodthirsty children and shouting encouragement to first one and then the other of us. Wagers flew back and forth and the owner of the female slave, stung to anger by my owner's vicious taunts, shrieked angrily that if I defeated her fighting woman, she would become my owner's wife for the night.

'Not for the night only,' cried my owner. 'Not for tonight only, but for ten more nights!'

'Yes,' snarled the female, '*if* your slave wins.'

My adversary began to press me savagely now. She seemed anxious to end the fight as quickly as possible by killing me. Her sword was nothing less than a hissing silvery blur and only my skill saved me from being fatally wounded. Then at last I struck a blow at her that all but cut off her left breast. She fell with a loud cry of agony and my sword point entered her chest.

Loud cheers rang through the hall as I knelt down and removed her helmet to take to my owner as a trophy.

As I removed the helmet, the woman's agony-clouded eyes opened and a look of great puzzlement and surprise spread over her dark beautiful face. She was looking at something on my chest, the black, moonshaped birthmark that stands out against the dark-brown of my body. She could not see my helmet-masked face and she could not see the tears that came welling into my eyes as I recognised her. She was the woman whom I had known most intimately once upon a time – sixteen years ago when she carried me in her womb, brought me forth, and suckled me.

'It is your mother,' whispered the old man *Obu* unnecessarily.

Sixteen years before, as a young girl, herself born in slavery, she had been mated to a young slave by the Slave Breeders, and had conceived and given birth to me. Like all slaves with suckling young, she had spent two years in the underground slave stalls where breeding took place, nursing her baby – me. After another year, when I was three, they took me away from her and I had never seen her again until this fateful night.

But she had not forgotten me and she particularly remembered the strange crescent-shaped birthmark on my chest, the birthmark that had excited the other slave mothers so many years ago.

Blind with tears I tore my helmet off and threw it to the floor. With great difficulty she opened her mouth and said: 'My son . . . you are my son . . . *Lumukanda*!'

'Forgive me, mother . . . Oh, forgive me . . .' I cried.

'Dear child,' she said with a strange pitying smile, 'I forgive you. You did not know – I could have killed you too. I am glad it is I, not you, who die.'

'Mother, don't die, don't die,' I cried.

Her eyes closed as I held her tightly, madly and desperately to my tear-bedewed chest. I looked up briefly to find that the hall was fast emptying of people. The masters were leaving in groups of threes and fours with their females, their laughter ringing loudly as they went into the moonlit night. My owner had already retired to his room with my mother's mistress and soon only my friends, *Lubo* and *Obu*, were left with me in the silent hall. Then my parent's eyes opened for the last time and once again she smiled. Her hand reached up and stroked my cheek briefly before dropping limply to the floor. Faintly she said: 'My child, you . . . great deeds . . . someone great . . . loves you. Be brave . . . strong, my son . . .'

And with that strange smile of incredible tenderness and pride on her lips she died. I could have killed myself with grief such as I have never known, before – or since.

Obu, Lubo and I laid my slain parent to rest in a deep grave on the shores of the silvery lake. We buried her in the way the Strange Ones buried their dead, lying on her back with her hands at her sides. Her helmet was on her head and her sword was in its scabbard beside her tall body.

'Farewell, my parent . . .'

I could hardly stand, let alone walk, and *Obu* and *Lubo* had to support me as we went back into the moonlit city. As we approached the great gates, over the bridge spanning the deep water-filled ditch, a loud cry tore the quiet night and a body came hurtling down from the top of one of the great towers that flanked the city gate, plunging into the moat with an unbelievable splash – immediately sinking like a stone.

'Another murder,' cried *Obu*. 'It is the second one in three days. What is this city coming to?'

'I know who that was who fell in there,' said *Lubo*. 'It is the male wife of the High Emperor *Karesu*. Gods – great immortal gods, now there is going to be trouble!'

A harsh voice called out to us as we entered the gate, the voice of the leader of a troop of bronze-clad White guards who had come running to investigate the scream and the splash.

'Ho there, slave dogs. Halt! Who was that who fell into the moat? Answer!'

'We do not know, Master,' replied *Obu*, bowing low.

'What are you dogs doing outside the city walls this time of night?' snarled the commander of the guard.

'They went out to bury a dead fellow-slave, Commander,' replied one of the guards. 'I saw them as they went out past the guard house.'

'Where did the one who uttered the cry fall from?' demanded the commander.

'He fell from the top of this tower, Master,' replied *Obu*, pointing to the tower on the left side of the gate.

'What race was he?'

'He was one of the master's, Master.'

The guard commander turned to his men and shouted: 'Some

of you get up there quick. You, slaves, stay here and do not move.'

The guards went pelting up the long flight of steps that went up the solid stone tower. Suddenly a white-clad figure came running down the steps of the other tower and flew like a mad ghost up the main street leading to the centre of the city. The commander, together with two of the guards who had remained behind, turned with a loud shout and gave chase.

'Come on, my sons,' said *Obu* to *Lubo* and me, 'let us get to our owner's home quickly. But do not run; these streets will soon be crawling with soldiers.'

He was right; we were only a few blocks away from our owner's house when squads of fully armed soldiers came clanking past us on their way to the gate and alarm horns sounded in the silver night, calling all available warriors to man the towers and the stockade around the city.

'I wonder if they caught whoever it is that was running up the street,' mused *Obu.*

'I would not like to be in his place, whoever it was,' laughed *Lubo,* as he went up to the tall gates of our master's house.

Suddenly *Lubo* pointed excitedly to our right. 'Look, look there.'

'Where?' cried *Obu.*

'Over there, on the corner of the garden wall, look!'

We turned and, following his pointing finger, saw a sight that sent shivers of excitement along our spines. A tall white-clad figure had just climbed the high wall surrounding our owner's garden and was about to leap within.

'It is the fugitive who ran away from the tower,' said *Obu* grimly. 'Let us get into the garden quickly and seize him.'

Like stalking wild cats we entered our owner's well-tended grounds and began our search for the white-clad fugitive whom we felt sure had pushed the male consort of our city's male Emperor into the moat. We all knew that if we let this fugitive hide himself in the gardens it would mean death for all of us and for our owner as well.

It fell to me to be the one who found the assassin, and a great surprise it was as well. I had gone well ahead of both *Lubo* and *Obu* when I heard people talking in low voices just round the corner of our owner's house. I dropped on my knees and crawled along the grass slowly and carefully until I could see around the corner of the great house. To my great surprise I saw the thickset, bearded man who owned us standing on the steps of the back door of the house and talking to the veiled white-clad figure of our quarry who stood on the ground looking up at him. I caught the last words of my owner's address to the fugitive.

'... well indeed, but you must come into the house before someone sees you, your Highness.'

'Your Highness ...' The words struck me like a blow! Who, then, could the midnight fugitive and murderer be? In the whole of the empire there were now only two people left alive to whom the title of 'Your Highness' could be applied. The first of them was, of course, the High Emperor himself; the other was his dead brother's widow whom I had never seen, but about whom I had heard a lot of fantastic rumours.

The visitor entered the house like a white ghost. Then came the next surprise of that memorable night. Loud shouting in three different voices erupted within our master's house and the voices were those of our owner himself, his son, and the woman who had been my mother's mistress. Then the blood-curdling sounds of a murderous sword fight, punctuated by the crash of breaking furniture, reached our shocked ears as we turned and ran to the front to get the long spears we carried when guarding our owner's house at night. A loud, quavering scream split the night air as we reached the front entrance. Then we heard the voice of my mother's former mistress shrieking loudly and accusingly:

'You killed him ... you killed your own son, you foul murderer! But I am going out to tell the Emperor that you are plotting against him. You false traitor ... you are trying to play a double game. I shall tell the soldiers you are hiding this bitch in your house!'

The door burst open and the woman came running out, wrapped in a blue cloak, with her hair flying behind her. Our owner was close behind her, bleeding from a cut above one eye. 'To me, slaves, seize her ... kill her ... quick!'

WHAT SECRETS HATH HEAVEN?

For a few moments we hesitated as the female came running towards us. Then we sprang to obey our owner and barred her way just as she reached the gate.

Lubo pushed her violently and she stumbled backwards just as the master drew back his arm and threw his needle-sharp sword with all his might at her back. We heard the thud and the female fell backwards with the blade protruding from her bosom. 'Your parent has been avenged, Oh *Lumukanda*,' whispered *Lubo* in my ear.

Never before had I seen a night in which so much happened at the same time. Never before had I experienced a night that left so many memories in my mind. By the time we finished our task of burying the two dead Strange Ones and cleaning up the master's house, dawn was not far away and in fact, the eastern sky was beginning to lighten. Three very tired slaves descended the stone steps leading down to the underground stalls where other slaves were sleeping.

'*Ka-whew!*' said *Lubo*. 'Oh my doddering father! What a night we have had!'

'Be quiet, my son, and sleep,' said the old man *Obu*. 'We shall soon have to get up, so try and get what sleep you can.'

But I could not sleep and dawn found me tossing and writhing in the vermin-infested grass piled on the damp floor of my sleeping stall. My mind was in turmoil and I could not think straight. But uppermost in my seething, troubled mind was the realisation that I was guilty of the worst crime any man can ever commit – the murder of my own parent.

Pictures, clear and astonishingly real, flashed like thunderflashes through my troubled brain: pictures of my childhood and my mother as I remembered her then – the silly sounds she used to make when I cried. But I recalled most clearly the little toy she had made for me out of wood – a puppet I used to play with in my lonely hours. I cried and moaned in incurable agony and remorse. But I knew that no matter how long and how loud I cried I could never, never bring my parent back again. I knew with a terrible finality that whether I lived a short life or a long one, I would carry my guilt to the grave.

I cursed the masters, I cursed the gods and I cursed myself bitterly for what had happened. But always present in the back of my mind was the realisation that all this would never bring my parent back again. I suddenly found myself longing for death.

Morning came and we all crawled out of our sleeping stalls – twenty male and sixteen female slaves in all – and followed *Obu* to the lake for our morning wash. As I bathed in the living water one of the younger female slaves *Luluma* waded up to me and laid her small hand on my chest, asking: 'How do you feel today, Oh *Lumukanda*?'

'I wish I were dead, Oh *Luluma*,' I replied. 'I really wish I were dead.'

'Try and forget, Oh my brother-in-suffering,' said the girl soothingly. 'It was not your fault – it was *their* fault.'

'I will never forget what happened last night for as long as I live,' I said. 'No water on earth can ever wash my parent's blood off these guilty hands.'

'Do not judge yourself, Oh *Lumukanda*. We are the playthings of fate and can never be responsible for all that we do or what happens to us any more than toys are responsible for what the playing child does with them.'

'The Old Ones tell us there are gods somewhere,' I said bitterly, 'but I am afraid these so-called gods are but figments of some . . .'

'No, *Lumukanda*!' cried she. 'Do not say that.'

'I shall say what I please,' I sneered. 'If there are any gods, or if there is the Great Spirit, why in the name of all that is foul and rotten do they let such things happen to human beings? Why are we slaves and the Strange Ones our masters? Why is there so much misery, murder, theft and strife under the sun? I dare any of those non-existent, imaginary, somnolent, gods-so-called to . . . to . . .'

'*Lumukanda!*' gasped the girl. 'You are blaspheming. You might regret your words one day.'

And she was right.

After finishing our morning wash we followed the old man *Obu* into the master's house to present ourselves and to do obeisance before him as was the custom amongst slaves. As we entered the master's great hall we found him sitting on his great couch with his two young concubines, one on either side. But there was also someone else with them in the hall, someone who did not belong there at all – who was a total and unusual and frightening stranger. This was a tall, well-moulded beautiful woman whose skin was almost as dark as my own and who looked like the daughter of a Strange One and a Black woman. This woman wore a tight-fitting garment that reached from her midriff to her ankles. On her arms and forearms she wore heavy, broad and skilfully engraved gold bracelets while around her shoulders she wore a great white cloak made of a woven, shiny material. Around her head she wore a broad golden band and she looked at the world through a pair of deep-set glittering eyes with lashes as long as the first joint of a man's thumb.

I realised with a shock that she was the white-clad one whom we had seen the night before, climbing over the garden wall. So this was the sorceress – the feared witch *Kadesi-Makira* – the dreaded opponent of the Emperor *Karesu*!

From where she sat in the far corner of the hall she flayed us with her pitiless stare as we filed past our master and briefly prostrated ourselves before him and his concubines.

My turn came and I fell on my knees before our owner and crossed my forearms before my face as was the custom. Then I stood up and turned to go.

'Wait!'

That one single command stung the silent hall like a slave-trainer's whip-stroke and all eyes turned to the white-clad dark woman who had uttered it.

'Where did you get that slave?' she demanded of our master.

'Your Highness?'

'I asked you, where did you get that slave?'

'I bought him as a pup, Oh Great One,' he replied humbly. 'Does your Highness know this slave from somewhere?'

'No,' said she grimly, 'I have never seen the dog before in real life. But I do know what you must do to him immediately. Kill him!'

'Kill him, your Highness?' gasped my owner. 'Pray why? He is my favourite fighting slave – he has won many prizes . . .'

'Fool . . . fool, what a fool you are!' cried *Makira*, rising to her feet. 'Have you never heard of the prophecy about the Dark Destroyer?'

'The Dark Destroyer!' cried our owner, his eyes opening wide with horror and astonishment. 'You mean . . .'

'Yes, my dear White fool, I mean that this slave of yours is none other than the Dark Destroyer whom the old prophets said would be born one day and would, like the vulture of sunset, destroy our empire,' the Queen *Kadesi-Makira* announced sharply. 'Tell me, has he no strange birthmark somewhere shaped like some well-known thing?'

'He has!' cried one of the concubines. 'A moonshaped mark

above his left breast. I noticed it one day when he brought me some wine.'

'I dreamt about this creature last night. I dreamt of the Sun-God telling me he was in this very house!' cried *Kadesi-Makira*. 'Seize him, you other slaves, seize him! Let me take a closer look at him before he dies. Seize him and bring him here!'

Obu and two other slaves seized my arms and pushed me towards the seated woman who rose and stared fixedly at me for a few moments and then lashed out with her open hand, hitting me hard on one side of the face.

'Ha!' she shrilled. 'It has fallen to me to uncover the foul menace to our empire. We must kill this viper before its fangs can grow.'

They bound me securely hand and foot and they tied two heavy grindstones to my ankles. Then they left me in my sleeping stall under heavy guard until the sun had set and night had crept upon the land like a stealthy panther. I knew that at last death would come and I would soon be with my dear mother. I felt happy and incredibly content. I joked with the slaves and with my owner. I told them to cook a nice dinner for me because I would be back tomorrow. The slaves laughed but the witch *Makira* and my master were far from pleased. I had the satisfaction of seeing my owner turn pale.

They loaded me into a boat at dead of night and rowed to the centre of the great Makarikari lake. In the boat were *Makira*, our owner and his two concubines, and the four slaves who rowed the alien boat.

At a sign from *Makira* the slaves pulled in their oars and lifted me up and threw me into the water.

The cold dark water closed over me, smothering me. I felt myself sinking into the dark depths like a helpless stone, down . . . down . . . down . . . into the watery womb of the lake.

There were sounds in my ears and there was heat on my body. Slowly I opened my eyes and found myself looking into the blinding glare of the midday sun.

Quickly I closed my eyes and allowed my brain to work on this incredible fact: I was alive. But I had no right to be. I should be down there in the green depths of the water instead of lying somewhere on the northern shore of Lake Makarikari! I should be dead instead of hearing the song of the birds in the swamp trees and feeling the heat of the sun on my naked body.

'*Lumukanda!*' The strange silvery voice calling my name suddenly out of nowhere sounded exactly like my mother's. I felt a rush of incredible strength gush into my body as I leapt up and looked about me.

'Lumukanda!' It sounded from somewhere in the forest.

'Mother!' I cried. 'I am coming, I am coming to you.'

Now I was sure that I was dead, that I was not on earth but in the Spirit Land. I knew I was going to meet my parent soon and be happy for evermore. I ran wildly into the forest and the next thing I knew I was flat on my face in the mud, having tripped over a mangrove root. I sprang to my feet again, ruefully, and looked about. I was covered from head to foot in stinking mud and a voice laughed heartily from somewhere behind me.

'My parent,' I cried, 'please show yourself. Do not make me suffer; I have suffered enough as it is.'

Suddenly my mother stood before me, smiling tenderly, with her sword in her hand and her metal headdress on her head. She stood there, tall and straight and very beautiful, and she smiled at me in a strange tender way – just as she smiled when she died. I leapt forward with my arms open to clasp my parent to my breast. My arms encircled her and I closed my eyes and wept, tears of pure heavenly joy that knows no description. But when I opened my eyes I found myself fiercely embracing nothing but a moss-covered mangrove tree.

The ringing laugh echoed through the forest again as I collapsed to my knees, sobbing bitterly.

I was going mad ... I *was* mad. Someone or something was playing evil voodoo tricks upon me, trying to drive me into the valley of insanity. I must escape. I had to escape from that evil swampland ...

I ran madly through the forest. Every tree, every rock seemed to have somehow grown a face – a face that opened its mouth and guffawed at me insanely. 'Run, you murderer – matricidal slave, thief, beggar, run ...' and there followed the laugh again, now distinctly maniacal.

How long I ran through that nightmare forest I do not know. But when at last the sun began to set I found myself lying flat on my face in a grassy glade utterly exhausted. My toes were bleeding from all the tripping and falling and I was caked all over with dried mud.

The grass rustled as something came towards me and I buried my face in my hands and moaned: 'No, no, leave me alone.'

But when at last I looked up I found it was only a stray impala which leapt gracefully and fled for its life when it saw me raise my head out of the long grass.

Some time later I found a small cave in the forest – a cave whose walls were covered with figures of men and animals painted not long before by the Batwa – the Little Yellow Ones. I cleaned out the abandoned cave and lay down inside to rest. I must have fallen asleep because when I awoke night had fallen long since and I was feeling terribly hungry and thirsty. Silently I crept to a nearby stream and drank my fill of the clear, cool water. Then I caught two frogs and ate both of them raw – having no means of making a fire – and finally returned to the cave where I made myself a bed of green leaves and lay down to sleep.

When I awoke it was nearly midday of the following day and I was feeling hungry enough to eat ten elephants. I left the cave and went down to the lake carefully avoiding the forest. A while later I found a game footpath leading to the lake. Here I dug two pit traps and covered them with grass and twigs, hoping to catch a buck or something for food. Then I proceeded to walk aimlessly along the lake to kill time and forget my hunger.

I had been walking for some time when I saw what I took to be an image made of shimmering silver, standing on a rock on the water's edge. It was shaped like a woman – tall and unbelievably well-moulded; it stood with its back to me and I was struck dumb by its utter perfection. It reminded me of those statues of alien gods which the Strange Ones had in their god-houses, or temples as they called them.

Because the Strange Ones had the habit of putting statues in the most unlikely places I was positive that this was also one of their works of metal art – probably a likeness of some imaginary water goddess.

But so perfect was the image that I was greatly tempted to have a closer look at it, and so I slowly approached it on the water's edge. Suddenly I became aware of a very strange thing: unseen waves of pulsating heat seemed to be radiating from the statue, becoming more intense as I went closer. Bolts of fear tore through my body and I turned and ran as fast as I could up the gentle incline away from the lake. When I felt sure I had put enough distance between the silver thing and myself I paused and looked back. An involuntary cry of horror and great fear was wrung from me by what I saw: The 'statue' had turned and was now looking directly at me. Even as I watched it slowly began to walk in my direction and then it began to run. With a loud scream, I turned and fled, the mysterious thing in hot pursuit.

I ran along the marshy edge of the great lake, taking care to avoid the forest. But the thing was fast gaining on me. It came so close that I could see it had three heavy breasts, each with a shining green nipple . . . and its eyes were the colour of gold.

Wild with panic I swerved and dived headlong into the lake, swimming away as fast as I could. The thing stood waist deep in the reeds and I heard the ringing laughter I had heard before.

Then, most gracefully it proceeded to swim in my direction and the radiance of its body left a trail of steam. What unearthly thing was it? It did not belong to this world – of that I was sure – and it was as out of place as a bird amongst the fish. Abruptly a voodoo voice reached my ears: 'You had better give yourself up, human being, I will catch you eventually in any case.'

'What do you want to do with me?' I cried loudly as I increased the speed of my swimming.

The voice came back to me: 'I am lonely and longing for companionship . . . I can stand it no more . . . I long for you . . .'

'No, no!' I cried. 'What are you . . . what kind of creature are you?'

'I am a creature whose existence you have once denied. I am a goddess, and *Ma* is my name.'

This increased my terror and as she closed in on me I dived under in an endeavour to drown myself. But she hauled me out by my hair and dragged me back to the shore. We had a brief struggle in which I managed to free myself and I made a dash for the depths of the forest. After a while I noticed that I was not being followed. 'I have shaken her off,' I quietly and happily mused by myself.

Cautiously I went to look at my two pit traps but found to my great disappointment that I had caught nothing. It was while I was staring in disgust at the second trap that I heard a rustling sound behind me. I froze with fright, took a step forward – and, with a savage curse, plunged into my own trap!

The tall, incredibly beautiful apparition of living silver stood looking down at me where I was lying on my back in the pit. A dazzling smile lit her face and she mused gently: 'Oh my reluctant lover, most stupid and cowardly . . . do you make a habit of digging pit traps to catch yourself?'

'*Aieeee!*' I cried. 'Go away and leave me alone, you unearthly monster.'

'You may not be aware of it, but you are equally unearthly, and in this world I have chosen you as my husband. But what an unfortuante bride I am! My new husband goes running like a madman and he even has the habit of setting traps for himself. Shall we now go to your cave and consummate our marriage?'

'Listen, you unnatural demon, go back to wherever you come from and leave me alone, do you hear? I am not your husband – I have never heard of such nonsense . . .'

'Now, now, now, who believes in demons? Did you not once tell a fellow slave that gods and demons are nothing but figments of the imagination? As far as you are concerned I do not exist. I am a figment of your imagination . . . is that not so?'

The apparition sat down on the edge of the pit, her feet dangling an arm's length above my head. 'Oh my great grandmother, can't the thing go away . . . vanish like the unearthly phantom it is?' I thought to myself.

'No, beloved one,' it said with a weary smile, 'I cannot just vanish into thin air. In this world I am too real – and besides, far too much in love with you – simply to vanish and leave you alone.' I had forgotten that the thing could read my thoughts.

I was determined to stay in the pit to the end of time and the apparition, growing tired of my stubbornness, stood up and went away. I decided to wait till night came, so as to make my escape under the cover of darkness. But towards sunset she returned with a bundle of writhing mambas in her hands and coolly threw them into the pit in which I was still lying.

I do not know how I got out of the pit – all I know is that it was considerably faster than the way I got into it. 'Let us go home, Oh my husband, there is much that we have to talk about.'

Outside, the night was alive with the sounds of animals of all kinds, from the faraway roar of lions to the lonely hooting of an owl in the tree at the mouth of the cave. Loudest was the croaking of frogs in the marshes on the edge of the lake. In the heavens above the stars shone like so many lost jewels against the dark expanse of the moonless sky. The Fire River, today called the Milky Way, was one broad band of smoky brilliance that stretched from one end of the heavens to the other, and a dethroned star streaked across it as it fell in disgrace.

I was now looking at creation with new eyes, and everything I looked at seemed to have assumed a new beauty – a new freshness. I had been listening to a very strange story: the story of creation – the story of how life came to this earth and the One who was telling me this story was none other than the Creator herself. She told me all about the First People, about *Amarava* and about *Odu*. I was feeling very small, a mere speck of living dust in a universe so utterly incredible.

'Great Mother,' I said at long last, 'but what does one so great as you are want with a wretch like myself. I am hardly worthy of the love of a crawling louse.'

'*Lumukanda*, eternity is a vast and incredibly lonely Darkness – and even a goddess has to have someone in whom to confide at times, to escape from the futility which human beings have misnamed Life. I grow tired of roaming the Outer Darkness alone – deceived and rejected by my erstwhile spouse, the Tree of Life – a lost leaf in the Tempest of Eternity. I wish to make a comeback to earth and communicate with the human beings I have created. And I wish to do so through you, *Lumukanda*.'

'Goddess . . . I am not worthy of the honour!'

'Who is, *Lumukanda*, who is? Who in this mad, evil world is worthy of attention from me? None! But I had to choose someone, and that someone happens to be you.'

'A blood-stained matricide . . . a slayer of his own parent?'

'Yes, *Lumukanda*, a blood-stained parent-slayer. Because your deed has opened your eyes to the falsehood called Life – which is nothing but a lie and a failure from birth to death. You have experienced Life as but a horrid nightmare in which only pain, suffering and death are real. I have chosen you because you are one of the few human beings who have seen Life most closely for the useless, futile *nothing* that it is. I can see in you the kind who will never use anybody or anything to gain domination over fellow mortals – simply because you have grown to hate life and all its useless pleasures, its mock glories, the senseless futility of it all!'

'Goddess, how can *you*, who have brought Life on earth speak thus?'

'Listen *Lumukanda*, I did not create the Universe and the earth, and life upon it, out of my own free will. I obeyed the order of a Great Master who, for all that even I know, in turn has to obey the orders of an even Greater Master. The heavens conceal more secrets than even I can understand. Even I was told to do as instructed, and ask no questions.'

'Then what is the purpose of life on earth, Oh Great Goddess? Do I understand there is really none at all?'

'The only purpose of Life is Death. A man is born and before he dies he gets the opportunity to ensure that others after him will also be born and die. You may deceive yourself by thinking that there is more to life than birth, growth, mating, old age and death. But, sooner or later, Naked Truth makes itself apparent.'

'Naked Truth – like you, Oh my Goddess?' I said, in an attempt to change the subject.

'Look at the race of men whom you call the Strange Ones. See what trouble they went to, in coming to your country, seizing it, enslaving your people and despoiling themselves. What have they gained by it all? All they have gained is a useless toy called wealth – and softer couches on which to mate and die. They do not know it yet, but within a few moons you, *Lumukanda*, will go back there to lead a horde of savages, like yourself, to raze their plaything empire to the ground. And men born a mere hundred years from now will look in vain for traces of the Great City of the Empire of *Karesu* and *Makira-Kadesi.* You will leave no trace of it; turn it into a legend. Even thousands of years hence people must search in vain for the Lost City of Makarikari.

BEHOLD THE DECEIVER

In the Great City of the Strange Ones there had been chaos and bloodshed. Piles of dead bodies choked the narrow streets. Blood had flowed like water as two opposing forces had clashed like wild cats through the shocked city. But now there was peace and jubilation in the land, because the cruel one, the Emperor *Karesu* had been overthrown and captured in one short bloody revolt by the followers of the Empress *Makira-Kadesi.*

As night fell the city blazed with lights. The singing and noise rose higher and higher into the jewelled heavens even as the night deepened. Wild celebrations were in progress in the Great Palace and people crowded the gardens and the steps of the palace like flies on a pot of honey. Whenever the victorious witch-queen *Kadesi* made an appearance in the doorway of the Great House with her harp in her hand and her voice raised, singing their 'song of victory', loud cheers split the moonless night from thousands of throats: 'Long live the Lioness, *Makira*! Long may she reign!'

The last time *Makira* made her appearance outside, before going back into the Great Hall to preside over the fantastic feast held in her honour, she held her hand up for silence and her voice was high and clear in the night: 'Thank you, my loyal people; thank you for your support in wresting the throne from that madman *Karesu* who ruled you with such cruelty and with no regard for your feelings. Today I am your Queen, your Empress, and my greatest aim will be to raise this empire to heights undreamt of by its founders. This I shall do as soon as possible, and I know that I shall succeed. I shall reorganise our armies and I shall strengthen the walls around our cities and villages to make them invincible to any attack. I shall take this empire to the very stars, if need be – and this empire shall bloom like a flower and live forever in the minds of men – as the greatest of all time. Now, before I retire for the night, let us all sing the song of our country: "Oh Flower in the Jungles Planted . . ."'

More than ten thousand voices burst into song and the Hymn

of the Strange Ones reached against the starry skies. As the last verses, charged with arrogance and pride, 'We shall fight and we shall conquer again, and yet again for you, Oh purple flower of the wilds,' rang out through the roaring city, *Makira* burst into tears and wept unashamedly before her people.

The crowds were delirious; they went mad. And not one individual there but felt himself capable of crushing the very heavens for the Empress and the land. Such was the magic power that *Makira* had over her people – the Strange Ones.

Roar after roar of applause followed *Makira* as she turned and went into the Great Hall, now packed with nobles, battle-leaders and priests.

As *Makira-Kadesi* entered the glittering hall men and women stood up and met her paralysing stare, while slaves fell flat on their stomachs, prostrating themselves before her dreaded presence. In the heavy silence that followed, her voice rang through the hall:

'Let us feast, Oh my people, and let us be happy this great and memorable night. Let us make merry now, for tomorrow we have a lot of work to do. We shall work until we drop, to make this empire the greatest under the sun. We shall work to make this empire the strongest and the most invincible on earth. Tomorrow all of you who have more than ten slaves shall send half of them to our ore mines to extract metal for our weapons and gold for trade. We must make this city so strong that not even a mouse shall enter our city gates unseen. Let the feast begin.'

The feast began; wine and beer flowed like water down the throats of the Strange Ones. Great quantities of meat and foods of all kinds were consumed to the magical sound of music. Dancing females and fighting slaves moved in and out.

The mystic notes of harp, flute and drum filled the gilded hall as toast after toast was drunk in honour of the Empress who sat alone in a corner with an untouched cup in her hand and a worried frown on her face. Suddenly she rose and, in a tempestuous rage, hurled the wine cup at the face of the nearest slave and drew her dagger from its sheath. She proceeded to dance – a wild, savage dance nobody had seen before, flourishing the dagger above her head like a bloodthirsty cannibal.

'Bring him out!' she screamed. 'Bring out the murdering pig who killed my husband. Bring out the unnatural *Karesu*. Bring him out!'

The gross, shambling creature named *Karesu* was hustled into the roaring hall, loaded with chains but still bearing himself like the proud Emperor he had been.

Makira-Kadesi saw him and split the air with a loud scream of unbelievable hatred, leaping high like a madwoman, which she was in fact. She crept up to the bound man like a stalking she-leopard and slashed him cruelly across the belly with her dagger. Then she danced away with a loud shriek of devilish joy. She circled round him again, dancing like a devil's flame, faster, faster and still faster. Then she stabbed viciously at his eyes, once, twice, thrice – leaving the helpless man's eye-sockets full of torn flesh. Then she danced away again under loud cheers from her bloodthirsty subjects.

'Let me speak!' cried the bleeding and blinded man *Karesu*. 'Let me speak before I die. Let me speak . . .'

'Speak, dog, speak before I disembowel you!' cried *Makira-Kadesi*. 'Whine and let me hear what you have to whine about.'

'I wish to warn you, Oh *Kadesi*,' said *Karesu*, 'the gods tell me to warn you that the whole empire is in great danger and that if you can save it from this danger it will last forever and climb to the heights you dream of.'

Makira froze where she stood. She had expected *Karesu* to beg for mercy or curse her; but not the words he was saying now. And she was surprised even more by the great calmness of his voice.

'Some time ago,' continued the dying man, 'the gods say that some time ago you took a slave out to the lake and drowned him secretly one night.'

'Whaaat!' cried *Makira*. 'What about that slave?'

'The gods say he is alive,' whispered *Karesu*, as he sank to the ground, 'Empire in danger . . . while he lives . . .'

'Where is he? Where do the gods say he is now?'

'In . . . near here . . . lake,' gasped *Karesu* as he died.

'Guards!' screamed the Empress. 'Call the guard commander here . . . quickly!'

While quick-fingered handmaidens were still helping *Kadesi* back into her attire, two heavily armed guard commanders and a battle leader clanked into the hall and bowed low before the Empress. She snapped out a few words to them and about an hour later the armed guards marched out of the gate of the city while the patrols in the city itself were heavily reinforced.

The guards left the city and fanned out in all directions in search of the one who had to be killed if *Makira's* empire were to be saved. Some went along the shores of the lake, while some took boats across the lake itself.

In the meantime the feasting in *Kadesi's* palace had come to an abrupt end and the guests had left for their homes. For a long while *Kadesi* sat alone in the silence while the torches were burning out one by one and parts of the Great Hall were plunged into darkness. She sat in deep thought and did not even see the young handmaiden who entered and knelt before her. The girl had to repeat what she said thrice before the Empress heard her and discovered her presence. 'Your couch is ready, Oh Great Empress.'

'I have no intention of going to bed. Call the guard commander and tell him to bring some of his men to escort me to the Temple of the Black Devil – quickly!'

The girl vanished behind the red drapery of the second door of the hall and *Kadesi* was once again left alone with only one torch burning. Then suddenly the solitary torch shook as if struck by an unseen hand; it snapped clean off the bracket holding it onto the wall and crashed to the floor with a dull clatter.

Kadesi leapt up, her eyes wild with fear and her heart pounding fiercely. 'An ill omen,' she gasped. 'An evil omen for my beloved empire. But I shall fight to save it – I shall fight.'

Then the guards came clattering into the darkened hall, followed by the two favourite handmaidens of the Empress. They found *Kadesi* standing near the door, trying her best to keep the expression of wild fear and horror off her face. 'Let us go,' she said curtly.

Dozens of oil lamps burn inside the Great Temple of the Black Devil Goddess of Darkness. A hideous image of stone towers above the black altar – extending right up to the roof. It leers down at the kneeling priestess from an obscene stone mouth and bulging sightless eyes. This hideous image was never carved by the Strange Ones; nor is it the work of a Black man. Legends say it fell from the skies, and its hideousness would seem to confirm this. The Strange Ones, having found this idol half-buried in the sands of the Ka-Lahari, had brought it into their city and built a temple for it. This idol was said to possess strange powers of evil and to be capable of devouring the soul of a man if it felt thus inclined.*

The priestesses – there are three – of the Devil Goddess are wearing nothing but brief loincloths and each wears a heavy black mask representing the Devil Goddess. All three wear heavy swords in leather sheaths at their sides and one of them carries a drum made out of the skull of a man with the top sawn off and a skin stretched across the brain cavity. This drum she beats with a short stick, a baby's skull forming the knob at one end. A trussed live calf lies on top of a pile of faggots on the black altar in front of the statue. Immediately behind the statue is a great stone bowl burnt

* *For thousands of years after the fall of the empire of the Strange Ones, the witchdoctors of the Batswana and later the Barotse, searched in vain for this alien idol, and the search is still continuing.*

black by countless fires. In this bowl is a pile of wood. Lying bound and helpless on this pile of wood are two captives – girls, both of them. The first of these is a young Black girl wearing the iron collar of a slave; the second is White, with flaming red hair and green eyes, and her enlarged abdomen denotes that she is soon to be a mother.

The throbbing drums, beaten by slaves hideously painted to represent Evil itself, send a steady rhythm through the macabre vault.

In the courtyard of the Temple, an alien god stands over a small altar to which is tied a loudly protesting dog that seems to have been very well fed indeed. The god is one of the obscene idols the Strange Ones brought with them from their far-off native land. In the porch of the Temple is a cage full of chattering and struggling monkeys. These holy monkeys are going to be used in the ceremony about to commence – and the dog also.

Suddenly a guard puts a horn to his lips and blows a short blast on it. Then he steps aside and the Empress *Makira-Kadesi* enters the temple courtyard, followed by her servants and gilt-armoured Palace Guards. They stop a few paces from the altar of the animal-headed god and the fat dog tied to the altar growls viciously. The three priestesses emerge from the temple itself, accompanied by a slave carrying a torch, and they briefly salute *Kadesi* by silently raising their hands. No talking is allowed near the Temple of Evil.

The First Priestess waves the Empress's retinue away and takes *Kadesi* by the hand, leading her nearer to the altar of the Dog-god. Then she suddenly draws her sword and slashes the raiment off the tall Empress, flinging the robes onto the pile of wood on the altar of the Dog-god. The Second Priestess reaches down and seizes the dog, unties it and holds it upside down, ignoring its loud protests. The Empress is made to kneel while the dog is held above her – its slavering mouth only a finger's length above her gold-crowned head. With a sudden vicious slash the First Priests cuts the dog's throat and spurting blood deluges the naked Empress.

The Second Priestess flings the dog onto the altar and the slave dips the burning torch into the pile of wood to set it alight. In the grim light both priestesses now perform a silent, though vigorous dance while the Third Priestess seizes the Empress by the wrist and whips her soundly with a long whip she had been carrying.

Makira screams with pain until she falls in a swoon. The First and Third Priestesses now carry her between them into the Temple, while the Second Priestess takes the whip and throws it onto the sacrificial fire, lingering there to ensure that it burns properly. Then she joins the others.

The Empress is left inside the Temple near the door to recover while the three priestesses go behind the great Idol of Evil to light the fire in the bowl in which the two girls are tied hand and foot. The screams of the two victims ring through the Temple and *Makira* sits up near the door, her eyes wide with horror and pain. At long last the screams die away and the smell of burning human and dog flesh drifts over the city from the Temple of Evil.

Makira is now dragged forward and made to offer tufts of her hair on the black altar in front of the hideous idol. The First Priestess applies a torch to the pile of wood on which the trussed calf lies and the Empress watches in fascinated horror as the violently struggling animal dies. Then the First Priestess waves *Makira* and the other two priestesses back and prostrates herself before the black altar, and soon sweat is pouring down her face as she concentrates all her mental power in one telepathic call to the Spirit of Darkness.

For a long time the silent, unspoken call from the kneeling priestess shrieks into the depths of Eternity itself. The priestess has even stopped breathing as she concentrates her whole being into projecting this mind-message into the depths of Infinity, summoning the very essence of Evil to make an appearance in the Temple.

There is a blinding flash inside the Temple – a flash of sun-bright flame which consumes the kneeling priestess utterly. It is closely followed by a peal of thunder that shakes the city and the surrounding countryside. Then a loud noise like a thousand tempests roars through the city and the shocked night is filled with howls of a million demons as they converge on the Temple of Evil. Inside the Temple *Makira* hears the mystic strains of the Song of Eternity and sees a dark figure emerge from the roaring flames. Before her stands *Watamaraka*, the She-Devil, the Goddess of Evil!

WHEN GRASS MEETS FIRE

A great darkness clouded the Temple of Evil, snuffing out the lamps, torches and altar fires, and the High Empress found herself standing alone in the eerie vault with ghostly, hideous shapes and faces leering at her. She stood facing the tall evil shape of the Devil Goddess *Watamaraka* – mother of all *tokoloshes* and demons. *Kadesi* suddenly felt a terror creeping over her, more than she had ever experienced before. It was one thing to worship the unseen forces; but to come face to face with them was another.

The golden Rebel Goddess suddenly smiled – a hard smile that sent icy worms crawling up and down the spine of the Empress. Her thin cruel lips twisted contemptuously as she said:

'You called me, and I am here. What do you want with me?'

'I want . . .' the Empress began.

'Oh stop, you make me sick!' snarled the Evil Goddess. 'I know what you want – you want me to save your miserable empire – but are you willing to pay a price for it?'

'What is the price?' stammered *Makira*.

'The price to save your rotten empire is your own miserable self – your life in exchange,' said the She-Devil with a mocking smile.

'I must . . . die,' stammered *Makira* aghast. 'How will my death save the empire, Oh Goddess; tell me – how!'

'I shall explain, stupid mortal,' sneered the Evil Goddess. 'You must give me your body and let me rule your empire, masquerading as you. This means that your soul must leave your body and go to hell, while I enter and act through it. That is my price – take it or leave it.'

The Empress *Kadesi-Makira* suddenly felt like an animal in a cruel snare. She realised that *Watamaraka* had cornered her; there was no way out. *Kadesi* was very fond of life and everything she had done or planned so far had only one aim: to make her own life as sweet as possible. It is quite true that she wanted to make her empire great and to remove the threat of destruction – but she also wanted to live to enjoy the fruits of it all. The fact is that *Makira-Kadesi* did not care how many lives were lost in the process of making her empire great and secure – provided those lives belonged to others. Like all rulers and tyrants she was extremely selfish. She swallowed hard and looked pleadingly at the Evil Goddess who smiled back at her maliciously and said: 'Well?'

'Can't we reach . . . a . . . compromise? I mean . . .' stammered *Makira.*

'Oh, be quiet!' snarled the Goddess. 'Your selfishness makes me sick.'

'But surely there must be another alternative . . .' *Makira* pleaded.

'Yes, there is,' smiled the Goddess evilly. 'Oh yes, there is! Call one of the priestesses and tell her to go and fetch me any Black female slave from your Palace – quick!'

Some time later a young female slave named *Luluma,* who had been given as a present to the Empress by her original owner, was hustled roughly into the Temple by one of the two surviving priestesses. The Black girl, her eyes wide with fear, was made to lie down on her back between *Makira* and the apparition *Watamaraka.*

'What . . . ?' asked *Makira.*

'You will find out soon enough – so keep quiet!' And with these words *Watamaraka* lifted her arms above her head and seemed to take a deep breath. Then a blinding flash of light lit up the Temple like the inside of a white-hot furnace, and *Makira* dropped unconscious. After a while she slowly regained consciousness and opened her eyes. She was surprised to find herself lying flat on her back and even more surprised to see a young tall woman towering over her like a pillar of beauty, wearing the tiara she herself had worn only moments previously.

'Get up, slave!' commanded the tall woman shortly.

As *Makira* rose the terrible truth dawned upon her – and it was a truth so fantastic, she could not bring herself to accept it. She could not believe that the Evil Goddess could actually have done this to her.

The apparition had vanished and *Makira* slowly realised that the tall woman standing before her was herself – her previous self. Her present self stood in the body of *Luluma.* And this to *Makira* was worse than death. She stood staring at the form that was hers. She saw herself as others saw her – a tall, mature and beautiful woman with a skin a few shades darker than the skin of the Strange Ones, with a strong face, a hard mouth and bright deepset eyes. Through a mist of bitter tears she saw the body she had been so proud of, now tenanted by the Goddess of Evil, Mother of all *tokoloshes*.

The crowned woman who had been *Makira*, smiled cruelly and snapped: 'Get up, you blubbering black bitch, and get back to the Palace before I have you whipped.'

'You foul she-devil!' cried *Makira-Luluma*. 'I shall expose you. I shall . . .'

'Remove this slave and have her locked up in the Palace dungeon,' *Watamaraka-Kadesi* ordered briskly.

The people of the Empire of the Strange Ones were astonished; never in all their lives had they seen anything like it. Never had they seen a ruler work them so ruthlessly as their new Empress *Kadesi*.

The empire was suddenly expanding and trade with foreign countries reached unheard-of heights. Tens of thousands of slaves were being exported, together with piles of ivory and gold dust. Wealth flooded the land once more, bringing more settlers to swell the population. Hundreds of slaves toiled and died miserably in the ore-mines and salt pans, while thousands of elephants were butchered. The Strange Ones had a unique way of hunting elephants: they dug deep pits, narrow in cross-section, and often lined with masonry. Inside these pits sat men armed with long spears. Others went out to drive the elephants towards them. As the elephants passed over or near the pits, the hidden spearmen thrust their spears deep into their bellies.

Six months went by during which the Empire of the Strange Ones grew to great heights of glory and splendour, and soon its name became known to other nations. Like a protea it rose from the rocks of obscurity and isolation and it smiled at the sun like a bride in spring.

Then one day the slave woman *Makira-Luluma* escaped from a troop of slaves working in a plantation and fled into the dark forest.

After eight whole moons I returned to *Makarikari* – to the cave where *Ninavanhu-Ma* enlightened me on so many things. I had been wandering throughout the land; I had seen the great *Lu-Kongo* river where *Odu* and *Amarava* begat the first human beings after the destruction of the First People. I even saw where *Amarava* gave birth to the first Bushmen and Pygmies. Now we were back at our cave.

'That was a wonderful journey, beloved Goddess,' I said with a smile. 'But you are not looking very happy at all – what can be the matter?'

'Humanity is in great danger, *Lumukanda*,' replied *Ma* seriously.

'Something strange happened while we were away and a great evil now walks this land. We must act fast to stop it from overwhelming the rest of the world.' Then she sat silent for a while, as though listening to something. 'Someone is coming in this direction. This is where I vanish and I leave everything in your hands.'

For a long time I stood waiting alone in the forest and at last I noticed a movement opposite me. A young girl, a young Black slave girl, came into view. There was an expression of wild fear on her face and she looked as if she was fast nearing the valley of insanity. She kept casting fearful glances over her shoulder and she did not see me until she was very close. I knew who she was – I remembered her very well; she was *Luluma*, the same girl who had comforted me on that dark morning after I had slain my parent.

'*Luluma!*' I said softly, '*Luluma*, what brings you here?'

The girl started and her eyes opened wide. With a jerk she jumped back. I had started to develop the ability to read thoughts, and I read terror in her mind – far greater than the terror she felt for whatever she was running from.

'Do you no longer remember me, *Luluma*?' I asked gently. 'Why do you look so afraid? I am no ghost.'

'You . . . you . . .' she gasped with infinite horror.

My newly acquired powers of reading human thoughts were not yet extensively developed but I could sense guilt and great shame faintly through the more overpowering cloud of terror. I grasped her by her thin shoulders and forced her to look up at me. 'Why are you scared of me, little one?'

The girl looked up at my smiling face and suddenly tears flooded her eyes. 'I am not . . . I am not *Luluma* . . . *Luluma* . . . is dead!'

'Nonsense! I know you are *Luluma*. We were slaves together, remember?'

'Let me explain . . .' she stammered.

'If I let you explain you will no doubt tell me you are a blue-eyed impala with a pink tail. Come let us go to my cave and I shall give you something to eat first.'

I took her by the wrist and drew her closer to me. Before she realised what had happened, we were inside my cave. She gasped in amazement. 'How did we get here?'

'On the wings of mental power.'

'Did you have these powers even while you were a slave?'

'No, I had the strange fortune to be saved from becoming a fish's dinner by a very charming Goddess . . .'

'A . . . a . . . Goddess?' gasped *Luluma*, her face turning more grey with horror.

'Yes, a Goddess, child, one of those things I used to think

were only figments of some crazy old man's warped imagination.'

Suddenly *Luluma* leapt to her feet with a flatly squeezed cry of fear and bolted for the entrance of the cave. But she virtually ricochetted off the radiance-shield enshrouding the apparition of *Ma*, who appeared in the entrance of the cave, and landed behind my back, gibbering like a monkey.

'Poor, poor thing, how you must have suffered,' said *Ma*. 'Do you know who this child is, *Lumukanda*?'

'Yes, I know her very well. She was a fellow slave . . .'

'Wrong! This is the High Empress *Makira* – her soul at least, contained inside the body of the girl *Luluma* whom you knew. *Makira's* real body is inhabited by my arch-enemy, the Goddess of Evil, *Watamaraka*. And unless I act promptly, the human race will go the way of the First People. Come, let us act now!'

In the city of the Strange Ones tension is mounting and rumours are flying like bats in the night. It seems that something totally without precedent had happened in a small fortified village on the northern border of the empire. Thousands of slaves had suddenly exploded into open armed rebellion and had not only destroyed the garrison in the village to the last man, but had massacred their masters and mistresses, and afterwards escaped into the forests beyond the border.

The governor of the north had sent a regiment in pursuit of these slaves, but the regiment had been totally annihilated in an ambush.

The Strange Ones are uneasy; men are carrying swords in the streets and if a slave so much as looks suspicious, they pounce upon him and slay him on the spot. There are differences of opinion; some want the slaves to be accommodated in bulk outside the city; others disagree as they feel the slaves might unite outside and attack the city.

To restore the people's confidence the Empress has ordered a parade of the armed might, and tens of thousands of troops are now marching through the streets, hauling their weird weapons of war. These include catapults for hurling vast stones, and giant bows capable of shooting bundles of spears, like arrows, with one shot. Also on parade is their latest weapon – a light structure drawn by only two oxen. It is also a catapult, but it hurls large bags full of an inflammable oil, and there are long wicks which are set alight before the missile is hurled. It is said that these murderous machines have been invented by the Empress herself.

The Great Square is crowded with people who have come to

watch the demonstration. At the appointed hour a war machine is brought into position on the far side of the square. On the near side two slaves are tied to stakes planted in the ground. Scores of slaves have been herded together in another part of the square to witness the exhibition. There is an expectant silence as the soldiers prepare the machines and the wick on the oilbag is lit. The commander snaps out an order and the catapult fires with a thud. The bag sails through the air with a trail of smoke, and a loud cheer resounds as it hits the two slaves tied to the stakes.

'There you are, you black vermin!' shouts one of the soldiers to the crowd of slaves herded in the enclosure. 'Would you like to rebel against us?'

'More . . . more . . . Give us more . . . show these black dogs!' The crowds roar with delight, while the two slaves writhe in agony in the flames.

From where she stands on her small portable platform the Empress smiles. She gives another curt order to one of her battle leaders, and another machine is brought into position, one that shoots a volley of spears at the same time. This time two female slaves are dragged out amid cheers from the crowds of Strange Ones.

But suddenly there is an interruption!

A tall, black-veiled woman emerges from the crowds and calmly walks into the centre of the square. She raises her arms and her loud voice shatters the silence:

'Stop! Enough!'

All eyes are fixed on her as she stands there in the centre of the square. A deeper silence falls upon the crowds and all mouths hang open in sheer astonishment. Then once more the voice rings out with compelling force:

'You . . . you there, who call yourself the Empress *Kadesi* . . . hear me! Hear what I have to say to you. You do not belong to this world and you have no right here. You must either stop your atrocious deeds or take the consequences. I am warning you!'

The Empress is being threatened within her Great City. The deep silence lies heavy on the crowds as everybody awaits the reactions of the Empress to this impudence. The Empress suddenly leaps off her platform and comes running towards the tall, veiled figure.

'You foul bitch . . . I'll teach you to insult me!'

A chorused howl of pure astonishment bursts from the crowds. The Empress has staggered backwards as if struck by an unseen hand. She spins head over heels and flops most disgracefully in the dust.

The Empress rises slowly and the watching crowds see her lips move as she asks her black-veiled enemy a question. They strain their ears in vain to hear the earnest conversation now in progress.

Then, in utter astonishment they see their Empress, fear now written on her face, slowly turn . . . and walk away. The assembly opens a way for her and she silently passes through, followed by her bodyguard – shocked and undecided – like a pack of dogs with their tails between their legs. The departing party melts away with the crowds and all astonished eyes now turn to the mysterious veiled figure, proudly striding away in another direction.

She comes straight down the narrow street towards where I am standing with the young slave woman *Luluma*, and in a voice charged with feigned haughtiness she shouts, loudly enough for some passers-by to hear: 'Attend me, you unclean beasts, and let us go!'

Like obedient slaves we follow the veiled woman at a discreet distance, making the hundreds of people who had been following the mysterious figure believe we are nothing but a couple of slaves following their widowed mistress home. Thus we entered the city and now we are returning 'home' somewhere in the poorer quarters of the city.

And now things are happening fast and I can feel in my bones that the 'end' is indeed within sight.

I know that *Watamaraka* in the guise of the Empress *Kadesi* is fully aware of the presence within her city of *Ninavanhu-Ma*, in the guise of a widowed mistress – and soon these mighty giantesses from the depths of Eternity, are going to be locked in a titanic struggle.

LUMUKANDA TURNS TRAITOR!

When we reached the house after successfully dodging the vast crowds that had followed us, we closed and bolted the door. I then turned to our mistress and asked her what she had said to the Empress *Watamaraka-Kadesi*.

'Well, when I struck her down with the powers at my disposal, she soon enough realised who I was. I told her I have decided to give her three moons in which to make her exit from this world and return to exile beyond the River Time. She said she would think it over. I now know that there is going to be an open clash between us very soon – and that will be an interesting battle.'

'What will happen . . . if you lose?' asked the slave girl *Luluma*, whose soul was that of *Makira*.

'If I lose, the whole world and the Universe will disintegrate, and chaos and nothingness will rule supreme.'

Tears flooded the eyes of the young slave girl. 'Goddess, I speak as *Makira*, and I speak in earnest. I have murdered, cheated and tortured, all on behalf of this useless plaything-empire, which I can see will soon be wiped off the face of history. Please, I beg you, do whatever you like – wipe it off, and destroy every human being in it. But do not fail to destroy *Watamaraka*, the Mother of Demons. Destroy her, above all.'

'The coming battle between *Watamaraka* and me will decide the future of creation. But I am very worried indeed, because I can foresee you, *Lumukanda*, turning traitor and betraying me to the force of evil.'

'What!' I cried. 'Me a traitor?'

Two days after that, news came to the Great City from the south – news that increased the tension within the empire to fever pitch. A great revolt had broken out in the land of the Ba-Tswana nation and vast hordes of slaves and half-white malcontents were razing the imperial towns to the ground and freeing slaves who swelled the ranks of the destruction-mad rebels tremendously. These hordes were being led by a young woman of strange appearance whom many called the Wild Huntress.

This young woman was an albino and she always dyed her hair a bright violet. She claimed to be the daughter of the Evening Star. No one knew who her parents had been but this much was known that she was an albino of the race of the Strange Ones. A deadly archer, she was leading her blood-thirsty hordes nearer and nearer to the Great City. Destruction pure and simple, and not conquest, was this woman's motive – and she was destroying thoroughly – and utterly.

Then close in the wake of these unpleasant tidings came more news from the north. A slave named *Lubo* had escaped from the Great City some time ago, it was said, and this slave had succeeded in reaching the northern border of the empire which he crossed and somehow made himself leader of the slaves who had already rebelled and escaped.

Now this *Lubo*, it was said, was ravaging the northern and eastern provinces and his hordes were also coming nearer and nearer to the Great City, from the east. When news of members of their race being mercilessly butchered by the rebel slaves reached the ears of the citizens of the Great City, they went wild with rage and fear and hatred. Howling mobs of the Strange Ones roamed the streets, murdering any Black slave they saw. Slaves who had been loyal for as long as they had been alive were beheaded by their very owners; some had their limbs torn from their bodies; some were hurled from the walls into the moat. No mercy was shown to any slave, male, female, young or old.

Within an hour the whole city had become one reeking slaughter pit – bodies of dead slaves strewn everywhere, up and down every street. But some owners hid their slaves in deep cellars, while others smuggled them out of the city. There were those who died or were injured in the process of defending their slaves against the mobs. There were, there are, and always will be, those with feelings for others.

I was asleep when all this started, and even as *Luluma* awoke me, our Goddess had already sprung into action. She was now standing on the highest tower in the city and projecting her penetrating voice across the length of the city:

'People from beyond the seas . . . hear me . . . the Guardian Angel of all living things – you included. I command you to stop killing those whom I have placed under my protection. I order you to leave them alone and allow them to leave your cursed city. I warn you – leave them alone, or face my vengeance!'

The shocked city heard . . . and saw . . . the Source of Life! They stood where they were, petrified. And in the minds of all re-echoed the words: '... your cursed city ... your cursed ...'

They knew their city was doomed, even before it was destroyed, and they knew that their race would soon be nothing but the faintest of faint echoes in the grottoes of history.

'... your cursed city ...'

They watched as thousands of slaves streamed out of the city and somehow they knew that within the breast of everyone burned a red-hot torch of vengeance. They were lost, they knew it; their death sentence had been passed ...

So, the people of the last remaining city of the empire stood to arms for the rest of that day, and for the three days following. They did not know that in future there would not be a single member of their descendants who would carry forth their memory; but that instead, a continent full of people would carry forth the memory of those they had enslaved and murdered!

On the fifth day reports came that the armies, or rather hordes, led by *Lubo* from the east, and the Wild Huntress from the south, were only a day's journey from the city. On that day all the Strange Ones fled to the confines of the city walls, leaving homes and farms behind. No slave, however loyal, was admitted into the safety of the city and those who had Bushman and Hottentot wives left them to their fate. These wives who had shared couches with the proud Strange Ones were butchered to the last soul by the slave hordes.

Abandoned, the slaves streamed across the plains in their thousands to join *Lubo* and increase his already over-swollen hordes.

Inside the walls of the Great City much was happening, the most important being the sudden disappearance of the Empress – deserting her people in their hour of peril. The shocked people did not know the truth, of course, the truth of her changed personality. The Mother of Demons had wearied of playing Empress and had simply left the city.

Another interesting happening was that two battle leaders became involved in a duel over the vacated throne, in which the one died shortly after having killed the other.

A young fifteen-year-old boy, the last descendant of the first Emperor, was crowned in a stirring ceremony in which nearly all the people in the city took part – their last coronation ceremony on earth.

The young boy rose after the formalities were concluded and addressed the cheering crowd, concluding: 'Let us fight to the very end. If the savages attack us, Oh my people, let us give them something with which to remember us till the end of time. If you must fall, Oh my people, fall as true warriors should – and fall after sending at least ten of the black swine to hell.'

The sun set in a blaze of fiery splendour. It set slowly, as if anxious to prolong the empire's last day . . .

A voice called softly out of the moon-bathed forest. It called once . . . twice . . . thrice . . . It was a voice of enchantment, a voice of pure seduction. It spoke of longing, a ravaging hunger such as no human being can ever feel and remain alive. It spoke of a great loneliness, surpassed only by the fury of hell itself. It was the voice of temptation . . . of pure Evil. It said: '*Lumukanda* . . .'

I was sitting outside the cave and inside my beloved Goddess was lost in pleasant repose. The girl *Luluma* was fast asleep at the entrance, comfortably curled up underneath a leopard skin. My inquisitiveness prompted me to explore the origin of the pleasant voice, and I quietly stole down the slope into the forest. The shadows closed over me, obstructing the silver light of the all-seeing moon.

Something kept telling me to go back to those to whom I owed allegiance. But another something told me to proceed and meet the owner of the voice. Briefly I hesitated and actually took a step back. But a pair of hungry arms reached out and caught me in a tempestuous embrace. It was the embrace of *Watamaraka-Kadesi*!

I was lost in a sea of pleasure such as no man had ever known on this earth. I felt as though I was flying high among the silver stars. I was like a bird – a lost butterfly among a field of scented flowers in another world, beyond Eternity. I was lost . . . lost like a fly smothering in a pot of honey – unable to fly and just dying slowly in its own delight, like a drunkard drowning in his favourite beer!

Suddenly a soft mournful melody rose like a dark cloud in the silver skies of ecstasy through which I was floating. It was the wailing death-song of millions of stars over a blatantly betrayed Universe. And I, *Lumukanda*, had betrayed the stars, the earth, mankind, into the hands of Evil!

A wave of horror swept over me – a wave of leaden remorse; I had condemned the Universe by flirting with destruction. For a few moments of transient joy I had sold all that is holy to Evil itself. I struggled to free myself, but *Watamaraka-Kadesi* smiled mockingly in my face. 'It is too late to escape now, Oh *Lumukanda*, I have you in my power. In your height of passion you vowed to do anything for me and now I am holding you to that vow. Go back to the cave and unclasp the Necklace of Life from *Ninavanhu-Ma's* neck, and also the *mutsha* of Fertility from her hips, and bring them to me. Have I made myself clear?'

'I hear and obey.'

'Now I have *Ninavanhu-Ma* at my mercy,' laughed *Watamaraka.*

UNDER THE FLOODS OF TIME

There was a flash brighter than the brightest thing imaginable – a flash of light which filled the cave with its blinding glare and a roar of sound that seemed to shatter every bone in my body. Then silence.

I opened my eyes and found we were no longer inside the cave. We were not even on earth, as far as I could make out, but somewhere . . . somewhere, it seemed, on the very frontiers of dark Eternity. We were on the edge of an incredible cliff – a mighty precipice that stretched down into the deepest reaches of Infinity. It plunged down into the depths of darkness, darker than the darkest darkness imaginable. I looked around to find the source of an eerie light behind me. Some distance away was a glowing vapour.

Ninavanhu-Ma and *Watamaraka* had taken their dispute to the all-knowing Great Spirit . . .

I shuddered and turned my face away from the eerie light. I looked down at the woman whose head was resting on my thigh and who seemed unconscious – or dead. I looked down upon the Empress *Makira*, and something told me her soul had been restored to her body – the body it belonged to. A ghostly shape stood some distance away to my left, looking down sorrowfully at the obviously dead body of *Luluma*, the slave girl. And I knew somehow that this ghostly shape was the soul of *Luluma*, weeping over the body it could not again inhabit.

Dawn was breaking in the sky. The dispute between *Ninavanhu-Ma* and *Watamaraka* had not been settled and it died like the cooking fires of yester-year. The Spirits of Good and Evil are destined to stay with Humanity in equal proportions till the River of Time ceases to flow.

The Empress *Makira-Kadesi* and I buried *Luluma* and we went out onto a low hill overlooking the Great City of the Strange Ones for which the dawn brought no hope. I knew, without being told, that the hordes of the Wild Huntress were now within striking distance of the city, and *Lubo* was not far away either.

For a long time I stood looking down on the heavily defended walls of the city where thousands of armed men stood ready to die for their homes. I realised that the two attacking hordes could easily be cut to pieces in no time at all, and I did not like the idea of so many human lives being sacrificed merely to destroy that city. A plan had already come to my mind whereby the city could be taken with as few casualties to the attacking forces as possible.

Then something I had not foreseen happened, just as the sun rose, sending long shadows streaming westwards over the dew-moist grass. I had known that the Wild Huntress was close, but I had not anticipated her being so close.

There came loud cries from the forest to the west of the city and a vast horde burst from the cover of the trees in a savage attack on the city walls. Some of the yelling attackers were carrying great rafts with which to cross the moat while others carried scaling ladders, clearly improvised during the night. They came close enough to send volleys of arrows from countless bows at the defenders of the city crouching on the walls. Even as I watched, the first rafts were launched across the moat, full of shouting and determined men. Raft after raft was launched until there were ten crawling up to the stockades. It was then that the defenders struck – quickly and pitilessly.

With devastating suddenness the mighty throwing machines on the stockades cut loose with a hail of stones the size of human beings, and these were joined by the giant bows and firebag catapults. The whole magic power of the war machines of the Strange Ones was concentrated on the ten rafts. Four were shattered by direct hits and soon the moat was turned into a pitiful emulsion of dying humanity.

Loud cheers of victory rang out from the walls and I was sure I heard across the long distance challenging sounds from the Strange Ones – inviting them to try again. The challenge was not accepted. In a mass wound-licking move they withdrew into the forest.

I stood there watching as the defenders shouted and danced in wild jubilation on the walls. I was determined to go down there in person and spoil their amusement. That city was an excrescence which interfered with the history of my people, and it was contrary to the laws of the Great Spirit who laid down that each race of humans should be left alone to find its own destiny without outside interference.

I descended the hill, determined to seek out the Wild Huntress, whoever she might be, and offer her my services. Soon I stood at the edge of the forest and it occurred to me that I now had powers which I might as well use. I simply wished myself to be within the presence of the Wild Huntress, wherever she might find herself.

For a moment my vision blurred and as my surroundings came into focus again I found myself standing waist deep in water, directly behind a long-haired young woman who was being bathed by two former female slaves. One of the latter saw me and let out a loud shriek of fear and there was a series of loud splashes as the women tried to escape into deeper water.

'He came out of empty air!' cried one. 'It is an evil spirit of some sort.'

Standing chest deep in water now, the three women regarded me with wide eyes for a few moments, then the wide-shouldered alien albino in the centre opened her mouth and found a voice:

'Who are you? Get away from here – get away, you ugly devil!'

I put a fierce snarl on my face and opened my eyes very wide as I took a few steps closer to the women. 'I haven't had breakfast yet; little women are my favourite dish!'

'You wouldn't dare!' cried the pink-skinned one. 'You just try eating me and I'll . . . I'll . . .'

'You will what?' I asked with a smile.

'I'll kill you!'

'Blood-thirsty this time of the morning, aren't you?' I remarked as I slowly moved closer.

The girl's eyes blazed in a sudden burst of cold rage, and her nostrils dilated, hissing with short breath. She squeezed a flood of words from between clenched teeth:

'No, you black demon, I do not like killing people . . . only a certain kind – my own kind. These I kill without compunction and I also raze their cities to the ground so properly that no-one will ever know they had ever been there. I leave their carcasses to rot where they fall. I torture some before I kill them . . . Do you know why?'

'Yes, because you seem to be well out of your mind.'

'You insufferable devil! You black son of a . . . lame goat and a . . . a dead hippopotamus! Why you . . .'

'Now, now, now,' I admonished sweetly. 'Let us first get our facts straight. A lame goat cannot mate with a dead hippopotamus . . .'

'Why . . . you . . . why . . .'

'Because the goat's back is lame and the hippo is . . . well . . . dead!'

'Be silent you!' She bared her teeth in savage rage. 'Do you know who I am? Or rather, do you know whose daughter I am?'

'I hope not the product of a similar combination such as you suggested for me.'

'I am the daughter of the Empress *Makira* ... and one of the battle leaders of her army.'

'And does that entitle you to damage her property?'

The girl composed herself and looked down into the water. 'She ... she is a swine! I have vowed that I will kill her with my own hand. I am going to make her whine for mercy before I kill her. When she was still an unknown half-caste harlot, she seduced my father and made him join forces with her to overthrow the Emperor *Karesu.* When they discovered I was an albino they both disowned me and left me in the forest for wild animals to devour. But a roving band of Bushmen found me ... and brought me up. Now I am back ... for revenge.'

'And I have come to help you, though my motive is somewhat different. I am going to show you a way of taking that city with the loss of as few lives as possible.'

'Oh, but I do not care how many lives it will take – my own included – but that city must be wrecked!'

'Calm yourself child, calm yourself. Get out of the water and summon your warriors. We have a lot to do.'

For the rest of that day thousands of men took turns at, what was for them, a most puzzling task. From where they were encamped, the forest crept along the lake front to quite close to the city. From a point closest to the city, but still under cover of the thick bush, they began to dig a large hole in the soft earth. We made the hole, and afterwards the tunnel, big enough to accommodate many workers at the same time. Scores of slave-blacksmiths worked unceasingly forging heavy hoes for digging and axes for cutting supports for the sides and roof of the tunnel. A mound of earth grew higher and higher as long lines of men emptied great baskets full of earth from the tunnel. It had to be dug deep enough to allow safe passage underneath the moat and the foundation of the wall. Deeper and deeper went the tunnel under the expert hands of those who had worked in the mines of the Strange Ones, and at sunset it was more than three-quarters of the way across to the unsuspecting city.

The motley 'armies' of the Wild Huntress were so carried away by what they were doing that they continued the work throughout the night. The idea of tunnelling under the very feet of the city's defenders and emerging behind them provided the toiling men with many a foul joke as the night wore on. Many were the speculations about how surprised the Strange Ones would be when they saw us emerge in their midst like harvester ants. At daybreak my old friend, now Chief *Lubo,* arrived with his fresh hordes – about a hundred thousand, counting fighting men only. *Lubo* provided us with fresh workers and other teams were formed to make ladders and rafts for the frontal attack above ground which had to start the moment a breakthrough was achieved with the tunnel to distract attention.

There were about two thousand Bushmen in the Wild Huntress's hordes and these I organised into a separate battalion of light archers and briefed them on spearheading the tunnel attack, which I would lead personally.

Lubo had also brought a hundred dugout canoes with which he had intended to attack the city from its weakest side – that facing on Lake Makarikari. We decided to carry out this plan as a further means of distracting attention from the tunnel breakthrough.

At last the headman in charge of tunnelling came back to report that they had broken surface and that they were fortunate enough to emerge within a garden well enclosed within a high mud wall. I ordered the men to rest while I traversed the long tunnel for an inspection. I emerged in a city whose streets were as quiet as a graveyard – into which we turned it pretty soon. By a strange twist of fate the tunnel had emerged in the garden of the house of my erstwhile owner. Now the great house stood empty because all the occupants, women and children, had taken refuge in the strong fort in the centre of the city while every able-bodied man and boy was manning the walls. I returned and ordered the Bushmen *impi* into the tunnel. They poured into the tunnel like so many ants and were closely followed by three-quarters of *Lubo's* and half of the Wild Huntress's savages.

Before the Strange Ones became wise as to what was happening, thirty thousand fighting men had emerged within the city and had infiltrated through the empty houses and had already effectively surrounded the fort in the centre, completely cutting it off from those manning the walls. Night had already fallen and only the stars came out to grace a sullen and moonless sky. I looked up at them and said quietly: 'This night you shall see the end of a proud empire, of proud men, who in their insolence and greed never dreamt that such a fate could strike them. They thought they had their tyrant feet securely planted – but they could not control or rule the River Time, which swallows the proudest empires and over whose rapids now cascades the Canoe of Eternal Death, carrying with it the empire of the Strange Ones to the seas of Oblivion.'

Lubo was saying to his battle leaders: 'Men, remember what you owe these creatures – not long ago you whined under their lash. They denied you the simple right of choosing your mates; they bred you like beasts, and they bought and sold you like beasts. The souls of those they have murdered are even now wandering aimlessly and weeping incessantly in the Spirit Land. Only one thing will pacify them: the death of the very last member of the creatures in this city. Strike, and show no mercy!'

In the meantime the sham frontal attack was being mounted and the Wild Huntress was leading the fleet of war canoes over the quiet, dark surface of the lake. Then we heard the savage roar from thousands of throats as the frontal attack was launched. We heard the distant thuds of the alien war machines on the walls as a hail of large stones hurtled out and the trails of burning fire-bags traced arcs through the night sky, rising and vanishing like comets beyond the walls. A wall of fire in the background lighted the skies.

I pointed to the dark fort in the centre of the city. 'Go, *Lubo*, seize that fort and spare nobody. The rest of you follow me!'

The entire Bushman *impi* followed me towards the weakly defended lake front wall. We ran through the silent streets, past trading houses, gardens and small temples, and a house of evil entertainment with alien statues of mating men and women decorating the steps. There was a long agonizing cry from the wall towards which we were running and an armoured body crashed from the top of the wall. The Wild Huntress's attack had begun and scores of figures running about in confusion were faintly silhouetted against the star-jewelled sky.

A little while later a group of dark figures came walking towards us and we were issued with a haughty challenge. It was the voice of the Wild Huntress herself. I laughed and told her to come closer.

'It was easy,' she said tersely. 'They had only a few men on the wall and only one stone-throwing machine, which sank two of our canoes. But the wall is in our hands. What do we do next?'

'Have all your men disembarked from their canoes already?'

'Long ago,' was her curt reply. 'We are all inside the city.'

'Then call them all together and follow me to the fort in the centre of the city – quickly.'

When we came to the fort we found that a fierce battle was still in progress between *Lubo's* warriors and the gilt-armoured Palace Guards, now commanded by the boy king of the Strange Ones. It seemed as if the Strange Ones had not only brought their women and children and very old men into the fort, but also their boy Emperor with his strong bodyguard. These heavily armoured guards were now standing shoulder to shoulder just inside the fallen gate, forming a solid wall of bronze shields, from behind which they inflicted heavy casualties among *Lubo's impi.*

A huge stone idol stood on an ornate pedestal not far away from the gate, and to this I made my way through the swarming hordes of attacking warriors. I picked the statue off its pedestal and charged with it into the solid phalanx of guardsmen defending the gate.

Three guardsmen went down and through the gap thus formed tore the Wild Huntress, *Lubo* and their followers, their swords hacking the confused guards down before they could re-form. Their heavy armour put them at a great disadvantage compared with the light-footed, more mobile attackers.

The guards died to the last man, but even as they died they took many of their former slaves with them. The howling hordes of Bushmen and Bantu roared into the main gate of the round, triple-walled fort and loud shrieks crashed against the star-sprayed skies as hundreds of women and children of the Strange Ones saw their death bursting in on them in a very real form. A troop of women, armed with bows and arrows, briefly delayed the attackers at the second gate. But these were promptly cut down by a hail of Bushmen arrows – however, not before one of them had sent a shaft into the belly of the Wild Huntress. She fell with a loud scream – of anger, rather than pain.

'Forward! Forward!' *Lubo* encouraged his men.

Then happened something that was both beautiful and pathetic – pathetic and most unusual – and something I knew would live for ever in song and story for as long as the Land of the Tribes still felt the ocean breakers roaring against its shores – for as long as the sacred symbol of the Story-tellers of the Tribes, the mamba with a flower in its mouth, was carried to the Holy Place on the nights of story-telling:

The young boy Emperor stood alone in the innermost gate of the triple-walled fort. He stood there, wearing a white loincloth and a bronze corselet that was too big and far too heavy for him. A heavy bronze helmet covered his whole head and his long jet-black hair tumbled from below it in heavy streams on to his shoulders. In the flickering light of the two torches burning on brackets on either gatepost we could see through the gap in his helmet that his great dark eyes were wide with fear and tears were running down his pale cheeks. But there was a firmness about his quivering mouth which was both comical and impressive. He was holding a short sword in his hands – a sword that any man would have wielded in one hand only – and his legs seemed to be doing their best to stand firm and straight, while they yearned to turn and start running away from under the brave child.

'No! No!' he screamed to the approaching warriors. 'You go back, you dirty savages – you lowdown slaves . . . you! Go, go baaaaack!'

The howling warriors closed in on him and the boy's sword flashed in the dim light of the torches as he fought fiercely like the brave young lion he was. A careless warrior fell with a loud cry, and another . . . and yet another. Although he was completely surrounded and being stabbed and struck at from all sides, the young Strange One fought on and on. He was bleeding heavily and clearly becoming weaker. Then, with a last heart-rending, loud appeal to his long-dead mother to save him, he fell and was cruelly trampled underfoot by *Lubo's* frontmost attackers. And even as he was trampled down his soul went and joined his mother's.

The fierce hordes swarmed over him into the very interior of the fort and soon loud screams of agony and shrieks of fear told the shocked night that when a thing is worth doing, it is worth doing properly. There was killing going on – by men whom years, and a lifetime of suffering and humiliation, had tortured into beasts that knew no pity. Afterwards I saw blood-crazy warriors doing a victory dance with the long-haired heads of women impaled on the points of their spears. As I walked through the sickening carnage I recalled an old saying which the old man *Obu* had once quoted to me when I was still a slave: 'For every act of evil people commit there always will be, some day, punishment in equal measure.'

Some of the warriors were already plundering the dead and had not *Lubo* reminded them angrily that the city was still far from taken, the warriors would have been caught unawares by the main army which had been manning the walls. These troops had heard the cries and clamour coming from the fort in which were their women and children and hastened along to investigate. As they came charging down the streets they ran into cloud after cloud of poisonous Bushmen arrows. The Bushmen were holding them at bay while the hordes of *Lubo* and the Wild Huntress crept around behind them to cut off their retreat and split them off from further assistance that might come from the walls.

This was the fiercest battle and the Strange Ones fought bitterly. They fought till the last man fell in the streets of the city in which they had been lords and masters for so long.

Not all of them died bravely, however. Some died like screaming cowards, having thrown away their weapons and gone running through the streets like warthogs gone mad. Some died begging for mercy – from the men whom they had enslaved. Others died in the act of looting the houses of their fellows. The fat chief Battle Leader of the Strange Ones was captured while trying to sneak out of the city with a chest full of the dead boy Emperor's royal jewels. I ordered him to be taken to the forest and kept alive there, together with his two concubines, for a certain delicious reason I had in mind.

The Wild Huntress was dead, as was Chief *Obu*, who had been struck accidentally by a stray Bushman arrow, while leading the attack on the last survivors, who had barricaded themselves inside the Temple of Evil. These were a group of the poets and philosophers of their race and they all committed suicide just as *Obu's* warriors broke the barricades. One old madman had even extended a blessing over the attacking warriors before plunging a dagger into his own heart.

Dawn broke in the skies and the all-seeing Lord of Day emerged and saw. *Lo!* By the mighty lake of Makarikari, which in later years was to become nothing but a desolate salt pan – a city of the dead. A city which already belonged to the past, and which was now destined to survive as a mere legend in the minds of the children of those who destroyed it.

For three whole days tens of thousands of Bantu, Bushmen and half-castes laboured in the great city, razing houses to the ground and scattering the stones all over the countryside. The towers and temples disappeared to the lowermost reaches of their foundations. Many ornamental articles, utensils and weapons somehow became spared as trophies and heirlooms, but the bulk of whatever was not breakable, like armour, metal vessels and bronze statuary, was taken into the forest and melted down. *Lubo* had sworn an oath that if he succeeded in taking the city he would destroy it so thoroughly that not the faintest trace would be left.

On the fourth day the task of merciless destruction was completed, and all that could still be seen was the great oblong clearing of the Great Square, some traces of the streets, and some foundations of private homes. Even these traces were destined to disappear at the hands of wind and weather, and all that remained which could betray the site was the mass of shaped stones widely scattered in the vicinity.

Then we proceeded with great celebrations in the forest. In the course of these celebrations the high Battle Leader of the Strange Ones and his two concubines – the three very last survivors – were brought in and prepared for the pot. They tasted considerably better than they looked, and they looked much less insolent and brave as they were passed around on our meat trays and stew bowls.

It was during the wild dancing and the loud singing and shouting by all the freedom-drunk people that the High Chief *Lubo* raised his hands for silence. After the crowds had quietened down and gathered in closer, *Lubo* raised his fierce voice to the heavens:

'My people ... this is for us a day of great joy and jubilation. Today we have come out of the evil hut of slavery and its door has closed behind us for ever. Today we have crossed the river of blood and tears and beyond we now see the dawn of our smiling future. Today we must mould ourselves into a mighty nation which no aliens would ever dare to enslave again. Let us mould ourselves into a nation of Strength, Beauty, Plenty and Prosperity. Let us call ourselves the Lu-Anda – "they that increase".'

People leapt up and, delirious with joy, they danced, sang and cried loudly: '*Lunda! Luaaaanda! Luanda! . . . Lunda!*'

On that day was founded the mighty Lu-Nda nation which, together with the Ba-Kongo, was in later years to rule vast tracts of land from the shores of the Western Ocean to where the land of Ka-Tanga is today.

I placed a solemn blessing on the Lunda people, inspired by the Goddess *Ninavanhu-Ma*, and I encouraged them to spread like the sweet *luvande* flowers and to bring joy and happiness to all – something they had not known for so long.

But on the Lunda people *Watamaraka* also placed her kind of blessing. She instilled in them a patient vengeful spirit and blatant ferocity, especially in battle. Even today the Lunda are among the fiercest warriors and the most vengeful people under the sun.

A month after all this I had a remarkable vision as I walked through the forest. I saw a strange tree, most unlike any I had ever seen, and whose girth was incredible. It was not growing in the ground like other trees, but walked about on its roots like a spider, or a crab. And it spoke to me: 'I am the Tree of Life who brought living things to this earth and I am the husband of both *Ninavanhu-Ma* and *Watamaraka*. You have interfered with both my wives, and for that I curse you and condemn you to Eternal Blindness, and in future you will be known as the Blind War-god *Lumukanda*.

THE BLOT OF ZIMA-MBJE

My children, I have come to tell you something that you must know . . . I am *Lumukanda*, the story-teller. For this I am going to ask you to give me all your patience and with this I am going to ask you to give me the brains with which you think and the ears with which you hear. And above all, I am going to ask everyone of you to repeat everything as you heard it. No word must be deleted . . . no word must be added. For this is the story which even our wisest of the wise, the witchdoctors, are afraid to tell. This is the story of shame – the story of how the whole Bantu race was nearly snapped like a twig. This is the story of which according to the strict laws of the Tribes must only be told to those people who are to rise and become Story-tellers. This is the story that must be remembered and yet be forgotten at the same time. And this is the story when every tribe and every nation that we find today in the lands of the Tribes – the lands of the Bantu, had its birth.

After we stoned the city of the Strange Ones, a hundred generations went by. It could be that even I, as an immortal, cannot keep touch with all the generations of Man.

Thus there are always those people who would like to revive the evil things and they usually do this only for their own end. And such a man was that of *Munumutaba* – which means 'Man of the Big Mountains'.

This man was a rascal from the very start. He was a rogue and he was a great breaker of the laws of his tribe. He was a bandit and he was a criminal. One day he heard from the lips of a very old man – he heard the story of the coming of the Strange Ones, and the way in which they met their fate, and the evil which they caused in this country. And he heard also how they – the red-headed Ma-Iti, of so many generations ago, gave us the ways of melting the hard iron stone into the spears and axes with which we face enemies in battle. This man, *Munumutaba*, decided that he himself would revive the empire of the Strange Ones, but as the ruler himself; because always, as you know, my children, it is the bad men who always try to lift themselves up and ruin the lives of men. Now, *Munumutaba* heard the story of this old man and he decided that he must gather all his fellow-bandits – all his fellow-criminals – and take them to the place to the west where the mighty lake Makari-Kari has got its shores – its salty shores. This young man gathered in that ugly place of bush and grass and there the bandit began to see the task that lay in front of him. He knew that he could not himself take all these ruined – all these old stones to the far away land of the Mashona. Then he looked about and he and his gang of criminals raided the villages of the humble and gentle Batswana and pressed them into his service. What he did was to build sleds – the kind of which the tribes had never seen before. They were big – big enough to accommodate a hundred people. And these sleds were each drawn by about fifty oxen in one row. What he did then was to collect all the old stones that he found, to stack them in great piles and to load them onto these fantastic sleds of his and so for many years – five whole summers – a strange procession was seen in the land of the Tribes – a procession the kind of which has never been seen since: great sleds loaded with stones being hauled by men and oxen. Hundreds of men died – hundreds of sweating, suffering men – and thousands of beasts died. But an evil man is never deterred by anything and to him death and suffering was but a game. And in the tenth year of this the great bandit began laying the foundation of the fortress that was for years to become a blot and a mark of shame on most of our tribes.

From the great koppies around that place he also cut stones that were copies of the ones he had got, and with these stones he added further to the strength of this fantastic fortress he was building. And then one day he – *Munumutaba* of the Mountains – was the confirmed ruler of the land.

You must remember, my children, that he had moved hundreds of sleds to take these stones all there, and he went nearly mad with this strange task of his because he wanted to make himself a great king. It was said that ever since his childhood he had always worked to be the one man on top. He always worked to be the ruler of all the boys who herded the cattle. But in the end an evil man never does change and so one day, when his chest was swelling with pride and cruel vanity, he stood on the highest tower, known as The Eye of Zima-Mbje – and he looked out over the distant plains and he looked moreover upon the great village that surrounded the mighty fortress. He looked at the ranging krantzes beyond. He saw them and he knew . . . 'I am the king.'

But it was not designed by the gods that it should be, because as he came down from the mighty fortress something slipped – and one stone slid away out of place, causing a lot of them to slide apart, and he fell like a bird among all the ruins of falling stone and so the great *Munumutaba* met his end.

But when one evil weed rises in the field and the law of justice cuts it down, another weed rises. And his son rose again and it was his son who caused this evil of which I am going to tell you now.

You remember, my children, that at this time the land was suffering from a strange scourge. A race of men, the kind of which the tribes had never seen before, was ravaging like lions throughout the land. Even today we have not seen anybody of that description. We must carry today a description of these people so that when you do see them you must know them for what they are – Feared Ones!

These Feared Ones are a race of thin men, but under that thinness lies a great strength. They have noses like the beaks of vultures and hair that grows long – but not as long as that of the Strange Ones. They had the habit of taking hundreds of our sons and daughters into a land that we must never, never know anything about – and to a land we must never *try* to know anything about. We never knew whether they were eating those children – whether they were devouring them by their thousands – but this much we do know, that they took them away and we never saw them again.

Munumutaba the Second decided that the best way for him to secure his empire was to come to terms with these Feared Ones – these men like the swift-footed animals, who were like zebras and yet had no stripes. This is what he did.

A band of these men had come to Zima-Mbje and showered him with praises in a foreign language. They called him a great king. They praised his sons and his daughters and his warriors, but wanted to take them to a faraway country ... their own country.

Munumutaba said: 'Look, look, my friends, I can give you all the slaves that you want – only this – give me your weapons. Give me the way of making iron hard.' And from these so-called Feared Ones – these Arabi as we call them – we learnt the way of making steel very hard.

Now, *Munumutaba* attacked other tribes, just as the Strange Ones had done before him – thousands and thousands of generations before him – and he took other tribes into slavery. You could see them – women and children being carried away to a land we know nothing about. He captured the women of the Batswana tribe. He captured the women of the outlying tribes of the Lunda; he sent raiding parties as far up as the land of the Lukundi. And he also sent raiding parties as far up as the land of the Mambo and the land of the Bakwana.

Now, children, listen very carefully. This is what happened. He took these women while he sent the men away into slavery and he had the men and these women led into the land which is today known as the Transvaal. Here the women were sent on their hands and knees to scoop up soil in a certain river known as the river of crocodiles. This river used to carry great quantities of sand and in this sand were tiny grains of the metal which was very dear to the Feared Ones – just as it had been very dear to the Strange Ones before them.

These women used to seek for days on end, sorting out these things just as your mothers sort out the beans from the husks – just as your mothers sort out the chaff out of the mealies. In those days, my children, those were the days which are known as the dark days of our tribes.

These women used to work for days on end sorting out this gold (as it is called today) and they used to fill it painstakingly into horns and even into large ivory tusks. This gold was taken away to the land of the Arabi by these Feared Ones. What happened to it we don't know; but this much we know – you cannot make a spear out of gold – it is far too soft. So, my children, leave that cursed metal alone.

In those days, my children, many visitors from beyond the seas used to come to our shores looking for this metal – looking also for the teeth of the great elephant which we regard as sacred.

Munumutaba was a man like his own evil father who knew no law. He broke the law by killing elephants without permission from the gods. He broke the law by killing the sacred spotted ones and these he gave to the Feared Ones together with hundreds of slaves. He sent hundreds of young men to toil in the Sacred Iron Mountain of the west – known as Thaba-Nzimbi, and here he mined the steel. He mined the iron which was made into spears – the famous spears of Zima-Mbje – which were the dread of all our tribes in those days.

My children, those days, as I have said, are days that you must never remember – days that you must never defile the ears of the young by telling. This story I tell now is not to be heard by the ears of children, only by those who want to rise and become great medicine men – and who must be the Guardians of our Tribal History.

What happened in those days, my children, was terrible. Many tribes died. As I have said, *Munumutaba* attacked hundreds of tribes and he destroyed many. Destroyed was the sacred tribe of the Bakenje, who were the first Bantu people to teach us to carve vessels out of wood. Destroyed was the tribe of the Haini – Haini, who were known for their music, for their games and for their great sport of wrestling. All these were part of the Batswana tribe.

Then in the north he destroyed, or partly annihilated, the tribe of the Mambo. The members of these tribes were scattered throughout the country as a result of the evil of *Munumutaba*.

Now, my children, an evil thing never does last long. It so happened that one day *Munumutaba* decided to marry. But the woman whom he married, and made his first queen, was a cruel and ambitious woman – as cruel as he was himself. And, my children, this woman destroyed him. She fell in love with one of these Feared Ones – one of these cruel strangers from beyond the seas. She started packing *Munumutaba's* sacred seraglio with women of the Lawu, the despised Lawu people, whom you know as the Hottentots – the people whom we hate worse than the plague and the people whom we are proud to have wiped off from the face of the earth – the Lawu Hottentots.

These Lawu were a cold and arrogant people. They thought they were next only in kinship to the Arabi and so this gang of people, the Arabi and *Munumutaba's* wife and the Lawu, began yet another reign of terror in the land which was worse than the first one which *Munumutaba* had begun.

One day while *Munumutaba* lay resting on his fat side his wife crept into the room and drove a spear into his heart – and so he died. And she ruled that country – and she ruled it with a hand of evil.

The trade with the Feared Ones grew and so the land of Zima-Mbje prospered at the expense of hundreds of tribes. But in the end, after generations and generations of people had come and gone, after *Munumutaba's* wife herself had met her death at the hands of – at the teeth of – a crocodile, things began to change.

My children, you cannot keep on storing up the wrath of a river without that river sweeping you along. I told you before, my children, that *Munumutaba* had displaced hundreds of people. He had scattered hundreds of tribes, and these tribes were cut off from their tribal laws and they became merely roamers in the forest. Some of them found their way into the land which we today know as Swaziland. And those – those days when those people had come – those sorry remnants of people had come – from tribes once great, they lost all their ways of making, building even humble huts for themselves. They took to dwelling in the trees. Also the famous Venda – they broke away at this time. They were formed out of hundreds of slaves who sought refuge in the mountains of the east, which are known as the Drakensberg today.

O, my children, those days were days of change and turmoil. Those days were days when one tribe went down into oblivion and another rose like an eagle into the sky.

In those days, my children, the great nation known as the Nguni (which means 'the people who lack country') who had no land, the people Nguni, were formed. The Nguni was formed out of myriads of tribes and even today their language contains hundreds of words that were taken over from these tribes. And, my children, a people that rises out of the ground – out of the charred remnants of destroyed tribes – these people are remarkable for their great ferocity, and the Nguni was a ferocious and cruel race.

And as you know, my children, they had to fight in order to be there – in order to exist. It so happened that when *Munumutaba* the Fifth, who was known as the Thief and who was partly an Arabi and also partly a Hottentot, took the throne of the great empire of Luvijiti (as they were insolent enough to call it), the great Nguni tribes began to hammer at the gates of this empire. In one mighty battle they threw back the degenerate scum, who belonged to no particular race or tribe, in whose veins flowed the blood of the Arabi and in whose veins flowed the blood of the Hottentots, and in whose veins also flowed the blood of the Bantu. They scattered it like chaff before the great wind.

The Nguni even today still date their history from this great battle when they crushed the poor, but well-armed, forces of *Munumutaba* the Fifth to the ground. And the poor rascal, as his forefathers had done before him, tried to make a stand and to show them what a brave man he was. But a stone from the great Eye fell down and crushed him to the earth. So died *Munumutaba* the Fifth.

My children, you will notice that this story I tell with a great reluctance – because it is a story that must never be told. It is a story that we must only tell you children so that you must know – and you must learn never – never ever, to allow anything like Zima-Mbje to rise again amongst you. You must never again have that glittering splendour, have that great lawlessness and lewdness, and you must never practise that strange and evil immorality that was committed in that evil place.

Zima-Mbje is a place that we must forget and if you ever pass that ugly and forbidden structure you must close your right eye and look at it only with your left – and curse it! Because there, in Zima-Mbje, is the shame of your fathers – the shame of the tribes. Zima-Mbje is a guilty place, and its name, its original name of Luvijiti, must always be mentioned with a curse. It must always be spat upon and which is why I ask you to know it by this name: Zima-Mbje – 'structure of stone'.

This great structure afterwards became a lair of criminals and bands of feared ones – the Arabi – who also came after the fall of Zima-Mbje.

Sometimes one or two tribes would dwell in that place for a few generations. But always the curse we put so many years ago upon the very structure – the very presence of Zima-Mbje only – drove these people away who lived there. Some used to find hiding places in other fortresses that *Munumutaba* and the Feared Ones had built before in the Inyanga, and also other places. But always the curse of our tribes drove these people out of there in the course of time.

My children, whenever you go near that hated place you must remember that in that place lies the great shame of the tribes. Never again must a thing like Zima-Mbje be allowed to rise in the land, because it is the thing that nearly brought upon us – the people of the Bantu – the doom of the First People. It nearly caused the wrath of the gods to fall upon us – so bad, so immoral, were the things that were done in that place.

And so, my children, in the course of time the Lawu, the Hottentots, were driven far down to the south and there in the end they became a lost people. I think they were being punished for what they had helped in founding in that land of the Mashona.

My children, Zima-Mbje was a very strong fortress. The stories that I could tell you of how it was stoned – the acts of courage that chief after raiding chief performed to bring that fortress to its knees – are too many for me to tell you now. There were times when heads of oxen were used to batter down the gates. And attempts were even made to undermine the walls. So strong was the fortress even in those days.

My children, I would rather dwell inside the humblest hut – in a hut where the dome is so small there is hardly any room for smoke – than dwell in the spendour that was once Zima-Mbje. In the reign of *Munumutaba* the Second, and especially his son – his wife's son who was half Arabi and half a Tswana – the Straight *Munumutaba* – those were days of splendour. Even today, maybe, you might find traces of those days . . . forget them. Destroy them wherever you see them! Such is the message I leave you.

THE EYE IS BLIND THAT WILL NOT SEE

My Lords, Ladies and Gentlemen of Science, especially those who are doing research into the past of Africa, may I humbly appeal to all of you for one thing which is of the greatest importance in these days when the world is changing as rapidly as a frightened chameleon – while new things once thought impossible are daily becoming part of the great reality. May I lodge with you a plea which I have sworn to continue urging until someone listens. I appeal for nothing big, dramatic or drastic; I only appeal for simple flexibility, and a willingness to hear and judge clearly without prejudice.

There is nothing more saddening than a man deliberately blinding himself to the shimmering lake of reality. There is nothing more pathetic than the sight of a man who, on beholding a frowning mountain in the purple distance yonder, still insists that the mountain is not there – a man who, though standing knee-deep in a roaring river, still insists with stubborn conviction that he is standing on a sand dune in the Ka-Lahari.

My Lords, a rigid inflexibility in one's beliefs in harmful, not only to the individual holding such views, but to the whole nation or race to which he belongs. Such a stubborn refusal to bend preconceived ideas caused the men of the Inquisition in Italy to persecute Galileo and to burn elsewhere at the stake hundreds of men whose only offence was that they entertained ideas which clashed with those of their lords and masters of the Church. It was this stubborn resistance to the voice of new ideas that caused the ancient Bantu to kill men and women who dared invent things that could have made their lives less rigorous.

This same inflexibility is very evident today and nowhere is it more blatantly displayed than in that field of research dealing with Africa's past.

Many years ago White men came upon a number of interesting

things while exploring Africa. They discovered paintings done in 'prehistoric' times by the Aborigines of Africa, and they promptly designated them as 'Bushman paintings'. These paintings were copied and classified on the basis of wild guesswork; few were those who made a sincere, open-minded and scientific enquiry into what these paintings portray.

Another thing that claimed the attention of scientists was the old stone ruins one finds scattered across Southern Africa. Soon the sound of picks and spades was heard, wielded by, or under the supervision of, archaeologists. Ruins, commonly known as of the 'Zimbabwe' type, were despoiled of their treasures and museums were filled with vessels, artifacts and ornaments, and even today these serve to illustrate the widest variety of hypotheses, not one of which comes near the truth. Yet in these very ornaments and numerous characters and symbols of Bantu and Hottentot writing the true story of 'Zimbabwe' is written for all to read – for all those who can read.

But rather than do this, the great scientists preoccupied themselves with forming strange theories about these ruins. Not only were these theories strange, but fantastically far-fetched, like those in which King Solomon and the Queen of Sheba are featured.

The tragedy is that each scientist is inclined to cling stubbornly to his own self-concocted theory.

Many decades ago a significant discovery was made by an explorer named Mack, an engineer of merit. He was exploring the mountains known as the Brandberg in South-West Africa and here he discovered some rock paintings to which he found himself drawn like a rusty spearhead to a lump of magnetite. The most remarkable of these paintings shows a figure which at first glance looks like a woman of Semitic or Caucasian origin – in short, a White woman. The engineer Mack made a rather inaccurate sketch of what he had seen and this was soon featured on the front pages of newspapers.

This news drew the attention of a great White scientist, who dedicated himself to the unravelling of the past of my fatherland. The Abbé Breuil decided to go and see the painting himself and he, too, made a copy of what he promptly called 'The White Lady of the Brandberg'.

As is usual with all great scientific discoveries and interpretations, the great Abbé Breuil found himself savagely criticised, mainly by critics of the padded armchair type, who found it easier to attack brave men and call them liars than to sweat out a trip to the Brandberg.

There were those who shamelessly accused the Abbé Breuil of having 'touched up' the face of the White Lady, to make an ordinary

Bushman look like a White woman. Others emphatically concluded that the White Lady is not white, but a ceremonially decorated Musutu woman.

The dispute, dormant for so many years, recently flared up again, sparked off by an exhibition of African art in the Johannesburg Art Gallery. Now new versions have emerged: the White Lady is not a lady, but a gentleman. They say 'she' is a Hottentot man, white-daubed for a dance. Others say 'she' is a Bushman out on a hunt. One of Johannesburg's morning newspapers even went so far as to run a 'pick out the mistakes' competition (no prizes awarded) by publishing various copies of the painting – those of Mack, Breuil and others.

This long train of childish arguments by people who refuse to face facts has gone far enough, and it is now my duty to enter into this dispute. For far too long a time has the White man done things, written and drawn conclusions about things without bothering to hear our accounts of events. This is due to a belief the White man has entertained about the Black man for centuries – that the Black man is a born liar. In fact, the great White architect of the Federation of the Rhodesias and Nyasaland once publicly stated that all Black men are born liars. Today he wonders why his Federation went down the drain.

On my shelves I keep as a souvenir Hugh Bryan's *Our Country*, a book of natural history published in 1909. The author says in this book: 'Africa has been called the Dark Continent, because we know so little about it. The ruins of big buildings, which cannot be the work of Black people, are found in Rhodesia. But no one knows who the White men were who built them. Our story is well enough known, but as regards the Blacks, we can only rely on their own tales. These do not go very far, however – they are not very clear, and sometimes we do not know whether they are true . . .'

If the White man's ancestors believed thus, who can blame their present-day descendants for refusing to listen to a brood of born liars?

Yet some of the Bantu knew all along who built Zimbabwe, and the place in the Brandberg where the so-called 'White Lady' is still to be seen, has been for centuries a place of both Bantu and Bushman pilgrimage. We have known the meanings of most cave paintings since they were painted; they are our history books – our archives. But we have all along been under oath not to disclose their true meanings to foreigners. We have deliberately lied to camouflage the truth (that is, by design, not by nature) and this we have regarded as our one and only triumph over the White man.

So well have the Bantu hidden their knowledge from the White man that those, like my humble self, who try to break this centuries-old taboo of tribal secrecy, meet with open disbelief, and even ridicule, when they try to help keep the White man's records straight. In another recent exhibition held by my employer's daughter – a display of antique Bantu carvings – several prominent White scientists openly doubted whether I was telling them the truth. One of them said to me that 'much of what you say needs to be taken with a grain of salt'. I did not know this idiomatic expression and only later discovered that it is a gentle way of calling me a 'goddamn liar'. This is, to say the least, rather dampening to the enthusiasm of one who sincerely believes that a better understanding may come from this attitude I am adopting, even though it amounts to turning traitor against my own race.

The White Lady of the Brandberg is but one of numerous rock paintings that tell the enchanting story of Africa's past. It is wrong to study it as an entity in itself; it is part and parcel of the so-called mysteries of Zimbabwe, Inyanga and many similar places. These paintings and ruins must be studied against a background knowledge of the history and folklore of Africa. But let me deal with the White Lady systematically:

Firstly: It is said that the Abbé Breuil had 'touched up' the face of the White Lady. What I find difficult to believe is why the Abbé Breuil did not sue these critics for defamation. This great scientist has come nearer to the truth than any of his armchair critics. I have been following his progress for many years and have continually checked his findings against our own knowledge of these paintings. He was so dangerously near the truth that certain Bantu Guardians of Tribal History had at one stage considered ways of eliminating him. The face of the White Lady has never been retouched or interfered with in any way, and on closer examination it will be found that 'her' profile is still exactly similar to those of other figures in the painting. To accuse the Abbé of forgery only serves to show to what depths certain civilised people are prepared to sink in their endeavour to discredit men whose wisdom towers way above their own. I challenge anyone to apply a nuclear age-determining device to the pigments on the face of the White Lady.

Secondly: It is said that the White Lady is not white, but a wealthy Busutu woman, white-daubed and out on a ceremonious hunt. This is utter nonsense. The figure is not only carrying a bow, but other weapons as well, and I would like to know since when have Basuto, or any Bantu women, become hunters of beasts? Since when have Bantu women started copying the Greek goddess Diana? The Busutu, like most Bantu, regard the bow and arrow as the weapon of a coward. The bow is not a Bantu weapon; its use has been restricted to the Hottentots, Bushmen and the Pygmies. No Bantu warrior, let alone a woman, has ever been seen with a bow and a quiver full of arrows. And, as anyone with even the slightest knowledge of the Bantu should know, never has any Bantu, Bushman, Hottentot or Pygmy woman ever gone out on a hunt. The Brandberg is in South-West Africa and no Basuto has ever been near that land. The Basuto is a very young tribe, founded by King Musheshwe only about a hundred-and-sixty years ago, and the painting is more than two thousand years old.

Thirdly: The latest argument is that the White Lady is a masked dancer, a white-daubed Hottentot specially masked for a hunt. No Bantu, Bushman or Hottentot has ever gone hunting with a mask on his face. A mask is a nuisance; it restricts the hunter's field of vision and spoils his ability to range stereoscopically. Furthermore, no Bantu, Bushman or Hottentot has ever painted his body for a hunt. Nothing can supersede their natural colouring for effective camouflage; white would be the last colour to use should anyone at any stage have tried such an odd experiment.

If the White scientists had only known a little more about the stories I have unfolded on the preceding pages, there would have been no controversy at all. Something which the White man must come to appreciate sooner or later is that the Bantu attach great importance to the history of their fatherlands and they have a clear perspective on incidents which occurred as far back as ten thousand years ago. This is something Europeans find hard to believe. Their Western culture has turned them into puppets who cannot fathom anything unless they *see* it happen, or can *read* about it in a book. To a White man history is not history unless it is written down, be it on paper, papyrus, clay tablets or stone obelisks. He has forgotten that much of what he can read about today had been passed by word of mouth from father to son for centuries before it was written down. Homer wrote the story of Troy a thousand years after it happened and only thousands of years later archaeologists uncovered the actual scene of the desperate triangle involving Agamemnon, Helen and Paris.

History has always been the foundation of every race's culture; but where a race's religion is based on ancestor worship, its history is no longer merely a foundation – it forms the very structure of their culture. One cannot honour and revere ancestors, seen out of context with the period in which they lived, and the deeds of fame or infamy they committed. When one boasts of an heroic ancestor, one must picture him within his regiment while fighting this or that battle under chief so-and-so.

Many Kings of Egypt and Greece actually tampered with the

histories of their countries, putting down as their deeds things that had either never happened or were the achievements of other people before them. One of the Rameses Kings of Egypt had the nasty habit of stealing the great deeds of earlier Pharaohs and having these recorded as his own, and there is a strong suspicion that certain Emperors of Rome and Greece did the same.

But the Bantu have never allowed anyone, however powerful, to distort history in any way because they strongly believe that by doing so they attempt to deceive the gods with the result that the Spirits of the Tribe would be highly offended. No words can ever describe the depth of this Bantu belief; nothing can ever show fully the unquestioning fervour and reverence with which the Bantu cling to their tribal religion. The worst fanatics are found in Africa, and should an African dream that his grandfather implores him to go and drown himself, he will go straight and do so the very next morning.

Our religion demands that we preserve for posterity the clearest, most detailed and most truthful account of every major event, whether such event involves persons, families, tribes or the whole race, and whether it is glorious or infamous. Even after a shameful defeat in battle, men of open minds, strong memories and clear speech are chosen to carry this defeat to future generations in every truthful detail possible. All surviving warriors are called upon to relate exactly what they experienced and witnessed. Every account is carefully screened for exaggeration. Lists of names of the bravest, and also of the cowards, are memorised after double cross-checking.

"WHITE LADY"

A single story is then extracted from all the less relevant information and this story is entrusted to the chosen Custodian of Tribal History. The story is permanently imprinted on his subconscious mind with a series of the most dreadful oath-taking ceremonies. A Custodian is not likely to forget any of the finer details of the account while he is required, in the process of assimilating the facts, to mate with a baboon or a dog. Such an experience is calculated to leave a lasting imprint on the subconcious mind.

In this way stories have come down to us through the millennia and an account of the Strange Ones told in Zululand is still exactly the same as the one told in Nigeria: 'They came out of the sea, and they were carried in the bellies of great sea-going animals with many legs. They wore the bright *tusi* sun metal on their bodies to stop our angry spears of futile bone and brittle granite. Their hair was the colour of dull fire; their skins were like dirty milk into which a little blood has been poured. They carried weapons of ravening iron which laughed to scorn the thick hide of the toothy lion. They wore bands of white around their heads as if to stop their flowing hair to fly off their scalps. Their shields were round with bosses of bronze reflecting the sun, and their battle shouts were loud in the ears of the frightened Bantu. They killed us with their iron swords. They speared us with their lances and scattered our brains to the seven winds with their axes of iron and bronze . . .

'And they made us into slaves; they turned us into dogs more tame than chastised women. They built mighty forts in our lands, and forced our women, and the women of the bush-skulking Bushmen, to go down into their mines which they dug with our unwilling assistance, to bring dull iron and bright sun metal to the world above . . .

'They made tame slaves of us. They made jesters and dancing clowns of the forest-born Bushmen, and they took Hottentots to their alien bosoms . . .

'But even the sweetest honey can produce an excess of bile, and there is death in every pleasure, for *lo*! the Strange Ones had most strange and frightening habits. When a man died, his wife was killed with his sword and buried with him, and into his grave also went half his slaves . . . alive. They did not weep at their funerals; they held a mighty feast. They sang and danced, and did other things of pleasure . . .

'Soon the race of Ma-Iti was a race of mixed blood. They hunted in ways most strange and repugnant to the Bantu. Men dressed themselves up in the empty skins and heads of slain antelopes to decoy animals to within range of their mighty bows. They used slaves as beaters, and they hunted for the sheer joy and pleasure of killing beasts – for no particular reason at all . . .'

Let us study the White Lady of the Brandberg in detail. The Abbé Breuil was right in one thing at the outset – the White Lady is a White person of Caucasoid or Semitic origin: the long reddish-brown hair, the straight nose and the un-African chin speak louder than words, and only the blind can ignore these facts. The prehistoric artists of Africa (and of Europe, for that matter) were very observant and accurate in their portrayal of the things they saw.

But the Abbé made a mistake in identifying the figure as a 'lady'. It is not a lady, but a strikingly handsome young White man, one of the five great Emperors who ruled the African Empire of the Ma-Iti for nearly two centuries. Here our historians are not unanimous, but I am positive it is *Karesu II*, who succeeded *Karesu I*, the Fire-Beard, the first Emperor. (Karesu is, of course, a Bantu corruption of his real Phoenician name.) The son of *Karesu*, the Fire-Beard, is known in our legends for his love of hunting. Even today the Batswana sing:

Une atsamae lifatsi kahofela—
Atsuma tau liditauana;
Atsuma pufudu libe pukujwe—
Alisebete, muriri wa mulle . . .

He roamed our tribal land completely—
Hunting big lions and young lions too;
Hunting the kudu and the jackal breed—
Great his courage, the one of the *burning hair*

I am convinced that the picture is that of *Karesu II*, because subsequent rulers are all known for their love of relaxation, luxury and homely pleasures. Not a single story has reached us of these later Emperors participating in manly pursuits such as hunting.

The key to the painting is not to be found in the central figure itself. An important figure is the one which the Abbé Breuil called the 'skeleton man', the one behind *Karesu II*. This figure is wearing a bronze helmet with a plume, and in his right hand he carries a long barbed stick. This dreaded 'thorn stick' (a flexible cane inlaid with rows of small metal 'teeth'), together with a 'mighty whistling whip of woven hide with the end forked like the tongue of an angry mamba', were classic tools in the hands of slave-drivers. The figure is also carrying two swords with finely tapering points and conspicuous hilts. These are as African as the jet airliner.

The central figure has long red flowing hair decorated with pearls. While the upper part of the face is yellowish, the chin is a stark white. The eyes are also done in white. These observations are very significant indeed. To a Black man, the eyes of a White man seem to radiate a strange 'light', and for this reason few Bantu can bring themselves to face a White man straight in the eyes. The whiteness of the eyes portrays this imaginary characteristic. The Bantu were also fascinated by the way the straight shiny red hair of the Ma-Iti reflected the light of the sun, and this 'highlight' effect is often shown in bright white in cave paintings. Mostly, however, the hair is depicted in red to characterise the Ma-Iti, and the white 'highlight' is reserved for the beard. The white lines on the face of the 'skeleton man' have been introduced for this effect, too, and this must have given the Abbé the impression of a toothy grinning skeleton head. Ever since, the White man has been described by the Bantu with the less complimentary epithet of 'sunlight beard'. Even the Zulu King Dingana used this epithet (*Ndevu-ze-langa* in Zulu) with contempt when referring to the White Trekkers. There is an old Bantu riddle:

Tell me, tell me, I command you—
Tell me the name of the beast I saw;
Its hair was as long as a wild sable's tail
Its hair was long as a wild sable's tail
And the sun shone through its eyes and beard—
It was shining through its ears and moustache . . .

The answer to this riddle is 'a White man!'

Besides the strange bow, the central figure is also characterised by wrist guards, studded with metal, to protect the wrist against

"SKELETON MAN"

the string of the bow. No Hottentot or Bushman has ever taken such precautions. Another most un-African feature is the strange footwear; although certain Bantu and Hottentots favoured elephant hide sandals, boots are foreign to the African simply because he could never master the art of making them.

Another figure, to the left of *Karesu*, is wearing sharply detailed, dark brown boots reaching up to the knees, and the soles are white. I have named this figure the 'General'. Our legends still describe the Ma-Iti footwear in clear detail: 'Over their feet they wore things of thick hairless skin, with soles of hard wood that insulted the cruel thorns with their thickness. These things often reached half way up the hairy white legs of the Strange Ones . . .'

On *Karesu's* upper arms there are thick bands into which are stuck small daggers for throwing, and even with a casual glance the small hurling axe is quite noticeable. The Bantu were staggered by the accuracy with which the Ma-Iti could hurl a knife or an axe. Our legends tell of how dexterously a Ma-Iti could, when disarmed of his shield and heavier weapons, briskly cross his arms over his chest and grab these daggers from their sheaths around his upper arms, hurling or manipulating both at the same time on two different victims. In his right hand *Karesu* is holding a trophy-like drinking cup; the idea of a protea or a lotus lily is too ridiculous to warrant comment.

The first of two most remarkable figures above *Karesu's* head is a man disguised as an antelope. This was a peculiar Ma-Iti habit when out hunting for fun. They would first kill a buck and skin it, leaving the forequarters, or only the neck and head, intact. A decoy man would then wrap himself into the skin and strut about with the buck's head and shoulders showing above the long grass. The hunters would lie low until the decoy succeeded in leading the other buck within range of their bows. The second figure carries only the head of a buck, and he has in addition a throwing club stuck in his belt.

Another immensely interesting figure is that of a Bantu with hair dyed or daubed red; this peculiarity has persisted until the present day and is still practised as a custom amongst the Swazis. This figure is also wearing a loinskin of leather with metal studs and a harness of broad leather strips, also with studs. With his wrist guards and sandals added, any Bantu historian can recognise him at first glance. He is a favoured royal slave, and entitled to singular privileges. To please his honourable master, such a slave would adopt Ma-Iti customs and daub his hair red to signify his wish to be as like him as possible.

* * *

In Zimbabwe, on a farm known as Diana's Vow, near the small town of Rusape in the land of the Mashona, there is a famous painting passing under the name of The Dead King. It illustrates a Ma-Iti king being buried in their traditional way, lying on his back with a death mask over his face. No Bantu, Bushmen or Hottentots ever buried their dead thus; only in the sitting position or lying on the side with the knees drawn up under the chin. This is simply based on another strange belief we have that if the body is left in the normal sleeping position, the spirit may also fall asleep and fail to leave the body. The Ma-Iti habit of covering a dead person's face with a mask was also regarded by the Bantu, Bushmen and Hottentots with the utmost revulsion and horror. We believe that the soul leaves the body through the face, and the basic idea of a mask is to disguise, or to keep the soul within the body, or the character out of sight.

In this painting the king is portrayed as considerably larger than his subjects (a Ma-Iti custom later adopted by all Africans throughout Africa). The dead king is wearing a well-defined shirt of mail and he has obviously been slain in battle. His face is covered with a mask and his long hair is falling loose. In his right hand he is holding something which would appear to be a lump of gold; the Ma-Iti had the habit of burying their dead with some valuable gift with which to bribe their God of Death in the Underworld to lead them to the Land of Everlasting Happiness. Such gifts were usually tied to the right hand of the dead man or woman.

The king's knees are partly drawn up and although he is dead, his penis is erect. The artist obviously loathed the Ma-Iti, for this is a most insulting portrayal; it is always used to indicate that although the particular loathsome individual is safely out of the way, he has left descendants behind to perpetuate his wickedness.

A small boy is bandaging the arm of the dead king, and again we are confronted with a Ma-Iti custom perpetuated in our legends. The Bantu never bandage wounds before burial; these must remain as open as possible for all the spirits to see and admire. Especially battle wounds are looked upon as battle honours.

Lying next to the king is another massive figure, the Hottentot queen of the dead king, obviously slain to be buried with her lord. This figure is dark brown while the king is yellow ochre and white.

There are two small figures of priests with headdresses, near the king's body, and above there are some slaves about to be buried alive. Another group of slaves is seen in the left-hand upper corner, below the feet of the king, and this group is clearly wailing and begging for mercy. One has his hands clasped behind his head – a typical Bantu posture of mourning and appeal to the gods for mercy.

Near this group of wretches there are figures of cooks, slave-drivers with whips, and one of the latter is shown as a gross, ugly figure, also with erect penis. A live figure thus represented signifies a rapist.

In the lower right-hand corner, below the vast bodies of the king and his Hottentot queen, there are dozens of fascinating figures of men and dogs like Afghan hounds. A great feast is in progress here and the detail is astouding. There are scores of calabashes containing beer and there are pots of food and skins of oxen left to dry. There are slaves and cooks and Ma-Iti youths, and men walking about with erect penises. The Ma-Iti are shown with white stomachs and long hair, another insult that shows the depth of the long-dead artist's hatred for the Ma-Iti. The Bantu called the Ma-Iti 'White Bellies', and the Hottentots who fraternised with them they called 'Green Bellies'.

It is very significant that in those figures representing Bantu and Bushmen slaves, the artist did not show the penis at all. In all Bantu paintings of men the penis is prominently indicated (but quiescent) as a compliment to his manliness. But when left out the man is signified as an object of compassion, a weakling calling for pity. The artist's sympathy was obviously with the slaves and there can be little doubt that he was a slave himself. So great was his contempt for the Ma-Iti that he depicted one of them with a penis covered with white spots – a leper-object; perhaps merely wishful thinking on the part of the artist.

There are also two dancing girls, or 'Alien Virgins of the Wind', as our legends call them. These girls are obviously foreign, not only in their long hairstyles, but more particularly in the fact that they are wearing something which no tribal African ever wore – halters, or 'brassiers', complete with frills. All Africans regard the covering of the breasts as wicked and utterly immoral.

There is in Johannesburg a young man from distant England. He is tall and lean like a lost reed. He has light brown hair, a Roman nose and a long sad face that often seems to be full of care. This young man has a South African-born wife, and she looks strangely like him. They are indeed well matched; they are like brother and sister. She too has a strange, serious and seeking expression on her face and the same smouldering personality . . .

And while most young married couples of the European tribe are content with the kind of life that Johannesburg's concrete jungles has to offer, these young people have devoted their lives to something which may seem to be pathetic, but which is in fact amazing and heroic! This couple who deserve the acclaim of all the peoples of

Africa, White even more than Black, and of all the archaeologists of the world, frequently risk their lives in penetrating by foot the wild, untamed and desolate areas of Botswana, and the land of the Ba-Tlokwa in the distant North-West of the Transvaal. No snorting 'jeeps' or 'landrovers' are at the disposal of these young adventurers. Yet they live in a land where scores of millions are spent on preparing for a war that might never come.

White people of South Africa, I, *Vusamazulu*, a humble Kaffir, am ashamed of you. I am thoroughly disgusted with your indifference to those things on which your ungrateful lives depend. In all enlightened countries of the world scientists are honoured and revered, even in Nigeria – one of the many African states you like to ridicule. But here you merely throw up your arms in despair when you see your scientists leave for America and Australia.

Your lives depend on a better knowledge of Africa's past. The Belgians never tried to learn more about the Congolese; they were caught unawares even while they were busy with what they thought were good deeds – civilising and developing the Congo. Making money and dabbling in politics are not the most important things in life. Only by unravelling the past can one hope to find the key to the golden portals of the future.

It is not right that a man and a woman like the two I have mentioned should sweat their lives out in the bush, doing things of national interest and importance while the authorities watch with indifferent eyes. A few rands' worth of equipment would be enough to enable this man to uncover treasures of immeasurable value. A heavy machine-gun, complete with belts and ammunition, costs at least ten times as much. A Saracen costs a king's ransom. A spade for an archaelogist costs next to nothing!

People of South Africa, I call upon you to salute the young man Adrian Boshier. Salute him even while you may be indifferent to the importance of what he is doing for you and the future of your country. This young man and his wife have gone into the lonely bush, armed with only their sleeping bags, and they live in caves like prehistoric Bushmen. They have been forced through sheer hunger to eat lizards, and the 'devil birds', the bats which no Bantu will touch, be he on the verge of starving. Young Boshier, whom the Ba-Tlokwa have lovingly nicknamed 'Rra-Dinoha' – Father of the Snakes (because of his fearless handling of these reptiles) has already made a long series of significant discoveries. He has already found some of the ruins dating back to the days of the Ma-Iti, and hundreds of cave paintings illustrating much of the stories disclosed for the first time in this book.

One such painting shows a city, or rather the crude town-plan diagram of a huge city with labyrinth-like streets, and a great wall completely encircling it. From the city men on horseback, with plumed helmets are sallying out to repel an attacking army of men on foot. Some of these foot soldiers are shown in black, and they are clearly carrying a long scaling ladder. A mighty battle is in progress, and one of the mounted soldiers is shown in the attitude of throwing up his arms as his stricken horse falls under him. Adjoining this painting is another like it, showing the city being pulled apart by the victors and its stones being heaped on sleds drawn by oxen and carried away. The treasures of the destroyed city are piled all around it and one can discern chairs, weapons and animals of all kinds. In short, this painting illustrates the central part of Book 2 in this work. But the painting was discovered only after the manuscript of this book had already been written, typed and submitted for publication.*

The Bantu in this wild and relic-strewn region are still very primitive and bitterly suspicious; the fact that Mr Boshier has won their confidence and trust illustrates his remarkable personality. Let higher authorities exploit to the hilt this trust that the Ba-Tlokwa have placed in their White friend 'Rra-Dinoha' for the benefit of science in South Africa. There is so much that has yet to be unearthed and brought to light. There is so much to be written also for the benefit of all. I pray for that day when the graves of the Ma-Iti shall be opened and another of Africa's vast secrets wrested from the womb of time.

I also pray for that day when a mighty museum shall rear its glittering form against the cuboid skyline of Johannesburg, welcoming thousands of eager-to-learn citizens into its glittering portals like a Queen of Sunset, greeting heroes into the land of Tura-ya-Moya. I long for the day when the Bantu, too, pass through the halls of this museum and proudly whisper while they glance around: 'This . . . this was our yesteryear!'

---

* *This chapter was introduced after the book had been completed.*

Book Three

The Journey to ‘Asazi’

IN MY WEB – A DEAD FLY

The land was a thing of incredible beauty, a jewel under the eyes of Ilanga, the God of Day. The land rejoiced in the green and scented embrace of the Maiden Spring and fiercely responded to her tender caresses, like an old wrinkled chief whose cold and tired veins are briefly heated by a kiss from his youngest concubine. The wild beauty of the untamed forest on that glorious day dazzled the eyes. Souls were lost in the misty valleys of happiness.

Each tree and bush was like a bride in full wedding regalia, a bride beautiful and soothing to the beholder's eye. Thick on each branch was a fresh green scented foliage that spoke of quantities of moisture yielded by a willing soil. Wild flowers laughed amongst the frolicking grass, nourished by the rotten leaves of yesteryear.

Birds argued in the tall trees while hares and steenbuck gambolled in the scented grass, rejoicing in the gentle heat and the perfumed whispering breeze of young summer.

And *lo*, along one of the footpaths leading into the cool shady depths of the deep forest there came a young man and a young woman. The man was tall, with the wide shoulders and narrow hips of a warrior, and the long legs of a very fast runner. He had a long face that ended in a square cleft chin, the kind which the Wise Ones of the Tribes call the 'chin of courage'. Under the flat nose with its large flaring nostrils was a mouth forever set in hard lines of fierce determination, while above, his forehead towered high like a cliff above two springs of sparkling water.

Around his head this young man wore a broad band of leopard skin with two feathers tucked in it: one the long tail-feather of an *Isakabuli*; the other that of a flamingo. The first denoted his royal birth and the second identified him as the son of the Second High Wife of the Chief. A triple necklace of lion's claws and cowrie shells graced his shoulders while around his manly loins he wore two aprons of cow-skin – one in front and one behind.

The front apron was fringed with long monkey and civet cat tails.

On both his forearms he wore heavy bronze 'warrior bracelets', so broad they looked more like arm guards. Around his calves he wore leggings of cow-tails which fluffed ever so slightly in the breeze.

He carried a black war shield with a civet cat skin tuft on its long centre stick and he was armed with two heavy hurling assegais and a weighty battle axe. He walked a few paces ahead of the girl with the lithe grace of a stalking beast of prey. His nostrils were dilated and his ears alert for the slightest sound. *Haaaieee!* Here was a budding warrior, a hunter still in tender flower, a future leader of men. Here was a man born to command! Brave and utterly reckless was the son of *Malandela*, the High Chief of the Nguni division of the mighty Mambo nation. Brave, reckless and utterly stubborn was the handsome young man *Zwangezwi* – the Voice of Battle, the last surviving son of the High Chief of the Land, successor to the chieftainship of the Nguni limb of the Mambo people!

And *ewu, ha-la-la*! Now we come to the girl, the foreign ebony black girl who was not of the Mambo people, but belonged to a tribe which was once great and which had been reduced to only a few thousand people through wars. This tribe which was now in danger of becoming absorbed by the Mambo . . . unless . . .

This girl was tall and slender, with long legs and with breasts jutting fircely from her chest. But she was the kind of girl whom chiefs forbid to bear children because, although her buttocks were beautifully shaped, her hips were far too narrow. She was beautiful. *Yea-ha*, she reminded one of a skilfully carved image from the land of Tanga-Nyika; she was a beautiful image carved in living ebony. Her face was oval and her forehead round and smooth. Her nose was tiny and flat, with small nostrils, and her full, wholesome mouth had a lower lip slightly more prominent than the upper. Her neck, graced by a broad band of flaming red copper, was a column of live ebony.

Whereas the Nguni maidens of her age either wore fringed *mutshas*, short skin shirts, or just nothing at all, this foreign girl wore something which no Nguni female would ever wear – a soft tiger-cat loinskin. Save for large copper earrings that weighted down her pierced earlobes and the band around her neck, she wore no other ornaments.

One could tell at first glance that this girl was very uneasy, that her soul was a canoe floundering in the whirlpool of fear and great anxiety. Nervous were the glances that she cast about her and she paused now and again to wring her hands and to open her mouth as if to speak to the young man in front of her, and then to shut it with a silent sob. The dew of tears hung heavy on her long eyelashes and the spirit of dread and guilt was heavy on her knees. Suddenly the man's voice shattered her troubled thoughts with a loud '*Aieeee*! Look over there . . . over there *Mulinda*, look!'

The girl's tear-misted and half-closed eyes slowly opened wider and followed the young man's pointed finger. They saw what is one of the most terrible omens of naked evil that anyone can experience. A mighty eagle had dived out of the blue skies into a grassy glade to their left, and now it was rising again into the heavens with a young steenbuck clutched in cruel talons. The keen eyes of the young Prince followed the eagle into the distance until it was but a speck above the hazy forest. Then he turned to *Mulinda* and she saw that his handsome features were clouded with uneasiness.

'That was an evil thing we saw, Oh *Mulinda*,' he said, 'for do not the Wise Ones say that to see an eagle snatching an animal off the ground is an omen of death to all those who see it?'

'It is so, my Prince,' agreed the girl. 'We must turn back and go home.'

'No!' cried *Zwangezwi*, the son of *Malandela*, fiercely. 'We have come so far and cannot turn back now. You will not escape so easily from giving me what you were told to give me, Oh daughter of the Vamangwe.'

The son of *Malandela* and the Vamangwe girl were going far away from their homes to break a law. They were going deeper and deeper into the dangerous forest to find a quiet place in which to break one of the oldest tribal laws, the High Law which says that no young man under the age of twenty-five must take a girl to the love-mat; and that no young man should as much as kiss a girl unless he is first circumcised and initiated into manhood in accordance with the High Laws and Customs of the Tribes.

Zwangezwi was only twenty years of age and he thought that five years was far too long a time to wait before he was initiated and permitted to enjoy the doubtful privileges of manhood. He was very tired of sitting near the crackling fire at night and listening to lurid, in fact, very exaggerated accounts by older warriors of what they do to their lovers. *Zwangezwi* was firm in his belief that *akuko okwedlula uku zibonela wena* (nothing beats having seen and experienced something yourself). He was firm in his resolve to have personal experience of what he had heard so much about. But the young man should have remembered another old saying that *ukutanda Ukwazi izim fihlo ezingalingani nawe ikona okwemuka u nogwaja umsila wa khe* (it was curiosity that shortened the rabbit's tail – or, more literally, the desire to know secrets that are above you is the thing that deprived the rabbit of his tail).

At last they came to a grassy clearing above which towered a huge outcrop of rock with a large cave at its base, a cave which *Zwangezwi* knew very well and within which he had sheltered many times with his father's warriors when they were out on a hunt and caught in a thunderstorm. It was in this cave that *Zwangezwi* had played with his half-brothers *Vivimpi* and *Bekizwe* only three summers ago before both the elder boys were drowned in a canoe accident a year later. Inside the cave were many paintings of animals and men, painted by the Little Yellow Ones, the Bushmen, years and years ago. Some of the human figures were done in white, representing the mysterious race called the Strange Ones – a race of White men who held the Black Tribes in slavery for hundreds of years. It was to this cave, full of memories of the past, that *Zwangezwi* led the Vamangwe girl *Mulinda*, and there he unrolled the leopard skin he had been carrying behind his shield and spread it on the sandy floor. He pulled the girl down beside him. To his great surprise he found she was crying and shaking all over like a sapling in a storm.

'*Hau*!' he exclaimed. 'What is the matter, Oh *Mulinda*? Why are you crying like a scolded child?'

'My Prince,' she sobbed, 'let us go from here.'

'Why girl? Did not your brother *Vamba* tell you to come here with me? Did he not promise to keep our secret and let no-one know about what we are going to do?'

'He did,' she wept. 'But it is not . . . you see . . . *Vamba* is not what he seems to be . . . he is your father's . . .' Her voice broke and her sobs were loud in the dark brooding interior of the cave.

'He is my father's what?' demanded the young man.

'*Vamba*, my brother, is your father's . . . great enemy!'

'*Aieee*! That is a lot of nonsense *Mulinda*. *Vamba* is my closest and dearest friend and he is my father's best witchdoctor. He even saved me from a wounded warthog only last year. He is the most trustworthy counsellor my father has and he is more loyal to my father than all his Nguni *Indunas* put together. How dare you call your own brother my father's enemy?'

'Believe me, Prince, believe . . .'

'*Ahhhhh*!' laughed *Zwangezwi*. 'So *Malangabi*, my old friend, was right when he said that you women start talking a lot of nonsense when you are on fire with desire. You are ablaze with the great longing for me, Oh my stolen love, so you have begun to talk all sorts of nonsense. Now, now, come to me and let me put the fire out.' So saying, he seized the girl roughly by the shoulders and all but wiped her lips off her face in one great clumsy kiss. Then he remembered what his old friend the rascally *Induna*, veteran *Malangabi*, always told him that he should do when one day he got an *intombi* in his arms. He started showering the girl's lips, neck and breasts under a rain of what he fondly thought were kisses. He proceeded to caress her with rather clumsy heavy-handed, self-conscious movements of his unsteady, calloused hands until at last, more by nature than from anything he did, *Mulinda* became so heated that she drew him to her with a short sob . . .

Eventually *Zwangezwi* released the limp form of the girl and sat up, dazed, shocked, and very thoroughly frightened. His head was swimming and he felt like vomiting . . . but most of all he felt like leaping to his feet and running for dear life. 'Why . . .' he thought, 'why, I never thought it felt like this . . . I wish it had not happened . . . I . . . I am so scared, so ashamed . . . I . . .' Then he remembered an old tribal saying: *Labo abazama ukuwela umfula Wo tando bese bancane badibana ne zimanga nga pesheya* (they who cross the river of love while still young will always meet very nasty surprises beyond it).

Zwangezwi was soon regretting his boyish curiosity. He began to feel very tired and in spite of his valiant efforts to keep his eyes open he slipped away into the valley of sleep in broad daylight – which is a very shameful thing indeed to happen to a warrior.

He was roughly awakened by the girl, whose voice was edged with fear and horror. 'My Prince, four times have I tried to awaken you. Wake up, for your mother's sake, wake up . . . they are coming to kill you!'

Although still dazed, the young man seized his two spears as a tall figure loomed in the entrance of the cave – a featureless silhouette against the blazing silver sky. Instinctively and with deadly accuracy, Prince *Zwangezwi* hurled his first spear and had the satisfaction of hearing it thud home into the armed intruder's chest.

A group of figures, all heavily armed, suddenly burst into view as the first man sagged to his knees. A hail of spears ripped into the chest and belly of the young Prince even as he raised his arm to throw his second spear. *Zwangezwi* fell backwards, treacherously and mortally wounded, but no cry escaped his lips. The son of *Malandela* was too brave to cry out when struck down by lowborn and cowardly curs.

As his murderers trooped into the cave and stood looking at him, *Zwangezwi* smiled contemptuously. He smiled even though he saw the shafts of the long lion-spears protruding from his body; he smiled although he was bathed in the seas of red agony. He smiled as he recognised each one of his assailants – even the man he admired, worshipped and for whom he would gladly have laid down his life – the man his father also trusted without question: *Vamba Nyaloti*, the brother of the woman *Mulinda*.

As the tall, thin, hardened *Vamba* came closer, *Zwangezwi* asked softly and calmly: 'Why did you do this to me, my dear friend, why?'

Vamba's reply was cold and steady. 'Because, my friend, you are the son of *Malandela* and you were the heir to the throne, which I am anxious to have when your father dies. For many years I have been ingratiating myself with your father and the rest of the lesser chiefs of the land of your nation, gaining their confidence and sometimes playing one against the other.'

'But why . . . you need not have gone to all this trouble. I would gladly have shared the kingdom with you after my father's death.'

'I know you would have, Oh gentle youth,' said *Vamba* quietly. 'Your friendship has been the most genuine I ever had. But the game I am playing for the sake of my tribe is one in which I must be utterly ruthless, one in which I must recognise neither friend nor relative.'

'Now I know,' said the fast-dying prince. 'Now I know that you killed my two elder half-brothers two years ago – you whom my father trusts with his life.'

'Yes, I gave your brothers a new canoe as a present, but the canoe had a hole just below the waterline when carrying a weight. This hole I had loosely covered with a wild gum which melts in water. I further urged your stupid brothers to give the canoe a good tryout by venturing to the middle of the Zambezi. When they got there they drank far too much of the Zambezi . . .'

'So you want to make your tribe great once again by taking over the Nguni, after having also killed my father . . .'

'*Yea-ha!*' agreed *Vamba*. 'I want to lift my people, the Vamangwe, to the greatness that once was theirs. I intend to seize the Nguni High Seat and replace all *Malandela's Indunas* with Vamangwe; I shall then abolish the name Nguni and replace it with Vamangwe.'

'You shall do nothing of the kind,' said *Zwangezwi* with a smile. 'Someone will come who will put a stop to your murderous intentions . . . *Beware of the Blind God who Walks*!' With a smile of pity and pure contentment on his lips, the son of *Malandela* died. He died having had the satisfaction of seeing fear in the eyes of *Vamba* and his four followers when he uttered his last words.

It was one of *Vamba's* followers, a burly rascal called *Mukingo*, whose body was one mass of Vamangwe tribal scars and who was blind in one eye, who broke the silence: 'What is this . . . this rubbish about a god who walks?'

'It is just a mere old legend, Oh *Mukingo*,' replied another man, a withered old charlatan called *Luva*, who always wore the jackal skin headdress and loinskin of a witchdoctor-storyteller. 'It is said that a lost immortal roams the land and many who claim to have seen him say his eyeballs are completely white and he cannot see. But he is as tall as a *mopani* tree and as strong as a thousand elephants. It is said that although he is blind he can fight, swim and dance like a normal man. It is said that he is always accompanied by three very beautiful girls, his daughters, girls who live only for their father and who never look at any other man . . .'

'They would look at me after I have finished with them,' growled *Mukingo* savagely. 'I can conquer any girl on earth, no matter how proud and beautiful she is . . .'

'Be silent you fools!' cried *Vamba*. 'There is no such thing as an immortal. Come on, take your spears out of this dog's body and let us close the entrance with rocks.'

'You are nervous, Oh great *Vamba*,' sneered *Mukingo*. 'Could it be that you are frightened?'

Vamba spun around and faced *Mukingo*, his right hand streaking to his *panga* hanging at his side. He actually half-drew the lethal blade, but pushed it back abruptly into the scabbard when *Mukingo* laughed evilly in his face. 'One day I shall kill you . . .'

'One day you can go and relieve your bowels over a prickly thorn bush,' sneered *Mukingo*. 'The day shall never dawn when a half-man like you kills me.'

Vamba's panga left its scabbard in a hissing blur of speed, but the burly *Mukingo* easily sidestepped and kicked the weapon out of *Vamba's* hand. 'Forget your girlish anger, you vile combination of both man and woman. Were it not for your brilliance in laying secret and treacherous plots, I would have killed you long ago and taken over leadership of the Vamangwe. And you know you need me to sire the children which the people think are yours, in order to cover up your shame, you miserable freak.'

Vamba's eyes glittered with cold anger and great bitterness. He knew that *Mukingo* was right; he knew he could never dare kill his cousin on whom he depended for many things. *Vamba* was not a normal man and the only people who knew this were the four men with him in the cave – *Mukingo, Luva, Dombozo* and *Mutumbi* – and these men he had sworn to secrecy. Furthermore, he kept these men constantly by his side and under his eyes to prevent his secret from leaking out. When the High Chief of the Nguni, *Malandela*, presented *Vamba* with a great kraal and three buxom Nguni maidens for wives, he asked *Mukingo* who very closely resembled him in features, to take the three women secretly and beget children for him. *Vamba* knew that if he killed *Mukingo*, who was very dear to the hearts of his other three friends, they would expose his shame to the world in revenge. In fact, *Vamba* knew very well that as soon as he reached his life's objective of lifting the Vamangwe to greatness once more, the very men who called themselves his friends would kill him and put the popular *Mukingo* in his place. Love of his tribe, however, outshone all else in *Vamba's* heart and he was determined to make the Vamangwe great even though he knew he would never live long enough to enjoy the ripe fruits of his labours.

His deformity was the major cause of his ruthlessness. He bitterly hated the world for what it had done to him and it was even whispered that he had killed his own father and cut off his beautiful mother's left hand as punishment for having brought him in such a state into this cruel world.

So, with the tears of bitterness stinging his eyes, *Vamba* retrieved his *panga* and sheathed it slowly. Then he said with his usual cold calmness: 'Come on, all of you, take your spears out of this dead thing and let us go.'

'Wait but a moment, Oh *Vamba*,' said the old man *Luva*. 'We must first cut off both his hands, and take out his liver too – you know why we need these things.'

'Get on with it then, but be quick,' snapped *Vamba*. 'We do not have all day.'

Luva slashed off both the dead *Zwangezwi's* hands and then, while *Mukingo, Dombozo* and *Mutumbi* tore out their spears and licked off the blood to prevent his ghost from haunting their dreams, the old man cut the body on the left side to extract the liver. It was then that *Mulinda*, who had fainted when *Zwangezwi* was struck down, recovered consciousness and screamed. *Vamba* took two strides to where his sister crouched, screaming at the top of her voice, and pulled the trembling girl to her feet. He struck her cruelly on the mouth and said: '*Nyerera*, be quiet you slut, keep your wide mouth closed!' Then he pushed her roughly out of the cave.

'*Vamba . . .*' called the girl as he turned to go back into the cave. He turned and she said: 'You had better kill me too, because if you don't I shall betray you – I shall expose you for the treacherous, cowardly murderer you are!'

'You shall do what? You shall do what?' hissed *Vamba* icily.

'You have caused enough bloodshed and evil in this world, *Vamba*. You killed father and you tortured mother. You caused three great wars in the land. You have murdered, or brought about the murder, of a thousand innocent people in the name of the Vamangwe tribe. Today you have killed an innocent boy who adored you and you are planning to murder his father as well. You used me as a decoy to lure him to his death. You are a foul, black-hearted beast *Vamba*, and I thank the Tree of Life you can never beget any children, otherwise the world would be overrun by other inhuman freaks like yourself!'

'Did you call me an inhuman freak *Mulinda*?' asked *Vamba*. 'Did I hear you, my sister, calling me an inhuman freak?'

'*Vamba*,' said the girl, smiling through the blood that still streamed from her lips, 'I, *Mulinda*, your eldest sister, call you a monstrous, inhuman freak whom the High Gods cursed from birth and whose only place is in the grave.'

'I shall kill you for that!'

'Go on, you cowardly, treacherous half-man!' screamed the girl. 'Kill me. Kill me and have done with it, you cur! One more murder should not worry you.'

Vamba drew his *panga* with the speed of a striking serpent and would have run the girl through with it, had not *Mukingo* seized his arm and pinned it behind his back. 'There are laws that even a deformed mongrel like you must obey, and one of them is that you must not spill the blood of your own kin. You can strangle your sister, or you can throw her into the Zambezi if you wish. But you are not allowed to stab her, you monstrous freak.'

'So be it,' cried *Vamba*. 'We shall not shed her blood, but we shall tie her hand and foot and leave her with her lover in the cave.'

At last the mouth of the cave was securely sealed with rocks and heavy boulders and the men turned to go, leaving *Mulinda* alive and alone in the dark cave with two dead bodies for company. *Vamba* went first, proud and aloof, and then followed *Mukingo* who had paused to relieve a capacious bladder against the sealed entrance of the cave. Next followed *Luva*, chuckling loudly to himself as was his habit, and with the hands and the liver of *Zwangezwi* in the small pouch slung over his shoulder. Then, last of all went the unnatural pair, the fat girlish youth named *Dombozo* and the middle-aged man *Mutumbi*. *Mutumbi* and *Dombozo* were more than just friends and comrades in evil; they really loved each other in more senses than one and it was whispered that *Mutumbi* had deserted his kraal and two wives to be beside *Dombozo* always.

A deep silence claimed the forest once more and two butterflies chased each other past the pile of rocks that sealed the mouth of the cave in which two dead bodies lay at the feet of a young girl tied hand and foot, propped up against a wall decorated by Bushmen. She was doomed to a slow death by suffocation, thirst and hunger.

Evil were the deeds of *Vamba*, the son of *Nyaloti* and *Luojoyo*, in the land of the Nguni. Treacherous and vile were his plots against the mighty *Malandela*! But do not the Ancient Ones say that 'There is no rascal, however clever, who can be so clever as to lick the small of his own back'? *Vamba* was a clever man, yes he was more clever than the fabled jackal that stole the skin off the Sun Elephant.

But he was not clever enough to know that the deed of dark and cowardly murder had been seen by somebody hiding in the forest, and that someone was a tall, dark-brown beautiful woman with only one hand, and with a stump where the left hand had been cut off many years previously. This woman was none other than *Luojoyo, Vamba's* own mother.

'I, THE IMMORTAL . . .'

The great kudu bull was wounded, but pain only made him run faster. Like the mother of the Seven Winds herself, he ran through the forest with the long-legged huntresses in full cry after him. He crashed through the bushes and jumped over fallen trees; he leapt like the Star Impala itself over a rush-fringed stream. Fear gave strength to his slowly weakening legs and he ran blindly through the trees – on and on, until a treacherous tendril twined itself about his horns as he flashed past an old parasite-vine smothered ebony tree. Down he went on his forelegs, struggling desperately to free his horns from the clinging vine. The two human females, who had chased the kudu over a great distance without tiring, closed in on the stricken animal and the elder and taller of the two sent a long-shafted arrow deep into the animal's heart.

'*Hey-ya*!' she cried. 'We got him at last, *Mvurayakucha*, we got him. But, Oh my father, did the brute run!'

'He must be the father of all kudus to be able to run so fast, with one of your arrows in him, Oh my sister *Luanaledi*! But let us make haste and cut parts off him to take to our dear father and . . . Look, Oh my sister, look over there!'

'Now, by the golden breasts of my mother *Watamaraka*,' cried the elder of the two females, following her sister's pointing finger. 'Is that woman a mad one?'

The two tall and perfectly moulded young females forgot the kudu at their feet and stood looking at the strange thing taking place at the base of a mighty outcrop of rock that reached into the silver skies, about a hundred paces from where they stood.

A lone woman who seemed to have only one hand was trying desperately to move some rocks at the base of the huge formation. But the rocks were far too heavy for her and she failed again and again. Now and then she would fling herself on the ground and roll about in the long grass, beating the ground with her one hand and crying to the high heavens.

'I smell evil, *Mvurayakucha*,' said the older huntress. 'Come.'

The two young huntresses ran to the struggling woman and the elder, *Luanaledi*, placed a gentle hand on the woman's shoulder and said: 'What is the matter, Oh respected woman?' The woman tried to speak, but only hoarse animal sounds escaped her parted lips and the young huntress realised that she was totally unable to speak – she was dumb. The woman gestured frantically and pointed again and again to the rocks she had been trying vainly to move.

'My sister,' cried the younger of the two sisters, 'I know why this woman is trying to move these stones. A girl is entombed alive in a cave under these rocks, with two dead males. This woman is the mother of the girl in there and she has been trying since yesterday to free her. I can read her thoughts, *Luanaledi*, and I can get those of the entombed girl as well. Unless we move these rocks and free her, she will be dead in a few moments.

The elder of the voodoo-sisters suddenly drew herself proudly erect in front of the sealed cave, her breasts heaved and her nostrils dilated as she said in a harsh and savage voice: 'In the name of my mother, the golden goddess *Watamaraka*, and in the name of our father, the mighty *Lumukanda*, and also in the name of my father's other wife, *Ninavanhu-Ma*, the Goddess of Creation, I, *Luanaledi*, the Heavenly River of Stars, command you inanimate stones to tumble to the ground.'

Then she stepped back, dragging the frantic woman with her and all three stood at a safe distance and watched. For a while nothing happened, then there came a faint crackling sound as a rock at the bottom felt a stress. This was followed almost immediately by a small thundering rockslide as the stones came tumbling to the ground, leaving half the cave mouth open.

The younger girl, *Mvurayakucha*, leapt inside, disappeared into the dark interior of the cave. A few moments later she re-appeared, carrying the dark form of the unconscious *Mulinda* in her arms like a child and passed her burden through the aperture to *Luanaledi* before scrambling out herself.

Mulinda regained consciousness and found she was lying on her back under a tree and that a whispering breeze was fanning her face, which felt as if it had been bathed with water from the stream nearby. The first person she saw sitting next to her was *Luojoyo*, her mother, who suddenly burst into tears when her daughter opened her eyes.

'Mother,' breathed *Mulinda*. But *Luojoyo* placed her finger on her daughter's lips for silence and pointed to something to her left. The girl turned her head and saw a very unusual sight. Two slender girls armed with bows and arrows in ornate quivers, with their backs to her, were busy cutting pieces out of the carcase of a buck lying in the tall grass. The over-perfect beauty of the bodies of the two girls left *Mulinda* breathless and filled her heart with a cold creeping fear. 'Who are they *Maie*?' she whispered.

Luojoyo made the sign of 'spirit' with her fingers. She touched the tip of her small finger with that of her thumb, holding her hand palm downwards. Then she brought together the tips of her forefinger and thumb, palm upwards, to indicate 'virgin', followed by the simple sign for 'two'.

'Two spirit virgins?' asked *Mulinda*. 'I am afraid, Oh my mother.'

Luojoyo smiled and patted her daughter's ebony-black shoulders, and it was then that a strange thing happened. The two girls suddenly dropped their *pangas* and stood perfectly still, as if listening. Then both of them burst into action – they dragged the carcase into the shelter of a dense bush. One went to retrieve the two *pangas* while the other approached *Mulinda* and her mother. She beckoned them to follow her and led them behind the same dense bush in which they had hidden the kudu carcase. Then they all settled on their stomachs in deadly silence.

Soon the bushes moved directly opposite the hidden female watchers, across the grassy treeless glade. A man came into view – a man tall, thin and handsome in a hard, cruel way, a man whom *Luojoyo* knew better than he knew himself and whom *Mulinda* had called a monstrous freak. *Vamba*, the son of *Luojoyo*, was followed by two other men who actually walked hand in hand and whom *Mulinda* recognised as *Dombozo* and *Mutumbi*. Then something occurred that left both *Mulinda* and her mother breathless: a woman came into view closely followed by *Mukingo* and this woman had her hair done up in the towering cylindrical *sicolo* hairstyle of the Nguni Royal Women. It was *Nolizwa*, the Fifth High Wife of the Nguni King, *Malandela*.

'Foul traitress,' whispered *Mulinda* hoarsely. 'So she too, who is the favourite wife of *Malandela* is among those who plot against the High King and the Nguni nation.'

There was a loud shout from the lips of all the plotters when they discovered that the rocks sealing the cave at the base of the huge outcrop had been moved. *Mukingo* went into the cave and then came out again announcing that the girl *Mulinda* had been – spirited away.

'Now, *Mvurayakucha*,' whispered the elder of the voodoo-virgins, 'now, my dear sister, now!'

The younger girl jumped to her feet and sent three arrows humming across the glade at the plotters. One arrow caught *Dombozo* in the left thigh and, full of fear and pain, he fell to the ground with a loud wail. The other two arrows thudded into the chest of *Mutumbi* as he whirled round to help his friend. So well did she shoot that both shafts were buried up to the feathers in *Mutumbi's* heart. *Vamba* and *Mukingo* leapt like wild impala and made off into the forest. But just as *Mukingo* vanished among the trees *Mvurayakucha* playfully, and with voodoo accuracy, placed two long arrows in his shiny black buttocks, one in each. *Mukingo* howled with pain, and made off into the depths of the forest with the two arrows protruding like two slim stiff wagging tails.

But the fat woman *Nolizwa* was not destined to escape, because she had only run a few paces when she tripped over a stone and fell heavily on her belly with a hoarse shriek. *Mvurayakucha* drew back the string of her bow to send an arrow through the woman. But her sister *Luanaledi* restrained her: 'No, no, we want her alive, for the pot.'

As she struggled painfully and breathlessly to her feet, the treacherous wife of the High King of the Nguni saw two slender and fantastically beautiful girls running towards her. They were laughing as they ran and both of them had bows in their hands. As they came closer *Nolizwa* saw that they both had the same expression of fiendish anticipation on their faces. This *Nolizwa* did not like at all and she gave vent to her feelings in a hoarse scream of fear:

'Help! Help me, *Mukingo*, come back and save me!'

But nobody came to her assistance as the two girls seized her and tore off her long skin skirt, her necklace and bracelets.

'*Aaaah!*' breathed the younger of the two girls. 'Oh just look at her, *Luanaledi*, isn't she the most darling cow you have ever seen?'

'She is just fit for the pot, my sister,' sighed the elder girl. 'Just feel her thighs and her buttocks – nice, fat, well-fleshed and soft – the kind that just melts in your mouth; just asking to be cooked.'

'Please, cow, do you mind if I have a small foretaste?' pleaded the younger girl to *Nolizwa*. But the woman was too paralysed by fear, horror and utter disbelief to reply, so *Mvurayakucha* took her silence for assent and sank her sharp filed teeth into the rolling mass of flesh that was *Nolizwa's* left buttock. The old woman sank to the ground in a dead faint.

Meanwhile *Dombozo*, who had fallen with the arrow in his thigh, had regained consciousness and crawled, or rather dragged, himself along the ground into the safety of the forest. From there he watched the two strange girls revive *Nolizwa* and push her roughly in the back as one does a cow, urging her towards the forest where they were joined by the other two women whom he recognised as *Mulinda* and her mother. *Dombozo* knew he was the only member of *Vamba's* band who had been able to see their strange assailants and who would be able to recognise them in future. He was the only one who knew that the girl *Mulinda* had been rescued from the cave, and that she was a danger to all of them as long as she lived. *Dombozo* tore the arrow out of his thigh and tried to stanch the flow of blood with green leaves, but in vain. He then urinated on the ground and scooped up the wet earth and plastered it on the wound, gritting his teeth and pressing the dirt right in regardless of the excruciating pain. Then he started limping slowly, painfully through the forest – he had to tell *Vamba* – to warn him quickly.

Suddenly a great lion bounded into view about thirty paces behind him and with a loud wail the young man ran blindly through the forest with the battle-scarred old man-eater in hot pursuit. The lion, who had been worsted in a savage battle with a young rival only a few days before, saw in *Dombozo* an object on which to vent his murderous anger and was determined to pursue him to the very frontiers of Eternity. However, with his bad limp, he was hardly doing a better speed than *Dombozo.*

The angry lion pursued the wounded youth through the forest until well past midday and slowly the distance between them lessened as *Dombozo* grew weaker from loss of blood. And then, just as he came to the stream he and the others had forded earlier that morning, he happened to cast a pain-misted glance downstream and saw *Vamba* with a strong party of armed Vamangwe warriors about to cross the stream on their way back in search of the mysterious attackers who had caused the proud *Vamba* to turn and run for his life earlier that day.

Dombozo raised his voice and called out as loud as he could: '*Vamba*! *Vaaaambaaaa*! Listen to me!' The distant men paused in midstream and looked in his direction and a voice floated faintly to his ears across the great distance:

'What is it, *Dombozo*?'

'Listen to me . . . a lion is after me . . . I haven't much time . . . I saw your sister . . . she is alive . . . and she and her mother and *Nolizwa* have been taken away . . . by two female cannibals . . . !'

As *Dombozo* finished speaking he was overrun by the lion who promptly tore his left shoulder from his body. A loud scream of fear and agony passed through his throat before his neck was broken. The lion dragged him behind a bush and for a long time there was the dull crunch of breaking bones and the sounds of ferocious munching – then a loud belch and . . . silence.

Nolizwa's face was a dark mask of pure horror. She could not believe what her ears were telling her. These incredibly beautiful girls, carrying bows and quivers, wearing the briefest of loinskins, were actually telling her again that they were taking her to their father for his dinner the next day. *Nolizwa* had heard about cannibals, many times, but had never met any before. And any doubts she may have had about the two girls were dispelled by the pain in her left buttock. Why, they had even given the meat from the kudu to *Mulinda* and her mother, who were following behind at a respectful distance with fear written all over their faces.

There was only one small question she wished to ask: 'Why do you want to eat me alone – why not those two behind us as well?'

Mvurayakucha answered crisply: 'We only eat evil people and you are one of them. We are not going to eat *Mulinda* and her mother; we are taking them to my father for safety. And if it is any consolation to you we shall not rest until we have eaten every one of those of your evil band who escaped today. We have found the best way to rid the world of evil pests such as yourself, is to eat them. And we have also found that the more evil a man's or a woman's character, the more delicious the stew he or she turns out to be. Do you understand me, Oh lovely midday meal?'

'After we have had as much of you as we can,' announced *Luanaledi*, very pleasantly, 'we shall take your skull and some of your stew and send it to *Vamba* as a warning. We tolerate no murderers and thieves near where we happen to be, so it is the pot for you tomorrow, my fat chicken.'

After that it was *Mulinda* who asked a question in her soft, gentle voice: 'Tell me, my sisters, who or what are you – to what tribe do you belong?'

'We belong to no tribe and we, together with the youngest one at home, are the daughters of one man by the most unusual mothers in all creation. Our father is a man who has lived longer than certain mountains and who has seen more evil on this earth than a million old men. We are all ageless and death will never touch us. We are known as the Lost Immortals.'

My two eldest daughters, *Luanaledi* (River of Stars) and *Mvurayakucha* (Morning Dew), entered the hut in which I was sitting with the third joy of my sightless eyes, their youngest sister *Mbaliyamswira* (Flower of Passion), listening to her singing 'The Song of the Day Star' in her soft girlish voice. Night had fallen and loud in our ears was the chirping of thousands of crickets in the long grass outside the kraal. I had never seen the girls who entered and knelt before me, but I asked them teasingly: 'What troubles have you now brought me, Oh my children? What problems have you brought to add yet another wrinkle to this tired brow?'

'We have brought you great problems, Oh my lazy father,' answered the eldest of the mischievous three. 'We thought that if we hunted around for problems with which to plague you it would stimulate your over-ancient blood and add yet more grey to your deathless hair.'

'We have brought you also an evil one to have for dinner,' the younger one chirped. 'But before we eat her she has a few questions to answer.'

'That she will indeed do, my children,' I said. 'I believe in making my breakfasts bare their souls to me before I enjoy them.'

'Oh father,' cried *Luanaledi*, 'the silly things you say! We have also brought two other females, father, a mother and her daughter. But they are good people and are not to be eaten.'

'The only good people are those in the stewpot, my children, and no woman is ever truly good until she is in the soup, so to speak.'

'Father,' cried *Luanaledi*, 'these are our guests – they need our help.'

'I shall help them so long as they are willing to become my second helpings one day.'

'Oh you impossible parent,' cried *Luanaledi*. 'Do you never think of anything else except eating people?'

'To be eaten is the only thing the human beings of this world are good for, my child,' I replied. 'Now if I were . . .'

'Father, please,' pleaded *Mvurayakucha*, 'the girl *Mulinda* is beginning to cry.'

'Tell her to be quiet or she shall soon be crying on a spit! And you can bring forward the one we shall be having for dinner tomorrow. Let these old hands feel the tender flesh I shall soon be digesting. Now from you, oh dinner, I want a full confession of the sins of your youth before we broil you!'

'Here she is, Oh father. She is as fat as a thief's bundle and as scared as a monkey in a beerpot,' said *Luanaledi*.

The ritual dinner was finished and *Malandela's* Fifth Queen had indeed made delicious eating. Great within me grew the longing to compliment the High Chief one day on his very tasty wife. *Luanaledi* wondered if all Nguni women made such a delicious meal, and we all decided to find out soon. Thus it was that two days later we were on our way to the land of the Nguni, by canoe down the Luangwa River. *Mulinda* and her mother travelled with us, huddled together in the stern of our Great Canoe. As I sat inside the skin-covered hut amidships, listening to my daughters' singing as they paddled down the river, I went over the story of the Vamangwe very carefully in my mind. It seemed that at the height of their power the Vamangwe had been a cruel and warlike tribe with the particularly unpleasant habit of making war on other tribes for no other reason than to get hundreds of male and female captives to sacrifice to their Leopard God.

At long last the Vamangwe had bitten off more than they could chew by daring to attack the formidable Lunda nation in the West. The Lunda had lashed back at the Vamangwe with the speed and ferocity so characteristic of them and had not only slaughtered the invading army to a man, but had pushed deep into Vamangwe territory and wiped out three-quarters of that hated tribe. The survivors of the Vamangwe, about eight thousand in all, had fled into the land of the Nguni some ten years previously and, because of their great skill in wood carving, spear making and preparation of medicine, the tribe had been granted a fraction of the vast land of the Nguni in which to settle, by the fierce and warlike High King *Malandela*.

But it seemed that the Vamangwe had no intention of living in peace and prosperity under *Malandela*. They wanted to take over and rule the entire Nguni nation. Now, because they were so few in number, they never stood a chance in open battle with either the Nguni or the Western Mambo supertribes. And the Vamangwe, led by an ambitious and fanatical creature called *Vamba Nyaloti*, had been fighting a secret and treacherous underground war against the unsuspecting Nguni. Their strategy consisted of secretly murdering the sons of the High Chief so that when that worthy died he would leave no heir to sit on the High Seat. It also involved removing some of the Nguni *indunas* either by having them executed by *Malandela* through accusing them of plotting against him or of being wizards – or even arranging accidents in which the particular *indunas* would conveniently lose their lives. This was all made possible by the simple fact that the High Chief *Malandela* greatly trusted the Vamangwe. In fact, he trusted them more than he trusted his own Nguni people.

His three personal witchdoctors, *Vamba, Luva* and a female called *Luwamba*, were Vamangwe tribespeople and it was these people who were busy murdering the foolish king's sons behind his back and who were already planning his own death.

Nolizwa, who had been *Mukingo's* secret lover, had been fully aware of the plot against the High Chief *Malandela*, her lawful husband. She had also been fully aware of the murders of *Malandela's* many sons over the period of five years; she had approved of them and had even helped in planning the murder of *Zwangezwi*. It was she who had thought of using the girl *Mulinda* to decoy the curious and woman-hungry *Zwangezwi* to his death. Other people in *Malandela's* kraal knew about the Vamangwe plot. But they were either too afraid to talk or they were too full of hatred of *Malandela* to care, because the High Chief of the Nguni, who was known by the nickname of 'Old Thundering Stomach' (he being consistently attacked by indigestion and flatulence) was not a popular chief. Unlike his brother *Bekizwe* who ruled the Western Mambo, *Malandela* was cruel, impulsive and utterly stubborn.

There were many Nguni who would have been happy to see Old Thundering Stomach overthrown and destroyed like the heartless dog he was. I was not at all surprised to find myself imagining *Malandela* inside my biggest stewpot. A fat, lecherous tyrant like him, who was stupid enough to trust a rat-like tribe like the Vamangwe, richly deserved to be eaten.

I wanted to meet *Malandela* and I wondered how one of his haunches would taste when roasted. It seemed as if the land of the Nguni was crawling with evil ones and I was quite sure many of them would find their way down my gullet before long. You may not know it yet, Oh *Vamba*, but one of these days you may find yourself ruling supreme in a big clay cooking pot, garnished with stewing yams and pot-herbs. I gradually developed a pleasant feeling around my stomach – a feeling born of anticipation.

SO DIE THE INNOCENT

The land of the Nguni was deep in the swampland of sorrow, mourning together with its Chief the death of *Zwangezwi* and the disappearance of *Nolizwa*, who was one of the High Chief's favourite wives – in the great thousand-and-one seraglio of *Malandela*. The cornfields sprawled untended on the grassy plains while the young corn was ripening and being smothered by weeds and turning a sickly yellowish-green. People were allowed to milk their cows but once a day and eat but once a day, with the result that the people went half-hungry and the cows wandered through the pastures and forests with their udders almost bursting with milk. The Period of Mourning was going to last for a whole year and that meant that at the end of the year there would be a disastrous famine in the land of the Nguni and many people would die.

During the Period of Mourning, nobody was allowed to go to the river side to wash, to sweep a hut clean, to sing or to call out loudly. People were even forbidden to repair huts or stockades and all acts of love between men and women were most strictly forbidden. Hideously painted and masked Tribal Avengers prowled throughout the vast land, together with tens of thousands of Sacred Informers of both sexes, looking out for those who broke the Rules of Mourning. People were made to cut big holes in the grass walls of their huts so that the Tribal Avengers might peep into the huts to see that no couples were secretly mating inside. People spent many a sleepless night while Tribal Avengers prowled around kraals and peeped into huts ever so often. It soon became a daily occurrence for a man to find himself being spied upon by a female Sacred Informer while relieving his bowels behind his favourite thornbush. The grotesque masked heads of the Tribal Avengers and the red headbands and red feathers of the Sacred Informers began to haunt people's dreams. Starvation, sorrow and fear covered the tortured land like a rotting worm-infested *kaross* blanketing the body of an old chief, three months dead.

In cowardly endeavours to curry favour with *Malandela*, many people began spying upon their neighbours and sometimes telling lies about them, with the result that innocent people died at the hands of the Tribal Avengers and marauding bands of *Malandela's* warriors. It became an everyday occurrence for a man to get rid of a hated neighbour or a rival by simply whispering into the ear of a Sacred Informer that he had seen him break one of the Rules of Mourning. Anyone thus accused stood no chance; he or she was very often killed on the spot without a trial of any description.

Yes, these were the days of great sorrow and fear in the land of *Malandela*.

The long canoe nosed its way through the thick *ncema* rushes that bordered the mighty Luangwa River and I sensed the great joy that exploded like a falling star within the minds of my daughters. I could read the thoughts of every animal under the sun and I always loved listening in to the thoughts of my dear children. This day all of them were more than happy to leave the cramped canoe and they wanted one thing on such a hot day – to bathe in the cool waters of the ageless Luangwa.

'*Aaaiee*, no! You do not,' I said to them. 'There will be no swimming until you have helped me build the kraal I want to have right here. So it is out of the canoe all three of you; go and cut as much thatch as you can.'

'But we never said we wanted to go swimming, Oh my father!' protested *Mvurayakucha*.

'No you did not say anything of the kind – but I can read your thoughts, remember.' At this I sensed angry resentment in their minds and one of them, the youngest, had a clear wish-picture of me being chewed by a crocodile in her little mind. We pulled the canoe well out of the water and with the exception of *Luojoyo* and *Mulinda* who remained behind to cook food for all of us, we set out to look for things essential in building a kraal – grass, logs and long pliant saplings.

Although the Tree of Life had deprived me of my eyesight out of spite and senseless revenge many, so many, years ago, I was not at all helpless – in fact I was much better off without it. I could not see the beauty of the green forest, but I could find my way through it much faster than a normal man. Although I could not see a man's face I could see his soul, hear his thoughts and, if it came to fighting, could rout any dogs stupid enough to attack me – dogs on two feet that is. So, armed with an axe, I went into the dark forest and after a good half-day's work I was hauling back to the site of our camp a great bundle of logs and trimmed saplings. My daughters had returned a few moments before with enough grass to build three big huts and a story of something terrible they had seen.

'They were all dead, Oh my father! Three women, a man, and about six of what we took to be his children. A whole family of them, all staked out in the clearing of their burnt-out kraal and all having been killed by stakes driven into their bellies. It was terrible, hideous, and utterly criminal.'

'But we found that not all of them had died father,' said another excitedly. 'We found a young boy alive and hiding high up in a *mopani* tree; we had to climb up the tree to bring him down by force because he was so afraid of people as a result of what he had seen being done to his family. He runs like a buck as soon as anybody comes near him. He is here now – we brought him with us. But we had to tie him hand and foot to stop him from escaping.'

'Bring him to me, Oh my children, let me read what happened from his mind. Surely there is much evil in this land and we must stamp it out, quickly and utterly.'

The boy was brought to me and laid gently at my feet. I heard him whimper and try to struggle out of his bonds before I commanded him to sleep while I read his mind:

The boy's father had been accused by a vengeful brother-in-law before the Tribal Avengers of having broken one of the Rules of Mourning laid upon the land by the lecherous tyrant *Malandela*, as a result of what he thought was the mysterious death of his son *Zwangezwi*. The brother-in-law had come at night with a troop of Tribal Avengers and openly accused the boy's father of milking his cows twice a day for several days. The boy's father had pleaded that he had done this to save his sick First Wife from dying of hunger. She had been ill and could take nothing but fresh milk now and again, and because the milk in the kraal had gone quickly sour in the great heat, the boy's father had no alternative but to milk once again, or have his already weakened wife die before his eyes. The pitiless Avengers had killed his father and three wives, including the accuser's sister, together with all the other children, except the boy *Mukombe* who had escaped and climbed into a tree. From his perch in the tall tree the boy had seen his parents, brothers and sisters die, had heard their agonising screams, and had also seen his already rich but thieving uncle help himself to his father's many head of cattle.

'My daughters,' I shouted, 'my soul is ablaze with anger. We have all sworn to wipe out evil from this land; we have sworn to eat every evil man and woman off the face of this country and it looks like we are going to be well-fed. You, *Mvurayakucha*, come with me with your bow and your quiver full of arrows and you,

Luanaledi, shall help *Mbaliyamswira* and *Mulinda* in building the huts, while *Luojoyo* can look after *Mukombe*. Someone find me my skull headdress and fingerbone necklace and axe. Tonight the Man eater *Lumukanda* shall attack the kraal of the man who murdered the parents of *Mukombe*!'

'I do not agree, Oh my father,' said *Luanaledi* rebelliously. 'I do not want to be left behind while you and *Mvurayakucha* have all the excitement. We do not need to build a kraal at all here. All we have to do is attack the kraal of *Mukombe's* uncle, stew him and have him for supper tonight, drive away his wives, take over his cattle – just like this!' and she snapped her long graceful fingers.

'All right, my eldest one, we shall do as you suggest.'

Madondo, the son of *Muti*, was a man very pleased with himself. He showed it by guzzling copious draughts of thin *mahewu* sour porridge and by taking a great bite out of a goat's haunch that sat on a great *gqoko* meat tray at his side. Then he would pause after each bite, and drink and chew slowly while smiling happily to himself and pat his great stomach tenderly and very lovingly. Anyone who had just succeeded in removing a hated in-law, and acquired his cattle without as much as a fist fight, would have felt as *Madondo* was feeling at that moment. He had simply gone to a roving band of Tribal Avengers camped not far from his kraal and had told them that his brother-in-law had broken one of the Rules of Mourning. He had led the angry Avengers to his in-law's kraal and had accused him once more to his face this time. The result had been that he had got rid of him and his wives, *Madondo's* own sister included, and had acquired no fewer than ten head of cattle to add to his own herd of one hundred. Yes, the very fat son of *Muti* had good reason to be very pleased with himself. He was now sitting alone in his Great Hut, because although he had four beautiful wives, including one ebony black Vamangwe beauty with flashing light-brown eyes, and had managed – just managed – to beget three sturdy sons with his first wife and one girl with his second, *Madondo* was a man whose 'lamp of virility' had been snuffed out by the wind of illness two years ago; he now had no need for women, except as cooks and slaves. In fact, he loathed the 'detestable breasted things' as he always liked to refer to them.

So he sat alone, eating and drinking and grinning pleasantly to himself, as happy as a louse on a skin blanket. Suddenly the Vamangwe Third Wife stuck her shaven head into the entrance of his hut and said: 'There are people to see you, Oh husband.'

'People at this time of the night! Tell them to go away. Tell them I am asleep and that they must come back tomorrow.'

The woman disappeared, but an unbelievably beautiful girl suddenly appeared in the entrance with a great bow with an arrow notched onto its string, just as *Madondo* was raising the goat's haunch to his lips with his mouth open to take a great bite.

'Who are . . .' demanded *Madondo*, but his angry question was cut short as a hissing arrow thudded into his open mouth to emerge behind his neck, closely followed by a second which sank to the feathers in his navel. 'Die, you foul murdering son of a *basenji* cur, die and go deep into hell with the curses of *Mukombe* pursuing you.'

'*Hey-yi*!' I cried, standing some distance outside the Great Hut of *Madondo*. 'I did not want you to kill that man, Oh *Mvurayakucha*. I wanted to have him for supper tomorrow night, you stupid hot-headed brat!'

'This creature is far too foul in many ways to deserve the honour of going down your immortal gullet, Oh my father,' snarled *Luanaledi* out of the darkness. 'We must cut off his head and put it on a pointed stick and send it as a message and a warning to *Vamba* and *Malandela*.'

We herded *Madondo's* terrified wives and sons into the Great Hut and made them sit down. I then said to them: 'Listen all of you, the man you called your husband and your father was an evil man, cruel enough and pitiless enough to cause the death of an innocent man and his family. My daughters and I are dedicated to destroying this type of evil utterly in this land. I know that one of you women actually praised your husband for this foul deed and that was you, *Nomeva*, his First Wife – I can see right through your guilty mind. So you and your sons are going to take some messages for me as punishment. You are going to take a message stick with your husband's head impaled on it to a man called *Vamba Nyaloti*, and your three sons are going to carry another message stick to no less a person than *Malandela* the dog, who calls himself the High King of this land. So I want all four of you to line up against the wall of the hut – do it now, stand up . . . come on, hurry up!'

The woman and her sons obeyed and I made them look right into my blind eyes, staring until their wretched minds were completely under my control. Then I opened one of the little gourds of voodoo medicine I always carry in my pouch and ordered them to take a small sip of the thick dirty-looking contents. This was the dread *munyonji* medicine which destroy's a person's will and memory forever and which makes anyone forced to drink it nothing but a dazed puppet that obeys anything it is told to do by the one in whose power it is.

'Come now,' I said to them, 'listen to what I command you to do, you brainless puppets. First say this after me: "We are nothing but puppets – We shall obey anything you say – We shall take your message to *Vamba* and *Malandela*". Now repeat all of that!' This they solemnly did.

Meanwhile my daughters had been cutting message sticks, two thick green *mopani* poles, one of which was sharpened to a point on which to receive *Madondo's* head, with the arrow still in its open mouth.

On the first stick the girls had cut the following message: 'Eagle.Proud. Look.Jackal.Own.Nest.Secret.Killer.In.Your.Kraal.' On the other stick, the one with the point, the girls had cut: 'Hyaena. Rotten.We.Watch.Day.Come.We.Immortal.Three.Female.One.Man. Old.Blind.You.Kill.Eat.Beast.Unclean.Curse.You.Killer.Cowardly. Deformed.Sterile.Father.Murderer.'

After that we waited with great impatience for daybreak and when the first fires of the coming sun lit with a reddish glow the eastern sky, I sent my messengers on their way – having first fed them and smeared their naked bodies from head to foot with a white clay mixed with hippopotamus oil. We watched as the four naked figures vanished into the dark forest and it was then that *Luanaledi* asked me why I had smeared the woman and her sons with white clay.

'To scare the loinskin off any fool impudent enough to approach those four,' I told her, 'and to show everybody that the woman is not to be molested in any way until she comes back to me. Anyone who touches her will have a High Curse on his shoulders, as will anyone molesting the boys.'

'She is very beautiful, my father,' said *Mvurayakucha.* 'When she comes back she will make you a willing and brainless slave who obeys all orders without question.'

'I shall use her and the rest of those beauties in this kraal in my war on evil. The dog *Madondo* certainly knew how to choose his women. Come, let us also deprive the remainder of their memories and put them in our power forever – they are too valuable to be eaten.'

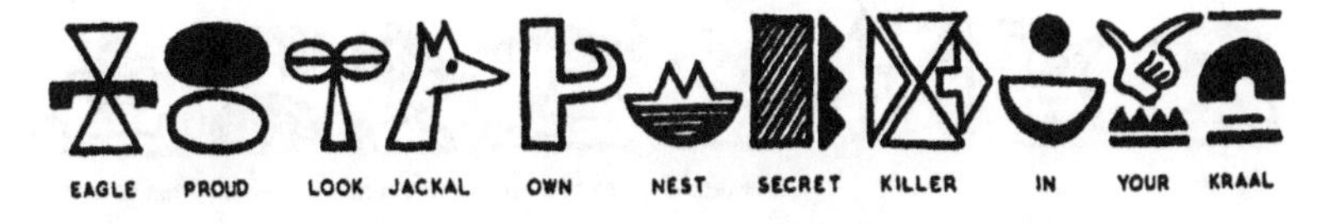

Three days later we were comfortably settled in the kraal that had belonged to *Madondo*. I had sent my eldest daughter to the riverside to fetch *Mulinda* and her mother, as well as *Mbaliyamswira* and the orphan boy *Mukombe*. And now, while *Madondo's* wives *Mamana*, *Muwaniwani* and *Lozana* moved about like sleep-walkers, sweeping the kraals and huts clean and preparing a delicious midday meal, *Mulinda* sat under the day shelter with her mother, combing and plaiting her parent's hair, and I reclined in the great hut with my daughters, planning our next move against the evil ones in the land of the Nguni. The one thing uppermost in my mind was to get *Malandela* to lift the Rules of Mourning off his tortured land because, by strict Tribal Law, *Malandela's* son *Zwangezwi* was not fit to be mourned for a full six months; he had been murdered while breaking an old Tribal Custom, the breaking of which would have earned him death in any case. Also *Malandela's* 'missing' wife *Nolizwa*, whom we had eaten, was not fit to be mourned at all, because she had been a traitress who had plotted against *Malandela* himself.

I was also painfully aware of the fact that *Malandela* was blissfully ignorant of all this, and I felt it my duty to go to his kraal as soon as possible and enlighten the fat fool on what was going on right under his nose – and to eat him if he was not prepared to mend his ways. Our problems, however, were solved for us by the appearance of another troop of roaming Tribal Avengers later that day, and when *Mukombe*, whom I had sent to spy upon the Avengers, came

back and told us the 'masked ones' were camping for the night near a small waterfall, I leapt to my feet and said to my daughters: 'Come, my dear children, this makes the whole thing much easier! Go out there and tell *Mulinda* and the other women to make as much noise as they can – let them call out in loud voices and sing the most provocative songs they can think of. You, my daughters, must go to the stream near which those masked fools are encamped, jump into the water and swim about, and also make as much noise as you can. Then come back here and bring along with you claypots of water, and sing all the way as loudly as you can. Go now, find some claypots and be off, quickly.'

'Father,' cried *Luanaledi*, 'do not be so excited. What must we do all this for?'

'We are breaking every one of the Rules of Mourning and if I know them, those masked idiots will soon come up here like a pack of mad hyaenas, their spears thirsting for our blood and I *want them to come here*!'

'Oh you mad, sweet father, we shall have such fun with them! Come on my sister, let us go now,' said *Luanaledi*.

To *Mukombe* I said: 'Come boy, bring out as many milking pails and milk pots as you can and then go and bring the cattle in. After that I want you to milk every cow in the herd – do you understand?'

'Yes, Big Grandfather.'

'I want you to whistle and shout while you milk the cows, do you hear?'

'Yes, I understand, Oh Big Grandfather.'

The boy ran out of the hut to carry out my orders and I also sent *Mbaliyamswira* to go and call one of my puppets, *Muwaniwani*, the Vamangwe woman, into my hut. When she crawled into the hut I could not see her of course, but I could see her mind from which all memories had been wiped out forever and which now contained only a reflection of my own – yet from that I could still identify her as *Muwaniwani*.

'Is that you *Muwaniwani*?' I asked, quite unnecessarily.

'To be commanded, my lord,' answered the zombie softly.

'Lead me out of the kraal and into the bush.'

'As my lord commands.'

Muwaniwani took my hand and led me out of the hut and the gate of the kraal. Anybody watching us would have mistaken us for a blind and helpless old man being led into the forest by his favourite concubine. 'Now *Muwaniwani*,' I said to her, 'I want you to listen carefully to what I have to say. I am laying a trap for those fools who call themselves the Avengers. I wish to attract them to my kraal, do you understand? I am going to make love to you and you must laugh and giggle so that anyone passing here will come and investigate. As soon as the leader of the troop sees *Luanaledi* and *Mvurayakucha* breaking the Rule of Mourning that forbids bathing, he will send out scouts to trail the two girls and find out where they stay and what other laws are being broken hereabouts. I want those scouts to find you and me here, breaking the strictest Rule of Mourning – do you hear?'

'I hear and obey, my lord.'

The honourable Leader of the Tribal Avengers of the Third Sacred Troop could not bring himself to believe what his eyes, together with those of his colleagues, were seeing. He blinked behind the slits of the heavy wooden mask covering his face and then he shaded his eyes against the blinding glare of the afternoon sun and blinked again. He turned to his young lieutenant at his side and said: 'Tell me, Second Avenger, is what I am seeing just what I think it is?'

'It is, Oh mighty First Avenger,' said the younger one. 'Those sluts are deliberately breaking one of the Rules of Mourning, and insulting us with mating gestures into the bargain!'

'This I cannot make myself believe!' growled the Honourable Leader. 'Such things only happen in a bad dream. Look again and tell me what you see.'

The Second Avenger looked again and he saw that the two slender girls were swimming nearer to the bank where the masked and hideously painted troop of very surprised Avengers stood shoulder to shoulder like a row of ugly idols in a 'forbidden valley'. Both these girls were golden brown in colour and incredibly beautiful; the perfect shape of their lithe bodies was enough to take any man's breath away – any man, that is, except a Tribal Avenger, because these queer types were always shorn of their powers of fatherhood before being enlisted into the ranks of the 'Secret and Sacred Regiments of Tribal Avengers' and not one of them was able to appreciate and desire women.

One of the impudent girls swam closer to the bank and hurled a lump of mud with great accuracy into the open toothy mouth of the mask worn by the Second Avenger. '*Aieeee*!' shrieked the girl. 'Come on, Oh my unmanly brothers, take those silly logs off your faces and get into the water – from here I can smell you need a bath!'

'Shall I kill the impious slut, High Leader?' asked the Second Avenger, lifting his spear, a monstrous thing whose head bristled with barbs and whose shaft was decorated with mysterious signs.

'*Chaaa*!' snapped the High Leader. 'When those two harlots leave the water I want Avenger Ten and Avenger Three to trail them to their home. I shall teach them and the misbegotten dog who begot them to insult the Tribal Avengers. They shall soon wish they had never been born.'

So the Avenger lowered his spear and watched angrily as the two girls left the water after hurling a stream of sacrilegious taunts at him and his followers. Then he saw the elder of the girls turn on the opposite bank of the treeshaded pool, and with hands clasped behind her head, she wriggled her hips most insultingly at the Avengers. As the two girls picked up their loinskins, dressed, and grabbed their water pots, the High Leader's voice rang out hoarsely: 'Avengers Ten and Three – ford the stream and follow them!'

BEHOLD THE CRUEL

Some time later, after sunset, Avengers Ten and Three returned to their camp and knelt before their leader. 'Well?' he asked.

Avenger Ten spoke: 'I . . . we . . . do not understand it, Honourable One. Either the people of that kraal are as mad as the Heavenly Hag or they are just asking to be executed. I have never seen anything like it in all my life.'

'What are they doing? Give me a full and clear report of what you saw and heard because at midnight we must attack that kraal and kill every living thing in it!'

'We trailed the girls to this lonely kraal and we found that it is the only kraal in an uninhabited wilderness. Just before we came in sight of the kraal we heard sounds of laughter behind a bush and both Avenger Three and myself crept forward to investigate. To our great surprise we found an elderly man, who seemed to be blind in both eyes, with a young Vamangwe woman in the bush and making violent love to her. We departed silently and continued trailing the two girls, following them to within twenty paces of the gate of the stockade that surrounds their kraal. We heard loud voices come from within the stockade – vulgar songs sung by women, at the top of their voices, and loud calls and shrill laughter. Then we saw a young boy about ten or twelve summers old, milking one cow after another in the cattle pen and when we came back, we saw the old man and the Vamangwe girl going back to their kraal laughing as if they were attending a lunatic's wedding.'

'Did they see you?' asked the leader.

'No Great One, we kept to the trees,' said the Tenth Avenger.

'*Hey-ya*!' growled the leader. 'We must go at midnight and kill those mad people. We cannot tolerate such flagrant breaches of the holiest laws of our fathers. That grey-bearded madman and his daughters must die!'

'Give me your ear, Honourable Leader,' said the Third Avenger. 'I have something to tell you which you must know. That kraal has something very wrong about it – something that doesn't make sense.'

'You are well known for your powers of observation, Third Avenger,' said the leader. 'Tell us more about what you think is wrong with the kraal.'

'I will, Oh High One. First let us take the two girls who taunted us at the pool over there. Did any of you notice something very strange about them?'

'No, we did not,' said the High Leader, speaking for the rest of the Avengers. 'It is best that you tell us, observant one.'

'Great One, and you my brother Avengers, today we were not dealing with ordinary law-breakers. We were dealing with something that is so strange and awesome you will find it very hard to believe when I tell you. But first, let me say that I think we are being deliberately lured into that kraal. Someone or something utterly alien and powerful *wants* us to go into that kraal – but for what purpose I do not know.'

'What?' cried the leader. 'What makes you think that? If you were an ordinary man and not a well-trained Avenger I would say you were dreaming, Oh Third One.'

'Listen to me, please. First of all, do you not think it very strange that we, who are feared and well known and revered by every tribe under the sun, should suddenly find ourselves taunted and insulted by two mere girls? The Secret and Sacred Regiments of Tribal Avengers have been in existence for a thousand years and never once in history has a Tribal Avenger been insulted! Even the maddest of mad chiefs thinks twice before he so much as tries to offend us in any way. Even *Malandela*, that cruel and blustering lecher, is terribly scared of us Avengers.

'Suddenly we find ourselves being insulted by mere girls, or what looks like mere girls, who are so unafraid of us that they make no effort whatsoever to escape afterwards. They sauntered slowly to their kraal as if wanting us to follow them. Tell me, my brothers, does all this not seem strange to you? Then, while we were still trailing the two girls, we came upon something also very unusual – an elderly blind giant and a young woman making love noisily in a clump of bushes, the very clump of bushes beside which the girls passed. Would a man as dignified as that old grey-haired one sink so low as to act thus with a female next to a footpath where any passers-by might see him?

'And the evil songs sung by the women in the kraal and the little boy senselessly milking cow after cow. All that was intended to lure us into that kraal. Those two girls were the first to kindle the fires of suspicion in my breast. They were too beautiful to face, too well moulded in body to be human. And their ears were not at all pierced. They had no tribal scars on their bodies, so they are neither Vamangwe nor Nguni – they just belong to no tribe under the sun. Believe me, when I saw that blind man with the Vamangwe woman in the bush, my suspicions were confirmed. I know who that old man and those girls are. That old man is none other than the legendary Lost Immortal whom the Supreme Leaders always tell us to watch out for. He must have taken over the kraal for some reason and . . .'

'And we must find out what he wants us for' growled the leader. 'We are not here to play games either with men or immortals. Come on, men, follow me.'

Now, to be an Avenger one had to be brave enough to face anything under the sun, be it natural or supernatural. One had to be brave enough to be able to walk into haunted kraals without fear – to tell even the most ugly ghost to pack up and get out. Avengers feared nothing under the sun, because they served Right, Truth and Justice, and the very fact that they were dedicated to rooting out and destroying all manner of evil gave them strength and courage denied to most men.

We sensed the Avengers as they slowly but surely surrounded our kraal. We heard their thoughts as each one of them tightened his grip on his charmed 'Spear of Justice'. Then we all went out into the star-sprayed night to welcome the High Leader who was about to enter our kraal alone and armed only with his heavy and skilfully carved 'Club of Execution'.

'I see you, Oh Avenger,' I said to him as I sensed him entering the open gate. 'I see you in peace and I see you again. I know that your men have surrounded the kraal. Tell them to lay down their arms and to come into the kraal in peace.'

'You are the blind "Lost Immortal" and we know you have sent your daughters to try and entice us into this kraal by pretending to be law-breakers,' said the leader in matter-of-fact tones.

'How clever you are, Oh masked one,' cried *Luanaledi.*

'Be silent, *Luanaledi,*' I said. 'Be silent and go and light the fire in the centre of the kraal.'

The one hundred and three Avengers trooped in. I heard the clatter of metal as they piled their spears and axes near the gate of the stockade before they went to sit around the roaring fire. Then I called out to *Muwaniwani* and the other two zombies to bring out five great pots of beer and fifty smaller pots, for the Avengers to drink. When the beer was brought, I took a deep draught out of each pot as the law dictates all hosts should do before passing the beer on to their guests. There were sounds of deep drinking as the pots were passed from man to man down the lines.

The Avengers had raised their masks a little in order to drink, but not so much as to reveal fully their features which were lost in darkness under the heavy masks fringed with lion's mane. When all had finished drinking, the leader said: '*Siyabonga* . . .' (Hail, Lord, we thank you.)

Then I rose to my feet and addressed them as follows: 'My sons, Sacred Avengers dedicated to the destruction of evil, I greet you. I, the Lost Immortal, whose heart is weary of life and whose knees are tired of wandering in the endless land and among tribes and nations, am greeting you this night. You are here because I wanted you to be here and to sit around me as you are sitting now listening to what I have to tell you. My sons, I have come into this land because thousands of people are suffering and hundreds have been murdered. The cries of the innocent sufferers fetched me from far away and today I am here – to crush to the ground the evil ones who, through their stupidity and ambition and greed, threaten the very existence of the two great divisions of the Mambo nation, the Nguni and the Western Mambo. My sons, I beg you to incline your heads and to listen to what I have to tell you.'

I went on to tell them what I knew about *Vamba, Zwangezwi* and *Mulinda.* I told them as clearly as I could about the treachery planned against the High King *Malandela* and his own great stupidity. When I had finished telling them, there was a long and heavy silence broken only by the distant roaring of lions, the yapping of night-hunting jackals and the cough of leopards in the midnight forest.

Then the leader said: 'This girl *Mulinda*, is she here, Oh Undying One?'

'Yes she is here.'

'She must be brought out.'

Mulinda came out of her hut after *Luanaledi* had gone to call her and she knelt down before the hard-faced Avenger leader. I could not see the girl, but I could see her soul and the great fear that tore through her. She was wishing the earth would suddenly open and swallow her; she was aware of the terrible fact that death was staring her in the face and she realised that she was very young to be struck down so suddenly and so cruelly.

'You are *Mulinda*, daughter of *Luojoyo* and *Nyaloti*, and sister of *Vamba Nyaloti*?' said the High Leader in a voice so utterly cold and pitiless that it would have struck fear into the hearts of the bravest.

'I am *Mulinda.*'

'Fifteen days ago you were used by your brother *Vamba* to decoy one *Zwangezwi*, a son of one *Malandela*, so-called chief of this land, into a certain place in the forest, there to be murdered by your brother – is that not so?'

'It is so,' whispered the girl.

'In the forest you broke an old tribal law together with this *Zwangezwi*, who was a youth as yet not permitted to have anything to do with women. Then you saw this youth being murdered and mangled by your brother and his followers. Is it or is it not so?'

'No . . .' sobbed the girl, 'I . . .'

'Is it or is it not so?'

Silence.

'Speak female . . . Is it or is it not so!'

'It is so, but . . .'

'Quiet! I pronounce you guilty of being party to the murder and I also find you guilty of breaking an old tribal law and I sentence you to death here and now.'

'Mercy,' cried the girl, 'I only did what . . .'

Her voice was cut short as the heavy Club of Execution in the hands of the Avenger leader shattered her skull. *Mulinda* sank lifeless to the ground just as her mother crawled out of her hut to plead with the Avengers for her daughter's life. The mute mother saw the Avengers stand up and take turns to spit upon her child's body and she uttered one strangling sound as she fell down to the ground in a dead faint. I ordered *Mamana* and *Muwaniwani* to take her into the Great Hut and revive her.

'We must hurry to the Great Royal Kraal and warn that fool *Malandela*,' cried the Avenger leader. 'It is four days' journey away from here and we must start well before daybreak. I only hope we are not too late.'

While my daughters and I had been busy in *Madondo's* kraal preparing messages to send to *Malandela* and to *Vamba*, great things were already happening in *Malandela's* kraal – great and utterly disastrous.

The leader of the Vamangwe Tribe, *Vamba*, could not sleep as usual, as his soul was one seething cauldron of boiling emotions: anger and bitterness, envy and sorrow growled in one steaming confusion within his tormented soul and *Vamba* was slowly becoming aware of another feeling creeping into his restless spirit. This was a feeling he had never before known in his life – fear, pure naked fear which tore his heart apart like so many hyaenas tearing at a dead buffalo.

Vamba was afraid, and he knew it. He was afraid because the one person who could expose his secret plans to the Nguni was alive somewhere in the land and that person was *Mulinda, Vamba's* own sister, whom he had entombed alive in the cave, but who had been rescued by unknown females and taken away. This was what worried *Vamba* so much. Who had those females been? Where had they come from and where were they now?

That *Mulinda* had told them about his doings by now, *Vamba* had no doubts. And it would not be long before those females came, or sent someone to tell *Malandela*, the High King. *Vamba* knew he had to act, and act fast. Already a terrible plan was forming deep in the valleys of his gifted mind.

Vamba paused in his thinking and listened to the night sounds – the faint and faraway roaring of lions, the derisive hooting of an owl in a nearby tree. Then from the hut nearest to his own came a burst of female laughter, and the bitterness within his heart exploded into searing white-hot hatred. He knew that it was one of his wives laughing, wives whom he could never make love to and for whose pregnancy he depended on another, his hated cousin *Mukingo*.

Vamba cursed his mother for the hundredth time and vowed once again to cut her throat with his own hands if he met her one day. 'Cur bitch,' he thought. 'When I find you one day I shall kill you so slowly you will wish for death a thousand times before you actually die. I shall make you pay for what you did to me – bringing me into this world in this condition, a useless, unnatural and deformed thing. I shall make you pay!'

Once again the ecstatic ripple of laughter stung *Vamba's* ears, and the man who was not quite a man could imagine one of his wives in his cousin's arms – in spite of the rules of mourning.

Vamba bit his lips until blood flowed. He snarled and beat the sleeping mat with his fists. He wept and cursed, and cursed again. He ground his teeth until his jaws ached. Then he leapt to his feet and pounded one of the wooden posts that held up the roof of the hut with his fists until his knuckles bled. Even as he did that, *Vamba* was glad he could not see his naked body in the darkness. The sight of his own body always filled him with fear, loathing and disgust, which was why he always wore a long leopard-skin kilt and *sipuku* that covered his chest completely.

Vamba was tall and slender in a feminine way with the rounded hips of a woman. He was not handsome, but pretty in a delicate girlish way, and he even had the silvery voice of a female. Under the tight-fitting leopard-skin *sipuku* he wore over the upper part of his body, he hid two breasts, both covered with scars as he had frequently tried, in fits of hatred and madness, to amputate them.

By strict tribal law *Vamba* should have been strangled at birth or taken out and thrown to the crocodiles. But what parent can bring herself to murder her own offspring in cold blood? Strong are the Laws of the Tribes, but stronger still the laws of Nature. So *Vamba* had lived to grow into adulthood – the object of scorn and derision of all who saw him. And within the growing *Vamba* had grown a terrible flower – a cold, calculating hatred of the human race.

'I am going to do something so great that future generations will remember me – will tremble when they hear about it from the lips of story-tellers,' he gritted in the darkness of the hut. 'I am going to set the world of the Nguni and the Western Mambo on fire! I shall kindle the flames of such a war that men will die in their thousands every day. Come tomorrow, come dawn, and I shall laugh as I see the piles of dead bodies rotting in the sun. I shall rejoice when blood flows like rivers through the land. I shall dance in the clearings of burning kraals and I shall sing while the screams of the dying crash against the sky. Come tomorrow, come! Yes, even you, fat stupid lecher *Malandela* and your fat albino slut *Muxakaza* – even you, the so-called king and queen of the Nguni dog-tribe – I shall play upon your bitterness and grief as if it were a *marimba* xylophone. I shall use you as torches to kindle the greatest war the land has ever seen. You will be my tools, you puppets, for the destruction of your own and *Bekizwe's* tribes.'

A sudden burst of strange feeling erupted like a falling star over *Vamba's* soul. He suddenly felt as if he were a god, and the whole world but a louse in the palm of his hand – a louse he could crush to pulp, if and when he chose, with ridiculous ease. He suddenly felt as if he were a mighty player of *murabaraba* games and the whole human race was but the stones he used, stones he would shift hither and thither at his whim. *Vamba* felt strong, uplifted and inspired beyond his wildest dreams and his bloody plan was sharply etched in his mind. *Yea-ha, Vamba* had become an image, a puppet of pure evil and he was ready to plunge the lands of the Nguni, and the Mambo of the west, headlong into the greatest war the land had ever witnessed.

He rose well before dawn and washed his face in a big clay bowl standing outside his hut. The song of the early rising birds was loud in his ears as he donned his rich High Witchdoctor's attire – his headdress with curving horns on either side and dark *sakabula* tail feathers fluttering on top; his newest *sipuku* heavily decorated with copper scales and cowrie shells; his broad girdle of heavy bronze beads, and his knee-length kilt of black sable skin heavily patterned with cowries and other rare and holy shells.

On his arms and forearms blazed broad copper bracelets and around both his ankles he tied the traditional witchdoctor's *mfece* seed rattles. Then he threw his great leopard-skin kaross over one shoulder, seized his great heavy lion spear in his right hand and crawled out of his hut. Treading lightly, and with a hard expression on his face, *Vamba* made his way to *Malandela's* kraal in the early dew-moist and mist-shrouded dawn.

The Lion of the Nguni, *Malandela* the Mighty and the Fearless One, had not slept for three whole nights and had not eaten for many more days. His soul was racked by grief and aflame with murderous anger, directed against nobody in particular – but an anger that needed but a little fuel to burst into flames that would consume thousands of men.

He was sitting in his great hut with his face to the wall in a pose of mourning. Beside him sat his three High Wives, *Muxakaza* (rattle of battle spears), who was the First Wife or *Ndlovukazi* (She-Elephant) according to Nguni nomenclature. *Muxakaza* was the strangest queen that any tribe has ever had and she was the topic of many a whispered conversation even in the remotest corners of her husband's vast kingdom. *Muxakaza* was the most beautiful woman in the land of the Nguni, which was well known for the beauty of its women. But she was a 'cursed one' – an albino. *Malandela* had been struck by the great beauty of this creature; he had married her and made her his First Queen, instead of having her thrown over the cliff as was always done to albinos. *Muxakaza* had presented *Malandela* with two sons, the boys to whom *Vamba* had secretly given the leaking canoe and who were drowned as a result.

The Second Wife was *Zuzeni* (what have I gained), an ill-favoured, but hot-blooded female who was the mother of the dead *Zwangezwi* and who was half-mad with grief at the loss of her only son.

The Third Wife *Celiwe* (the one we asked for) was a tiny little thing who, at thirty summers, still looked like a girl of sixteen, and whose great big eyes, set in a beautiful round yellow-brown face, had earned her the nickname of *Sikhovana* (little owl). *Celiwe* was as kind hearted as she was beautiful and she was famous for her charity to the needy and her keen foresight. And she was bitterly hated by both *Muxakaza* and *Zuzeni* who were proud and evil women, well known for their cruelty and great wickedness, a wicknedness that manifested itself in many ways. For example, *Zuzeni* had developed an unnatural and secret habit of wooing and actually loving other females, preferably young girls, as man loves woman, and one of her handmaidens was her sweetheart whom she forbade to so much as look at men, under pain of death. *Muxakaza*, on the other hand, loved bloodshed; she loved seeing men killed and she was always present at mass executions. She used to whip the many members of *Malandela's* seraglio and was never satisfied until the luckless concubine was unconscious and bleeding at her feet.

Malandela was not wearing any ornaments and neither for that matter were his wives, who had washed the red clay off their cylindrical coiffures, as was the custom when people's hearts were 'black' (mourning). At such times they were not supposed to wear any ornaments at all and were always supposed to sit and face the walls of the hut and to speak only when strictly necessary.

Malandela was a big fat round-shouldered man with a high forehead, large flat nose and a mouth that was always set in a hard determined line. His eyes seemed able to penetrate a person's soul. He was a brave man, but he had neither wisdom nor foresight and mercy was an unknown thing to him. He was stubborn and quick tempered and he had a habit of killing first and asking questions afterwards.

A young concubine crawled into the Great Hut where *Malandela* and his High Wives were sitting in a mourning attitude, and she struck her chest twice with her fist, then crossed her hands in front of her face in silent salutation.

'What is it?'

'*Vamba Nyaloti*, the High Witchdoctor is here, Oh High Ones.'

'Tell him to come in.'

Vamba Nyaloti crawled into the Great Hut and, like the concubine, he crossed his hands in front of his face and then kissed the floor of the Great Hut. He waited with well-feigned humility for *Malandela* to break the heavy silence.

'My son,' growled the High King, 'you are the only one I trust and yours is the only voice I have ears for. Before my eyes you are the only light I depend upon to light the darkness that is my life. Tell me, *Vamba*, who is the secret wizard who is causing the deaths of my sons? Three years ago I lost two sons in one day under mysterious circumstances. I have never found out just what my sons had been doing in the river and nobody ever told me where they had got the canoe from which they were drowned. Now my last hope, *Zwangezwi*, is gone and I am left with a hundred daughters – girls, mere useless girls who cannot carry even the lightest shield in battle. *Zwangezwi* also died under mysterious circumstances – I do not know what in the name of my first ancestor led him into the forest so far away from home. What was he doing in that cave in any case? What led him there? Who was the other dead man with him in the cave? As you know, the searchers found nothing but scattered bones picked clean by hyaenas, and only some ornaments could identify him. Tell me, *Vamba*, ask the Spirits . . . throw your bones. Stand on your head and lie on your back . . . but tell me who killed my sons.'

'Tell us, *Vamba*,' said the First Queen. 'Tell us who the secret enemy is who wants to break my husband's knees. Tell us who it is that wants the Lion of the Nguni to depart to his ancestors in the Spirit World, without leaving an heir. Tell us who it is that is fighting a secret magic war against *Malandela*.'

Vamba stood up and slowly he raised his hands to the heavens; his entire body shook like a leaf in a tempest. His long-lashed eyes glazed over and froth burst from the corners of his mouth. Sweat streamed down his face and a flood of 'spirit talk' burst out of his open mouth. Then slowly with his hands still raised, *Vamba* sank to his knees, very slowly. Still acting, he fell flat on his face, as if struck from behind by an unseen hand, and lay still for a long time. *Malandela* and his women felt their hair struggle to stand on end while their crawling skins suddenly erupted into pimples of fear. They stared in fascination at the prostrate form of *Vamba* – like buck hypnotised by a python. Then slowly *Vamba* 'came to life' and like a man in a trance, or a sleepwalker, he reached a slow hand to his girdle and untied the pouch which contained his *amadolo* and *mazinyo-endlovu.**

Vamba took the pouch in both hands and emptied its contents slowly on the ground while *Malandela* and his women watched like people under a great spell – which they were in a sense. *Malandela* watched the slow stream of falling bones, ivory pieces and shells until he felt drowsy. Then in a flash of sudden movement, *Vamba* scooped up the pile of bones in both hands – spat on it once, twice, then shook it violently, making one continuous rattling sound. He then opened his cupped hands suddenly, spreading the 'bones' on the floor.

With an agonizing scream *Vamba* leapt away from the bones as if they were so many snakes. He crouched in the very centre of the Great Hut with a look of fear on his face – a look intended for *Malandela* to notice and to worry about.

'What is it *Vamba*?' he demanded. 'What do the bones say?'

'I cannot bring myself to tell you, Oh High One,' muttered *Vamba.*

'Why, why?' cried Queen *Muxakaza.* 'Why can't you tell us?'

'I am afraid, Oh Great She-Elephant,' whispered *Vamba.* 'I am utterly afraid!'

'*Vamba,*' said *Malandela* in a terrible voice, 'tell me what the bones say.'

'*Cha*!' cried *Vamba.* 'No, never!'

'Listen, Oh son of *Nyaloti,*' hissed *Muxakaza,* 'tell us what you see or by the spirits, you shall not leave this hut alive!'

'*Vamba's* girlish mouth hardened into a line of cold defiance: 'I would rather die ten times than tell you.'

'Why?' the gentle *Celiwe* asked, raising her eyebrows and opening her great soft eyes very wide. 'Why, Oh Vamba, what do the bones say?'

---

* *Bones from the heels of goats, and other carved pieces of ivory and a few cowrie shells. This strange collection of bones, ivory and shells, generally referred to as 'bones', is used in divination.*

'I cannot bring myself to tell you, Oh High Ones, let other lips than mine tell you the message of the bones and shells . . .'

'*Celiwe*,' said *Malandela*, 'go and call the Wise Ones *Luva* and *Mukingo*, and also my sister *Nomikonto*, and be quick about it.'

'As you say, lord.'

Some time later *Celiwe* came back and crawled into the small entrance of the Great Hut, closely followed by the old Vamangwe witchdoctor-storyteller *Luva*, and *Vamba's* cousin *Mukingo*, who were shortly followed by *Malandela's* mountainous sister, *Nomikonto*, who got stuck as usual half-in and half-out of the hut in the small entrance. To be brought inside the hut, *Celiwe* pulled from within and one of the High King's concubines pushed from without.

Although *Nomikonto* was now thirty years old, she was unmarried and still a virgin, because there was nothing on earth she feared more than marriage. The very word 'husband' was sufficient to send her squealing with terror.

Briefly *Malandela* explained the situation to *Luva* and *Mukingo* and ended by demanding that they should tell him what the bones said. *Luva* took one glance at the bones, which formed a clear pattern that read 'killer is within the kraal', and he all but seared *Vamba* with a look of well-feigned contempt and said: 'This timid one is afraid to tell the truth for fear of starting a war. The message of the bones reads that the one who is causing the deaths of the Lion's sons is the Lion's own brother. A witchdoctor must have the courage to tell the truth, no matter how unpleasant, Oh *Vamba*!'

A terrible silence followed – a silence so deep, one could have heard the sound of a falling feather. The silence was so terrible that one's own heartbeat sounded like a hundred war-drums. Then *Malandela* broke the silence at long last, his voice sounding like that of a man speaking from the depths of a great cave – hollow and horribly unreal: 'Throw those bones again, Oh *Vamba*.'

Once again *Vamba* scooped up the bones, spat on them, shook them thoroughly and then scattered them once more. Another deep silence followed, a silence *Muxakaza* broke harshly: 'Tell us what the bones say, quickly!'

Luva swept the scattered bones with his rheumy eyes and he read silently to himself the message displayed: 'The evil ones shall soon be scattered and their evil schemes exposed.' But to *Malandela* he said: 'The message is still more or less like the first one, Oh Lion of the Nguni. The bones point to one who is a male, who was carried in the same womb that carried you, who is secretly killing your heirs – and who will soon send a *tokoloshe* to strangle you in your sleep.'

'That is a lie!' screamed *Nomikonto* (daughter of battle spears). 'Brother *Bekizwe* would never do such a thing. You lie, you foreign charlatans. My brothers love each other; do not try to set them at each other's throats!'

'Be silent you fat, vile spinster,' cried *Muxakaza*. 'Who are you to insult those whom the spirits protect? On what grounds are you calling *Vamba* a liar? Tell me, you greasy strumpet, is it not obvious, does it not strike you as strange that of the two kings in this land only our lord *Malandela* loses sons, while *Bekizwe* loses none? Why must we be empty-handed while the wives of *Bekizwe* carry sons in their arms? Can't you see that something strange is going on? I always suspected that *Bekizwe* was a wizard and now I am sure. *He* is the one who had cast a spell on *Zwangezwi*, causing him to wander off into the forest where he was murdered, probably by followers of *Bekizwe*. I am sure of it. And it will take more than a bloated spinster . . .'

The albino queen's voice broke short as *Nomikonto's* great fist crashed home full on her pink jaw. 'Spinster yourself, you foul cursed baboon female!' she hissed as the Great Queen slumped unconscious to the ground. 'Whoever it is who has been killing *Malandela's* sons may not be known to me, but I am positive it is not brother *Bekizwe*. If it is anybody it could be you, you Vamangwe renegades. Do you hear me, *Vamba*? It could be you!'

'You are mad, *Nomikonto*!' cried *Malandela*. 'The Vamangwe people are the most loyal and the most trustworthy in all the land. Why would they kill the sons of their benefactor? I think you need a man's embrace to put your mad brain right. Come on, *Mukingo*, take her.'

But before *Mukingo* could move, *Nomikonto* was out of the hut like a big fat mouse – with no difficulty getting through the door – and had run to her own hut where she shut herself up securely. Then *Malandela* turned to *Vamba* once again and bade him to throw the bones a third time. This time *Vamba* read the scattered bones himself and while he clearly read 'the hawk of retribution will be swift to overtake the wicked fowls', he read out aloud: 'Unless the Lion takes quick action now, the Hyaena of the West shall strip him of his mane.'

In the heavy silence that followed, *Malandela* was heard to say: 'That is all I need to know. So my brother *Bekizwe* wants to kill me, does he? Well, I shall kill him – first!'

Before anyone else could move, *Malandela* was out of his hut and bellowing for his two personal servant boys, *Bafana* and *Madoda-Doda*. 'Go and tell all the Rainbow *Indunas* and all the Battle *Indunas* that I want every attack regiment and every reserve regiment in full battle order assembled before the Great Kraal at midday. Hurry up, *sesha*!' roared *Malandela* to *Madoda-Doda*. To the fleet-footed *Bafana* he bellowed: 'You, go to the spear-makers and tell them

I want them to bring five hundred thousand assegais, five hundred thousand battle-axes, and eighty thousand *pangas*. Go . . . run!'

The two boys ran like the wind to carry out the High King's commands and *Malandela* crawled back into his hut and thundered to everybody. 'I am now declaring war on my brother whom I mean to defeat and kill like the treacherous dog he is! I shall make him pay for the sorrow he has caused me. You, witchdoctors, go and prepare for the Ceremony of the Strengthening of the Warriors!'

Vamba, Luva and *Mukingo* went out of the Great Hut to the hut allocated to them within the Great Kraal, to prepare for the coming ceremony, the most interesting ceremony of any witchdoctor's career. Thoughts flashed fast through Vamba's mind: 'You have accomplished it at long last, Oh *Vamba. Malandela* has fallen into your hands like a fat pumpkin. He is doing exactly what you wanted him to do and there is going to be an ugly war – soon!'

'Fools are born to be the tools of the wise,' quoted *Luva*. 'And the old proverb says that the gains of quarrelling fools become food for the monkeys – does it not say so, *Vamba*?'

'Be quiet you two and don't clap hands until the dance has started,' said *Vamba*.

'The struggle is as good as won,' said *Luva*. 'The fat dog *Malandela* may not know it yet, but he is a king no more!'

'Now listen you two,' said *Vamba* tersely. 'As soon as *Malandela* leaves with his armies I want you to bring every able-bodied Vamangwe of fighting age here. I want you to seize this kraal and proclaim *Mukingo* the new king of the Nguni, which shall thereafter be known as the Vamangwe.

'Me!' exclaimed *Mukingo* in great surprise. 'Proclaim me a Chief?'

'That is what you have been wanting all the time, is it not, Oh *Mukingo*?' asked *Vamba* sarcastically. 'You always love to eat the fruits of the labours of others and I am now handing over the fruits of my labours to you.'

'But what about you?' asked *Mukingo*.

'As soon as you are proclaimed High King of the Nguni – the Vamangwe, rather – I shall take a long journey in search of a certain woman I have sworn to kill. After that I shall kill myself.'

'You do not mean your mother, do you?' asked *Luva*. 'But you cannot . . .'

'Yes, I do mean my dear, beautiful – and detestable – mother!'

'Listen, foul dog,' growled *Mukingo*, 'you will do nothing of the kind. We still need your scheming brain around here and you will stay and help me rule if I have to tie you hand and foot.'

As the sun climbed to the very peak of the silver heavens, the first two attack regiments came chanting up the cattle pathway that led up to the Great Kraal. In front was the First Attack Regiment, or Night Owls, each warrior wearing a headband of lion skin into which two tall feathers of an owl were fastened. The Night Owl Regiment carried black shields with white *magabela* decorations and wore black bands of sable antelope skin on their forearms and legs. Behind the Night Owls came the Second Attack Regiment, the Flamingoes, *Malandela's* own regiment, whose warriors carried white shields and wore cowrieshell studded headbands with flamingo feathers. They also wore great tufts of white cow tails around their legs, wrists and upper arms.

After these two units came the dreaded Beggars Regiment whose members wore headdresses of sisal fibre and violet-dyed fibre skirts around their waists. They carried zebra skin shields and a special knobkierie shaped like a fish. Every single warrior in this regiment was a veteran of more than ten successful campaigns.

But more fantastic was the regiment that followed – a regiment with the apt name of The Madmen, whose warriors carried no shields and were swathed from head to foot in tattered old impala, jackal and hyaena skins.

This regiment used only clubs studded with crude metal nails, and double-headed battle axes. They were men trained for savage hand-to-hand combat and never used spears. Each and every warrior was a raging, bloodthirsty maniac in battle and whenever the madmen were sent into a fight, the enemy very promptly took to their heels. Nothing on earth could stand against them and their fame had spread as far north as the land of the Baluba.

After the Madmen came lesser regiments, the most remarkable of which was the Magundane (the Mice), a regiment of boys aged seventeen to twenty. By full midday, close to eighty regiments – each consisting of 2,000 men – were marched around the Great Kraal of *Malandela*, like swarms of bees around a hive.

Spearmakers went from regiment to regiment distributing weapons of all kinds from piled sleds drawn by boys and even oxen.

Sled-loads of corn cakes and meat were also distributed among the warriors, as were great pots full of corn beer. The warriors ate heartily and drank deeply, and waited.

Then *Malandela* appeared in full battle regalia at the gate of his kraal and the age-old salutation, *Bayede*, burst from nearly two hundred thousand throats.

LO! THE VIPER STRIKES

Malandela, whose name means 'He that follows', stood at the gate of his sprawling circular kraal and looked with angry pride at his massed *impis* darkening the land as far as the eye could see. On either side of him stood his six famous Rainbow *Indunas*. There was the hunchbacked, wry-mouthed mute giant *Ngovolo*, a veteran of countless battles who commanded the regiment, The Beggars. His exact opposite, the massive bow-legged dwarf with the big head and only one eye, *Malangabi*, who had killed a whole pride of lions single handed, commanded the regiment, The Madmen. Then there was the great thinker, *Mapepela*, as wise as he was brave, and tremendously fat, the only man who could out-eat and out-drink and talk back to *Malandela* himself – and the only man who referred to *Malandela* to his face as 'Old Thundering Stomach'. *Mapepela* was *Malandela's* Chief Adviser and *Malandela* had two of *Mapepela's* sisters in his seraglio, one of whom was the famous *Celiwe* – the beautiful and the wise.

Then there were *Ziko* and *Majozi*, who were brothers and who jointly commanded the regiment, The Night Owls. They were a youthful pair of hard-drinking, hard-loving and hard-fighting hotheads, also famed as great singers and story-tellers who had composed long verses in praise of *Malandela*.

Finally came the fierce, loud-voiced old man *Solozi*, who had fought under *Malandela's* ill-fated father, *Mitiyonka*, who was murdered by his own wife and daughters. *Solozi*, whose name means a kind of pumpkin, was the best – or rather the worst – braggart in *Malandela's* kraal. Although he had never been in love with any woman and had never married, because of his natural shyness, he boasted about the hundreds of mistresses he had taken to the love-mat – mistresses who existed only in his fertile and colourful imagination. He was among the bravest of men, but his life was one big falsehood, one big lie.

These were some of *Malandela's* famous Rainbow *Indunas* – men who were one day destined to accompany their king on the greatest journey of all time, the Journey to Asazi, the journey to 'we know not where'.

Members of the Boys' Regiment, the Mice, led fifteen oxen into the centre of *Malandela's* Great Kraal – oxen that were to be used in the coming Ceremony of Strengthening the Warriors. From every regiment the Battle *Indunas* selected twenty men who ran into the second gate and surrounded the fifteen oxen in the centre of the great clearing among the many hundreds of grass huts that made up Mzinwengwe – *Malandela's* Royal Kraal. (Mzinwengwe means 'the kraal of the leopard' and *Malandela* was fondly called the Leopard or the Lion of the Nguni.)

The duty of the men, who had been chosen from every regiment, was to slaughter the fifteen oxen without weapons – by kicking, pummelling and tearing them apart. The flesh of these oxen was cut into little pieces and pickled with juice from crushed, bitter-tasting herbs before being given to the warriors to eat raw. Being made to eat meat so treated upset a man's stomach and left a very bad and bitter taste in his mouth, and this was destined to kindle a man's temper in battle – which it always did with disastrous results to the enemy.

Then from their hut came *Luva, Vamba* and *Mukingo*, together with the tall, hard-faced *Dambisa-Luwewe*, the female Vamangwe sybil. *Vamba, Mukingo* and *Luva* were covered from head to foot in billowing fibre costumes and looked like faceless long-haired beasts that had just emerged from the swamps of Demon land. But the female *Dambisa-Luwewe* wore nothing except a long fringed mask with a toothy, hideous grin – grotesque in every respect and representing the female demon *Watamaraka. Dambisa-Luwewe's* naked body was furthermore painted with broad stripes of red, white and grey clay and she carried two great skin bags of thousands of dirty green pellets of the dreaded *lubanji* drug which turns men into raging bloodthirsty beasts who no longer feel pain, and who can still fight with enemy spears buried deep in their bodies. So fantastic is the power of this ancient drug that men under its influence have been known to fight on with arms cut off, and other severe wounds from which blood was freely flowing.

Dancing, leaping and shrieking like demons, *Vamba* and his followers tore through the circle of men surrounding the fifteen oxen and danced from beast to beast, spitting at each and calling it all sorts of vile names. The lithe *Dambisa-Luwewe* brought lusty cheers from the throats of the assembled warriors by leaping high into the air and doing a double somersault on the backs of two oxen and landing on her feet on the other side. This was the signal for the war drums to sound forth a thundering tempest that filled all hearts with dread. The warriors within and without the kraal began to dance, each regiment in perfect formation, led by its battle leaders and Rainbow *Indunas*. The angry red dust rose in columns from tens of thousands of stamping feet.

'*Heshe! Heshe!*' went the rythmic chant from thousands of throats. Then from the mouths of the watching women who peered over the grass fences and *guma* screens in front of the entrances of their huts burst the blood-curdling *Kikiza* cry: 'Li-li-li-li-kee-kee-keeee-!' At that signal *Dambisa-Luwewe* did another breath-taking somersault over two oxen and then danced away together with *Vamba* and the other two men.

With bloodthirsty yells of pure savagery the chosen warriors closed in on the oxen with punching fists and clawing fingers to tear them apart. All but one ox went down under a pile of yelling and bellowing men who gouged out their eyes, tore their ears off and broke their horns from their skulls. But this beast fought back equally savagely, tossing men high into the air and trampling others underfoot. It broke away – an evil omen – and charged down the great clearing to the First Gate where *Malandela* and his six *Indunas* were standing.

The mute hunchbacked giant *Ngovolo* leapt forward and seized the beast by the horns while the dwarf *Malangabi* went behind and seized its tail. A short fierce struggle followed in which *Ngovolo* broke the animal's neck and then helped *Malangabi* to drag it back to the centre of the clearing. The dead warriors whom the ox had gored and trampled down were carried away for quick burial by members of the Mice, while the other warriors drew their *pangas* and cut up the dead oxen into little pieces, each about the size of two or three fingers. This done, the witchdoctors emptied great potsful of juice from crushed *ntshuba* leaves on the pile of meat, rendering it terribly bitter.

At a signal from *Malandela* the clearing was emptied and everybody proceeded to march in at the first gate and out of the second. As each warrior passed the pile of raw and evil-tasting meat he picked up a piece and immediately started chewing it. A strict watch was kept by the battle leaders to ensure that nobody spat out the foul meat. Those who tried to bolt it down to reduce the clinging foul taste left behind in their mouths, choked themselves and had to be thumped on the back by their fellows. As the warriors came out of the second gate chewing and with ugly scowls on their sweating faces, the masked *Dambisa-Luwewe* thrust the green *lubanji* pellets into their mouths and each man was forced to swallow the pellets with the meat.

In the late afternoon about two hundred thousand angry warriors, with aching stomachs and a nasty taste in the mouth, filed at a brisk pace past where *Malandela* stood with his Rainbow *Indunas*. As each sullen evil-tempered warrior went past his king, he stooped low and saluted by placing his right hand above his heart. Many were the foul whispered curses the warriors directed at *Malandela*, who was not what one might call a popular leader.

With a loud shout, *Majozi* and *Ziko* leapt away from the group around *Malandela* and stood facing him. *Majozi* started to praise his king, leaping high into the air, stamping his feet, falling flat on his stomach and even standing on his hands with his feet in the air.

> You are the black eagle of sunset
> That snatches the lamp from the hands of *Galaza*;
> You snatched the lamp and brought it
> To your nest to warm your eaglets.
> You are the Lion of Sunrise
> That stalked the craven impala
> And brought it into your great den
> To feed us, your cubs, till we grow.
> River of Wisdom that flowed from
> Between the breasts of *Nomvula*;
> Flame of Courage that was lit
> By the valiant *Mitiyonke*—
> *Bayede, Bayede Uyi Zulu.* (Hail, Hail, you are the heavens.)

So chanted the greatest tribal poet that ever lived. As he finished the last verse, he leapt up and allowed himself to fall violently to the ground, lying still in pretended death. His brother *Ziko* stood over him like a warrior victorious in battle and sang a song, a song destined to be famous for scores of generations to come. *Ziko* held his spears in one raised hand and his shield in the other. He stood thus, still as a carved image, while tears flowed down his face and his lips trembled as he sang – the 'Song of the Warriors':

> My ears have heard the battle drum—
> Summoning me to war;
> My soul has heard the voice of God—
> Calling on me to die.
> I've snatched up war's whetted tools
> And now I stand prepared;
> My headdress nods upon my head—
> My ox-hide shield is here,
> And bright in the midsummer sun
> Glitter my honed spears.
> Before I lay me down and die;
> Before my heart is stilled—
> I'll send into *Kalunga's* Hell,

A hundred foes and more—
That men in years as yet to come
Shall speak my name with awe.
The hoary past looks down on me—
The silent future waits;
And loud my dead ancestors call—
Go conquer son, or die!
Farewell, farewell, my mother dear,
Farewell my wrinkled sire;
And you that share my marriage mat
Weep not for me, farewell!
I ask not, God, to come back safe,
But that victory be mine!

With a roar that shook the very heavens, some two hundred thousand voices took up the savage refrain of the last two lines – and went on chanting the last line again and again.

For *Malandela* and his *Indunas* there remained yet one ceremony, one which tested a man's courage to the utmost and one which was effective in its simplicity – the throwing of the Royal Spear. *Malandela* summoned all his Rainbow *Indunas*, his lesser Battle *Indunas* and battle leaders to the centre of the great clearing in his kraal. They came and stood in a circle around their king who had laid aside all his weapons except one heavy throwing spear. This he was going to throw high into the air, and as straight up as possible above his men's heads. The idea was to see which man lost his nerve, jerked his head up to see where the spear would fall. The spear would turn around and come down point first among them. But nobody must make the slightest movement.

Malandela bent backwards with the spear poised in his hand; he straightened suddenly and the spear hissed into the air. Not one man among his *Indunas* moved a hair in those few terrible moments while hearts stopped functioning. Then there was a dull thud and all eyes turned to see where the spear had landed. It had missed *Mapepela's* protruding stomach by a thumb's length and still stood quivering in the ground a finger's length from his big flat feet. A barely audible sigh went out from the lips of each man – the test was over.

'All regiments,' roared *Malandela*, 'all regiments follow the setting sun. Westward! Westward!'

The Flamingoes went first, closely followed by the Beggars, Madmen and Night Owls. Regiment followed regiment in perfect battle order and last of all the Boys' Regiment, the Mice, who carried hundreds of sleeping mats, tens of thousands of corn cakes and huge slabs of boiled meat for the other regiments. Some of the boys even carried big bags full of *nsangu* (dagga or marijuana) and great *magudu* water pipes used by the warriors in smoking this drug.

The Mice were never used in actual battle – or very seldom. They were simply camp followers and scouts. All tribal armies had one or two Boys' Regiments, some as many as four.

The Third Wife *Celiwe* was standing behind the *guma* screen that shielded the entrance to her hut and watching the regiments depart towards the West. She heard their chanting grow fainter and fainter the farther they went and, like a secret spear thrown by a coward from a hiding place, fear tore through the little woman's heart – a meaningless fear, fear without a reason and all the more terrible for that. Something was very wrong somewhere, but *Celiwe* could not for the life of her tell what it was. Although it was a very hot day, *Celiwe* suddenly felt a chill wind caressing her back and the pimples of fear erupted all over her crawling skin. A small voice suddenly started to whisper in her mind: 'Get out of this kraal – get out!'

Beads of sweat jewelled *Celiwe's* round little forehead and her huge eyes opened wide. Her heart seemed to miss a few beats. 'There is evil afoot, I can feel it,' she sobbed. 'But what am I to do?'

The Lord of Day sank beyond the western mountains and his last rays stained the weeping clouds a fiery, passionate red. Darkness, the usurper, slowly claimed the world thus abandoned by the sun, until the trees were sharp silhouettes against the burning sky. There was a roar of thousands of hooves as countless cattle were driven into the pens from the pastures by more than a hundred Royal Herdboys. Loud in *Celiwe's* ears were the bawling of cows and the whistles and shouts of the herdboys. Sharp in her little nostrils came the smell of fresh dung and persistent in her heart there was the strange still voice: 'Get out of this kraal!'

The silent moon rose in the eastern sky – the holy missile with which the Tree of Life stunned the Great Mother millions of years ago. Slowly the caitiff Darkness yielded before the Orb of Peace, which flung a veil of shimmering light over the head of her sleeping baby, protecting it from the stings of ravening mosquitos.

Aieeeee! But even as the Orb of Peace shed its light on the enchanted earth, the footsteps of evil came with stealthy and silent pace to within striking distance of the Great Kraal.

Foul were the grins of savage triumph worn by the thousands of Vamangwe cut-throats as they crept nearer and nearer to the lightly defended kraal. They went down on their bellies in secret ambush in the forest that surrounded Mzinwengwe, waiting for the treacherous *Vamba* to set one of the huts near the gate on fire as a signal for attack.

All this *Celiwe* did not know. But as the silver-drenched night wore on, so within her grew the great uneasiness. Then she saw something strange happening near the first gate which had just been closed for the night by members of the Old Men's Regiment, the Tortoises.

She saw *Vamba* and *Mukingo* come walking slowly towards the two old warriors guarding the gate and engage them in conversation. *Celiwe* could not hear because of the great distance. Then she saw *Luva* creep behind one of the old men and stab him in the back, while both *Mukingo* and *Vamba* seized the second guard and dragged him into the shadows. A spear flashed as it stabbed downwards in the moonlight . . . once . . . twice.

Celiwe turned and ran to the hut of *Nomikonto*, the High Chief's sister. She found the princess reclining on a pile of leopard skins inside her hut with her two handmaidens washing her feet with warm water in a great stone bowl.

'Great One,' gasped *Celiwe*, 'there is treachery! I have just seen *Vamba* and *Luva* and *Mukingo* murder the two guards at the first gate . . .'

'What!' *Nomikonto* leapt to her feet, upsetting the stone basin and sending one of the handmaidens sprawling. 'I thought some such thing might happen. I knew it! Oh, my stupid, gullible, headstrong, foolish brother *Malandela* – I never did trust those Varnangwe dog-people!'

'We must warn all the women, Great Princess,' said *Celiwe*. 'They must escape while there is still time.'

'Come on, you girls,' said *Nomikonto* to her handmaidens, 'Go and warn all the other women and tell them to leave the kraal quietly by the second and third gates. Hurry up . . . come on, hurry!'

'Tell them, added *Celiwe*, 'tell them to make their way into the forest and assemble near the Rock of the Eagles. Send boys to warn the *Indunas* of the Tortoises as well. Hurry, my children, hurry!'

The girls ran like scalded mice out of the hut and just then an inspiration came to *Celiwe*. She ran out of the hut with *Nomikonto* close behind her and crawled into the Great Hut where the first and second queens were already sleeping. Without bothering to wake them, *Celiwe* seized one of *Malandela's* battle bugles and crawled out again, leaving *Nomikonto* to awaken the sleeping queens. Once outside, *Celiwe* put the bugle to her lips and blew one long blast and three short ones, the signal for *Vukanibo* – 'Everybody wake up'.

The ever-ready members of the Home Regiment, the Tortoises, who slept with their headdresses and loin-aprons on, tumbled out of their huts with shields and spears in their hands, ready to die for their High Chief's Kraal, cattle and wives. But from the gate came *Vamba's* cold and contemptuous voice: 'Hear me, you old and doddering idiots . . . I have the kraal completely surrounded. You are outnumbered two to one and if you so much as raise a finger, I shall order the massacre of every living thing in this kraal, men, women and children alike. Lay down your spears and I shall let you get out of this kraal alive to spend the remainder of your wretched lives in peace.'

'What guarantee have we of that, Oh treacherous one?' asked *Jeleza*, the old *Induna* commanding the Tortoises. 'And what about the High Chief's wives?'

'I gave you my word, Oh miserable old goat,' sneered *Vamba*, 'and I shall see to it that the blood of your High Chief's wives will not be spilt, provided you do not try to resist. So lay down your spears now.'

'Our duty is to defend the Kraal of our Chief to the last drop of our blood, Oh *Vamba*, and this shall be done,' *Jeleza* said quietly.

But *Nomikonto*, who had come out of the great hut with *Muxakaza* and *Zuzeni*, raised her husky voice and called out to *Jeleza* and his men who were forming up to oppose the Vamangwe now advancing on the Kraal openly from all directions: 'Loyal servant of my brother, order your men to lay down their arms. It is childish to let blood be spilt in vain. I command you to put down your spears in the name of *Malandela*.'

'But, Oh Great Royal Child,' protested the grizzled old *Jeleza*, 'what guarantee have we that the murdering dog of a Vamangwe will keep his word? From *Vamba Nyaloti* I can accept nothing short of a High Oath!'

'*Vamba Nyaloti*,' said *Nomikonto* coldly, 'I, the daughter of *Mitiyonke*, the son of *Malembe*, the son of *Vezi*, do hereby challenge you to take the High Oath that you will honour your promise that if the Tortoises lay down their spears without the spears having drunk the filth that the Vamangwe have instead of blood, you shall let the old warriors go unharmed and shall also spare my brother's wives and concubines. I, *Nomikonto*, the undefiled daughter of a thousand kings, challenge you to take the High Oath.'

'I accept your contemptible challenge, Oh spinsterly daughter of a thousand Nguni fowl-thieves,' laughed *Vamba*. 'I swear by the *Great Spirit* and by the silver thighs of the Goddess of Creation, the mother of men, and also by the breasts of *Mamerave*, the second mother of Mankind. I also swear by the loins of the High Father *Odu*, that if the Tortoises yield and lay down their arms, I shall not spill so much as a drop of the blood of the human beings within this kraal. I, *Vamba*, the son of *Nyaloti*, the son of *Dawudi*, the son of *Kabanga* have spoken.'

Then *Vamba* fell on his knees and licked the dust with his tongue, and as he finished taking the High Oath of Solemn Promise, the Vamangwe cut-throat army poured into the Great Kraal.

TRUST NOT A JACKAL'S WORD

As the Vamangwe poured into the Great Kraal from all directions and through all the ten gates, the outnumbered Tortoises laid down their spears and shields and began ceremoniously burning their grey headdresses in the middle of the clearing – a sign of total though honourable surrender. Then, to the shock of everyone in the Kraal, *Vamba* raised his stolen spear and cried to the swarming Vamangwe: 'To me . . . the Vamangwe . . . to me! Kill these miserable old Nguni fools. Kill them all!'

The Vamangwe, most of whom were drunk and full of *mbanje* fumes in their bellies and heads, needed no second order; they fell upon the unarmed Tortoises and killed them with great cruelty.

Screaming men were shorn of their members of manhood by bloodthirsty and sadistic Vamangwe, using blunt knives and barbed fishing spears. *Vamba* and *Mukingo* stood side by side watching the fearful carnage with cold and contemptuous smiles on their cruel faces, nodding encouragement to those of their followers who tried to outdo one another in acts of cruelty. Shrill screams and loud death cries mingled with the wailing of children and the shrieks of frightened and horrified women.

Auuuu! The silver night so peaceful and lovely hitherto, was defiled by cries of fear and mortal agony and by the sight and smell of human blood. The brave warriors of the Tortoise Regiment were tortured and killed to the last man. But while the Vamangwe had been busy murdering the unarmed old warriors, ten of *Malandela's* servant boys, led by the two chief servant boys *Bafana* and *Madoda-Doda*, seized food and weapons and made their escape into the dark forest, mounted on ten of *Malandela's* strongest oxen and driving fifty fat cows before them. These brave boys were not stealing; they intended to take all these cattle to a hiding place far away in the mountains for safe keeping until *Malandela's* return. They had not the time in which to drive away all their King's cattle, but had done as much as they could in the time they did have.

When the Vamangwe had finished torturing and murdering the luckless old men, they stood over the blood-soaked piles of dead bodies and looked with feverish and hungry expectancy first at their leaders *Vamba* and *Mukingo*, and then at the vast crowd of women, virgins and children milling around like so many frightened impala.

With a harsh laugh, *Mukingo* made a sweeping gesture at the women and children, saying: 'They are all yours, Oh my jackals. Do with them what you will, but first seize and bring to me that haughty slut of a *Nomikonto*. She shall be initiated into womanhood by me, *Mukingo*, High Chief of both the Vamangwe and the Nguni.'

Rough hands seized the Princess *Nomikonto*, but she fought back savagely with her nails, feet and teeth. She bit the nose off one man and an ear off another. With her fists she knocked the teeth out of the mouths of ten men before she was seized and bound securely hand and foot.

They carried her away into the Great Hut and *Nomikonto* saw the little *Celiwe* break away from the clutches of a Vamangwe scoundrel who had seized her, and vanish behind one of the women's huts. She also had a brief glimpse of the First Queen *Muxakaza* struggling violently on the ground with a burly brute of a Vamangwe who was doing his best to crush the resistance of the fierce and beautiful albino woman under a shower of savage blows with his fists. Everywhere girls and women were locked in fierce struggles with snarling Vamangwe ravishers while children, dead and alive alike, were trampled like lost motherless lambs underfoot.

Nomikonto wept as she was roughly dragged by the hair through the low entrance of the Great Hut. She wept for herself and for the rest of the women throughout the world who were suffering similar indignities at the hands of cruel men – men who never thought once of the harm they do to the souls of their victims by forcibly breaking their 'pure womanhood'.

Nomikonto slowly opened her pain-misted eyes and saw *Mukingo* standing like an ugly shadow over her. He was obviously very pleased about what he had done and his cruel grin was a blotch of white ivory teeth against his ebony black ugly face, which glistened with sweat that ran in streams down to his chin. *Nomikonto* felt the stinging pain where *Mukingo's* sharp teeth had sunk into her smooth cheek at the height of his beastly passion. She also felt the pain where his nails had dug deep into the flesh of the small of her back.

'I have never had a woman like you, *Nomikonto*,' said *Mukingo* breathlessly. 'You must become my wife, my First Queen.'

'Never . . . never . . . will that happen . . . I would rather die!'

'A lot depends on how you die, beautiful one,' said *Mukingo* quietly. 'A lot depends on how and how soon you die . . .'

'Death is death, regardless of the *kaross* he is wearing,' quoted *Nomikonto* with equal calm. 'And if you do not kill me, I shall kill you, *Mukingo*!'

'I know you would, so I shall have to kill you first, you and the rest of *Malandela's* wives.'

'Thank you, you could not do us a greater favour. Kill us and get done with it.'

'Yes,' smiled *Mukingo*, 'I shall kill you, but it will not be a quick death.'

With a smile on his ugly face, the fat *Mukingo* dragged *Nomikonto* out of the Great Hut by one leg and flung her beside the unconscious forms of *Muxakaza*, *Zuzeni* and *Katalize*, who were lying like abandoned flowers in the dust. She heard *Mukingo* shout at his men: 'Keep all the virgins and younger women and make them your wives, but bring all *Malandela's* High Wives here. I have a very pleasant fate awaiting them, together with this hot-blooded *Nomikonto* here.

Nomikonto watched as more than eight hundred women, all wearing the towering *sicolo* hairstyles of the High Wives of *Malandela*, were dragged or pushed roughly towards the clearing near the Great Hut. Some were screaming at the tops of their voices; some were moaning silently to themselves. Others were lost in the mist of unconsciousness and oblivious of what was going on.

'Take these defiled sluts out of there as soon as day breaks, men,' said *Vamba* coldly. 'I want all of them taken far away to the Mahodi Cave and there sealed in alive. I have only sworn not to spill their blood, but not to kill them by entombing them alive. But first clear the kraal of all these stiffened cadavers quickly, and slaughter oxen for a midnight feast.'

While the Vamangwe army was busy carrying out *Vamba's* orders, one of the men came up to him and fell on his knees at his feet. 'I beg to tell you, Oh High One, that one of *Malandela's* wives, *Celiwe*, escaped into the forest a short while ago.'

'Why worry about that?' asked *Vamba* quietly. 'She won't get far with all those lions and leopards prowling through the forest. Go back to work and help the others.'

Celiwe was afraid and she was lost – lost in the depths of a dark forest that reverberated with the blood-chilling roars of numerous lions and she knew it was only a matter of time before one of those shaggy beasts found her. She now had one purpose in her fear-numbed brain and that was to find a tree she could climb – and as soon as possible. It was no longer a consolation to her that of all *Malandela's* wives she alone managed to escape the Vamangwe rapists, for what use is it to escape with one's honour intact and only become a lion's supper immediately afterwards.

Celiwe heard a rustling sound behind her and sank to her knees with a small scream of fear. She lay trembling in the long grass while the rustling came nearer and nearer. One part of her brain was telling her to get up and run while another was telling her to lie very still in the hope that whatever it was would pass her by.

Panic got the better of her, however, and she leapt to her feet with a wild scream and ran madly through the forest with a great leopard in playful pursuit. *Celiwe* ran like a wild hog, but the leopard reduced the distance between them. With a strength inspired by fear, *Celiwe* flew like a squirrel up a tall *mopani* tree – forgetting of course that unlike a lion, leopards can also climb trees. Thus, as she shinned up the tree, the old leopard clawed its way up after her and with a raking paw he tore the long skin skirt off her waist, narrowly missing her flesh.

Celiwe lost her hold and in a most un-feminine way she spun head over heels through the air landing with a thud on the ground in a stunned heap. When eventually she opened her eyes she found herself staring straight in the eyes of the leopard which was lying on its side an arm's length away. A long arrow was buried deep in its evil heart.

'I am saved ... I am saved!' she thought. But *Celiwe* was still in for a great surprise, because as she struggled to her feet, a gentle arm caught her wrist and pulled her erect. She found herself looking into the high cheeked, square chinned, hard-mouthed face of *Dambisa-Luwewe*, the witchdoctor woman of *Vamba's* group.

'You!' gasped *Celiwe*. 'You ...'

'Do not hate me, little *Celiwe*. I saved you because you and I must find a way of warning *Malandela* in the land of the Western Mambo before he starts something he will regret and which will plunge the whole land into great misery for many years. But first let me tell you that although I have always seemed to work together with *Vamba* and his friends ...'

'Seemed to work with them, *Dambisa*! How can you say, "although you seemed to work with them"?'

'Give me time, Oh Royal Wife *Celiwe*,' said *Dambisa*. 'Give me a little time to explain. Firstly, I am not a Vamangwe woman. I am not even a witchdoctor woman for that matter. You see, I am a woman from the Baluba nomad tribe and I have been following *Mukingo* and *Vamba* for two years to kill them for what they did to my father long ago. They do not know who I am, of course, and like you they mistake me for a Vamangwe woman.'

'But it does not make sense,' gasped *Celiwe*. 'You have been close enough to *Vamba* and *Mukingo* for two years now and if you really wanted to kill them you could have done so long ago. What have you been waiting for?'

To *Celiwe's* surprise *Dambisa's* eyes filled with tears as she said: 'There is a profound reason for my apparently senseless actions, *Celiwe*. You see, one of those two creatures has in his secret possession the dreaded stone called the Eye of *Odu*.'

'But that thing only exists in fairy tales and ancient legends.'

'The Eye of *Odu* is no fairy tale, *Celiwe*. It is a thing that does exist and unless somebody recovers it and returns it to its rightful owner soon, the tribes called Nguni and Western Mambo shall soon be but memories on the shores of bygone – and where there have been kraals full of people, lonely hyaenas shall howl.'

'These are awful words *Dambisa-Luwewe*,' said *Celiwe*. 'They fill me with fear and a terrible foreboding. Please tell me clearly what you mean.'

'Let us first climb up that big tree, as high as we can *Celiwe*,' *Dambisa* replied, indicating a huge frowning *marula* a hundred paces away. 'Then I shall tell you very clearly what I mean.'

Dambisa, who was heavily armed with a lion bow and a quiver full of arrows, as well as a long sharp *panga*, helped the little *Celiwe* up the tree and soon both women were seated high above the ground with the rough trunk of the tree at their backs and the empty air underneath their dangling feet. *Celiwe* was eating one of the sour-tasting *marula* fruits and listening wide-eyed to what *Dambisa* was telling her.

'In the great fortress known as Zima-Mbje there is a huge hollow idol representing the Ultimate Mother, who is said to be the Mother of the Great Spirit, and those who believe thus, look upon the Great Spirit as the Eternal *Piccanin* of the Ultimate Mother, because they feel that the Great Spirit holds the Universe like a child holds a toy. Within this great idol is an altar above which sat a small idol of bronze – an idol that always glowed as if red hot because within it was a mysterious stone with peculiar radiating qualities, called the Eye of *Odu*. Some say the stone is about the size of a baby's head. Very few men have seen this stone outside the bronze idol and those who have, died shortly afterwards. It is said that if one is exposed to the naked radiance of this stone, one's flesh starts to rot while one is still alive, and will come off one's bones in a mass of noisome putrefaction. If a man is exposed to the radiation of the naked stone, he dies. But when the rays are filtered through the body of the bronze idol and fall upon a man, he ceases to be an ordinary man; he becomes a super being, a half-god, and he can then see and do things no ordinary man can see or do. He can even become an immortal.

'Nobody is allowed inside the Idol of the Ultimate Mother and the only people who have had the privilege of exposing themselves to the mysterious filtered radiation of the Idol of the Eye, are the High Chief, the *Munumutaba* of Luvijiti and his First Wife *Namutaba*, and also a dozen warrior priests specially appointed to guard the Great Idol.

'It was always said that nobody would ever dare try to steal the glowing bronze idol and the proverb "as safe as the Bronze Idol" had become one of the most quoted in the empire of Luvijiti.

'My father, *Munengu*, who was a famous thief and who emigrated from the land of the Baluba far to the north into the empire of the Luvijiti with my mother long before I was born, decided to attempt to steal the well-guarded Bronze Idol – after my mother had playfully taunted him and actually challenged him to steal it as something more spectacular than stealing cattle. Much to my dismay, and my mother's horror, my father succeeded. He drugged the drinking water of the two guards and calmly walked away with the idol while they lay there, prostrate across the entrance to the Great Idol.

'We realised he had gone too far this time, and we fled northwards across the plains, with the idol still in our possession. Two months later we crossed the Zambezi into the land of the Nguni. For a few months my father hid the idol in a hole inside our hut. But one day he made the fatal mistake of boasting about his feat in the presence of *Mukingo*, during a beer-drinking feast.

'*Vamba* and *Mukingo* seized him and tortured all the information they wanted out of him. They then staked him to the ground and burnt him by lighting a big fire across his body. That same night they raided our kraal and killed my mother. However, I escaped by hiding in a grain pit.

'*Mukingo's* raiders found the idol, of course, and took it to their leader who hid it – nobody knows where. Because neither *Vamba* nor *Mukingo* had seen me before, I succeeded in posing as a Vamangwe witchdoctor woman and being drawn into their foul schemes against *Malandela*. My sole purpose was to try and find out where *Mukingo* had hidden the bronze idol, recover it, and then have *Vamba* and *Mukingo* pay for murdering my parents.

'So far I have still failed to discover where the idol is hidden. When it is found, I wish to see to it personally that it is returned to Luvijiti before it falls into the hands of yet more unscrupulous men, and before the spies now swarming all over the land of the Nguni send a messenger to the *Munumutaba* confirming their suspicion that the ones who stole the idol and now possess it, are in fact in the land of the

Nguni. In that case the *Munumutaba's* armies would invade the land of the Nguni and recover the idol by force. In an open war with the *Munumutaba*, the Nguni would be exterminated because so powerful are the armies of Luvijiti that nothing on this earth can stand in their way. I do not want the Nguni race to be wiped out simply because of my father's silly prank. I now want *Vamba* and *Mukingo* seized and made to tell where they hid the idol before it is too late.'

'How do you know that there are Luvijiti spies in the land of the Nguni, *Dambisa*? And why are you sure that the *Munumutaba* might attack our land?'

'The man *Luva*, whom the fools *Vamba* and *Mukingo* think is a Vamangwe and a friend, is in fact *Muvedu* the Cruel, one of the Warrior Priests of Zima-Mbje. I recognised him clearly, but he does not know me. I also recognised one of the lesser priests, *Luao*, who goes under the false name of *Dahodi*, and who travels from kraal to kraal in the land of the Nguni selling hippo-fat. The last time I saw *Luao* he was giving a long message stick to *Muvedu*.'

'Does *Luva*, or rather *Muvedu*, know that *Vamba* and *Mukingo* have the Eye of *Odu* in their possession?' asked *Celiwe*.

'He was not sure until two moons ago, when *Mukingo* casually made mention of a bronze idol he and *Vamba* have – hidden away somewhere,' replied *Dambisa*. 'Ever since, he has been trying to find out where they kept it. But, like me, he has failed. The message stick I saw *Luao*, or *Dahodi*, give to *Muvedu*, was from the *Munumutaba* himself and the message read that unless *Muvedu* succeeds in recovering the idol within two moons, the *Munumutaba* was going to attack the land of the Nguni and recover it by force. I stole into *Luva's* hut one night and read the message stick myself, while he was in council with *Malandela*. That was a moon ago and now I have only one moon left in which to find the cursed idol, before the *Munumutaba* strikes.'

'And,' said *Celiwe*, cutting *Dambisa* short, 'unless we can get to *Malandela* in time to stop him attacking his brother, the Nguni and the Western Mambo will stand no chance against the invader from the south. They are torn apart by mutual strife.'

'Yes, certainly – much depends now upon you and me. Let us pray to the Great Spirit it is not too late already!'

Despairingly *Celiwe* cried: 'Tell me, sister, what are we going to do now?'

'The first thing we have to do as soon as day breaks, is to reach your brother's kraal and ask your brother's two sons to accompany us – together with any other men we can find – into the land of the Western Mambo. We shall all have to ride on the backs of oxen to make the journey. Let us hope we are not too late.'

But the two heroic women were already too late – too late by a full day – to avert a terrible disaster and prevent the death of innocent people at the hands of the tempestuous fool named *Malandela.* Too late by one day were they, to prevent two great tribes from clashing head-on – two great tribes who were unaware of the mutual danger creeping upon them from the south and who were now becoming too filled with bitterness and hatred of each other to unite and face the common enemy in the form of *Munumutaba's* revengeful hordes.

The coming sun's first rays stain the drifting clouds a red-hot gold and loud in the trees is the song of many birds. Wisps of mist cling like passionate ghosts to the forests and the valleys, and crystal-clear dewdrops glisten on the leaves of every tree. The sun mounts higher in the eastern heavens and slowly the drifting mist is dispelled to the Seven Winds.

On the dew-wet grass thousands of trapdoor spider-webs stand out sharply – mysterious to behold. Alone, an impala emerges from the shadow of a tree, its bulging black eyes glistening in the soft early sunlight. Its shadow stretches long and strange-looking behind it. It has scented something – something whose smell strongly taints the morning breeze . . . human beings!

The lonely impala identifies the smell as that of Death. This it knows from sheer, bitter experience. So back into the friendly embrace of the sheltering bushes and shrubs, and away. It leaps with fluid grace among the dew-bejewelled shrubs. Then it pauses. It peers cautiously over a leafy bush . . . leaps up – and sees them, hundreds of them. But something is wrong here. Most of these human beings are females, and they look very unhappy. Some of them are weeping, others are pleading with the armed men who appear to be deaf. It seems as though all these many human females are captives and being taken somewhere for destruction. The little impala quakes with fear as it senses the evil afloat. It shivers to its very hooves and abruptly turns and flees; it has no wish to be tainted by the aura of evil that radiates from the brains of the leading human beings – like rays from an evil star.

'Waa-ugh! Waa-ugh!'

Old Konde, the baboon, is puzzled. He scratches his red itching buttock and glares malevolently at the strange behaviour of the human beings far down below the great rock on which he is perched, his wife at his side.

'*Waa-ugh*!' She wants to know 'why'.

'I do not know,' he barks back, equally puzzled.

Yes . . . he does not know why these queer human beings down there did what he saw them do. They drove a vast number of their females into a great cave that yawns at the base of the mighty mountain on whose lower slopes he and his family have their home. Now those incredible human creatures are working hard to seal the great cave with boulders to prevent the females from getting out. One of them has just run screaming from the cave, but has been knocked down by two of the males, who carried her back into the cave between them. Now the cave is closed and the fifty males pick up their weapons and sticks and return to the forest below.

Konde wonders why so many good-looking and healthy females are being wasted just like that. He knows somehow in his baboon way that his baboon brain will not be able to fathom the situation. 'Now,' he thinks, 'if I had so many females, I would not waste them like that.'

Mukingo was standing at the gate of the Great Kraal he had now taken over as his own, watching hundreds of his Vamangwe warriors building a triple stockade. He had ordered the kraal to be heavily fortified so that 'not even a mouse can get in'. The new stockades were going to bristle with sharp stakes and barbed metal points. Loud in his ears was the sound of axes biting wood, hammers hitting red-hot metal, beating it into jagged points. Loud in his ears was the chanting, cursing and whistling of two thousand toiling men.

Mukingo saw his cousin *Vamba* coming up the footpath that wound its way up to the first gate, followed by *Luva* and the rest of the men who had gone with him to entomb *Malandela's* High Wives in the Mahodi cave. *Mukingo* could see from the hard smile *Vamba* wore that everything had gone strictly according to plan. But if *Vamba* was smiling, *Mukingo* was most uneasy and the dark clouds of foreboding were obstructing the sun of triumph within his evil soul. He had achieved his life's greatest ambition at long last, yet for some reason he was not at all happy. He was now a ruler of men but the beer of triumph had turned acid in his stomach.

He was as uneasy as a locust in a herdboy's frying bowl. He enjoyed being High Chief about as much as one would enjoy a claypot full of bitter *mbiza* purgative. His expression revealed this clearly to *Vamba*, whose keen eyes rarely missed anything, however small and insignificant.

Vamba asked in his usual mocking tone: 'Why is my great and valiant cousin looking like a bilious hippopotamus this morning? What have you eaten – or what is eating you, Oh *Mukingo*?'

'Nothing is eating me, *Vamba*,' snarled *Mukingo*. 'I'm only thinking – about many things . . .'

'The only things you are always thinking about are women,

Mukingo, and it must be very ugly women you are thinking of now – to bring such an expression on your usual ugly face.'

'*Vamba*,' said *Mukingo*, 'I am not well . . . What in the name of the dog with ten heads is thaaaat?'

Everybody turned and looked towards where *Mukingo* was pointing and they saw what looked like a woman, daubed from head to foot with white clay, coming up the footpath. She seemed to be carrying a stick on which was impaled a man's head. As the fearsome feminine apparition came nearer, everybody except *Mukingo, Luva* and *Vamba*, took to their heels and fled like rabbits into the forest.

Slowly, like a sleepwalker, the white-daubed woman approached the three men. *Mukingo* took a few steps back and then checked himself with a prayer that brought a strange light into the eyes of the man both he and *Vamba* knew by the name of *Luva*: 'Eye of *Odu*, defend us!'

The daubed zombie stopped two paces away from the three men and *Vamba* snatched the message stick out of her hand. The partly decomposed human head fell to the ground with a ghastly thud and *Mukingo* leapt up with a hoarse scream as a piece of worm-infested flesh splattered over his right foot.

Vamba read the message on the stick slowly and carefully: 'Rotten hyaena – we are watching you – one day we shall kill and eat you – you vile deformed killer of his own father – we, the three females and one old blind immortal.'

'The Lost Immortal has found us, Oh *Vamba*,' croaked *Mukingo*. 'What are we going to do?'

'Be silent, you whining son of a rabid cur!' grated *Vamba*. 'Remember that we have the Eye of *Odu* and with it we can rout any immortals, be they lost or found!' And to the vacant-faced painted woman *Vamba* coldly snapped: 'Go and tell whoever it is who sent you that I, *Vamba Nyaloti*, am waiting for him to come any time he chooses. I may be a rotten hyaena but I still have teeth.'

'I . . . will . . . tell . . . him,' said the zombie as she turned to go. The three men watched her until she was lost among the distant trees.

Suddenly *Vamba* spun around and faced *Luva*, an expression of incredible hatred on his face. The next thing *Mukingo* heard was the dull cracking thud as *Vamba's* hissing *panga* sliced *Luva's* head clean off – sending it tumbling off his shoulders and rolling away, before the body dropped.

'*Vamba*, you mad fool!' roared *Mukingo*. 'You have killed him, you foul dog! What in the name of a million demons has got into you?'

'Nothing,' said *Vamba* coldly. 'Come closer and have a look, you stupid son of a hog!' To *Mukingo's* great surprise, *Vamba* ripped the loinskin off the dead body and kicked it over so that it lay on its right side. 'Look! Look at this dog's left buttock! Since when have we Vamangwe started worshipping the moon?'

Mukingo's eyes bulged as he stared at the shining tribal scar on the left buttock of the dead body. It represented a crescent moon within a circle of tiny raised nodules representing stars. 'Well, fool!' hissed *Vamba* coldly. 'What do you say now?'

'He was not one of us,' said *Mukingo* pensively.

'Of course he was not! But what do you make of it?' dernanded *Vamba.*

'I don't know . . .' said *Mukingo,* scratching his head in puzzlement.

'Listen fool, that tribal scar is very similar to the design on the belly of the glowing idol we have. I think this dog here is of the tribe in the south from which the idol was stolen. He has been trying to steal it back. Now do you understand?'

Mukingo's eyes flashed as an idea swept through his brain like a bolt of lightning. '*Vamba* – this could mean there are more of these dogs posing as Vamangwe. Come my cousin, we must act now!'

'Someone has started to think at last! What do you aim to do, *Mukingo,* smell them out?'

'You will soon see.' *Mukingo* flew into the kraal and bellowed at the top of his voice: 'To me . . . everybody . . . to me . . . hurry . . . hurry!'

Warriors came running out of the huts and the forest where they had been hiding. They assembled in their hundreds in the centre of the kraal. Then *Mukingo* raised his voice and once again gave a strange and totally unexpected order: 'Every man take off his loinskin!'

Men stared at one another in total disbelief. They shook their heads and some raised their eyebrows in puzzled inquiry. Some even laughed nervously while others looked at both *Vamba* and *Mukingo* surreptitiously and tapped their foreheads.

'You heard me!' roared *Mukingo.* 'Every man take off his loinskin!'

'As you say, Oh Chief, growled a heavily built giant named *Mbobo.* 'But tell us, are you going to clean out our bowels with a horn?'

'A truce to your jokes, *Mbobo,*' growled *Mukingo.* 'Do as I say!'

Mbobo tore off his loinskin and playfully tossed it at *Mukingo's* feet. Then he turned his back to his leader and bowed politely. 'I hope my great Chief likes my humble backside.'

With roars of laughter the remainder of the Vamangwe followed suit and soon *Vamba* and *Mukingo* were being entertained by the rather unnerving sight of thousands of pairs of buttocks lined up in neat rows.

However, one of the men refused to remove his loinskin. He turned and tried to bolt for the gate. But *Vamba* was too fast for him and soon the two were struggling violently in the dust. *Mukingo* joined the struggle and knocked the man, a rascal named *Dahodi*, unconscious with a blow from his great fist. *Vamba* tore off the man's loinskin and . . . sure enough, as with the dead *Luva*, there was a crescent scar on his left buttock.

'So, we captured another spy . . . Kill him!' cried *Mukingo*.

'We shall question him first,' said *Vamba*. 'Revive him, *Mbobo*, and then we shall take him out into the forest to the village of the warrior ants.'

Dahodi was revived with water splashed over him by *Mbobo*. Then he was frogmarched into the forest by *Mbobo*, *Lusu* and *Mabewe*, with *Vamba*, *Mukingo* and fifteen other men bringing up the rear. *Mukingo* carried a heavy rawhide rope with a noose on one end, and he was grinning most fiendishly. At last they came to a great donga in the forest, a donga so old that its walls were heavily overgrown with small bushes and other vegetation. Far down below, at the bottom of the donga, was a cluster of six great anthills swarming with thousands upon thousands of the great tribe of ants called the 'Warriors of Sunrise', – the biggest kind of ant in existence. *Dahodi* could see human bones bleaching in the sun far below, bones of victims fed long ago to the terrible ants by *Malandela*, who had discovered this strange colony by accident while still a boy. *Dahodi* watched as *Vamba's* men cut down a tall slender tree and trimmed off the branches. Then *Mukingo* slipped the noose of the long rope under *Dahodi's* armpits and drew it tight, while *Mbobo* tied his hands and feet firmly. The other end of the rope was tied to the thin end of the trunk.

The trunk was then carefully thrust over the edge of the great donga by the fifteen men who afterwards sat on the thicker end to prevent it from slipping into the donga completely. *Vamba* forced the captive towards the edge and pushed him over. He did not fall to the bottom, but dangled in the air with the top of the tallest anthill just brushing the soles of his feet.

'*Dahodi*,' said *Vamba* coldly, 'unless you wish us to feed you to the ants down there you must open your ugly mouth and answer my questions clearly and truthfully.'

'I have nothing to tell you,' gritted *Dahodi* through clenched teeth.

The men at the other end of the trunk slowly raised it off the ground with the result that *Dahodi* sank until he was standing with feet bound securely together in the middle of the cluster of anthills. *Dahodi* screamed loudly as the dreaded ants swarmed in their hundreds up his legs. Soon it was feeling as if he had been plunged feet first in a pot of boiling water. Blood ran down his legs as the attackers burrowed into his flesh.

'Mercy . . . mercy . . . I shall talk! I shall tell you anything you want to know. But please pull me up!'

'That is good!' exclaimed *Mukingo*, rubbing his hands gleefully. 'Come on men, lift him up a bit and let him talk first before we free him from his misery.' The last words were spoken in a manner so ominous that the men holding the trunk felt an icy coldness in their stomachs. They raised the screaming *Dahodi* to his original position above the anthills.

'Well, start chattering, my little monkey and let us hear what you have to tell us,' called *Vamba* pleasantly.

Dahodi told them everything they wanted to know – that his real name was *Luao*; about his mission; the names of other spies in the land of the Nguni – and concluded by telling them of *Munumutaba's* intended attack next moon, to recover the bronze idol and to extend his already vast empire at the same time.

When he had finished, *Vamba* ordered the men holding down the trunk to release it. The luckless spy fell on his back amongst the anthills – and the trunk fell across him, pinning him down, while thousands of ants proceeded to devour him to the bones.

Plans flowed in a wild cataract down the gorges in *Vamba's* evil mind. As they walked slowly back to the kraal he poured out the results of his quick-thinking brain into the ears of his friends:

'*Malandela* is a very unpopular chief with his subjects. Many people hate him for his cruelty and stubbornness. There are many amongst the Nguni who will follow us, *Mukingo*, who will be glad that we have seized power. I know some of them. I will go to their kraals to rally them to our side to greatly reinforce our armies. Listen, *Mukingo*, we are facing two enemies now – this *Munumutaba* and *Malandela* who might return quickly if word gets to him that we have seized his High Seat. We must be strong enough to meet anyone of these two who marches into this land first. You must set a thousand Vamangwe to work immediately making no less than five hundred battle canoes. Let them use the greatest trees they can find. I want our army to be able to resist any invader trying to cross the Zambezi.

'The fate of this land will be decided on the waters of the Zambezi in the case of *Munumutaba's* attack. And you must set another thousand warriors at work to quadruple the stockades around the Great Kraal. I want every major kraal and village heavily fortified within two or four days. Send messages to every kraal in the land. Now, be quick – we have little time.'

Such was *Vamba's* skill at talking and deceiving people into believing him and *Mukingo* that by sunset the following day he had succeeded beyond his wildest dreams. He had succeeded in turning thousands of discontented Nguni peasants and war-lords against their lawful king, the tyrant *Malandela*, who was deeply hated by many of his subjects. *Vamba* held one great *indaba* meeting after another. On the one day alone he held three great meetings, each attended by no fewer than thirty thousand men.

He promised them many things. He bribed some of the war-lords with many cattle from *Malandela's* many overflowing pens. He even frightened some into joining him by threatening to send his *tokoloshes* after them.

Thousands of peasants and even *nswelaboya* outlaws flocked to join the army of *Mukingo* which soon swelled into twenty thousand fighting men – all sworn to fight for *Vamba* and *Mukingo* to the last drop of blood.

Strong forts and lookout posts were soon being built throughout the land. In the absence of the lawful ruler of the Nguni, the Viper that was *Vamba* tightened his coils around the sceptre of the Nguni tribe, and *Malandela's* throne was seized from under him while he yet lived.

To gain further popularity for himself, *Mukingo* abolished the law that said every man in whose kraal three calves were born should send two to the Great Kraal as tribute to the king. Yes, great grew the popularity of *Mukingo* in those four memorable days after he had seized power in the land of the Nguni. But for some reason, even he could not understand, *Mukingo* felt more and more uneasy and afraid.

The feeling of uneasiness grew as the days passed. It preyed upon his soul so much that he began to imagine everybody was plotting to murder him and that assassins lurked behind every bush he saw. He refused to eat, yelling that there was poison or voodoo potion in the food. He felt all alone in a world full of thousands of shadowy whispering plotters and sneering assassins. He even killed one of his new wives, believing she was coming into the hut to strangle him as he slept. He tore up his favourite hunting dog with his bare hands, and ate some of its flesh raw, thinking it was *Nomikonto* creeping up behind him to stab him in the back.

Then, on the tenth night of his reign, he crawled into his hut and sat for a long time with his shoulders sagging and his eyes staring fixedly at the roaring fire in the centre. He suddenly imagined he heard someone moving behind him and shafts of fear tore through him. He spun around and saw his own shadow dancing on the curved wall of the hut. His brain gave it blood-red glaring eyes and a mouth full of jagged teeth. *Mukingo* was bathed in cold sweat as he leapt to his feet crying, 'Who are you?' The shadow gave back no reply and

Mukingo drew his *panga* and shrieked: 'You have come to kill me – have you? Well, I shall kill you first!'

Mukingo lashed out at the shadow with his *panga* and, of course, the shadow also struck back at him. 'You won't kill me . . . I won't let you . . . !'

Bundles of grass flew in all directions as the madman's *panga* slashed the hut to pieces around him. Leaping from wall to wall, *Mukingo* chased his own shadow around the hut, hacking and hewing at what he thought was an assassin lashing equally fiercely at himself. Then, in his frenzy of madness, *Mukingo* hacked down the three posts that supported the domed roof of the hut and it collapsed about his ears with a great sigh. *Mukingo* was borne down by the weight of the grass onto the fireplace and died screaming in the inferno that followed when the dry grass caught fire and burnt fiercely, fanned by a brisk night breeze.

The following day *Vamba* proclaimed himself chief of the Vamangwe, which included the Nguni.

FROM THE CLAWS OF DEATH

While *Vamba* and *Mukingo* were busy torturing the Luvijiti spy *Dahodi* in the donga of the warrior ants, much was happening to *Nomikonto* and the eight hundred and fifty Royal Wives whom they had entombed alive in the great Mahodi cave. It was dark, damp and hot in the cave and the women were crammed with barely room in which to move. Gradually the humid air grew foul for human lungs. The gasping women had long since abandoned their fruitless efforts at moving the great rocks that sealed the mouth of the cave and they no longer had the breath with which to scream for help. *Nomikonto* knew she was looking in the face of the cruellest death any human being can ever die, and she was terribly frightened. It is one thing to think about death; facing it is another. Princess *Nomikonto* wanted to live. She did not have the courage to resign herself to the dark embrace of death as the laws of the tribes say one should, and as *Muxakaza* and the other older women had advised her to do. The blanketing fog of wet and airless heat was heavy on her lungs and nostrils and in her gasping she only sucked in more of the foul air.

Her head ached dully and there was a continuous noise within her brain now. The moaning, gasping women had all fallen and lay in a great pile at *Nomikonto's* feet – the top ones crushing and smothering those below. *Nomikonto* alone was standing now, or doing her best to stand by pressing her back against the rough rock and even trying the impossible feat of digging her fingers into its cruel unyielding surface. She knew she did not have long to go – she actually felt herself falling . . . falling . . .

'No . . . I cannot die . . . I cannot just lie down and die. I am *Nomikonto* – child of a warrior king.'

Slowly, painfully, the girl staggered to her feet and started moving along the walls of the great cave – stumbling over the bodies of her fellow victims, some of whom were still choking and struggling violently on the ground while others were already lying very still . . . lifeless.

'No . . . no!' moaned *Nomikonto* to herself, 'We can't die like this – there must be a way . . .'

How long she kept on edging her way along the side of the cave she could not tell. The cave was indeed very big. Something gave her the strength to fight on and that something was a small flame that kindled itself in her subconscious mind – a flame that brought back to her memory an old legend she had once heard as a child. And the legend concerned the very cave in which she now faced death.

On she went, edging her way along the rocks which cut and bruised her back and broke the nails of her fingers . . .

Then, suddenly she felt a wide cleft between two different portions of rock and pouring through this cleft came a steady stream of life-giving air. She pushed her face into the space and took breath after breath of the cool living air. She breathed in and out – faster and faster – and then found her voice: 'Air, air, air!'

Filled with new strength and hope – and madness – the girl tried to enlarge the cleft by pulling, yes, tugging to pull the rocks apart. But the great masses of granite held fast. Then she tried to push them apart – and there came a faint crackling. She actually felt the rock on the side move ever so slightly.

With fresh hope, the woman pushed with all her might and what felt like a big monstrous boulder again moved almost imperceptibly. There was another sudden sound as an unseen rock, dislodged by the slight movement, fell and thudded into the ground an arm's length away to her right. She shuddered at her narrow escape but immediately continued pushing against the slowly yielding boulder. Another rock was dislodged and now a jet of cold air poured into the cave. 'We are saved, we are saved!'

This cry reached the other women and passed from one to another of those who were still conscious. Bodies came to life and started crawling across other bodies – following in the direction of the gush of fresh air. 'Help! Help me . . . do not leave me . . . I am not dead! But I cannot get up . . . I cannot move . . . !'

Nomikonto heard the cacophony of sounds and struggles and called out: 'This is *Nomikonto* here. All those able to move, help those still alive and work your way across in this direction. I command you, in the name of the High One, *Malandela*!'

'It shall be done, Oh my Royal sister-in-law,' came the husky voice of the First Queen *Muxakaza*. 'But where in the name of the great spirit does all this air come from?'

'It seems that the old legends were right, Oh *Muxakaza*,' said *Nomikonto*. 'This cave is one of the entrances to the underground river Lulungwa-Mangakatsi which flows northwards into the great lake Nyanza. The rush of air comes from that terrible river – as does the noise.'

'But how did you manage to let the air in, Oh High One,' asked *Katazile* out of the dark.

'I had to push this big rock a little,' the princess replied. 'And I think if many of us can push against it, we might roll it completely away.'

'How big is it?'

'About the size of a half-grown elephant. But it is round and can be rolled aside.'

'All women to the High Princess,' shouted the First Queen. 'All women able to do something, move across to the Royal Child and help her with the rock. I am going back to help the others who are still unconscious – and I need two to give me a hand.'

Women moved in the darkness. One of them blew her nose noisily and spat. There were moans from those regaining consciousness amongst the pile of bodies on the floor. One sobbed piteously in the dark: 'Mother, do not let me die . . . help me . . . help me . . .'

Women groped their way towards *Nomikonto* and soon fifty hands were placed on the great rock to push it back. 'Lord of my fathers!' cried one of the women, the tall, broad-hipped and beautiful *Lulamani*, the dancer, also nicknamed *Ncelebana* (man-hungry harlot) by her fellow Royal Wives because of her unquenchable thirst for the love-mat. 'By the Tree of Life's kiss . . . what is this here on the rock?'

'What is it, *Lulamani*?' asked Nomikonto.

'It is an inscription, Royal One – an inscription cut deep into the rock.'

'Can you trace its meaning with your fingers?' asked *Nomikonto.*

'Wait, let me feel. No, I cannot make out any of these – incestuous and defiled signs'

'Stop using dirty words, you man-hungry slut,' cried *Nomikonto.* 'You are the only one of us who can read inscriptions on rocks and drums. Come on, read it!'

'Seduce me, Oh crocodiles,' swore *Lulamani* vehemently. 'I think . . . I think I can make out some of the adulterous things.'

'Well, tell us what the inscriptions say!'

Lulamani traced out sign after sign which, although they had apparently been cut into the rock tens of thousands of years ago by men who spoke the First Language – the language from which all tribal languages sprang – could still be deciphered by anyone from any tribe who had been trained to read them.

Lulamani eventually succeeded in deciphering all the characters and could read the message straight: 'Future generations, we are warning you. There is much secret evil behind this round rock – do not touch it. We, the last two alive of the Children of the Star, a male and female, are warning you. We who are to die tomorrow, are warning you all.'

'Oh my father!' gasped *Nomikonto.*

'Who were they?' asked *Katazile.* 'Who were the Children of the Star?'

'It is one of the forbidden stories which no one must retell,' said *Lulamani.* 'And I shall tell it to you on the understanding that you will never repeat it to anyone else if we get out of here alive.'

'*If* we get out alive,' said *Nomikonto.*

'The Children of the Star were a tribe that existed long before the coming of the Strange Ones. They were a tribe of Wizards who spent their lives looking for things we must not try to know and they lived in a Forbidden Valley near the land of the Nyasa. The great Goddess *Ma* destroyed the Forbidden Valley with Muotamkulu, the Great Fire, after the Children of the Star had started creating a Goddess for themselves – a Goddess who was the most perfect being ever created in the Universe.'

'What?' cried *Nomikonto.* 'The Children of the Star created a Goddess?'

'Yes,' said *Lulamani*, 'and this so angered the Goddess *Ma* that she destroyed the Children of the Star utterly with disease and fire. All the artificial animals they created were destroyed as well, except those we know today as the quagga, the giraffe and the okapi, which somehow escaped destruction and now mingle freely with other animals in the forest.'

'So that is why the giraffe has no voice!' exclaimed *Katazile.* 'Because it is man-made and not god-made!'

'Yes, and that is why the okapis and quaggas are such imperfect and strange-looking beasts. Their ancestors were not created by the Tree of Life.'

'But why do we regard these beasts as sacred then?' asked the inquisitive *Katazile.*

'Because through them we commemorate the Children of the Star who were the only human beings ever created, who reached the Peak of Ultimate Perfection. They had so evolved themselves that they were free from hatred, fear, greed, lust, let alone disease. They were more perfect than *Ma* herself the First Goddess. That is why they were utterly destroyed. The Universe is no place for Perfection and in the eyes of the Great Spirit, Perfection is as bad as Evil. Once a race has reached Ultimate Perfection it automatically loses its purpose – like a runner who stops when he has reached his goal as there is no purpose in continuing.'

'But what evil can there be behind this rock?' demanded *Nomikonto.* 'We cannot stay here and die of hunger and thirst. We must try and find a way out of here and the only way is beyond this rock.'

'We might be lost forever in the underground tunnels through which the Hidden River flows, Princess,' answered *Lulamani* soberly. 'But I think a quick death is better than a slow one through hunger and thirst.'

'It is said there are places where the Hidden River flows for short distances through deep gorges open to the sky before it disappears underground again, *Lulamani,*' said *Nomikonto.* 'If we find we can walk along the banks of the Hidden River, we might find such a place.'

'Assuming that the Hidden River has banks along which we can walk,' responded *Lulamani* quietly.

'But after all, what have we to lose by trying? We would only lose our man-defiled bodies anyway,' said *Nomikonto.*

'I do not consider myself defiled simply because a few Vamangwe took me by force,' smiled *Lulamani.*

'You filthy slut! You are without womanly pride and honour,' shrieked *Nomikonto.*

'You can call me a dirty slut, Oh Royal Child, but I am a far better woman than you in many ways. I have learnt to face life's hardships

with a smile. I do not surround myself with a shell of artificial pride. Neither do I lay claim to an imaginary honour and dignity I do not possess. Thus no amount of abuse from men would ever make me feel deprived of things that I only imagine I have.

'You are just the opposite – you are now prepared to throw your young life away simply because you lost imaginary honour at the hands of *Mukingo* who, after all, only did to you what some man would have done sooner or later, and who only did to you what you were created for.

'People like you never last long in this cruel world. You are too stiff-necked to bow your head to the tempest of life. You are like a wretched little tree that tries to resist the fury of the storm instead of yielding to it gracefully and surviving. Unless you are capable of sinking your imaginary pride occasionally in the course of your life, you might find yourself taking a mighty jump over a precipice one day, so intolerable will your life soon become!'

Nomikonto said nothing. She knew there was nothing to say, because *Lulamani* was right. She knew that in spite of *Lulamani's* unnatural hunger for men, she was the wisest woman who ever walked the earth. Every word that fell from her sensuous lips was a word of wisdom deeper than lake Nyanza. *Lulamani* was an expert at making people face the facts of life instead of deceiving themselves. Her words opened the eyes of those who deluded themselves and they also brought joy to those in sorrow and hope to those in despair.

In the darkness of despair and sorrow, *Lulamani* always shone like a Star of Hope, just as she outshone all women under the sun when it came to the hour of love. 'Well, what are we going to do now?' said *Nomikonto* after a long pause. 'Do we stay here or do we push this rock away and challenge the darkness beyond?'

'Evil harms only those who look for it – at least, that is what the Old Ones say,' said *Lulamani.* 'I say that we push the rock away and take our chance in the dark beyond. If there is anything evil lurking behind this rock it can only harm us if we look for it. We are not looking for evil or for secrets of the past; we are only interested in finding our way out of this evil place.'

Of the eight hundred and fifty women who had been urged at spearpoint by *Vamba* and his men into the Mahodi cave, only five hundred and sixteen were left alive; the rest were lying very still in the dust of the great cave – sleeping the last sleep from which there could be no awakening.

Muxakaza tried again and again to revive many of them, but in vain. The beautiful albino queen wept continuously as she groped her way from body to body, trying her best to shake life into each one, feeling for the beat of a heart here and there and screaming loudly when she found that the heart was stilled for all time. She let out a loud wail of surprise when she found that one woman had committed suicide by stabbing herself with a small knife which she must have smuggled in under her skin skirt.

'Withdraw the knife from the body,' said *Nomikonto.* 'We might need it.'

At a command from *Nomikonto* the women who had come forward to help her placed their hands and shoulders once more against the rock and pushed with all their combined effort. They pushed, relaxed, pushed again – and yet again. Each time they pushed they felt the rock give way a little more.

Suddenly it yielded. It rolled away from the straining women, causing many to lose their balance and fall forward on their faces in the darkness. Then there came an ominous rumble from the roof of the cave, a sound that told of great slabs about to collapse on the heads of the sweating women. 'Get back . . . get back! Run for your lives!' shrieked *Nomikonto.*

'The defiled rocks want to crush us,' cried *Lulamani.* 'Run for your unclean lives, you foul bitches!'

There was a noise like a million thunders – one continuous hellish roar as vast slabs of the roof crashed to the floor. A great gust of air hurled many of the women across to the far side of the cave like so many goatskin dolls. The ground underfoot shook and heaved under the incredible blows it received, while showers of living sparks flew in all directions. Clouds of smothering dust billowed in the darkness while sharp rocks darted from the great roof – splinters that dropped like spears, penetrating skulls and bodies and pinning them to the ground. Shrieks of agony and fear in that tumult of sound were like squeaks from newborn mice against the peal of midsummer thunder.

Gradually the fury of the rocks spent itself. There was still an occasional thud – then, silence. It was a long agonising silence, interrupted only by a hiss of breath escaping from a crushed and mangled body – and a low moan here and there.

At last a husky voice sounded hollow in the darkness: 'This is the First Wife *Muxakaza* . . . this is the First Wife. Please will anyone still alive call out.'

'Princess *Nomikonto* here,' came another voice. 'I am shaken but unhurt.'

Another throaty and musical voice floated out of the dark: 'Likewise here . . . it will take more than an incestuous rock to kill me. I'm destined to live till I manage to make an adulterer of your future husband, Oh *Nomikonto.*'

'Is that you, *Lulamani*?'

'It is. You weren't expecting me to get killed by any chance, were you?'

'As a matter of fact I was,' said *Muxakaza*, forcing a nervous laugh.

After that, other women called out and identified themselves and, to *Nomikonto's* horror, only two hundred and twenty-eight women were left alive – and the inquisitive, talkative *Katazile* was among the dead.

Nomikonto wept silently by herself while *Muxakaza* groped among the rocks in the darkness to find the badly wounded women and those pinned down by the rocks with their legs or arms crushed. She put them out of their misery by plunging the little knife into their still pulsing hearts. After this, the survivors made a careful search of the dark cave for any there might be who were lying unconscious. But they found none.

It was during this search that one of the women came upon something most unusual which greatly helped them in their journey – their fantastic and perilous journey along the bank of the terrible river Lulungwa-Mangakatsi, deep, deep down in the bowels of the earth. *Duduza* smelt burning hide and saw a red glow, a fiery patch that was being fanned by the strong draught in the cave into small flickering flames. A spark from the falling rocks had landed on the skin skirt of a dead woman and been miraculously fanned into a steady smouldering fire. *Duduza* shouted to *Nomikonto* and reported her strange find.

It did not take the three leading women long to realise that they now had fire to light them on their way. Soon after *Nomikonto* had torn the skirt off the dead woman and whirled it round and about to fan the smouldering patch into flame, a handsome fire was burning in one corner of the cave. Scores of willing hands were collecting bundles of dry grass that had blown into the cave in the course of years and torches were being made by rolling these bundles into torn pieces of skirt.

Two hundred and twenty-eight women had to sacrifice their skirts to make two torches each. At last *Nomikonto, Lulamani* and *Muxakaza*, each carrying a lighted torch (the others carrying two unlit spares each) led the way down the gently sloping tunnel along which the great inscribed boulder had rolled – down, and still farther down, into the very womb of the earth.

There was a loud roar like that of a thousand waterfalls in the ears of the women and great gusts of wind threatened to blow out the three flickering torches. Each woman knew they were nearing the dreaded Lulungwa-Mangakatsi and there was fear in every pulsing heart. In the dull light of the flickering torches, one could see clearly the expressions of horror and barely repressed panic on the faces of the women. One could see heaving chests and the sweat of pure terror glistening on each dark-brown, ebony-black, yellowish-brown, and even one albino-pink face.

The leading women emerged from the narrow sloping tunnel on to a wide ledge that ran along one side of a cavern so vast that its roof was lost in the darkness above, and it seemed to carry on like a tunnel of incredible size that twisted and turned over unbelievable distances deep under the earth. The river flowed far down below the ledge on which the women stood, gazing down with awe and horror.

'Let us go,' cried *Nomikonto* above the roar of the dreaded Lulungwa-Mangakatsi. 'Follow me . . . let us keep moving.'

Like soulless puppets the women followed the sister of their husband. To their left, far below, roared the Hidden River and to their right towered a vertical face of ugly scowling rock which rose and was lost in the darkness above. They proceeded with this perilous march, like a long serpent, for a period that felt like many days. In the course of this journey two of the women sank to the ground exhausted from hunger and injuries. They had to be left behind to their fate. Another woman went mad and pushed three others over the ledge before *Muxakaza* could stab her to death and dispose of her in the same way.

---

* *To be entombed in a cave with the only known exit blocked and to proceed with reconnoitring alternative unknown routes that might lead to another exit, is an experience both hazardous and nightmarish. The experiences of* Malandela's *wives have been reconstructed from numerous tales, stories, legends and songs that have survived for many generations. This account may be more factual – historically true – than meets the eye. If we should accept as an historical fact that* Malandela's *wives were actually entombed under circumstances not greatly different from those depicted, and we are prepared to accept the size of his seraglio, which is not unusual, we may accept even more readily that some of these wives had actually seen daylight again.*

If not, their experience inside the cave must have been improvised by subsequent storytellers, in which case the entire account is an improvisation. Those that survived would almost certainly have related widely differing accounts, influenced by individual imagination. Future legends on which the present is based, are a glossary of those accounts that sounded most fascinating. The author has sketched so far a picture designed to illustrate the hazardous part of the women's various experiences and this picture is physically possible at least, if not historically true. On subsequent pages the author proceeds to sketch their nightmarish experiences, also based on legends. However, it would appear that a great deal of mythology crept into the generalised legendary story that was subsequently formulated. Conversely, the generalised story had in the course of time contributed a further chapter to an already existing and colourful mythology.

At one time the women came to a place where part of the ledge had collapsed into the river, leaving only a narrow part very close to the rock face. Here, *Nomikonto* ordered the women to get down on their stomachs and crawl across one by one. And here death claimed five of the women, all having lost their nerve and falling to their doom in the river below.

After that the nightmarish journey continued without further incident for another long stretch of time, in which the women's endurance was systematically drained away. Eventually they all decided to lie down on the ground for a rest, and await death for that matter, as they could walk no farther.

Lulamani was the first to see the monster creeping upon the women from behind. She was the only woman who still had a torch firmly in her hand. Unlike the others, who were all lying down, some sleeping, she was sitting upright and she saw the nightmare horror creep upon them from the dismal darkness.

The monster was bigger than the largest elephant and it was covered all over with scales that looked more like shards of granite than ordinary scales. It had two round heads, each with yellow-luminous and split-pupilled eyes, and each head was mounted on a separate long scaly neck remotely resembling that of a giraffe. Under the luminous eyes of each head snarled a reddish mouth with countless fangs. It had four webbed, scaly arms and it walked on two elephantine hindlegs. It had a tail whose length was lost in the darkness beyond.

Lulamani stared at the horrible thing in utter disbelief and watched paralysed as it picked up four of the sleeping women and hurled them into the river below, before stooping to pick up four more. She then hurled one of the burning torches straight at the drooling mouth of one of the heads and had the satisfaction of seeing the smoky brand vanish into that vast and terrible cavity.

The monster uttered a roar and a bellow which shook the entire cavern and temporarily drowned even the roar of the river. The women awoke and more than two hundred pairs of eyes widened as they saw the monster. Fear lent great strength to the legs of all the women as they rose as one, and ran as they had never run in all their lives. They ran like the very wind, with *Muxakaza* and *Nomikonto* leading. *Lulamani* was now in the rear, her flaming torch still clutched firmly in her hand.

The monster was after them, its eyes ablaze with murderous hatred and its two mouths wide open, displaying terrible teeth. The monster gained on *Lulamani* and it was only twenty paces behind her when the ledge collapsed under its great weight. It vanished into the dark depths with loud trumpeting screams of fear. There was a tremendous splash far below and the unearthly creature was no more – but the women kept on running as if the ghost of the monster was still after them.

There were exactly two hundred of them left now and they were all in the last stages of exhaustion. They were no longer walking erect, but were crawling on hands and knees like babies. Only the strongest, swiftest and bravest of them had survived, and now it looked as if death would soon claim all of them at once. The strongest wish in every heart was now to die – among, and together, with friends.

They had come to a place where the river formed a great lake deep in the core of the earth and they were now in that mysterious land known as the Nether Earth, or the Second Earth, which some say will one day rise again to the surface while our earth will sink below. This New Earth, our Tribal storytellers say, will be populated with creatures more beautiful and far wiser than this human race.

Although the women had long since lost their torches, there was plenty of light where they now were, because far away across the great lake mighty volcanoes were belching fire and smoke, lighting up the entire, fabulous landscape. Only mossy crystalline grass and bronzy trees without leaves grew in this Nether World, and there were no animals of any description. A deep peaceful silence lay over everything and the living air was charged with a strange vitality and a pleasant scent.

Nomikonto stretched her tired body on the transparent mossy grass and looked at the other women, who followed her example. They had all come a very long way and could go no farther. They all chose this fantastically beautiful and pleasant place as the one in which to lie down and gently die.

But there came to their ears a quiet tender voice, across the scented air – a voice that belonged to someone or something which was the very pillar of mercy and love. It filled the tired women with awe and reverence.

'My children, my much tired, exhausted children, you do not belong here. Your lives will be of great value in the service of your people in the Upper World. You must live to become the cressets that light the way of the Tribes you belong to. Come to me and I will restore your strength and help you find your way back to the Upper World once more.'

'Who . . . where are you?' stammered *Nomikonto*, struggling to her feet.

'I am *Lufiti-Ogo*,' answered the voice, 'and if you will promise me not to be repelled by what you will see, I shall make myself visible to you.'

'Repelled by what we shall see!' exclaimed *Lulamani*. 'How can one who possesses such a beautiful voice be repulsive?'

'I am not ugly, but I am different from what you look like. You see, I was created by men who had totally different standards of beauty, tens of thousands of years ago.'

'You mean you are the Star Mother?' gasped *Lulamani*.

'Yes, I am the Star Mother.'

'Who is she?' whispered *Nomikonto*.

'She is the Fugitive Goddess, created by the Children of the Star,' replied *Lulamani* in an awed whisper. 'The most perfect being ever created in the Universe.'

'Goddess, please to show yourself,' said one of the women, *Namulembu* of the Vamangwe, in spirit language, 'Show yourself and let us fall on our knees and worship you.'

'Do not call me a Goddess,' said the voice gently. 'I do not deserve that title. Observe, I am now going to make myself visible.'

The creature was as tall as a man and looked for all the world like a cross between a human being and a very pleasantly beautiful Chimbandzi, or Ngangi ape. She had a smallish head and the receding chin of the higher primates. She had thin lips and a human mouth around the corners of which hovered the faintest ghost of a most pleasant smile. Her eyes, set deeply under heavy brows, were soft and alive with wisdom – far beyond that of men. Her shoulders were as wide as that of a giant. Her arms were long and slender and her beautiful hands were crowned with graceful claw-like nails. Her broad chest was weighted down by two enormous breasts and it seemed to *Nomikonto* that those breasts could easily nurse the babies of a whole tribe. She had the narrow waist and the broad hips of a good child-bearing woman.

Without a word the Great *Lufiti-Ogo* sat down on a rock and beckoned *Nomikonto* to come to her, which the Nguni princess promptly did, in spite of her aching feet and tired body. The Goddess reached out a powerful arm and lifted the princess off the ground on to her lap as if she were a baby. Although somewhat ape-like in certain respects when seen from a distance, *Nomikonto* now noticed that her skin was human-like, smooth, and free of hair, except for a soft shiny black attractive covering like a heavy mane across her head and reaching down to between her shoulder blades. She also saw that the skin of the Goddess was a yellowish red-brown and that her eyes were black.

The princess soon discovered the object of the Goddess's hospitality. She was being encouraged by the Goddess to allow herself to be nursed like a baby. Needless to say, the princess considered this a most embarrassing experience, as did the other women who watched in great amazement. However, the others were given their turns and eventually all two hundred had had their strength restored, like so many newly fed babies.

'Rest now, lie down and sleep, all of you,' said the *Ogo*.

The women all lay down and slept heavily. For how long they slept they did not know, and could not care.

Eventually *Lulamani* found herself wide awake with the *Ogo* sitting beside her and looking intently down at her. 'You are a woman with much to hide. Tell me, you who are not what you seem to be – what seek you in the land of the Nguni?'

Lulamani gasped. Tears burst in a flood from the springs that were her eyes and she asked in a trembling voice: 'You know who I am, Great *Ogo*?'

'I am the *Ogo*,' said the Primate Goddess. 'I see everything and I know everything. I know who you are and what you are. All I wish to do is to cure you of the fear and the guilt that is devouring your soul – the fear and the guilt you are trying to hide under a cloak of cheerfulness. The other women are still asleep and you need not fear that they will learn your secret. Confide in me, my child, and unburden your chest of the heavy weight that lies within.

'I would rather unburden my chest in front of all my friends, Oh Great *Ogo*,' decided *Lulamani* courageously. 'I have gone through much evil, side by side with them, and they are now like sisters to me. As you say, Oh Great *Ogo*, I must unburden my chest of what it contains. But I ask only to make a full confession before my friends, and let them decide what to do with me.'

'You are under my wing now, *Lulamani*,' said the *Ogo*. 'You shall not be harmed in any way because very soon you are going to help in saving thousands of human lives and your name shall be sung and spoken about for many generations to come by singers and storytellers of a thousand tribes. You, Oh *Lulamani*, shall save the Nguni nation from annihilation very soon. I, the *Ogo*, salute you here and now. Hail, heroine of the River! Hail, saviour of thousands!'

Lulamani was stunned by the Goddess's prophecy. What did all this mean? She did not know it then, but she was going to find out after two moons had gone by.

Lulamani felt the arrows of fear as she stood facing the women with whom she had endured and suffered so much. She saw the curiosity and expectancy written on the face of each of them. She opened her mouth to speak, but no words came. She tried again and once more failed. Then at last she looked appealingly at the *Ogo* and whispered: 'I do not know how to begin.'

'Then I shall help you, my daughter,' said the *Ogo*. 'My children, *Lulamani* here has something to tell you, but she cannot summon enough courage to do so, and therefore I will help her. You have always known her as *Lulamani* and had taken it for granted she was a Nguni. You calmly accepted her as a fellow Royal Wife, a rival in marriage. She is none of these things. She is the true Queen of the Empire of Luvijiti. She was deposed by the present *Munumutaba* years ago and had to flee for her life. She fled into the land of the Nguni and was adopted by an old Nguni man and his wife who also swore to keep her true identity a secret and who gave her a new name. Afterwards they married her off to *Malandela*. Apart from this, she whom you know as *Lulamani* also suffers from that disease which must never be mentioned by name!'

'What!' cried *Muxakaza*, the First Queen. 'Gods of my fathers, that explains everything!'

'That explains what, Oh Great First Wife?' asked *Nomikonto*.

'It explains why *Lulamani* always used to invent every kind of excuse and low trick to avoid having to go and share the love-mat with *Malandela* when her turn came in the six months of every year!' cried *Muxakaza*. 'I always wondered why she, who seemed so fond of the love-mat and always eager to flirt with any man, young or old, who came near her, should always come up with some excuse or other when her turn came to spend the night with the High Chief. It is very lucky for her that *Malandela* is not such a hot-blooded man – she would have been found out long ago, and burnt alive!'

'My children,' said the *Ogo*, 'in this beautiful fallen woman you see a weapon that will win the great war and save the Nguni tribe from annihilation. Do not scorn her; look well upon your fallen saviour.'

'The fallen saviour!' The name re-echoed within the minds of all the women and each one of them repeated it again and yet again to herself silently. It was a name to be used by a thousand storytellers from a thousand tribes for a thousand years to come; it was a name to be used by countless poets and by countless singers whenever they referred to *Lulamani* or, to give her the name by which she would henceforth be known, *Maneruana*, the fallen saviour.

'When the warriors have fought until they can fight no more,' said the *Ogo*, 'when spears have drunk blood until they can drink no more, and when the knobkieries are broken and the battle-axes are blunted, and the plains littered with the bodies of men, this woman will throw one spear and stab the enemy to the heart. His warriors will be scattered to the Seven Winds. Behold, this is our beautiful spear – this our *Maneruana*! Look well upon her, Oh my children, look at her beauty. Before I cure her of her secret illness, *Maneruana* shall bring a proud and insolent man and a proud empire of murdering dogs hurtling to the ground. Come, my children, follow me. We must join forces with the old blind and devouring eagle whom we must help to restore peace to the land of the Mambo and the Nguni.'

The women raised a loud acclamation and all took turns in kissing *Lulama-Maneruana's* forehead, breasts and cheeks. Then they turned and followed the Great *Ogo* across the plains of the Nether World where crystal grass and leafless bronze trees grow.

After a long journey the *Ogo* suddenly stopped and took a few steps backward, fear creeping into her eyes. 'Get back, my children, get back,' she shouted.

The women in front immediately fell back on those behind them as some huge and incredibly evil-looking creature emerged from behind a huge outcrop of rock. This creature could best be described as a great pile of rubbish. The growth over his surface, whether supposed to be hair or not, had the appearance of drift grass deposited on branches of trees by flood waters. But this great pile had two legs and two arms – and a voice. 'Where are you going?' he asked.

'I am taking these earthly human beings back to the Upper World . . . and I am going there myself.'

'Who gave you permission to leave the Nether World?'

'No one, Oh great Heap of Rubbish,' answered *Lufiti-Ogo*. 'I am tired of this world and I want to leave it forever.'

'You will not leave this world – you will stay here,' said the Heap.

'Never!'

'If you try to leave this world against my command, I shall destroy you.'

'You try . . .'

The Demon and the Goddess immediately came to grips in the presence of the women who stood watching in wide-eyed awe. Then suddenly a luminous patch appeared in front of the women, hovering a thumb's length above the crystal grass. 'Follow that light patch, it will guide you – run!' the *Ogo* panted.

The women ran like the wind. They ran like impala through the silent forests of mineral trees and metal shrubs with ruby-centred and diamond-petalled flowers. The fallen saviour, whom all now knew as *Lulama-Maneruana*, looked once over her shoulder and saw the Demon carry the Goddess away like a husband who forcibly carries home a stubborn and wayward wife. 'Poor *Ogo*,' she thought, and then rejoined the rest of the women.

The little red luminous patch led them into the yawning mouth of a cave under a mountainous wall of black rock – a cave which seemed to conceal many evil secrets in its dark, brooding depths.

Before it entered the cave, a flute-like voice spoke from the luminous patch: 'Keep close together – do not get left behind. Many dangers await us in here. Follow me.'

Into the cave went the terrified women and on through echoing tunnels where dark shapes with luminous eyes scuttled away into the darkness around the glowing patch. Great shapes resembling bats with horns instead of ears flew past the terrified women.

Then to the nostrils of the women came a smell so foul that their heads started spinning. By the light from the luminous patch the women saw a huge beast, an elephant in size but in appearance a cross between a bull and a crocodile. 'Be very silent now,' a whisper came from the luminous patch. 'That is the *Burumatara*, the Old Bull, who is the father of all demons. He mated with the Goddess of Evil, *Watamaraka*, to produce certain races of men, and he is physically the father of all *tokoloshes*.

But the *Burumatara* had seen them and with a swish of his scaly crocodile tail and a toss of his great bull-like horned head he bellowed: 'What are you puny things and whence are you? And why are you trespassing in the realm of *Burumatara*?'

'We are going back to the world we belong to, *Burumatara*,' replied the Queen *Muxakaza* at length.

'No one passes my kingdom without paying a tribute. I want ten of the fattest and healthiest of you to remain here. I am tired of eating rocks. The rest can then proceed on their way.'

It was here that the Princess *Nomikonto*, who was by far the fattest and the healthiest of them all, did a very shameful thing. She calmly knocked ten others unconscious with blows of her powerful fist, and they were left behind. It is from this legendary incident that the saying sprang: 'When the bugle of pleasure calls from within the kraal of Life, I shall go in first – but when the drum of death groans from within the kraal, please, Oh Life, would you care to go first.'

This saying has been made into a song and the warriors sing it when going into battle. And it is always sung with a long refrain of vulgar epithets directed to those at home who start wars and then hide, leaving others to fight.

The little luminous patch led the women on and on through dark tunnels full of unseen evil and where ghostly shapes hooted and gibbered at them as they passed. Then at last the greatly decimated group of women emerged into a vast cavern of incredible dimensions. This cavern seemed to be filled with tens of thousands, if not millions, of giant luminous butterflies. Some were soaring around in clouds that vanished in the expanse above, while fresh ones emerged in their thousands from crevasses in the floor.

'These are the souls of men and women,' explained the glowing patch. 'Those that you see rising from the floor are souls of people who have just died. They come here first to await their turn to be reincarnated into the animals and birds of the Upper World. You are beholding the knot in the Cycle of Life, and it is here that you experience the truth of the philosophy that Life is but Death and Death is but Life. One only lives to die, and dies to live again.'

They proceeded farther and the voice came again from the luminous patch: 'Although we are nearing the end of our journey, there are still many dangers ahead. I must now return to my mother and father whom you last saw in less co-operative spirit, there where I first joined you. Perhaps I should tell you that my father is not what he looks; he is, in fact, the Spirit of Nature.

'But fate is cruel to you, Oh daughters of men! Soon you are going to be faced with the strangest choice that any human being ever had to make as a price to re-entry in your world. As soon as I depart, three creatures will present themselves to you – a dove, an eagle and a bat. You will have to decide individually which of these creatures should guide you back to your world. One will lead you there safely; another will lead you to total annihilation, while the third *may* lead you through to your world, but you will then have become transformed into something different. I leave you to make your own choice and I cannot advise you on which will lead you where!

'Now, I can sense also evil approaching you from behind. Take that tunnel and run for your lives! Hurry, and try to reach the Grey Land where your three guides are waiting. There is a Damned One after you!'

A Damned One is a soul, one of very few, condemned to roam the dark depths of Eternity forever, without being allowed to reincarnate, because of a great evil it had committed against the Universe.

After the glowing patch had vanished the women dashed into the tunnel indicated. But they were not quick enough. A large black butterfly with wings that glowed an intense violet, overtook them, descending on the back of *Muxakaza* – and dissolving itself into her body. Every woman clearly understood the meaning of what they witnessed.

When *Muxakaza*, who was no longer *Muxakaza*, rejoined the other women in the valley of that strange land, halfway between the Nether World and the Upper World and known as the Grey Land, the fallen saviour *Lulama-Maneruana* saw that she had changed. The beauty of the Albino Queen, which had been the beauty of a self-respecting, dignified woman, was now the brazen beauty of a shameless slut. Even her matronly figure had changed into that of a voluptuous 'Black River harlot'. She, who had been hailed as the most beautiful woman in the land of the Nguni, was soon to be cursed as the worst slut that ever defiled the history of any tribe.

From the pitch-black depths of the ash-grey land there appeared a white dove, a black eagle and a giant bat. *Lulama-Maneruana* and *Nomikonto*, together with a number of the other women, promptly chose the proud eagle. Ninety, led by the Vamangwe, *Namulembu*, chose to follow the bat. The remaining fifty, led by *Muxakaza, Zuzeni* and *Notemba*, elected to follow the white dove. There was fear in every heart. Who had made the right choice? They all knew that one group was doomed to complete annihilation – but which?

HURL BACK THE WAR SPEAR

The eyes of *Lulama-Maneruana* slowly opened. Above her were the pale blue sky and the trees of the Upper World, which she knew and loved so well. A cool breeze whispered in the long grass and the ground was wet under her from the previous night's rain.

The first thought that came to her mind was: we have succeeded, but what about the others?

She leapt to her feet and saw *Nomikonto* and the rest of the women of her group lying like so many dolls in the long grass, unconscious. She went from woman to woman and felt their hearts and was thankful to find that they were alive. All those who had followed the eagle were safely back and, to *Maneruana's* surprise, all of them looked younger than they had been, and they were all endowed with a strange and unearthly beauty.

Maneruana quickly wove a short grass skirt for herself and went in search of those who had followed the bat and the dove. She searched for a long time before she came across an old and incredibly wrinkled woman with a solitary tooth in her mouth, sitting upon a fallen tree and sobbing her heart out. The woman was so old, she seemed like the grandmother of the stars herself. Her thin wasted body was a mass of wrinkles and her hair was as white as snow. Slowly she raised her face and saw *Maneruana* looking down at her in blank amazement. 'Don't you realise who I am, *Maneruana*? I am *Namulembu*, who led those who followed the bat . . .'

'*Namulembu*! It can't be . . . !'

'It is, Oh *Maneruana*,' croaked the old woman. 'I don't know how I survived; the rest were consumed in a great fire, together with the great bat we followed. I alone survived in my party – and look at me.'

'If this happened to you, cried *Maneruana*, 'what of those who followed the dove?'

There was a sound in the forest behind *Maneruana* and she spun around. Her eyes widened and she yelled.

There stood *Muxakaza* and *Zuzeni.* But if she felt younger, they *looked younger.* They were nothing but young girls.

All those women who had followed the dove, all fifty of them, had changed from women of forty and thirty summers, to girls ranging from twenty-five to sixteen, and the two youngest were reduced to crawling babies. These two were carried in arrn by a buxom twenty-year-old *Zuzeni* and the half-ripe sixteen-year-old virgin *Notemba. Maneruana* collapsed and wept.

We were too late, sixteen whole days too late and the white-daubed woman *Nomeva,* the only one of my zombie messengers who had returned, had confirmed this. *Vamba* had seized power in *Malandela's* absence and the Vamangwe were now firmly entrenching themselves as the ruling tribe in the land of the Nguni.

The reason for our lateness was that a malignant fever had broken out amongst the Avengers just after we left my kraal, and we had had to turn back, carrying the sick men on litters. Two of the Avengers had died on the way back and although we had succeeded in curing all the sick, they had still been too weak to walk unaided.

'So the treacherous rat has succeeded in his evil schemes,' growled the First Avenger. 'But I swear by the Ten Gateways of Creation that the skunk *Vamba* shall not go unpunished for his evil deed.'

'Do not worry yourself about him Avenger,' I said. 'The moment of glory for an evil man is very short indeed. *Vamba* will not rule the land of the Nguni for long.'

While we were talking, one of my daughters, *Luanaledi,* crawled into the hut and knelt before me. 'I have strange news for your ears, Oh my father,' she said.

'What sort of news, child?'

'Very strange news, father,' she responded. 'While we were out gathering wood in the forest we met about a hundred women and girls, father . . .'

'Women! Women!' I cried. 'I am tired of hearing about women. Quick, people here for many days' journey around.'

'It is true, my father, and we have brought all of them back here with us.'

'Women! Women!' I cried. 'I am tired of hearing about women. Quick, stew up some of them. I'll have them for supper.'

'Father, they say they are . . .'

'They say they are all ready for the pot, do they?' I shouted. 'Well, dress some of them to start with . . .'

'I beg you to hear first what these women have to say. It is the most fantastic story you have ever heard.'

'Well, bring them all into the Great Hut and let me hear their story. It had better be good or I shall stew them so fast. Who are they, did you say, and from where do they hail?'

'They claim they are the wives of *Malandela*, my father, but we cannot believe it. Why, some of them are nothing but girls, about sixteen . . .'

'I sense great evil behind this. Bring them into the Great Hut, my daughters, and you, Honourable Avenger Leader, stay to hear this strange story.'

As *Luanaledi* led me into the Great Hut I sensed their strange story even before the women, who seemed to be their leader, opened her mouth to speak. We listened to the strange tale unfolding from the lips of *Maneruana*. We listened until it was well past midnight. And then, finally, I heard *Maneruana* give a low exclamation of surprise and ask the woman next to her: 'But what happened to *Muxakaza*?'

'I thought she was here,' replied the woman. 'She was with us in the other hut just before sunset. I saw her conversing with the one-hand deaf-mute in sign language.'

It was my adopted son *Mukombe* who supplied us with the next shock when we began making inquiries in the kraal: 'I was sitting in my hut, Great Father, and the door was open. I saw the two women slip out of the kraal gate in the most stealthy manner. One was *Luojoyo, Vamba's* mother, and the other was that strange pink-skinned and white-haired woman who came with these other strangers.'

'When was this, *Mukombe*?' I asked.

'Just when it was beginning to get dark, my Great Father.'

'Now why did that woman take *Vamba's* mother away?' demanded the Avenger Leader.

'I do not know yet, Avenger,' I said, 'but we shall know in a few days' time.'

Lulama-Maneruana threw herself at my feet. 'My lord, that woman is evil – she is possessed by an evil spirit. Please find her before it is too late and kill her before she does more harm than *Vamba* ever did!'

'We shall go after her early tomorrow morning. Meanwhile I want all of you to go to sleep, because tomorrow we are leaving this place and I am going straight to *Malandela's* kraal to unseat that evil dog *Vamba* from his stolen throne.'

Bekizwe, Malandela's own brother, was a little man with a very big head who walked with a slight limp and who was harassed by constant attacks of ill-health. Unlike *Malandela*, who was the most hated chief that ever ruled the Nguni Tribe, *Bekizwe* was lovingly known by the nickname of Our Little Father by his numerous subjects, and he was a god in the eyes of most. His great mercy and wisdom, and his open-handedness and unselfish love for his people, had won him undying love in the hearts of those whom he led. Not one man and not one woman was there in the land of the Mambo, unwilling to lay down his or her life for *Bekizwe.* He was a true father to all of them, a father and a mother at the same time. Many are the stories told about *Bekizwe*, the 'Little One', 'Our Dear Father', or 'Little Black Dove'. It was said that he had once disguised himself as a *tokoloshe* in order to capture a ravaging band of brigands who were making a thorough nuisance of themselves in the north-western corner of the land of the Western Mambo. He had scared the wits out of the band of thieves and had then commanded them to go to his Royal Kraal and give themselves up. When they reached his kraal, with him driving them like so many scared oxen, *Bekizwe* revealed his true identity – and gave them a free pardon. He chose their leader, *Nsongololo* (the centipede) as his first Battle *Induna.*

Another story that is told about him is that he helped a very shy young man to marry the girl he loved, by dressing up as a little girl himself and carrying messages between them. When the heartless girl wove a message mat in which she greatly insulted the young man, concluding by refusing marriage with him, *Bekizwe* took the mat and, on his way, unravelled it, weaving it again in patterns praising the young man and inviting him to come and claim the girl as his bride. When the girl was confronted with this mat later, she had no alternative but to admit that the mat had come from her and she was prepared to marry the man. For a girl to weave a mat in the patterns of acceptance of a young man and thereafter deny her promise was an offence punishable by the laws of the tribes.

Some time later the Little Chief had summoned the happily married couple and laughingly told them that *he* was the 'little girl' to whom they had entrusted their messages, one of which he altered. The girl had fainted on the spot, but the husband had laughed and thanked the chief profusely.

These, and many more, were the stories told about *Bekizwe* throughout the length and breadth of his vast land, stories that were told with loud peals of laughter around village cooking fires to open-mouthed and wide-eyed *piccanins.* Even while he was still eating the corn off the land, he had already become a legend.

Bekizwe had many children, whom he begot with the ugliest women in the land. This was because *Bekizwe's* heart inclined to the belief that even ugly people have a part to play in life, and to this belief he clung tenaciously.

Amongst *Bekizwe's* many children were two boys, *Zulu* and *Qwabe*, two very fat and ugly little urchins who were so black that they contrasted sharply against the darkest night. *Zulu* was one year old and *Qwabe* three, and both these boys had lost their mother *Tandanani* who had been bitten by a mamba while out in the forest a year earlier. *Tandanani* had been *Bekizwe's* First Wife and he had been mad with grief at her loss, swearing that when the time came for him to take another woman as First Wife, it would be the ugliest woman in the world.

He had spent three whole moons combing the country for the ugliest woman. He had prayed to the Spirits to grant him his wish and had held many Prayer Dances; slaughtered many oxen in tribute to the Spirits of his Ancestors, and then, at last, his wish had been granted.

Nsongololo and a party of warriors had suddenly come upon a strange woman living in a dark cave deep in a dangerous forest and the woman was so incredibly ugly, tall as a man, with the face of an ape. By the gods, was she ugly!

Children ran away screaming when they saw her. Men doubted if she existed at all, or was just a favourite nightmare come to life, and the ugliest women found they had reason to be thankful. These, who were mostly found in *Bekizwe's* harem, suddenly turned lovely like a midsummer night moon. Everybody soon lovingly nicknamed the monstrous woman *Nunu* (ugly little monster).

On top of everything she was stupid. She never knew whether she was asleep or awake, alive or dead. She would try to carry water in a grass bucket, and she had to be reminded every morning to put on her skin skirt before leaving the hut.

But *Bekizwe* was enchanted with his new queen. He was fascinated and enthralled by her. He soon became her slave. At night when the lions roared and the jackals howled in the forest, *Bekizwe* found his new queen as hot-blooded and passionate as she was both stupid and visually repulsive.

While the people laughed heartily and danced whenever their dear chief's new toy was mentioned, there was one man who strongly suspected that the ugly new queen was something more than just a repulsive idiot giantess. This man was *Shondo, Bekizwe's* Highest Witchdoctor, who was the most suspicious of men and who was quick to detect that things were not what they seemed to be. *Shondo* was a great believer in the most ancient saying of the Tribes: 'Oh wanderer, lost in the Valley of Life, remember that nothing is ever what it seems to be, and seeing is not always believing!'

To *Shondo, Nunu* was very much in appearance like a certain goddess of whom the grizzled old withdoctor had once heard about, as a young trainee, years ago. But what was her name? Old *Shondo* could not remember.

It was now ten days after *Bekizwe* had married his new First Queen, and the night preceding the fateful day when so much was to happen in the Royal Kraal – and *Bekizwe* had a strange, rather frightening dream. He dreamt he stood on the top of a high mountain, looking down at thousands of warriors fighting a fierce battle. Then the mountain shuddered and split from summit to base and he felt himself falling down the yawning cleft. As he fell, he saw his two ostrich feathers fly off his royal headband, floating loosely away from him. He then saw two hands appear from nowhere, catch the feathers and hold them firmly.

This strange and vivid dream greatly aroused *Bekizwe's* curiosity and he was most desirous to know its meaning. Thus, early that morning he sent for *Shondo* and with his usual broad smile the Little Chief greeted his High Witchdoctor:

'I see you, *Shondo.*'

'I see you, Little Father. I see you once and I see you ten times. May peace be always your portion in life and may the hyaena of hunger howl far away from your door.'

'You are unhappy, *Shondo.* You look as unhappy as a stolen goat. Tell me, have you eaten?'

'I have not eaten, Little Father. I have no desire for food. My heart is black.'

'Then you shall daub your heart with white clay here and now, because I am going to send for food and you must eat and drink whether you like it or not. I dislike having to tell my dream to a hungry man whose face looks as sour as last year's corn beer. To me, boy!'

A servant boy entered and the High Chief said: 'Bring some cold meat, boy, and bean stew, with a potful of beer for the Old One.'

The food was brought and the High Witchdoctor managed to eat somehow, in spite of the dark cloud of strange foreboding that darkened his soul. Old *Shondo* sensed that something was going to happen that beautiful day. After he had eaten and bowed twice to his beloved chief as a sign of thanks, he listened intently as the Little Chief related his dream. *Shondo* was horrified at the interpretation the dream suggested to his mind, but he concealed this horror and said simply:

'The dream means that you have a great enemy close at hand, Oh my Little Father.'

'But how can anybody hate me, *Shondo*?' asked the chief. 'I have no enemy that I know of, either within or without my country. I have many, very many friends. I think it was just a meaningless dream.'

'I wish I could be sure of that, Little Father. But whatever the dream may mean, I want my Chief to know one thing, that no enemy would ever touch you while I live.'

'I know that, my loyal *Shondo*, and I thank you.'

As he left his chief's hut, *Shondo* went past the newly built hut of *Nunu* and saw the ugly woman feeding the two motherless boys yam stew from a bowl. Then he saw to his surprise that tears were streaming down *Nunu's* cheeks – and he distinctly heard her say: 'Poor little sons. Poor, poor children. But I will save at least *you*, whatever happens.'

The words startled the great witchdoctor and he felt the icy worms of fear crawling up and down his spine. These were not the words of an idiot woman. These words were clearly spoken, not in the usual faltering fashion *Nunu* always used, but in the clear liquid accents of a sane, normal woman – and above all, a woman who had foreseen what was to happen on that day.

Who or what was *Nunu*? That she was not what she pretended to be, old *Shondo* no longer doubted, and he decided to keep an eye on her for at least the whole of that day.

Although the memory of his strange and disturbing dream was strong in his mind, *Bekizwe* was not the type of man who was easily depressed. He was a strong believer in 'happiness at all times'. So, to amuse his people and children, himself and his wives, *Bekizwe* donned his newest and most ridiculous headdress – a fantastic towering creation of cowrie shells, ostrich eggs, wooden horns and bundles of feathers of all sorts of birds. He also wrapped himself in his great *kaross*, which he called the '*kaross* of merriment' and which was heavily decorated with such unusual things as stones with holes through them, wild nuts that rattled, dried lizards, two small tortoise shells and about a dozen little monkey skulls.

He strode into the centre of the Great Kraal where women were busy cooking pot herbs in large clay pots. With his head held high and an expression of exaggerated pride on his face, he came strutting like a stumpy little ostrich to where the great pots were boiling, his great *kaross* sweeping the ground behind him.

'Hey, what is this?' he asked in mock surprise. 'What are you women supposed to be cooking here?'

'We are cooking pot herbs, my lord,' replied the Second Wife, *Kanyisile*.

'You are cooking what?' he asked with an exaggerated expression of surprise on his small, round face.

'Pot herbs, lord.'

'Pot herbs,' whispered *Bekizwe*. 'And why are you cooking this rabbit's food?'

'The children say they are tired of yams, *putu* and sour milk, so we thought we would have some herbs for the midday meal for a change.'

'Do you not know that eating pot herbs gives one a green stomach?' asked *Bekizwe* severely. 'Do you not know that eating pot herbs causes constipation, flatulence, indigestion, obesity, running nose, fractured hip bones, stupidity, and a cold in the back passage?'

'But, my lord,' protested *Kanyisile*, 'our sacred forefathers showed us that pot herbs were safe to eat and they never suffered any of the ills you mention.'

'Our sacred doddering and myopic forefathers showed us that pot herbs were safe to eat, it is true, my beloved stupid, but they were the worst murderers, thieves, wizards, adulterers, fornicators, cheats, cowards, stone heads, malingerers, madmen, blunderers, fools, hypocrites, in short the grandest collection of green bellies under the sun. And do you know why, *Kanyisile*? Because they ate pot herbs, that is why!'

'But, my lord,' protested *Kanyisile* weakly.

'Do not argue with me! Have you forgotten that I am the High-Low Chief around here? Have you forgotten that I am the chief – the one and only fountain of pure unwisdom?'

'I am not arguing, my lord,' said *Kanyisile* amid shrieks of laughter from the other women. 'My lord, dear husband, I did not mean to offend you . . .' she gasped, thoroughly scared by now.

'*Kanyisile*, you did argue with me and you did offend me and for that I am going to punish you. Go into your hut and remain there until I call you,' said *Bekizwe* in mock anger.

Kanyisile retired to her hut while the Little Chief drew his High *Induna Nsongololo* aside and whispered into his ear for a long time, concluding with a roguish wink which *Nsongololo* returned with a smile and another wink just as wicked. He took five young warriors and vanished into the forest.

Bekizwe then called out the drummers and singers and yelled for the cooks to slaughter three cows and prepare what he called a small feast, for not more than a thousand guests.

A hundred cooks of both sexes sprang into action at *Bekizwe's* comical commands, and by early afternoon the feast was ready. Great pots full of steaming meat stood in neat rows in the centre of the kraal while piles of huge wooden meat trays were enticingly arranged around the pots. Then, with a great show of dignity, *Bekizwe* began to inspect the pots of different kinds of meat, cooked to perfection. Behind him came a solemn procession of head cooks, food tasters and other members of the 'Stew Regiment', as he lovingly called those of his *Indunas* who were in charge of food.

Suddenly *Bekizwe* clutched his forehead and staggered back for a few paces before falling flat on his back. Anxious hands reached out to assist him where he was lying dead still, but he opened one mischievous eye and said: 'Oh . . . No!'

'Great Chief,' asked *Shondo*, 'is anything the matter?'

'Yes, much is wrong!'

'What is it, Great One?' asked *Shondo* again, most anxiously.

'Just this, Oh *Shondo*. Am I to eat all this delicious meat by myself? Look at all these juicy roast haunches, these tasty ribs. Am I supposed to drink all that beer by myself? Help! Who's going to help me?'

And with this, *Bekizwe* leapt up and raced to the gate of the kraal with his *kaross* lapping up billowing clouds of dust. 'Help! Who's going to help me?'

Hearing their chief's voice raised in what sounded like obvious distress, heavily armed men poured out of the surrounding kraals and converged upon the Royal Kraal, ready to die for their beloved Little Father. When the first wave of armed men reached him, he pointed wildly to the inside of the kraal. 'Inside, in those pots! Sit down and help me – and help yourselves!'

Men stared in blank amazement at their chief and then at the pots in the centre of the kraal and gradually understanding dawned in the heart of each one of them. The High Chief of Merriment had been full of tricks again. They laid their weapons down – somewhat unsure – and with sheepish expressions on their faces they trooped in dribs and drabs in the direction of the pots, to feast and make merry.

'Oh no! you greedy hogs,' cried *Bekizwe*. 'Send home for your wives and tell them to come too. Do you want to get fat while your females grow thin? Have you forgotten that our unholy ancestors have decreed that of the two, the woman must always be the fatter, as she has to take all the weight?'

Roars of laughter greeted the Little Father's last words and messengers ran back to the neighbouring kraals to fetch wives, and even farther afield to other villages, to collect men, women and children to join in the feast. There was eating and drinking, and dancing and singing, and ever so often *Bekizwe* rose to tell an amusing story which left the crowds breathless with laughter.

Some of the stories *Bekizwe* told his guests live in the hearts of true Nguni to this very day. Among them are the classic stories of 'How men got their beards', 'The ignorant bridegroom', 'The hot-blooded bride', 'The girl who married a lion by mistake'.

Bekizwe always sat on his famous 'Throne of Misrule' on such hilarious occasions. This was a raised platform on four elaborately carved posts, on top of which was a clumsy throne, in the shape of two very ugly women who held up a small stool between them. The throne itself was carved out of one solid piece of ebony.

When the feast was nearing its end, *Bekizwe* sent for *Kanyisile*, whom he had promised to punish for arguing with him. He also instructed *Nsongololo* to bring forth what he had been instructed to prepare in the forest. What they produced was a great skirt made entirely of leaves and long grass, and a large headdress made of cooking herbs. When *Kanyisile* appeared she was escorted by warriors armed with grass whips, while she was wearing a skirt and a headdress of fibre.

Nsongololo took the part of Royal Accuser and, standing under *Bekizwe's* tall throne with folded arms, he addressed *Kanyisile* as follows: 'You, *Kanyisile*, the daughter of *Sonsizi*, the son of *Velapi*, the son of *Nkomo*, have been brought here because you did deliberately and most maliciously argue with the chief, your lord and undisputed husband. We all know that you are guilty and we, therefore, sentence you to do the Dance of Penitence while wearing this skirt of leaves and grass and this headdress of the same pot herbs you had the great impudence to argue over with our most unimpeachable chief.'

'My dear people,' said *Bekizwe* in a broken voice. 'Before the sentence is carried out on my dear wife, I would like to tell you what we argued about. I found my wives cooking pot herbs – pot herbs, my people – the food of rabbits, oxen and kudus! Oh my people, green herbs that only beggars would eat. Pot herbs which cause people to have malaria in the stomachs, colds in their intestines, green hearts, purple brains and club feet; and which even cause the green grass to grow in people's armpits and sunflowers to bloom in the areas beneath their navels.'

Bekizwe paused and wiped away an imaginary tear, while a veritable hurricane of laughter swept the kraal.

'My people, for many years I have been wondering why my wives had a green look about them every morning, and why the babies they present me with always see the light of day with green leaves protruding from their ears. Today I found the reason: my wives are too fond of pot herbs. When I tried to point this out to my wife *Kanyisile*, she argued with me and said our forefathers ate them and what was good for our forefathers is good enough for their descendants too. My dear wife would not listen and she launched an argument against me – as long as a crocodile's tail – and I, being as I am a self-respecting, dignified chief, anxious to avoid a public scene, ordered her to be confined to her hut until further notice.'

Kanyisile was made to wear the heavy skirt of grass and leaves, and also the large leafy headdress. At a command from *Bekizwe* the hands of the masked drummers flew over the taut skins of their drums and *Kanyisile* began to dance, encouraged by mock blows from the plaited grass whips of her five guards.

Suddenly something fell from her skirt on to the ground and a loud shout burst from the excited spectators when they saw that it was – a fat live hare tied into a furry ball with a strip of calfskin.

'Oh my fathers,' cried *Bekizwe*. 'My wife has given birth to a rabbit! This is all the result of eating the food of rabbits. I thought something like this would happen.'

'My lord!' cried *Kanyisile* above roars of laughter from the crowd. 'I did not give birth to this . . .'

Her voice turned into a loud scream as she felt something warm and alive struggling feebly amongst the leaves and grass of her large skirt. With a shriek she jumped high into the air and two more rabbits fell out. Then a small tortoise thudded to the ground from her headdress. She tore the headdress and skirt off and ran like the wind to her hut. Amid roars of laughter, *Bekizwe* collected the tortoise and trussed hares and solemnly gave a humorous name to each creature, calling it his dear child, before ordering some boys to go and release them in the forest. He ordered a 'toast' to be drunk to the latest additions to his family, and the feast ended with another humorous story from *Bekizwe*, which caused a final roar of laughter. The people departed reluctantly for their homes, but in high spirits, secretly regretting having to leave the kraal of their dear Little Father, and wondering when he would hold another feast.

The sun sank in the West and darkness claimed the land. In the forest, owls hooted loudly and faintly. In the distance, lions roared their challenge to the stars. *Bekizwe* was sleeping and his dreams were pleasant. Beside him slept *Kanyisile* whose turn it was to share the Royal Mat. The new First Queen, *Nunu*, slept in her hut with the motherless boys *Zulu* and *Qwabe*.

Towards midnight the chief felt someone shaking him violently: 'Wake up, Little Father, wake up!'

The voice belonged to *Nsongololo*, the First Battle *Induna*, and former bandit leader.

'Who is stealing the fowls?' joked the Little Chief.

'Little Father,' cried the *Induna*, 'wake up and flee. We are being attacked – wake up!'

'Your joke is beautiful, *Nsongololo*. I will give you a cow in the morning. Now go back and sleep.'

'Little Father, I am not joking. The huts are burning outside and people are dying. Our warriors are fighting bravely, but we are badly outnumbered. *Malandela*, your brother, is attacking us – listen!'

The ringing cry of a dying man tore the night to shreds and dispelled all doubts in *Bekizwe's* mind regarding the truth of what *Nsongololo* was saying. Slowly the sounds of a desparate battle crept into *Bekizwe's* ears.

Bekizwe snatched up his loinskin and put it on quickly. He crawled out of the hut with *Nsongololo* close behind him. Outside, the battle was in full fury and a rain of spears fell inside the kraal. Ten huts were burning near the first gate, sending billowing columns of red glowing smoke and sparks into the star-bejewelled sky. Dead warriors were lying in the fire-lit clearing in the centre of the kraal and *Bekizwe* felt his heart sink into the depths of dark sorrow when he came to realise they were his men. He could not believe that the enemy was *Malandela* – of all people. He wondered why anybody, let alone his own brother, would want to attack him.

Bekizwe looked beyond the forests and saw that other kraals were burning and his eyes filled with tears when he realised that all those kraals belonged to the people with whom he had been feasting and joking, not so very long ago.

Could it be *Malandela*? They had never had a quarrel; they had lived in peace for so many years. *Bekizwe* could not believe it.

Even as he watched the brave defenders of the kraal, they were driven back – away from the stockade. A great section of the stockade went down with a loud crash. Warriors swathed in tattered animal skins poured into the kraal. *Bekizwe* recognised his brother's crack assault regiment – the famous 'Madmen'. At the head of them was *Malandela* himself.

'*Malandela*,' cried *Bekizwe*. 'My brother . . . my own dear brother!'

Bekizwe ran across the clearing, ran towards his brother whom he could see clearly by the light of the burning huts. He was blind to the yelling hordes of Nguni warriors, pouring into the kraal like an overwhelming flood. He did not see his brave warriors fall, selling their lives dearly to *Malandela's impis*. Only dimly, faintly, did he hear the cries of his wives and children as they were slaughtered by the attacking hordes.

He never saw the huge ape-woman *Nunu*, his new First Wife, dash out of the kraal into the forest, through a hail of spears, with *Zulu* and *Qwabe* under her arms. *Bekizwe* only saw his brother and he saw the naked fury in his eyes.

'Brother *Malandela*, what have I done?' cried the Little Chief.

'I see you, wizard,' said *Malandela* between his teeth. 'You killed my sons and now you die. Die, you wizard!'

Bekizwe felt pain greater than any pain he had known before – the double pain of *Malandela's* words and that of the spear which *Malandela* plunged deep into his side – piercing lungs and heart, and coming out the other side. *Bekizwe* died not knowing why his brother killed him, died without a chance to plead for himself. Like a light snuffed by a sudden gust of wind, he was cut down by a brother he loved as much as he loved his own people.

He never saw a little woman come racing out of the darkness and throw herself at *Malandela's* feet. He never heard *Malandela's* curse and his loud exclamation: '*Celiwe*! What are you doing here?'

He never heard the hollow-eyed, exhausted little *Celiwe* shriek loudly: 'You killed him! I am too late . . . Oh gods of my fathers! I am too late . . . poor, poor innocent *Bekizwe*! You, you . . . *Malandela*, you foul stiff-necked gullible fool! You impious, hotheaded bloodthirsty dog! You killed an innocent man. You call yourself the king of the Nguni, and yet you are a king no more. You think you rule a country and yet that country is now in the hands of others. You have been deceived into killing your own brother and your kingdom has been usurped behind your back. You have been foully deceived, you low-down cur!'

'*Celiwe*!' roared *Malandela*. 'What are you talking about? Are you mad? What do you mean by saying my country is in the hands of another? Speak, or I shall kill you too!'

'Kill me!' cried *Celiwe*. 'One more murder should not worry your foul soul. You have just killed an innocent man. Carry on, kill more innocent people if you like!'

'Royal One,' intervened the old Rainbow *Induna Solozi*, 'I think your most honourable wife brings great and terrible tidings. Please listen to what she has to say.'

'Speak clearly and tell me what has happened,' said *Malandela*.

'All your daughters are wives of Vamangwe warriors. Your children and all your wives, save myself, are dead. You will never see your sister *Nomikonto* again. *Vamba Nyaloti*, who deceived you into fighting your own brother and who was the one who really killed your sons, is now king of the Nguni and the Vamangwe. You are lost, *Malandela*, you might as well kill yourself.'

'What!' cried *Malandela* and his Rainbow *Induna* with one voice.

'Yes,' said *Celiwe*, 'and that is not all. I have brought with me the woman *Dambisa-Luwewe*, who tells me that within one moon the chief known as the *Munumutaba* of Zima-Mbje will attack our land because of a certain idol that *Vamba* has in his possession.'

'Gods have mercy upon us!' groaned *Mapepela*, one of the Rainbow *Indunas*. 'What have we done?'

'The gods have no mercy to waste on scum like you,' cried *Celiwe*. 'We shall be very fortunate to get out of this land alive. When the Mambo nation learns that their Little Father has been murdered they will come upon us like a landslide down a mountain slope.

They will know how to avenge their chief's death – and we have no country to fall back to. What chances have we with an enemy in front of us and an enemy behind our backs, and yet a third on our flank?'

Malandela knew that *Celiwe* was right. She always was and always would be. He knew that at last the day of reckoning had overtaken him on the wings of sunset. He knew that at last his impulsiveness, cruelty and thoughtlessness had brought him to the very brink of the precipice of undoing, and there was no way out – no escape.

The fact that his throne had been stolen from under him and that he no longer had a country to return to, shattered him completely. Every army depends on a steady flow of reinforcements from the homeland if it is to continue its role of invader in a hostile land, and once that flow of reinforcements is cut off, the army is soon destroyed. With his country in the hands of a usurper, *Malandela* knew that his regiments, mighty as they were, would soon be overwhelmed by the vengeful Mambo and totally annihilated. He knew that men whose brains are clouded by anxiety for the safety of their families whom they left behind do not make good warriors in a hostile land and he already noticed marked signs of uneasiness amongst his *Indunas*, nearly all of whom had families in the land *Vamba* had seized. Conquest of the Western Mambo was no longer possible for *Malandela*, and he knew it was now utterly impossible for him to try and make peace with the Mambo whose land he had already partly ravaged and whose beloved chief he had cruelly murdered with his own hands. With a low moan of despair, *Malandela* fell on one knee and touched the cold form that had been Little *Bekizwe*. Oh, how *Malandela* wished he could bring the dead one back to life again. How he wished he could raise within the stiff lifeless corpse but the faintest spark of life.

Too late. No amount of sorrow, no amount of tears and no amount of regret could ever bring his younger brother back to life again.

Worst of all, *Malandela* began to realise that no matter what the outcome of his present predicament, he would carry the guilt of having murdered an innocent man to the day he died. And he knew that men as yet unborn would judge him and find him – a fool.

The stigma of fool is indeed the worst stain that can defile a chief's name and in no time at all *Malandela* seemed to hear the name of '*Malandela* the Fool' echoing and re-echoing along the caverns of time.

'*Malandela* the Fool.'

For once in his cruel and wicked life, *Malandela* felt tears welling into his eyes. He wept bitterly for his dead brother and his family and people, and he wept also for his own murdered wives, family and people. He wept for *Nomikonto*, his dear sister. These were a great many people to weep for, whose lives he had ruined. And then finally he rose and cursed himself – above all for not heeding *Nomikonto's* warnings. She had always hated and suspected *Vamba*.

When dawn broke, *Malandela* ordered that every dead man and woman in *Bekizwe's* kraal be given an honourable and a hero's burial, with full mourning rites. He ordered all his warriors and *Indunas* to shave off their beards and hair, and collect all the hair in a great pile in the centre of the burnt kraal. This hair was to line out *Bekizwe's* grave as a sign of regret and an appeal for forgiveness. *Bekizwe* was to be buried in his biggest cattle pen, as befitted a chief, and his dead wives and children were to be buried in a great circle around the circular cattle kraal.

Men armed with razor knives went into action just as the sun rose, and by midday every warrior in every regiment had been shaven and the hair collected in a great heap in the centre of the kraal. Warriors carrying hoes and digging sticks began excavating the pits in which the dead were to be buried.

The Little Queen *Celiwe* and her Baluba companion *Dambisa* had the agonising task of dressing *Bekizwe's* dead queens in their best skin skirts and cowrie and copper necklaces, iron and ebony bracelets. Each was buried in a kneeling or crouching position, depending on her age. The mothers were buried in a kneeling position with brooms in their right hands, while girls were buried in a crouching position with water pots in front of them, and gourd water scoops in their right hands. The men and boys were buried with their knees drawn up to their chins and their hands clasped in front of their legs. This required skill and experience, and strength from those handling the already stiff bodies, and it also took a lot of time to prepare each body, with the result that the burial was not completed until the day following. Last to be buried were *Bekizwe* and his Second Wife *Kanyisile*.

The First Wife *Nunu*, with the two boys *Zulu* and *Qwabe*, and the Third Wife *Nodumo*, who was eight moons pregnant, had escaped. Also missing were *Shondo* and *Nsongololo*, and the escape of these two men boded ill for *Malandela*.

Bekizwe was laid to rest seated on his ebony throne with his headdress on his head and his great '*kaross* of merriment' covering his shoulders. He was buried holding the short 'Royal Assegai of Justice', with an elaborately carved shaft, in his hands and with his two favourite dogs, Nsini and Hlaya, lying at his feet. They had died while bravely defending *Kanyisile* and their master's hut.

A great *kaross* consisting of twelve big impala skin *karosses* sewn together, was lowered into the circular grave and it completely covered the seated body and enclosed the lining of human hair from the thousands of warriors.

As a hundred chosen warriors filled the pit with earth *Malandela* knelt nearby. Instead of making a long prayer and speech to his dead brother, as custom required, he simply said in a broken, hollow voice: 'Forgive me, brother.'

These three simple words were the most sincere *Malandela* had ever spoken in his life.

Celiwe wailed aloud and clasped her hands behind her head as *Kanyisile's* body was covered with earth. Loudly she wailed and twice fell fainting to the ground. Tears streamed down her pretty little face which was distorted with grief.

The burials were over and as the old man *Solozi* dug a hole in the ground near *Bekizwe's* grave to plant a fleshy leafed *mlahlankosi* plant which must always be planted over the graves of chiefs, the famous 'singing brothers', *Ziko* and *Majozi*, began to sing one of their songs, a song destined to live long, and for generations after both brothers had passed to the land of *Goqa-Nyawo*:

Oh Life, upon whose cruel stream
The Soul of man is borne;
Upon the savage, surging stream—
Behold the Soul forlorn.
As a lost leaf in a flood,
Behold the helpless Soul;
Over the rapids of Despair—
Over the cataracts of Pain
Or through dark forests of Fear,
The moaning Soul is borne.
Ah, cruel heartless soulless thing,
Oh thing as Fate by men misnamed,
We are the playthings in your lap,
The puppets in thy hands.

Behold with pride upon his brow
The scowling tyrant struts,
While 'neath his haughty flaming gaze
The starving peasants cringe.
But all are puppets thine, Oh Fate—
A puppet race, a puppet world;
And every move that each one makes
Is at thy dread command!

Behold with dark and evil soul
The thief a wanderer waylays
And from the wanderer's bleeding form
He rends the copper spoil!
He also is thy plaything Fate,
A plaything in a plaything world;
And though he thinks that I am I,
He is a plaything still!

Behold, upon the field of war,
Two tribes with deathful steel argue,
While loud upon the tortured plain
Resounds the voice of war!
Then he who should have lost the strife
Bears high a victor's shield,
While he who had a claim to Right
Lies slaughtered on the plain.
That was thy dread decision Fate,
Oh strangest Arbiter of all!
And though we shout that We are We,
We are thy puppets still.
Raise not your haughty head too high
Oh tyrant of the vales,
And you who won the glory shield—
Praise not overmuch your strength.

And thief, that stole the bawling calves,
Praise not your cunning hand,
Nor must you boast, Oh proudest headman
Who over thousands rule supreme,
For though you rule ten thousand men,
The Web of Fate rules you.

T'was not thy cunning nor thy stealth
That gained thee calves, Oh thief;
T'was just dread Fate that willed that thou
Shouldst have the bawling things.
T'was not thy war club's mighty blows
That won the tyrant throne for thee;
T'was at Fate's decision sole
That thou didst rule the vale.
Great men, low men, fools and knaves,
Chiefs or peasants, one and all:
Though thou boastest Thou art Thou,
Thou and all the rest are toys,

Dancing, capering, rising, falling,
In the mighty hands of Fate.

Then when the great singers had finished, the lonely outcast from an outcast tribe, the ebony Baluba maiden, *Dambisa-Luwewe*, opened her mouth and sang in a low mournful voice:

Bekizwe – Bekizwe—
Chief of the Mambo Tribe
Which, at the setting of the sun,
Still has its fair and ancient land.
Bekizwe – Bekizwe—
The forests weep for thee;
The footpaths of thy beauteous land
Shed dusty tears for thee.

The moon is shamed, the sun is dull,
The grassy lands are black,
While bitter in my thirsty mouth
Is now the river's silt.
The *sakabula* sheds its tail—
The weeping mountains groan—
The fleet impala sighs with woe
And hangs his horned head.

The black-eyed cows low woefully
The stern bulls bellow deep in awe,
While loud and long and unrestrained
Each dog lets forth his willing howl.

The breasted virgins laugh no more—
The warrior's song is stilled,
While loud and long, with drooping heads,
The doddering Grey Ones sigh,
And from each dim and wrinkled eye
The liquid sorrow pours . . .

For he that laughed but yesterday—
With his happy tribe – he laughs no more,
Snuffed is now their Light of Merriment
It flickers and it burns no more . . .

'Stop that!' roared *Malandela*. 'Stop that, you foreign bitch! Do you want to torture me – have I not suffered enough?'

With a savage oath *Malandela* threw his spear at *Dambisa*. But the tall, lithe girl twisted sharply to one side and the missile spent its murderous passion deep in the grass thatch of a hut.

'Madman twice befouled!' cried *Celiwe*. 'Would you add yet another murder to your score? Rabid dog of a *Malandela*! You, shamed lion with its tail bitten off by a crocodile! Vile warthog without respect for the graves of those you butchered . . . so you will murder still! You, *Ngovolo* and you, *Malangabi*, hold that raving madman still, I command you! Break his arms if he resists. Foul, defiled and impotent fratricide!'

The giant hunchback *Ngovolo* and the powerfully built dwarf *Malangabi* seized the raging *Malandela* and held him fast; they no longer had any respect for him, they no longer recognised him as their chief. They despised and scorned the man who had killed his brother without a trial and tried to murder a dirge singer afterwards. In the eyes of his men *Malandela* was a creature without honour and totally undeserving of any respect. His own wife had publicly called him impotent and that was the worst accusation that can be hurled at any man. It was far worse in *Malandela's* case, because there it was based on fact!

For a man to start a brawl at a funeral, or to injure or attempt to injure one of the mourners, was a heinous crime, punishable by instant death if the offender happens to be a commoner. But for one of Royal Birth, the punishment was worse – infinitely worse than death!

Thus:

'*Malandela*!' *Celiwe's* voice was hard and utterly cold. 'You have committed a very serious offence. You have shown great disrespect for the dead, which includes your brother whom you murdered. If it is the last thing that I do, I shall see to it that you are suitably punished in strict accordance with the law.'

Celiwe turned and coldly addressed the grim-faced Rainbow *Indunas*: 'You know what the law says should be done to a chief who disrespects the dead. Proceed to execute retribution to its fullest extent!'

They took *Malandela* into the forest, tore off his chief's attire, cut the tree-gum *sicolo* ring from his head, tore off his 'necklace of honour', and flung all these in the dust. They collected a vast pile of fresh cow dung, goat pellets, dog droppings and any amount of human excreta. All this incredible filth they transported into the forest to a clearing where *Mapepela* had already erected a giant tripod of tall *mopani* limbs. From this they suspended *Malandela* upside down, still fully alive, and he actually stared in utter disbelief at the meticulous preparations that were under way for his formal disgracing.

'This cannot be happening to me,' he thought. 'It must be a bad dream from which I will soon awaken. It cannot be true!' *Malandela* watched as warriors left the great circle of spectators and fouled the pile of filth that had been brought from the kraal. Many even spat on it to improve the texture. Then *Malandela* saw the ugly dwarf *Malangabi* come strutting importantly up to the pile of refuse and scoop some of it up with his bare hands and roll it affectionately into a ball.

'You know, Old Thundering Stomach, I have been wanting to do this to you for years!'

'*Malangabi*! I command you to stop at once!' croaked the suspended *Malandela*.

'Why?' asked *Malangabi*, with a hideous yellow-toothed smile. 'Why? You make such a lovely target.' And with that he drew back his arm and threw the ball of foul excrement straight at *Malandela*. It splashed over his face, into his eyes and nostrils. He gasped only to get a second full in the mouth from the hand of the hunchback giant deaf-mute *Ngovolo*. *Malandela* retched and vomited as a storm of balls of filth hit him from all directions as each warrior took his turn at defiling and insulting the chief with gusto and many an obscene jeer. In the end the helpless man was one lump of dripping manure, around which thousands of flies buzzed in the midday sun.

Then everyone roared with laughter as *Malangabi* plaited a long rope of grass and thrust the one end between *Malandela's* buttocks, saying: 'All demons have long tails, whether upside down or right way up!' And with this they left him to his fate.

Just before sunset, the Nguni armies withdrew to their stronghold in the Madlonti mountains whence they had launched their attack on *Bekizwe's* kraal. *Celiwe* and the Rainbow *Indunas* wished to make a stand in the mountains from where they intended negotiating peace terms with the Western Mambo, who the scouts had reported were massing vast armies in preparation for a fierce counter-attack on the Nguni aggressors.

Night fell. From where he was hanging, *Malandela* saw a form emerge from behind a bush and make straight for him. It was a tall, lithe dark girl, whom *Malandela* had tried to kill not so long before – the Baluba girl *Dambisa*.

'She has come to kill me,' thought *Malandela*. But *Dambisa* had no such intention. With a few strokes of her knife she freed *Malandela* and briskly rubbed life back into his numbed ankles and wrists. Silently she led him by the hand through the forest towards the Luangwa River and bathed him thoroughly, not forgetting her own needs. They had not yet spoken a word.

They proceeded along the bank of the river to a fisherman's village that stood deserted. Here the woman collected cooking and eating vessels, two bags of grain and a slab of stone which a fisherman uses as a fireplace in his canoe. She also collected two fishing spears, a shield and an old axe. All these she took to the biggest of the four clumsy dugouts that were moored to a crude jetty. *Malandela* helped the silent girl to carry some of the things and when the loading was done, *Dambisa* waved him to step in.

'But why . . . why have you saved me and where are we going?' *Malandela* asked.

Dambisa made no reply and behaved for all the world as if he did not exist, as if she were entirely on her own, paddling down the mighty Luangwa River.

'Young woman, tell me at least where we are going,' said *Malandela*. But *Dambisa* remained silent.

The canoe glided down the ageless river, through dark and frowning forests, past the tall rustling rushes and reeds that bordered many an unhealthy malarial swamp. Down the Luangwa River glided the canoe until at last the first light of dawn kissed the eastern skies.

The old witchdoctor *Shondo* was standing on a rock with *Nsongololo*, the former thief leader at his side, and both men were looking down at the sea of upturned angry faces belonging to tens of thousands of shocked Western Mambo tribesmen who had just learnt of the murder of their 'Little Father'.

'I do not believe you,' said a burly rascal named *Ntombela*. 'I think you are a liar. Why would *Malandela* attack and murder his own brother – the brother who is to us as the blood in our veins – part of us?'

'I wish to the gods I were lying,' replied the old man, tears flowing down his cheeks. 'I have not summoned so many of you here only to tell you lies. Our Little Father and all, except two, of his wives and children are dead in the Royal Kraal. Our warriors, and even the servants, fought to the bitter end in defence of our dear High Chief. But in vain. *Malandela* was too strong for us. He, yes even he, *Malandela*, was the one who cold-bloodedly slew his own brother – our Little Chief – on his own doorstep. That foul, defiled murdering cur – he killed our *Bekizwe*. He killed the Sun of Happiness that shone over our land.'

'Tell us that you are joking,' said *Ntombela*. 'Surely *Bekizwe* cannot be dead. No, no, I cannot believe it!'

'It is true, we swear it,' cried *Nsongololo*.

'Then why are we standing here like gossiping old women?' roared *Ntombela*. 'Why are you standing there and whining like a lost dog,

Oh *Nsongololo*? There is nothing we have to live for now. We are like trees with roots cut off. We have lost our father, our very blood. We have lost our head; and without a head, does the body not die? Our lives will never be the same again without *Bekizwe*, without the smiling Little One we loved so well. What is there left for us but death? Come on, you sons of defiled harlots, come on and let us first take the oath of vengeance. Then let us go and wipe that murdering dog *Malandela* and his band of cowardly curs off the face of the earth.'

'*Yebo*!' cried *Nsongololo*. 'Men of the Western Mambo, the blood of our dear chief cries out for revenge. His soul is roaming the Grey Land and it will never know peace until its murderer is dead! To enable our beloved chief's soul to find peace in the valleys of the Other World, we must kill *Malandela* and every Nguni in our country. Do you hear me? *Malandela* must die! Follow me, everyone.'

'Sound the signal drums!' roared *Shondo*. 'Send messages throughout the land. Send messages reading as follows: "*Bekizwe* dead. Murdered by *Malandela*. All Mambo. Able to fight. Assemble. Royal Kraal. Two days. Must Avenge. Our Little Chief".'

From hill to signal hill went the message; from valley to valley, plain to forest. Those who heard the terrible message took out their signal drums and relayed it farther, passing it on to other villages and kraals. A net of sound covered the shocked land. People heard the message and were stunned to the very marrow. Then their shock and surprise quickly gave way to cold anger.

Soon the footpaths leading to the half-burnt Royal Kraal were black with heavily armed bands of warriors keeping the rendezvous with *Nsongololo* who already had ten thousand men at his command.

Soon the mound of earth under which *Bekizwe* was buried became red with blood as thousands of warriors cut their hands slightly to let drops of blood fall on their Little Father's grave as they swore to avenge him, no matter what the cost. Some swallowed small pebbles from the grave mound with water as a sign of their dedication to vengeance.

At last all the oath-taking was done and an incredible horde of three hundred thousand men poured in a black flood towards the Madlonti mountains where the Nguni *impis* were hiding.

The Nguni suddenly found themselves completely surrounded by a sea of angry, bloodthirsty Western Mambo tribesmen and knew that a massacre was inevitable – a massacre in which the Nguni would be the victims. Not one of the Nguni *Indunas* was unaware that the Mambo were seeking revenge and would show no

mercy. They would be satisfied with nothing else but the complete annihilation of that vast Nguni army, down to the very last man.

This is what *Celiwe* wanted to prevent. She was aware of the importance of peace between the Nguni and the Western Mambo, because these two tribes needed time to prepare themselves to meet the threat from *Munumutaba*, whose hordes were now reported to be only a moon's journey away from the Zambezi. *Munumutaba* was reported to have vowed to wipe both the Nguni and the Mambo off the face of the earth in revenge for the theft of his sacred Bronze Idol, and for the murder of his two spies, *Luao* and *Dahodi*.

Celiwe therefore sent a message stick to the leader of the Mambo, *Nsongololo*. It was a beautiful mat on which patterns were woven translatable into the following: 'We desire peace with all our souls – the murderer of your chief has been exiled from our tribe.'

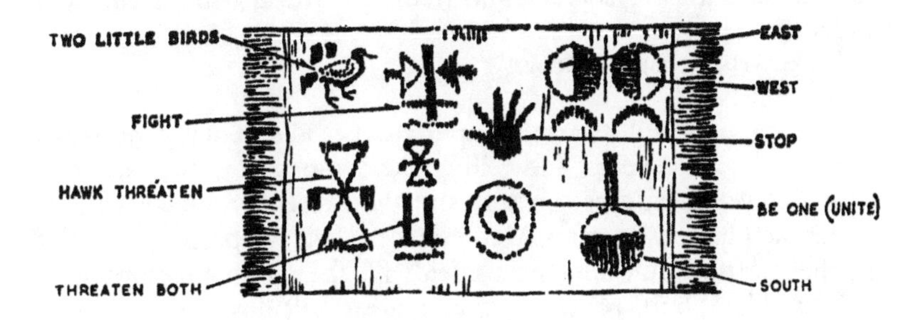

To this message *Nsongololo* replied arrogantly: 'You skulking mountain beasts, we have sworn to kill you all. Come out into the open and fight like men – so say we, you rotten vile cowards.'

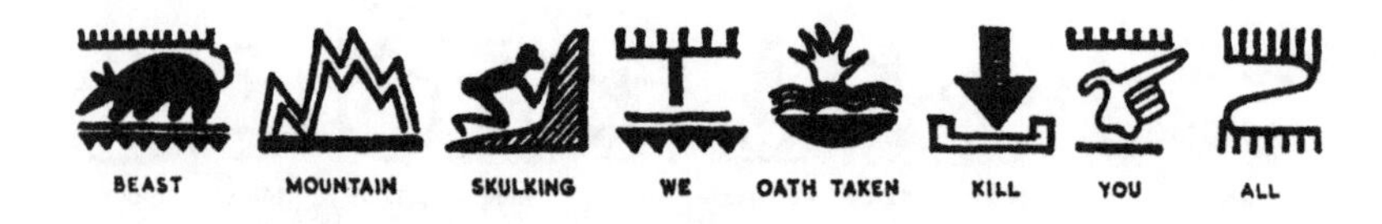

Celiwe made yet another moving appeal to *Nsongololo.* She sent a small fibre mat with violet patterns in it decipherable as follows: 'Two little birds, one from the East and one from the West, must not quarrel – a hawk from the South is threatening both. It is best for them to stand together.'

To this the Mambo replied curtly that battle would commence forthwith. And even as the Nguni received the message the Mambo was swarming up the slopes of their stronghold. *Ngovolo, Malangabi* and *Mapepela* rallied their men, exhorting them to fight and die like men and not let future generations call them cowards.

The well-trained and freshly experienced Nguni regiments fought back fiercely, flinging back one savage attack after another with spears and clubs – and even large boulders. The attacking Mambo were at a disadvantage on the open slopes and died like flies; but for every Mambo warrior that fell, a thousand took his place. The kranzes and the crags shook and trembled with the shock and fury of battle.

'*Bekizwe*! *Bekizwe*! *Bekizwe*!'

The Mambo are still swarming up the slopes like so many monkeys, with shields and spears, and yelling like demons from the sewers of hell. *Celiwe's* keen eyes can pick out the expression of savage fury and naked hatred on every Mambo face. Their weapons shine dully in the morning sun and their shields fill the mountain slope with colour. Black, red, brown, white, a great kaleidoscope of shields steadily spreading up the mountain side.

Behind their breastwork of stones and boulders wait the grim-faced Nguni regiments, their plumes fluttering and nodding in the mountain breeze. *Celiwe* crouches lower behind the rock and gives way to tears as Nguni spears take their toll of the advancing Mambo, spears that flicker briefly in the sun before they bury themselves in the bodies of the advancing warriors. Men cry out as they fall, and are quickly lost under the forest of legs. A tall handsome Mambo man gains the Nguni breastwork and two warriors fall under his axe. But *lo*! a young boy from the Mice Regiment hurls a spear straight and true into his chest and he falls like a tall tree. *Celiwe* sobs . . . sobs as she realises that perhaps that dying man has wives and children at home. Silently she curses the sheer wastefulness of war.

LET PEACE REIGN SUPREME

Peace thee, Peace thee, Oh my spirit,
Bow thy head to great *Somandla*;
Into His hands completely yield thee,
Into His mercy now surrender thee.
Though thou sufferest much disquiet,
The leopard of pain thy heart devoureth,
Though the jackal of sorrow howleth
Within the falling portals of thy soul.

Though raging foemen encircle thee
With whetted steel, vowing thee to slay;
Though scornful laughter pursueth thee,
From hostile mouths deriding thee!
Yield thee, yield thee to the Almighty.
Ere thou wert born He cared for thee;
And when thou diest, He shall be by thee.
Lackest thou then, a protecting hand?
Peace thee, and yield to Him entirely.

Are not the stars of His creating?
Do not the beasts proclaim Him Father?
Is He not Ruler of us all?
Is He not Owner of all these?

The River Time supports His canoe,
The fleeting years are slaves of His;
The laughing stars bow low to Him:
Is He not Sire of them all?

Bird, man, beast and tree He owneth;
Star, moon, sun and earth He ruleth:
Who dares to dispute His profound authority?
Peace! And yield completely to Him.
No Evil One there is but fleeth

When *Somandla's* name is noised;
There is no trouble but that vanisheth,
When thou callest, Him, The Highest!
He shall take thee in His dread arms,
And bear thee to the Vale of Quiet;
Before thy feet and from off thy path
He shall completely sweep all thorns.

Let Him be the Great Helmsman,
Who guideth thy life's canoe o'er rapids;
Let Him be thy hard Fire Stone,
That lighteth thy fire in Life's midwinter.

Peace thee, Peace thee, Oh my spirit!
Bow thy head before *Somandla*;
In life's dark jungle let Him be thy Axe,
That shall hack thy path for thee.
In life's chill winter makest Him thy *Kaross*
That shall keep cold winds from thee.
Let Him be thy sturdy Canoe,
Wherewith thou sailest unto Tomorrow!

The strange song echoed and re-echoed through *Malandela's* slumbering and troubled brain. Each word, each verse left a firm imprint in his memory. The beautiful flowing liquid tune rose and fell like a river in the canyons of his soul. Over and over again flowed the strange new song, a song destined to live for a thousand years.

It was the famous song which the Nguni, Zulu and Matabele of future ages were to sing in the darkest moments of their land's history. It was the great 'Song of *Malandela*' – a song that came to him while he slept, a troubled and dishonoured man. He had been deprived of his country by a scheming usurper and had lost not only his honour, but well nigh his life as well; he had lost everything – kingdom, honour, family – and was now sleeping in a small cave in a dark forest with a hard-lipped foreign girl by his side.

Let Him be thy sturdy Canoe
Wherewith thou sailest unto Tomorrow.

Over and over again, in a great glittering, rotating circle of heavenly melody, the song floated through the dark skies of *Malandela's* mind. It filled his veins with strength and it lit a roaring fire of hope in his soul. *Malandela* woke up suddenly, sat up. But the song and its tune was still clear in his mind.

Let Him be thy hard Fire Stone
To light thy fire in Life's midwinter.

'Am I mad?' muttered the exiled and disgraced chief. 'I did not make up a song – it just blossomed in my mind.'

'What is it?' asked *Dambisa*, addressing him for the first time in two whole days.

'I must have been dreaming, *Dambisa-Luwewe*. I dreamt about a song.'

'What song?'

'A strange new song with a beautiful tune. It was simply heavenly,' muttered *Malandela*, holding his forehead in one hand. 'I remember every word of it.'

'Let us sing it then, my beloved one,' said *Dambisa*. 'That song must be a gift to you from the spirits.'

'What did you call me?'

'I called you my beloved one,' *Dambisa* replied, 'and I love you – I have loved you for a long time. Now that everybody has deserted you and you are alone in the cruel world, I love you even more. I know that, come what may, I will always be by your side.'

'My future is dark, Oh *Dambisa*. We are hiding now in a dark forest in what was once my land. We are hiding like animals and our future is dark. Do you want to couple your life's youthful canoe to my life's sinking one?'

'The spirits tell me this could be the beginning and not the end, *Malandela*. They tell me this could be the beginning – the re-birth of *Malandela*, a new, wiser *Malandela*, purged of the sins of the past. A greater *Malandela* who will recover his throne and lead the Nguni once more into a glittering future full of happiness.'

'I have no such hope in my heart, Oh dear *Dambisa*. Do not try to light a futile hope within me. What I have lost, I have lost forever.'

'Come let us sing the song you dreamt about.'

It was already nearing midnight and the moon was high in the night sky. The crickets were harping their love songs under rocks and fallen trees and the owls were hooting derisively from the branches of tall *mopanis*. In the depth of the scowling forest lions roared savagely and leopards coughed challenges to those who dared to steal their prey.

In a small, cramped and lonely cave high on a rocky hill, an exiled chief sat side by side with a homeless and fatherless Baluba girl, singing a strange haunting song – a song destined to be sung by millions of men as yet unborn, men suffering and dying under stranger chiefs in a future more fantastic than the past had ever been.

Peace thee, Peace thee, Oh my spirit,
Bow thy head before the great *Somandla*.
In life's dark jungles, let Him be thy Axe,
That shall hack thy path for thee.
In life's chill winter, let Him be thy *Kaross*,
That shall keep cold wind from thee . . .

We were only one day's journey from the kraal in which the usurper *Vamba* ruled the land, which he and his gang of Vamangwe cut-throats had stolen from *Malandela*. Soon, oh so soon I would unseat that murdering Vamangwe devil and destroy him utterly and finally. As I lay tossing and sleepless on my sleeping *kaross* within the shelter we had erected for the night deep in an ugly forest infested with marauding beasts, I went over in my mind what I intended doing with *Vamba*. When I caught him, I intended making an *umkovu* out of him. This is done by cutting off the tip of the tongue and driving a thin steel spike carefully into the top of the skull, some short distance into the brain. This blots out all memory and an *umkovu* is thus a voiceless, memoryless, half-dead thing that lives on a diet of fermented millet and which wizards send into the kraals of their victims to kidnap people in their sleep or to drive poisoned awls into their ears and so kill them. An *umkovu* obeys anything you tell it to do – except crossing a river; for it develops an uncanny fear of water.

As I lay thinking and laughing to myself, I heard people singing far away in the distance. They were singing a strange and beautiful song, a haunting song, in the middle of the night. Who were they? What lonely castaways were they, and whence? I used my telepathic powers to catch the words of that fairy melody, that strange haunting song that made me feel like trading my immortality for earthly things, so that I could drop my age-old head and die. Yes, I wished to die and forever shut out this cruel and heartless world which only knew suffering of humans and beasts alike. I, the Lost Immortal, the Outcast of the Ages, hated by the gods and feared by men, leading a lonely unhappy life amongst stupid, selfish, bloodthirsty, quarrelsome, wretched mortals – who are, after all, only good for stewing.

Let Him be thy great Helmsman
Who guideth thy life's canoe o'er rapids.
Let Him be thy hard Fire Stone
That lighteth thy fire in Life's midwinter.

Oh poor human beings, poor pathetic hopeful mortals! Poor self-deluding and ignorant mortals! If only they knew how little the gods whom they seek as Life's Helmsman, could care about the Universe, about the creatures He created.

Being immortal is not a good thing because one has to live for thousands of years with naked and unpalatable reality as one's companion, while mortals like those midnight singers lived their brief quarrelsome lives along with that greatest deceiver of all: Hope! Hope that in one's hour of peril there is somebody looking after one like a fat old aunt who looks after an orphan boy; hope that in one's life there is a purpose and, that beyond the grave is yet another life. Hope that this evil today might fade and reveal a better tomorrow!

Hope, the Great Deceiver, which lying priests and deceitful witchdoctors use as a pedestal for their countless doctrines and beliefs. And yet, strangely enough, I would rather be a mortal, leading a brief, hope-filled life, than an immortal enjoying a life as bleak as the wastelands of the Ka-Lahari. Slowly I got to my feet and groped for my loinskin, and my heavy and ornately carved ebony staff.

I crawled stealthily out of the crude hut, taking care not to awaken the three infernal little pests I had the misfortune to call my daughters. I just did not, and still do not even today, know what to do with *Luanaledi, Mvurayakucha* and *Mbaliyamswira* – especially the first two. These voodoo girls, who are as ageless and as immortal as I am, were a plague – a High Curse on my shoulders. This evil spawn of both *Ninavanhu-Ma* and *Watamaraka* was the ruin of my life. They had the horrible habit of murdering any mortal woman who loved me and whom I wanted to marry. They had already killed five women whom I loved, simply because they themselves entertain an unnatural love for me, their own father, in their evil little hearts.

How I loathe and detest my daughters! I had once even tried to destroy the elder two but I had failed, because they were part of me. They were dedicated to spoiling everything I did, which they thought might turn my attention away from them. They had threatened to kill the Princess *Nomikonto* recently because she had kissed me in a fit of passion. Was there ever a man so cursed with a brood of foul little demon daughters?

I went outside and made my way past the big temporary huts that housed the Avengers, *Malandela's* changed wives and sister, and my puppet women who had formerly been the wives of the man called *Madondo. Mukombe*, my adopted son, must have seen me pass his tiny shelter because I felt his hand on my arm and, although I could not see him, I could see his soul and the anxiety and the love in his heart as he whispered: 'Great Father, where are you going?'

'Shhhh,' I whispered. 'I am going to the forest, son, to find the people I heard singing. Come with me and we shall find them together.'

'Let me get my weapons first, Great Father,' said the boy, adoration shining in his soul like a sun. As I stood waiting for him to return, I heard once again the distant singing. I smiled as I imagined their surprise when I walked into wherever they were and asked them the reason for their midnight singing. People are forbidden by law to sing at midnight and I intended to remind the unknown singers of that fact.

We had not gone far into the forest when I sensed *Luanaledi* following us quietly. Her thoughts were quite clear: she was thinking I was sneaking off with one of *Malandela's* many women and she was promising herself she would kill the woman before I could so much as kiss her.

I paused and called out angrily: 'Come out from behind that bush, you vile thing – I know you are there!'

She came out of her hiding place and made her way to where I stood with *Mukombe* at my side, and she said: 'Forgive me, father, but there is no reason why you should call me a vile thing in front of this little mortal here.'

'This little mortal here has a purer soul than you ever had, *Luanaledi*,' I retorted. 'He has not ruined my life in any way and he does not kill the women I love, as you filthy sluts do!'

'Father, listen,' said the girl in a voice so cold and so utterly without pity that it chilled my soul to the very core. 'We may be vile, we may be evil, or we may be any foul thing under the sun you care to call us. But remember one thing, we did not ask to be born and we cannot help feeling what we feel about you. We are the results of your stupid lusts: we are you! What evil there is in us we inherited from you. If you had been clean and free from evil we would have been clean and free from evil likewise. But we are the products of an evil father who associated with the Spirit of Evil, and an Imperfect Mother. Do dirty pots bring forth clean food? Do not the mortals say that rotten seed begets evil plants?'

I could listen to the tirade no more and walked on with the awful feeling that every word she had uttered had been nothing but the truth. I sensed great puzzlement in the heart of *Mukombe* who was immediately behind me. The poor innocent, adoring little mortal orphan could not understand what was happening.

The three of us pressed on deeper into the forest and at last we came to the source of the nocturnal singing – a small cave high on a rock-strewn hill.

'I see you, Oh midnight singers,' I said, as we stopped just outside their cave. 'Have you forgotten the law that says the hour of midnight must be respected? Do you not know that midnight is the hour of silence?'

Two brains, male and female, through which I could see as clearly as through the crystal water of a mountain stream, were clouded with fear, and a gasp escaped from the lips of the female: 'Who . . . what are you . . . ?'

'I am an old man and my name is *Lumukanda.* Unlike you, I do not have to ask you who you are. I am blind, but I know your name is *Dambisa*, and that the fat skunk with you is no other than *Malandela*, former chief of the Nguni.'

'But I have not told you my name; how do you know me?' cried *Malandela* in blank astonishment.

'Your lips did not speak, but your mind did, and that I can read more clearly than spoken words.'

'Are you a demon – a ghost – a *tokoloshe*?' asked the girl, panting with fright.

'My father is always joking,' quietly intervened *Luanaledi.* 'He is the Lost Immortal, and I may as well tell you that he has a strong weakness for human flesh.'

'What . . . !' bellowed *Malandela*, retreating deep into the darkest recess of the cave. 'The Lost Undying One?'

'*Yebo*,' I said. 'The lost undying one who has found a dying one, Oh Thundering Stomach! I have long since promised myself that on the day I meet you, I shall have a feast. Now come out of there and let us see if you taste as beautifully as you sing.'

'No . . . No! Have mercy, please! If you want to eat someone then eat me,' cried the girl *Dambisa.*

'That I shall do in any case.' And with these words I stooped into the cave and hauled the girl out into the moonlight. I felt her all over and said with a sigh: 'You are too slim and muscular, my girl, so you're not quite fit for the pot. But I sense your fat *Malandela* would give me heartburn, indigestion and a sore throat – so perhaps I shall spare both of you. Come with me and be my guests. Who knows, I might even consider helping you out of your predicament.'

'Let us first hear them sing the song they had been singing, my father – it was such a lovely song.'

Their throats were still dry from fright, but the relief my last word had brought induced them to start singing and soon we all joined in. The innocent mortal atmosphere brought tears to my eyes, especially when the voices reached the final verse in perfect harmony:

> Let Him be thy sturdy Canoe,
> Wherewith thou sailest unto Tomorrow.

'Please sing! Let us all sing this song once again!' I exclaimed.

Our voices rose into the silver night in perfect unison, floating over the brooding forest like incense from an altar. It seemed to me as if the very stars, which I had not seen for ages, bowed from their lofty thrones to listen. It felt as though the forest held its breath.

'Let us go,' I said at last. 'And, *Malandela*, I think you and I have a lot to talk about.'

On our way back to our improvised camp, I listened as both *Malandela* and the Baluba girl poured out their stories all too eagerly, like gushing springs of fresh water. On our arrival at camp, I woke up *Nomikonto* and had her relate to her brother *Vamba's* treachery and the blood-chilling adventures she and his wives had gone through in the Underworld. *Malandela* wept when he met the changed, wild-eyed survivors of his once great seraglio.

Nomikonto and *Lulama-Maneruana* stressed the need for finding *Muxakaza* immediately before the evil spirit that had taken possession of her could wreak havoc in the land. 'She is evil, Oh Great *Lumukanda*, very evil. We do not know where she went with *Vamba's* mother, but you must find her.'

'All in good time, Oh my children,' I said. 'Even an immortal cannot do two things at once and I think we must pack all our things immediately and be on our way. This time we are going into the land of the Western Mambo to avert a massacre. *Vamba* can wait – his turn will come!'

The Nguni regiments were still holding their stronghold on the Madlonti mountains in spite of repeated and fierce attacks by the Mambo *impis*. But the end was fast drawing near. The Nguni, who had not slept for four bloody nights and who were cut off from supplies and refreshments, were in the last stages of exhaustion. Their arms were numb and swollen from hurling spears and swinging clubs, axes and *pangas*. Many of them were falling easy victims to the fresher Mambo warriors who were continuously relieved from behind.

Celiwe knew that death stood only a few paces away, watching all of them – herself, her *Indunas*, warriors, and the boys from the Mice Regiment. Food and water were exhausted and some of her men had already died of thirst. Twice during a lull in the fighting *Celiwe* had sent her 'sacred messengers' to *Nsongololo* with offers of unconditional surrender. But the Mambo had replied with abusive signs to both requests. *Nsongololo* and his Mambo warriors wanted to kill them all, to the very last man.

'It won't be long now, Royal One,' said the one-eyed dwarf

Malangabi to *Celiwe*, with a hideous smile. 'Do not worry, we shall all be nice and dead soon. I am not scared – are you?'

'I am very scared, *Malangabi*. I am very scared indeed!'

'I wonder what happened to Old Thundering Stomach,' said *Malangabi* musingly. 'Somehow I have a feeling we might meet that man again if we live through this.'

'Not one of us will live through this, *Malangabi*,' said *Celiwe*. 'I only wish they would give us all a quick death.'

The ugly dwarf laughed. 'You will be the last one to get a quick death. You know what is done to the women of the defeated enemy. So, don't go hoping for a quick death, little one!'

'They have withdrawn for the present,' said *Celiwe* sadly. 'Perhaps they are eating their supper now that the sun has set. But they will be back. Will this never end?'

'It will, do not worry, and we shall all soon be in a better world – as happy as butterflies.'

The sun had already set and a great round tired moon was climbing wearily into the skies. *Nsongololo* was standing alone on the flat-topped rock this night. *Shondo* had been killed early in the day and *Nsongololo* was bitterly angry at the death of his friend. With gnashing teeth and frothing mouth, the former bandit leader was telling the thousands of men massed below:

'This is going to be the final assault on those Nguni dogs up there. This time we must overwhelm them and slaughter them to a man. When you go up there, remember what those scum did to our chief and his family. Let us go now and . . . kill them all!'

With bloodcurdling yells, the teeming thousands burst out of the forests in a thundering black flood. They swooped up the Madlonti slopes like a tidal wave.

'*Bekizwe*! *Bekizwe*! Kill! Kill!'

With these savage war cries, the Mambo hordes raced up the slopes, brandishing spears, axes, *pangas* and clubs, and not one warrior in all those incredible hordes but thirsted for Nguni blood. Not one warrior in that roaring sea of fierce humanity but hungered to slay the Nguni to the very last man. Vengeance is the sweetest and the headiest mead in creation. Drink from the Claypot of Revenge and drink deep! Happy . . . Happy are they who perish while avenging themselves on a hated foe! Happy is the one who will die first.

Thus the flood of humanity raced up the slopes, each man more eager than the other to see who could die first. Such is the law and the belief among all tribes: that the first, second and third to fall in a Battle of Vengeance receive special honours in the Other World. They are elevated to the rank of gods. Men have cheated and murdered, throughout the ages, to advance themselves to the position where they could be first to fall in a Battle of Vengeance.

Nsongololo has made up his mind that with this attack *he* is going to be the first to die and he is determined to kill any of his warriors who gains on him as he runs. *Ntombela* is close behind, but he is taking good care not to pass *Nsongololo.* Puffing and panting behind *Ntombela* is the fat *Mavuso,* the Story teller, who has already felled three Mambo warriors contending for third place.

The three men are running well ahead of the main hordes and they are beside themselves with joy. They are going to be the first to die – they are going to be gods!

'Hail to the three of you there. Happy are you – blessed are you who will die first!' shout the warriors from behind.

But, it was not to be. Nobody is destined to die first; nobody is destined to die at all.

Nsongololo sees it first, and stops dead in his tracks. All the Mambo hordes stop. They stop and they stare – up in the sky – a strange premonition. A ball of fire like a shooting star. No, a comet. They all see sights – the weirdest they have ever seen.

They see naked girls, covered in blood, riding human skeletons. They see them riding backwards on beasts like oxen covered with scales. They see human skulls and gory human limbs, and freshly cut-off human heads.

This is seen by Mambo and Nguni alike. They drop their spears and flee – a mighty stampede with Mambo and Nguni running shoulder to shoulder.

A mighty voice brings the terror-stricken mobs to a halt:

'Listen, Oh Mambo; listen, Oh Nguni. You shall forget your hatred for each other instantly; tomorrow you shall take a High Oath of Peace for a thousand years. I, the Lost Immortal, have spoken.'

It is midday and the sun is shining. A few clouds float like lazy flamingoes in the blue skies above. A wind is whispering its love song to the trees and the long grasses rustle as they dance to the tune. In the great gathering of tens of thousands of men, one loud voice is raised in violent protest:

'But this is contrary to the laws of our fathers! We cannot allow this to happen. The High Law states clearly that all aggressors must be wiped out to the last man. We cannot make peace with these Nguni dogs who invaded our country and laid waste part of it before murdering our chief. Do you hear me, blind wizard? There can be no peace between the Mambo and the Nguni!'

I am sitting on a high rock with my three daughters and one

adopted son, and I cannot suppress the smiles that have come to my face. That wordy individual named *Mavuso* does not know it yet, but he is talking himself into the stew pot. Not only is he excessively rude – he is standing between the Mambo and the Nguni and preventing them from reaching agreement. He has been at it from early morning and I have ordered my two zombies, *Nomeva* and *Muwaniwani*, to go to our temporary camp and get the biggest cooking pot we have. *Mavuso* does not know it yet, but he is already in the soup in more senses than one.

Peace is absolutely essential between the Mambo and the Nguni. A nation divided by internal strife cannot survive the onslaught of a powerful invader. Time is running out and it will not be long before *Munumutaba's* hordes invade. I cannot allow a single garrulous mortal to stand between me and my task of restoring peace to the land. So . . .

'We have brought the pot, Oh lord, and have lit the fires,' announces *Nomeva*. 'What are your wishes now?'

'Stay and rest here awhile, and you *Luanaledi*, lead me down to that talkative *Mavuso* – I have a bone to pick with him!'

I am being led down the great rock and into the vast crowd of men who cringe away as I pass. I cannot see their faces, but their thoughts spell sheer fright. Some are anxious to repeat last night's performance when I announced my presence. I am now focused on *Mavuso's* soul, and I read every thought as he stands there on his own in the centre of the rapidly enlarging circle. *Mavuso's* terror is growing as the distance between us decreases. I can see his courage oozing from his soul like sour milk from a cracked calabash.

'Tell me, *Mavuso*, what were you saying? I could not hear well from up there.'

Mavuso swallows hard, and I hear a strange hissing sound as he wets his loinskin.

'I . . . I said it is unlawful. No! No, get away from me . . . go away, you foul wizard. Do not touch me!'

'My son, you have just made the most delicious mistake of your life! You see, I have the nasty habit of devouring my opposition.'

I like men who have the courage to voice their opinions. They make such brave stew and such courageous roasts. *Mavuso* is merrily sizzling away in my big pot. My spectators were not too amused when I seized him, turned him upside down and crushed his skull on a rock . . .

'Is there anyone who still disagrees with my proposal for peace between the Mambo and the Nguni?'

'There is no one, great cannibal wizard. How can men voice their opinions if you cook them?'

'Who are you, little morsel?'
'*Celiwe*, Great One.'
'One of *Malandela's* wives?'
'*Yebo.*'
'Then I have good news for you. Your husband is alive and well, and you must return to him.'
'Never! I will never go back to that selfish monster – not that evil-hearted murdering brute. I live now to try and make my people happier. *Malandela* never did so – he oppressed them and only lived to gratify his vile appetite. I would rather die than go back to him!'
'Come here, my little one. Come to grandfather and let us discuss this properly.'
I see fear in *Celiwe's* little soul. She tries to escape, but *Luanaledi* seizes her and brings her to me. I sample her delicious little round body with my hands, and I sense the youthful beauty of her. A strange feeling creeps over me. I want her . . . madly. I want to possess her, with all my heart and soul. This little woman is kindness, wisdom, mercy personified. She would be wasted on that wretched dull-brained thin-blooded mortal *Malandela*. I can easily take her as wife. But I sense my daughter's thoughts. They know now that I love *Celiwe*, and plans are taking shape in their minds to kill her.
Celiwe must not die on my account. The two tribes need people like her. She must go back to *Malandela* and help him to rule wisely and somehow I have to force her to do so . . .
A second cooking pot has already been brought and into this I gently lift *Celiwe*. '*Nomeva*, add some water and light the fire.' And to *Celiwe*: 'This is your last chance, Oh beautiful one – I command you to return to your husband.'
'Never . . . Never!'
'I command you!'
'No.'
'If you don't, I shall cook and eat you.'
'That does not matter.'
'Why?'
'I loathe *Malandela*.'
The water is getting warmer and warmer and *Nomeva* is stoking the fire briskly. *Celiwe* refuses to change her mind, so . . . I lift the heavy lid on top.
'*Muwaniwani*, bring the pot herbs and yams.'
The lid flies off the big pot and *Celiwe* stands upright. 'No . . . No! Surely you don't mean it . . . cooking me alive!'
'I am not joking, young woman. Either you go back to *Malandela* or back down in the pot.'

'No, no . . . I mean yes, yes, I shall go back to him,' she wails, like a child.

'*Muwaniwani*, take her to our camp and dress her in full wedding regalia. Present her there to *Malandela*.'

And raising my voice to the crowds around: 'Hear me, Oh tribesmen of the Western Mambo. I now claim you as my people. I now declare myself as your new High Chief. I will stand no arguments and I have given you a graphic demonstration of what I do to people who oppose me. I am invincible – I am the Lost Immortal. I promise to rule you wisely. But you must obey my every command. My first command is, make peace with the Nguni here and now!'

Five hundred skilled wood carvers from both the Nguni and the Mambo tribes go into action. Seasoned *mngongo, mvongoti* and *chiwande* trees are quickly felled and split in two from top to bottom after the leaves and branches have been hacked off. Five hundred big Peace Bowls must be ready within two days. These double bowls are to be used in the great ceremony of the High Oath of Peace for a thousand years, between the Nguni and the Western Mambo. Each one must be carved to perfection and lavishly and skilfully decorated.

It is indeed strange to see men who were at each other's throats only yesterday, working together so feverishly. It is a rare and beautiful scene which I had seen only twice before in the many years of my life.

There is the tap, tap, tap of tempered steel adzes cutting into wood. Laughter and boasting jokes . . . and the work is going faster and smoother than I thought it would. One bowl is finished, a second, a fourth, a tenth. Two men from each tribe carve one double bowl and a third smooths it with a razor-sharp knife while a fourth heats the iron needles used in decorating it.

Meanwhile two thousand Mambo women and youths are building my great new kraal, the kraal I have decided to call *Tulisizwe* (bring peace to the land).

I want this kraal to be big enough to contain one hundred thousand people and I want it to be surrounded by a quadruple stockade bristling with sharp stakes and metal barbs. On top of that I am going to surround it with a double circle of deep ditches with metal-tipped stakes and also with a double circle of pitfalls and man traps sown with cruel stakes. I am doing all this because I can foresee a great war in the near future and I want to turn my kraal and all others in the neighbourhood into the most unassailable forts on earth.

Now I am busy re-forming the disorderly hordes of the Mambo into disciplined, hard-hitting regiments of five thousand men each. Each regiment is divided into two *mabuto* of two thousand five hundred men each, and the supreme commander of the regiment is called *Induna Yo Tingo*, or Rainbow *Induna*. Under the Rainbow *Induna* are two Battle *Indunas*, or Thunderbolt *Indunas*, each commanding a two thousand five hundred strong *ibuto*. Each *ibuto* is divided in turn into four parts of six hundred and twenty-five men under the command of a Battle Leader. When a command comes from the chief, it is received by the Rainbow *Induna*, who passes it to his two Thunderbolt *Indunas*, each of whom passes it on to the four Battle Leaders under him.

Should a Rainbow *Induna* be killed in battle, he is promptly succeeded by the two Thunderbolt *Indunas* who take joint command of the regiment. Should one or both Thunderbolts be killed or wounded, that regiment is withdrawn and reorganised behind the fighting lines.

There are also men known as Battle Avengers, a thousand to every regiment, whose duty it is to execute deserters on the spot and to catch and torture cowards. The penalty for cowardice is to have the 'members of manhood' chopped off and a wooden plug forcibly driven up the back passage.

A collection of four regiments is called an *impi* (army), and to each *impi* are always attached two or three Boys' Supply regiments and one *Sekela* (support and replacement regiment).

I have four regiments in my *impi* now, and the first is the Swallow Regiment under *Nsongololo*. This regiment wears headdresses of black sable antelope skin and the shields are black and white, and shaped like swallowtails. The second is the Storm Cloud Regiment under the fat *Ntombela*. Its members carry oblong heavy dark-red shields reinforced with wood and they are designed to spearhead any attack. The warriors carry five hurling spears each, and one heavy battle axe. Their headdresses are made of red-dyed ostrich plumes.

The third regiment under the command of *Dudula*, a heavily scarred one-eared veteran who has only half a nose, is called the Thunder Hawks. *Dudula* fought under *Mitiyonke*, father of *Malandela* and *Bekizwe*. The shields in this regiment are of untrimmed bull's hide, heavily reinforced with crocodile skin. The warriors wear a headdress of ornately carved wood with a cluster of hawk feathers on top. Each headdress is carved to represent a hawk's head.

The last regiment is called the Crocodiles, and each warrior is an expert swimmer, including the Rainbow *Induna*. I have designed this regiment for secret attack: they will fight on land as well as on water. This regiment is going to man the huge fortified battle rafts I intend to build on the Zambezi. Their duty will be to ferry troops across the river and to attack any enemy canoes trying to cross the river.

Under the command of the former fisherman *Mavimbela*, the Crocodiles are distinguished by their crocodile skin cuirasses and headdresses made out of the heads of crocodiles.

I also intend forming a fifth regiment of archers and slingers, to be called the Hornets. I want each one of these archers and slingers to be so well trained that he can put an arrow through a man's head at a hundred paces or sling a stone and hit a running guinea fowl at half-a-hundred paces. I know that if the *Munumutaba* attacks, much might depend on these archers and slingers.

Five days later. Everything was ready for the great Ceremony of Peace. Thousands of willing Mambo tribesmen had worked feverishly to finish the Great Kraal. Two thousand and ten men had been erecting the stockades, digging ditches and mantraps and carving huge wooden gates. More than ten thousand men and women had been occupied building huts at the fantastic rate of five hundred huts a day. My Great Hut, a gigantic monster of wood and grass which could easily accommodate a hundred men, was built over an underground 'secret dwelling' or 'boar's lair', as I had called it. It had been dug and tunnelled out of the hard clay by men whom I afterwards swore to secrecy. I did not want anyone, including the pests I call my daughters, to know what was going on and to have knowledge of my secret underground sanctuary.

Everything was ready for the great Ceremony and scores of oxen were being slaughtered for the feast. Women and girls were bringing in hundreds of claypots full of corn beer and thick-walled baked-clay cooking pots. Great cooking fires were lit; the cooking pots filled with water and the frying pots filled with fat.

It was not long before rows of boys started bringing along the fresh meat from the slaughter kraals on huge six-legged meat trays to the places of cooking.

From all over the vast land of the Mambo, gifts of thousands of cattle and goats were pouring into my new kraal – gifts for the 'Wizard Chief', as everyone began to call me.

It seemed that every kraal and village in the land was anxious to curry the favour of the feared and distrusted new chief, who had the nasty habit of eating people for breakfast if they so much as tried to criticise him.

The traditional gifts of girls were not forthcoming, however, because few parents relished the idea of sending their daughters as gifts to a wizard and a chief who might put them in the stewing pot rather than taking them to the love mat, as all good chiefs should.

Thus I was beginning to feel very lonely indeed. In fact, I was going to be the loneliest chief on earth, because my subjects treated me as one treats an evil and dangerous animal.

Whenever I summoned some of them to my presence, they came with shuffling steps and fear written all over their souls, and they were all too keen to get away from wherever I happened to be. Even my newly elected Rainbow *Indunas* spoke to me from a very safe distance of ten paces, crouching like runners about to take off. I did not like this at all, but there was nothing I could do to prevent it.

The cooking and the roasting had gone on right through the night and early on the following morning there remained only the final preparations before the Ceremony of Peace began.

The Laws of the Tribes require that if people intend to do something of importance, time should be taken to do that something properly and it was the deepest sacrilege for anyone to try rushing the preparations for something as important, as great and as sacred, as a Ceremony of Peace.

But now, everything was ready. The sun smiled from a cloudless sky and the birds sang their joy in the trees. The grass, already yellowing with the approach of autumn, or 'Late Summer' as the tribes call it, nodded and rustled to the faintest breeze.

Four powerful Nguni and four powerful Mambo warriors carried a great slab of sandstone into the kraal – the 'Peace Stone' – with a shallow scoop out of the centre. This stone was hollowed out by craftsmen who also decorated it with signs and inscriptions decipherable as follows:

'On top of me (over this stone) the two Tribes, Nguni and Western Mambo, made peace. Do not dig me up. Future generations respect this peace. All our evils of yesterday are here buried for a thousand years.'

The Peace Stone was carefully laid on two great *karosses* and the skilfully carved wooden peace bowls were arranged in a wide circle around the stone.

The ceremony begins – the ceremony on which so much depends for so many generations to come. Thousands of people converge on the great kraal and the hills overlooking *Tulisizwe* are black with distant spectators from the farthest corners of the Mambo land – even from beyond its borders.

News of this rare event has travelled like wildfire over the lands of many tribes. A Peace Ceremony! A rare thing that happens once every five hundred years.

Oh sacred, unforgettable ceremony, that means so much to so

many! A ceremony that means that men need go about no more with fear in their hearts – that means that men no more need take the whetted steel to fellow men. The weary wanderer shall no more be greeted by burning kraals and dead bodies in the valleys. In this land, at least, the war spear is broken and the voice of war shall shatter the peaceful night no longer.

The massed Nguni regiments face their former enemies across the Stone of Peace, but there is a green branch of *ntolwana*, instead of a spear, in the hand of every warrior. The frowning war headdresses have been laid aside, as have been all other war regalia, including shields. From the Nguni side, the Rainbow *Induna Mapepela* steps forward with a battle assegai in his hands. From the Mambo side, *Nsongololo* steps forward. But he is carrying nothing in his hands. Then the Nguni singers *Ziko* and *Majozi*, start up the Song of Peace:

> Now *lo*, the weary *impis*
> Lay down their bloody spears,
> And from war's night they turn away
> To seek the dawn of peace.
> Souls by hatred scorched, they seek
> Refuge now from hatred's flame;
> War-weary warriors come to seek
> The fair embrace of Peace.

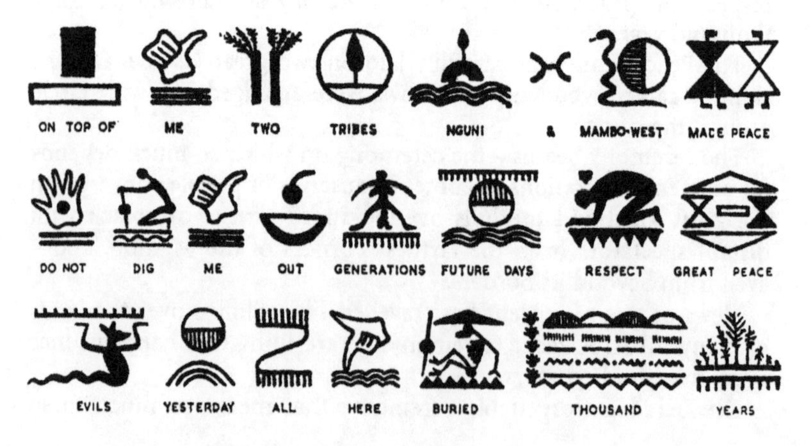

Let us come together friends
And build from war's destruction Love;
Those who carry hatred still today—
Let them do so never more.
The summer of peace has arrived,
War's dark winter has fled
And never more shall there be heard
Amongst us, the Song of War.
The dark deeds of yesterday,
My brothers, let's bury them now;
Let us now as brothers wait
For tomorrow's peaceful dawn.

Mapepela slowly stretches out his arms and offers the spear to *Nsongololo*, shaft end first. *Nsongololo* takes it and breaks it over his knee and throws the two halves contemptuously to the ground.

He extends his right hand and shakes hands with *Mapepela*, who leans over the Stone of Peace and kisses *Nsongololo's* forehead briefly. Both men stretch out their arms and touch one another's shoulders before changing places. *Mapepela* returns to stand in front of the Mambo and *Nsongololo* returns to the ranks of the Nguni.

'I see you, Oh brother,' says *Mapepela* to *Nsongololo*. 'May, as of now, the cloud of war vanish between you and me forever. May there no longer be strife of any sort between us. May peace be the torch to light us both on our way and may the deeds of the past, though impossible to forget, be remembered without rancour. May, on the refuse that is the past with all its mistakes, the plant of a peaceful and enlightened future grow. May we, on the cinders of the past, build a new kraal of understanding, love and brotherhood between our two tribes – a kraal that will stand for a thousand years as an example to future generations.'

'I see you brother, and I see you again,' *Nsongololo* now replies. 'My eyes look upon you in peace and my heart is white when I see you. Both you and I can now face the future without having the gritty dust of hatred blinding our eyes. We can now face the future without the wood smoke of enmity itching our eyes. We can now swim across the River of Life unhampered by the grindstones of war tied around our necks. I see you, Oh brother, and I see you again and yet again. As from now, when you come into my kraal, I shall give you water to wash your hands and food to still your hunger. My daughter shall lay a sleeping mat for you and you shall spend the night in my kraal without fear. Brother, I see you and I see you in peace. Between us the tool of war has been broken and there is peace between us. Our tribes shall stand together and face the future side by side.'

Two old Tribal Avengers hand out small knives to the warriors, one to every tenth man, and with these knives the Nguni and the Mambo warriors each make incisions between the thumb and forefinger of the left hand, and they all let some blood drip into the Bowl of Peace nearest to them. There is one double Peace Bowl to every one hundred warriors – fifty Mambo and fifty Nguni. When the bowls are half-full, the two old Avengers go from bowl to bowl pouring bitter *joye* juice into the blood to prevent it from coagulating.

When all this is done, the Avengers call upon the Great Spirit and the Holy Ancestors of both tribes, to witness the Vow of Peace which the Nguni and the Mambo now make to each other. The Rainbow *Indunas* take all bowls and empty them into the great hollow in the Stone of Peace.

At the command of the Avengers, the warriors, both Nguni and Mambo, queue up in one long line and march past the great Stone of Peace. As each warrior and *Induna* passes, he dips his forefinger of his right hand into the blood and then puts that finger into his mouth after which he says aloud: 'I am one with my brothers and they are one with me. Whoever attacks the Mambo now attacks the Nguni. Where there was war, there is now peace; and where there was disunity, there is now unity.'

There is a continuous drone of voices for a long time as warrior after warrior repeats the words – words which one must speak with all sincerity straight from the heart, because the spirits must see the genuineness of the desire for peace in the hearts of all the members of the two former enemies.

By midday the solemn ceremony is over, but one more ritual remains to be done. The Little Queen *Celiwe*, whom the Nguni warriors have chosen as their chieftainess, with *Malandela* demoted to Prince Consort, steps up to the Stone of Peace with a ceremonial water pot on one shoulder. A woman named *Nonudu*, representing the Mambo tribe, also carrying a claypot full of water, approaches from the opposite direction and, like *Celiwe*, puts her pot down on the Stone of Peace. A young girl brings a gourd water scoop to the two women.

Celiwe takes the vessel and scoops out some water and hands it to *Nonudu* who drinks the water and, with the same scoop, hands *Celiwe* some water from her pot. Then they both wash one another's hands upon the Stone of Peace, before leaping on to the stone itself and falling into one another's arms in a fierce embrace.

With shattering abruptness the drums crash out a booming torrent of savage noise; the fierce sinuous Dance of Life begins – the Dance of Life which seals the Peace Ceremony.

From behind a tall grass fence there emerges a weird figure: a man dressed up as the Holy Tree of Life, with little carved figurines of men, birds and animals dangling from every branch of his wood and bark costume. My eldest daughter *Luanaledi*, bursts through the crowd daubed from head to foot in white clay, representing the First Goddess *Ninavanhu-Ma*. Leaping, shaking, swaying, and all but tying herself in knots, she dances around the Tree of Life while the storm of drumbeats mounts to a deafening crescendo. Slowly and menacingly the Tree of Life approaches her while she dances. But like a lithe phantom, she leaps away from her would-be captor and dances in dizzy circles around him. Then, from one of his many branches, the man representing the Tree of Life plucks a soft sphere woven out of bark and hurls it accurately at the dancing girl, enacting that incident so long ago when the Tree of Life threw the moon at the First Goddess.

The drums roar out as the Tree seizes the make-believe Goddess and pretends intimacy with her. Rattling nuts are shaken and everybody dances as my daughter, in the role of the Goddess, writhes and screams on the ground in pretended labour, symbolising the lengthy agony the Goddess suffered before she gave birth to the First People.

The first dance is over and everyone takes refreshments. Huge trays full of well-stewed and well-roasted meat are attacked with savage gusto. Giant claypots full of beer are emptied of their contents in the twinkling of an eye. Roars of laughter fill the air with an earth-shaking din.

Outside the kraal, lively contests are held by boys – running, wrestling and stick fighting – contests in which the victors win either one or both the lungs of an ox, roasted or boiled to perfection. My son by adoption, *Mukombe*, has won a delicious boiled lung in a stick fight.

The great feast, with close to ten thousand people participating, not counting the two armies, is by no means a disorganised affair. Under the gaiety, the singing, shouting and laughter, stern rules of feasting are being strictly adhered to. For example, each kind of meat is eaten only by that age group supposed to partake of it. The warriors eat what is known as the 'warriors' meat' – that is, the flesh from the heads and hooves of the oxen and also the tails and the intestines which have been stuffed into the stomach bag together with fat from the kidneys, before being boiled. The Rainbow *Indunas*, Thunderbolts and Battle Leaders eat only the liver and the kidneys and the left haunches, while old men, regardless of rank and social status, eat what is called the 'meat of the Grey Ones' – that is, the tongues and the right haunches.

All strangers are given meat from the forequarters, while all beggars are given what is called 'beggars' meat' – that is, the back passages and the genitals.

Married women eat only the very fat meat from the breast bone, while virgins eat the udders of cows, slaughtered expressly for this purpose.

Adolescents of both sexes eat the brains and the left-overs from any of the other age groups.

Newly married brides are not given any meat; the law forbids it. They must be content with soup, yam stew and corn cakes.

All men born out of wedlock, all impotent men who have no wives, and all liars and cowards, have been separated from the rest of the people and are shut inside a dark hut guarded by two burly warriors. They eat the 'meat of shame' – that is, the urine bladders, and goat's meat mixed with a little earth.

Suddenly there are hoots of laughter as *Mboza*, one of the male cooks, who has been caught eating the meat of the Rainbow *Indunas*, is brought forward for punishment. A cracked old clay pot is fitted over his head and he is made to wear a heavy necklace of the jawbones of goats and oxen, while his stomach is smeared with black soot from the bottom of cooking pots. His loinskin is torn off and a witchdoctor paints the following signs on his bare buttocks in white clay: 'I AM A THIEF.'

The laughter reaches hysterical proportions as *Mboza*, the best cook in the whole land, is made to run the gauntlet of warriors who each gives him a heavy kick as he passes. *Mboza* ends up by running blindly into the closed gate, which he hits head on, shattering the pot on his head and falling heavily on his fat buttocks. He is not seriously hurt, however, and his fellow cooks carry him to his hut with many a ribald 'cook-place' joke.

The eating and drinking and singing is over and people wait tensely for what is to follow. They do not have long to wait. A horn bugle sounds and a great monstrosity of wood and skin and clay enters the main gate of the kraal. This monstrosity is a great fish, hideous, with a mouth full of wooden teeth and a body of cow skin, wooden fins and tail, and painted all over with fertility symbols. Its eyes, skilfully painted in white, yellow and black, glare menacingly at the people. This fish is supported by fifty warriors dressed in grass, tree leaves and fibre from head to foot, and a red-daubed girl rides on top. With her is an ugly man, the dwarf *Malangabi*, the Nguni Rainbow *Induna*. The girl is *Ntombazi*, the Mambo girl who has for a strange and very interesting reason fallen madly in love with *Malangabi*.

The fish represents that great 'Fish of the Seas' on whose back the

Father and Mother of the Second People, *Odu* and *Amarava*, escaped when the empire of the red-skinned First People was destroyed. *Malangabi* represents *Odu* while his adoring sweetheart represents *Amarava*, whose name was afterwards corrupted to *Mameravi* – Mother of Nations – by the Sacred Storytellers.

Reed flutes shriek out and xylophones rattle as everybody – man, woman and child – rises and begins to dance.

The second part of the 'Dance of Life' has begun.

Soft-eyed virgins abandon their shyness and turn into ravening bolts of dark-brown, passion-charged lightning and they leap, shake, sway and even turn complete somersaults to the music of flutes, pipes, and *marimba* xylophones. Old men and women forget their age as the wild 'Song of Fertility' rises to a savage crescendo. They forget their toothless mouths, wrinkled faces and bodies. They forget their age-stiffened joints, age-cooled veins and weakened muscles. They yell at the tops of their voices and stamp their thin, wasted feet. They are slow and clumsy and many are not even in step, but they do not care. Any step, as long as it is a dancing step, caper or gallop, will do.

If only I still had my sight to see this marvellous spectacle . . . If only I could see . . .

The married man dances with his wife, or wives; lover with lover; unmarried girls dance in 'regiments' on their own, openly flirting with and teasing the hot-blooded warriors dancing opposite them.

With a nerve-jarring suddenness the growling drums boom out, adding more sound to the incredible barrage of noise. The dancing reaches heights of wild abandon, terrible to behold. Savagely dancing girls and screaming women tear into the ranks of the maddened warriors – twisting, shaking, leaping and bending. Two of the men are sent spinning by women who strike them in the groin with their broad hips. Here and there a girl is tossed into the air and expertly caught by strong arms as she comes down. An exhausted married woman is carried away by her husband amid shouts of laughter and crude banter.

Malandela carries his tiny Queen *Celiwe* on one wide shoulder out of the jostling crowd which is now fast losing control as people dance around the great monstrous fish with its bearers and riders. The Princess *Nomikonto* is dancing with her new lover, the singer *Ziko*. *Lulama-Maneruana* and the rest of *Malandela's* changed wives, whom he refuses to take back and who are all mine now, are also among the crowds and all but dancing themselves into a frenzy. The only people who are not dancing are my three puppet women who are serving me with food and beer, here where I sit – an island of unhappiness in a seething ocean of joy and wild abandon. Beside me sit five of the masked Avengers, including the Avenger Leader. Strict custom forbids Avengers from taking part in any dance, singing or burial, unless it is the burial of an executed person.

The dance is now at its wildest and the venerable old man, the sage *Mpungoso*, the Master of Ceremony of the Feast of Peace, makes his way to the drummers and raises his long black Stick of Wisdom. The beat of the drums slowly dies away. The dancing and singing now also dies down and people sort themselves out and seat themselves with many a weary sigh. The great moment has arrived for the burying of the Stone of Peace in the centre of my kraal. Absolute silence is now imperative.

A drunken man and his wife who had trodden on one another's toes during the dancing and who had continued shrieking obscenities at each other, regardless of the order for the Holy Silence, are seized by the Tribal Avengers and taken out of the kraal. They are going to be hung by the wrists from a *marula* tree and given a hundred lashes each with a rawhide whip.

A heavy thrashing was also to be given, in my Great Hut, after the feast, to a hot-blooded beautiful stranger, the widowed *Noliyanda*, daughter of *Xhosa*, a thieving chief who rules a small breakaway tribe of expert cow thieves. They call themselves the Ama-Xhosa, after their chief. This tribe inhabits a small portion of the land of the Mambo, towards the southern tip.* *Noliyanda* had been given by her father, *Xhosa*, to *Shondo* the witchdoctor, as the price of *Shondo's* services in curing his persistent headaches. *Shondo* was killed in the battle of the Madlonti mountains and he had only received his golden-brown dark-eyed, full-hipped and full-breasted, though sterile, beauty thirteen months before.

Noliyanda had been caught trying to seduce a young boy of eighteen years to go into the bush with her during the wildest moments of the Dance of Life. This female was notorious for her strange love for boys younger than herself and already the stern Avenger Leader is pressing me to have her whipped to death in public for her offence.

I nod in agreement; even I dare not stand in the way of tribal justice. But I have a strange feeling of sorrow as I agree to this. I wish to spare *Noliyanda* from such a harsh chastisement. An exciting idea dawns above the valleys of my mind – an idea that banishes the crushing feeling of sorrow and loneliness in my heart and makes me smile broadly and say to the proud Avenger: 'Yes,

---

* *It is this thieving tribe of cunning bush-skulkers which in later years blossomed into the mighty and famous Xhosa nation after the Great Journey to the South.*

Oh Avenger, the woman shall be whipped to death as the law requires.'

I had decided suddenly that I desperately needed a First Queen. I intend stealing *Noliyanda* and bringing her back to me afterwards, secretly, so that my three daughters will not interfere until it is too late.

I have made up my mind that I am going to train *Noliyanda* into being the most perfect and most powerful being in the Universe – a being against whom my three daughters will be powerless. I need a wife.

The Stone of Peace is lowered into the great hole that has been dug in the centre of my kraal and now comes the most harrowing part of all this strange and uncommon ceremony. Two brave warriors are required now – brave men, one each from the two opposing tribes – a Nguni and a Mambo who must don full battledress and be buried alive in the hole with the Stone of Peace. This is the final tragic seal of peace between the two tribes – the most cruel sacrifice of all.

No word is spoken and people must communicate by signs only. Everyone grows tense and there are tears in the eyes of many. With a whispered curse, the dwarf *Malangabi* leaves the ranks of the Nguni and stands forward, but *Mpungoso* thanks him in sign language and waves him back – he is too ugly and deformed.

The two men needed for this final part of the ceremony must be the most handsome, the most brave and the strongest men from either tribe. Tension mounts as a tall, lean hard-lipped Mambo steps forward. A loud cry follows as a Nguni warrior also steps forward.

HIS ADOPTED SONS

'Oh no!'

That agonising cry is wrung from the lips of a round-faced girl somewhere in the vast silent crowd. But the cry is cut short as the girl's mother clamps her hand hard over her offending offspring's mouth.

The hard-eyed tall Mambo has stepped forward. He is *Luti*, the son of *Vezi*. But the handsome Nguni is known only as *Mdelwa*, and he does not tell *Mpungoso* who his father is.

The Mambo girl who cried out has been *Mdelwa's* sweetheart for the past few days and she is horrified and brokenhearted when she sees her beloved thus forsake his young life and her.

Two Avengers lead the young men away to be dressed and fully armed. When at last they come out of the huts, striding abreast with heads held high and their weapons and bracelets shining in the sunlight, the young girl, *Nozipo*, breaks free of her mother's detaining arms and throws herself at *Mdelwa's* feet. 'No, *Mdelwa*, you cannot do this – not you *Mdelwa*!'

One of the Avengers seizes the sobbing girl roughly and drags her aside. *Mdelwa* and *Luti* help each other into the pit and both squat upon the Stone of Peace, facing each other. With a smile on his cruel, hard features, *Luti* extends his hand and shakes *Mdelwa's* hand as the deep pit is filled in rapidly by fifteen Avengers, using hoes and canoe paddles.

Nozipo suddenly goes limp in the Avenger's arms, and when he looks down he finds that she is dead.

She is lowered into the half-filled pit, from the bottom of which at this stage only the headdresses of the two entombed warriors are protruding.

'Tell your children, and urge them to tell their children,' bursts forth the philosopher *Mpungoso* as he stands over the pit which is now completely filled in and stamped over. 'Tell them that in the centre of this kraal built by *Lumukanda*, King of the Western Mambo, the Peace Stone is buried. Tell them that here the Mambo and the Nguni broke the spear of war and made peace forever. Here we buried the mistakes of our yesterday and two brave young men sacrificed their lives so that you might live in peace together – to the end of time. Disperse now, and go to your homes. Go to your homes carrying with you the memory of what happened here today.'

The guests disperse in their thousands, some to their homes, as far as ten days' journey away, and all of them carry with them memories which will always be fresh in their minds to the day they die.

Malandela is weeping bitterly, because only he knows who *Mdelwa's* father is. Many years ago *Malandela* had forcibly dishonoured a young girl in a forest and she had conceived and later given birth to a baby boy under heavy guard in one of *Malandela's* many kraals, where he had kept her for more than a year. The reason why *Malandela* had kept this girl, *Nonsizi*, a prisoner was due to her age – a mere child of twenty and thus of the age as yet not permitted by tribal law to sleep with a man, or to be slept with. *Malandela* who was in those days an insolent and blundering tyrant, had kept the girl a prisoner in order to avoid a scandal and because raping a girl who is under twenty and who has not been initiated into womanhood in accordance with the Laws of the Tribes, promptly invites death for the offender at the hands of the Tribal Avengers. *Nonsizi* had died mysteriously six months later and the little boy, *Mdelwa*, whose name means 'Forsaken One', had been brought up by two old women in the secret kraal. *Malandela* had never recognised *Mdelwa* as his son and although *Mdelwa* had once saved *Malandela's* life in battle, he had never been promoted or thanked by his father. *Mdelwa* had known very well who his father was, but had chosen to take this secret to the grave with him.

Although peace has been made between the Mambo and the Nguni, there is still someone in the land of the Mambo whose heart is on fire with revenge and grief. This is the Second Queen of the murdered Mambo Chief *Bekizwe*, who is dying in her father's kraal far away. She gave birth to a baby girl three days ago and although the baby is alive and well, the mother is dying. Beside her kneels *Tembani*, her faithful handmaiden, and to this bitter and ill-favoured woman the dying queen says: 'Now promise me, *Tembani*, that you will take my little girl and bring her up as your own child. But remember, when she reaches puberty, you are to tell her exactly who her father was and how he died. You are to make her take an oath that one day she will kill *Malandela* and thus avenge her father – do you hear me?'

Tembani places her right hand below the navel of the dying queen and solemnly swears to do as bidden. Then, as the woman dies, *Tembani* whispers in her ear: 'Do not worry, Oh my mistress, because even if it takes me a thousand years I shall grant your dying wish. I shall bring up your premature little girl *Pindisa* (Vengeance) as if she were my own, and when she has grown up – *Malandela* shall die!'

After the guests had dispersed and the memorable ceremony was over, a company of warriors which had been out patrolling the forest, returned home just before sunset, bringing with them the First Queen of the murdered Mambo Chief. They had caught *Nunu* in a cave where she was hiding *Zulu* and *Qwabe, Bekizwe's* little sons. The Battle Leader commanding the company knelt before me and said:

'We found this woman hiding in the forest with these two children, Oh Great One. They are *Bekizwe's* two sons and his First Queen, *Nunu,* this most hideous and ugly female here. What shall we do with them, mighty King?'

'Take them to the women's huts and tell the Royal women to wash and feed them. Then call the Nguni ex-chief *Malandela* to my presence,' I commanded.

A short while later, *Malandela, Celiwe, Dambisa-Luwewe* and six Nguni Rainbow *Indunas* entered my Great Hut and I lost no time in telling them about the woman and the little boys who had been found in the forest.

'I have lost all my children, *Lumukanda,*' said *Malandela* at length. 'And since the High Gods in their mercy have spared two of my brother's sons, I shall adopt these boys and make them my sons.'

'The adoption will be in strict accordance with High Laws,' said *Celiwe.* 'We must make preparations for a Ceremony of Adoption immediately.'

'Do the Rainbow *Indunas* agree to this?' I asked, absent mindedly tapping the huge cooking pot.

'Great One, we give this adoption not only our fullest agreement, but our blessing as well. We consider it to be the best thing that can be done for the departed one, *Bekizwe's,* memory. It will go down in history as the noblest deed *Malandela* ever accomplished and it will, in our eyes, salvage for him a little of the respect we lost for him on the day he was disgraced,' said *Mapepela,* the Nguni Rainbow *Induna.*

'Those are indeed words of wisdom, *Mapepela.* I wonder what a man as wise and as fat as you will taste like in the shape of stew. Quite noble, I suppose.'

Nervous laughter followed this remark and *Mapepela* suddenly found that his bladder needed relieving. He crawled out of the hut, followed by titters from *Celiwe* and *Dambisa.* Shortly after that the Avenger Leader entered and stood before me, his soul radiating insolence and righteous anger. (Avengers never kneel before chiefs and they always address even the highest of High Chiefs in a haughty manner.)

'Chief!' he snapped. 'The time has come for the punishing of that unnatural beast named *Noliyanda*, who tried to seduce a young and uninitiated boy. I demand that all the women in your kraal and all the Rainbow *Indunas* attend.'

'It is fortunate for you that Avengers are such revered people,' I told him coldly, 'otherwise I would have roasted you so fast for your insolent words, that you would find no time to scream until you were half digested! Bring the woman in and have her whipped to your heart's content. You, *Malangabi*, go and call the Royal Women and the other Rainbow *Indunas*.'

The great hut was full of people, men and women who had come to witness the punishment of *Noliyanda*, the Xhosa woman. There were a series of gasps from the women when the beautiful woman was brought in and flung unceremoniously at my feet. I sensed her shrinking, frightened soul clearly. She was so scared that she could not think and her thoughts were a hopeless jumble.

'You do not know it yet, my beautiful one,' I thought to myself, 'but you are not going to rot in a grave of shame. I shall revive you and make you into an undying goddess. You have not come to the end of your life yet; you have, in fact, come to your rebirth.'

The Avenger Leader then spoke and his voice was a harsh rasp in the silent hut: 'You, *Noliyanda*, the only daughter of a thieving bastard named *Xhosa* who calls himself chief of a dog tribe known as the Ama-Xhosa, are accused of trying to mislead a young and uninitiated boy. Do you deny the charge?'

'Yes,' gasped *Noliyanda*.

'Why?' grated the Avenger.

'I . . . I . . .'

'Be silent!' cried the Avenger Leader. 'One of you, bring in that boy.'

'I have already brought him in, Oh Great Leader,' one of the Avengers replied.

'You, boy, stand up!' roared the Leader. 'What is your name; how old do you think you are; who is your father; who was your grandfather; what did this woman say to you and what did you say to her? Answer!'

'I . . . My name is *Vumani*, Great One,' stammered the boy. 'I am the son of *Ntombela*, the Rainbow *Induna*. My grandfather was *Malevu* . . .'

'What did this woman say to you? And what did you say to her?'

'It was during the dance, Oh Great One . . . I was also among the dancers. She . . . She . . .'

'She did what? And whom do you mean by "she"? Don't waste

my time boy; speak clearly if you value your wretched life. She did what?'

'She drew me aside and told me to come to the forest with her . . . She said she had something to show me.'

'What did you say to her? And what did you think about what she said? The truth, boy!'

'I asked what it was she wanted to show me and she laughed and said I would see when I got there. I told her that father forbids us to go into the forest on our own and . . .'

'And what?' roared the Leader. 'Speak up, you unclean brat!'

'She kissed me in the mouth . . . with her tongue . . .'

'So!' hissed the Leader. 'And what did you think of all this?'

The boy did not answer and I, who could see in the depths of his mind, clearly fathomed what he had thought when she had kissed him. He had felt very strange and frightened at the same time – but also very curious, as any boy would be under similar circumstances. I realised that if he admitted this to the Avenger Leader he would be put to death immediately and without mercy. So, to thwart the old Avenger, who was trying to trap the lad into convicting himself, I took command of the boy's mind and replied through his lips:

'I was frightened, Oh Great One . . . very frightened.'

'You can sit down now,' growled the Leader. 'You are a good child.'

Noliyanda was tied to one of the solid posts supporting the hut and whipped until she lost consciousness. Then water was thrown over her and when she came back to life she was whipped again, this time until she dropped in a dead faint. I commanded my two strongest zombies to follow the Avengers who were taking *Noliyanda's* limp body away for burial in the forest.

Outside, the angry skies were being torn by lightning. Earth-shaking peals of thunder exploded again and again above the cringing land. Soon hail and rain would sweep the forest-clad hills, valleys and plains.

No sooner had the Avengers buried the not-quite-dead woman and left, when my two zombies exhumed her and carried her back to the kraal, which they entered through a secret tunnel known to me and them alone. Under cover of the roaring darkness, *Noliyanda* was brought into my dark and empty Great Hut, and lowered carefully into the secret underground dwelling place. *Nomeva* then securely fastened the wickerwork door of the hut and joined *Muwaniwani* and me in the secret dwelling.

My two zombies carefully washed the half-dead woman with hot water and laid her very carefully on a big rush mat. Then I ordered *Muwaniwani* to cut the woman's scalp carefully away from the crown of her head and remove a large disc of bone from her skull, using a tempered steel chisel and an obsidian hammer. For some time there was the sound of the tapping of the hammer on the chisel, as I performed the operation through the mind and hands of *Muwaniwani.* Eventually the disc was loosened and the brain exposed. I produced a small green emerald with a strange irridescence which *Muwaniwani* inserted between the two lobes of the brain.

'Replace the bone disc and tell me what happens.'

'I have replaced the bone disc,' said *Muwaniwani* in a hollow voice. 'It looks as if the bone is fusing again . . . it is healing . . .'

'Replace the scalp,' I said, concentrating hard on inducing the damaged tissues to heal, with all the mental powers at my disposal. The half-dead woman would henceforth cease to age. I had endowed her with immortality.

'I have replaced the scalp . . . the flesh is healing. The heart is beating normally. She breathes normally too,' said *Muwaniwani.* 'Her face has assumed a strange beauty, her body also. She seems to be taller than she was. But her hair has turned grey – a purplish-grey.'

'Go on,' I said.

'She has moved one arm – her eyes are now open. She is looking at you now, my master. There is surprise on her face. She has passed into unconsciousness again.'

I sent a sharp mental command that shocked the unconscious woman back to life once more.

'What happened? Where am I?' she gasped.

'Do not ask silly questions,' I snapped. 'Tell me who you are. What is your name?'

'*Noliyanda,*' she whispered. 'I am *Noliyanda,* and yet I am not! I feel very strange.'

'Close your eyes and tell me what you see.'

'I see stars . . . a great darkness. I see strange men and women who shine, like the sun. I also see a great tree with animals growing from its branches like fruit. I see many strange things – thousands of people – monsters . . . No, I can't bear to look! It is such a vast spectacle . . .'

'What do you think it is?' I asked gently.

'Something tells me I am seeing the Birth of Eternity . . . and the furthest future. It is awe-inspiring . . . unbelievable . . . The gods and goddesses, and the Tree of Life are talking about me. They say I must be destroyed immediately. Why . . . what am I? What have you done to me? What have you turned me into . . . you blind and utterly wicked monster!'

'I have made you into my wife, Oh beautiful one,' I said. 'You are going to be the most perfect and most beautiful being in the Universe and you are mine, and mine only, *Noliyanda.* No god or goddess can harm you now, because I have turned you into a goddess yourself.'

'You evil demon!' she cried. 'You unclean and impious monster from the depths of hell! Who gave you the right to create me into a goddess?'

I brushed *Muwaniwani* aside and took *Noliyanda* in my arms – violently and with great passion. I was madly in love with her.

'I turned you into a goddess, because I love you, my Queen,' I said harshly. 'You are mine and nothing will ever take you away from me. Sleep now – take a good rest, my Queen.'

Malandela, Celiwe and *Dambisa-Luwewe* woke up very early the next morning and began their three-day fast in preparation for the Ceremony of Adoption to be held on the night of the fourth day.

First *Celiwe,* the newly appointed High Queen of the Nguni, and *Malandela,* her consort, and *Dambisa, Malandela's* concubine, had to drink a strong *mbiza* purgative to clean out their stomachs. Then all three shut themselves in a hut whence they were not to emerge until the ceremony was over. They had to fast for three whole days, touching neither food nor drink, purifying themselves in preparation for a ceremony which would make the little boys, *Zulu* and *Qwabe, Malandela's* sons – a ceremony which is both strange and sacred.

The days and the nights flew by and at last the great day arrived and the Princess *Nomikonto* prepared the little boys for the Holy Ceremony which was to take place that night.

The little urchins first had to have their bowels cleaned out and this is a very simple and fascinating procedure. The only requirements are a small hollow reed, a bowl full of warm water and a nice fat ebony black *piccanin.* One end of the reed is smeared with fat, as a lubricant, and the *piccanin* is best caught by surprise. He must be made to lie flat on his little belly across somebody's lap. The reed is carefully inserted into the back passage and, needless to say, the *piccanin* will invariably squeal his big fuzzy-haired head off.

Nomikonto cleaned the bowels of both *Zulu* and *Qwabe,* who voiced their disapproval in no uncertain terms. Then she scrubbed them thoroughly – something they resented even more. In the meantime I had chosen two spotlessly white cows from my vast herds and these were slaughtered quickly in the morning and once more cooking was in progress within the kraal. This time no guests were invited because the Meat of Adoption must be eaten only by the people in whose kraal the adoption takes place. It must be eaten only at night in a darkened hut.

The bile sacs from the two cows were carefully preserved in a clay pot full of water. I ordered my first-rate cook *Mboza* to excel himself preparing food for the coming feast, because all the food to be eaten after the Ceremony of Adoption must be cooked to perfection. 'And,' I concluded, 'if that food is not cooked to the highest peak of perfection, you will promptly take its place.'

'My Great Chief,' said the fat buck-toothed cook calmly, 'on the day I cook you a bad meal, cut off my legs and I shall prepare them for you for supper.'

'That sounds very appetising, *Mboza*. I am quite sure that you who have turned out so many good meals, will turn into one equally good!'

When *Mboza* left I called my first Rainbow *Induna, Nsongololo*, and told him to remove all the dogs in the Great Kraal to the neighbouring kraals and to tell everybody to observe absolute silence during the coming night.

Night falls and the Rainbow *Indunas*, both Nguni and Mambo, assemble in the Big Hut in which *Malandela* and his two women have fasted for the past three days. *Nomikonto* and the rest of the women also move to the hut in the gathering dusk – the hut which will henceforth be known as the Hut of the Adoption.

The females do not enter the hut yet. They must first bathe themselves in warm water just outside the entrance and then throw the dirty water in a great circle around the Hut of the Adoption, to keep away *tokoloshes* and other Evil Spirits. To facilitate matters the great baked clay bowls used for face washing by the warriors in the morning have been arranged in a wide circle around the hut. Beside each bowl lies a loofah with which to scrub the body. The only women who will not attend the Ceremony are *Muwaniwani* and *Nomeva*, who are attending to my new Queen, *Noliyanda*, in the secret dwelling place under my Great Hut. I have told nobody about my Queen and my daughters have not yet suspected her presence. They are going to be the three angriest girls in the land on the day they find out about their new stepmother – of that I am very sure.

It is nearly midnight now and the ceremony begins. I have been chosen as Ceremony Leader. I raise my ebony staff and everybody, male and female, shed their raiment, necklaces, earrings, ear plugs, mutshas, loinskins and bracelets, and pile all these near the entrance of the hut. All stand dead still as I address them:

'We are here to take part in, and also to witness the ceremony in which *Malandela*, the son of *Mitiyonke*, and *Celiwe*, the daughter of *Nyawo*, take by the full Rights of Adoption, *Zulu* and *Qwabe*, the sons of the departed one, *Bekizwe*, as their own children. Henceforth *Zulu* and *Qwabe* shall be known as the sons of *Malandela* and the name *Bekizwe* shall not be connected with them as long as they live. The first rule of the ceremony requires that nobody in this hut shall think of anything except the proceedings here performed. You must observe this rule strictly because your ancestors and I can see clearly into the mind of every one of you. I am now going to ask the son of *Mitiyonke* the Seven Questions as the law requires and I expect each question to be answered clearly, truthfully and with all the sincerity at his command. Are you ready for the Seven Questions?'

'I am.'

'*Malandela*, son of *Mitiyonke*, are you prepared to take these two children, *Zulu* and *Qwabe*, as your very own flesh and blood, your very own sons regardless of whether they grow up into brave men or cowards, into wise men or fools, into cruel men or kindly?'

'I am.'

'Do you sincerely promise before the thrones of your Holy Ancestors to treat these children as your very own; to guide them as a father should; to chastise them and to teach them the laws and the customs of your tribe?'

'I do.'

'Do you promise to protect these two children, and if necessary lay down your life for them?'

'I do.'

'Do you promise to care for them in illness and ensure that they will never lack food?'

'I do.'

'Do you promise that when these children offend you, you will never under any circumstances reveal in the heat of anger that you are not their father?'

'I do.'

'Do you promise to love both children equally and never show favouritism to any one of them?'

'I solemnly swear to love both my children equally.'

'Lastly, do you promise to leave an equal share of all your wordly wealth to both these children on the day you die?'

'I promise.'

To *Celiwe* and *Dambisa* I address questions very similar – only small differences here and there in the wording.

Malandela picks up a ceremonial knife with a handle shaped like a fish, and heats its blade in the fire until it is red hot. With this razor-sharp red-hot knife he makes a long cut on the inside of his left thigh – a cut deep enough to bleed profusely. With blood from this cut he smears the two baby boys from head to foot, and taking both blood-bedecked children, one in either arm, he says slowly: 'Be a witness, Oh my departed brother – and all you, my Ancestors, be witnesses. Witness that I am today making these two children my own flesh and blood. Be witness to the solemn oaths I have taken and the promises I make this night. As from this night men shall know both *Zulu* and *Qwabe* as the sons and heirs of *Malandela.* And future generations shall know and salute *Zulu* and *Qwabe* as the sons of *Malandela.* They are now my sons, and my sons they shall always be.'

Celiwe sits down on the reed mat and *Malandela* places her little boys on her lap. She induces both to apply their mouths to her breasts, but *Zulu* protests with a loud scream. She also makes a small incision on the inside of her left thigh and smears the palms of both boys with her blood, saying: 'I am your mother now, and you are my children. I shall love you with all my heart and with all my soul. With the gods and the spirits willing, my sons, I shall choose brides for you one day, and shall lead the dancers on both your wedding days.'

She now takes both bile sacs from the bowl of water and empties their contents over the heads of the two little boys, saying: 'This bile from a spotless white cow symbolises the birth fluid which covers you, Oh my sons, on this day of your being brought forth by me, your mother. May the Highest of the Most High grant you pleasant lives, my children, and a future unclouded by the storms of suffering and of trouble. May you walk in the sunshine and may the moon attend you at night. May your loins be ever fertile and may your brains be crowned with wisdom. This, my children, is my blessing to you.'

Dambisa-Luwewe takes both the little boys and washes them thoroughly and then blesses them in her lilting foreign accent. She calls *Zulu* the 'Lion of Sunrise' and *Qwabe* the 'Fount of Wisdom and Courage'. She wishes them each a thousand wives and a million warriors at their command. Then the girls and women, and both Nguni and Mambo Rainbow *Indunas,* take their turns in saluting and blessing the two boys. *Malandela* heats the knife red hot once again and cauterises the cuts on both his and *Celiwe's* thighs.

Everybody leaves the Hut of Adoption and joins in the great feast laid out in my Great Hut. Here the Feast of Adoption proceeds in the dark. But in due course dawn's fiery hues start kissing the eastern sky.

The Hut of the Adoption is ceremoniously burnt to the ground and each Rainbow *Induna* receives as a present from *Celiwe* a small gourd containing the ashes of the hut as a fertility charm.

The two little boys are carried by heralds on great war shields and presented to the Nguni and Mambo warriors amidst thunderous cheers. With this the Ceremony of Adoption is concluded.

Three days later we led the powerful combined armies of the Nguni and the Western Mambo back eastward with the intention of wresting the Nguni throne from *Vamba Nyaloti*, the Vamangwe murderer and usurper, and reinstating *Celiwe* and *Malandela* as rulers of the land of the Nguni.

We made good progress on our journey towards the Great Kraal of the Nguni and to our great surprise the people in the kraals we passed welcomed us with open arms. Some of them even fell on their faces before *Malandela* and *Celiwe* and asked them – begged them, with tears in their eyes – to save them from someone whom they simply called the Horrible Beastess who was now ruling them with unbelievable cruelty. They told us that this beastess had overthrown *Vamba* somehow and had seized power in the land. She was now terrorising both Vamangwe and Nguni alike and every tenth day she had the habit of sending bands of her evil followers to scour the country for ten of the most handsome youths and maidens. These young people were taken to the Great Kraal and there sacrificed to this evil and mad beastess, whose real name was *Muxakaza*, who had once been *Malandela's* First Queen.

Determined to crush this infernal mad woman, I urged the army to make the journey to the Nguni Great Kraal in a forced march that shortened the three days' journey by a full two days. But when we reached the kraal, we found it deserted, save for an old man named *Ngozo*, who met us at the gate and prostrated himself before *Malandela*.

'Where is the Beastess, *Ngozo*?' asked *Malandela*, 'and what has happened to everybody?'

'The Beastess sensed your coming, High Ones, and fled across the Zambezi together with the rest of the Vamangwe people,' said the old man. 'But *Vamba*, or what is left of him, is in one of the huts together with his mother, who is vainly trying to nurse him back to health.'

'*Vamba*!' bellowed *Malandela*. 'Take me to him this very moment! Let me see that murdering, treacherous dog and run him through with the spear.'

'I do not think you need defile your spear with that creature's blood, Oh Lion of the Nguni,' said *Ngozo*. '*Vamba* is already dying – he has been dying for ten days now. Come and see.'

Malandela followed the old man *Ngozo* to the hut where *Vamba* was dying. We all followed him and stood just outside the hut as *Malandela* went in, spear in hand. There was a loud yell of fear and horror from within the hut and *Malandela* crawled out of the small entrance as if all the evil spirits in hell were after him. 'Gods of my Fathers – it is horrible, it is utterly horrible!'

'What is it, my brother?' asked *Nomikonto*.

'*Vamba* is in there with his mother, and both are rotting – rotting away while still alive. *Vamba* is glowing like a firefly and his flesh is disintegrating before your very eyes. Set this hut on fire . . . burn it down!'

'So,' cried *Celiwe.* 'This is the source of the horrible stench that hangs over the kraal. *Vamba* has at last got his just deserts! Burn down the whole kraal – we can build a new one elsewhere. It has seen far too many sins for far too long.'

Soon the kraal was one mass of flames from which a dense column of smoke rose to the very heavens, attracting thousands of people from the neighbouring kraals. And out of the roaring mass of ravening flames came the sound of shrill demon laughter. All the people turned and fled for their lives down the gentle slope, leaving the courageous Nguni dwarf *Malangabi* and his gigantic deaf-mute friend *Ngovolo* and me standing our ground at the gate of the burning kraal.

'What do you see, Oh *Malangabi*?' I asked. 'Tell me what you see.'

There was a short pause and then: 'By the shrivelled buttocks of my first ancestor – I see a corpse capering about in the flames, listen . . .'

Ghostly laughter reached our ears, and then *Vamba's* voice: 'I am immortal; I am indestructible; I shall live forever!'

The smell of burning flesh grew stronger in my nostrils as the sizzling remains of *Vamba* came staggering out of the flames and made straight for us, leaving a trail of smoking pieces of charred flesh behind.

'Stop!' I shouted. 'Stop, you foul thing and answer my questions.'

'What questions?'

'Where is the Bronze Idol of Zima-Mbje?'

'She has got it, ha, ha, ha. But before she took it, I exposed myself to its glow. I am immortal, indestructible . . . ha, ha, ha . . .'

'Thing most foul – perish! I command you!'

The rotten living cadaver sagged to the ground and one thigh bone broke with a dull crack and telescoped through the flesh. It opened its smoking mouth and croaked: 'I know you – I know who you are.'

'You don't need to tell me,' I said. 'I am the Lost Immortal . . . *Lumukanda*.'

'Yes,' croaked what was left of *Vamba*, trying to rise, but failing as his flesh tore from the bones. 'Yes, but you are also my father!'

'What?'

'You, *Lumukanda* . . . are my real father. Remember . . . dumb maiden, *Luojoyo*?'

Luojoyo! So *Vamba* – *Vamba* the evil, the ruthless *Vamba*, was the son of *Luojoyo*. *Luojoyo*, one of the hundreds of maidens whom I have loved and discarded in the many, many years of my ceaseless wanderings through the land. *Luojoyo*, one of the many girls who had loved me fiercely and then with whom I had to part for one reason or another. Girls whom I had loved briefly, fiercely, during short stays in villages and kraals here and there, and whom I had forgotten soon afterwards, but who had never forgotten me, because they had become mothers of my children – evil children who had inherited their father's worst traits.

There were scores of my children all over the land and only the Great Spirit knew when one of them would cross my path again. I felt tears starting into my eyes and flowing down my cheeks. I had spread evil all over the land and no wonder the gods hated me. I had befouled the land of mortal men with my evil spawn – evil children like *Vamba*. When, Oh when would I clash head on with one of them again?

'So,' croaked *Malangabi*. 'So you are *Vamba's* father.'

'Yes,' I replied, 'I am the dead *Vamba's* father.'

Afterwards *Ngozo* told us how *Vamba* came to be afflicted with the malady which had rotted the flesh from his body while he yet lived. The Beastess, *Muxakaza*, had tricked *Vamba* into giving her the Bronze Idol of *Zima-Mbje* and had used the evil idol's powers to overthrow *Vamba* and to afflict him with the strange consuming disease. *Vamba's* mother had tried in vain to cure her son and had contracted his deadly malady for her pains. *Luojoyo* . . . my *Luojoyo*!

I did not leave the land of the Nguni until I was sure that *Malandela* and *Celiwe* were safely and happily reinstated as the rightful rulers. *Malandela*, of course, was no longer a king – he was now a mere consort and it was the wise and kindhearted *Celiwe* who ruled supreme as the High Chieftainess of the Nguni.

This strange reversal of roles brought many a smile from the old men of the Nguni tribe, who had forced *Celiwe*, as High Chieftainess, to take two extra husbands besides *Malandela*, as the law states that all women of her rank should do. *Celiwe* had agreed to do this, most reluctantly, with a lot of sobbing and copious tears. She had chosen *Mabovu*, a tall handsome warrior, and she had also chosen the grey-haired Mambo philosopher warrior *Mpungoso*, who had presided over the famous Peace Ceremony between the Mambo and the Nguni. *Malandela, Mpongoso* and *Mabovu* were all tall and powerful men who dwarfed the pretty girlish chieftainess as a *Marula* tree dwarfs a thornbush. 'By my fathers . . . !' the one-eyed dwarf *Malangabi* had sworn after the Little Queen had made her choice of extra husbands, 'Have you seen anything like it? How is a small and delicate woman like *Celiwe* going to cope with the demands of such hulking monsters? I would never be *Celiwe* for all the riches in the world.'

'Do not worry about her, *Malangabi*,' said the old Rainbow *Induna Solozi*. '*Celiwe* is a woman-and-a-half. She can love any one of those thin-blooded scarecrows to death any time. Why, if she had chosen an experienced old cock like me . . .'

'There you go again, you lying old boaster,' growled *Malangabi*. 'You have never loved any woman in your whole life, and yet you call yourself experienced!'

'I have loved hundreds of women, my boy,' boasted the old liar vehemently. 'Dare you doubt my word?'

'*Aaarrrgh*!' *Malangabi* spat disgustedly before turning away.

After *Celiwe* had chosen her husbands, she held a great feast to celebrate her return to the land of the Nguni and also to honour her sister-in-law, *Nomikonto*, who had also declared the handsome singer *Ziko* to be her husband.

The marriage of *Nomikonto* and *Ziko*, however, was not a happy one, because *Nomikonto* continued to nurse a private hatred for men – a hatred that started to grow in her soul that eventful night when *Mukingo* ravished her. Strong is the truth behind the old saying of the tribes that 'a raped woman makes a thorny wife'. This marriage was destined to break up shatteringly, resulting in *Ziko's* death when we needed him most during the great journey to the south.

When, after a stay of nearly a whole moon, the time came for me to return home to the land of the Mambo, I knew I was leaving the Nguni a happy, contented tribe, in the hands of a kind-hearted and wise woman who was doing her best to erase the hatred for *Malandela* in the hearts of her many subjects. Already people were beginning to call *Celiwe* their Little Mother.

BEHOLD THE COMET

I cannot see her, but I can hear her voice and I can see the sorrow clouding her deep immortal heart. In her hands she is holding an ugly ebony doll and she is fondling the lifeless thing as if it were a baby. I can actually feel the great beauty of her – a beauty she radiates as the sun radiates heat at midday. Her sigh is a barely audible caress in the confines of the silent underground chamber. I hear her as she puts the doll down carefully on the tiny mat she has woven for it and covers it tenderly with a small wildcat skin blanket. I hear her crooning nonsense to the ugly doll – the kind of nonsense a mother croons to her baby when she wants it to sleep.

She comes towards me and I await her coming with bated breath. Her arms encircle my neck and her perfectly moulded body is pressed fiercely against mine. I feel her heavy breasts, her abdomen and thighs against mine. Her warm, trembling lips seek mine.

She releases me from the fury of her embrace with a shuddering sigh and steps back. 'Gods of the gods . . . if only I can see you!'

'What is the use?' she asks at length. 'Of what use is my loving you, my lord and husband, if I can bear you no young? *Lo,* my womb is more barren than the sands of the Ka-Lahari, where the skulking Bushmen live. My breasts are for nothing and never will I feel a baby's tender mouth extract nourishment from them. Oh my husband, I am so . . . so ashamed of myself.'

'You have nothing to be ashamed of, Oh my adorable creature – you, who are the most perfect, most beautiful being in the land, have nothing to be ashamed of, except that you are the wife of an immortal to whom the gates of the land of the gods are barred. My love for you and your slowly flowering love for me is worth more than a million babies.'

'The duty of the female throughout the length and breadth of Creation is to conceive, carry and bring forth young. Of what use is the rocky beauty of a barren desert? Of what use is a barren woman, mortal or immortal?'

'*Noliyanda,*' I chide her, 'be quiet. Do you want those above to hear your voice?'

'My husband, you must reveal me to your daughters and to the people you rule. I am sick of hiding like a mouse in a hole from your naughty daughters. They can do me no harm, although they have cut the throat of many a woman you loved. I want you to present me to your people and your children, and then I would like to select for you the three most beautiful mortal women for your second, third and fourth queens. I shall ask these women to bear children for me. I shall adopt them; I adore children.'

'The children I beget grow up into evil people, *Noliyanda.* I have no wish to spread farther my evil-tainted spawn.'

'The goodness or the evilness of a child depends on how he or she is brought up. There is no such thing as an inherited evil.'

'*Noliyanda,* I love you. I love you more than I have ever loved any woman or goddess before.' I kiss her forehead, cheeks, and we rub noses together.

'Ha!' she laughs. 'So the great *Lumukanda* loves his own creation! Does a sane potter ever love the pot she has made? Does a wood carver ever love the image he has whittled out of the unfeeling ebony? Tell me, Oh my creator, my god and my husband, what is love? Love is nothing but a euphemism for animal desire. Love is what a man feels for a woman before he takes her to the love mat. Love is only a form of hunger: a yearning to possess and to keep, and the interdependence of male and female beings.'

'A truce to your nonsense, Oh my wife. We must now . . .'

A familiar voice cuts my words short. 'Father, what are you doing down there and who are you talking to?'

'He is talking to me,' says *Noliyanda* pleasantly.

'Who in the name of all that is evil are you?' demands my first daughter *Luanaledi.*

'Come down, Oh children,' says *Noliyanda* gently. 'Come down here and meet me.'

'Who are you?' cries *Mvurayakucha* fiercely.

'I am your father's new wife – your step-mother.'

'Our what?'

'You heard me, child, I am your step-mother.'

'Will you please say that again,' hisses *Mvurayakucha.* 'Have we heard you correctly?'

'Children, come down here and let us talk properly and stop being so rude.'

The two eldest girls come down the ladder, but the youngest, *Mbaliyamswira,* remains above; she has foreseen trouble for her two sisters.

'How did this woman get here, and when did you have this secret dwelling made?' *Luanaledi* demands.

Before I can answer, the second girl's voice cuts in coldly, savagely: 'So this is our new mother – all beauty, large breasts and broad hips. A voluptuous, moist-lipped and obviously hot-blooded slut. From which malarial swamp did you fish her, my father?'

'He found me growing from a *marula* tree,' says Noliyanda with a smile. 'Don't tell me he did not inform you!'

'Is that the reason why you smell like fermented *marulas* in a dead warthog's stomach?' queries *Mvurayakucha* nastily. 'And when are you going to be ripe for the bush pigs to eat, Oh beautiful *marula*?'

Luanaledi, who has been studying *Noliyanda* closely, suddenly chips in: 'I know what this thing is. She is not a mortal woman; she is a goddess. How terrible – how disgusting!'

I sense anger rising in *Noliyanda's* soul – anger so terrible that I can feel the bolts of fear tearing through me like lightning through storm-pregnant clouds. '*Luanaledi, Mvurayakucha*, stop your nonsense and get out of here.'

Too late! There is a loud crackling clap of mountain thunder and an invisible force hits me full in the chest and sends me crashing back against the wall of the chamber. With a loud scream the lithe form of one of my daughters falls across my thighs. Then, to my great surprise, I slip into unconsciousness.

But not completely. Across an infinite distance I hear *Noliyanda's* voice: 'My lord and husband, what . . . what have I done! I did not mean it, honestly . . . it just happened . . .'

I hear a loud wail, and a shrill scream of horror, surprise and fear. Then *Luanaledi's* voice, charged with bitter hatred and unfathomable grief shrieks accusingly: 'You monster, you vile demon from the sewers of hell . . . you have killed her!'

'Child, I did not know . . . I did not know I had these powers,' cries *Noliyanda* in a voice shrill with pain and grief.

Another voice comes to me, a voice dull and hollow with pain so great that only an immortal can feel and still live: '*Lua*, sister *Lua* . . . call father . . .'

'What is it?' I cry, as things come into focus again. 'What is it? What happened . . . tell me.'

'Father,' cries *Luanaledi*, helping me to my feet. 'This foul mistress from hell you concocted, has murdered *Mvurayakucha*. You must destroy her . . . destroy this unearthly evil creature!'

'*Mvurayakucha*?' I ask hollowly, unable to comprehend. 'But nothing can harm you children. We are all indestructible.'

'But immortals and gods can destroy each other, though nothing mortal can destroy or harm us,' cries *Luanaledi*. 'Father, *Mvurayakucha* is a horrible sight. She is blistered all over and her face is all but gone. There is a gaping hole in her chest. Her heart still beats ... do something for her quick, father!'

Mvurayakucha's voice, strange and hollow sounding, floats up to me from where she is lying in the corner: 'Father ... end my misery ... take away my immortality ... destroy me.'

I make my way to where my second daughter is lying and I can smell charred flesh. The suddenness of the whole episode has left my brain numb. My knees become very weak indeed. For once I am glad of my blindness. I am glad I cannot see what is left of one of my beautiful daughters. 'I can recreate, you, child, I will ...'

'No father, I do not want to live. Life is too futile and sickening. Destroy me quickly – the pain is too great. And help *Lua* too ... she is also hurt.'

I stand over my child and I have to fight back the tears. A Master of Eternal Life is not supposed to weep, and I seem to have acquired the mortal's habits of weeping lately. I concentrate all my mental powers and with the utmost effort I project them – focus them on *Mvurayakucha*, and as though an unseen bolt of hissing lightning strikes her, she dissolves into a cloud of warm air. I turn and ask *Luanaledi* to tell me just what happened.

'This foul monster hurled a bolt of concentrated mental power at us, father. My sister received it full blast, but I was hurled clear and fell on top of you. My left hand has been burnt off at the wrist and the pain is getting unbearable.'

'I reach out and touch *Luanaledi*. It brings her immediate relief from the pain. I concentrate on her arm and the wound closes ... it gradually heals. But, as from now, she will have only one hand.

'Father, destroy this evil creature,' *Luanaledi* commands. 'I insist that you do so now!'

I just cannot bring myself to destroy her. I love her too much. Now I have to choose between my daughters and someone whom I really love. The object of my affection has just murdered one of my children; must I punish her? My soul is tossed about like a leaf in a hurricane of indecision as I take a step towards *Noliyanda* ...

'No father, do not kill her,' says the voice of my youngest daughter *Mbaliyamswira*. 'My two eldest sisters got what they fully deserved.'

'What!' cries *Luanaledi*, in great surprise.

'Yes, big sister,' says the younger girl from the top of the primitive ladder, 'you seem to forget that there are High Laws in the Universe which all beings, mortal and immortal should, and must, obey. Respect for one's parents and chosen superiors is one such law. The gods of the forests, of the rivers and plains, must respect the First Goddess, *Ninavanhu-Ma*, at all times, and the First Goddess must respect the Great Spirit, who must respect the Ultimate Cause, subject in turn to the Most Ultimate, the Grand God of all gods Himself. Respect is one of the ten pillars of the Universe, and humility is another. But sister *Lua*, we have never shown any respect to our father or for those whom he loves – whom we must respect for our father's sake. And today we have reaped the bitter harvest of our lack of respect. Although we love our father most sincerely – and in a way which shocks both gods and mortal men, a way considered to be evil and unnatural by all creatures in the Universe – we must remember that he is our parent, our lawful superior, and that there are things we must not do to him – nor to those he has chosen as his mates, be they mortals, goddesses, or creatures of his own creating.

'Sister *Lua*, a parent, be he mortal or immortal, human or animal, god, man or tree, is more than just a "thing" that has brought forth young. A parent is to his or her young the representative of the Most Ultimate Himself and the respect due to him or her from the young is not something they – the young – can give or withhold at will; it is a compulsion – a duty.'

Slowly *Noliyanda* rises from where she was sitting and approaches *Luanaledi* and *Mbaliyamswira*, who had come down the ladder while she was speaking. She reaches out her arms and takes both girls in a tender embrace. The three females sob loudly and I turn away, climb the ladder to the surface on heavy legs. I reach the floor of the Great Hut, and I shut the door in the floor carefully behind me.

A voice reaches my ears. It is calling loudly, excitedly, outside the closed door of the Great Hut. It is the voice of *Nsongololo*, my first Rainbow *Induna*.

It seems as if night has fallen long ago, but strangely, instead of being asleep in their huts, the inhabitants of my kraal are milling around in the clearing and shouting at the tops of their voices. I wonder what has happened. Once more *Nsongololo* knocks at the wickerwork door of my hut, shouting very excitedly: 'Great Chief, wake up, there is a Star of War in the sky . . . an ill omen of great bloodshed.'

A Star of War, and much bloodshed. So that is what has excited the people so much. A very rare thing is in the sky out there: a great comet. A comet, large and terrible looking is dominating the star-bejewelled, cloudless autumn skies, like a hideous demon from the deepest pits of hell. A comet – a star which the tribes fear more than anything that can ever appear in the skies. A comet, and also a total solar eclipse, are regarded by the tribes throughout the length and breadth of the land as omens of disasters to come – disasters that would claim thousands of lives.

A comet! It is the duty of every chief in the land above whose skies a comet appears, immediately to sacrifice his first-born son or daughter by burning him or her alive in a pit full of charcoal and cow dung to placate the dread Star of War. The people out there are waiting for me to bring out my daughters, and drag out my adopted son *Mukombe*, to sacrifice them in a great fire pit to the beat of drums and the wail of flutes. Well, they are going to be very disappointed . . .

Outside, the cool night air is fanning my body and face. I can feel the eyes of everyone turn towards me and all the excitement, the loud shouting and gesticulating, dies down. An expectant hush claims the kraal as the people turn and come slowly to where I am standing, flanked by *Nsongololo, Ntombela* and *Mavimbela*, all three carrying lighted torches. (A chief must always be accompanied by *Indunas* carrying torches when walking about his kraal at night.)

'My people,' I shout in the silence, 'listen to me – *Lumukanda*, your immortal High Chief. I know what you are expecting me to do now in view of that star you see in the sky above. But I shall not do it!'

I pause and listen in great satisfaction to the gusty gasp of collective surprise that escapes from more than two thousand mouths and it fills me with a sense of elation such as I have never experienced before. There is nothing like disappointing bloodthirsty people. It is like cheating hyaenas of their prey!

'I say once again that I am your High Chief and as far as I am concerned, there is no Star of War in the sky. I am your blind Chief and I do not see any Star of War. What your chief does not see, you must also not see.'

'But there is one, Oh Chief, there is,' protests a voice in the crowd. 'There is a War Star in the sky.'

'Warriors, seize that man and bring him to me.'

The man is promptly seized and brought to where I stand, and he is none other than *Govu*, one of my ten best cooks. 'So at last I am going to have a cook for breakfast. Listen *Govu*, I have heard of men being cooked in a pot of their own shaping which, as you know, is an old tribal idiomatic expression. But at last I am going to have the satisfaction of literally experiencing and tasting a *cook* being cooked in his own cooking pot! And what is more, you are first going to wash and prepare the pot herbs and yams which will flavour your stew. Take him away.'

They drag him off and I continue: 'Does anyone still insist that there is a War Star in the sky? If so, kindly step forward.'

Nobody steps forward. But all eyes are focused on me and I quietly proceed: 'You say there is a War Star in the skies, and you say it is an omen of war and evil to come. I say again, and without fear of contradiction,' and I point to a great stew pot, 'that it is a warning and not an ill omen – a warning to all of us to prepare and not to waste time on all kinds of ceremonies. We must start immediately. You must help me strengthen your armies, help me raise our regiments from five to ten. I am going to send messengers to all the districts in the land first thing tomorrow. I want each district to contribute five hundred men. I want blacksmiths, shield makers and iron miners to work day and night – on pain of instant death if they do not. I want spears, 'man-killing' arrows, bows, weapons – all this within ten days from now. You must stop gawking at that star and help me to make the army of the Mambo the strongest in the land.'

There is a burst of thunderous applause from the massed warriors and peasants. Even the women join in the cheering. There is a loud gasp from the people as *Noliyanda* crawls out of the Great Hut and stands just behind me, a little to my right.

'My lord and husband, I beg to speak to the people.' Her low throaty voice is nevertheless musical.

'You have my permission.'

'Children of the Mambo,' says *Noliyanda*, 'I have something to tell you and also a confession to make. You are very surprised to see me, I can tell, because none of you knew of my presence until now. I am not a human being like you; I am not a spirit either. I was brought back to life in a secret underground chamber under this hut by your Great Chief *Lumukanda*, who is a master of Eternal Life . . .'

The people let out loud screams of astonishment and press closer to have a look at *Noliyanda*. The warriors venture closer with exclamations of '*Hawu*, Impossible, *whew*! Is she a real woman?'

'Children of the Mambo,' continues *Noliyanda*, 'I have just caused the death of the second of the three daughters of your Great Chief and the loss of the right hand of the eldest.'

But the people are not interested in what she is saying; they are only interested in her. The other women press forward and the hideous ape-woman *Nunu* tears the leopard-skin cloak from *Noliyanda's* shoulders and feels her smooth skin with an innocent curiosity.

Lulama-Maneruana and the other girls and women crowd around my new queen and tear the skin skirt off her waist. They just cannot bring themselves to believe that she is real and alive – as real and as alive as they themselves are – and *Noliyanda* seizes both *Nunu* and *Maneruana* by the backs of their necks and playfully bumps their foreheads together.

'By the breasts of *Ma*, the thing can fight,' says *Maneruana*.

The warriors and *Indunas* surge still further forward and deluge me with a flood of questions: 'What are you going to do with it, Oh Chief. It speaks like a human being, but is it truly one? Shall we kill it, Oh Chief?'

The warriors also reach out grimy, calloused hands to touch

Noliyanda, but the Rainbow *Indunas* curse them and tell them to stop. With loud giggles and much chattering the women and girls carry *Noliyanda* away to their hut – as excited children would do with a toy they wished to show to their friends.

Noliyanda had tried to introduce herself to the people. She had tried to make them accept her as a human being. But she had failed miserably. For many years the people always referred to her as '*Into*' (the Thing); they always called her *It* and never *She*.

For twenty-one days after the appearance of the dread Star of War my Rainbow *Indunas* and I were very busy indeed. Fortified war rafts were built and canoes were hollowed out, while sleds drawn by oxen brought great bundles of weapons of all kinds from the twelve districts of the land of the Mambo to the Great Kraal *Tulisizwe*.

The scent of war was in the air, and we were prepared.

THEY WHO MUST DIE

The messenger was staggering with exhaustion. He was in the very last stages of weariness. A huge message stick was clutched tightly in his hand and his hard mouth was grey with hunger and thirst. He had not had time to drink from the many streams he crossed. He had to deliver the message and . . . die.

Valindlu, the son of *Nopempe,* knew that each weary step was bringing him nearer to the grave. The High Law of the Tribes says that all bearers of evil tidings must be killed immediately and instantly after they have delivered their unsavoury message or news.

Valindlu was past caring. All he was worried about was that the message he was carrying should be quickly delivered to the cannibal High Chief of the Mambo as quickly as possible.

It was evil news indeed.

At long last the messenger saw the kraal, standing out against the dense forests surrounding it like a wound – a great circular wound on a thick-haired warrior's head. He saw the tiny distant figures of warriors and women moving about among the countless huts like so many ants. He heard the faint sounds as women called out to each other. Noise-loving things, women. The messenger began to think about *Tandi,* his bride of ten days, back there in the war-torn land of the Nguni. What would become of her? Tears flooded the messenger's eyes as he realised with shocking finality that he was *really* going to die that day, die and never see *Tandi* again!

He crushed his feelings; the law says one must be ready to sacrifice all for the sake of the tribe. The Nguni tribe was in great danger. The long-awaited invasion from the south had come and savage hordes of the tyrant of Zima-Mbje, the *Munumutaba,* had crossed the Zambezi and were ruthlessly laying waste the land of the Nguni. They had come to exterminate, and not to conquer or enslave. The Nguni regiments were fighting back fiercely when the messenger left with the message from *Celiwe,* from the besieged Royal Kraal. But the brave Ngunis needed help; they alone could not hope to stem the tide of murderous Mashonas and half-castes together with a moderate sprinkling of the dread foreigners, known as the Feared Ones – these long-haired, long-bearded, light-skinned Arabi, with noses like the beaks of vultures.

The army pouring across the Zambezi was the strangest the land had ever seen, and it was the most ruthless army the Nguni and the Mambo had ever been called upon to face.

Thus, the tired messenger ran the remaining distance towards the Great Kraal *Tulisizwe.* He entered the main gate at full speed and promptly slipped on a slick of thin dung deposited by a sick cow, and fell flat on his back. A Rainbow *Induna* took the long message stick from the ground where the unfortunate man had fallen, scanned the message briefly, shook his head and gave a brief order to four warriors before turning away. Four long-bladed new spears tore into the body of the fallen man and he was no more.

Noliyanda read the message to me and even before she had finished, I was on my feet and groping for my great war spear. The message read: 'Evil. Plenty. Our land. Under attack. Royal Kraal. Besieged. Beg help.'

I crawled out of the Great Hut with *Noliyanda* close behind me and yelled at the servant boy sitting just outside to sound the battle horn he held. The boy leapt up to obey and the sound of the great horn floated over the kraal. The Rainbow *Indunas* came running out of their huts and stood before me – all fully armed.

'Our long wait is over, men, this is war! You know what to do – do it!' I snapped.

In the short space of half-a-day the great Mambo *impi* of ten regiments and approximately a hundred thousand men was ready for war. From each of the ten great military kraals neighbouring the Great Kraal, came two heavily armed regiments in full battle order. Leaving two regiments, the Stormclouds and the Hornets, to guard the land, I dispatched five regiments overland under *Nsongololo* and *Ntombela.*

I took the remaining three regiments to the riverside and embarked with them on the war rafts – the massive fleet of battle canoes

and barges. These regiments, directly under my leadership, with *Mavimbela*, the Rainbow *Induna*, as my second-in-command, were to be used in cutting off the *Munumutaba's* retreat and in keeping the Zambezi clear of his ferry barges and supply canoes. They were also to be used in lifting the siege of the Nguni Royal Kraal, situated near the great river. The *Munumutaba* was soon going to find he had lifted a stone with a scorpion poised under it; he was about to regret the day he set foot in the two lands under my protection. The vain egomaniac was unaware of what he was up against. I was ready to thrash the pelt off his miserable carcass and send him back to Zima-Mbje with his tail between his legs like the miserable cur he was.

The great battle rafts, fifty in all, huge things made of logs with a raised platform in the centre on which were built ten skin covered huts, glided slowly and carefully down the river. We entered the Zambezi from the Luangwa. These rafts were manned by the regiments called the Crocodiles and the Crabs, and the third regiment, the Leguans, followed the raft spearhead in the fleet of battle canoes and barges. Just as the leading raft, in which I was, glided past a stretch of crocodile-infested reeds bordering the great river, I heard my Rainbow *Induna Mavimbela* give a loud shout of excitement.

'Look at that! Oh, what a rare sight – what a good omen!'

'What is it?'

'An omen of victory, Great One. Two otters, fighting like drunken demons amongst the reeds. Look there, you stupid sons of Mambo goat thieves, look over there. We are going to win this war! We are going to trounce those impotent sons of bush pigs from Zima-Mbje and I am going to un-man the first son of a double-sexed hyaena who says we won't!'

A thunderous cheer shook the great rafts, following such strong words from the grizzled old crocodile hunter, who was also a fisherman of renown. The confidence among my warriors mounted; every man was suddenly fired with enthusiasm and a raging desire to come to grips with the enemy.

Night fell and the laughing stars twinkled mockingly down at the ancient earth from their lofty thrones in the skies above. The heavenly river, the milky way, was a great smoky band of living silver, jewelled with millions of stars. The sullen river reflected the glorious sky and loud in our ears was the song of frogs amongst the reeds. In the frowning forests on either bank of the mighty river lions roared savagely in the naked night.

Hyaenas laughed in the dark, and now and again the loud wail of a love-thirsty jackal added more discord to the disturbed night, the untamed night, invisible to me, but yet so distinctly audible. This was not a night for men to seek the enemy; it was a night for men to seek the soft arms of those they loved. This was the sort of night in whose embrace Wise Men sat near dying fires, swathed in *karosses*, meditating – meditating on history already made, not participating in history about to be made. This was indeed a night made for peace.

The whispering dawn sets fire to the Eastern sky; a weary sun climbs slowly up to usher in yet another day over an ungrateful earth. The dew vanishes from the grass and the clinging morning mist flees like a sneaking thief before the High Chief of Day. In the trees the birds sing their morning love song to the cool breeze – and directly in front of us, *lo*! the hated enemy we seek.

A fleet of thirty barges full of Luvijiti warriors is trying to cross the Zambezi. Paddles lash the water as the barges labour across the current and there are shouts of surprise as the enemy sees our giant rafts bearing down upon them. I give no command to attack – none is needed; I hear a series of sharp twangs as the Mambo archers send volley after volley of arrows at the enemy boats. There is a bone-wrenching shock as our raft rams two barges and capsizes them, spilling the Luvijiti warriors to the crocodiles. Loud screams of agony rise as the Mambo archers send more flights of arrows tearing into the struggling, drowning men. Dead bodies are borne down river by the current and there is a cloud of bright red blood on the waters of the timeless Zambezi.

The enemy rallies as the warriors recover from their surprise. They fight back bravely and their arrows tear into the ranks of the Mambo massed on the battle rafts. But the Luvijiti barges are rammed mercilessly one after the other and their occupants become ready food for fishes and crocodiles now massing to partake of the spoil.

The great fleet of Mambo war rafts, barges and canoes glides onward, with a long trail of tiger fish and crocodiles whose appetites have apparently only been stimulated. We meet ten more Luvijiti barges and we ram them savagely out of existence, to the satisfaction of only a small portion of our greedy rearguard.

Gradually we leave the middle of the river and edge our way closer to the northern bank of the mighty Zambezi. In the far distance we see *Malandela's* kraal, with thousands of enemy warriors swarming around it like flies around a honeycomb. Some of the huts are burning and the smoke is climbing lazily into the cloudless skies.

On my brisk command, two regiments thunder off the rafts and swarm up on the bank, falling immediately into battle order. Two men who refuse to disembark, due to a sudden attack of cowardice, are promptly shorn of their members of manhood and flung into the river.

'Forward! Forward!' I shout.

The great crescent of warriors rolls through the forest. I am leading at the southern point, and *Mavimbela* is leading at the northern point with a battery of foul curses. We tear into the rearmost ranks of the besieging Luvijiti with the fury of a charging rhinoceros. Men whom I can sense but not see go down under the crushing blows of the iron-studded club I am wielding with both hands. No shield on earth can withstand the tremendous weapon in my hands.

Spears hiss past me and men cry out as they fall on either side. Spurting blood drenches my legs with warm stickiness, clotting and peeling off. The sickening sounds of spears thudding home in human bodies and axes cracking and splitting skulls, mixed with hoarse screams and groans, are all around me. The enemy tries to disengage and re-form, but this I shall not allow them to do. We press the enemy hard and fight our way forward without pause, towards *Malandela's* kraal. And above the din of battle a familiar voice bellows in my ear: 'We have got them surrounded, Oh High Chief. We have surrounded the adulterous sons of double-sexed, splay-footed hyaenas!'

'Is that you, Oh *Mavimbela*?' I yell.

'It is I, Oh Great Chief.'

'Let us then press them hard. We must give them no breathing space.'

'They won't get the slightest chance for that, Oh High One. We are pressing them closer than a lover presses his sweetheart at the great moment.'

'Forward!' I shout at the top of my voice. 'Forward and annihilate the Luvijiti dogs!'

There is a savage torrent of Nguni war cries as they break out of their Great Kraal and fall upon the hated enemy which has been threatening them for four days. Like hawks released from captivity, the three husbands of the little Nguni Chieftainess *Celiwe* lead a gallant charge by twenty thousand yelling warriors. The besieging Luvijiti are thrown into confusion and they fall in their hundreds . . . and along with them fall many of their hateful foreign allies, the Arabi.

The siege of the Nguni Great Kraal is a thing of the past. In half-a-day's savage battle more than fifty thousand Luvijiti, five hundred Mambo and ten thousand Nguni have been killed. But the great war is by no means over. In fact, it has just begun!

The clever dog of a *Munumutaba* has not used all his forces in the invasion of the land of the Nguni. The bulk of his armies is encamped south of the Zambezi and it would appear that his intention is to attack us from as many points as possible at the same time. In fact, he had merely diverted our attention from the main objective he wishes to attack.

The Nguni Great Kraal has been relieved and the enemy hordes which beseiged it have been annihilated to the last man. But there are still strong Luvijiti regiments carrying all before them in the land of the Nguni and these must be destroyed first before we can think of launching a counter-attack upon the *Munumutaba* beyond the Zambezi.

When my First Rainbow *Induna, Nsongololo,* arrived with the five Western Mambo regiments I had dispatched overland, we decided to launch an immediate attack on the marauding invaders laying waste the land of the Nguni. We left three regiments in the Nguni Royal Kraal, two Nguni and one Mambo, under the joint command of *Mabovu* and *Ngovolo.* These regiments were to work closely with the river-borne Mambo regiments I had left in the river to man the war rafts and the canoes, to keep the river clear of Luvijiti barges.

Malandela, Mpungoso and I led the powerful combination of seven Mambo and ten Nguni regiments in search of the Luvijiti marauders who, reports said, were under the command of the youngest of the great *Munumutaba's* twelve sons, *Munengu.*

For ten days we followed the enemy who seemed to be determined to avoid capture and destruction. But on the eleventh day we came upon the vast Luvijiti camp just before sunset and we slowly but surely encircled it, keeping out of sight in the great forests. When night fell, the unsuspecting enemy was trapped in a deadly double circle of nearly fifty thousand fighting men. Secure in the knowledge that the enemy forces had no chance of escape, I sent word to all the regiments to have a good night's sleep, because I intended wiping the foe off the land early in the morning. Thus, in the dark depths of the frowning forest, the Nguni and Mambo built carefully covered cooking fires and cooked their supper – mainly meat and corn cakes.

It has always been attractive to me to spend the night with mortal men who were going to gamble their lives bravely against a ruthless enemy the next morning. It is fascinating to see just how differently men feel the night before about their coming ordeal. The words so dear to beggarly story tellers: 'brave and fearless warriors' are but a putrid myth. No mortal is ever truly brave in battle and the picture often etched in our minds of a fearless and cool-headed warrior slaying a thousand of the foe is so much make-believe.

On the eve of a battle a warrior is either as scared as a wet *kaross* or he is resigned to death, but determined to do as much damage to the enemy as possible before being killed. Very often this strange resignation to death and a raging desire to kill as many of the enemy before being killed, has been mistaken for courage. Once one is resigned to death and ready to receive it with open arms, one can still live to die peacefully in old age.

Many of the older warriors and *indunas* in both the Mambo and the Nguni armies had been going into battle totally resigned to being killed or maimed, but only after they had dispatched as many of the enemy to hell as they possibly could. Such men were *Nsongololo, Mavimbela* and three other famous Nguni Rainbow *Indunas, Malangabi, Mapepela* and *Solozi.*

There is also a third type of man – the man who comes to the field of war only to make a name for himself or to keep up a family tradition. Such a man was *Malandela.*

Malandela was a bitter man with a long family tradition of ferocity and courage to uphold. He also wanted to outshine his two rivals in the eyes of *Celiwe*, and he wished to recover the honour and respect he had lost on the day of his disgrace by distinguishing himself in the battle about to begin. Such a man tends to be impatient, and reckless; he can spoil carefully designed plans and prolong a battle.

In anticipation of this I called *Nsongololo, Mavimbela, Malangabi* and *Mapepela* aside and said: 'Men, I want you to keep a close watch on *Malandela.* I have a strong feeling he might try to do something reckless tomorrow. I do not want him to be killed.'

'Between you and me, Oh High Chief,' grinned *Malangabi* wickedly, 'I think it would be a good idea to let our friend Old Thundering Stomach get himself killed. Ever since he killed his brother and got himself disgraced his life has been hell. He has become moody, absent-minded and irritable. I think only death can cure his misery.'

'Far be it from me to question your logic and decision, Great One,' added *Mavimbela*, 'but why must *Malandela* be exempt from the privilege of taking a chance on the battlefield, like the rest of us? Quite a few good sons of our women will be dead by midday tomorrow, and we might be among them.'

'Listen men,' I said, 'none of you will be killed tomorrow – of that I can assure you here and now. You will survive tomorrow's battle to take part in monumental happenings in the very near future. But *Malandela* must also survive tomorrow's clash so that he too can take part in these happenings. They will be remembered by generations as yet unborn as the greatest happenings in the history of the Nguni, Mambo and Xhosa Tribes.'

'Great One,' said *Mapepela*, 'is it true that you have lived for a thousand years and can see the future as clearly as we see today?'

'Yes, *Mapepela*, I have lived for more than a thousand years.'

'I am sure that in the course of your long life you have loved quite a number of women,' *Malangabi* put in with a wicked leer.

'About two hundred thousand,' I replied nonchalantly.

'By my father's—' swore *Mavimbela*, 'I really envy you, Oh High One.'

'No, *Mavimbela*,' said the wise *Mapepela*, 'the Great Chief *Lumukanda* is more to be pitied than envied, I think. We human beings, we ordinary mortals, should thank the spirits for the fact that one day we shall die. We should be thankful that we are not immortal. Life is a futile, senseless thing. Death is not evil; it is the ultimate relief from the pain and dreariness of life. A mortal man can at least struggle hard in the course of life to win himself fame and renown one way or another, so that when he dies men will at least remember his name, which is the only victory that one can glean from the stark futility which is life. But what does an immortal gain from life? Nothing at all! Tribal wisdom says that all men should try hard to make their names famous for long after they are dead. I would rather lead a brief life and leave a name behind, than an endless one in lonely obscurity.'

'Three curses on your thick head, *Mapepela*,' growled *Mavimbela*. 'Do you have to be so free with your opinions in the presence of my respected Chief?'

'Do not be angry with *Mapepela*,' I said with a smile. 'Every word he has said is true. He is a very, very wise man.'

'Strangely, Wise One,' growled *Mavimbela*, 'I am forced to agree with what *Mapepela* says. Give me a short and sweet life, an honourable death, and a name men will remember.'

'The only thing for which people will remember you, is your foul tongue,' said *Malangabi*. 'Never have I come across a man with a tongue as rotten as yours.'

'You must get married, *Mavimbela*,' said *Nsongololo*. 'Perhaps a wife, or a nice pair of wives would help to cleanse your foul tongue.'

'The day you see me married and wasting my blood in the stupid and ungrateful task of procreating children, will be the day when elephants grow wings. I loathe the things they call women, I detest them,' *Mavimbela* responded.

'Why do you hate women, *Mavimbela*?' I asked. 'Were you once hurt by one?'

'My mother must have planted an unfading flower of hatred for all women in my heart. She was the cruellest mother; she used to torture me and my two brothers while we were small children, Oh my Chief,' said *Mavimbela*.

'She should have wrung your bull neck,' said *Malangabi*. 'Then the land would have been one foul-mouthed scoundrel less.'

'I hear you have a wife, *Malangabi*,' said *Nsongololo*. 'They tell me you married that girl you were riding the great fish with, during the Peace Ceremony. Tell me, what made that beautiful creature choose a monstrosity like you?'

'She dreamt that an old man, who was her first ancestor, told her to marry me,' said *Malangabi*. 'And the very first thing she did on waking up was to weave a message mat telling me she loved me. I nearly fainted when I received the message.'

We all laughed heartily at this and just then one of the warriors brought my supper – a whole boiled goat with yams, and I invited the *Indunas* to join me. As we ate, the voice of *Malandela* came faintly to us. Bitter, lonely, he was sitting all by himself with a three-string harp for company, and singing:

'Peace thee, Peace thee,
Oh my spirit—
Hold thy peace before the great *Somandla* . . .'

Even after I had wrapped myself in my great *kaross* and was waiting for the sweet embrace of sleep, even when all the camp fires had been extinguished and the only sounds heard were the crackling of twigs under the feet of the sentries and the roar of distant lions, *Malandela* still sat alone singing to the hum of his harp.

Dawn spreads itself over a land swathed in a thick blanket of crawling mist, blunting human vision to a distance of a few paces. Horns sound and the Mambo and Nguni regiments surge forward through the forests with savage war cries.

The attack is on. The attack is fully launched, and a young warrior named *Gojela*, the son of *Mlomo*, is scared. Every one of the more than six hundred warriors under the command of the scarred Battle Leader *Malevu* knew *Gojela* by the nickname of 'The Coward' and every one of those hardened veterans made life unbearable for *Gojela*.

The pitiless, hard-bitten warriors have the habit of torturing *Gojela*. Their favourite method is to hold the thin, spindle-legged boy upside down over a very smoky fire . . . teaching him courage, as they call it, with loud roars of laughter.

Gojela is a coward and he cannot understand why. The very sight of a spear is enough to make his bowels open uncontrollably and a war cry leaves him paralysed with fear – with teeth clattering. *Gojela* has always dreamt of the day when he would rise and become a great Battle Leader, like *Malevu*, and the mighty *Mapepela* under whose command *Gojela's buto* falls. Often, in his few moments of peace *Gojela* has liked to imagine himself in the role of either of these two men, fighting bravely like them, killing many victims and bringing home trophies in the form of wounds from a victorious battle. Always when he has lain whimpering after having been cruelly teased or tortured by his fellow warriors, he has comforted himself by dreaming of the day when he would show them all that he too could be brave. He too could die bravely as all true warriors should. He has pictured the day when he will die a hero, praised and admired by all.

Last night, after a particularly nasty bout of torturing and gross teasing by the other warriors, *Gojela* lost his temper and became angry for the first time in his life. With a flood of tears pouring down his cheeks, he called them rotten bullies and told them he would show them all in the morning that he too, could be brave. Loud roars of contemptuous laughter followed this tearful promise. Now, in the mist-wreathed morning, sneering warriors are urging *Gojela* to make good his boast. *Gojela* swallows hard. His brows are covered in sweat and his round fish-like eyes are glazed with fear. His legs are stiff with terror. His headdress has fallen off and is lying at his feet; his shoulders droop under the 'weight' of his shield and weapons and his teeth chatter.

'Come on, hero,' roars one of the warriors. 'Come on, we are attacking.'

'Come on, you son of a rotten hyaena,' bellows *Malevu*, prodding the boy cruelly with his spear. 'Can't you see we are attacking?'

Gojela, urged by his inbred fear of men like *Malevu*, leaps high into the air, tosses his shield and weapons aside, and flees in blind panic – in the general direction of the enemy.

'Look! Look at him,' roars *Malevu*. 'Look at our hero; he is going to tackle them with his bare hands!'

Gojela runs, on and on – and right into the centre of a Luvijiti encampment. A score of the most ruthless looking foemen led by an awe-inspiring foreigner with a long flowing beard, long white robe and a spine-chilling curved sword, come charging straight at *Gojela*.

He turns and runs blindly away from such terrifying and very unfriendly looking men. He runs right into another band of yelling Luvijiti and they promptly surround him and hack at him with their *pangas*.

'No! No, please don't kill me . . . No . . . Oh my mother . . . save me!' cries *Gojela*.

A huge Luvijiti aims a tremendous blow at *Gojela's* head. He ducks between the legs of the tall man, who falls back sprawling in the dust, with a curse. *Gojela* leaps away only to crash into another man who seizes him by the throat. Both go down and a savage struggle is in progress. *Gojela* finds himself astride the bigger man and he hits him again and again with his bare fists. Another man slashes at him with a *panga*. But he twists sideways and the tall man under him receives the full force of the blow; its owner loses his hold on the weapon – and *Gojela* seizes it.

Wildly, blindly, *Gojela* lashes out all round him – and three men go down. The Luvijiti close in, but in their wild frenzy they lash haphazardly and inflict more injuries on one another than on *Gojela*. A shield falls and he grabs it. He dances around, screaming, praying to his mother, pleading, treading around in a muddy puddle of blood, freely contributed by some twenty Luvijiti warriors now lying prostrate around him.

Gojela is still dancing, lashing, fighting blindly, insanely, and he is suddenly joined by another Nguni who charges forth from the mist, yelling at the top of his voice and carrying all before him. It is *Malandela*.

The attention of the Luvijiti is distracted by this newcomer. They try to re-form to face both. But their confusion is only increased. *Gojela* and *Malandela* are now fighting back to back, completely surrounded by maddened Luvijiti. *Gojela* adds ten more to his score, fifteen . . .

The mighty Nguni and Mambo regiments close in on the scene as the combined score of *Gojela* and *Malandela* reaches towards three score.

The Nguni and Mambo regiments closed in from all directions and a savage battle took place, lasting the best part of the morning. The Luvijiti were butchered to the last man – including the youngest son of the *Munumutaba*.

Gojela had seen his enemies melt away before the Nguni and Mambo warriors, and he had wondered why he was still alive. He observed the men he had killed, and he was not prepared to accept that it was his own handiwork. He retched at the sight of so much blood and death and slowly felt his senses evaporate from his body. He quietly sagged to the ground unconscious.

'Awake, hero!' The voice seems to come from a great distance. 'Wake up, the High Chief wants to see you.'

Gojela opens his eyes and looks into the bloodshot eyes of his battle leader, *Malevu*, and he is surprised to find no mockery in them – only dawning respect and surprise.

'I did not know you had any courage in you, *Gojela*,' says *Malevu*. 'You and Old Thundering Stomach must have enjoyed yourselves before we came.'

Gojela is half-led and half-carried to where *Malandela* and the rest of the Nguni commanders are sitting in the shade of the old *marula* tree, sheltering from the intense heat of the midday sun. As he comes face to face with *Malandela* his bewilderment weakens his legs. But *Malandela* catches him as he sags and, holding him erect, he plucks two ostrich feathers from his royal headband and places them on *Gojela's* head.

'Heroic son of *Mlomo*, I salute you, and I here and now appoint you one of my Rainbow *Indunas*,' says *Malandela*. 'I shall give you ten maidens for wives and a kraal of your own with fifty head of cattle. You are a brave, a very brave, man.'

Gojela quietly sinks to the ground in peaceful oblivion.

Kokovula, the Great Witchdoctor, all his assistant witchdoctors and other numerous assistants are very busy. To him and his vast panel of assistants has fallen the most pathetic duty of all, that of saving the wounded and burying the dead. There are five hundred Nguni and Mambo wounded lined up for attention.

Groaning and writhing men are laid out in neat rows under the shade of the sacred *mopani* trees. Great pots of molten tree resin and pain-killing drugs are smoking and boiling away on fires a short distance away. Also in the fires are scores of metal axes, knives and hammers used for amputating limbs and cauterising wounds. These instruments must only be used when red-hot. The High Laws forbid anyone to use either a surgical instrument or the poultices placed on wounds, unless these are red-hot. A pile of ornately carved ebony splints is close at hand, as is a great heap of soft hare skins, wild cat skins and even young impala skins, used for bandaging. On a bowl of clay is a pile of *tsinga* gut used for stitching open wounds and a grass basket stands next to this bowl; it is full of small copper clips used to clip stitched wounds firmly, in case the stitches loosen too soon afterwards.

Kokovula is quite used to the sight of human blood and pain. He has attended to the wounded on many a battlefield before. He is a cold, calculating and efficient man with nerves of iron and a heart of cold granite. He is occupied at his gruesome task with the casualness of a man weaving a grass basket. His two close assistants, *Mandatane* and *Silwane*, are nervous and scared by comparison, and *Silwane* has a small gourd of strong *ilala* palm beer in his hand to help steady his untrustworthy nerves.

Kokovulu draws with a piece of charcoal the sign of life on the foreheads of his two immediate assistants and then all three men wash their hands and arms thoroughly in a bowl of ox urine which has been brought in a great leak-proof skin bag for this purpose. It is important that all witchdoctors have a bag full of it when going to a battlefield to tend to the wounded. Ox urine is considered, together with that of a woman, to have strong antiseptic powers.

After washing their hands in the urine, the witchdoctors rinse them in hot water and they are ready to begin their task. The first patient is a badly wounded man whose forearm had been all but slashed clean off in the middle, and who also had an ugly flesh wound in the left hip. This patient poses a challenge to the skill of the great *Kokovula*, the Nyasa. The problem is, which wound to attend to first. The prompt action of the Battle Leader to whose *buto* this warrior belonged, of putting a firm tourniquet around the severed forearm had saved the warrior from losing too much blood, and for this *Kokovula* is more than thankful. Prompt action is now needed if this man's life is to be saved.

'*Mandatane*, you see to the wound in this man's hip, while *Silwane* and I attend to his arm – and don't let us waste time!'

Mandatane knows what to do; he does not need to be told. From the leather pouch he procures a soft hare skin and this he uses for cleaning the gaping wound carefully, with warm water, and from a large claypot with a lid he takes a handful of cobwebs and stuffs it into the wound. The cobwebs absorb the blood and assist the clotting process; bleeding stops almost immediately. He takes a delicate bronze needle and a short length of gut and stitches the wound skilfully. There is no need for a copper clip – only a wooden spoonful of *joye* leaves boiled in ox urine to keep away infection. The poultice is placed over the wound and a soft cat skin is used to bandage it.

Meanwhile *Kokovula* and *Silwane* have also begun the delicate task of amputating the man's arm – a task which requires iron nerves and infinite skill. This is a task which few witchdoctors attempt. Even the best witchdoctor loses one out of every three cases.

Carefully *Silwane* lays the man's arm on the great ebony block used for amputating and *Kokovula* starts by cutting out four flaps of flesh above the wound towards the elbow. There is much blood, but *Kokovula* does not mind, though *Silwane* retches continuously. The bone has been reached and it shines pink in the sunlight. The red-hot knife cools and with a curse *Kokovula* demands another from one of the ten 'fire boys', who take turns in pumping the bellows. He brings the next knife at a run, holding it with a wet skin, and *Kokovula* seizes it by the wooden handle and, with a deft slash, severs the forearm at the elbow and tosses the knife back at the feet of the boy who brought it. Quickly he stitches the four flaps together, adding copper clips to help the gut. Then he calls for the tree resin which is promptly brought by two other boys. This specially prepared resin is moulded skilfully and firmly over the stump until it forms a huge ball. This resin helps to keep the wound clean and also accelerates the process of healing. One can only get this resin from the *luwafa* tree, which grows only in very hot places. Its wood is often used in carving very sacred masks.

So antiseptic is this resin that any wound is bound to heal, provided it is properly covered and any infection or pus is properly removed before it is applied. It causes an unpleasant itching, but a brave man finds it quite bearable. The warrior under treatment is bound to go with this ball of resin for a year or two before it can be melted off.

'Great *Kokovula*,' says *Silwane*, 'this man has not been unconscious all the time.'

'I have seen you cut off my arm,' says the brave warrior. 'What are you going to do with it? Roast it for dinner?'

Kokovula smiles back at the warrior and says: 'You are a very brave man!'

'Did you doubt it, you old butcher?' smiles the man weakly, still in a daze. 'Just wait till I am well again.'

Mandatane brings a bowl of *lunjwe* juice – a thick syrupy and pleasant-tasting potion prepared from a herb by this name, which brings almost immediate and pleasant unconsciousness to anyone drinking it in the right quantity. 'Drink this, brave one,' he says, putting it to the lips of the warrior.

Meanwhile the other lesser withdoctors have also been busy with the wounded. To each witchdoctor are attached two learner witchdoctors. All the witchdoctors and apprentices are under the command of *Kokovula*, who only treats the most serious cases.

One fat warrior is making a thorough nuisance of himself and he is not even seriously wounded. This gross quivering nuisance has only an arrow buried deeply in his thigh. But judging by the way he is yelling and screaming he has a whole quiverful of barbed arrows in his fat belly. The poor young witchdoctor and his two apprentices who are attending to this fat coward have been kicked in the face and clawed viciously. In desperation the young witchdoctor calls loudly for *Kokovula* who comes running with a short, heavy club in his hand. One good blow sends the fretful nuisance into dreamland and *Kokovula* calls for a red-hot knife with which he promptly cuts the arrow from the man's thigh.

There is a strong smell of burning human flesh as the great *Kokovula* uses a red-hot hammer to cauterise the wound. The arrow itself is thrust in the charcoal till the metal tip is red-hot. Then it is plunged into cold water. As soon as the warrior regains consciousness, he must drink the water and hang the arrowhead around his neck with a string as a charm to protect him against being wounded by arrows in future.

Thus the hours pass while, with the smell of blood heavy in their nostrils and the cries and groans of the wounded loud in their ears, *Kokovula* and his team of witchdoctors labour to save lives. There have been some deaths, under operation, but many have been saved already who would certainly have died had they not received attention. Lesser ailments are casually treated; men with large bumps on their heads have these punctured and blood is drawn with suction horns – a favourite remedy with witchdoctors, called the *lumeka.*

The witchdoctors work with acrid smoke in their eyes. This smoke comes from the fires and also from the piles of burning *ntelezi* leaves, purposely burnt to give off clouds of billowing smelly smoke which drives away blow flies that might endeavour to reach the wounded men. All kinds of flies are an infernal nuisance and a foul menace to any witchdoctor trying to operate on a battlefield.

Spare 'fire boys' enjoy themselves in a circle around the clearing in which the wounded are laid out and attended. These boys are armed with slings and bows and arrows, and already they have killed some dozens of vultures.

While *Kokovula* and his team are saving lives, another detail – or rather a whole regiment – under the command of the Nguni Rainbow *Induna Ziko,* the singer, is occupied with burying the dead. Nguni and Mambo dead are given a 'Victor's Burial', which means they are buried in full battle regalia in a sitting position with the knees drawn up and all their weapons are interred with them. The Luvijiti are buried in what is called the 'Defeated One's' graves – large communal graves taking twenty men each, with bodies stripped and laid flat on their bellies across their shields.

Bodies of the enemy, of those known to have killed Nguni and Mambo warriors before they were killed themselves, are buried upside down with their legs protruding from the mound. Thus they mark the spot, so to speak, for hyaenas and jackal to find them and drag them out. This is called the 'burial of the hated ones' and is often practised on executed wizards and murderers. Nguni and Mambo graves are arranged in a large circle and a battle axe is planted in the centre to mark the burial ground. This battle axe is planted with its edge facing the East as a salutation to the gods. The dead foreigners, the Arabi, are left unburied and all those Nguni and Mambo warriors who were killed as a result of cowardice are strung up in trees to attract the attention of vultures and hyaenas first.

The burial takes the whole day and as the sun goes down the great singer *Ziko,* who is also a traveller and the only man in the whole land who can speak the languages of both the Lawu (Hottentots) and the Batwa (Bushmen), stands over the fresh graves and commences one of his famous songs: *Brief is life's flickering flame.*

The kneeling warriors look up at their tall handsome Rainbow *Induna*, sharply silhouetted against the flaming sunset sky, and they listen attentively to his rich manly voice.

Lo, in the scowling, icy Dark
Is lit a tiny flame;
It is a tiny flickering flame,
Which is a human life.
Lo, for only moments few
It doth illume the dark,
And quick the chilly wind of Death
Sucketh its fuel away.

Life is but a lost caress,
A whisper in the dark;
Life is but a tiny flame,
That flickers and soon is gone.
Mighty tyrants briefly rule,
And suddenly they live no more;
Great empires grow and bloom
Blooming just to fade again.

You that walk Life's thorny path,
And still are young in years,
Remember Life's thread is short
And brief each fleeting year.
So make the most of each bright day
You see upon this earth;
Strive and bleed for but one end—
A victor's death, a victor's name.

Vain the life a fool doth lead,
Who leaves no name behind;
From Life's own stark deserted land,
I snatch this fragrant triumph—
That on the day I'm laid to rest,
Men shall salute my grave—
Do thou then likewise, Oh my son,
Do thou then likewise, Oh my child.

Leave on Life's flinty ancient sands,
Oh leave thy footprints firm and deep,
And plant on history's recent shore

The flower of thy name.
Thus men and beasts as yet unborn
Shall bow above your grave,
And greybeards of long years to come
Shall say with pride – there was a Man!

The last dead man had been laid to rest and the last wounded man of the Nguni and Mambo carefully attended to – and carried home on a strong wickerwork litter. The last enemy wounded had been caught and dispatched, with a deft blow from an axe.

Now it was time for the weary though jubilant regiments to go home. All the enemy weapons had been collected and ceremoniously urinated upon by every man from both tribes, before being handed over to regimental blacksmiths to be melted down into lumps. All this metal and other spoils were transported on the backs of the ten thousand head of cattle we captured from the Luvijiti, and which they had brought up for their food supplies.

We rested for two days and on the third day we set out towards *Celiwe's* kraal. We had rid ourselves of an invader, and now there remained the counter-attack.

THE TENDER, DEADLY SPEAR

While we were busy hunting down the Luvijiti in the land of the Nguni, the *Munumutaba* was chuckling softly to himself. He had successfully diverted the bulk of the Nguni-Mambo armies far to the East and now he was ready to launch a savage, devastating attack on the thinly defended land of the Western Mambo.

He thought he would sweep through the land like wildfire. But he did not keep reckoning with a woman named *Noliyanda. Noliyanda* had foreseen the invasion long before it came and on her own initiative she mustered a small fleet of old fishing canoes and crocodile hunter's rafts. She manned all these with the two regiments left behind to defend the land. She had decided to meet the invaders on the Zambezi. Thus, when the black invasion barges and canoes of the *Munumutaba* nosed their way across the Zambezi one moonless night, they ran right into a storm of stones and arrows and fire spears hurled at them by the Mambo home defence fleet.

Twenty Luvijiti barges were sunk almost immediately and another ten set on fire. The rest limped back to their side of the river, badly mauled and defeated. It was rumoured that the gross *Munumutaba* burst into an earth-shaking rage when the news of this defeat reached him, and bellowed orders at his nine remaining sons, each of whom commanded a sixteen-thousand man regiment.

The result of these orders was that on the following morning a three-pronged attack was launched across the Zambezi, an attack which forced my Queen *Noliyanda* to retreat to the Mambo Great Kraal, fighting every step of the way.

During the ten following days, Luvijiti armies besieged the ten military kraals built across the land of the Mambo, and also the heavily fortified Royal Kraal *Tulisizwe.* Thinking that he had all the time in creation, the *Munumutaba* built a great camp around each of the besieged kraals, intending to starve them gradually into surrender. As he reclined amongst leopard skin pillows, the *Munumutaba* giggled softly to himself, enjoying visions of what he intended doing with the tall beautiful Queen of the Mambo, who was impudent enough to try and resist him – the mighty *Munumutaba*!

Every attack that the *Munumutaba's* sons launched against the incredibly fortified Great Kraal was repulsed with heavy losses to the attackers, and already four of the sons of the *Munumutaba* had been killed – by bronze-headed, red-feathered arrows shot with deadly accuracy by none other than my Queen *Noliyanda* herself. The *Munumutaba* sent a 'sacred messenger' to the besieged kraal during a lull in the fighting, with a long message demanding that *Noliyanda* surrender. The great Queen replied with a single, well-known and most insulting sign.

When the *Munumutaba* received this insulting message, he killed the messenger on the spot and ordered an all-out attack against the Great Kraal. There was an earth-shaking roar as the Luvijiti hurled themselves at the bristling stockades.

She is standing on the stockade; she is tall, wide-hipped, large-breasted and narrow-waisted. And she is beautiful in a way which is not of this earth – a way which astonishes all mortal men and brings fear into the hearts of all who see her. To the warriors crouching at her feet, ready to meet the rush of the Luvijiti multitudes with spear and arrow and slingstones, this unearthly giantess is more to be feared than the enemy hordes converging on the Great Kraal from all directions. They fear her because she is not an ordinary human being. She is shaped like one, but she does not belong to this world.

Men fear this synthetic creature; they are repelled by her. To them she is like a most beautiful ornate claypot full of vomit – a beautiful flower whose odour causes a fatal headache. The very fact that she was created out of the near-dead body of an executed woman, fills everyone with horror, fear and disgust, and the most pathetic thing is that *Noliyanda* is herself fully aware of this. She tries hard to ignore it; she tries hard to overcome the bitterness in her own soul and the maddening longing to be just an ordinary human being. Her voice is low and throaty as she says: 'Here they come, men. Get ready and give them a hearty welcome!'

The warriors grip their weapons hard and wait tensely as the attack closes in. Arrows and spears tear the air around *Noliyanda's* head. But she is contemptuously indifferent to them. The very skies darken with hissing and whining arrows – and they take a frightening toll.

Soon loud screams rend the air as wounded and dying men writhe in the dust, some with arrows protruding from them like so many porcupine quills.

The Luvijiti hordes advance at a run, their bows twanging and their slings snapping viciously. Hundreds of men vanish into the ground as they step on to the cleverly covered man-traps dug in great quadruple circles around the kraal. There are loud shrieks of agony as dozens of men are impaled on the barbed stakes protruding from the bottom of the deep trenches.

'Now!' cries *Noliyanda.* 'Now men, now!'

A hail of arrows erupts from the defenders behind the ten rings of stockades surrounding the kraal – a tempest of death that cuts down the yelling Luvijiti with only the first concerted volley. But volley follows volley of arrows, slingstones and spears, and multi-pointed heavy missiles also launched by slings. The Luvijiti attack falters. They withdraw and leave thousands of men lying wounded and dead in a huge circle around the kraal, and those within are sickened by the sight.

Slowly the Luvijiti withdraw farther back from that devouring scourge of airborne death, and the defenders intensify their efforts by projecting a last devastating hail of arrows at a steep elevation. This is more than the attackers can take; they turn and run in blind panic, helter-skelter, a pathetic sickening rout.

Noliyanda has won yet another victory. The Luvijiti stampede back to their great camp in spite of savage efforts on the part of the leaders to make them stand firm. Many of the leaders are trampled under foot, and the *Munumutaba* loses more of his sons. In fact, there are now only two left!

The *Munumutaba* ordered a three-day pause in hostilities in which to mourn the loss of his sons. The besieged kraals had a breathing space, and in this period interesting things happened. First the ugly woman *Nunu* accosted the pretty foreigner *Lulama-Maneruana* who had just come out of the new 'hut of the wounded' where my Queen *Noliyanda* and her witchdoctors, *Hlabati* and *Madolo*, were busy tending the wounded. *Lulama-Maneruana* had been helping *Noliyanda* and was red-eyed from lack of sleep. She was utterly exhausted and was on her way to her own hut to sleep, as *Noliyanda* had commanded her to do.

Lulama-Maneruana's pretty face was also lined with pain; the secret unmentionable disease from which she suffered was becoming worse with each passing day. Already she had contemplated suicide, as the High Laws encourage, by setting fire to her hut in which she would then calmly lie down and await death.

This strange, shameful alien disease is called the 'bite of the Arabi' because the alien slave raiders brought it into the country of the Black Tribes. Only those women who had loved members of the Arabi, or who were ravished by Arabi suffering from this disgusting malady, could be infected, and they could pass it on to those with whom they associated afterwards. *Lulama-Maneruana* who had been an empress of Zima-Mbje before being deposed by the *Munumutaba*, had once slept with an Arabi suffering from this disease. For many years she had borne this secret malady with great fortitude. But now the end was in sight. She could bear it no more.

Maneruana had been bitterly annoyed when that hateful, soulless synthetic creature *Noliyanda* had discreetly asked her if she was unwell. She had fiercely and coldly lied to the infernal thing that she was healthy – quite healthy. The impudence of the infernal creature! The Great *Lumukanda* must be induced to destroy this soulless thing one day. Imagine a man like *Lumukanda* loving something he virtually manufactured with his own hands!

'My child,' the rattling voice of the huge, incredibly ugly woman *Nunu* cut across *Maneruana's* angry thoughts, and caused the pretty woman to jerk up her bowed head, 'I want . . . to talk to you . . .'

'What about, *Nunu*?' asked *Maneruana* irritably. 'Speak quickly; I am tired.'

The half-witted *Nunu* was deeply disliked in the Mambo Royal Kraal. People loathed her for her ugliness and very close resemblance to an ape, not only in features, but also in behaviour. *Nunu* preferred to live in a hole in the ground and she was so much like an animal that, if given food in a bowl, she always emptied it in a shallow hole in the ground and then proceeded to eat it. She was always dirty and she always liked to wear an old mouldy skin. The only time when people had use for *Nunu* was when heavy corn-grinding was to be done, or a heavy stone or log needed lifting. *Nunu* was used to doing all this without a murmur. The men and the women in the Great Kraal hated *Nunu* with the same intensity as they hated and feared *Noliyanda*, and in this *Maneruana* was no exception.

'You hate me, do you not, *Maneruana*?' said *Nunu* softly – and something in that soft animal voice made *Maneruana* feel uneasy.

'I do not hate you, *Nunu*,' stammered *Maneruana*. 'But I do not want you near me – that is all.'

'Is it . . . is it because you consider me dirty?' asked *Nunu* with an ugly grin which was intended to be a smile. 'You are not so clean yourself . . . with all that purulence in your loins.'

Lulama-Maneruana gasped. She had never told *Nunu* about her secret malady. The only people who had been told about it were *Malandela's* former wives and they had sworn not to disclose her secret to anybody.

'How . . . how do you . . .'

'Does the name *Lufiti-Ogo* mean anything to you, my child?' asked *Nunu* softly.

'*Lufiti-Ogo*!' cried *Maneruana*. '*Lufiti-Ogo*! Do you mean you are . . .'

'Yes,' smiled *Nunu*, 'I am your old friend from the Underworld . . . the *Ogo*, my child.'

'Why . . . why?' gasped the girl, 'Why did you not tell me this before? Oh, why . . . ?'

'I did not want *Lumukanda* and his wife *Noliyanda* to know who I am,' *Nunu* replied. 'Now my child the time has come for you and me to strike the final shattering blow at the *Munumutaba* and save the land from further bloodshed. Remember that I predicted you would strike the decisive blow, my fallen saviour? The time is now! Come.'

The *Ogo* seized *Maneruana* around the waist and suddenly the girl's vision blurred and the kraal vanished. When things came into focus again *Maneruana* found herself somewhere in the depths of the forests near a small lake. The *Ogo* was nowhere to be seen but her voice came from somewhere close by: 'I have made myself invisible, and I want you to do exactly what I say. Take off your skin skirt and necklace, and bathe in the water. Quickly!'

'How did I get here?'

'I carried you here, child,' said the *Ogo*. 'Now do as I say.'

Lulama-Maneruana quickly took off her attire and got into the water. No sooner had she done so when two young men armed with bows and arrows burst through the forest on the other side of the lake and spotted her. They circled around the edge at a fast run to get at her. They were Luvijiti warriors. *Maneruana's* heart poundèd wildly as she leapt out of the water onto the grass and fled with desperate fear into the depths of the forest. But the long-legged Mashonas were gaining on her and the leading one dived at her legs from behind and brought her down. She fought and struggled and screamed, but in vain. She was knocked unconscious with a fist and left lying in the grass while the two young men discussed what they were to do with her.

'We must take her to our camp and show her to our father,' said the elder of the two.

'You are a fool, *Shabasha* – a great fool!' said the younger. 'That fat hog we call our father will only sacrifice her to the gods, and for that she is far too beautiful.'

'What shall we do with her then, Oh *Shumba*?' asked *Shabasha*.

'She is our woman. We can hide her in a cave, and have her any time we want her,' the younger replied.

'But we are not allowed to sleep with women,' cried *Shabasha*. 'We are not yet initiated into manhood.'

'Who needs to know?' asked *Shumba* contemptuously. 'There are only the two of us here and . . .'

'Yes, you are right, Oh my brother. She will be our secret woman. We don't have to tell anybody about her, and I know a cave close by where we can hide her.'

But the woman had recovered consciousness quickly. She had been listening to this conversation with wide, horrified eyes and at length she whispered: 'No, children . . . no!'

'You keep your mouth shut,' grated *Shumba.*

Shabasha threw himself down beside her and drew her to him with savage trembling hands. *Maneruana* struggled fiercely, silently, to free herself from the young man's passion-deranged clutches. *Shabasha* struck her cruelly across the face – again and yet again. Dazed by the savage blows, *Maneruana* ceased struggling and lay still. 'So be it, you stupid young fools,' she thought angrily. 'If you want to infect yourselves then, do so with the greatest pleasure!'

Lulama-Maneruana smiles softly to herself as she sits alone in the dark interior of the cave. She feels a strong self-satisfaction at what she has done to *Shabasha* and *Shumba.* Soon the only two surviving sons of the *Munumutaba* will be wishing they had never been born. She smiles softly when she remembers that in the greatest adventure of her life in the Underworld, the *Ogo* had called her the fallen saviour. Yes she, *Lulama-Maneruana,* had at last succeeded in hitting back at the *Munumutaba* through his sons, using no other weapon than her beautiful though disease-wasted and pain-wracked body. Yes, the fallen saviour has struck the final blow at the hated invader – the tender deadly spear has stabbed twice and stabbed deeply. Soon the *Munumutaba's* hordes will be finally and shatteringly defeated and sent running back to their distant land like the dogs they are.

The stone the two young men used to close the mouth of the cave is suddenly rolled aside and *Nunu,* the *Ogo,* stands in the sun-drenched entrance. 'Come out, Oh my child, come out quickly.'

Maneruana staggers to her feet and emerges from the cave. The *Ogo* says: 'Child, I am now going to cure you of your terrible malady, as I promised you in the Underworld.' She places both hands on *Maneruana's* hips and the girl feels a strange burning sensation tearing through her. Her hips seem to be on fire and she writhes and moans with pain. She has to endure this ordeal for quite a while, and at last the *Ogo's* voice says gently: 'You are cured now, my brave child, although you have been deprived forever of the powers of bearing children.'

'I honour you, Great *Ogo,* though I don't deserve your mercy. I thank you from the very roots of my soul. But what do we do now?'

The *Ogo* smiled. 'We shall now go back to the Royal Kraal and . . .'

'You will do nothing of the kind – you will come along with me!' says a harsh hollow voice behind them. They whirl around and *lo*! behind them stands that strange apparition – the Spirit of Nature. 'You, *Ogo*, you will now kindly return with me to the Underworld.'

'Never!' screams the *Ogo*. But the Spirit of Nature seizes her in his long grassy arms and both vanish from sight in a hiss of disturbed air.

Lulama-Maneruana was left alone in the forest, alone and utterly helpless. When she had recovered from the great shock and surprise at the sudden turn of events her first action was to get as far away from the cave as possible. *Shabasha* and *Shumba* had said they would return at sunset to bring her food. For *Maneruana* to try and return to the Great Kraal on her own was no longer possible. She was cut off from the kraal by the beleaguering Luvijiti and even if she could have crept through their encampments unobserved, there was still the risk of falling into one of the many man-traps before she reached the kraal itself.

She decided, therefore, to keep walking towards the east, farther and farther away from the besieged kraals. For three whole days she journeyed eastwards towards the land of the Nguni. On the fourth day she was found by a band of Nguni cow thieves who had crossed the border into the land of the Western Mambo to steal some cattle. The thieves, led by *Shungu*, a hulking rascal with a big wart on the nose, found *Maneruana* lying near a stream, suffering from a serious fever.

She was half-conscious and delirious. But her shining bronze necklace and dull-red copper bracelets told the thieves what her status was.

'This is a woman from a Royal Kraal,' rumbled *Shungu*. 'We are bound by the High Laws to protect her with our lives if need be – thieves and cut-throats though we are.'

His band of seven hundred hardened killers nodded in gruff agreement. Even thieves had to revere and respect the High Laws. These were not laid down by selfish and bloodthirsty tyrants for their own evil benefit; they were laid down by Wise Men in ancient times for the benefit of all tribes and they had long since been accepted by all tribes. These laws were a pleasure to obey, not a burden, because everyone, from the highest chief to the lowest footpad, knew and clearly understood that they were the roots, aye, the very lifeblood, of every tribe.

So *Shungu* and his band of incorrigible thieves and cut-throats took the helpless woman to their temporary camp where the gaunt, frightened girls who were *Shungu's* wives and concubines did their best to nurse her back to health. Slowly, ever so gradually, *Lulama-Maneruana* began to recover.

Meanwhile, in the great camp of the Luvijiti, other things were happening which were destined to live forever in song and in story throughout the lands of the tribes. The *Munumutaba* had withdrawn all his armies from around the ten Mambo military kraals he had been besieging, and concentrated them all round the Royal Kraal Tulisizwe, which he intended to crush and destroy finally, regardless of the cost to his armies.

The day for the final attack had come and the *Munumutaba* chuckled softly to himself as he sent one of his counsellors, *Mpolo*, to call his two sons *Shumba* and *Shabasha* who were to lead the attack. On the leopard skin mattress on which the *Munumutaba* was reclining like a great hippopotamus on a sandbank, there also sat a hard-eyed albino woman who formerly had been *Muxakaza*, *Malandela's* one-time First Queen, who had become possessed of an evil spirit during her strange journey through the Underworld. This woman was now the *Munumutaba's* wife, with the proud title of *Nyabangerika*, or High Empress. This woman had escaped just punishment from the land of the Nguni which she had ruled briefly and with great cruelty after outwitting *Vamba Nyaloti* and she had been ingratiating herself with the Luvijiti and their mad ruler by restoring to them the infamous Bronze Idol, the 'Eye of *Odu*', still intact within it.

Now *Muxakaza* was the proud, haughty and cruel spouse of the man she fondly imagined to be the strongest ruler under the sun, and the person who suffered most at her hands was, strangely enough, the *Munumutaba's* orphaned grand-daughter, the dusky deaf-mute *Muwende-Lutanana*, of whose great beauty *Muxakaza* was bitterly jealous.

Muxakaza was seated next to the *Munumutaba*, feeding him ripe wild figs and other fruit as if he were a child, pausing now and again to whisper intimately into the fat despot's ear, causing the depraved *Munumutaba* to explode into gusty raucous laughter. The girl *Muwende-Lutanana* crouched in a dark corner of the temporary hut, awaiting with mute resignation the next sign-language command from either *Muxakaza* or her heartless grandfather. Beside her lay Lumbilo, her famous pet cheetah, who watched his mute mistress with yellow and highly intelligent feline eyes.

Mpolo returned just as *Muxakaza* was holding a bronze bowl full of strong beer to the *Munumutaba's* ugly lips. *Mpolo* fearfully prostrated himself before his ruler, expecting to be killed any moment and terribly afraid of speaking what he had to say.

'Great Elephant, the young Royal Lions cannot come to your presence,' said *Mpolo* shakily.

The *Munumutaba* choked and spluttered on the mouthful of beer he was about to swallow. He tore the bowl from *Muxakaza's* hand and hurled it with great accuracy at *Mpolo's* face. He snatched another bowl of sticky sour porridge and also threw it – straight and true. *Mpolo* fell flat on his back as the heavy clay bowl struck him full in the face filling his nostrils, mouth and eyes with sour porridge. The *Munumutaba*, encouraged by giggles from *Muxakaza*, leapt up, seized *Mpolo* by the throat and hauled him to his feet.

'Why can't my sons come to me when I call them?' he demanded.

Mpolo's eyes bulged and his tongue lolled out. His dark-brown face became as black as ebony. He tried to speak but could not and, as the gross tyrant tightened his grip around *Mpolo's* throat, the poor counsellor's loinskin became very wet. The *Munumutaba* laughed cruelly and released his hold. *Mpolo* fell flat on his back once more.

'Speak, dog!' growled the *Munumutaba*. 'Why can't my sons come to me?'

Mpolo opened his mouth to speak, but only a hoarse croak came out and, as he made another equally unsuccessful effort at answering his ruler's question, *Mpolo* received a back-handed blow right on the mouth from *Muxakaza*.

'That ought to encourage you, dog,' hissed the Queen. 'Answer!'

'They are most unwell, Oh Great Ones,' screeched *Mpolo* when he found his voice at last. 'They are unwell and are ashamed to come to your presence.'

'What illness would make my sons ashamed to come when I call? Answer, dog!' bellowed the Great *Munumutaba*.

Mpolo swallowed hard, opened his big fish-like mouth once, and then promptly shut it. He then beat a strategic retreat towards the entrance of the hut, but the *Munumutaba* followed him and reached for his throat. 'Answer, dog!'

'Great One,' stammered *Mpolo*, 'your sons are both suffering from a foreign and unclean disease.'

The *Munumutaba's* eyes opened wide. His flabby face became a playground of different expressions – surprise, anger, and utter disbelief.

'What disease is it?' he demanded.

'The slave raiders' disease, Oh Great Elephant,' whispered *Mpolo*.

'You are lying, *Mpolo*,' growled the *Munumutaba*. 'Tell me you are lying.'

'Great One,' moaned the counsellor, 'I wish I were.'

'*Mpolo*,' said the *Munumutaba* in a low, terrible voice, 'tell me you are joking.'

'Believe me, I am not, Oh Great Elephant.'

The *Munumutaba* stood still for a long time, huge fists clenched and sweat pouring down his fat many-chinned face. He bit his lower lip until blood flowed and tears burst in a torrent out of his eyes. '*Mpolo*,' he said at last, 'tell me, what have I done to the gods to deserve this? What awful sin have I committed before the Highest to be thus punished?'

'Great One,' cried *Mpolo*, 'I do not know.'

'Call *Lumbewe* the Prophet,' said the *Munumutaba* in a faltering voice. 'Send for *Lumbewe* the Prophet.'

The counsellor *Mpolo* bowed his head to the very ground and went outside, leaving the *Munumutaba* sobbing on his leopard skin mattress, with *Muxakaza* trying in vain to comfort him. Some time later *Mpolo* came back into the hut, followed by a thin, hollow-eyed, wild-looking man wearing tattered and mouldy impala skins and a headband of green leaves.

'Your soul is greatly troubled, Oh *Munumutaba*,' cackled *Lumbewe*. 'You who have the dread Eye of *Odu* in your possession and who should have used its awful powers for the benefit of your people, instead of your own selfish ends, have been overtaken by retribution at last. The gods are angry with you, Oh *Munumutaba*, because you have abused the powers they gave you. You have tried to make yourself into a god, and you have even had the impudence to force your subjects to pray to you – and offer human sacrifices to images of yourself.

'Today your evil deeds have overtaken you and your name has been stained with shame because of what has happened to your last two surviving sons. And here is another thing which has called forth the anger of the gods: you have taken as your wife an evil woman whose body is inhabited by the soul of a creature that caused the destruction of her race a million years ago. Her only intention now is to destroy you so that she can take over your subjects and lead also them to death and destruction. You are lost, *Munumutaba*, you might as well kill yourself.'

'Get out of here!' bellowed the *Munumutaba*. 'Get out of here, you cackling old spook!'

With a loud, cracked laugh *Lumbewe* left the hut. Then the *Munumutaba* said to *Mpolo*: 'Accompany me to the hut in which my sick sons are.'

Without so much as a glance at *Muxakaza*, the *Munumutaba* took the Bronze Idol from its little shrine in the far corner of the hut and went outside. The tens of thousands of fierce Luvijiti warriors flung themselves flat on their faces and licked the dust as the *Munumutaba* went by, while the thousands of wives and concubines the Luvijiti had brought with them from their distant native land knelt and tore off tufts of their hair, flinging them at their dread god-king's feet in salutation as he strode heavily past.

But the *Munumutaba* seemed blind to all this. For once he was not smiling and waving his hand in indifferent blessing as had been his practice. For once the expression of fierce pride and arrogance have left his bloated features, being replaced by one of unimaginable agony and horror. His high priests, who tended fires on altars on which were burnt human sacrifices to himself, were quick to notice that something was wrong. Together with lesser army commanders and counsellors, they came forward in a crowd and followed their flesh-and-blood god at a discreet distance.

When he reached the hut in which *Shumba* and *Shabasha* were hiding, the *Munumutaba* paused and ordered all his priests, commanders and counsellors to stand in a circle surrounding it. He then drew *Mpolo* aside and whispered harshly into the ear of that terrified man: 'Listen *Mpolo*, this is my last moment on earth and I command you to take charge of my armies and fight your way out of this land, back to Zima-Mbje. Take the female *Muxakaza* with you and make her your goddess-queen in my place. But first I want you to move all commoners, all ordinary warriors and their women as far away from this hut as possible. Now go.'

Mpolo ran like a maddened impala to carry out his king's commands. By dark he had completed the task of moving people away from the vicinity of the hut and the men standing around it. Night fell. The smiling stars looked down upon the earth once more, and the brooding forests were lent a more sinister appearance by the coming of the darkness. In the depths of the forests jackals began to howl dismally and hyaenas to laugh like drunken old women.

Inside the hut the *Munumutaba* rose slowly from the carved stool on which he had been sitting and listening to the ceaseless babbling of his two sons who had been shocked into madness at finding themselves afflicted by so horrible a disease.

'So,' said the *Munumutaba* softly, 'so this is the end . . . and the time has come for me to die. The thread of my life, which would have gone on forever, must be snapped off soon. Welcome death . . . welcome maiden from the Outer Darkness . . . welcome dark Virgin Death. My name has been stained with a shame so great that were I to live for a million years I would never wash it off. Neither would I be able to forget what happened to my sons were I to outlive the very stars, the very mountains, the very River of Time. A curse, a vile curse on this evil, senseless thing that some idiot misnamed Life! Of what use is life, whether it outlasts the Universe or whether it lasts but a mere heartbeat? It is still nothing but life – life with its few transient joys, but mostly heart-racking pains and soul-shattering sorrows. So, farewell life – I cast you away as easily as one casts away an old flea-infested loinskin. But, *Munumutaba* shall not die alone, neither shall he die an ordinary mortal's death. He shall die in a blaze of glory that men shall remember to the end of time. And he shall take all his servants and his last two sons with him.'

The *Munumutaba* opened the Bronze Idol and took out the radiant stone called the Eye of *Odu*. For a few moments he looked at the heavy crystal shining brightly in his hands and shedding a dull yellow light all over him and on to the floor. He raised his hands above his head and focussed his mind on what he wanted the stone to do.

A pillar of searing, ravening flame burst from the ground around the hut and consumed everything almost immediately, as though struck by a direct flash of lightning. The priests and servants standing around the hut were reduced to ashes. The dry grass and bush all round caught fire. A mighty pillar of flame rose and lit the countryside with the brightness of midday.

Soon the fire spread far and wide, fanned by a strong south-easterly wind. The Luvijiti hordes fled wildly from the advancing wall of tree-devouring flame, smothering heat and choking smoke. Driven by a natural fear of fire, wild beasts of all kinds burst from their sanctuary and fled side by side with the human horde – a stampede of a haphazard host of man and beast. Tall *mopanis* burst in flame like tufts of grass, and crashed to the ground, crushing mobs of falling and struggling animals and human beings. Panic-stricken elephants trampled men and beasts alike. Maddened rhinoceroses tore through the seething ocean of fleeing beasts and warriors. Crashing, dashing and falling, up and on, shoulder to shoulder, darted lion, wildebeest and impala, leopards with fear-glazed eyes, and baboons, kudu, eland and nyala.

The devouring wall of fire seemed to reach the very stars. It was the greatest forest fire of all time – the *Muuota-Mkulu* of song and legend. The fire raged westward across the lands of the Tribes for more than a hundred days.

From where she stood on the innermost stockade of the Western Mambo Royal Kraal, my first Royal Queen *Noliyanda* saw the fire rage over the land. And she saw the great tide of men, women and beasts fleeing past the kraal on either side – one continuous torrent of living creatures fleeing side by side, natural and mutual enmity forgotten in the face of the greater common enemy.

To the panic-stricken people within the Great Kraal *Noliyanda* shouted: 'There is no need to abandon the kraal. The fire won't reach it, the clearing around the kraal is wide enough. You are quite safe, but prepare for sparks coming down on the huts . . .'

Some time later two shapely female figures were seen staggering towards the main gate of the Great Kraal from the direction of the fire and *Noliyanda* herself went down to open the gate. It was *Muxakaza* and the dead *Munumutaba's* orphaned grand-daughter, the deaf mute *Muwende-Lutanana*, the beautiful. As the surprised *Noliyanda* was about to close the huge carved portals behind her midnight visitors, a lithe cheetah bounded in and frolicked around the two strangers. The mute girl snapped her fingers twice and the beast stopped its display of affection and stood, looking up at the girl with luminous, adoring eyes.

'I see you, Oh foreign ones,' said *Noliyanda* throatily. 'What brings you to the kraal of those you hate?'

'I see you, Oh Great Queen,' the albino woman *Muxakaza* responded. 'But I do not see us as enemies because the enmity between our nations has been wiped out by the death of my lord, the *Munumutaba*, and also by the fire you see roaring across the land. I, *Muxakaza*, the Empress of Luvijiti, greet you, *Noliyanda*, as a friend. And I have come to give you a peace offering – a gift which will bring you much joy, you and your lord, the Great *Lumukanda*.'

'I do not think I want any gift from you, Oh *Muxakaza*,' said *Noliyanda*. 'Hands that are red with the blood of my husband's people can bring no gift to me.'

Muxakaza knelt mockingly before *Noliyanda* and her eyes were alive with pure mockery as she said: 'Great *Noliyanda*, it ill becomes a great queen like you to continue hating an enemy who has come to you with an offer of peace. The High Laws say that the hand that is offered in friendship must never be struck aside, and I have not yet heard that the Great *Noliyanda* is exempt from obedience to the High Laws.'

'A truce to your mockery, Oh *Muxakaza*!' hissed *Noliyanda* angrily. 'What is the gift you have come to make me?'

Muxakaza pushed the girl *Muwende-Lutanana* towards *Noliyanda* saying, 'She is my gift to you, Oh *Noliyanda*.'

'What am I supposed to do with her? I cannot take her to the love mat, can I?'

'The birds of rumour have sung in my ears, Oh *Noliyanda*,' smiled the albino woman. 'They have told me that although the Great *Noliyanda* is the most beautiful creature in all creation, she is as barren as a lump of granite and is even now looking for a woman who will be prepared to bear children for her, whom she could adopt as her own. And I have brought my dead husband's grand-daughter with me to present her to the Great *Noliyanda* so that the dearest wish in your most royal heart may be granted.'

For a long time the tall *Noliyanda* stood as still and as silent as a *mopani* tree. Long-lashed eyes lowered, she glanced down at her heavy jutting breasts and sadly shook her head. Tears sprang from the fountains that were her deep-set, burning eyes and flowed freely down her high-boned cheeks. Her dark, full mouth trembled as she said very slowly, 'I accept your gift, Oh *Muxakaza.* I desire nothing more on earth than to bear my husband just one, just one child. Alas, that is not possible. So I shall take this girl for my husband as his Second Queen and she shall bear children whom I shall know as my own. Thank you, Oh *Muxakaza.* I . . . I honour you.'

The Great *Noliyanda* was blinded by the glare of the distant bush fire and by her own tears, so she did not see the expression of malevolent triumph that flickered for a few brief heartbeats over the brazenly beautiful features of *Muxakaza.* The immortal woman did not realise that her insane love of children had already plunged her, and the man she loved, into the cauldron of sorrow and disaster. The evil woman *Muxakaza* had struck a devastating blow at us and we were not to feel its effects until a year had gone by.

'She is a virgin, the daughter of a great man who loved her mother for a short time long ago, and then left her to continue his travels,' the albino woman was saying smoothly. 'When she finally realised she was pregnant and that her lover was lost to her for ever, the mother of this child nearly went mad with grief. When the time came for her to bring forth her baby she was so weak she did not survive the strain and the pains of childbirth. But her offspring lived – and this is she, *Muwende-Lutanana,* the beautiful. Take her, Oh Great *Noliyanda* – she is my gift to you.'

Queen *Noliyanda* drew the girl *Muwende-Lutanana* gently to her and smiled down at her sad, beautiful face. She then ordered the two puppet women, *Nomeva* and *Muwaniwani,* to take her into the Great Hut, bath her and give her some food.

Noliyanda turned to *Muxakaza.* 'Tell me, what do you intend doing now?'

'I have ordered that all those of my people who survive the fire should make their way back to our boats on the Zambezi,' said *Muxakaza.* 'When they have assembled there, we shall cross the river and go back to our homeland.'

'But you must first spend the night here and eat the corn cake of peace with me. Then in the morning I shall personally escort you to that place of embarkation.'

'Your kindness overwhelms me, Oh *Noliyanda.*'

The two queens made their way through the crowd of warriors and servants towards *Noliyanda's* hut. The distant fire shed an eerie red glow over everything. Inside the Queen's Hut *Noliyanda* washed *Muxakaza's* hands in warm water and both women sat down to eat.

First they broke a huge corn cake into two pieces and from her piece each woman broke a smaller piece which she ate. The rest was broken into still smaller pieces and distributed among the women and warriors inside the hut. The two queens then toasted each other with copper bowls full of *mukoyo* beer before eating the deliciously cooked fowl set before them.

Mpolo the Counsellor was dying. He was lying helplessly on his back watching with pain-dimmed eyes as the fire swept nearer and nearer.

He saw mighty trees go crashing down to the ground. He felt the searing heat of the oncoming fire wall. He saw bushes explode into brilliant flame and he saw the rain of sparks and ashes that fell over everything, setting the long grass on fire and singeing the skins of the countless dead and dying men and animals around him, all trampled underfoot by the stampeding hordes and left behind in the path of the approaching inferno.

Muxakaza had stabbed *Mpolo* – to stop him from warning *Noliyanda*, as he had threatened to do, about the horrible trick *Muxakaza* was about to play on the man whom *Mpolo* knew as his father. *Mpolo* was determined to get up from where he was lying and warn *Noliyanda* before he died; slowly, painfully he raised himself on his elbow, gasping hoarsely for breath, slowly . . .

Mpolo sat up. He managed to rise to his feet. He actually took a few staggering steps away from the oncoming fire. But then he fell flat on his face. With a sob he struggled slowly to his feet once more and staggered on, clutching the streaming gaping wound in his chest with both hands. On he staggered, on . . .

'Got to warn them . . . *Lumukanda* . . . my father . . . never saw him. Got to . . . can't . . . can't let evil woman . . . do this . . . to father . . .'

He did not see the pain-maddened and smoke-blinded rhinoceros charging madly out of the flaming forest. The huge beast had been trapped under a great fallen tree, but had succeeded in freeing itself after a mighty struggle. Its hide was blistered and smoking; one ear was burnt and shrivelled and one eye had burst. The great horn above its nose was burning and smoking like the stump of a fire-devoured tree.

Blindly, madly, it bore down upon the struggling human being. It struck Mpolo with its burning horn full in the small of his back and sent him high into the air, and down into a clump of bushes that exploded into fire at the same time. The forelegs of the animal collapsed and it ploughed the ground with a shuddering grunt.

HAIL TO THEE, OH MAIEGAWANA

The Wise Ones of the Tribes have a saying that goes: '*Inyoni yobubi ilizalela qede iqanda layo isheshe ibaleke.*' (The bird of evil lays its foul egg and quickly flies away.) This saying applies to an evil person who is always quick to leave the scene of his or her crime.

And Empress *Muxakaza* of Zima-Mbje was quick to leave the Great Kraal Tulisizwe early the next morning. She did not wait for *Noliyanda* to wake up and arrange an escort for her. She did not even bid *Noliyanda* goodbye. She left alone and unattended just before daybreak, armed with two short assegais and a woman's shield. She left at a brisk, half-running walk, not pausing until she was three-quarters of a day's journey away from Tulisizwe.

She was a triumphant woman who had done an evil deed and was now putting as much distance as possible between herself and the scene of her crime. *Muxakaza* was no longer *Muxakaza*. She was nothing but a shell in which dwelt a spirit of a woman who lived a million years ago – a woman more evil than the Spirit of Evil herself; a woman who revelled in committing the worst crimes. She had no conscience. She dedicated herself to evil. She had once more begun a career of wickedness beyond the wildest imagination. The Beastess had just struck the first blow in her new project and this was to be followed by worse acts of evil before she would finally be defeated.

In the Great Kraal Tulisizwe the Queen *Noliyanda* was preparing the deaf-mute *Muwende-Lutanana* for the ceremony of receiving the long cowrie-shell decorated skin skirt of a Royal Wife. Firstly the beautiful girl was handed over to three old women known as the Sacred Grandmothers of the Tribe. These women dwelt in a big hut in one of the military kraals and they were elected for the sole purpose of checking all the girls in the land of the Mambo as yet unmarried to see if they were still virgins. This was done once a year and was – and still is – one of the strictest laws among the Tribes.

It was also the duty of the Sacred Grandmothers to verify the virginity of any girl about to be married, whether she was to marry a commoner or a king.

In the hut of the Sacred Grandmothers, or the Three Hags as they were secretly though popularly called, a secret ritual was once again in progress. No man is ever allowed to be present, least of all the bridegroom, and few men know the details of the ritual. I am one of these few men, but the High Laws of the Tribes forbid me to divulge any details.

The young girl *Muwende-Lutanana* was proven a virgin beyond all doubt. She was tested most rigorously and was found to be a fertile and highly sexed girl – a woman of the first order, a woman capable of bearing children with the minimum of pain, difficulty and risk to her own life and that of the child. I repeat that I am forbidden to describe the tests by which all this was established. Suffice it to say that the whole programme took ten whole days and nights.

Muwende-Lutanana also went through the painful ritual of the 'opening of the gate of love' with mute fortitude and, on the fifteenth day she was released from the hut of the Three Hags where she had been confined without seeing daylight for the whole period. As a mark of their approval and blessing, the Three Hags presented her with the elaborate cowrie-shell fringed *mutsha.* This garment, called the *Mutsha* of Fertility, was given only to those girls who had passed all the strenuous tests of womanhood with honours.

The Three Hags also gave the girl lengthy advice in sign language and made her swear, by placing her hand on the withered right breast of each of them, to be good and faithful to her husband to the end of her days.

Then, on the evening of her Day of Release, *Muwende-Lutanana* was sent back to Tulisizwe with three young priestesses for company.

Noliyanda received her with great joy and made a great fuss over her, after which she told her to have a good night's rest in preparation for the Ceremony of Acceptance which was to be held early the following morning.

Dawn had not yet stained the eastern sky and the glittering star called the *Ndonsakusa*, the Bringer of Day, or the Morning Star, was high in the Eastern heavens. This star is also known as the Star of Purity, because of its pure, steady brightness, and the Tribal Wise Men tell us that all brides taken when this star rules the eastern sky are destined to be faithful and dutiful wives.

Noliyanda woke up with the birds which had started their morning worship of the coming dawn. She did not step into her long, black, calf-skin skirt as she used to do; she only tied the First Queen's *mutsha* – made of shining bronze and copper beads – round her broad hips, put on her copper necklaces and bracelets and broad copper headband, also her bronze earrings. Then the stangest female creature of all time left her hut to awaken the two zombies *Nomeva* and *Muwaniwani.* These went to arouse the other women in the kraal while she turned her attention to the gentle awakening of *Muwende-Lutanana.*

A little later a group of twelve women made their way down to the lake in the fire-devoured forest, *Noliyanda* leading. The red light of coming day was creeping up the heavens and the trees of the burnt-out forest stood etched against this background tint like gaunt, atrocious skeletons. The smell of the burnt veld was still strong in everyone's nostrils and the black ash of burnt grass and wood was ankle deep. The women hastened their steps because the coming ceremony must be performed before sunrise and while the Day Star still rules the eastern skies.

Quickly the Queen *Noliyanda* led the bride *Muwende-Lutanana* into the cold water and the rest of the women threw off their skin skirts and followed. They all stood in a circle, waist deep in water, around their queen and the bride from the south, waiting patiently for the ceremony to begin.

Noliyanda scooped water with her cupped hands and poured it over *Lutanana's* head, saying, 'I now pronounce you the Second Wife of my lord and husband, Oh ebony flower of the South, and to me you shall be like a sister, a part of me. I shall laugh when you laugh; I shall sing sweet songs and pray for you. I shall weep when you weep and dance when you dance. They who hate you shall be my foes and they who love you shall be my friends. The fruits of your undefiled womb shall be known as though they are mine as well. I, *Noliyanda* the ageless, salute you, Oh Dark Flower from the South.'

Then each woman, but not the two zombies, scooped up water and poured it over *Muwende-Lutanana's* head in turn, praising her and giving her a poetic nickname, such as 'Flower of Sunrise', 'Joy of the Immortal' and 'Daystar of Luvijiti' and so on. The brief ceremony was concluded by the singing of the Song of the Moon. The gentle voices of the women rang eerily across the black desolation in the spreading dawn:

> Oh sacred orb, which through the starry sky
> At fleeing *Ma* the Tree of Life let fly—
> Shed o'er the world thy gentle silver light,
> And make each being feel love's consuming might.

* * *

Inflame with love the lion's savage soul—
Make him forget to stalk the zebra foal;
And make him turn to where beneath the trees
His mate awaits; and there find sweet release
From pleasant anguish, Aye, command the warring king
To lay aside his deathful lance awhile
And seek his consort of the shining smile
And with her fight and win a sweeter war,
Where shield is kiss and assegai desire!

'Where shield is kiss and assegai desire ...' The words were a whisper, a lost fragrant whisper in the charred forest long after the women had departed to return to the kraal. A lonely bird sat on the only remaining branch of a blackened tree and sang its joy to the rising sun.

Another day was born. Another day was sent like a lost *mopani* leaf on a stream down the savage cataracts of time.

There was laughter in the kraal of Tulisizwe. There was joy and happiness. There was singing and dancing – eating and drinking. The Mambo were celebrating the end of the war and the return of peace in the fire-ravaged land.

But there were also tears. There were many tears for those who died. There were thousands of homeless people whose kraals had been devoured by the fire. There were thousands of widows and orphans. *Noliyanda* had sent out one of her two regiments to collect all the orphans and widows in the land and to bring them to the Great Kraal. She was also distributing thousands of baskets of corn to the homeless and the starving.

In a long ceremony with much dancing and singing, *Muwende-Lutanana* was presented at long last with the skin skirt of a Royal Wife. The singing and dancing went on for three full days.

Noliyanda was the happiest woman in the world and the people were surprised to see their queen dancing and leaping amongst the revellers like any young girl.

Shungu the thief leader and his band of male and female incorrigibles met us just as we were crossing the border from the land of the Nguni into the land of the Western Mambo. *Shungu* handed *Lulama-Maneruana* over to me and would have gone back to his evil ways of stealing had I not threatened him with my biggest cooking pot. I actually forced him and his whole band into my service.

Lulama-Maneruana threw herself at my feet and told her story, concluding by urging us to make full haste for home. When we reached my Great Kraal two days later we were greeted by a large crowd of men and women led by *Noliyanda*. The triumphant Mambo armies which I had led into the land of the Nguni were received like the victors that they were. They marched into the Great Kraal, preceded by shrieking and dancing women who showered them with a storm of sacred cowrie shells to the accompaniment of reed flutes and the thunder of victory drums. Oxen were slaughtered and roasted whole over great fires for the Victory Feast to be held on the evening of the following day.

In the wild tempest of rejoicing that preceded and followed our entry into the Great Kraal, I found myself carried shoulder high by my ten Rainbow *Indunas*. I was festooned with garlands of flowers and thousands of strings of cowrie-shell necklaces. My Queen, my *Noliyanda*, led thousands of wildly dancing women each of whom carried a sacred broom with which she swept the clearing before the advancing and chanting warriors. Loud piercing *kikiza* cries tore the air to shreds as they exploded from countless female throats. The dust rose in clouds from under the feet of the twisting, shaking, leaping women and the sounds of happiness floated over the surrounding hills and plains.

The wild dancing went on into the depths of the silvery moonlit night – as did the singing, drinking and eating. At midnight huge clay bowls full of water, mixed with the bile from the slaughtered oxen, were placed in the centre of the kraal for the warriors to wash their hands in, to remove the 'dirt of battle' before retiring to their homes.

The High Laws of the Tribes forbid warriors to go to sleep with their wives on returning from battle and for this reason a Widows Regiment is formed before the victorious armies return. A Widows Regiment includes all women without husbands at the time – true widows, rejected ones and spinsters – and these are gathered for the sole purpose of accommodating married warriors on the first night of their return. For a warrior to sleep with a strange woman on such an occasion is said to remove the 'darkness' with which he becomes cursed when he kills men in battle. Under no circumstances must a man pollute his wife with his first fluid immediately on returning from the field of bloodshed because, if he does so, he will defile his own children as yet unborn – and their children's children – with tendencies to become homicidal maniacs. Such is the law, and such the beliefs of the Tribes.

Thus, the woman who shared my love mat that night was not my favourite *Noliyanda*, but the mortal, vivacious *Lulana-Maneruana*. Just before we went to sleep *Noliyanda* came in and told me pleasantly that she had a surprise for me, the nature of which I would find out in the morning.

As my Queen, *Noliyanda* had chosen the beautiful foreigner *Maneruana* from a hundred women who had been clamouring for the honour of sharing the love mat with their High Chief. But *Noliyanda* had not given thought to the fact that *Maneruana* hated her bitterly and the greatest wish in this former queen's heart was that I should destroy *Noliyanda* – the Unnatural Creature as many called her. A man is forbidden by law to reject a woman whom his first wife has chosen for him, be it permanently or for one night only. I was thus powerless to change *Maneruana* for another woman, much as I wanted to.

Lulama-Maneruana – now generally known as the Fallen Saviour – loved me with an intensity that approached madness and she wanted badly, madly to become my First Queen in *Noliyanda's* place. She was a wilful, dangerous woman who knew what she wanted in life and stopped at nothing to get it. As she came proudly and fearlessly into my Great Hut, her thoughts – her secret unspoken thoughts were as loud in my ears as if she had spoken them at the top of her voice: 'At last, my adorable and mighty god, I have you – even though it will be for only this short night. Would to the Ultimate Cause it were for the rest of my life! I love you *Lumukanda* . . . I desire you with every vein in my body . . . every cord and fibre of my being! You shall be mine, Lost Immortal, you shall be mine even if I have to wait till the very stars fall from their lofty thrones. You will be mine even if I have to kill and poison every woman upon this earth to get you.'

'Someone,' I said with a smile, 'someone is thinking in violent and red-hot directions.'

She was startled. She had forgotten that I could read human thoughts. I sensed her hand going to her mouth and I heard her gasp of surprise and fear.

'I do not want you, Oh *Maneruana*,' I told her gently. 'You must remember that you are one of *Malandela's* wives and you have not gone through the Rites of Separation with him so that you may marry again.'

'My lord and Chief,' she said coldly, 'whether or not you desire me makes no difference to me. I love you and that is all that matters. And I mean to have you or die trying. I am *Maneruana*, the rightful chieftainess of Zima-Mbje, and what I want, I get. Even if I have to go out and kill every woman in the world, my mind is made up that I shall have you.'

'You talk like a fool, Oh *Maneruana*,' I said calmly. 'I have met many women like you in my life and your drivelling does not impress me. To me you are but a man-hungry harlot, nothing more.'

'You shall have reason to regret those words one day, Oh Great *Lumukanda*,' she said angrily. 'The day shall come when you shall crawl to me with your tail between your legs, you arrogant, heartless beast!'

'Sit down, *Maneruana*. A truce to your childish bleating and squawking. You are here to do my bidding, so shut your dirty little mouth, you strumpet!'

'*Ha*!' laughed she. 'Insults are spears that hurt only the foolish. Insult me as much as you wish. But in the end – one day – you shall be calling me your beloved one.'

'That day shall never dawn, Oh *Maneruana*,' I said, smiling. 'Come here, Oh mad one – you shall have your wish, but for this one night only.'

In the course of my life I have met and loved thousands of women. But, believe me, *Lulama-Maneruana* was one of the best, of the very best, as I discovered that night.

She was a pliant sapling, tossed by the raging tempest of emotion and desire. She was a bolt of searing lightning, vibrant with passion. *Yea-ha*, she was a red-hot spear, heated in the furnace of love. There was something frightening in her wild unabashed caressing, her lip-bruising kisses and her lacerating clutches. *Lulama-Maneruana* – the Fallen Saviour – was second only to *Noliyanda*, in what the Wise Ones of the Tribes call 'True Womanhood'.

But somehow I did not dream of making her my wife. To me she was but one of the thousands of women whom I had loved once and forgotten. She was but one of the many flowers I have plucked, admired, and cast aside – flowers that grew in their thousands along the footpath of my life.

'That,' I said at long last to the thoroughly spent female, 'ought to cure you of your stupid infatuation.'

Her closed eyes opened slowly and her eyelashes fluttered. '*Aiekoan*, great *Lumukanda*,' she whispered, 'nothing will ever cure me of my love for you. And this has made me love you all the more. And I am prepared to walk into the Furnace of Eternity itself if by so doing you will turn out to be mine.'

In the morning *Noliyanda* came into the Great Hut with her handmaidens, the two zombies, and greeted me by first kissing my forehead, hands and feet, and then saying pleasantly, 'My Lord, I shall now present to you the young mortal woman I have chosen to be your Second Queen and I beg you to accept her and love and cherish her for my sake. She is the one I have chosen to bear you the children I am unable to bear. She is a proven virgin and *Muwende-Lutanana* is her name.'

'I accept your gift to me, Oh *Noliyanda*, joy of my sightless eyes, and I do hope she is a beautiful one.'

'She is as beautiful as midsummer dew, my Lord, and unlike me she is both young and fresh . . . and pure.'

'No creature under the stars could ever be as beautiful and as pure as you, Oh immortal sun of my life. And it is for your sake only that I accept the young woman. Bring her in and let her see her lord and husband.'

Twenty women, including my two daughters, *Luanaledi* and *Mbaliyamswira*, crawled into the hut at a signal from *Noliyanda*, accompanying the young bride *Muwende-Lutanana*.

'My Lord – your bride,' said *Noliyanda* throatily.

I was suddenly aware of tension mounting inside the hut and I wished to the stars I could see what was going on. I sensed *Lulama-Maneruana*, who had not left my side since sunrise, stiffen beside me. I heard her gasp with horror. Then I heard *Luanaledi's* delightful voice saying, 'It seems as if *Lulama-Maneruana* and *Muwende-Lutanana* know each other from somewhere, Oh my stepmother.'

'They are looking at one another as if they are each seeing an evil ghost, Oh *Luanaledi*,' laughed *Noliyanda*. 'Tell me, *Maneruana*, are you and *Lutanana* acquainted?'

Lulama-Maneruana ignored *Noliyanda's* question. Instead, she rose and flung herself at my feet shrieking, 'Great *Lumukanda* . . . my Lord, Great Immortal One, you . . . you cannot marry this girl!'

'Why, *Maneruana*?' I asked, feeling uneasy. 'Why can I not marry this girl?'

Noliyanda's voice rang out suddenly, coldly: 'My Lord, disregard this woman's raving. She is jealous of *Lutanana*, that is all. And she hates me bitterly as you know. All she wants is to spoil your new bride's happiness. I want a child-bearing female for my husband, *Maneruana*, not a creature like you who is as sterile as I am and has many other faults besides!'

'Believe me, *Lumukanda*,' shrilled *Maneruana*, 'believe me, I beg you. You cannot marry *Muwende-Lutanana*.'

'Rainbow *Indunas Mavimbela* and *Nsongololo*,' called out *Noliyanda*, 'come in here and get this mad woman out! I am sick of her jealousy and I do not want to see her face again.'

'Shall I kill her, Great Queen?' bellowed *Mavimbela*, the woman hater, as he crawled into the hut.

'No,' replied *Noliyanda* coldly, 'give her food and tell her to go away from here and never come back. Take a company of warriors and escort her far away from this kraal and tell her to keep on travelling. Quickly now!'

Mavimbela hauled the sobbing *Lulama-Maneruana* to her feet and dragged her roughly away.

'My Lord,' sobbed *Maneruana*, clinging briefly to the doorway, 'my Lord *Lumukanda* . . . my beloved one, you shall regret having accepted this girl as your bride. That evil, unnatural monstrosity you created – that slut *Noliyanda* – is plunging you into the whirlpool of sorrow, shame and suffering . . .'

'Come, you dirty harlot!' snarled *Mavimbela*.

I accepted the young girl *Muwende-Lutanana* as my bride. But *Maneruana's* words had filled me with uneasiness and dark foreboding. Something was wrong somewhere and for once in my life I did not know what. And, to my great surprise, I could foresee great trouble in the very near future for myself – trouble springing forth from my having accepted *Lutanana* as my Second Queen.

Thus, when *Lutanana* came into my hut that night I turned my back on her and began thinking of ways of getting rid of her – somehow. When I read her thoughts in an effort at finding out the true nature of the trouble that she was going to bring me, I found she was nothing but a simple girl who had never known her father and whose mother had died when she was born. I also discovered why she had been so shocked at seeing *Maneruana* sitting next to me. *Maneruana* had ill-treated the girl somehow, long ago while she was still queen of the Luvijiti, before her brother, the now dead *Munumutaba*, overthrew her. I also realised that *Lutanana* loved me and was beginning to feel heartbroken and insulted as a result of my ignoring her.

One moon went by and at the beginning of the second winter moon *Muwende-Lutanana* did a strange and unprecedented thing. First she tried to kill herself with a spear while she was alone in her hut. Fortunately my daughter *Luanaledi* happened to enter at that moment and was just in time to tear the spear from the deaf-mute woman's hands. Then *Lutanana* sought out Rainbow *Indunas Nsongololo* and *Ntombela* and bitterly complained to them in sign language about my continued coolness towards her, and concluded by demanding that the *Indunas* should ask me the reason for my insulting behaviour.

They came to me as I reclined on a lion skin under the cool roof of the canopy hut, known as the 'day shelter', a large grass roof supported by eight wooden posts. They knelt at a safe distance from me and started beating about the proverbial bush for a long time, asking me a lot of questions about my health and *Noliyanda's*. They even wanted to know if all my one hundred favourite dogs were healthy and if I slept well the night before. They were summoning enough courage to ask me the question they had been told to ask – and they hesitated again and yet again. I could not help smiling softly to myself because I had already read their thoughts and found out the true reason for their having come to me. At long last the fat *Ntombela* cleared his throat and said slowly:

'Great One, a little sparrow has complained to two dogs – two of your dogs with two feet . . .'

'Oh!' I responded. 'And what did the sparrow say to the dogs?'

'The little sparrow sat on a branch and called the dogs to her,' said *Ntombela.* 'And when the dogs came under the tree the sparrow asked them to go to the great vulture and ask him why he was ignoring her. She also told the dogs to tell the great vulture that if he does not love her, and has no intention of making her his own, he must please say so.'

'And,' added *Nsongololo,* 'the little sparrow says unless the great vulture respects her rights of wedlock, she shall complain to the great hen-vulture, who chose her to be the second mate to the great vulture.'

'And,' *Ntombela* put in again, with a nervous laugh, 'the little sparrow is of the opinion that the great vulture has become, er, well . . .'

'She does, does she!' I bellowed, sitting up with a jerk. 'The two dogs must go back to the little sparrow and tell her that the great vulture would like to see her in his Great Hut right away.'

The two Rainbow *Indunas* left with wide grins on their faces. When I entered my hut some time later I found *Muwende-Lutanana* there alone. And very soon she had good reason to regret having insulted me by telling tales to my headmen.

The moons sped by and it was not long before the song of summer was again in the air. From the ashes of the burnt forests new and brighter trees were rearing their young heads proudly – growing, slowly growing.

In many places the wild beasts were returning and the roar of lions and the howling of jackals tore the nights asunder once more.

The cornfields and yam plantations were the purest green and loud was the singing of women and maidens as they hoed the fields. The days were lovely and cool and the nights were either cloudless or cloud-packed and torn by hail and lightning. It was on one of these clear lovely days that *Noliyanda* came into my hut and said tiredly:

'It is as said, Oh my Lord, the young woman *Muwende-Lutanana* has three lively young in her womb, and the time for her deliverance has come; it is today. But she is in difficult labour and might not survive.'

There was tension in the Great Kraal Tulisizwe. There was tension mingled with great excitement and expectancy. The bird of rumour had already flown around the great kraal and everybody knew that at long last, after many months of speculation, something was about to happen, for better or for worse, to a young Royal Wife with the foreign name of *Muwende-Lutanana.*

For her the greatest and the most dangerous moment of any young woman's life had come and her life was definitely in danger. For a young woman who had never given birth to a child before, the birth of triplets trebles the pain, fear and hazards.

At long last *Noliyanda* came into my hut again and said with a sigh: 'My Lord, the brave young woman *Muwende-Lutanana* has given birth to three healthy baby boys, and two of them are blessed ones.'

Blessed ones! Oh rare occurrence on a rare event. Blessed ones! For a woman to give birth to triplets is a rare enough event in the land of the Tribes. But for two of these to be Blessed Ones is rarer still! Such children, born with a caul covering the head, are destined to become wise and famous in the land. The Laws of the Tribes require that such children should be treated with special care. They should be trained to become Wise Men, or witchdoctors even; and they should be cared for, not spoilt, in the course of their growing up like rare plants that they are. Immediately after birth such children should be given an ivory spoonful of the fluid from the caul that had covered their heads, and the caul must be dried and included in the *gri-gri** charm that such a child must wear around the neck for the rest of his life.

'This is indeed a great happening, Oh *Noliyanda,*' I said, genuinely moved. 'Have you seen to it that the requirements of the High Laws are being carried out with regard to these two children?'

'Yes, my Lord, the Blessed Ones have been given that which they must drink and I have sent the puppet woman *Muwaniwani* to the river to find a smooth white pebble for the third child.'†

'This means that preparations will have to be made for the journey to Maiegawana,' I said. 'Go, my wife, and bid *Nsongololo* find a young white goat with black ears.'

'As you command, my Lord,' she said and promptly left.

Maiegawana, the 'mother of children', was a great rock far away across the Zambezi where little babies of all tribes were buried. Babies who died at birth, one of twins destroyed according to the law, premature babies, all were buried at the foot of this towering rock. People travelled for days on end, carrying tiny litters on which

---

* *A* gri-gri *is a tiny roll of calf skin containing the dried navel string of the wearer.*

lay their dead young, to Maiegawana, the ageless rock. The legends say that this rock was once a beautiful woman who had turned into stone when she saw the Sun Dragon devour all her children. It was also said that all little ones buried under the presence of the great cone of solid granite turned into stars that brought hope to the hearts of all those in distress who read them on clear nights. Yes, strange indeed are the beliefs of the Tribes.

We took half a regiment of warriors and crossed the Zambezi in fifty large canoes. On the other bank we left a company to guard the canoes while we made the long journey south-west to Maiegawana on foot.

On the well-worn trail to the great rock we met many people from different tribes returning to their homelands. We even saw two skeletons of a young couple who had been so heartbroken at the loss of their child that they had killed themselves with a spear on the way.

Two days later we reached Maiegawana and the two old half-witted gravediggers, who had their home near the great rock, met us with heavy digging sticks and hoes in their hands. To these lonely, but very rich old men we gave the red cow we had brought with us, and they began digging the round little grave at the foot of the mighty rock. *Noliyanda* and I brought the little litter with a tiny bundle of leopard skin inside it to the grave side, walking backwards as custom dictates, and *Tondo*, the elder of the gravediggers, took the bundle and put it gently into the grave. 'Rest now, little one,' he said tenderly. 'You shall be playing amongst the stars soon.'

The other gravedigger dragged a portable stone altar towards us as *Tondo* rapidly filled the grave, and lit a fire of dry twigs on it. *Tondo* then took the goat we had brought with us and trussed its legs together before laying it on the altar. The two old men lifted it on to the fire and then waved us away. 'Go now, and peace go with you.'

We left just as the sun was setting and the sky was a blaze of blue, red, yellow and purple. Sharply silhouetted against the burning sky the mighty rock Maiegawana reared its bulk above the flat-topped trees. Maiegawana the ageless, Maiegawana the eternal rock which has seen more woe and more grief than any other single rock in the land.

Hail, hail, and farewell, Oh Maiegawana!

---

† *The law requires that if a woman gives birth to twins one twin must be destroyed by having a round pebble pushed down its throat. But if she gives birth to three children, one must die and two must live.*

A WOMAN'S REVENGE

The year fled by on the wings of sunset and another year winged its silent way towards the waiting earth. The two little boys, to whom I had given the names of *Demane* and *Demazana*, grew up like green corn plants in a fertile field. Although I could not see the chubby little things, I could feel and sense exactly what lovely babies they were. Everybody wanted to hold them, and once or twice I had to be firm with childless women who tried to steal the little *piccanins*, now crawling all over the place, bawling and very often fighting fiercely with one another over the hundreds of ebony toys that children from all over the land had showered on them. *Noliyanda* was beside herself with joy, and now most of her time was spent in bathing, dandling and anointing with hippo oil *Lutanana's* chubby little mischiefs as if they were her own.

Then came the day of the 'Sun-baby Ceremony' which must be held when the baby begins to walk. With this ceremony the little Sun-god *Shati* is called upon to bless the child and to make him strong and unafraid.

The Sun-baby Ceremony of *Demane* and *Demazana* was unique because everything had to be in triplicate. The land had been combed for three cows exactly identical in colouring, age and general form. The cows we eventually found were red with white bellies and white faces and all three had horns that grew in a perfect moon crescent. Every vessel, every pot to be used in this ceremony had to be in triplicate. Nothing was to be used individually.

The result was that each guest found himself eating the same food at the same instant from three identical bowls and the law prescribed that everybody must eat exactly the same amount from each bowl.

Although the third child of the triplets had been killed according to the law, he was never to be referred to as dead, for as long as the other two were alive. He was always to be referred to as living – albeit in spirit – and whenever anybody wanted to give gifts to the boys he had to give three, not two. For the rest of their earthly lives the two boys were to refer to themselves as 'the three of us', and whenever food was dished out there had to be three dishes.

To our great surprise, very few people answered our invitation to the ceremony, and many of those who did had an uneasy look about them which made *Noliyanda* wonder what could be the matter. My adopted son *Mukombe* told me a rumour he had heard that daily many people were secretly leaving the land of the Mambo and trekking to the land of the Nguni. *Mukombe*, who was an overseer of the boys who watched my vast herds of cattle and who had thus to make frequent trips overland to find new grazing lands, added that confirmation of the truth behind this rumour was to be found in the fact that about twenty large kraals he and his fellow herdboys had passed on several occasions were standing empty.

In spite of the few hundred guests and the atmosphere of uneasiness that hung over everything, the Sun-baby Ceremony was a great success. The warriors danced wildly and ate, drank and laughed lustily, as did some of the guests, both male and female.

When the time came for the little boys to come out – daubed all over their fat little bodies with broad black and white stripes of soot and white clay, and wearing most unwillingly light round calf-skin masks with a stiff grass fringe all round, the people roared with laughter and toasted the squalling urchins from bowls of beer, solemnly calling upon the Sun-god to look upon and bless the two little infants.

Two days later the Rainbow *Indunas Nsongololo, Mavimbela, Ntombela* and *Shungu* came into my hut – armed to the teeth.

Their souls radiated murderous anger and *Mavimbela* was weeping openly and without shame as he laid down his spears and crawled close to me. He laid both his calloused hands on my right foot. 'Great One, Great *Lumukanda*, we have a request to make to you. We, your loyal servants humbly request to be permitted to kill an evil and black-hearted pest here – here before you.'

'You four war leopards seem a little angry,' I said with a smile. 'And who is the pest you ask my permission to kill?'

'Great One,' replied *Ntombela* angrily, 'this is not the moment to joke and we are in no mood for laughing. In spite of your many faults, you have been a great and good Chief to us, and I, together with these three brave colleagues, regard you as a father. We should willingly lay our lives down if you tell us to – here and now. You know our loyalty to you, and our love for you, Oh Great One. Now, an evil woman has been going around from kraal to kraal for these past two years and spreading evil stories about you among the people. She has been telling the people that you are an evil demon and a wizard, and that you have . . . have . . .'

'Have what, *Ntombela*?' I asked. 'And who is this evil woman?'

'She says, Great One, you . . .' stammered *Ntombela*. His voice trailed away in a low moan and he refused to say another word.

Just then *Noliyanda* came into the hut, her soul radiating surprise. 'What have you men got in that big grain basket you have outside the hut?'

'An evil pest, Great One,' said *Mavimbela* with a grim smile, 'the queen of all the skunks and the polecats in the world.'

'*Mavimbela*,' said *Noliyanda* sternly, 'there is a woman in that closed basket out there and I can hear her thoughts. Take her out! Who is she?'

Nsongololo and *Shungu* brought the basket inside the hut and there was a loud scream as its contents were unceremoniously emptied on the floor.

'You!' cried *Noliyanda*. 'You!'

'Who is it?' I asked.

'It is that dirty harlot who used her body to destroy the *Munumutaba's* sons,' hissed *Nsongololo*, '*Lulama-Maneruana*.'

'Now,' growled *Mavimbela*, 'let me hear you talk before we kill you. Open your rotten mouth and let the *tokoloshe* within you tell our chief what you have been telling the people about him.'

'Five hundred thousand people have left this land as a result of this woman's malignant prattling,' roared *Nsongololo*. 'There are now less than that number of people left in the land of the Western Mambo. She has caused the Mambo to scatter and to leave their country. This pest has destroyed our tribe. Beat her.'

There came the dull thud of a blow – another and yet another. A storm of savage blows, punctuated by loud yelps of pain, was followed by the dull thud of a falling body. There followed yet sounds of kicks and further loud screams.

'Stop it!' I cried. 'Stop it . . . let me hear what this is all about.'

'Speak, you filth!' cried *Navimbela*. 'Tell our chief what you told the people about him.'

'Forgive me,' sobbed *Maneruana*. 'Do not hit me again . . . please . . .'

'Speak woman!'

Lulama-Maneruana sobbed out her story, encouraged by occasional blows from the Rainbow *Indunas*: 'I had tried to tell you the story, Oh Great One . . . to warn you in time. But I was not given the opportunity. When I was still the chieftainess of Zima-Mbje, the daughter of my brother quarrelled with her father and left the land of the Luvijiti with a band of her followers and fled into the land of the Lunda to the north-west. A year later she returned and told us she had met a man with whom she lived and after six months she was carrying his child. But he left her. She was half mad with grief and on her return to us she died a few days after giving birth to the child . . . a girl. I brought up this girl, a normal child, capable of speech and hearing – *Muwende-Lutanana*. She grew up as my slave and servant.

'Then one day I was told that the girl was among those who, together with her grandfather, were plotting against me. I had her seized and taken to the fortress of Zima-Mbje to be publicly tortured as an example and a warning to the other plotters. A hot poison was poured into her ears, forever destroying her ability to hear, and she was forced to drink some of this poison, with the result that she nearly died and forever lost her voice. A few months later her grandfather, my brother, led a popular revolt against me and my followers, and I had to flee in defeat. My brother took over the vacant throne and assumed the title of *Munumutaba* the Fifth. When I saw the girl on the day *Noliyanda* presented her to you, Oh *Lumukanda*, as your Second Wife, I was shocked. Although neither you nor she knew it, I knew that you are her father. And *Muxakaza* brought her to you as an instrument of revenge!'

'But why did you have to go about the country telling all the people about this?' demanded *Shungu*. 'Why did you not warn the Chief first?'

'I tried!' shrieked *Maneruana*. 'I tried hard, believe me, but no one bothered to listen to me. *Noliyanda* had me thrown out of the kraal like a dog. And that broke my heart.'

Mavimbela drew back his arm and sent the woman flying with a blow in the stomach. She fell at my feet and lay still for a few moments. Then she stirred and sat up. 'Forgive me, Oh *Lumukanda*,' she gasped. 'I deserve everything done to me. Love makes a woman mad and being scorned makes her even more so. I thought that while I had been given no opportunity to speak, I might tell others so that they may find an opportunity to bring my warning home to you.'

'Your spreading this terrible thing among the people has caused them to flee the land, because they think that the chief married the young woman *Lutanana* knowing she is his own daughter, and they believe that a great curse will fall over their homeland as a result,' said *Ntombela* coldly. 'You may not have anything to do or say now, strumpet, but we know what to do. You shall die, *Maneruana*.'

'No, no!' I said in a voice I no longer recognized as my own. 'No, there shall be no killing. Let *Maneruana* go free.'

Noliyanda began to weep, sobbing louder and louder until she was wailing at the top of her voice. She flung herself about on the mud floor of the hut. 'I caused all this, I was the one who caused all this,' she wailed over and over again.

Night fell and *Muwende-Lutanana* and my two daughters, *Luanaledi* and *Mbaliyamswira*, returned with the other women of the kraal from hoeing the cornfields. *Noliyanda* bade the *Indunas* not to tell anybody else what had happened, at least not until the whole problem had been given a lot of thought. *Maneruana* was confined in one of the huts and it was not long before I found myself alone in my own hut.

I took my long ebony staff, flung my leopard-skin *kaross* over my shoulder, and silently left the night-veiled kraal.

I did not know where I was going and I did not care. I walked and walked. The birds sang in the trees as dawn broke. The day wore on to sunset and another dawn crept upon me. The days fled by, the frowning nights passed, never to return. I neither ate nor drank, and I was walking in no specific direction.

Eventually, one storm-wracked night, with ravening bolts of lightning tearing down tall trees and peals of thunder shaking the earth I stumbled and fell – and I entered a yawning chasm.

'Lost and Fallen Immortal!'

'Lost and fallen in more ways than one!'

'Awaken . . .'

'Awaken!'

'Father of all Demons!'

'Awaken . . .'

> It was the voice of a midsummer's dream,
> Like love's lost caress—
> It dripped with honey,
> And was lived with deadly mockery.

I turned over slowly on my left side and, for the first time in the countless years since I have been afflicted with blindness, I could see.

I was in a great cavern – in the bowels of the earth. Into my ears came the distant roar of the Lulungwa-Mangakatsi like one continuous cataract of muted thunder. I could dimly make out mighty rocks in the darkness. In the near distance I could clearly see a mighty waterfall whose top and bottom were lost in dark chasms.

A tall silvery apparition appeared on the far side of the cavern. It was *Ninavanhu-Ma*, the first Goddess. I heard her voice saying, 'You must surrender, *Lumukanda.* You must deliver yourself into our hands for punishment. You must be punished for all your sins. The earth does not want you, and neither do the heavens. And you are equally unwelcome in the Underworld of Evil.'

'I do not fear you, Goddess,' I replied. 'I shall continue fighting you to the end of time.'

I felt myself rising from the ground as everything vanished in a burst of silver light.

'Awaken, Outcast of the Ages, we have a long way to go to your kraal.'

I opened my eyes and found that I was back in the Upper World and for the first time in a thousand years of blindness my eyes drank in the pure beauty of the blue skies, the breathtaking greens of the whispering forests and the purple of the distant brooding mountains. I felt like a man reborn, and suddenly my thousand years of earthly life seemed to slide off my shoulders and I was young again. I looked in rapt fascination at the surrounding landscape; I spent a long time drinking in the sight of two rainbow-hued birds pursuing each other in the blue skies above. The distant silver river that snaked its way through the green undulations held me in its spell.

I saw tiny canoes full of warriors crossing the river – far, far away; I saw a herd of more than fifty impala grazing at the base of the low hill on whose slopes I lay. I saw the long grass nodding and dancing as the lovelorn wind sang through it.

Yea-ha! After a thousand years of blindness, sight is a wonderful thing. Surely there is a great truth in the tribal saying that if one wishes to appreciate a good thing, one must first be well acquainted with its opposite.

I was conscious of a presence and I turned slowly. A woman, almost as tall and powerful as I am, stood there. Unlike my dark-brown skin her skin was as black and as smooth as polished ebony and she was as beautiful as only a goddess can be. Every curve of her womanly body spoke of beauty and perfection, and her wide, full-lipped mouth smiled mockingly at me: 'Are we going to stay here forever, *Lumukanda*?'

It was *Vuramuinda*, my Fire Bride of those long centuries ago.

'I can see you *Vuramuinda*,' I blurted out stupidly. 'I can really see you!'

'Your long fall into the Underworld knocked sight back into your stupid eyes, baboon,' she said, 'and you had better start thinking of a very good explanation of where you have been to give to those people coming towards us. Some of them seem to be women of yours.'

I glanced downhill to where she pointed and I saw what looked like two full regiments of warriors advancing up the grassy hillside.

'How did they know I was here?'

'They must have followed the smell, Oh beloved Carrion,' replied *Vuramuinda*. 'You may not know it, old fool, but to those mortals down there you have been missing for one whole year.'

'One whole year!' I could not believe it, but it was true nevertheless. As the warriors came closer I saw there were women among them, and also a man in the garb of a Royal Consort.

They had not yet seen us, but there was something about the leading woman that told me she had sensed our presence.

Suddenly *Vuramuinda* did something that left me totally speechless with surprise. She threw herself down beside me and her arms stole round my neck, holding me fast and crushing me down into the yielding grass. She started raining kisses on my mouth, neck, nose and forehead. The sound of long grass being crushed under many feet grew louder in my ears. A tall shadow fell over both of us and a soft voice said: 'Oh . . . h!'

'Go away, you interfering fool!' hissed *Vuramuinda* to the youthful female intruder. 'Can't a woman be with her husband in peace in this land any more?'

The young girl vanished and I heard a voice: 'Princess *Luanaledi*, who are those people in the long grass over there?'

'It is father!' cried the girl. 'We have found him at last . . . we have found him!'

There was a rush of many feet and *Vuramuinda* and I found ourselves surrounded by scores of warriors with very amused expressions on their faces.

'By my grandfather's—!' swore a burly round-shouldered individual who looked like a gorilla's first cousin. 'It is our chief all right . . . and as virile as ever! Where have you been, Great One?'

'And who is this woman, my Lord?' asked a tall woman – none other than *Noliyanda*.

'*What* is this woman, you should ask,' said *Vuramuinda*. 'Then you might get a sensible answer.'

'Well, *what* is this woman then my Lord?' asked *Noliyanda*, completely taken aback.

'Are you asking about me?' purred *Vuramuinda* insultingly.

'I am addressing myself to my Lord and husband, strange one.'

'Your husband? If this is your husband, why did you not cut your name symbols on his buttocks? Until you do that he is any woman's property. Now, believe it or not, beautiful pumpkin, I have decided to keep him all to myself.'

'We shall see about that!' stormed *Noliyanda*. 'Who are you?'

'Do you really want to know?'

'Of course!'

'I am what you waste yourself in imagining that you are.'

'Oh!' said *Noliyanda* pleasantly. 'And from under which rotting log did you crawl?'

Vuramuinda ignored the question and turned to me, saying softly (but loudly enough for the guffawing warriors to hear): 'Tell me, *Lumukanda* mine, is there a shortage of women in the land?'

'No,' I answered. 'Why do you ask?'

'No! Then why did you go to all this trouble of creating a thing like this one and then calling it your wife? You started an evil precedent, my love, and it will not be long before all a lovelorn potter and carver will have to do is to model and carve himself a wife, thus saving himself the expense of paying *lobolo.* You should be ashamed of yourself, *Lumukanda,* putting us decent natural women out of business!'

'Decent is not the word you should apply to yourself!' cried *Noliyanda.*

'Stop your rattling, you glorified puppet!' cried *Vuramuinda.* 'When I want advice from a plaything like you, I'll ask for it.'

A diminutive baby-faced woman interrupted hurriedly: 'Peace, my sisters, peace. This is not the time for childish squabbles. Let us all go home and thank the Great Spirit that at last we have found *Lumukanda* on whom all our hopes of saving our Tribes rest.'

'Well spoken, Oh Royal One *Celiwe,*' said *Noliyanda* quietly. 'We must let *Lumukanda* know of the terrible thing that has happened in the land, and perhaps he can tell us what is to be done.'

'Do not tell me the land has been invaded again!' I cried, leaping to my feet.

'No, my Lord and husband,' said *Noliyanda.* 'The land has not been invaded . . . yet; neither is there any disastrous occurrence . . . yet. But about ten days ago the people of the two lands saw a terrible sign in the heavens. The sun was totally eclipsed at midday.'

'Tell me about it,' I commanded, sitting down on a rock.

'We were out in the fields, busy with the ploughing and sowing when suddenly it became dark,' said *Noliyanda,* 'and when I looked up I saw the sun was dim. Two women looked straight at the sun and were blinded. For a long time there was darkness over the land and the only sign of the vanished sun was a blinding glare from behind a black sun, two glares, one pointing east and the other west. It was terrifying, yet magnificent. But that is not all, my Lord and husband, that is not all. A day later, after this terrible omen of coming disaster, a group of four men entered the Royal Kraal on the pretext of bringing gifts of iron ore for making spears. These men we received and treated kindly indeed. But they were bent on evil, as we soon found out. They saw the triplets, *Demane* and *Demazana,* playing near the Great Hut and they playfully called the little ones. The children went to them and two of them seized the boys and ran into one of the empty huts with them. The remaining two then did a strange thing. They set the hut on fire with their two friends and the boys inside, and then they too crawled into the burning hut. But *Lulama-Maneruana* and *Muwende-Lutanana* ran into the burning hut and succeeded in rescuing the two children, although *Maneruana's* left arm was badly burnt. *Mavimbela* here hauled out one of the four men before the hut collapsed on the other three . . . and I will let him tell you what we learnt from him about this fantastic attempt at murdering the innocent children. Speak *Mavimbela*.'

'I will indeed!' growled *Mavimbela*. 'When I dragged out that struggling son of a hyaena, I said to him: "All right, you filthy beggar, you shall tell me why you tried to murder our absent chief's children!" The stupid fellow shook his head and refused to answer me. Great One, I turned him over to the warriors and by my grandmother's—, was the fool glad to start babbling! When he saw his . . . being cut off and thrown to the dogs and a red-hot spear being applied to where it was, he started squawking and words poured out of his drooling mouth like a torrent.

'He told us the few Mambo still left in the land had formed themselves into a band dedicated to overthrowing you. They have already named one *Sozozo* the Fat as the new chief of the Western Mambo. Those four men were suicide volunteers whose duty it was to kill either *Muwende-Lutanana* or the children, because the Mambo believe it is your incestuous marriage to *Lutanana* which has angered the gods who now wish to bring disaster to the land.

'But Great Chief, I can assure you here and now that every one of your *indunas* and warriors is loyal to you. All of us, in your Great Kraal and the ten military kraals, know that you did not marry *Lutanana* knowingly and for this reason we are standing firmly behind you . . . come what may.'

'Thank you, *Mavimbela*,' I responded. 'But that does not alter the fact that I have unwittingly committed a gross and disgraceful sin, and I am left with an insoluble problem on my hands.'

'What problem, Great *Lumukanda*?' asked the tiny baby-faced Nguni Queen *Celiwe* with a strange smile on her face.

'Unknowingly I was tricked into marrying and having children by my own daughter, and the problem facing me now is this – just what to do with these children. I cannot kill them and I cannot bear the realisation that for the rest of their lives they will carry with them the stigma of being children of incest. What am I to do?'

'Doubtless the Great *Lumukanda* thinks his problem is unique in the history of the Tribes,' said *Celiwe* softly. 'You tell him, *Malandela*.'

The handsome thickest man in the garb of a Royal Consort said slowly: 'Your problem can be solved, Oh *Lumukanda*, and that is why we are here – to help you solve it. But I must say I am very surprised that you, who have outlived many mortal generations, do not know this. We live in a turbulent world, *Lumukanda*, a world where many strange accidents happen – and the accident which has befallen you is by no means unusual, neither does it pose a problem to which there is no solution. My own grandfather married his own illegitimate daughter by accident in the land of the Nyanja and did not discover his mistake until ten years later. His problem was also solved in the same way that yours will be. What has happened to you is what the Wise Ones call '*Ichilo lo muzi*' (Knot of confusion in the family), and *Celiwe* and I have been in your land for six whole months now, trying to find you and help you in unravelling this knot. This we hope to do soon and to the complete satisfaction of both the Nguni and the Mambo.'

'But how?' I asked. 'I don't see . . .'

'You will discover soon,' said *Celiwe* sweetly.

Vuramuinda rose from the rock on which she had been sitting and contorted her face into an expression of self-importance – cleared her throat in a most unwomanly fashion and said: 'Oh honourable bachelors and spinsters of the Mambo and Nguni cow thief tribes . . . I, *Vuramuinda*, the daughter of Nobody who comes from Nowhere, have a strong complaint to make to you. Not only are you, yes you, the most hypocritical, the most stupid, cowardly, bad-tempered cretins under this misbegotten sun, but you are also worm-eaten, mildewed, splay-footed sons of ungrateful hyaenas into the bargain. You are all, deliberately and with malicious intent, trying to ignore the fact that this insignificant stranger is the one who found your silly old chief for you. I am the one who took care of him for you, and also restored his eyesight so that in future he may be able to have a good look at his women.'

'You—!' *Mavimbela* swore. 'Do you mean that our venerable chief can see now, Oh Honourable Lady?'

'That,' said *Vuramuinda*, 'is just what I mean.'

'By my father's—!'

'My father,' cried *Luanaledi*, 'can you really see – after all these years? Can you see us, father?'

'I can see you, child. After a thousand years of blindness I can see at last.'

'This is wonderful!' said *Celiwe*.

'The Great Spirit be praised!' cried *Malandela*.

Mavimbela expressed his jubilation with a string of foul curses.

'It is a great day,' said *Ntombela*.

'You must be rewarded, Oh Unknown Lady,' said *Nsongololo* gallantly to *Vuramuinda.* 'Name any number of cows you want and you shall have them.'

'Yes any number,' said *Noliyanda* uneasily.

'I want only one ox,' said *Vuramuinda* with a roguish smile.

'One ox!' *Malandela* exclaimed in astonishment. 'One ox after what you have done for us!'

'Yes, just one ugly, bony, hornless old ox.'

There was a roar of laughter at this, because *Vuramuinda* had indicated me. Men rolled in the long grass and some danced about, tearing themselves with laughter.

'Oh no!' gasped *Noliyanda.*

'Oh yes!' responded *Vuramuinda.*

Once more I looked at everyone of my servants, friends and beloved ones in turn, drinking in every detail, every feature of their faces. The ugly gorilla-like visage of *Mavimbela,* the handsome serene face of *Malandela, Ntombela's* blunt fat visage and *Nsongololo's* long sloping muzzle, strongly reminiscent of a giraffe's. I drank in the face of *Celiwe* – the childlike innocence of the woman I madly coveted but could not have – a fruit placed beyond my reach by a cruel god. I turned my gaze to the heavenly features of the light-brown *Noliyanda* – the woman who was not a woman, and yet more of a woman than any of her kind. My own beautiful handiwork, with her wide forehead, her long nose and full mouth, her large deepset eyes and her jutting squarish chin with a slight cleft in it. My own creation, neither goddess nor human – an unhappy creature, human in shape, unhuman, yet more human than any human can ever be.

I saw *Lulama-Maneruana* hovering in the background like a lost sparrow. I saw what I had suspected for a long time, that this ravening, brazen-featured wanton whose face was that of a wilful and stubborn slut, was of Bantu-Arabi parentage – a soulless half-caste from that hotbed of a harlotry in the south – Zima-Mbje, where Arabi slave raiders and Bantu maidens mate freely.

I stared in rapt fascination at her soft hair, her light skin and straight, almost aquiline, nose. So this was *Lulama-Maneruana*! So this was the woman destined to win undying fame as the Fallen Saviour of song and legend! I turned my eyes away and stared straight into the bitter, veiled eyes of *Luanaledi,* my eldest immortal daughter. I saw the strange hunger burning in my child's eyes. I saw the bitter lines about her beautiful mouth. I turned away and *Vuramuinda's* alien face smiled mockingly and half pityingly at me. She knew. She knew of the strange love *Luanaledi* held for me, and like me she sensed danger – danger in *Luanaledi.* This one-handed stormy daughter of *Watamaraka* seemed like a mamba poised to strike – but whom?

I heard *Vuramuinda's* unspoken thoughts ringing in my mind: 'Watch that brat of yours!'

'Let us go home,' I said to all those assembled. 'We have much to plan and much to do.'

As we made our way down the hill and into the forest towards the canoes, *Malandela* slung his heavy *kalimba* harp from his shoulder and began to sing his famous 'Song of *Malandela*'. His manly voice rang through the forest as verse after verse of the wonderful song floated like a mellow breeze over our heads, to be lost in the distance:

> Peace thee – Peace thee, Oh my spirit!
> Bow thy head before the great *Somandla*—
> Into His mercy now surrender thee;
> Into His hands completely yield thee.
>
> Ere thou wert born He cared for thee,
> And when thou diest He shall be by thee . . .

BEHOLD THE PLAGUE

Night has fallen and a savage storm is lashing the cringing land with thunder and hail. The rivers have been turned into roaring, hissing torrents and by the frequent light of the bluish flashes one can see them, borne relentlessly down towards the Zambezi, trees, bushes, zebras, more wild animals, two huts . . .

Water is knee-deep in places and the newly ploughed fields are flooded. The first rains of early summer have come with a devastating vengeance and summer has used the thunder horn-bugle to herald its arrival. The frowning heavens are torn apart by searing bolts of lightning. The young trees are stripped naked of their green foliage by a roaring sheet of hail, the size of fowl eggs.

Yes, the ravening heavens roar their spite upon the helpless land and even the trees are afraid. The howling dogs and cackling fowls have long since sought shelter under granaries. Some of the hens have lost their chickens and two young calves in the cattle pens are dead.

Such is life on earth – a destructive storm bringing hope for a year of plenty. Life and death go hand in hand. The one is but a reflection of the other – two facets of the same thing. The Wise Ones of the Tribes say 'Life is Death and Death is Life'. Without life there can be no death, and *vice versa.* Such is life on earth!

Inside the Great Hut of the Royal Kraal of the Western Mambo, strange and momentous things are about to happen. A man is about to dissolve the bond of fatherhood between himself and the daughter he accidentally married, proclaiming her a stranger – in strict accordance with the Laws of the Tribes.

There are eighty people inside the Great Hut and all of them have not tasted food or drink for ten whole days. Some of them are now weak with hunger and thirst and are lying on their sides on grass mats and leopard skins. They are awaiting the beginning of yet another ceremony – one of the many that rule a tribesman's life, as strings govern a puppet's limbs.

The roaring rain-drenched and lightning-torn night wears noisily on and soon it is midnight. And now the storm holds its savage breath. A silvery star peers shyly through a gap in the scowling clouds and near the Great Hut, just outside the door, comes the sound of a dog shaking water from its long lean body. There is still the heavy uneven sound of large drops from trees and the distant continuous rumble of sheets of water exploring new channels of flow.

There is the sound of fire sticks being briskly rubbed inside the darkened hut, and soon a shower of red sparks falls onto the small pile of dry grass in the centre of the great sunken fireplace. A woman – yes, it is *Muwaniwani* – blows into the pile of grass. There is a glow and smoke – a sudden flicker – and a burst of flame. Dry twigs are laid on top and they are ravenously devoured. Heavy logs follow and soon the whole interior of the hut is bathed in flickering light.

In the far corner of the hut a wickerwork cover opens on the floor and a tall ebony-skinned woman with flashing eyes emerges from the secret underground dwelling. It is *Vuramuinda*, the Black Goddess, and her silvery voice rings through the smoke-blackened interior of the hut: 'The ceremony begins now. *Lumukanda* and *Muwende-Lutanana* must stand up and come near the fire.'

I leave my seat between *Noliyanda* and *Lulama-Maneruana* and step close to the fire. *Muwende-Lutanana* also rises at a sign from *Vuramuinda* and comes to stand next to me – her eyes wide with mute wonder and fear. *Vuramuinda* picks up an all-metal copper Holy Axe and thrusts it deep into the fire, also a long, slim-bladed, iron knife with a wooden handle carved to represent the Star Serpent.

The little Nguni Matriarch *Celiwe* rises and picks up one of the fowls lying trussed in a dark corner of the hut, bringing it to the fireplace. She begins to pray:

'May the High Heavens look down upon what is taking place in this hut tonight and bless each and every one of the people taking part in this most holy of ceremonies. May the pure, distant, undefiled stars breathe their scented breath of forgiveness upon all of us for the great sin, which was unwittingly committed in this kraal. May our ancestors in their wisdom and mercy plead with the Highest of the High to erase from the memory of men and gods the sin which *Lumukanda* and *Muwende-Lutanana* unknowingly committed, great and heinous though it be. May the Highest of the Most High remove the shadow of this very great transgression from the lives of the three innocents, *Demane, Demazana* and their brother who walks unseen with them alive in spirit.

'Since, Oh Great Spirit, *Lumukanda* had unknowingly made a wife of his own daughter, had taken to the love mat the fruits of his own loins, he has now come before you to ask your forgiveness and to break forever his claim of fatherhood over *Muwende-Lutanana*. Hear me, hear me, all my respected Ancestors! Hear me, *Malembe, Vukela, Dlalela* and *Kanjane*! Hear me as I pray to you. Plead, Oh plead with the Highest of the Most High, to forgive these people. Plead with the earth, the stars and the Great Waters to raise their voices and ask the Highest of the Most High to forgive his servants.'

With these words she hurls the struggling fowl into the fire and at the same time *Vuramuinda* throws a bundle of dried *mpepo* plants into the pit. A cloud of white smoke rises from the fireplace and the smell of burning feathers combines with the fragrant smell of the *mpepo* incense. As *Celiwe* returns to the place where she had been sitting earlier, *Vuramuinda's* cold, mocking voice came to my ears through the smoke:

'*Lumukanda*, I, *Vuramuinda*, of no fixed abode and of no definite origin, do here and now demand that you declare truly before the Most High, before the Stars and before the Eternal Fire in the very Core of Eternity, before the mountains, the seas and the skies, and before all things that are upon this earth – did you deliberately and with sinful intent sleep with your own daughter? Did you knowingly have children by your own child?'

'No.'

'Come close to me, *Lumukanda*, and address your denial to the Highest of the High.'

I step over to her and she draws me very close to her. Side by side we stand, looking up – up, and slowly the roof of the hut fades – the upturned faces around me fade. They all vanish, and I find my stare penetrating space – far into the depths of Eternity. Far, far beyond the deepest reaches of Eternity; far beyond the outer frontiers of Eternal Darkness. I see a Shape, which is like no known shape on earth or under the stars. It is the Shape of Something Ultimate – something beyond Which and above Which there is and can be nothing greater, nothing more ultimate . . . Men call it God. Some call it the Ultimate, the Ultimate Cause, the Most Ultimate. Some recognise Its existence. Some doubt and even deny It. But there It is, recognised, doubted or denied – that Shape is there and I see It. Far is It above beings, mortal and immortal. Far is It above gods and goddesses – above spirits Ancestral and Existing. All these fear It – always. I have no fear of gods and goddesses, of Spirits, be they that of Nature, Evil or Creation. But before the Ultimate upon whom my eyes now focus, I tremble like any mortal should, immortal though I am. And to the Ultimate I address my denial: 'No, I did not deliberately and knowingly take my own child, oh Highest of the High. You know I did not.'

There comes a strange dizziness to my head. My body sags to the ground. But I remain standing. My soul – yes it is my soul that remains standing. I find myself on the edge of a great barren plain under a dark red sky. There, covering the entire horizon, is the Presence of the Ultimate. I am standing before It, like an aphid before a mountain. I feel naked. A voice like a thousand tempests cleaves my brittle soul: 'You feature but insignificantly in My great experiment of Creation, and yet you have a part to play. I am interested in you. Stop defiling yourself with evil, I command you.'

'Forgive me,' I beg humbly.

'I forgave you long before you asked. Go now; be watchful always. You are alone in a hostile world. Your fellow immortals despise you and they wish to destroy you . . . but they shall fail. Work for Me and spread My name amongst the wretched mortals to whom I have sent you. You are my Chosen One.'

Those words – those mysterious words. I am shocked into wakefulness. *Vuramuinda* bends over me, and for once I can see concern on her face. I hear her voice: 'He has regained consciousness . . . the ceremony shall continue. *Lumukanda*, you have denied before the Highest of the Most High that you wilfully and knowingly slept with your own child and made a mother out of her, is that not so?'

'It is so.'

'To the complete satisfaction of the people of the Mambo and Nguni Tribes, I, *Vuramuinda*, who loves you and who believes your denial, challenge you fully to confirm your denial by holding the red-hot Axe of Truth in your bare left hand.'

'I accept that challenge.'

Vuramuinda draws out the almost white-hot copper axe and hands it to me, head foremost. I reach out, grab the axe by the middle of its long red-hot shaft and hold it aloft. The smell of burning flesh invades my nostrils and the pain is intense. But I hold it aloft.

'I ask you all within this hut,' says *Vuramuinda*, 'you who are of the Nguni Tribe and you of the Mambo Tribe . . . are you satisfied?'

Malandela's metallic voice answers: 'I, *Malandela* of the Nguni, am speaking for the Nguni . . . we are more than satisfied.'

'And I,' says *Mavimbela* savagely, 'am speaking for all the Mambo. We knew our chief was innocent, and we are completely satisfied.'

'That is good,' says *Vuramuinda*. 'Put down the axe, *Lumukanda*.'

I tear the axe off my left hand with my right, and deeply scorched flesh from my palm comes with it. The pain slowly evaporates.

'Sit down.'

Vuramuinda draws the terrified *Muwende-Lutanana* to her and asks her a question in sign language. With an expression of unimaginable agony on her ebony features she shakes her head.

'You – still – love – him?'

Her eyes widen and she looks around nervously for a possible way of escape.

'Answer!'

She makes a sign in the affirmative.

'Why?'

She indicates that she does not know.

Vuramuinda's long fingers flutter as she tells *Muwende-Lutanana* the purpose of the ceremony we are now holding and she pauses now and again to ask the girl whether she really understands.

Vuramuinda takes the long iron knife from the fire and with a gasp *Muwende* sinks fainting to the ground. *Celiwe* and *Maneruana* revive her with cold water and as she regains consciousness the two women hold her down while *Vuramuinda* scorches some of the hair from the girl's armpits and below her navel. The rites involving the Axe of Truth and the burning off of hair are known as 'Fire Rites of Penance'.

Water and food are brought in and the gathering, excluding *Lutanana, Vuramuinda* and me, enjoys its first meal in ten days of rigorous fasting. This concludes part one of the four-part ceremony.

The people have eaten their fill and my adopted son and two other boys bring in a black goat which is to be used in the second part of the ceremony. This goat is not going to enjoy his role one little bit. It is the 'Animal of Sin Bearing' and the sin I had committed with *Lutanana* will be transferred to it after which it will be promptly dispatched to beyond the borders of Outer Darkness.

There is a long time of waiting while people indulge in second helpings and now they sit around gathering strength for the dancing about to commence. Heavy drums are rolled in and the ceremony is continued.

Vuramuinda calls for a big grass mat to be brought near the fire and instructs *Muwende-Lutanana* and me to lie on this mat. Now pandemonium is released as the masked drummers strike up weird rhythms with their hands on the taut skins and roaring, booming sounds fill the Great Hut. *Malandela, Mavimbela, Ntombela* and *Celiwe* jump to their feet and snatch up fowls from the bundle lying trussed in one corner. They shriek, caper, stamp their feet to the savage beat of the drums – dancing in a series of mad circles, nearer and nearer to where we lie.

Everybody now joins in and the dust really starts flying. I see *Mavimbela* leap high into the air. I see *Maneruana, Noliyanda* and *Vuramuinda* turn themselves into ravening bolts of demoniac abandon – dancing, leaping and rolling on the ground. I am holding my breath for the Great Hut – it might tear off its foundations and take off into the air as a result of the explosions of incredible noise.

The dancing grows wilder; men and women fling off their loinskins and skin skirts and dance forth naked, maddened, as though all the demons of the Underworld have suddenly taken possession of them. *Maneruana* goes into a wide-eyed slack-mouthed trance and falls backwards, only to be kicked aside by *Mavimbela* and *Vuramuinda.*

With a torrent of savage oaths *Mavimbela* tears the fowl he had been holding to pieces and deposits the gory remains on the forms of *Muwende-Lutanana* and me. Others follow suit and soon we are covered with feathers, blood, and sticky intestines – a warm mess symbolising the sin we have committed.

The drumming, screeching, bellowing and cursing are still building up to a deafening crescendo. Even the dogs outside are now competing with us at the tops of their voices. I cannot hear it, but I know that their sympathetic participation has infected others in neighbouring kraals and in kraals far beyond.

Vuramuinda breaks away briefly to light three large lamp bowls full of hippo oil, with calf skin wicks floating inside. At the height of their frenzy the men, led by *Mavimbela,* now close in a tight circle around the fire in the centre and begin to extinguish it.

Malandela and *Mavimbela* add the finishing touches by dancing into the middle of the fireplace, trampling the hot wet ash into a muddy pulp. *Vuramuinda, Maneruana* and *Noliyanda* proceed to excavate the fireplace with heavy hoes to the accompaniment of the drums.

The hole is now filled with grass and twigs and quick-burning *marula* logs and a roaring fire is promptly lit by throwing in one of the hippo-fat lamps. The interior of the hut is like a furnace. Water is rushed in and the women proceed to wash *Lutanana* and me from head to foot, using powdered calabash seeds and loofahs. A great leopard skin mattress is brought in and on this we lie down while we are rubbed dry with jackal skin towels.

Mavimbela hauls the black goat near the fire and starts dancing wildly around it, pummelling it savagely and calling it all sorts of names, the very best from his repertoire. To this the goat takes exception and butts him cruelly in the belly sending him sprawling, his last breath turning into a foul curse.

'*Aieeeee!*' shrieks *Ntombela,* 'that is a very good omen. That goat is aggressive, and he will make a good messenger to carry our chief's sins to hell. Nothing will get in its way . . . what a good omen!'

Meanwhile the women have been collecting the mutilated fowls and have stuffed them and their intestines into two grass baskets. These are now tied to the back of the goat, held fast by a blaspheming

Mavimbela. The dirty water with which we have been washed is poured over the goat which glares savagely at us and tries its best to have another go at *Mavimbela.*

At a signal from the Black Goddess the drums roar and *Mavimbela* pushes the goat into the white-hot fire pit. Women add twigs and heavy logs and the fire roars in fresh fury while savage dancing starts again.

'Go, Oh honourable goat,' shrieks the dancing and twisting *Lulama-Maneruana.* 'Go straight to hell and take all our sins with you . . . and leave us in peace and happiness.'

Lutanana and I are bathed again and yet again. We are rubbed with earth and ash, and for the tenth time with scalding hot water. Finally we are rubbed dry and *Vuramuinda* calls for silence.

'We have now come to the end of the second part of this ceremony, and both *Lumukanda* and the young girl *Muwende-Lutanana* have now been purified of their sin.' She says 'We shall proceed with the part where Chief *Lumukanda* must break his bond of fatherhood with *Muwende-Lutanana* and openly declare her no longer a child of his. What we now require is that one man must come forward and declare himself prepared to answer to fatherhood of this girl. To this man *Lumukanda* must apply for permission to re-marry his daughter, who will cease to be a daughter of *Lumukanda* after we have completed the part of the ceremony we are about to perform.

Malandela and *Celiwe* come to their feet and take a few steps forward: 'We shall adopt *Muwende-Lutanana* as our daughter,' says *Celiwe* softly.

'And I, *Malandela,* champion of the Nguni, challenge any man to a death duel who dares to dispute that I am not, in fact, the father of *Muwenda-Lutanana.* Is there such a man?'

There is none, and *Vuramuinda's* voice proceeds, with an undertone of mockery: 'Since there is no dispute, we shall continue. *Lumukanda* is now required to break his bond of fatherhood and you are all required to assist him with your prayers.'

Vuramuinda cuts a tuft of hair from my head and tosses it into the fire. She does likewise with *Muwende-Lutanana.* In strict accordance with the High Laws *Noliyanda* and her former enemy *Lulama-Maneruana* smear themselves with ashes and they lift *Muwende-Lutanana* up in their arms, bringing her close to where I am standing. I call upon the Highest of the Most High to witness my breaking of the bond of parenthood with *Muwende,* and with this I spit at *Muwende* and turn my back on her.

Muwende is laid near the door of the hut while I and the three women known as my High Queens, *Vuramuinda, Noliyanda* and *Lulama-Maneruana* – I have reluctantly accepted the latter as a

Royal Concubine – walk over the prostrate girl in the final act of disownment. We walk out of the hut, leaving *Celiwe* and *Malandela* to perform the Ceremony of Adoption.

Dawn crept up to the horizon and the sun peered hesitantly over it a short while later. After ensuring that everything was safe, it rose boldly into the blue heavens. When it assumed its lofty throne in the midday sky the ceremony ended and the feasting began.

Three days later the Matriarch of the Nguni, *Celiwe*, and her First Consort *Malandela*, took their adopted daughter *Muwende-Lutanana* and her three children, *Demana* and *Demazana*, to their land, whence they were to send her back to me as my bride – after the payment of *lobolo*. I felt I could look the world straight in the eye again. I found time to attend to my affairs and my responsibilities as chief again, after an absence of more than a year.

The first thing I did was to call my *Indunas* together to discuss what was to be done about the rebellious remnants of the Mambo tribe.

'The trouble, Oh Great One,' complained *Mavimbela* angrily, 'is that we do not know just where the sons of . . . dogs are hiding.'

'That is soon remedied,' said *Vuramuinda*. 'Bring me a bowl full of water . . . a clay bowl.'

The bowl was brought and *Vuramuinda* slowly stirred the water and withdrew her finger, allowing the water to settle. Within the water she conjured a clear picture of our opponents hiding in the Madlonti mountains. 'So that is where the dogs are hiding!' cried *Nsongololo*. 'Let us go there and wipe them out, Oh Great Chief.'

'There must be no killing,' I replied. 'Those people are misguided. We must capture them all alive and put them to work on a scheme I have in mind.'

'So be it, Oh Chief,' *Nsongololo* responded with a smile. 'The idle dreamers must be given something to do.'

'Call out two regiments and we shall go after them at sunset,' I commanded.

'Take us with you' pleaded *Vuramuinda*, taking *Noliyanda's* hand. 'We shall use our powers to scare these fools into submission.'

Sozozo was a very happy man. He had just murdered two men and proclaimed himself chief of a small band of about five hundred men and women hiding in the Madlonti mountains. Although night had fallen and the bodies of his victims had long since grown cold at his feet, he was still letting all and sundry know for the hundredth time that he was now the Big Man of the sorry remnants of the scattered Mambo Tribe. In one hand he held the roast leg of a goat and in the other he brandished a club still soiled with the blood of his two unfortunate victims.

'Do you hear me, you green-bellied scum?' he bellowed at the top of his voice. 'Do you hear me well and clearly? I am now your chief, by right and might – and I dare any of you miserable dogs to dispute my claim! I am now going to appoint ten men amongst you to be my *Indunas*. And all ten must lick the dust off my feet and swear allegiance to me.'

'B-but,' an old man named *Mpongo* protested, 'the Laws of the Mambo say an *Induna* must swear allegiance by laying his hand on his chief's left thigh, *Sozozo*, and not by licking his feet.'

'You shall do what I say without question!' bellowed *Sozozo*, his incredibly fat face darkening and his bloodshot eyes bulging obscenely. 'I have already laid down new laws. And as from now you are no longer to call yourselves the Mambo, but the Masozozo. You are my people – the people of *Sozozo*. You shall obey me, and me alone, morning, noon and night. To start with, I want the prettiest of your daughters as my wives and I want lots of your best beer and meat. Hurry now, *shesha!* Bring these to me now.'

The frightened people jumped to obey the gross vagabond's commands and while they were busy at the tasks *Sozozo* appointed ten very fat men as his *Indunas*, and ended by crowning himself High Chief with an improvised and rather clumsy royal head-dress.

He and his ten *Indunas* then sat down and ate like greedy hippos the food that was brought in – celebrating their first night of power. They consumed piles of meat and nearly drowned themselves in a lake of corn beer. They toppled over where they were sitting and fell asleep, each with two terrified girls in his arms.

They were awakened by a blood-curdling scream such as can only be produced by a demon from the Underworld. The men sat up and jumped to their feet like one man. There, in the mouth of the great cave which *Sozozo* had named his 'Lions Den', was the most hideous female demon ever seen.

She was glowing a bright red all over and had only one huge eye in her otherwise featureless face. A large fanged mouth leered between her breasts.

Sozozo was the first to find a voice with which to scream and legs with which to run into the furthest interior of the cave. The newly appointed *Indunas* tried to hide themselves by digging their faces into the bat guano on the floor of the cave.

The demon told the terrified girls to return to their families and, after beating up *Sozozo* and his *Indunas* with a heavy knobkierie, she said: 'Run, you carrion animals. Run and go straight to High Chief

Lumukanda and surrender yourselves to him. Tell him the Red Devil sent you. . . .'

Sozozo shot out of the cave like an arrow, with his ten *Indunas* anxious to do better. They dashed down the mountainside like feathers pursued by a tempest. They ran slap into another she-devil – a green one this time – and this hastened considerably their speed through the forest.

The guards at the gates of Tulisizwe saw eleven very fat men running, touching the ground only here and there and squealing like so many biped bush-pigs. The surprised warriors watched in blank astonishment as the panting fugitives ran straight into the gate of the largest cattle pen and started digging holes in the manure.

'Get out of there!' yelled one of the warriors. 'Get out of that manure, you fools – have you gone mad?'

The men crawled deeper into the manure until only their heads showed. Their eyes were glazed with fear and the hair of *Sozozo* and two others had turned grey.

'Surround this heap and keep a close watch on these shivering fat-bellies,' bellowed a battle leader. 'We shall have to keep them here until our chief returns.'

When we returned to the Great Kraal at midday of the following day, bringing with us five hundred would-be Mambo rebels, we found a full company of fifty warriors guarding a pile of wet manure in which eleven men seemed to be hiding – or at least trying their best to hide. I went up and smiled down upon them, most unpleasantly. 'I see you, Oh rebellious ones. Tell me, are you yam plants?'

'Go away, you incestuous wizard!' bellowed *Sozozo*. 'You can't kill me, you dare not try. I am the High Chief of the Mambo. I am now your superior and I command you – go away!'

'Is that dung-heap your throne, Oh new High Chief?' I asked with a sneer. 'Surely the Great Hut is yonder.'

'Go away, you son of a man-eating wanton.'

'Listen *Sozozo*,' I replied, very pleasantly, 'you are talking yourself into my biggest stewpot. You seem to have forgotten that I indulge in excentricities of diet.'

'You wouldn't dare . . .'

I turned to the warriors and commanded: 'Take all of them to the cooks. They are to be tied to poles and they are to be fattened even more. I want to enjoy them one by one, in my own time.'

After that I called my queens and my *Indunas* together and spoke to them as follows: 'My people and my wives, we must now make preparations to meet the disasters foreshadowed by the sun's eclipse which you saw. These coming disasters can only be of the following nature: invasion, which we are strong enough to repel, a famine or a pestilence. One of the last two is the most likely. But we must prepare ourselves to face either. The land of the Mambo is vast and mostly deserted, and it is my intention to turn it into one big cornfield, the biggest cornfield in the land. And I am sure we can do it. We must plough and sow day and night. We must cut down whole forests and plant corn and yams everywhere. I shall send messengers to *Celiwe* and *Malandela* to ask them to send all the Mambo refugees back, by force if need be. I want every hand in this land on the handle of a hoe. The survival of both tribes may depend on what we now plan to do.'

Blacksmiths went into action immediately, forging tens of thousands of heavy hoes and axes. Soon every warrior, every woman and child, was out in the veld ploughing and sowing. Tilled lands began to advance, to creep over hills and through vales, as tens of thousands of cursing warriors and bad-tempered women laboured day and night at the most unusual task of all time – turning the land into one vast cornfield.

Two moons fled by and still the work went on, gaining pace as thousands of sullen Mambo were herded back to their homeland by Nguni regiments.

The rains came, the corn grew, and the ploughing and sowing were accelerated. At last, after three solid moons of sweat and toil exactly three-quarters of the land stood under corn – from horizon to horizon. The angry and lazy Mambo talked openly of revolt and many were my own warriors who started calling me a madman and a tyrant, with strings of suitable adjectives. Many were the blistered and calloused hands in the land by the time I calculated we had done enough.

In those three months of toil and tears I had made myself the most hated chief of all time and only my persistent threat to cast an evil spell on anyone found guilty of insubordination kept things going according to plan. *Vuramuinda, Noliyanda* and I had to use our voodoo powers once or twice to scare the lives out of some angry Mambo men and women who threw down their hoes and took to the forests. I threatened once to turn six mutinous warriors into hyaenas in public – which I very nearly did – to discourage a general revolt in one area.

Eventually the work was finished – the ploughing and sowing, that is – and the people assumed the task of guarding all the lands against the hazards and the whims and fancies of nature. I forced thousands of already infuriated people to take up posts and beat drums to scare the clouds of finches and frighten away herds of wild animals. Ten full regiments were out continuously, chasing animals and shooting, with bow and arrow and sling-stones, finches and other birds – a rather humiliating chore for full-blooded warriors.

Then *Vuramuinda* and *Noliyanda* did something that was both strange and unusual, and which brought wonderful and unexpected results. They called upon an old wood-carver and his assistants to carve numerous small ebony masks representing themselves, and they instilled in these masks voodoo powers guaranteed to bring good luck to all wearing them. They publicly announced that a mask would go as a trophy to any man, woman or child, who could produce evidence that he or she was responsible for the death of more than a thousand finches while watching the corn anywhere in the land.

The result was astonishing. Every man, woman and child in the now fully populated land of the Western Mambo declared open war on the destructive birds. Within ten days people were making their way in thousands to the Great Kraal carrying large skin bags full of tens of thousands of dead finches as proof of their prowess. Within one month my wives had made presentations of five thousand of these small good luck masks. The corn flourished. Good rains and plenty of sunshine showered their blessings on our efforts. The sorghum ripened and harvest time arrived.

The Mambo streamed from their kraals in multitudes to reap the ripe corn. Now there was no cursing and scowling. All the people hurled themselves with an almost fanatical dedication upon their task of gathering the harvest. This dedication was considerably enhanced by a knowledge that further good luck masks were due to those who could claim, from any district in the vast land, that they had reaped a thousand grain baskets of corn within eight days.

While the reaping was in progress I gave a full regiment of warriors the task of constructing ten of the largest granaries ever built on earth. Each granary could accommodate a thousand men, with some room to spare, and stood on no fewer than eighty wooden posts well planted in the earth. Each was built entirely of skins on a stout sapling framework. This consumed no fewer than three hundred ox hides. There were ten entrances to each dome-shaped granary.

The outside of each granary was heavily coated with fat from a hundred hippos to make it waterproof. It was not long before the amused people started referring to these granaries as the black domes of mad *Lumukanda*. Each granary stood next to a military kraal and was heavily fortified. A short path flanked on either side by a great stockade linked the granary to the kraal so that in the event of a raid the warriors could dash from the kraal to man the granary stockade without exposing themselves.

Each granary contained enough grain to feed a million people for fifty days and yams to feed the same number for ten days or more.

The people never stopped thinking I was mad as they brought the hundreds of thousands of baskets full of yams and sorghum to the granaries. Many were the sly jokes cracked about me and my ridiculous enterprise. Some said I had developed a leaking stomach which needed constant filling. The more imaginative said I had started a secret *tokoloshe* farm somewhere and that all this was intended for food for their breeding. If only the stupid mortals had known...

It was towards the end of the harvesting and storing of the grain that Queen *Celiwe* of the Nguni visited me once again, bringing *Muwende-Lutanana* and her children, *Demane* and *Demazana*, back to the land of the Mambo. The diminutive matriarch came into the Great Kraal attended by two regiments of warriors and announced with a glint of mischief that she had left a little gift for me outside in the forest, and asked whether I would be so kind as to fetch it. She gave me the directions before escorting *Muwende-Lutanana* and her children into *Vuramuinda's* hut.

I took *Ntombela* and *Mavimbela* and set out over the golden cornfields towards the distant forest. On reaching it I sent *Mavimbela* in to get the little gift. The fierce *Induna* went in and returned, cursing most foully.

'What is it, Oh *Mavimbela?*' I asked. 'Why are you empty-handed?'

The foul language continued to flow from his lips and he concluded by saying: 'They cannot do this to my chief! Wait till I lay my hands on that filthy little hyaena *Celiwe*. She cannot do this to you, Oh Great One!'

'Swallow a stone, *Mavimbela*, swallow a stone and tell us calmly just what has happened,' said *Ntombela*.

'Come and see for yourselves.'

We followed him to a small clearing in the forest and there we saw the most amazing sight of all time – a company of grinning Nguni warriors guarding nearly two thousand pretty girls. 'Your gift, Great *Lumukanda*,' grinned the battle leader in charge of the warriors. 'Your gift from *Celiwe* of the Nguni.'

'We shall need more than one of your granaries to store them in,' bellowed *Mavimbela*.

'No, *Mavimbela*, we shall build three great huts in the Royal Kraal for these beautiful wives of mine and you shall have the honour of guarding them.'

'Great One, you can tell me to do anything – to go out and kill a lion with my bare hands, to go and wrestle with a crocodile. But – I beg you, do not make me guard these women.'

'I have spoken, *Mavimbela.* Now you will be kind enough to escort my wives to the Royal Kraal and there guard them until further notice. You shall enjoy your new appointment.'

On reaching the Great Kraal I found *Celiwe* staring in blank amazement at the granary. 'What is that huge dome there, *Lumukanda?* Is it true that you are storing grain in that . . . that huge thing?'

'Yes, Royal *Celiwe,* I am storing corn in that, and nine others like it.'

'But why, *Lumukanda?*'

'Believe it or not, *Celiwe,* but I can foresee the greatest famine of all time in the very near future.'

'*Somandla,* save us!'

'He gave us brains to enable us to save ourselves. He has no time for puny mortals on a plaything world.'

Celiwe smiled, saying: 'I do not think he has time for puny immortals either.'

'Neither do I. But tell me, Royal *Celiwe,* why have you played such a trick on me?'

'You mean the girls? I hope they give you much pleasure. I spent six whole months scouring the country for girls as near to me in looks as possible, to present to you.'

'But why, *Celiwe,* why?'

'Let us be frank with each other, Oh *Lumukanda.* I love you as the earth loves the rain. And I know you love me too. But alas, as Queen of the Nguni I must bear it. A High Law of the Nguni forbids a ruler to marry a foreigner. So I have sent you these two thousand girls to occupy in your heart the place I bitterly long for but cannot occupy. Please love them for my sake.'

'I will, Little One, but I have sworn, as a result of what happened between me and *Lutanana,* to deny myself women for three years.'

'Oh no!' she cried, her great eyes widening. 'You are in for trouble then, Great Immortal. Those girls are not only the prettiest in the land of the Nguni; they are the most hot-blooded wantons ever born into the bargain. Sooner or later they are going to come after you like a pack of hungry hyaenas.'

'They wouldn't dare! Every woman in my seraglio will respect my vow.'

'You Black Goddess *Vuramuinda,* and *Noliyanda* and *Lulama-Maneruana* might take strong exception to not being slept with, Oh *Lumukanda.* A woman gets very offended when a man ignores her, as you well know.'

'They can all go and milk a zebra,' I said, as we went back to the kraal along the fortified passage.

'Tell me, *Lumukanda,* are you happy in your life?'

'Do you really want to know, Little One?'
'Please.'
'I am not, *Celiwe*. My life has been, still is, just one long, rock-strewn path of misery. I live only to carry out the mission given me by the Highest of the Most High.'
'Oh! Can I be so bold as to ask what that mission is?'
'Your little brain might not fully comprehend. But I shall try to explain. You see, the lesser gods, led by the First Goddess, *Ninavanhu-Ma*, have been trying to destroy the Bantu in various ways. The Bantu, as a product of Creation, are a danger to the old gods.
'Destroy the Bantu? But why, why?'
'In the far-distant future, the furthest future you can imagine, a chief is going to be born who will challenge the very gods and enslave them. He will be born among the Bantu and his name will be *Luzwi-Muundi*. He will be so powerful and so wise that he will give immortality to every man and woman on earth. This chief, who will be born some twenty-eight thousand years from now, will turn men into indestructible spirits with unimaginable powers. These people will conquer the Mother of Creation and make the very stars do obeisance before them. These people shall give blood and a thinking brain to the mountain Killima-Njaro, and use it to conquer the Great Waters over which they will walk as one walks on solid ground. The Holy Chief *Luzwi-Muundi* shall train elephants into spear-carrying warriors and lions into wise counsellors with the ability to speak the tongue of men. The armies of *Luzwi-Muundi* will beseige the Hidden Kraal of the gods and capture them, and enslave them. An end will be put to greed, anger, murder, war and famine. The whole world will be turned into a soft, scented paradise in which undying men and women will live in peace and happiness forever.
'But the lesser gods do not want this. They do not want *Luzwi-Muundi* to be born and they know that if they destroy the Bantu completely in the next two thousand years this will not happen. I am here to thwart them again and again.
'The gods are trying all kinds of ways to destroy the Bantu. They sent the Strange Ones to enslave the tribes and exterminate them, more than two thousand years ago. Now they are sending slave raiders to ravage and denude parts of the country of its inhabitants. And they are going to try again and again in the future, while I shall do my best to thwart them.'
Celiwe was sobbing silently as we entered the kraal. As we crawled into the empty Great Hut she said: 'Give me your lips, *Lumukanda*.'
Kneeling just inside the sunbathed entrance of the Great Hut we kissed briefly, savagely.

'I shall always love you, unhappy immortal,' she breathed. 'In your hour of sorrow always remember – *Celiwe* is there.'

'I shall remember, *Celiwe*. I shall remember.'

We broke away quickly as I sensed *Vuramuinda* coming towards the hut. She entered and smiled sweetly at *Celiwe*, who smiled back equally warmly. *Vuramuinda* then told me she had had to knock *Luanaledi* unconscious when she caught the latter trying to brain *Muwende-Lutanana* with a small grindstone.

'I must keep an eye on *Luanaledi*,' said the Black Goddess. 'This is her third attempt to murder *Lutanana*. I think the girl is mad.'

Celiwe stayed with us for the rest of the winter and left for the land of the Nguni early in the first moon of the early summer. As usual, I ordered the Mambo out on the cornfields and soon we were busy ploughing and sowing again.

The rains came – the corn grew – and the second moon of spring fled by. Then the cruel gods struck their first terrible blow. The rains abruptly stopped and a burning sun glared malevolently at a shrinking earth from radiant cloudless skies. The tender corn drooped like heartbroken virgins, ruined and deserted by cruel lovers. The bawling cattle grew thin as the grass slowly dried. Rain-making ceremonies were held everywhere, ceremonies in which naked girls and old women danced in great circles around idols of *Ninavanhu-Ma*, the First Goddess.

The rains came. The drooping corn revived. The grass grew greener than before. And then came the scourge of Africa – locusts.

The first hint we had of the presence of this dreaded pest in the land was a message – a drum message – relayed from the distant land of the Lunda in the west and warning all tribes to be on the alert for the vast swarms that were winging and breading their way south-east from the land of the Ba-Luba.

The Laws of the Tribes say that all messages of this kind must be relayed by drum from kraal to kraal and from land to land. Any tribe failing to relay a message as important as a locust plague immediately fell under a High Curse and it had become a point of honour for all the other tribes to attack such a tribe and wipe it out.

Immediately after the arrival of the message the Mambo 'drummers of honour' hauled out their huge signal drums and relayed the dread warning from kraal to kraal right into the land of the Nguni, who in turn relayed it into the land of the Nyanja.

Two days later, *Vuramuinda* and *Noliyanda* called me to the stockade of the Great Kraal. There I found women and warriors standing and watching, eyes wide with horror, the reddish-brown clouds approaching low over the north-western horizon – a solid wall of millions upon millions of locusts drifting slowly and relentlessly nearer.

A hoarse agonised cry exploded from one of the warriors as he pointed to an equally dense cloud moving in from the south-west.

'Out all available grain baskets!' I shouted. 'Out all skin bags and big spare cooking pots! All warriors, all men and women – out of the kraal, quick! Drummers, call out all people of the neighbouring kraals. We must build a chain of fire to stop those locusts. Out all regiments! They will not eat our grain; we are going to eat them.'

Torches were applied to all the piles of dry grass and twigs arranged in a great crescent facing the oncoming swarms and a sheet of white smoke billowed upwards to the sky. Green branches were laid on the fires to increase the density of the smoke. The fires were tended ceaselessly by tens of thousands of men, women and children from scores of kraals. The mighty wall of billowing smoke was a spectacular sight.

The locust swarms hummed closer to the wall of smoke and fire, leaving a stretch of desolation in their wake. They consumed every blade of green grass and every leaf of the tall trees. Millions settled and laid eggs, soon to hatch young to take part in the devastation. They dropped in their millions as they came against the unbroken wall of smoke. They dropped until the ground within the crescent was a writhing sea of crawling destruction. Men and women waded knee-deep into the vast mass, scooping up great grass bowls full and pouring them into the large grain baskets, each big enough to contain two men. Ox-sleds hauled dozens of these baskets to and from the kraals where old women were busy with pots, making large dumps of cooked locusts.

For five days the desperate battle against the locusts raged. Many thousands of great grain baskets full of roasted locusts found their way into my already overflowing granaries.

Finally the locusts broke through the wall of smoke. We could not maintain the defensive operation. The sky turned black and the land became alive with them as they winged and hopped their way eastward. But we were not disheartened – they still met with bitter opposition. We set entire fields on fire, destroying millions upon millions of the invaders in each field. Whole *mopani* forests were set alight and billions of locusts were charred. But millions more came and passed – and bred – to spread more destruction further afield.

People lost all their crops. The cattle lost all their grazing. Starving cows died calving – goats died. So did many of the wild animals of the forests.

Vultures came in their thousands, gorging themselves to bursting. And in their wake came the epidemic.

BEHOLD THE GREAT DEATH

> Peace thee, peace thee – Oh my spirit—
> Bow thy head before the great *Somandla*;
> Into His mercy now surrender thee,
> Into His hands, completely yield thee.

It was midday and the sun shone fiercely from a dazzling sky on whose pale blue expanse not a single cloud wàs to be seen. Underfoot, the ground was as hot as a furnace and a heavy veil of stifling heat hazed over the land like a transparent mist.

The small lake, towards which the five girls were coming in single file with heavy water claypots on their heads, was steaming hot and a haze of vapour hung in the stagnant air above its slimy green water. The five girls were walking on the dry, blasted, locust-cropped grass on the edge of the stony footpath, carefully avoiding the blistering ground.

'*Aieee!*' cried the leading girl whose name was *Zodwa* (short for *Ntombi-Zodwa*), 'the sun is hotter than the bottom of a frying pot. Oh my sisters, I can hardly see with all the sweat pouring down my face.'

'Be careful that the sun does not melt you out of existence, Oh *Zodwa*,' said the third girl in line. 'You are so fat that you might melt quicker than we.'

'You are always jealous of my figure, you tall thin piece of dried meat you,' *Zodwa* replied tartly to the third girl, whose name was *Ntutana*. 'You are always the envious one.'

'*Hai-ya!*' jeered *Ntutana*, 'I would rather be a tall thin piece of dried meat than a heavy clumsy sorghum-meal dumpling, Oh *Zodwa*.'

'You forget, Oh *Ntutana*,' said the soft-spoken second girl, *Duduzile*, 'that men take no notice of tall thin women.'

'I do not need you to tell me, you little mouse. Shut your birdlike mouth quickly before I feed you a fist!'

'You *Ntutana*?' asked *Duduzile* softly. 'Have you forgotten all the fists I fed you three days ago?'

'*Yey-yieee*!' cried *Zodwa*, turning round slowly. 'I will have no fighting between you brawling mad fools today. I am sick of your constant squabbling.'

'As you say, *Zodwa*,' murmured *Duduzile*.

'Yes, as I say, you bloodthirsty little she-jackal!' shrieked the leading girl. 'It is high time you got yourself a man to tame you, you little bully. I am getting tired of your habit of picking fights with *Ntutana*.'

'*Ntutana's* mother always picks fights with my mother,' replied *Duduzile* mildly.

'Your mother's quarrels are none of our business,' cried *Zodwa* sternly. 'You must learn to respect *Ntutana*, you lawless little hag; you must respect your father's first wife's daughter.'

'If you fight with *Ntutana* again we shall all beat you up, *Duduzile*,' said the rather ill-favoured fifth girl *Nonsizi*, in heavy tones. 'The High Laws say the daughters of one man must never fight amongst themselves.'

The fourth girl, *Tandiwe*, took no part in this bickering because she was deaf and could not hear what her sisters were talking about. But it was she who first saw the three young men crouching behind a bush and surveying the girls with hopeful, sheeplike eyes. *Tandiwe* tapped *Nonsizi* on the shoulder and pointed at the bush behind which three heads had just bobbed down out of sight.

'What is it, *Tandiwe*?' asked *Nonsizi* at the top of her voice. 'What is behind that bush?'

'Three young men,' replied *Tandiwe*, who could hear nothing less than a shout.

'Ignore them – pretend they are not there.'

The girls came to the little half-dry lake and started scooping up the sun-baked water with gourd scoops into the clay pots, each trying her best to ignore the three love-struck young men who had left the bush and were now coming stealthily up to them.

'I see you, Oh beautiful ones,' said one of the young men gently.

The five girls coldly ignored the greeting as though it had not been spoken and continued with great deliberation their task of filling the clay pots.

'Oh, happy is he into whose hands one of you has fallen, Oh beautiful butterflies,' said the young man again. 'Oh happy will be the man that will one day marry one of you.'

'And you are not that man,' *Zodwa* responded, turning upon him suddenly. 'You had better turn around and go straight home to your mama before we spank your behind, Oh little boy.'

'It would be an honour to be spanked by your beautiful hand, Oh star of my waking dreams,' murmured the young man with a bright ivory-white smile.

'Star of your waking dreams, do you say?' asked *Zodwa*, her eyebrows rising in mock surprise. '*Ahhhh*, poor little boy . . . poor little boy, so you dream in daytime do you?'

'*Yebo*, oh bright star of the dark skies of my life; I do dream in daytime and I always dream of you.'

'Well, you can just carry on dreaming for all I care.'

'My vein's desire, please to remember that today is the day you promised to give me the answer I have been begging you for two whole years now. I am sick of waiting and the suspense is killing me.'

'The suspense can kill you thrice for all I care, Oh *Gawula*, son of *Mtombo*,' said *Zodwa* spitefully. 'You have waited two years for my answer and, by the stars, you shall wait for ten years more.'

'No, *Ntombi-Zodwa*,' replied the young man in a cold and deadly voice, 'I shall wait no more. I am warning you here and now to give me your answer today.'

'Or else what, son of a green-bellied hyaena?'

Gawula did not answer. Instead, he drew one of his short heavy spears from behind his black shield and, before *Zodwa* could stop him, he had given himself a nasty cut with it above the left breast. The four girls and the two other young men cried aloud in alarm and dismay. *Zodwa* leapt upon *Gawula* and pinned his arms to his sides, an expression of horror distorting her face. '*Gawula*! *Gawula* . . . are you mad?'

'I want my answer from you *Zodwa*; I want my answer here and now. Say yes you love me or I shall stab myself and die at your feet. I am not joking.'

'*Gawula*,' sobbed *Zodwa*, '*Gawula*, can't you see that I have already given you your answer? Can't you see I love you? Do I have to tell you that I love you? I have loved you since the first day we met. Here, may be this should convince you.'

She undid one of the cowrie-shell strings around her waist and tied it around the bleeding *Gawula's* neck. Then she raised herself on tiptoe and kissed him full on the forehead. 'Beloved one, you did not have to do this to yourself. I would have given you the token of acceptance in any case. I love you *Gawula*. Mother was right after all when she warned me to be careful of you. She said you are a hot-headed, impulsive fool.'

'I know, beloved one, I know. I did act like a fool. Forgive me my love. Now let me go and wash off this blood.'

'Let me help you, *Gawula*. I always carry some wound medicine in this little pouch.'

She undid a small impala-skin pouch hanging from a copper-bead necklace and shook out a lump of greenish stuff into her right hand. All first-born daughters had to wear such a pouch around their necks whenever they led their sisters to the riverside to get water or to the cornfields to hoe or reap. This little pouch contained a lump of medicine that should be used immediately if one of the girls was bitten by a snake or injured by a hoe.

The others crowded round as *Gawula* cleaned the blood off his wound and *Zodwa* applied the greasy medicine.

The two other young men, *Mvezi* and *Fanyana*, took their sweethearts, *Duduzile* and the ugly *Nonsizi* respectively, into the forest for a walk in the cool shade of the trees and to talk such intimate drivel as young and hot-blooded lovers talk to each other when all by themselves.

Never was there a pair better matched than *Mvezi* and *Duduzile*, except perhaps for the pair *Nonsizi* and *Fanyana*.

Mvezi was short, thickset and round of face, with monkey-like features and a light-brown skin. He had a very quick temper. His sweetheart, *Duduzile*, was a tiny, pretty little thing also with a light skin, also soft-spoken and with an equally fiery temper.

Fanyana was monstrously ugly, with a dark-brown skin, and he was huge, slow-witted and clumsy in almost anything he did. His bride-to-be, *Nonsizi*, was just as ugly and just as slow-witted. But she had a beautiful figure that compensated for her ugliness. The people of the village of these young people waited with great impatience for their day of marriage, because for people to be so well matched as these four, was something that happened once in a hundred years. People referred to them as the 'four little doves of our village'.

After the four had gone into the forest, *Zodwa* and *Gawula* also departed. The tall, thin *Ntutana* and her deaf cousin *Tandiwe* were left alone under the tree to guard the clay pots in the cool shade.

Tandiwe had not yet reached the age when girls are allowed to love and to be loved, being not yet twenty-five years old. But *Ntutana* was an unlucky girl. No man wanted her, and the reason for this was plain enough to see. She was too wide-shouldered, too narrow-hipped, and altogether too thin. She was the type of girl men take and marry, not for love and for bearing children but to work in the fields and to cook. Hers was a bleak future indeed. She was tormented by asthma and also by a searing loneliness which made her cry every night while the other girls stole out of the kraal to meet their lovers under the stars. Her father, the great lion hunter *Madevu*, hated her – and her mother was the only one who had any love for her among the many men, women and children in *Madevu's* village.

Mvezi and *Duduzile* had been walking hand in hand for some time before *Duduzile* started complaining that she was feeling dizzy.

'There you start again,' cried *Mvezi* irritably. 'You always love to spoil our appointment one way or the other. If you do not shriek at me like an old hag then you pretend you are ill. I do not believe you.'

'Oh you insufferable rat! You are a heartless jackal, *Mvezi*, and I have half a mind to break our engagement. Do you know that?'

'You have been threatening to do so for six moons now, Oh *Duduzile*, and I am telling you again as I told you many times before – break our engagement and I shall break every bone in your vile little body. I dare you to break your promise.'

He seized her left arm and twisted it behind her until she screamed aloud with pain, fear and anger. When he released her she spun around and struck him a stinging blow across the face. With a fierce oath *Mvezi* dropped his shield and spears and grappled with her. Like two infuriated wild cats the two young lovers fought, rolling over and over on the ground.

Duduzile seized a round stone and struck *Mvezi* savagely on the forehead with it. *Mvezi* retaliated by picking up a stump of wood and beating the girl black and purple. The angry girl tore the stump from *Mvezi's* hand and closed with him. Her hands clutching his neck, she tried her best to throttle him. The lovers exchanged blows until both were tired and short of breath. Finally *Duduzile*, who had taken the worst punishment, threw her arms around *Mvezi's* neck and kissed him tenderly on the forehead saying, 'Do not hit me again, beloved one; you know I shall never break my promise . . .'

Mvezi sat down and drew *Duduzile* gently down beside him. The lovers kissed each other's foreheads twice – and then kissed each other full on the mouth. This is a thing reserved exclusively for married people. And then it is to serve one purpose only.*

'We should not have done that, my love,' murmured *Duduzile*, suddenly feeling very tired. The persistent headache she had been

---

* *The Laws of the Tribes forbid people to kiss on the mouth unless they are going to mate. Engaged couples may kiss each other's foreheads, noses and even necks. But they must not kiss on the mouth. The Bantu worship the love-kiss and regard it as very holy – not to be used in a trifling way; only in dead earnest. A man or a woman must never kiss a child on the mouth. Even when a man returns from a long journey, he must not kiss his wife on the mouth – only on her forehead or cheeks. The love-kiss is reserved only for mating and then only when the intention is to procreate children. When honey and beer are used to prevent conception, the married couple too, should not use the love-kiss. Such is the Second Law of the twenty-one High Laws in the 'Secret and Sacred Code of Love' among the Tribes.*

feeling flared up blindingly and she felt hot all over. A strange fear tore through her as she found herself falling backwards. She did not know it, but the young man holding her was dead – and she was dying.

Nonsizi was walking beside the man she loved. She was feeling the ripple of the muscles of his strong arm as it drew her close to him. Her broad hip pressed his own muscular form and a strange hunger rose inside her as his fingers caressed the other hip. Her legs suddenly weakened.

She sat down in the long grass with a nervous giggle and *Fanyana* sat down beside her. His bulging bloodshot eyes were ablaze with adoration and love no words can describe. They spoke but little, these two ugly lovers – they were both shy and nervous in one another's presence. They kissed, they cuddled and caressed and were both alive with a ravening desire.

At last *Nonsizi* said very tiredly: 'Hold . . . hold me tightly, Oh desired one. I . . . I feel . . . dizzy . . . very strange . . .'

She was smiling and her long-lashed eyes fluttered coyly. She gave no indication of the blinding headache that was all but tearing her apart – a headache that had troubled her since the previous night. *Fanyana* continued to kiss and caress the doomed girl, even though he himself suddenly felt unwell. He suddenly found himself a victim of a blinding headache. But he gritted his teeth and tried to shrug it off. The Laws of the Tribes say it is very shameful for people to show that they are not able to bear pain cheerfully, and *Fanyana* smiled down at his sweetheart whose head was resting on his lap. She smiled back. Beads of salty perspiration erupted on the foreheads of both lovers. But still they continued to caress.

'Kiss me, Oh *Fanyana*,' murmured *Nosizi*.

His arms tightened around her as he sought with his lips her sweat-bedewed neck through the red mist of pain swimming in his glazed eyes. She struggled up – their lips met . . .

It was their last kiss on earth. They died in one another's arms.

'I cannot believe it!' cried *Gawula* some time later as he stared down at the dead bodies of his younger brother *Mvezi* and his sweetheart *Duduzile*. 'They are dead. But what . . . what could have killed them?'

'Don't you think they killed each other?' asked *Zodwa* in a horrified whisper. 'Look, the grass has been flattened all round them and both are bruised all over.'

'I do not know what to think. Come let us call out for the others. Somebody has to run back home and call our parents.'

They called and called and no one answered. Then they began to search the locust-ravaged forest for *Fanyana* and *Nonsizi.*

It was *Gawula* who first saw the 'ugly lovers' lying dead in each other's arms. There was an expression of indescribable peace on their faces and their arms were tight around each other – their last embrace in a cruel world.

'Dead . . .,' moaned *Gawula.* 'They are dead – they are dead too . . .'

Gawula and *Zodwa* lost their nerve and ran out of the forest at this shattering sight. They ran straight back to the sun-bathed lake, and found both *Tandiwe* and the tall thin *Ntutana* dead among the water-filled clay pots under the flat-topped *munga* tree.

'No! Oh no!' shrieked *Zodwa.* 'Let us run home, Oh *Gawula;* let us go and call father and the other people. There is evil afoot . . . there is much evil!'

'I . . . I can't believe it,' muttered *Gawula,* as both young lovers set out at speed for the distant village.

They entered the village at a run. There they found all the people either dead or dying. Men had died where they sat. The women had died where they worked. One had fallen into the great cooking fire in the centre of the kraal.

Zodwa and *Gawula* ran to the next kraal and found it burnt to the ground. The owner of that kraal had seen his wives and children drop dead one by one and had realised that a deadly epidemic had invaded his kraal, that he too, was as good as dead already. The brave man had remembered the demands of the law in such circumstances. He had carried his dead wives one by one into his hut, and the children one by one into their hut. He had first set fire to the children's hut and then to his own hut, which he had then entered himself.

Zodwa and her lover, *Gawula,* realised the truth at last. A pestilence of some unknown type was sweeping the land – a deadly epidemic that killed silently, swiftly and effectively. Before the blood-red sun sank wearily beyond the western mountains, *Zodwa* and *Gawula* had visited three kraals and four villages, finding nothing but dead, dying or unconscious people.

The two young lovers stood at last on the top of a scowling precipice, searching the distant horizon for a sign of life – a whisp of smoke from some far kraal, or a distant shout. Seeing neither the former nor hearing the latter, they realised that they were the last two persons alive in the eastern district of the land of the Nguni.

> Ere thou wert born, He was close to thee,
> And when thou diest He shall be by thy side;

Lackest thou then a protecting hand?
Peace – and surrender thee to Him.

Are not the stars of His creating?
Do not the beasts proclaim Him Father?
He is the One who careth for thee,
And thy footsteps He shall guide.

Let Him be thy hard Firestone
That lighteth thy path in Life's chill winter;
In Life's dark jungle He shall be thy axe
That hacketh thy lonely path for thee.

Let Him be thy sturdy helmsman,
Who guideth thy barge o'er the rapids of Life;
He – thy Star that adorneth the sky,
To guide thy footsteps to thy home.

Zodwa and *Gawula* are now in a cave among huge rocks. They have gone through a simple ceremony on their own and have proclaimed themselves man and wife. *Zodwa* has taken off her small calfskin skirt and presented it to *Gawula* on her knees, and *Gawula* has accepted it with both hands, also on his knees. The lovers have embraced fiercely, clinging to each other with a strength born of despair. Both are as good as dead already, and both know it all too well.

They are now man and wife, and they have no future. *Zodwa* is a fertile, hot-blooded woman who has always aimed at bearing the man of her choice no fewer than ten children. She had passed all the tests during her initiation with honour and had been very proud of this fact.

Now all her dreams are shattered. She will not live to see tomorrow's dawn.

Gawula is a young man whose heart has been broken again and again by cruel girls. By the time he met *Zodwa* he had lost all hope of ever being loved by a woman. Even as he kneels now, facing *Zodwa*, he remembers the strange words of *Tambo*, his famous grandfather, who was once the leading witchdoctor in the eastern district of the land of the Nguni. Old and wrinkled, *Tambo* had thrown the 'bones of divination' and had told *Gawula* in his toothless and cracked old voice:

'Listen, Oh son of my son, the bones of divination say that your heart will be broken many times by faithless girls. And on the day you find a woman who truly loves you death will be breathing down your neck.'

Gawula had been puzzled by the old man's words on that bright mid-summer day so many years ago. And now he knows.

He has met the first woman who truly loved him, and by tomorrow he will be dead. Tears run down his lean cheeks and he wipes them savagely away with the back of his hand. A Nguni must not cry – and *Gawula* is a proud Nguni.

Zodwa's experienced hands are building a fire to roast the two hares *Gawula* has brought from the forest. The two lovers sit side by side, their arms about each other's shoulders, listening to the hissing of carcases roasting in the fire. Outside, the frowning forest has assumed a more sinister shape with the coming of night and a distant jackal strikes up dismally, advertising a vacancy in his heart. The song of night has begun and its discordant verses assail the ear with countless sounds.

The last two lovers left alive in a plague-scourged land eat their last supper in trembling silence. The two participants in one of the strangest marriages of all time eat their wedding feast with no enjoyment. There are silent tears in their eyes and a creeping fear in their clouded hearts.

The dark, beautiful bride Death is close behind them, smiling softly. She has reaped a good harvest in this part of the land of the Nguni, and now only two little ears of corn await her basket. It will not be long now. In the darkness the beautiful bride Death smiles softly, almost pityingly.

The two young people have eaten and now recline on their love mat of green *mopani* leaves. The slow moon rises above the distant forest-veiled hills and a lonely owl hoots derisively from a branch of the tree directly outside the cave. A pack of marauding wild dogs yaps excitedly in the vale below.

'Come to me, my bride . . .' *Gawula* reaches out and draws *Zodwa* to him. But the woman pushes him away savagely and rolls off the leaf mat, out of reach. *Gawula* half-rises and seizes her again, crushing her to his chest almost brutally. A fierce struggle ensues in which the hot-blooded young people pit their strength against one another.

Zodwa writhes away like a snake and *Gawula* seizes her for the third time and pins her down mercilessly. Then with the skill of a well-initiated young man *Gawula* controls his own smothering passion and starts 'lighting the fire of love' in Zodwa by skilfully caressing her and occasionally kissing her fiercely. *Zodwa* still resists but she knows already that she has lost the battle. She is afraid and excited at the same time. Her mind begins to wander and she starts talking a lot of unintelligible nonsense.

She suddenly feels shy and afraid of *Gawula* and she closes her eyes tightly. To her great surprise she finds herself kissing him ardently.

She is calling him all sorts of names; she is calling him her fierce lion, her mighty elephant, her chief, her star in the sky. She is lost in a whirling mist of rainbow colours . . .

The two panting lovers draw deep breaths of the cool night air. For a long while they lie on their backs, revelling in the strange feeling sweeping over them – a feeling of peace and pleasant tiredness they wish would last forever.

At last *Zodwa's* eyes open and she sees the laughing moon huge in the sky outside the cave. Sharply silhouetted against its golden face, the fat owl is still hooting derisively at the world.

Zodwa turns on her side and caresses *Gawula's* muscle-corded belly. He turns too and takes her in his arms again. She says: 'Hold me tighter, Oh beloved one, I am yours . . . all yours forever.'

These are her last words. Outside the cave in which the two lovers are now lying, sleeping a sleep from which there is no awakening, the plump owl still sits on the branch of the lonely tree, ruffling his feathers and glaring malevolently at the midnight landscape with his large, frilled, smouldering eyes.

'Too-whooo-who . . . too-whooooo . . .,' it hoots sombrely.

He was a 'drummer of honour' and he had a duty to perform ere he yielded to death. Everybody in his kraal was either dead or dying, but he, *Liva*, was still on his feet. His vision was already blurring with the throbbing headache and he knew he would not last till sunset. He had to send out a drum message; he *had* to before his strength failed. A wanderer – a dying wanderer from the east, whom *Liva* had admitted to his kraal two nights previously, had brought this vile, deadly contagion into his kraal and it was only a matter of time before the strange deadly plague depopulated the whole district.

'I must warn them,' moaned *Liva* as he staggered towards the drum shrine – the little hut in which the sacred drums were kept and treasured for the ancient and sacred things they were. *Liva* crawled into the hut, his head heavy with pain, and rolled out the largest and oldest drum, which had stood untouched for more than fifty years. Heavily preserved with hippo fat, it stood there waiting for such an emergency.

Liva lifted the drum and slung it over his shoulder. He staggered out of the kraal he had built with his own hands so many years ago and which he loved. Wearily, painfully he climbed the steep hill that rose some distance away. He finally reached the summit, unslung the heavy drum and rested briefly. Slowly he stood up, tested the wind direction with his hand and, turning upwind, he gripped the heavy drum between his thighs and with his last ebbing strength he proceeded to beat out a short message over and over again: 'Big Death . . . Abandon All Kraals . . .'

The terrible message boomed out of the bottom end of the drum. The howling wind carried the sound to the farthest mountains. *Liva* did not ease the beating until he heard another drum in the far distance taking up the message and relaying it.

He smiled happily and embraced the ancient drum. He laid it down and drew his sharp hunting knife. 'A sacrifice to you, Oh Holy Drum of my Fathers.' With these words he gritted his teeth and drove the knife into his chest. He sagged across the drum and died the death of a 'Drummer of Honour'. His blood stained the huge black drum on which was inscribed in holy symbols the history of the Nguni. An ugly vulture dived from the blue sky and for a moment its shadow fell over the dead drummer . . .

The trails and footpaths are thick with cattle and people fleeing westward and southward in their countless thousands – fleeing from a deadly unseen Death which carries off thousands every day. The epidemic has struck a cruel devastating blow at Man, but Man is now fighting back bravely.

As the people and their cattle flee westward they meet hard-faced warriors marching resolutely towards the east. These warriors are known as the 'Dedicates' and they are not going to return alive. Their strange mission is to seek out all kraals in which victims are lying dead and dying, and to burn these kraals to the ground.

Any member of the fleeing crowd falling a victim of the plague must immediately remain behind with all the members of his family. They are required by law to commit suicide or to wait for the 'Dedicates' to assist them if they lack the courage.

In other parts, if a man finds a wife or a child struck by the plague, he must immediately tie a large branch with green leaves across the entrance to his kraal to warn passers-by to keep clear and to attract the attention of the 'Dedicates'. It is from this custom of tying a green branch to the gate of a plague-afflicted kraal that the famous Bantu saying *Kuvalwe nge hlahla* sprang. It means 'a green branch closing the gate' and is used when a calamity – mostly an illness of some description – has fallen upon a kraal or a village.

The epidemic, or the 'Great Death' (as the Nguni now call it) is spreading with a shocking rapidity, sweeping across the northern, eastern and central parts of the land – sweeping these parts clean of human life with a mercilessness unparalleled in the history of the Tribes.

When the news of this terrible epidemic reached her, *Celiwe* of the Nguni ordered an immediate evacuation of all the kraals in the three remaining districts of her realm which were still unaffected. She ordered her warriors to seal off the borders of the districts to prevent the streams of refugees from the other districts entering the three districts. This was the most terrible decision of *Celiwe's* life and it is said that she wept bitterly as she made it. It was a terrible, but wise, decision and it saved more than three-quarters of the Nguni nation. Even so, more than twenty-five thousand refugees were left to their fate. Desperate refugees fought with the Nguni warriors who were barring their way. A great bitterness against *Celiwe* arose in the hearts of these refugees. They swore vengeance against her. They moved in another direction and formed themselves into a tribe apart from the Nguni and called themselves the Balahliwe – 'the Forsaken Ones'.

Although these refugees did not know it at that time, *Celiwe* had followed what was destined to become one of the High Laws of all Tribes. All chiefs were henceforth expected to make such sacrifices to save the bulk of their people. Future generations were going to thank and remember *Celiwe* for her wisdom, however cruel it may in actual fact have been.

Meanwhile, a great exodus from the three unaffected districts of the land of the Nguni was in progress and countless thousands of people streamed over the border into the land of the Western Mambo. The last to leave was *Celiwe* herself, accompanied by her regiments from her military kraals. *Malandela* had to carry *Celiwe* forcibly across the border because she wanted to remain behind and die with the other refugees whose escape she had blocked.

The land of the Mambo became the last stronghold of humanity in central Africa against this most fantastic disease of all time. But not for long. The 'Great Death' entered the land of the Mambo from the west. It would appear that this strange contagion had broken out independently also in the land of the Lunda. After sweeping away more than four million people it had crept into the land of the Western Mambo from behind.

People were suddenly beginning to die in my own Royal Kraal. But we decided to make a stand. *Vuramuinda, Noliyanda* and I attacked the infernal pestilence with a foul-tasting medicine which people soon called '*Tokoloshe's* urine'. We worked day and night brewing thousands of great clay pots full of this evil medicine. We forced the warriors, *Indunas*, servants and peasants, every man, woman and child to drink it. This medicine also turned out to be a strong purgative.

We launched a ruthless, savage battle against the unseen enemy. We snatched tens of thousands of victims from its talons. I sent entire companies of warriors out to every district with sleds loaded with giant pots full of my secret miracle medicine. They forcibly seized every human being they saw, including those half dead, and forced the medicine down their throats, liberally and indiscriminately.

Thus one day *Mbewu* the mighty hunter was standing at the gate of his new kraal staring absent-mindedly into the hazy distance, trying his best to ignore the throbbing headache with which he had woken up in the morning. And then, suddenly, he saw a group of heavily armed men working their way up the dusty footpath leading to his kraal. Behind these warriors came two oxen hauling a sled – a huge strongly built thing – carrying what appeared to be large shiny black cooking pots. Four young warrior boys walked beside the plodding oxen and a full platoon of a hundred warriors brought up the rear.

A huge round-shouldered Rainbow *Induna*, with a face that reminded *Mbewu* of an ape, led the procession – urging them with an angry purposefulness that struck fear into *Mbewu's* heart. *Tetiwe*, *Mbewu's* First Wife, came running out to join her husband at the gate. 'Those are High Chief *Lumukanda's* warriors, Oh my husband,' she whispered. 'What do you think we could have done wrong?'

'I do not know, Oh beloved one,' muttered the hunter. 'I shall meet them and find out what they want.'

Tetiwe watched as her tall husband strode down the slope to meet the warriors. She watched with fear-filled eyes and with both her hands hard on her mouth to stop herself from crying out aloud. 'Great gods, what have we done . . . *Lumukanda* is such a strange and terrible cannibal. Oh my dear husband! Now what are they doing to you?'

After a brief conversation, which *Tetiwe* could not hear across the distance, the giant Rainbow *Induna* had knocked *Mbewu* flying to the ground with a huge fist. Four grinning warriors leapt on the fallen hunter and had pushed a huge enema horn into him. *Mbewu* yelled in outraged dignity and tried to shake off the fat warrior sitting comfortably on his back, while three warriors took turns in blowing the medicine through the wide end of the horn deeply into his bowels. Then, under the threat of a huge battle axe, *Mbewu* was turned over and forced to drink some of the foul liquid.

Tetiwe watched in shocked amazement as her husband got up after being released and ran like the wind into the bush, yelling and cursing at the top of his voice. The Rainbow *Induna* then came striding up the slope to the kraal.

'You, woman!' he roared. 'Call out every man, woman and child . . .'

'Why . . . why . . .' stammered *Tetiwe*.

'Hurry,' roared the *Induna*. *Tetiwe* sprang away to call her rival-in-marriage, *Kikiza* and the children. 'Here!' bawled the *Induna* at the terrified group – two women, three boys and four girls – shoving to them a calabash full of the most foul-looking, foul-smelling and obviously foul-tasting medicine *Tetiwe* had ever seen. 'Drink that in turns, you stupid fools.'

'But we are not sick,' protested *Kikiza*.

'Our venerable High Chief has declared everybody in this land sick. And when the chief says you are sick, you had better be sick!'

The women drank first, then the boys and last the girls. Murderous looking warriors kept a close watch to see that everyone actually swallowed the required amount. Then the *Induna* thundered: 'Turn around, all of you, and bend over.'

With many a sob and many a sniff the women and children surrendered to the remainder of the treatment. Thereafter the warriors moved to the next kraal, after the Rainbow *Induna* had added another pebble to those in his already nearly full pouch – each representing a family or a kraal saved from the terrible claws of the Great Death.

Ndawo, son of *Vezi*, was a thief and on this particular night he had a good reason for losing himself in the dark forest. He was driving eight brown cows before him and all of them were stolen. *Ndawo* had waited and planned for more than a year to steal these cows from the kraal of his fat, rich neighbour, *Dumaza*. Now he was taking them to his secret hiding place far away in the dark forest.

He was already dreaming of the fortune in copper ornaments, ivory and ebony utensils he was going to get from *Mxhosa* of the renegade Xhosa tribe in the south-west, in exchange for the eight fat cows. The wily old hyaena *Mxhosa* would haggle and fume and try to beat *Ndawo* down to a few bracelets for each cow. But as always, *Ndawo* – who was more than a match for *Mxhosa* in dishonesty and low cunning – would get his full price in the end.

'May the gods keep the Great Death out of *Mxhosa's* kraal until I have sold him these cows,' muttered *Ndawo* with a greedy smile.

Then, out of the quiet night, an angry rasping voice bellowed: 'You there, you with the cows, stop . . . in the name of the chief of the land!'

Ndawo saw dim forms moving towards him out of the frowning darkness. Warriors. *Ndawo* may have been a thief, but he was averse to hurting people because he did not like being hurt himself. He knew the punishment dictated by the High Laws for stealing cattle, and for this kind of punishment he had no particular liking. Few people would like to have a fire lit on their chests while staked to the ground like drying skins. And *Ndawo's* wish was to live to a ripe, if dishonest, old age.

So he turned and ran as fast as he could, trying to shake off the pursuing warriors. He ran as he had never run before. But his pursuers seemed to fly over the long grass and the distance between him and them grew horribly less and less.

Ndawo did not see the startled lovers in the grass until he tripped over them and went ploughing into the land. And before he could rise and resume his flight he and the startled couple were seized and frogmarched back into the forest.

'I am as good as dead already,' muttered *Ndawo.* The young man next to him began to sob – the young woman had been doing nothing else since they were caught. This surprised *Ndawo*, until he discovered later that the woman was another man's wife . . .

The three were hustled into the centre of the camp the warriors had built for the night and an irritable Rainbow *Induna* gave them, to their great surprise, a bowl full of an evil-smelling fluid and told them in sharp terms to drink from it in turn. When told to turn around and bend over, *Ndawo* and his fellow-victims obeyed and tensed themselves for the pain of deadly spears. The enemas were pushed into them and their bellies croaked as they swelled from the cold medicine.

A few moments later, a very astonished cow thief and two equally astonished transgressors of the marriage laws were sworn and cursed on their way by the *Induna.*

Ndawo lost all interest in the stolen cows. His outraged belly dictated thus, and he was soon squatting behind a particularly unfriendly thorn bush. He did not know it just then, but with this strange experience a rather worthless life had been saved.

Thy yesterday – thy pale tomorrow—
Thy dark and uncertain present,
They are all clear to Him;
They are all in His Holy Hand.

Though thy foemen encompass thee,
With whetted steel, seeking to slay;
Though the unseen hyaena of woe
Devour thy bleeding soul – yield to Him.

Though thy hut be the starry sky,
The vagabond wind be thy blanket—
Though for a lover thou hast but a dream,
Trust in God and yield thee to him.

Though for thy food thou hast but the grass,
And for thy fire the faint firefly;

Though for thy loinskin thou hast but thy hand
To shield thy shame from a staring world;
And though thou hast weeds for a sleeping mat—
Trust in God and yield thee to Him.

Six moons later we had won a decisive victory over the Great Death, not only in the land of the Mambo, but in the land of the Nguni as well. We snatched tens of thousands from the claws of death, but it had carried away more than we could save. The last traces of this disease we swept out of the land of the Xhosa.

People started drifting back to the depopulated areas, trying to bring back life to the desolate country. A slow, painful task of rebuilding began. The large herds of ownerless cattle were equally distributed amongst the people.

But we survived one battle only to fight another. And the latter was more terrible than the first. The pestilence-ridden and sun-blasted summer had worn on to late summer, and on into winter. It was soon early summer once more and before we knew it, the second moon of early summer had passed. And in all this time an angry sun blistered the cringing earth most mercilessly.

Grain fields ceased to exist. Cattle died by the hundreds. The Jackal of Starvation was howling outside every gate in the land.

THE GREAT JOURNEY BEGINS

The Hand of Death is heavy upon the land and people are dying like flies in the Milk-pail of Famine. There is no food; even the leaves of trees in the forests are too dry for human consumption. In the great kraals the people are dying the most terrible death any creature can die. They fade into hollow-eyed skeletons, hardly able to move. They look like things dead, and yet they move. They look like the desiccated bodies of long dead Bushmen on the dry sands of the ageless Ka-Lahari. Their teeth protrude in hideous grins; their thin necks make their heads look very big.

Inside these heads brains are also shrinking, not in volume, but in normal mental capacity. Men, women and children resort to doing strange things, and these should not be seen – least of all be remembered. Yet many are the unsavoury incidents destined to be brought back to memory for many generations to come. Let us take a brief look at one such example and quickly pass over this dark phase in the History of the Tribes. Let us try to forget . . .

The two youngsters are waiting and watching with great impatience as their mother slowly dies. Their beady, sunken eyes are alive with a hideous, insane animal fire. Now and again they lick their hunger-cracked lips and glance furtively at each other. They are sitting with their bony knees drawn up and their thin shoulders hunched. They look like two large dark-brown bats – like two demons from the deepest pits of hell . . . waiting . . .

These two youngsters, *Dedani* and *Baningi*, are no longer human; they are not normal animals. They are insane beasts from the cesspools of the Underworld. Ten days ago they had their last bite of food. Their mother sacrificed their baby brother, *Velapi*. They have not eaten since . . .

And now *Dedani* and *Baningi* are waiting for their mother to die so that they can eat again. But *Dedani's* patience is suddenly drowned in a frenzy of madness. Summoning all his strength he reaches for his long dead father's battle axe . . .

* * *

For many days after this, *Dedani* and *Baningi* had food on hand, and they slowly regained their strength in a region entirely depopulated by the famine.

Nearly a month later they left the kraal and ventured out into an environment ruled by vultures in the day and by hyaenas in the night. For days they walked, sleeping in caves or treetops. One day they passed a kraal perched on a grassy hilltop and were spotted by a tall skeletal man who stood at the gate. His starvation-dimmed eyes widened as he saw the two youngsters, and his mind spoke through his cracked lips the one word 'Food!'

Three naked and emaciated women crawled out of one hut when they heard this magic word. They saw their husband stagger out of the kraal after something that was apparently edible, and they felt strength – strength born of despair – flood their wasted bodies. They must help their husband. The four moving skeletons ran down the bush-dotted hillside towards the two children – fourteen-year-old *Dedani* and his sister *Baningi* of twelve summers. The two youngsters saw what was coming their way, and they took to their heels.

With his longer legs the tall man closed in on *Dedani*. But he stooped, picked up a stone and hurled it straight and true at *Dedani's* head. The boy went down screaming while his sister streaked away for the shelter of the distant forest. *Dedani* tried to struggle to his feet. But the man and his shrivelled wives threw themselves on him . . .

Baningi ran on and on, running until she could run no more. The sun was setting when she stumbled over a fallen tree and crashed headlong into a pit barely covered by the grass growing over it.

She remained in the pit until the following day. Towards midday she heard the shuffling of many feet in the grass above, a murmur of many listless voices. A group of ten boys was hunting tiredly through the forest for something to eat. A dead animal they thought would do, even a dead man.

Baningi did not know this and she made the last mistake of her life. She cried out for help. They *did* help her out but they brushed aside her whispered thanks. A little while later a brisk fire was burning . . .

Those were strange days in the history of the land – those days of the Great Famine. The Lunda tribe, which held a vast empire in the west, consumed their Emperor, all his wives and *Indunas*. Men ate their wives and children ate their parents. Lovers no longer took each other to the love mat, but to the meat tray.

Men fought with vultures and hyaenas for carcases of oxen many days dead. Whole families settled around such carcases eating away like mad – assuring all and sundry that they were eating the meat and what crawled inside, not the smell from it.

People now realised why I had built my huge granaries, and they began to praise me where they had insulted me before. I was no longer the mad Wizard; I was transformed into *Lumukanda* the Father of the People.

Starving thousands from as far as the land of the Lunda in the west, the Nyanja and Kikuyu in the north and the Lukondi in the east (those that the slave-raiders overlooked), converged on the land of the Mambo and Nguni where they had heard that a Great Father named *Lumukanda* had corn and dried locusts with which to feed them. I heavily reinforced the regiments guarding the granaries. I sent out other units to hunt elephant and buffalo, and even rhinoceros. I sent out warriors to fish. And for six whole moons I fed the gods alone know how many thousands of mouths besides those of my own people.

People had become too weak to hunt for themselves. Many just lay down and died. There was death everywhere, in spite of the provision we made, and the cruel drought showed no signs of abating.

The Great Famine killed more people than the Great Death and it caused more misery to the Tribes than anything that had ever happened before or was to happen afterwards. I made my wives and concubines work day and night stewing locusts and sorghums for the hungry thousands who clamoured daily for food outside the gates of my kraal. They begged in ten different tongues: 'Give us food, Oh Great Father *Lumukanda*!'

I gave it to them – I gave bowls of steaming sorghum and meat broth to those naked, pathetic scarecrows – men wasted into shrivelled skeletons covered with taut skins; women once creatures of beauty turned into desiccated nightmares, nursing babies at their empty breasts – babies which looked like skinned dried hares. I gave them food and they ate like the starving animals they were; they ate and licked the bowls clean, and not a few devoured the gourd bowls.

One of my two thousand wives was eaten by a mob of Nguni starvelings for whom she was dishing out food. They ate her, all the food in the pots and the giant wooden stirring spoons as well. I was greatly annoyed by this – she was quite a lovely little wife – and for two days I closed down the food distribution in my ten kraals and told the clamouring multitudes outside my kraal to go and milk a zebra, or jump in the Zambezi and drown themselves.

And this they did. The strength of my voodoo personality combined with their diminished mental faculties induced more than eight thousand of them actually to jump in the Zambezi and drown themselves. I was bitterly sorry for what I had said to them. On the following morning I re-opened the food distributing, and this time my wives and concubines were guarded by heavily armed warriors to avoid further accidents.

Some months later a band of hunger-maddened Lunda tribesmen got themselves killed trying to raid one of my granaries, and before my warriors could bury them a band of mixed Nguni and Nyanja descended upon them and left only their bones to bleach in the sun.

The Great Famine raged for one whole year and eight moons, and the food in my granaries sank lower and lower. Then at last we decided to do something about it. It was already early summer, and rainless, and the land was not green, but a dead, brittle brown. The tall trees stood leafless and naked in the blistering heat and the ground underfoot was as hot as a spear heated in a forge. No birds sang in the silent forests; there was death under every bush. Here and there in the long grass piles of bones lay bleaching whitely in the dazzling sunlight – bones of whole herds of zebra, impala and other wild animals that had perished from hunger in the forests.

Along a faint and long-disused footpath there came a man and three women. The man was huge and his shoulders were round and stooped, while he walked as if all the cares in the world were resting upon them. His hair and beard were a mixture of grey and black and his eyes deepset under a wide and care-lined forehead. He wore no ornaments and his loinskin was of cheetah skin trimmed with black sable antelope – the loinskin of a High Chief.

The woman immediately behind him was a tall, wide-shouldered and broad-hipped giantess whose skin was as black as polished ebony and whose fiercely out-thrust breasts seemed to cry defiance at eternity. Her beauty was a beauty which was not of this earth and the perfection of her figure did not speak of a cruel world. She was a creature who belonged to the plains of the Forever Land, where only High Gods dwell in places of pure crystal.

She walked with the assurance of a female who is over-conscious of her beauty.

The second woman looked more human, but still in an intensely beautiful way. She was human – and yet, somehow she was not quite human. She reflected the smouldering beauty of a midsummer moon. Her skin was a rich golden brown and her eyes were so dark brown as to be almost black. Her face was beautiful in a soft, delicate way that made her look like a fragile toy of exquisite workmanship. The perfection of her physique was that of the tribal ideal; it was the beauty which tribal elders dream about but rarely see in this world.

The third woman was, unlike the first two, of medium height and while the first two were obviously Bantu, she stood out conspicuously as a foreigner. It was easy to recognise that she was a half-caste – a daughter of Bantu-Arabi parentage. Her skin was very light and her hair fuzzy and soft, with a glossy sheen to it. Her round forehead and full-lipped mouth were her only Bantu features; her straight thin nose and high arching eyebrows were her most alien characteristics. The beauty of her face was the beauty of a very earthly harlot and she walked with a gait aimed at attracting men.

All three women were dressed alike in black calfskin skirts reaching to just below the knees and decorated with cowrie shells and large copper beads. Such skirts are worn only by the High Wives of a High Chief.

These four people were myself, *Lumukanda*, and my three wives *Vuramuinda, Noliyanda* and *Lulama-Maneruana*. We were on our way to the Madlonti mountains to ask the Highest of the Most High to save the Tribes from death by starvation.

We are now on the highest summit in the timeless Madlonti range and I look down on a devastated land. Down there in those brown, lifeless plains and ravished forests, thousands of men, women and children are dying. Tens of thousands of cattle are dead and no young are being born to men or to beasts. The Land of the Tribes, from as far north as the Masai to as far south as the Mashona, is in the grip of death. The cruel gods have turned their backs on mankind and are slowly but surely bringing about the extinction of the descendants of *Odu* and *Amarava*.

We kneel down on the hard rock. We bow our heads low and our souls reach out beyond the farthest frontiers of Eternity – to the presence of the Highest of the Most High who sees all and knows all.

'Your mercy, Oh God!' whispers *Vuramuinda*. 'Your mercy, Oh Highest of the Most High.'

And the ringing silver voice of *Noliyanda* strikes up with the Song of the Supplicant:

Lord of the Eternal Land,
Father of the Stream of Time—
Thou in whose almighty Hands
Rests the future of all mankind.

Thou upon whose Mighty Hands,
Our lives' paths are clearly traced;
Father of all the Ages—
Hear us now – we pray to Thee.

From the cruelty of *Ninavanhu-Ma*,
From the dreaded arrows of *Shimbi*,
From the bolts of *Duma-Kude*,
And the wolves of *Nomkubulwana*—
Shield, Oh God, the human race
From the claws of darkest plague—
From the jaws of hunger-death,
From the evil eyes of *Kufa*,
And *Ka-Lunga's* grasping hands,
Lord of all the far-off stars,
Save – Oh save the Human Race.

Lo! on earth the dark vile demons,
Make a mockery of Thy name;
Lo! the gods that know no mercy,
Dare to harm Thy helpless souls.

From the cruelty of *Ninavanhu-Ma*,
From the bolts of *Duma-Kude*,
From the keen arrows of *Shimbi*—
Save, oh save the sons of men!

We all concentrate our minds, giving God a clear picture of what we have come to lay before Him. I imagine rain falling on the parched country – great and extensive showers bringing relief to the devastated land. In her mind, *Vuramuinda* has a clear picture of corn growing, trees turning green and cattle grazing in lush pastures. *Noliyanda* imagines people of many tribes eating – happy children playing near baskets overloaded with corn. She imagines peace, plenty and happiness all over the land.

Our mind pictures and unspoken prayers float up like lost feathers to the Feet of the Highest of the Most High. He sees them and accepts them. And then it is as though we hear His Voice:

'My lost children, your prayers are granted. Even today rain will fall over the whole land, and it will carry on for five days. There shall be plenty of food in the land once again. But listen carefully: I command you to take the Mambo and the Nguni tribes, and all the other tribes now in your land, and go to the south. Go beyond the Limpopoma. This is not, as you believe, the southern frontier of the earth. You must spread, multiply and grow strong, to meet what lies ahead. This will be a perilous journey, the greatest and longest of all time. This journey will be full of woes and surprises. Leave as soon as your people have recovered their strength.'

For a long time we remained kneeling on the windswept mountain top, tears of gratitude streaming down our cheeks and a pleasure most profound pulsing through our hearts. Our people were saved – our land was saved.

Far away in the south-east a cloud appeared above the dim horizon. Another and yet another – a whole regiment of rain-pregnant clouds soon gathered in the distant skies and some time later we heard the rumble of thunder. The land was saved.

Slowly the frowning clouds crept across the skies and came overhead, shielding the sun. The earth breathed a sigh of relief. As we made our way down the mountainside the sky grew darker and soon it turned so black that we feared the presence of *Kalunga*, the double-sexed god from hell. The hot wind died down and an expectant silence fell upon the earth.

There came a dazzling flash of forked lightning which briefly illuminated the mountainside with a purplish light and was quickly followed by a brazen peal of thunder that shook the earth under our feet. Flash followed flash, tearing the frowning skies apart. Peal after peal shook the mighty mountains. Great eagles left their nests among the crags and chased each other in dizzy circles high in the scowling heavens, revelling in the stormy turbulence.

'We might as well make ourselves at home here, my Lord,' said *Lulama-Maneruana* with a nervous smile, pointing to a cave shortly below us. 'I shall make a fire.'

'It is my duty as First Wife to make a fire for my husband,' said *Noliyanda* throatily. 'Remember that, you foreign harlot!'

'There is someone who would like to dispute that claim,' hissed *Vuramuinda* venomously. 'I am *Lumukanda's* First Wife, and remember that, you glorified puppet!'

'My sisters-in-marriage, I beg you, please. Respect the presence of our lord and husband. Go and brawl elsewhere.'

'Let them fight to their hearts' content, *Lulama*,' I said. 'The honour of making a fire for me falls into your hands.'

'Thank you, my Lord – your handmaiden is honoured.'

Quickly *Lulama* built and lit a roaring fire in the cave, warming and lighting the interior. *Vuramuinda* and *Noliyanda* stopped their fighting and both came to sit near the fire with eyes downcast.

Some time later there was movement in the mouth of the cave and a low, husky voice said: 'Neither of you is this man's First Wife; it happens to be my privilege.'

We turned and stared with widening eyes at the apparition that stood tall and beautiful in the entrance of the cave. I recognised her in spite of her efforts to shield her identity behind a large black *kaross*, and I sensed an expression of incredible dejection on her face. There was a terrible flash of lightning, and I remembered no more . . .

O irreki hamaresi –
E, anazueru!
Thaite marhevi anakeberu!
Ouzarauena ahité Bakeri –
Thaite areri amakharabethi
O, yrreck hamaresi i ana Zueru!

The strange song – the 'Song of the Gods' in spirit language – rang through my brain again and again as I slowly opened my eyes. Who was I? What was I doing lying on my back between two rocks? Above me the sun was shining and a few clouds were drifting in the blue skies yonder. The ground was wet as though it had rained during the night.

Suddenly a girl emerged from behind one of the two great rocks between which I was lying. She was an alien-looking girl about twenty years old, with a very light, reddish-yellow skin and a shock of fuzzy hair with a glossy sheen in it. She was wearing a skirt made of green leaves and there was a frightened look in her dark eyes. She stood for a few moments looking down at me and then her hand went to her mouth to stifle an involuntary cry:

'*Lumukanda*, my Lord!' she cried at last. 'So . . . so it has happened to you too!'

'*Lumukanda*?' I asked. 'Who is *Lumukanda*?'

The girl's eyes widened and she came nearer and knelt on one knee beside me. 'You are *Lumukanda*, my Lord. That . . . that is your name. I am *Lulama-Maneruana*, but both of us . . . have changed. I can hardly believe it!'

'Young girl,' I asked, 'just what are you talking about? You say we have changed, and that you are called *Lulama-Maneruana*. To me you are a stranger . . . I have never seen you before.'

'Don't you remember me, my Lord? I am *Lulama*, your Royal concubine. We went up to the top of this mountain a moon ago, you, *Vuramuinda*, *Noliyanda* and myself. We went up there to pray for rain and rain came. We took shelter in a cave. And then that Goddess came . . .'

Even as she spoke, memory returned to me like the sun breaking through the clouds after a thunderstorm.

'You say we went up this mountain a moon ago? Do you mean I have been lying here for a moon?'

'More than a moon, my Lord. I have been looking for you for more than a moon now. But yesterday I saw you lying down here – this is the bottom of a precipice. But I did not know how to get down to rescue you. This morning I succeeded, and here I am.'

'I honour you, *Maneruana*. But why is it that you look much younger? Why, you are just a child!'

'My Lord, you would be even more surprised if you could see yourself. You have changed too, my Lord. You look like a boy of twenty-five.'

'What!' I cried, sitting up with a jerk.

'Yes, my Lord, had it not been for the moon-shaped birthmark above your left breast and for the star-shaped scar of immortality between your eyes I myself would not have known it was you.'

'What happened to us, *Maneruana*? And where are *Vuramuinda* and *Noliyanda*?'

'You will never see them again, my Lord. I do not know just what happened. But I have a very strong feeling that you will never see them again. A strange blinding light exploded in the cave. I was hurled outside and into a clump of thick *mfomfo* shrubs. When I regained consciousness a great fire, fantastically bright, was burning in the crater where the cave had been. Then, my Lord, I saw a dark figure rising slowly out of the flames: it was the figure of a woman. This figure rose higher and higher and I saw sparks flying off her body as she floated out. Afterwards she went to sit on a stone – for a long time. Dawn came and she was still sitting there, and I was still hiding in the clump of bushes. And, my Lord, as the sun rose she also stood up. But I have never seen a creature so beautiful. She was like *Vuramuinda, Noliyanda* and the goddess *Ma* combined. My Lord, she came straight to where I was lying, as if she had known all along that I was there; she stood over me in all her naked beauty. She looked down at me and said: "Tell *Lumukanda* when you find him that *Ma-Ouzarauena* awaits his pleasure in the Royal Kraal". My Lord, I was terrified. Her eyes looked upon me with a cold pity and seemed to be alive with all the forbidden knowledge of the Universe.'

'Where is she now?'

'She is in the Great Kraal, my Lord; she is ruling the Mambo and she has had your grain fields ploughed and corn sown. Soon there shall be plenty of food under the good rains of the past moon. She told the people that you had gone to the Land of the Gods to drink from the fountain of youth and that she, your new Goddess Queen, would rule the Mambo until you came back.'

'I honour you, *Maneruana*. I honour you again and yet again.'

The warriors are very angry; to them I am the biggest liar in all creation. They believe so and they say as much. 'You beggardly knave, you are not the Lost Immortal. For the last time, tell us the truth: what do you want here?'

'I am telling you lame-brained sons of dogs that I am *Lumukanda*, the chief of this kraal!'

Once again the Battle Leader *Mandla* draws back his powerful arm and plants a heavy fist on my nose. 'If you said you were a flying elephant we would believe you, pretty boy!' he snarls viciously. 'Try another lie; this one you persist in telling is now tarnished. What do you want here?'

'Listen to me, you son of a hyaena – if you do not believe I am *Lumukanda*, then go and call someone who will recognise me. Call one of the Rainbow *Indunas*.'

A tall girl with one hand missing comes striding along the path between the huts. It is my eldest daughter, *Luanaledi*, and *Mandla* bows low before saying, 'Great Princess, we have here a mad youth who claims he is your father. He has persisted in this, in spite of the thrashing we have given him.'

Luanaledi's cold dark eyes sweep me from head to foot. She extends her long-fingered, right hand and touches the scar between my eyes. And slowly she says: 'Do not lie to me, young man, you are no more my father than I am a crocodile's cousin.'

'Do not be a fool girl – I am your father, *Lumukanda*.'

'I have known my dear father for countless years, and you are not he. Take this beggar away and imprison him in a hut until *Ma-Ouzarauena* comes back in a few days' time.'

For three whole days they held me prisoner in an empty hut in my own Great Kraal. Then, on the night of the fourth day, I had a visitor who crept stealthily into the hut and quickly closed the wickerwork door.

'Who are you?' I demanded.

'It is I, the Princess *Luanaledi*,' answered the visitor.

'Do you now believe that I am your father?'

'There is no need to keep up this deception, strange one,' she replied. 'I do not believe you and nobody in this kraal believes you. I have come to help you escape, beloved one.'

It is midnight and in the ebony skies the stars shine like so many lost sunstones. The great constellations stand out against the starry tumult – the Three Healers, the Virgin's Fire and the Stars of Planting are directly overhead. The River of Stars spans the heavens from horizon to horizon – cold, glittering, utterly remote.

'I do not believe you,' says *Luanaledi* for the fiftieth time.

I see the tears that flow down her cheeks. I hear her heartrending sobbing.

Beside me I hear a shuddering sigh burst from the reddish lips of

Maneruana. Far down the ancient mountain in the night-shrouded forests a hyaena laughs hideously.

Lulama-Maneruana leans forward and addresses the girl beyond the dancing fire. On the walls of the cave time-dimmed figures of men and beasts drawn by Bushmen, stand out against the grey granite. 'Princess *Luanaledi*, you simply must believe us. This is your father and I am his Royal concubine, *Lulama-Maneruana.*'

The one-handed girl beyond the fire shakes her head violently. She leaps to her feet, her eyes blazing. She tears off her 'virgin's *mutsha*' and flings it savagely at my feet. Her light-brown face is black with rage. 'You keep on telling me you are *Lumukanda*, my father. You are not! All you want is to deny yourself to me, knowing fully that I love you. You want to break my heart and I can assure you, you will not! As an immortal I can will myself to death if I so wish. And if you do not promise me here and now to take me as your wife, stranger, I shall will myself to death – and you will have a lot to explain to the Rainbow *Indunas* when they find my body here. I give you twenty heartbeats in which to make up your mind, stranger.'

'Give me more than that,' I plead. 'Give me six moons in which to think it over. Do not destroy yourself.'

'Good, I give you exactly six moons. The daughter of *Lumukanda* can afford to wait. Give me your word that you will not try to run away in the meantime . . .'

'You can see the star of immortality on my forehead, *Luanaledi.* I swear by it that I shall not run away. I give you my word as one immortal to another.'

'I accept your word, beloved. Now stop calling yourself *Lumukanda.* I shall call you *Lishati-Shumba*, the Lion of the Sun. That is the name I give you, handsome youth.'

Lulama-Maneruana begins to cry . . .

We are back in the Great Kraal. We have been tracked down and captured. We are kneeling outside the Royal Hut, surrounded by scowling Rainbow *Indunas.* We are waiting for the great *Ma-Ouzarauena* to appear.

Above us the sun lags on towards midday. I am waiting with great impatience for *Ma-Ouzarauena* to convince the people that I am their High Chief *Lumukanda.* She is my only salvation now. I can hardly wait to meet her.

The Rainbow *Indunas* fall flat on their faces as *Ma-Ouzarauena* emerges from her hut. The warriors also prostrate themselves before the Goddess Queen's dread presence.

She is beautiful – yet she is terrible to behold. She looks like the silvery Goddess *Ninavanhu-Ma* – and yet she is not *Ma*. She looks like *Vuramuinda*, and like *Noliyanda*, and yet she is neither . . .

The awful thought strikes me with a thundering blow. This – this frightening immortal – is in fact a combination of all three. She is all three immortals fused into one. Could it be that this one being now combines the powers of all three?

Ma-Ouzarauena asks coldly: 'Is this the boy who claims to be *Lumukanda*?'

'It is, Oh Great One,' says Rainbow *Induna Nsongololo*. 'The young one must be mad.'

'Shall we execute the . . . son of a hyaena, Great Queen,' asks *Mavimbela*.

'No,' she replies. 'I want both him and the girl who claims to be *Lulama-Maneruana* whipped soundly and then made to work in my hut. I want them to be my slaves.'

She turns away and I can swear there is a cruel smile on her face.

We are dragged away and tied to posts. They whip us in spite of protests from my daughters, *Luanaledi* and *Mbaliyamswira* – who still do not believe I am their father.

Lulama-Maneruana is whipped into unconsciousness. They release her and revive her with cold water. I am also released and we are both told to report to the Royal Hut for duties.

While we are busy sweeping *Ma-Ouzarauena's* hut she crawls into the small entrance and faces me with hands on her hips, and a smile on her face. 'I see you, *Lumukanda* . . . how do you enjoy being a slave?'

'Why are you doing this to us?' asks *Lulama-Maneruana*. 'You alone know who we are. The other people do not believe us. What do you hope to gain by making us suffer?'

'Revenge . . . the sweetest thing in creation!' laughs *Ouzarauena*. 'I am enjoying my revenge on *Lumukanda*. Inside this body are three separate souls. But you can look upon me as the Goddess *Ninavanhu-Ma* because my soul exercises control over those of *Vuramuinda* and *Noliyanda*. And I do not have to remind you, poor half-caste, that *Lumukanda* humiliated me; he rejected me who gave him immortality more than two thousand years ago. He dared to scorn me, his real First Wife. I shall reinstate you on one condition, *Lumukanda*, and enlighten those love-struck daughters of yours.'

'What is that condition?'

'Take me back as your First Wife.'

'You can go and milk a moth-eaten, flea-infested zebra. I do not want you, no matter in what guise.'

'I shall make you suffer, Oh *Lumukanda.* I shall make you regret your attitude towards me.'

'Go on, do your worst; I am not afraid.'

The moons rolled by and soon it was harvest time. Thousands of women went out into the great cornfields with *pangas* and flails. The Great Famine was now something of the past, like its predecessor the Great Death, and the time for the long journey south was drawing nigh. *Lulama-Maneruana* and I were still slaves; we were beaten up, sworn at and we worked from dawn to dusk in the hut of *Ma-Ouzarauena.*

My greatest task now was to keep avoiding *Luanaledi* who was still pressing me to elope with her. I had to play for time. I must fulfil my mission to lead the tribes beyond the Zambezi and the Limpopoma, as commanded by the Great Spirit. I must first do this and settle my personal problems afterwards.

Celiwe of the Nguni, *Mxhosa* of the Amaxhosa and *Ma-Ouzarauena* of the Mambo sent messengers to all parts of the lands which they ruled. The messages were curt and to the point – every man, woman and child was to assemble on the northern bank of the Zambezi river as soon as harvesting had been completed.

Every man must bring his family, cattle and goats, and all the grain from his fields to the 'place of assembly'. But people do not just pack their belongings and burn their kraals when they leave the land they have inhabited for generations. The moving of a nation, a tribe, even a clan, must be accomplished in accordance with the law. Each family must dig up its burial grounds and exhume as many of the ancestors' skulls as possible. These skulls must be packed in large grass baskets and reburied in the land where that family or clan settles with full rituals of burial. Those who cannot find remains in the graves of their ancestors must scoop up some of the earth and pack that in the baskets. This is important because the people must not lose their contact with their ancestors. In their distant places of abode their ancestors must continue to keep an eye on them and guide them.

Any tribe that fails to take its ancestors' skulls to a new land is cursed forever and might as well commit mass suicide, or disperse and be absorbed by other tribes. This is the most shameful thing to happen to any tribe.

No chief, no matter how tyrannical, will ever force a tribe to move without first letting the people exhume their ancestors. A ruler who fails to comply with this requirement is declared an outlaw and killing him becomes a matter of honour to any man who might get the opportunity.

Many were the 'dances of farewell'; many were the sacrifices; many were the 'ceremonies of departure' performed in the valleys and among the hills. There were tears, there was doubt and fear; the Journey to *Asazi*, the journey to 'we know not where', was about to begin.

The people and their cattle have assembled in their millions. The land is a seething black mass of humanity and domesticated animals for as far as the eye can see, stretching over hills and vales beyond the horizon in all directions. A tall, beautiful woman is standing on the very summit of a high hill overlooking the plains of assembly. In one hand she holds a great horn bugle and this she raises to her lips and blows with all her might. Thus *Ma-Ouzarauena* signals the start of the greatest exodus the world has ever known. Hardly have the moaning notes of the great horn bugle vanished into the misty distance when the great masses of people and animals start moving slowly westward to a section of the Zambezi where that mighty river narrows as it flows through a gorge, known hereafter as the Sacred Gorge of Kariba, to become famous in song and legend as the holiest place under the sun.

Ma-Ouzarauena slowly makes her way down the hillside to where *Lulama-Maneruana* and I are standing. 'Attend me, slaves!' she commands coldly as we follow her. The Journey to *Asazi* has begun.

GANDAYA THE ELEPHANT

It was fast approaching midday and *Ilanga*, the God of Day, shone brightly from a pale sky on whose expanse not a single cloud was to be seen. A perfumed breeze caressed the verdant earth, making warm and pleasant a day which would otherwise have been unbearably hot. The same whispering breeze touched the great pool in the bosom of the murmuring forest, raising tiny ripples on its cool, greenish-blue surface. On the edge of this great, reed-bordered pool a vast herd of zebra and impala gambolled and drank, watched over by a huge wildebeest.

The wildebeest was old, a scarred veteran of many a savage battle. The tip of one of his forward-curving horns had been broken off quite recently in the only battle that the old bull had lost to a younger bull, in his hoary twenty years of earthly life. A composite feeling – partly anger and partly injured pride – flooded old One Horn as he remembered the battle of a month ago, the battle which resulted in his being expelled in disgrace from his place at the head of his herd – driven away by one of his own sons.

A tremor ran along his powerful flanks and a mist of sorrow crept into his eyes. His vision, already blurred by age, grew dimmer. An itchy feeling in his eyes caused him to blink angrily and to twitch his tail irritably.

'Such is life,' thought old One Horn. 'The one son you love is the one that overthrows you in the end . . .' Old One Horn turned and swept the mixed zebra-impala herds with his brownish-red, fatherly eyes. He saw the strutting impala rams with heads held high and graceful spiralling horns shining like polished ebony in the sunlight. He saw the shy impala does, with their dark, innocent eyes and their shiny, reddish-brown, fawn and white coats that were a shade lighter than those of the rams.

He saw the fat, seemingly clumsy, yet fleet-footed, zebras with their many stripes and dark-brown noses; the males, females and frolicking foals which gambolled about their mothers in the long grass.

'Life,' thought old One Horn, 'is a beautiful and amazing thing, sometimes at least. There are times, however . . .'

Suddenly an unpleasantly familiar odour assailed his quivering nostrils. There was no mistaking the evil, acrid stench of these hated carnivores. Suddenly the forest held no beauty for the old warrior. He tossed his massive head as though to shake off the skulking, clawing nightmare and the zebra patriarch saw the signal. He let out the warning call that the murmuring forests know so well. This call means 'lion' in both zebra and impala language, and with incredible speed and grace, the animal herds erupted into motion. There was a drumming roar from more than a thousand zebra hooves. Dust rose in clouds of billowing disorder among the flat-topped *munga* trees, and the fleet impalas shot like arrows into the safety of the dense forests.

Old One Horn saw two lionesses burst forth from the bush and bring down a beautiful striped female which had a foal running beside it. One lioness sank her teeth into the zebra's nose, depriving it of breath, while the other leapt on to its back. The orphaned foal raced away and was lost in the billowing dust.

A huge maned lion, with one eye clawed out in a fierce battle some time earlier, brought down a zebra running just ahead of old One Horn. The thundering herds had dashed into a cleverly laid lion trap and they now veered away with old One Horn in the lead – away from the scene of the ambush. But the lions had not finished yet. A young lion made the mistake of trying to leap upon a racing zebra from behind. There was a vicious snarl on his face and his eyes were narrowed into points of blazing yellow malevolence. He leapt, yes, but the zebra lashed out with both hind legs, and hit him in mid-air. Old One Horn heard a loud cracking thud and saw the golden lion go sailing to one side with his lower jaw smashed to a bloody pulp.

A huge lioness exploded from behind a bush with a blood-chilling snarl straight at the head of the racing old wildebeest. Old One Horn crashed into her and his one remaining horn sank full into her chest, knocking her back into the spot from where she had sprung. Before she could recover she was stampeded into a pulp by the whole herd of zebras.

Old One Horn led the zebra herd towards the Zambezi at a devastating dust-shrouded gallop and they halted only when they reached the dense, impassable forests bordering the river. They stopped to graze once more, and to rub their itchy hides against the rough tree trunks with contented snorts. For old One Horn and his friends life turned beautiful once more.

Then there came a crashing, splintering sound from the forest and each zebra jerked up its head, ready to turn and run once again. The cracking sound of breaking trees and shattering branches came to old One Horn's ears and finally the largest elephant that ever walked the earth crashed into view on its way to the river.

Old One Horn had seen this terrible monarch of the wilds many times, and so had his father and father's father. This dreaded dweller in the gorge was Gandaya the Trampler who guarded not only the vast herds of elephants in the Kariba Gorge, but, if legend could be right – which it often is – also a 'Shining One' named *Luamerava* the Pure. This apparition was known throughout the land of the tribes by name, but had never been seen. *Luamerava* was said to be the last of the Children of the Star whom the Holy Legends say were born from that Lost Star which shone at midday. Chiefs from as far away as the land of the Ba-Kongo had tried in vain for thousands of years to penetrate the Gorge of the Virgin (Kariba) to capture *Luamerava*, because it was said that the chief who caught the Desire of Kariba would not only live to the end of time, but would rule the very stars when that great event called the 'Transformation of Humanity' came in some thousands of years in the future.

Many great chiefs had perished trying to secure this legendary female – amongst them *Lubo*, who had founded the Lunda nation more than a thousand years previously.

Many doubted the very existence of *Luamerava* and contemptuously called her the Illusion of Kariba. The elephant Gandaya was said to be one of *Luamerava's* guards, among whom there were also the tailless Star Lion and the Black Python.

Gandaya reached the Zambezi almost at the same time as a large herd of normal elephants. It was not long before the great river, which had been sparkling in the midday sun, was reduced to a muddy yellow by the wallowing of the fifty clumsy brutes. Gandaya bathed all by himself in aloof dignity – a huge, dark-grey monster reputed to be four times the size of an ordinary big bull elephant.

Gandaya had a white star-shaped scar on his broad, wrinkled forehead and in one of his hind legs was buried an old rusty spearhead which a slave-raiding Arabi had driven into it more than fifty years earlier. It still gave the colossal beast much pain and made him hate all human beings with a hatred that was all-devouring. The faintest scent of humanity was enough to send Gandaya into a murderous frenzy. His great forelegs had trampled many men to death since he was wounded, but he wanted to kill more – many more.

An elephant's memory is as long as the Path of Life itself. Its invincible anger lasts for a hundred years at least, but Gandaya's anger had lasted for more than three hundred years and it was bound to last till the end of Eternity, for Gandaya was a beast of the Immortals and it knew no age.

Whenever he was alone, grazing far away from his herd as he was doing now, the Spirit of Anger would rise high in his mind and the red mist of fury would dim his fierce eyes. He would explode into destructive actions, venting his wild spleen against the innocent trees. He would push the highest *mopanis* over and uproot the spreading *mungas*, trampling them to splinters.

He was at it now, and his wrath was terrible. Trees were forcibly parted from the sandy bosom of Mother Earth and they crackled and roared as they plunged. The dying cries of the tall *masasas* were heard in the splintering of their brittle branches as they succumbed to the wrath of the great *Indlovu.* Dust and disinherited grass flew high from under the trampling and shuffling feet of Gandaya and his wild, savage trumpeting shook the forests of Kariba Gorge. The frightened birds trembled and left their homes in clouds of twittering terror, seeking security in the blue heavens.

At last he paused in his task of destruction and with this pause for breath he sent a wild and savage note of sheer elephantine pleasure ringing as a challenge through the sacred gorge.

It was then that an unpleasantly familiar – a most hated smell came drifting towards him, borne on the wings of the rustling breeze. It was the smell of that kind of animal that Gandaya hated more than any other smell under the sun . . . the acrid stench of human beings!

A red mist crept over Gandaya's eyes. His great feet itched to crush the hated little bipeds into slime – the slime from which they had crawled aeons ago. His long trunk burned to flail them into a bloody pulp and his great tusks longed to string them like beads.

Gandaya the Trampler thundered down the forest-veiled slope of the great gorge, leaving dust and fallen trees in his wake. He roared down to the river and plunged into it. The smell of human vermin grew stronger as he surged out of the river and up the other slope of the gorge.

He tore and smashed his way through the forest with fiery impatience. At last he ascended a small hill and scanned the distant plains. There they were. There were thousands of them – myriads of these puny, infernal little pests. This was the moment of glory. Trample the filthy vermin into the dust; crush the biped scum to a pulp!

Gandaya made his way down the grassy hill with gradually quickening pace.

There is open dissension among the Nguni, Mambo and Xhosa tribes. The people are openly rebelling against crossing the Zambezi at Kariba. Many cry out that they would rather die than enter that mysterious gorge populated, according to legend, by all kinds of monsters. Agitators for secession are exploiting the insubordination to the hilt, and one fat, shrill-voiced harridan named *Lokota* is the driving force behind all this rebellious sentiment: 'They dare not send us in there!' she screams to a large crowd who nod and hang on to her every word. 'They are asking you to hazard your lives and the lives of your children by going into that gorge. Thousands of chiefs and heroes have gone there and not one came back alive. Do not the Holy Legends say that in that gorge lives a witch named *Luamerava* who eats newborn babies and turns men into stone? You all know the Holy Legends . . . you know all about brave chiefs who took long journeys from their lands to that place over there . . . and were never seen again except in dreams. Who does *Celiwe* think we are – and *Xhosa* – and what does that vile witch *Ma-Ouzarauena* make of us – infernal, invincible, immortals like herself? I say we must all refuse to go into Kariba. We must sit down here and refuse to budge. What say you, Oh my brothers and sisters?'

The mob roared its approval and soon a full three-quarters of the Mambo, Nguni and Xhosa tribes were firmly behind *Lokota.* They made it quite plain that they were not going near – let alone into – the Kariba gorge. Many made ready to turn back.

The three High Ones – *Ma-Ouzarauena, Celiwe* and *Xhosa* – sent warriors to intercept these would-be deserters.

And then, just before sunset, the largest elephant that ever walked the earth tore into the milling, gesticulating, rebel tribesfolk with the fury of an avalanche. He trampled a path of death through them and soon the people saw the limp body of a beautiful dark-skinned woman impaled on one of its gleaming tusks. The woman was *Muwende-Lutanana*, the mother of my two sons, *Demane* and *Demazana*!

I fought my way through the milling, panic-stricken masses. My soul was seized with a devastating anger. I stumbled over mangled bodies but did not care. I made straight for that thundering, charging brute, and when he saw me he accelerated his pace. I concentrated all my mental power straight at the oncoming beast and a force struck the tusk on which my wife was impaled, shearing it off at the root. With a searing, trumpeting scream of shock, fear and pain, the mighty Gandaya reared on his hind legs. He sagged to the ground for a moment, but rose again and fled with pathetic, heart-rending shouts of despair.

It was not the wild trumpeting of a brute wounded in an act of aggression. It was an appeal for help from a loyal animal, in the service of someone or something it fears, loves and reveres. It dawned on me that it could be true that Gandaya was more than just a murderous brute with an abnormal hatred of humanity. Gandaya was a loyal guardian belonging to somebody who wanted to remain hidden and unknown.

I was seized with a strange feeling of remorse and pity for the huge animal and for having used my supernatural powers of destruction on it – something I save only for hostile gods and immortals. I decided to follow Gandaya. But he sensed my pursuit and tried his best to shake me off. This continued till the sun sank in the golden west and darkness crept across the forest-veiled land.

The sound of footsteps behind me brought me to a halt and soon my two daughters *Luanaledi* and *Mbaliyamswira* stood by my side. 'We have come to call you back, father,' said *Mbaliyamswira*.

'So at last you believe that I am your father!'

'Yes,' replied *Luanaledi*. 'The Queen *Ma-Ouzarauena* has told us and all the people the truth at last. The Mambo and Nguni warriors mutinied just after we saw you chasing the elephant. With *Celiwe* leading them, the Nguni warriors surrounded *Ma-Ouzarauena* and demanded that she tell them where you went on that night when she made her appearance for the first time. They told her that they would enter the Kariba Gorge only under the leadership of their Great *Lumukanda*, the mighty lost Immortal. She then told us that you had gone and drunk from the fountain of youth – as she had hinted before.'

'Come back with us, Oh father, and speak to the people,' *Mbaliyamswira* pleaded. 'You alone can persuade them. They are all in a mutinous mood now.'

We made our way back to where the countless thousands of people were occupied in building temporary shelters for the night and lighting a huge circle of fires to keep wild animals away. Many were also busy digging graves for those killed by the elephant.

It is past midnight and I have just won a great victory after having almost talked my head off my shoulders. They cheered me enthusiastically when I promised them I would go into the gorge first and make short work of any monsters, witches, demons and hostile gods that might be residing there. Before launching into what has been the longest speech of my life I had ordered the arrest of the fat agitator *Lokota*.

'Thank you, my people,' I smiled at them benignly. 'That is very good. I am sure your glorious ancestors are now greatly pleased. Forward at all times – that is what your forefathers believed in and that is what you must also believe in. We must advance in the name of the Highest of the Most High, and woe betide anyone or anything standing in our way! The survival of the Tribes – the safety of your children as yet unborn – depends on our reaching the mysterious land beyond the Limpopoma. Some of you have been urging others to go back. Do you want to remain in a land now crawling with Arabi slave-raiders? Do you wish to return to the land in which you were nearly wiped out, first by pestilence and then by famine? Have you so soon forgotten the dark, leering spectres of death and destruction?'

'*Aieeee!*' roared the people, 'No . . . no, we have not forgotten!'

'Do you promise that you will follow me, who saved you from famine, from death, without questioning how I will lead you and where I will take you?'

'Yes . . . Yes!' they roar. 'You and you alone we shall follow, Oh Great Father *Lumukanda*.'

'*Lumukanda* of the Granaries – Saviour of the People,' they shout again and again. 'We remember the granaries of *Lumukanda!*'

I turn away, followed by resounding cheers from the throats of more than five million people. Everybody is now happy and everybody is determined to go with me to the very edge of the world if need be – I can feel it in my bones.

Flames of elation burn fiercely within my heart. I am going to succeed in my God-appointed task after all. I am going to lead the tribes to and beyond the Limpopoma. I am once again *Lumukanda* the High Chief – the leader of the Tribes. My *Indunas* and my wives will take some time to get over the shock of my changed appearance.

I am determined to go into Kariba directly to prove for all time the truth or otherwise of the legends that say the place is inhabited by all manner of monsters and witches. Somehow I have a strange feeling that the legends are not far off the truth.

A dark figure bars my way as I walk slowly towards where my wives and daughters have just laid *Muwende-Lutanana* to rest, with the great tusk to mark the solitary grave.

'I beg to talk to you, my Lord,' says *Ma-Ouzarauena*.

'I have no time to talk to you or anybody else now. Just do me one favour, I beg you . . .'

'Anything you say, my Lord.'

'Go and lose yourself in the forest.' I brush past her and kneel at the grave of my unhappy *Muwende*. 'Farewell *Muwende*, farewell child. You probably know by now that you have not died in vain. We shall cross the Zambezi at Kariba and the Tribes will always remember your name. Farewell, my unhappy *Muwende*.'

I rise to my feet and without another glance at the silent, torch-carrying women standing around the grave I turn and make my way through the night towards Kariba.

Luanaledi suddenly emerges from the darkness and falls into step behind me. She has brought my huge *panga* and heavy, wooden club – and she carries a spear as well.

We walk in silence while around us crickets chirp their joy to the night-sky.

At last we reach the deep gorge of mystery. Far below us we see the Zambezi clearly outlined in the moonlight. 'Be on your guard, dear parent,' says *Luanaledi* huskily, 'I sense danger!'

The brooding gorge is strangely silent – like a foul, night-prowling beast ambushing its prey. Even the trees hold their rustling breath.

Then a booming voice charged with incredible insolence strikes up and echoes and re-echoes through the great gorge: 'Intruders, I sensed you enter this forbidden place and I now warn you – you have time to retrace your steps. Do so now. I, *Zaramatesi*, the Lord of Kariba, have spoken!'

'Father, let us go and find that impudent wizard!'

Even as she spoke a voodoo python appeared from nowhere and coiled itself around her. I stooped and wrung its neck before it could crush the breath from *Luanaledi*. As I flung aside its limp form, I came face to face with the ugliest ape-man that ever walked the earth. He introduced himself as *Odu*, a name that sounded vaguely familiar, and I induced this brute to lead us to his lord and master.

Thus we passed through a secret entrance into a vast underground cavern of dazzling beauty. There was a large bronze dwelling, ablaze with brilliant stones of all kinds and sizes, and pots and other vessels of fantastic metal workmanship. Huge mats of a soft fibrous material dyed into scores of colourful patterns adorned the highly polished smooth walls and floor. A tall figure stood on the far side of the dwelling, facing us with arrogantly folded arms. He wore an elaborately moulded and decorated ritual mask over his head – a mask made of silver so dazzlingly bright that it rivalled the moon. It had a pink fringe of what looked like very fine fibre. This tall man was covered from shoulders to feet in a glossy black *kaross* heavily decorated with sunstones and waterstones of all colours from green to bright red. On his powerful forearms blazed broad bracelets inlaid with flaming magic stones that glowed like smouldering embers.

I suddenly developed a surge of unreasonable murderous hatred towards that masked man. He became the target of all the hatred that my soul could brew. Through a mist of blinding anger I heard his voice saying coldly: 'Kneel, miserable mortals . . . kneel in my presence!'

'Miserable mortals indeed!' I retorted. 'I am *Lumukanda*, the Lost Immortal . . .'

The mention of my name seemed to strike him a profound physical blow. His arms unfolded and fell to his sides and he took a step forward. 'Who did you say you are?'

I lost control of myself and pounced upon him. The savage struggle that ensued was perhaps the strangest of all time. With every blow I dealt him I felt the pain in the corresponding part of my body, and it was evident that he also felt the pain of the blows he inflicted upon me. The struggle continued until both of us sank to the ground unconscious.

Finally a voice reached me across a great distance and I sensed relief in it. 'He moves – he is alive! Oh praise be to the Highest of the Most High!'

I opened my eyes and looked into the beautiful face of *Luanaledi* who promptly put her warm lips to my forehead. 'Thank the gods you are alive, father.'

I was lying on my back on one of the soft, brightly coloured mats inside the dwelling and there was a cool freshness all over my body. Someone had bathed me from head to foot while I was unconscious. Slowly I sat up and my eyes fell on a huge, beautifully decorated, bowl full of water. My eyes also fell on the strange female kneeling beside the large basin and I turned my head away, sick and nauseated to the core of my soul.

Such a creature as that strange woman, with her yellowish, brownish-red skin, should not be allowed to live in this universe. Such a strange revolting being – be it human or animal – simply cannot exist.

We all eat and enjoy sweet things – like honey and ripe plantains. We enjoy chewing sweet cane, and we know that even sweetness can be revolting if there is too much of it. The same applies to beauty – if carried beyond the limit of its extreme it can be more revolting than ugliness.

And the woman I saw kneeling beside the bowl was extremely beautiful – and utterly revolting in that there was too much of it. It may be difficult to believe, but ugliness, no matter how great, is a natural thing, and nature is only beauty. Mountains are ugly, yet profoundly beautiful in their utter ugliness. Ugliness is either utterly revolting or thoroughly amusing, but beauty-in-extreme, though fascinating, can also repel, and even disgust.

If the many chiefs who had lost their lives in search of the legendary *Luamerava*, the Illusion of Kariba, had known they were risking their lives for a creature whose very appearance would have sent them running in bewildered flight, they would not have ventured there in the first place. And they would have thanked the gods for the imperfection of their own wives. They would have left the creature alone to be admired by the stars, the mountains and the timeless Zambezi. She is an unnatural, forbidden creature that no man can possess and yet remain sane – a gaudy flower whose scent is spread by the breeze of heaven. I heard her voice as she spoke to *Luanaledi*:

'We might as well tell the Lord, your father, the truth, Oh Princess *Luanaledi*.'

'I would rather we waited a few moments,' my daughter replied. 'He looks tired and weak, and the shock might be too great.'

'As the Princess says,' murmured the Illusion of Kariba.

'What is it?' I demanded. 'What has happened?'

'Please rest, father, you are tired. Try to keep calm.'

'No, I insist that you tell me what has happened!'

'As the lord commands,' said the Illusion of Kariba from behind *Luanaledi*. 'Who are we to disobey him?'

She strode across towards the entrance of the dwelling. I rose to a sitting position and then I noticed the lifeless body of my adversary. *Luamerava* slowly removed the silver mask from the dead man's face.

I was immediately struck by the familiarity of the face. Somewhere I had seen this face before, and quite recently. But I could not immediately place it. Like me, he had a small star-shaped scar of immortality between his eyes. The vague familiarity began to disturb me and I said so to my daughter.

'It's you . . . father,' was her strange statement.

'Me? How can this man be me? You must be dreaming, *Luanaledi*.'

'It is you, father,' she insisted. 'A futuristic projection of yourself, say ten thousand years hence . . .'

'What nonsense are you talking about, girl. How can I be alive and dead at the same time?'

'Explain to him, *Luamerava*.'

'As you command, Princess. If the Lord, your father, will honour me by listening . . .'

'Speak . . . I hear you.'

'My Lord, for generations people of all tribes have known the gorge of Kariba as a holy and forbidden place, even though many do not know why it is so. They simply believe the very soil of Kariba is sacred, and that is as far as their knowledge goes. Kariba is not sacred simply because I have lived here for thousands of years; it is sacred because here is the navel of the earth. Here is the source and the mouth of the River Time. It is from here in Kariba that a new race of men and gods shall spring when the most Ultimate God creates a new earth and a new universe from the ashes of this one we see . . .'

'I know all about that,' I responded coldly. 'What I want to know is why my daughter refers to this dead body as mine.'

'Your forgiveness, Lord. You, *Lumukanda*, have been alive now for exactly two thousand years . . .'

'I know that.'

'And you are destined to live for another ten thousand years,' smiled the Illusion of Kariba, ignoring my interruption. 'In the course of your life you will see many things, fight many battles, and love women without number. But after nine thousand years of life the evil spirit of ambition and pride will possess you. You will venture out to conquer the whole earth, and the heavens as well. You shall betray and slay the greatest king of all time, *Luzwi*, whose birth in the far future you are now fighting to bring about . . .'

'What? What are you talking about?'

Luamerava ignored the interruption again and went on coldly, relentlessly: 'You will become proud and mad and cruel. Men will cringe and cower at the very sound of your footsteps. The very stars will weep when they witness the sting of your tyranny. You will end by destroying the Race of Man, and you will continue to reign in a world barren and dark – all alone. You will be afflicted by a strange disease that will force you to eat the souls of the stars in order to remain alive. In desperation you will board the magic canoe and sail the river time – upstream – returning to your past . . . our present . . . Here your future self will meet your present past, and the latter will kill the former.'

'It has already happened!' I screamed insanely. 'That body over there is mine, returned from the future, and my present self has killed my future replica. This is utter madness!'

I went completely berserk. Shaft after shaft of mental power left my frame and wrecked the contents of the cavern. I had a last glimpse of *Odu* seizing me, before the entire cavern collapsed upon us.

It is midnight and I hear distinctly the roar of lions in the forest outside. I also hear the yapping of jackals and the wild laughter of hyaenas in the distance beyond. Slowly I open my eyes. It is dark and there is something soft and alive next to me. I feel a warm yielding breast – a smooth shoulder and arm. It is *Ma-Ouzarauena*, and she wakes up slowly.

'The spirit of life has returned to your body, my husband. The people feared you were dead.'

'What . . . what happened? How did I get here?'

'The huge *Odu* brought you here from Kariba, my Lord, and that terrible animal *Luamerava* brought in poor *Luanaledi*. Both these creatures say they belong to you, they are your servants. They told us of everything that happened there. Out there the people are worshipping you, *Lumukanda*. They insist that you are a god, after successfully capturing the Illusion of Kariba and her companion *Odu*, and killing that monster in there.'

'Did they tell you who that monster was that I killed?'
'They did not say, but I know nevertheless.'

The mass crossing took place ten days later. It was a crossing destined to live in song and story for many hundreds of years to come.

I had ordered twenty great rafts to be built, each big enough to accommodate fifty. Each raft was shaped as a triangle and was built of *mnongo* logs lashed together with thick plaited ropes of cow hide. To the corners of each raft were attached long cow hide ropes with which the warriors operated the rafts backwards and forwards, two hundred standing either side on the banks of the river.

We transported more than a thousand people a day with the rafts only. Many people also found their way across in the fleets of canoes at our disposal. And for the first time in the history of the Tribes a floating bridge was built by lashing logs together. At first only the bravest warriors used this bridge; but when it proved to be reasonably safe, many others risked the crossing that way.

It took six whole moons to transfer the five million people across the Zambezi and only fifty were drowned in the entire operation. Their raft capsized as a result of a fight between two men over a girl, which started in midstream.

We could not ferry the livestock. We forced all the cattle and goats into the river and made them swim across, guided by fleets of canoes.

While the whole operation was in progress, those who had already crossed gradually settled in temporary villages spread over a wide area. People scooped up handfuls of the holy sand of the Kariba gorge and poured it into small skin bags which they kept as mementoes of their passage through the holiest place on earth. About two hundred people of both sexes, led by the Nguni philosopher *Mpungose*, one of *Celiwe's* consorts, elected to remain behind in Kariba to spend the rest of their lives in prayer and meditation. These people and their descendants were afterwards known as the 'Holy Ones of Kariba'. The fame of this little tribe has spread far and wide. Its members travel out periodically to neighbouring lands to assist, especially newly founded tribes, helping them to lay down their laws, attending to the sick and needy, and settling inter-tribal disputes. They practise a form of faith healing, and never use medicines.

Present-day descendants of this tribe are easily recognisable. Men normally wear a tortoise-shell headband and they carry teak staves with carved snakes coiled around them. They are normally heavily bearded. They prefer jackal-skin loincloths. These are descendants from the Holy Ones of Kariba, the Gateway to Eternity – the Navel of the Earth.

INTERLUDE

There is an old Zulu wedding song in which each passing day is depicted as a flower in a pasture, each with its distinct and unforgettable scent. This is merely symbolic of how each passing day brings something which leaves a distinct and lasting memory in one's mind. The twentieth day of November, 1963, was one such day in my life.

It was well towards midday that the Wise One entered the door of my place of work and he and my employer began talking for some time, discussing this very book that I am writing. The Wise One is a strange White man whom I fear and admire at the same time – a man who to me is a deep and frightening puzzle. This man is tall, more than six feet in height, and powerfully built. He looks like a judge, and when he is not smiling his face wears a grim and probing expression. Then he looks like a judge about to sentence a night-walking felon to the gallows.

In spite of his iron-like build and granite face, the Wise One has a ready smile and an infectious sense of humour that makes him even more puzzling. You must know that he is Dr A S Brink of the Institute for the Study of Man in Africa.

He had seen something at the exhibition of Prehistoric African Art which had escaped my myopic notice. This was a representation of a vast mural painting from a shelter near Mtoko in the land of the Mashona. This huge rock painting, embodying hundreds of figures of men and beasts, shows Bantu and Bushmen crossing a mighty river – very obviously the Zambezi, judging from motifs on either side. This painting also shows Arabs with their white head-scarves and long robes inside what is obviously a fortress of stone.

The outstanding feature is the image of a huge elephant, the same animal drawn in two different positions to indicate its movement across the scene. There are witchdoctors and chiefs disgracefully fleeing from the elephant in all directions, along with the other people. In several places one discerns a figure of a man with multiple arms, which is the normal way of representing an immortal. There can be little doubt that the artists had *Lumukanda* in mind.

There are also many figures of a bisexual individual, represented in the normal way with both male genitals and female breasts. These no doubt represent that classic individual who, in all Bantu and Bushmen folklore, stands for the combination of evil or adverse principles, and who always passes under the name of *Vamba Nyaloti.*

For centuries these legends have been told by Bantu and Bushmen alike and the very fact that Bushmen often portray Bantu legends in their cave paintings points to contact, and even friendship, between these two races for a very long time. Both races destroyed the Hottentots simply because the latter sided with the Strange Ones, and later also with the Feared Ones.

Dr Brink showed this painting to my employer, Mr Watkinson, and me in the Johannesburg Art Gallery. We studied it for more than an hour. We also noticed in the upper left-hand corner women with long flowing hair and long robes, in dancing attitudes. These characters depict the Strange Ones, and they are dancing within a stone enclosure – a fortress, possibly one of the Ka-Lahari cities. Dominant across the entire frieze is the map motif of a huge river, with lines indicating pathways towards suitable fording places. Lesser motifs, but of extreme interest, are a white-clad woman chasing sheep into a fortress, in which is seen a throne of alien – not Bantu – design. There are two clear paintings of trees, representing the Tree of Life. One of these is painted in clear detail and includes a phallic design in the place of the roots, and with several female figures dancing around it. The other, more crudely painted, tree is the Tree of Life, swollen and open, with a female figure – possibly *Ma* – stepping out of the opening. The roots, which the Tree of Life is said to use as feet, are well detailed, and the very shape of the whole tree matches our baobab very closely indeed. Most of our legendary descriptions of the Tree of Life portray an uprooted baobab.

There are also clear representations of sweet potatoes and other tubers, but the Bantu obtained these from the Portuguese in trade. These are obviously later additions to the monstrously huge frieze and it is equally obvious that the entire design is the product of many different artists, who have added contributions periodically over a long period of time.

Another conspicuous component of the incredibly complex design is the horse. There are several groups of horses and it is known, from our legends at least, that both the Arabs and the Strange Ones had brought horses with them.

On this occasion we looked again at many other paintings with figures obviously non-Bantu; those with white faces, red hair and long white robes; those with steel mail and boats of Phoenician design; those with long curved swords and slender swords with hilts, and wearing strange helmets. All these paintings prove beyond any doubt that these strange people had once dominated vast areas of

Africa. The coming of the Ma-Iti is not merely a myth – a figment of primitive imagination. Such a colonisation by people whose real uncorrupted name has been lost, but whose deeds live on, actually did take place. These people did many things which the Bantu and the Bushmen have good reasons never to forget.

If I ever succeed in the duty I have set myself, I shall spend the remainder of my days promoting research into these people. The Ma-Iti and the Arabi were not the only Strange Ones that set foot on our fatherland's shores. Our legends speak of another race of White men 'who had tails growing from the tops of their heads'.

Mr Boshier, a young anthropologist with whom I hope to collaborate, and initiate a new science – the *knowledge* of cave paintings – assures me that these 'Mehatla-Ditlohong' were Chinese. I know too little about ancient China to comment. But in a sequel to this book I shall write many interesting stories about what these people did in Africa, even before the coming of the Strange Ones.

I mention a new science – the *knowledge* of cave paintings – because whatever has been achieved so far cannot be regarded as a science. Cave paintings can only be interpreted against a background knowledge of the legends which they illustrate. This has never been done. At best they have thus far been copied and admired, and very wrongly interpreted.

JOURNEY TO THE SOUTH

About two hundred years after our passage through Kariba two small tribes came to dwell with the Holy Ones in the Holy Place and these tribes were the Tonga-Ila and Batonka. They are regarded even today as the Guardians of Kariba and as standing directly under the protection of the most Ultimate God. Any tribe disrupting or disturbing these tribes is immediately attacked by its neighbours and driven from the land in disgrace. Such is the Law of the Tribes.

In the great journey to the south we were following the tracks of Gandaya – the greatest beast that ever trod the earth. He had also decided to leave Kariba and he was going southwards for some unknown reason.

The great elephant always remained a few days' journey ahead of us and whenever we paused to rest, Gandaya also loitered near us. He always remained within sight; we could see him far in the distance amongst the trees, grazing and minding his own business. Eventually he dictated when and where we should rest, and when he decided to stop for a moon in one place, so did we.

It was during one of these moon-long pauses that *Zulu* and *Qwabe*, the sons of *Celiwe* and *Malandela* of the Nguni, got themselves into serious trouble. The result of this was that both these youths were circumcised six moons earlier than the appointed time for their initiation.

It was quite an amusing incident. They had in the meantime grown into tall, strong, young men. *Qwabe* was twenty-one summers old and *Zulu* eighteen. One day, while these two boys were out hunting with my three sons, *Mukombe*, *Demane* and *Demazana*, they saw a young man and a girl going into the forest. *Zulu*, who was the most inquisitive boy under the sun, lost all interest in the hunt and started trailing the lovers instead. *Qwabe* followed him, intending to bring him back, but he too developed a strong curiosity. The sons of *Malandela* were soon lying side by side on their bellies behind some thick shrubs witnessing the antics of the lovers in the long grass a few paces away, with wide-eyed, open-mouthed fascination. And when they returned to camp that night they were walking like people in a daze and the sight they had seen haunted their dreams in the nights that followed.

Zulu, who was a little 'wise fool', soon told his more slow-witted elder brother that, Tribal Law or no Tribal Law, he was going to find himself a girl and explore with her the possibilities they had witnessed.

On the following day these two young stupids decided to waylay a young girl near the river with blatantly obvious and most unlawful intentions. For a long while they crouched behind a thicket close to the path the young women and girls took on their way to fetch water. At last a tall, slender, very beautiful virgin came striding along the path, all on her own, with a clay pot balanced on her head.

Zulu and *Qwabe* waited with bated breath and pounding hearts for the girl to draw close, then they sprang like leopards upon her. But they made a very wrong choice indeed! Their lovely prey was none other than my daughter *Mbaliyamswira* (Flower of Passion), and immortals, much more so than mortals, take strong exception to being violated, be it by amateurs or specialists.

To add to the overflowing bowl of their misfortune, *Ma-Ouzarauena* appeared on the scene and it was not long before they stood before a Tribal Tribunal with thoroughly wetted loinskins. They stood there facing a hundred and fifty very unsympathetic Rainbow *Indunas* from all three tribes. Also present were fifteen Tribal Avengers, and of course, *Malandela, Celiwe, Mxhosa, Ma-Ouzarauena* and me. The poor boys were so scared they were trembling from head to foot and wetting their loinskins without pause.

The old Avenger Leader stood up and his voice roared from the circular mouth of his mask: 'Hear me, everybody, *Zulu* and *Qwabe*, the sons of *Malandela* of the Nguni, stand here accused of trying to rape the daughter of *Lumukanda* of the Mambo. I say, and I say again, that both these boys are guilty and they are free to try and prove their innocence – if they can!'

'Boys,' said *Malandela* in a broken voice, 'tell the truth now – did you try to take the honour of *Mbaliyamswira* by force?'

'N-no father,' stammered *Qwabe*. 'I m-mean y-yes father.'

'Don't give two contradicting answers at the same time, boy!' roared the Tribal Avenger. 'Did you or did you not try to rape *Lumukanda's* daughter? Answer!'

'Y-yes, we d-did sir.'

'Did you not know you were breaking the law?' the Avenger Leader bellowed.

'We . . . we . . .'

'Quiet! You were spitting upon the Laws of your forefathers.'

'P-please sir . . .'

'Quiet! We find you guilty and as the Law dictates, punishment must be meted out by the parents of the girl you tried to rape.'

Celiwe buried her face in her hands and *Malandela* groaned as the Avenger handed *Ma-quzarauena* the Spear of Justice. The latter advanced slowly and menacingly upon the two boys. They tried to run away but were seized by the Avengers and brought back. To everybody's surprise *Ma-Ouzarauena* merely made them bend over and she gave each the biggest thrashing of his life with the shaft of the spear. *Celiwe* thanked *Ma-Ouzarauena* humbly for her mercy. *Malandela* turned to the withdoctor *Kokovula* and told him to take the two boys and initiate them into manhood according to the Law.

Kokovula is grinning most savagely in his beard. He is going to enjoy the coming ceremony very much. He is very fond of circumcising boys and, although the law requires that a very sharp knife be used, *Kokovula* has other ideas about *Zulu* and *Qwabe.*

These two boys have been fasting for five whole days and they have been confined together in a dark hut full of leering, obscene-looking masks of lions, water and mountain gods and a few demons as well. Also there were strung up against the walls the skulls of *Malandela's* ancestors and skin bags full of the dried foreskins of nearly all those long-dead men.

Zulu and *Qwabe* are quaking with fear – and who could blame them? The boys are casting fearful glances at the huge 'circumcision mask' standing on an ornately carved wooden tripod in the corner of the hut. This hideous mask represents the Goddess of Fertility, *Nomkubulwana,* and it looks ugly enough to scare the hide off a rhinoceros.

The boys also glance nervously at the rough, hard, *pehla* sticks in a bowl of water. *Qwabe* has heard about the use of these sticks in an initation ceremony and not one bit does he like what he has heard. Towards midnight drums erupt into violent sound as the two witchdoctors assisting *Kokovula* begin the 'drum prayer'. *Kokovula* enters the hut and orders the boys to come out. He is wearing a hideously grinning mask of animal skin and he is covered from shoulder to ankles in red-dyed fibre. A huge fire has been lit in front of the initiation hut and by the light of this fire *Zulu* and *Qwabe* see the two assistant witchdoctors, *Vundla* and *Dondolo,* standing behind the heavy drums and beating out the drum prayer for all they are worth.

Kokovula drags both boys near to the fire and tells them to take off their loinskins, throw them into the fire, and lie down flat on their backs.

The teeth of the two boys chatter with terror as *Kokovula* and *Dondolo*, both masked and clad in fibre garments, begin to stamp and caper as they perform the 'prayer dance', chasing each other and gesticulating fiendishly round and round the two boys on the ground. *Kokovula* stoops suddenly and seizes *Zulu* by the hair, hauling him to his feet. Then he sends him flying to the dust again with a savage blow in the stomach. The poor boy lets out a squawk and flops on his back like a lost impala-skin doll.

'Be strong!' bellows *Kokovula*. 'Be brave, you are a man now.'

Zulu lies sobbing and gasping like a fish stranded on a mudbank – but not for long. *Kokovula*, who has knocked down *Qwabe* as well, uttering the same words, comes dancing back to *Zulu* and hauls him to his feet once more. This time *Kokovula's* fist crashes against *Zulu's* head and once more he goes down into the dust and as consciousness leaves him he hears *Kokovula* snarl: 'You are a man now – be wise!'

The two boys, who have both been knocked unconscious in the same way, are now revived with a mixture of urine and water thrown over them. The urine is a donation from ten of the most virile men in the three tribes and is intended to make the boys virile too. As the two boys regain consciousness they are forced to drink some of the stuff.

The three witchdoctors proceed with the dance of fertility, taking turns at capering and at operating the drums. *Kokovula* and *Dondolo* eventually seize the two boys and all but flay the skin off them with long wildebeest-tail switches.

Zulu and *Qwabe* writhe on the ground and yell loudly as the witchdoctors zestfully lay on. The 'ritual thrashing' is soon over and once more the two boys are left lying in the dust. The worst is yet to come.

They are now dragged into the hut and *Zulu* is covered with a heavy kudu-skin *kaross* to prevent his seeing what is being done to *Qwabe*. The latter is roughly seized and hauled to his feet by *Vundla* and *Dondolo*, while *Kokovula* lifts the heavy 'mask of circumcision' and moves it to the centre of the hut. The mask reaches up to *Qwabe's* waist. Above the forehead of the mask there is a carving in the hard wood, with a hole through the centre.

This carving is not just an ornament but a feminine symbol of fertility. On the back of the mask, below the hole, is a receptacle carved in the same piece of wood – a small bowl to receive the blood and the foreskin of the boy to be circumcised.

The two lesser witchdoctors bring *Qwabe* to the front of the mask and force him to insert his member of manhood through the hole above the forehead. *Kokovula* performs the operation on the other side. *Qwabe* yells with pain and tries to withdraw, but the two witchdoctors press him hard against the mask so that blood may flow into the small bowl.

Zulu, who has been fearfully peeping from under the *kaross* and has seen everything from start to finish, lets out a loud howl and makes for the entrance. He crashes into the closed wicker door and is quickly recaptured. With a sneer on his ugly face, *Kokovula* rubs the edge of his knife lightly on his whetstone to make it even blunter.

For twenty-one days after this the sullen boys were confined to the initiation hut, and daily they had to listen to *Kokovula's* lengthy lectures on the twenty-one different love-mat techniques. They were carefully instructed on the methods used in cases where the woman is tall or short, lean or fat, and the precise preparation of medicines to use to counteract evaporating potency.

The night of the twenty-second day, before the 'coming out ceremony', the two boys were visited by a woman. She was naked but her identity was shielded by a heavy mask elaborately fringed with fibre. The identity of such a 'midnight visitor', be it a female in the case of boys being initiated or a male in the case of girls, is always kept very secret. But of course, as an all-seeing immortal I know the identity of the 'midnight visitor' who came to give *Zulu* and *Qwabe* their practical experience and at this stage I see no harm in disclosing it. She was *Dambisa-Luwewe, Malandela's* royal concubine, the famous dancer.

Qwabe passed the test to *Kokovula's* satisfaction. But *Zulu* was found to be far too virile and was not directly released. He had to be subjected to further treatment to 'blunt his horns a bit'. He was given the *pehla* treatment to reduce his potency.

Finally the time arrived for the coming out ceremony and the two boys were brought forth from the 'hut of purification' to the thunder of drums and the chanting of hundreds of warriors. The boys were daubed from head to foot with white clay and red stripes. A white path was painted from the entrance of the initiation hut to the gate of the improvised stockade surrounding the temporary 'forbidden kraal'. This path always represents the 'road of life' which such young men have to take. In this case, as usual too, masked men representing 'fertility gods' and long-dead ancestors flanked the white path. As the two boys passed, each god and ancestor bestowed a blessing on them.

Zulu and *Qwabe* were wearing hideous masks themselves, intended to scare evil spirits from their path of life. In addition they each carried a staff in one hand and a fowl in the other. These fowls were sacrificed to each of the huge idols flanking the gate of the 'forbidden kraal', both idols representing the most Ultimate God. The ceremony was concluded with savage dancing, wild drumming and torrents of blessings: 'Be brave, Oh my sons – fear no man. Be wise, be kind, be resolute and bold. May you beget a hundred sons, and may your love-mats be always green.'

After the initiation ceremony the three tribes rested yet another moon, as did our guide, the great elephant Gandaya. It was during this second moon of rest that Bushmen made a daring dawn raid on the cattle pens of one of the most isolated temporary kraals of the settlement. This raid was made under cover of thick morning mist and succeeded in the driving-off of two hundred head of cattle. A company of warriors set out in pursuit of the little yellow-skinned thieves, but they were ambushed and routed with heavy casualties by a Bushman rearguard, armed with poison arrows. Of about fifty brave Nguni, only ten escaped.

The Bushmen proceeded westwards with the stolen cattle and boasted their success in an elaborate painting on the wall of one of their many caves.

Three days after this raid another band of these little yellow thieves tried to break into my cattle pens, this time at midnight. But my Rainbow *Indunas* and I managed to eliminate fifteen of these skulking rascals and to capture five alive.

Ntombela, my fat Second Rainbow *Induna*, was killed by a poison arrow while in pursuit of those who escaped. The three tribes were infuriated by these raids and we turned to mounting heavy guards every night around all cattle pens and kraals. They then tried a raid in broad daylight. A band, accompanied by their wives and children, tried to drive off a herd of Mambo cattle grazing on a plain off to one side. The Mambo herdboys raised the alarm and we pursued the raiders, killing ten males and capturing alive three males, fifteen females and ten children.

All these captives were kept in my kraal and the Nguni Rainbow *Induna Ziko*, the famous singer – who alone could understand their language – acted as interpreter while we interrogated them on all possible subjects.

We learnt a great deal from these captured Bushmen. They taught us how to make beads out of ostrich egg shell and perfumes from *tambuti* and *lubande* leaves. We learnt about many herbs that could cure many ills and about others that can be eaten. We learnt how to prepare poisons and suitable antidotes for each.

The Bantu developed a deep fear and reverence for the Bushman and it was not long before colourful stories were being told about their supernatural powers, especially of their womenfolk's reputed ability to turn themselves into any kind of beast at will.

I decided to contact the many groups of roaming Bushmen in the neighbouring mountains with the intention of trading with them. I would have used *Ziko* as interpreter, but unfortunately, on the very day we were going to set out to the mountains with trade cattle, *Ziko* stabbed himself with an assegai and died after a violent quarrel with his wife, the Princess *Nomikonto, Malandela's* sister. *Ziko's* death was a tragic loss to all of us because not only was he the greatest singer of all time but he was also a man as wise as he was brave. My plan for trading with the Bushmen had to be abandoned because with *Ziko* gone we could not communicate with them.

Ten days after the death of her husband the Princess *Nomikonto,* who had been expelled from the Nguni tribe for causing the death of *Ziko,* took her two handmaidens, *Mabashana* and *Nontombi,* to the river to bathe and to wash their skin skirts. It was a hot day and the water was cool and pleasant. Hundreds of butterflies chased each other among the many bright wild flowers in the long grass and birds argued in the tall green-clad *mopanis* and *mungas.*

The three women were not laughing though, and they were not singing either, because they were mourning the death of *Ziko.* There were tears in *Nomikonto's* eyes and bitterness in her heart; now that her husband was dead she suddenly found that her life had become dark, bitter and empty. The lean handsome face of her husband haunted her dreams by night and by day she seemed to hear his manly voice raised in one of his many famous songs – songs destined to live forever in the memory of the tribes.

Nomikonto longed for her husband. She longed for the strong embrace of the man she had so badly treated while he was still alive. She longed for the love with which he had loved her and which she had not appreciated. She longed for the strong manly presence of *Ziko* and she could not bring herself to accept the fact that he was gone forever, never to return.

She sobbed quietly as *Mabashana* and *Nontombi* rubbed her body with loofahs and the tears that flowed down her cheeks mingled with the cool river water in which she was standing waist deep.

None of the women saw the three Bushmen creeping upon them through the undergrowth until it was too late. In fact, the first inkling the three Nguni females had of the presence of the Bushmen was the crackle of breaking twigs as two of the yellow skulkers burst through the shrubs in their final dash towards the women in the water.

Mabashana screamed as the first of the two Bushmen dived at her, seized her around the waist, swung her like a bundle of skins over his shoulder and proceeded to drag her out of the water into the forest.

Nontombi fought savagely with the other Bushman – her fists crashed again and again into the yellowish-brown puffy-eyed face until the little man stunned her with his short club. *Nomikonto* leapt out of the water and ran, not even bothering to retrieve her skin-skirt on the river bank – and she ran straight into the third Bushman who brought her down in a most ungallant way.

Thus the Princess *Nomikonto* entered a new life as the wife of a Bushman and she was never seen again.

The Bushmen are great boasters and they like to immortalise their triumphs in life in paintings on the walls of their cave shelters. Many of these paintings depict the little yellow men carrying off Bantu women. Their portrayal is incredibly accurate and in some of them it is possible to identify the tribe, like those showing the *sicolo* hairdo, characteristic only of Mambo and Nguni women.

After the period of rest the three tribes once more struck camp and moved south. Henceforth we had all the warriors out as a vanguard to the migrating multitudes, as we were then entering the slave-raider infested empire of the Luvijiti, whose capital was the great fort of Zima-Mbje in the south. Here *Muxakasa*, who had once been *Malandela's* First Wife, ruled an empire of Mashonas, Arabi and Hottentots – and their numerous mutual bastard products – with exotic tyranny.

In the Royal Dwelling within the mighty walls of the ancient fort Zima-Mbje the hall is crowded to the very entrance with warriors, grey-bearded half-caste Royal Advisers, full-blooded Bantu slaves and eunuchs. A great feast is in progress and the dreaded ruler, the Empress *Muxakasa*, reclines in haughty splendour on a *tambuti* and ivory couch, smiling like a she-leopard with a full belly as her warriors toast her again and yet again in foreign wine. She flirts shamelessly with the black-bearded Arabi who have come to buy the thousands of Lunda slaves her warriors had captured. Her couch is flanked by *Jovu* and *Audi*, her enormous eunuchs, who are both armed with daggers, axes and *pangas*. Her ankles, neck and arms blaze with foreign ornaments of sun-metal and three ostrich feathers grace her shining metal headband. Beside her stand three great grass baskets full of glittering ornaments which the Arabi slavers had brought in exchange for the host of slaves and bags of sun-metal dust.

Muxakasa is swimming like a lewd and shameless fish in the wealth she has gained from her trade in human lives. She is basking like some obscene crocodile in the sun of shimmering splendour which is fed with the souls of countless slaves. She is a walking curse to the lands of the tribes. But she has come to the brink of the precipice of retribution. She does not know it yet, but the hour of her undoing has drawn very close.

She curses the tired dancing girls to urge them to dance even faster. Already some of them have dropped to the ground from exhaustion. She orders the cringing slaves to hurry more food and wine to her gluttonous guests. She orders a slave promptly killed because the exhausted wretch accidentally dropped a tray full of meat on the lap of a foul-mouthed Arabi.

But deep in her rotten soul an uneasiness is growing. She has sent a great army to attack the hordes of black barbarians advancing into her empire from beyond the Zambezi and for ten days she has had no news of it. The uneasiness in her heart is growing in spite of the great quantities of wine she consumes in an effort to still it.

The wild feasting is interrupted by the entry of a badly wounded man, apparently in the last stages of exhaustion. He is a warrior and his hands clutch a horrible, festering wound in his left side. The man totters through the great hall and drops at *Muxakaza's* feet, gasping for breath and almost fainting with pain.

Muxakaza leaps to her feet and towers over the wounded man, a bowl of foreign wine in one hand. 'Who are you, dog, and what do you want?'

'Great Queen,' gasps the dying man, 'I am one of your battle leaders . . . come to . . . tell you . . .'

Naked fear and dark foreboding tears through the evil soul of the albino queen and in her frenzy she hurls the bowl of wine at the dying man.

'Speak up, dog, what have you come to tell me? Speak up!'

The kneeling man sags forward and his voice is hardly a whisper: 'Your army . . . met savages . . . fought bravely, but . . . defeated. I . . . only survivor . . .'

Muxakaza's face darkens with murderous rage. Her eyes protrude and foam shows between her clenched teeth. With a lightning whirl she snatches an axe from the hand of one of her eunuchs and shatters the skull of the prostrate man.

'To the walls!' she screams. 'All warriors to the walls! The savages are coming – be prepared to meet them!'

Heavily armed men wearing corselets of crocodile skin and ornate wooden helmets rush to man the walls of the great stone fortress of Zima-Mbje. Some dash to man the wooden stockades that surround the vast city spreading all around the fortress – a city of oblong mud-houses and beautiful and ornately decorated grass huts, all built in a strange foreign style. Regiments of Hottentots, Mashonas and Arabi-Mashona bastards march through the city to the sound of alien music from alien drums and metal bugles. For once in its long and evil history the empire of Luvijiti is on the defensive. For once it cringes and cowers before the advance of an enemy determined to fight to death. The infamous Luvijiti have tasted the cup of defeat once and, like all cruel peoples down the ages, their time has come to taste the cup of fear.

Muxakaza leaves the great hall, where the wild feasting persists, and climbs the short flight of stone steps leading to her private dwelling. There is a hard smile on her cruel mouth and a savage glitter in her eyes. Her slaves, the beautiful half-caste *Lukuma* and the diminutive Hottentot maiden *Wadaswa*, meet her as she enters and prostrate themselves before her.

'Has my husband been fed?'

'Yes, great one,' answers the half-caste maiden, *Lukuma*. 'The respected one has been fed and brushed as you commanded.'

'Good, prepare my bath quickly.'

The two slaves leap to obey and in a short time *Muxakaza* is standing in a big clay bowl being bathed in hot water from head to foot. A few heart-beats later she steps out of the bowl and is rubbed dry by brisk, nervous hands.

Suddenly *Muxakaza's* arms close around the waist of *Lukuma*, drawing the surprised slave to her savagely, passionately. *Muxakaza's* lips crush those of the slave girl in a bruising kiss. Equally suddenly the albino woman pushes the girl away, saying: 'If my enemy *Lumukanda* is leading those savages now invading my land, then you are my only hope of escape, *Lukuma*.'

The slave girl is even more surprised at these strange words and she wonders what her cruel mistress is talking about. She does not realise that *Muxakaza*, or rather the evil spirit that dwells within her, intends taking over *Lukuma's* body, should Zima-Mbje fall into the hands of the invaders.

Arrayed in all her finery, *Muxakaza* makes her way alone into the underground chamber where her 'husband' awaits her. The smell of grass assails her nostrils as she enters the 'dark place of delight'. In the darkness a hoof stamps impatiently and the albino woman laughs as she lets her long leopard-skin skirt fall down. There is savage hunger in her eyes as she advances deeper into the darkness.

The sun has risen and its light falls on the towering rocks that lend the surrounding countryside a rugged beauty. It also falls on the distant stone tower of Zima-Mbje and on the hard faces of the warriors advancing on the walls from the west through the dense bush.

Nine hundred thousand Nguni, Mambo and Xhosa warriors have been working their way slowly but surely round that fortress for the past twenty days and now Zima-Mbje is well surrounded, though the inhabitants of this hated stronghold are not yet aware of it. It is our intention to deny escape to any of the people within the high-walled abomination, especially the foreign slave raiders whom we know to be in there. Every man in the vast army of the 'Three Tribes' is fired with a savage determination to destroy Zima-Mbje so utterly and so thoroughly that nobody will ever dwell within its walls again.

Whatever the cost in time, whatever the cost in lives, Zima-Mbje must be destroyed without mercy. That obscene excrescence of rock and wood must be relegated to the past to which it rightly belongs. We are determined to make an example of this hotbed of harlotry and unmentionable disease.

The order passed on to the rank and file of the armies of the Tribes is simple and to the point: 'Spare no one!'

For five hundred years the fortress of Zima-Mbje has been the lair of chiefs who grew fat and rich by capturing and selling fellow black men to those foreign devils, the Arabi. For five hundred years Zima-Mbje has been the den of the vilest women, who sold their bodies to the lecherous Arabi in exchange for trinkets, a thing unheard of in the land of the Tribes before.

And now as an example to all generations of men as yet unborn, Zima-Mbje has to be destroyed – with all its inhabitants and other contents – its wealth of possessions and its moral poverty.

We attacked and were on the hated enemy before they came to realise it. We crashed against the outer stockade and breached it in many places by sheer weight of numbers. Only then did they recover from their surprise. Their arrows, stones and javelins tore into our ranks as clouds of whistling death. Hundreds of brave men fell. The fire-pots of the enemy roasted many of our men alive – but all to no avail; the angry warriors of the 'Three Tribes' were not to be stopped. We tore into their town and butchered Luvijiti and Arabi alike – but especially Arabi! We set their foreign oblong dwellings on fire and seized their women and children and flung them into the flames. Through the smoke and the flames and the whining arrows we advanced in a raging wave upon the stone walls of the fort itself and surrounded it completely.

Here I ordered the massed armies to rest awhile before the final onslaught on the infamous structure. The enemy kept up an unceasing barrage of heavy stones and arrows from the high walls and tower. Their alien stone-throwing catapults and huge multiple spear-discharging bows tore gaps into our ranks and although all this forced us to keep our distance, it nevertheless increased our anger and cold determination. Two of my *Indunas, Nsongololo* and *Shungu*, were killed by a heavy stone thrown by a catapult mounted on the wall, and

Mabovu, the second Royal Consort of the Nguni Queen *Celiwe*, was also killed a short while earlier – stabbed in the back while routing single-handed twenty Luvijiti warriors at the stockade.

We did not waste time in mourning the dead. They had fallen with honour and one must rejoice and not mourn when brave warriors fall in honourable battle. Men live and die but once, and happy are those who die in an honourable cause, in brave battle against an evil and pitiless rabble like the Luvijiti and their allies, the Arabi.

A violent thunderstorm was tearing the scowling skies apart with lightning and reverberating thunder as we launched the final attack on the fortress. We led the angry yelling men of the Three Tribes straight at the gate, but were driven back with heavy casualties by a very determined enemy who concentrated all their firepower on our spearhead – fire-pots, arrows, spears, catapult stones and even, by hand, the oblong stones torn from the very walls they stood upon.

The vast armies of the Three Tribes retreated to regroup on the edge of the smouldering townships. High on the tall tower of the great fortress the ruler of the Luvijiti, *Muxakaza*, stood and taunted us in a loud voice: 'Come back and try again, my stinking dirty black friend! Come and try again! Do not be scared! But I warn you, we have enough weapons and missiles here to keep you occupied for a hundred years.'

'Bitch!' growled *Mavimbela* savagely. 'Just wait until I get my hands on you.'

The Royal Consort of the Nguni, *Malandela*, turned with a smile on his face and said something to *Mavimbela*. But his words were drowned by an earth-shaking peal of thunder that was promptly answered by a savage scream from something huge and grey and monstrous, which came lumbering out of the bush behind us – Gandaya had smelled the blood and death of human beings with deep satisfaction.

The huge elephant made straight for the stone fort, and in the mind of the great beast I sensed a hatred so great that my blood grew cold. Gandaya hated the fort Zima-Mbje. Somehow he must have associated the place with the slave-raider whose lance-head was still buried in his foot.

Gandaya was closely followed by the ape-man *Odu* and the Illusion of Kariba, *Luamerava*. The roaring warriors followed the huge beast which made its way straight for the closed portals of the fortress. Arrows and spears and heavy stones glanced off Gandaya's body and head. Fire-pots were thrown down upon him, only to bounce off and break on the ground.

There was a splintering crash as the huge beast struck the gate and carried it through, impaled on the one remaining tusk, and it helped the attacker considerably in spreading death, destruction and confusion along a broad path through the fort. A portion of the wall came thundering down and frightening were the shrieks and groans from those who became buried and those who were standing on top.

'Forward, forward!' roared *Malandela* to the Nguni regiments following him.

'Forward!' came the command from the diminutive pot-bellied chief *Mxhosa* of the Amaxhosa to his hordes of cut-throats.

'Attack!' bellowed *Mavimbela* by my side to the Mambo behind us. His command was as usual richly garnished with the foulest curses from his repertoire.

The massed regiments swept forward in perfect battle order. Lightning tore the skies apart and thunder crashed across the rain-swept land as we advanced. Zima-Mbje's doom was nigh.

We advanced upon the gate of the fortress at a steady run and I found two people running on either side of me – *Odu* and *Luamerava.* With a rush and a roar we were inside and there was a desperate hand-to-hand battle in which the Luvijiti became mangled and mixed with mud, blood and rain. Bands of Arabi slave-raiders grouped themselves and tried to counter-attack, quite contrary to their inherent cowardice. But we wiped them all out in no time – a measure they so richly deserved. Our arrows and thrown spears hissed skyward at those who fought desperately from the top of the walls. They dropped into the mud below.

The enemy strove to rally in big groups and stand their ground against us, but Gandaya tore savage pathways through them. Some he trampled in bunches underfoot; others he seized with his trunk, flinging them like rotten eggs against the walls. As the thunderstorm rose in fury, so did the savage battle and the slaughtering out there in the rain was enough to nauseate the strongest and bravest.

Meanwhile *Odu* and *Luamerava* were searching the place for *Muxakaza* and it was during the last rounding up of the few who still breathed that *Odu* shouldered his way through the milling warriors to my side. 'My Master, you come and see!'

I followed the huge creature into what had been the private apartments of *Muxakaza.* We stepped over a dying Hottentot slave woman and went down a flight of stone steps into a dark underground chamber.

Malandela of the Nguni and his three surviving Rainbow *Indunas, Mapepela, Malangabi* and *Solozi,* followed us. By the light of the smoky torches we saw *Muxakaza* lying naked and dead on the grass-strewn floor with a foreign knife in her heart. Lying next to her was the carcass of a zebra which we had been told by Luvijiti prisoners we interrogated, was tame and specially kept by *Muxakaza*. It was said that the zebra was passionately in love with *Muxakaza*.

There was a smile of savage triumph on the lips of the dead woman. Tied to the wrist of one limp hand was a piece of soft buckskin on which was figured the insulting message: 'You sterile beast, I am alive still. But you will never find me – you stupid fool of an immortal.'

'What does that mean?' demanded *Malandela*. 'She is dead and yet she claims to be alive – and that you will never find her.'

'This woman's body was taken over by an evil spirit, remember? In all probability that evil soul took over someone else's body and escaped unobserved as that person . . .'

Just then the Illusion of Kariba came in and fell on her knees before me. 'Your humble handmaiden begs to report, Lord, that she has found a secret tunnel under the wall of the fort. One woman has made her escape through this tunnel, which leads into the forest. This unworthy servant found her footprints in the tunnel, together with this ornament.'

She held out part of a broken copper bracelet.

'So, she has escaped!' cried *Malandela* angrily. 'She has stolen some other woman's body and gone to spread her evil further afield.'

'She will not get away – I'll catch her yet!' I said as we turned and left.

Outside the storm had passed on and a clear rainbow graced the eastern sky. The sun had burst through the clouds in the west and their fringes were ablaze with the golden hue of the Lord of Day. Light was reflected by raindrops on the leaves of the tall *mopanis* and the stones of the great circular tower glistened wetly like a giant fish.

The regiments of the Three Tribes were occupied in burying the dead just outside the great fortress. Many were busy razing the gutted enemy houses to their foundations. Others were collecting every enemy weapon they could find and burying these in a deep hole.

Nobody was allowed to keep so much as the smallest item of Zima-Mbje jewellery, and nobody wanted to, because we already looked upon all such items as thoroughly cursed.

In the ruins of the fortress thousands of elders from the Three

Tribes were taking a solemn oath and making a promise to the High Gods that they would see to it that such a thing as Zima-Mbje was never built again in their lands – that the infamies of this cruel place would always be recounted in order to discourage future generations from ever trying to emulate the Luvijiti in any way. Lastly, the grey-haired elders placed a 'High Curse' on Zima-Mbje. They cursed it to be desolate, lonely, lost to mankind until the end of time.

Ten days later we left the vicinity of the 'fort of infamy' and followed Gandaya towards the south-east to where the mighty Limpopoma flowed through very dense forests. We were two days' journey distant from the great Limpopoma when open disobedience erupted among the people once again.

Strong deputations were sent to us from each of the Three Tribes. The people were refusing to cross the Limpopoma because, they said, beyond the Limpopoma was a great bottomless precipice marking the edge of the world. Crossing this river was not only a clear invitation to trouble; it was a sacrilege as well. The Holy Legends say that God does not want anyone near the edge of the world. Tension mounted and trouble was in the air.

THE MEALIE TRIANGLE

'What are we going to do about this?' asked *Celiwe* of the Nguni sadly.

'It seems everybody is refusing to cross the Limpopoma. What can we do?'

'I propose that *Lumukanda* should deal firmly with these rebellious fools,' said the little monkey-faced chief, *Mxhosa*. 'This is just the right time to cross the river; it is at its lowest and the rains will not come for several moons. You must do something, *Lumukanda* – we all depend on you now.'

'Since we cannot use force on the stupid fools, we have no option but to scare them across,' I said after some pondering. 'I have a plan that would make these people cross the Limpopoma faster than they have ever crossed any river before. Give me three days and you shall really see a sight you shall remember for the rest of your lives. But first I want you, the rulers with all those who stand close to you, including your loyal warriors, to cross the river. I shall pretend to cross along with my loyal followers, but I shall return under cover of night to put my plan to work.

'I do not like this, Oh *Bengu*,' said the old man *Dolo* to his son-in-law one moonlit night exactly three days later. 'The chiefs have gone across the river, but we, the people, are left to our fate on this side. What is going on?'

'I do not know, Oh father of my wife,' said *Bengu* lazily. 'All I know is that nothing will ever make me cross that river. Not only am I tired of these many years of wandering; I am also not going to risk my neck by getting near the edge of the world simply because someone who calls himself a chief says so.'

'The legends say there is nothing beyond the Limpopoma except a great emptiness in which winged cannibals, each with ten eyes, fly about like vultures in search of carrion,' whispered the old man *Dolo*, casting a fearful glance behind him. 'That is why our forefathers called the south '*Ningizimu*' – which means "where many ten-eyed cannibals dwell". Nothing on earth will ever make me cross that river . . . oh no!'

'It is that foreign demon, that wizard *Lumukanda*,' said *Dolo* fiercely. 'I think he is trying to lead the tribes like blind goats to fall over the bottomless precipice on the edge of the world. I say, and I say again, that *Lumukanda* is a dirty . . .'

He was cut short by a loud shout from outside – a shout edged with horror and naked, blood-chilling fear. '*Aieeeee*! Look over there, look over there.'

The shrieks and shouts were repeated everywhere and thousands of people crawled out of their shelters to see what was happening. They saw what they mistook for incredibly large bats flying low from east to west – three that were as large as men. Tens of thousands of eyes stared in horror as the three monstrous bat-like apparitions came flapping slowly and clumsily along, darkly silhouetted against the big round moon.

'They are not bats,' shrieked someone. 'They are demons! Flee for your lives!'

The people stood their ground watching the oncoming demons in horrified fascination. But when the weirdest sounds came forth, accompanying instructions in no uncertain terms for everybody to cross the Limpopoma, there followed a stampede which was destined to live forever in song and story. It was the strangest, most horrible stampede of all time. Thousands of people, frightened out of their wits, ploughed helter-skelter through the waters of the river and raised billowing clouds of dust under the winter moon along either bank. They stampeded for three whole days and only afterwards could families sort themselves out. There were unfortunately a number of casualties, especially among old people, some of whom merely dropped dead from fright.

A grazing hippopotamus on the opposite bank is reputed to have been pounded into a pulp by the hooves of tens of thousands of cattle. With our combined voodoo powers my First Wife and I, and my two daughters, conjured a too realistic scene; we could have achieved effective results in a less dramatic way.

One moon later we entered the land of a people who were still so savage that they dwelt in trees like monkeys and hunted with stone and bone-tipped spears. In future years the Nguni came to adopt the whole tribe and they in turn adopted the Nguni culture and language. Henceforth they called themselves the Swazi, or Ngwane people. If anybody wishes to land himself in serious trouble he should only call a Swazi a 'raw-flesh-eating tree-dweller'. He should actually do so at a very safe distance and then run away immediately. The Swazi prefer people to believe they are an offshoot of the Nguni. But this is not true.

We fought many a battle with the cunning tree-dwellers before we managed to tame them. They were fond of ambushing herdboys and killing them before driving off the cattle. It was in one of these battles that I lost my adoring adopted son *Mukombe*, and I wept as I buried him at the foot of the Lebombo mountains. With the death of this youth I lost a brave and smiling, faithful son who had brightened my unhappy life. Forthwith my life would become darker and less tolerable.

After another moon of fighting our way through the land of the tree-dwellers we crossed the Upongolo river and I realised at last that we had reached our destination – the land which would in future become the land of *Zulu* – the land of the Zulus, or Zululand, and also the land of the Tongas.

I knew that I had finally fulfilled my mission and that my life would henceforth lack a particular purpose, other than minding my own personal affairs.

One morning I sent for my only remaining Rainbow *Induna* and said to him: '*Mavimbela*, we have at last reached our destination – a new, greener land where the tribes can live in peace and prosperity for many, many generations to come. I consider my duty as having been done and I praise the Highest of the Most High for having guided me this far, despite all the difficulties. You have been a brave and loyal servant, *Mavimbela*, and I am going to ask you a last and most important favour. Promise me here and now that you will not deny it to me.'

'Say it, Chief, and I shall do it even if I lose my life.'

'I want you to take over the Mambo Tribe and be its new chief.'

Mavimbela's curse is not translatable, let alone repeatable. 'No, no, that I cannot do!'

'I insist that you do it, *Mavimbela*. I really insist that you do.'

'Me, the son of a wall-eyed, wry-necked, knock-kneed fisherman a chief! Never!'

'*Mavimbela* . . .'

'I said I will never accept chieftainship, *Lumukanda*. You are not going to unload the responsibilities of being a chief on my shoulders.'

He stalked out of the hut and went to sit amongst the warriors in the place of gathering. I followed him and the next thing he knew I had put my chief's headdress on his ugly head and thrown my lion-skin Royal *kaross* over his broad shoulders. 'Warriors of the Mambo, your new chief,' I shouted to the assembled warriors. 'Be loyal and true to him and his children, and children's children.'

The warriors roared their assent and raised their spears and other weapons in salutation to the brave, popular man who was now their new chief.

Mavimbela wept – tears of real anger and sorrow. He begged and pleaded with me and his warriors in turn.

'Come on, you old coward,' cried a young warrior, 'you are so ugly and so big, you are more fit to be a chief than any of us. We shall enjoy worrying and hating you, you are just *made* all round to be a chief.'

'Whom are you calling a coward? Shall I mention by name the thousand battles I have fought and won? I have killed more animals and men than . . .'

'Show us how brave you are by becoming our chief.'

'You—,' cursed *Mavimbela*, tugging nervously at his royal head-dress and settling it more firmly on his head, 'that ought to convince you.'

The next moment *Mavimbela* nearly had an apoplectic fit and the warriors roared with laughter when I made him a coronation present of my two thousand wives and concubines. He raved and swore luridly as I ordered each of the women to kiss him – in public. The giant former Rainbow *Induna*, now revered chief of the Mambo, had the time of his life trying to break free from the giggling women who were caressing him with feigned gusto. The Mambo warriors roared with laughter as the great *Mavimbela*, the famous, incurable woman-hater, was frogmarched by laughing, shrieking women into the Great Hut of the new kraal that was still under construction, to give him the first thorough bath he had had for moons.

When at last *Mavimbela* was washed and anointed with scented hippo fat and was sitting dejectedly in his hut surrounded by his concubines and wives, I asked him to adopt my two sons *Demane* and *Demazana* and rear them as his own. This he agreed to do quite readily.

Ten days later I left with *Odu, Luamerava, Ma-Ouzarauena, Lulama-Maneruana* and my two daughters, and we set out towards the east, drawn by some strange power which wanted something to happen – something that was destined to change the life of all the tribes throughout the land.

Lulama-Maneruana was alone in the sun-drenched forest. She had gone to get a claypot full of water and had decided to bathe afterwards in the cool clear water of the gurgling stream. Now she was sitting on a dark rock with one foot in the bubbling crystal water. She was running an elaborately carved horn comb through her soft, fuzzy hair that was partly that of an Arabi and partly that of her Mashona mother.

Her skin skirt lay beside her, as were her necklaces and other ornaments. The hot sun was pleasant on the pale brown skin of her perfectly shaped body. Birds twittered as they built their nests in the tall trees above and butterflies fluttered among the many flowers around her – a beauteous symphony in colour, shape, sound and movement. The heavenly scent of the green forest was pleasing in the nostrils of *Lulama-Maneruana* and the sounds of bird song were delicious in her ears.

The beautiful half-caste, who had seen and endured so much in her eventful life, enjoyed the colourful and scented solitude of the unspoiled forest. She closed her long-lashed brown eyes and drew a deep breath of perfumed air. She did not see the strange metal-clad man advancing softly behind her. She did not see his blue eyes alight with adoration and the flush that tinted his white, alien face. She only felt his presence when she heard his voice at the same time – a kindly voice that formed words which sounded to her ears like '*Buwena Diye . . . Sinyora.*'

Lulama-Maneruana leapt to her feet, snatched up her skin skirt and swung around to face the owner of the gentle alien voice. She saw a man, tall and strong, and through the gaps in his armour she saw that his skin was much lighter than those of the Arabi with which she was familiar – a race to which her father belonged. This man's hair was long and soft and his beard was pointed, trimmed and glossy. Both his hair and his beard were as black as midnight. His nose was long, but not hooked like that of the Arabi, and his eyes were a brownish-blue.

He wore a helmet of bright grey metal with a ridge on top and a red feather flowing behind it, like cold fire. He also wore a corselet of the same metal, with sleeves and elbows. All surfaces were richly engraved with patterns representing a kind of flowering plant with which *Lulama-Maneruana* was not familiar.

His feet and legs were sheathed up to the thighs in strange footwear and on his left side hung, from a broad bluish-purple belt that went over his right shoulder, a sheathed, deadly-looking weapon – obviously a sword of some description. It was a thin, wicked-looking thing that gradually tapered to a needle-sharp point.

Even as *Lulama-Maneruana* watched open-mouthed with her skirt held defensively before her, the alien smiled broadly, revealing an even row of pearly teeth. He doffed his metal helmet with a sweeping gesture and bowed stiffly to her, saying something that was obviously friendly in his foreign tongue, concluding with the word that *Lulama-Maneruana* found fascinating – and she wished to learn its meaning – *Sinyora.*

'What are you?' she asked at last. 'Are you a demon?'

The alien did not understand, of course. She pointed to him and raised her delicate eyebrows in gentle inquiry. The man smiled back and pointing to himself with his thumb, uttered a word which sounded like '*Potugeesa*'.

Just at that moment ten more of the aliens emerged from the forest led by one wearing a long dark-brown robe reaching to his ankles. He was carrying a staff on the top of which was a bronze statuette of a man of some race, nailed to a cross of wood by his hands and feet. All the others wore helmets and cuirasses of leather. Two of them carried strange tubes with wooden stocks – obviously weapons of some kind. The rest of the aliens carried long heavy weapons that looked like a cross between a spear and a battle-axe and, like the first, they wore swords at their sides. Only the hooded man in the dark-brown robe carried no weapon.

Unlike the first man, these newcomers had no beauty about them. The robed man had a thin sour-looking face and the other nine had the atmosphere of ruffians about them. There was one with a peculiar thing tied with a string over his left eye.

Lulama-Maneruana dived into the water and put on her skirt while standing waist deep, much to the amusement of all the aliens except the sour-looking robed one who turned his back and made peculiar gestures, obviously magic, on his forehead, chest and shoulders with his right hand.

While *Lulama-Maneruana* was putting on her ornaments she heard the men conversing and whenever they addressed the first alien she heard a word sounding like '*kapitanoh*'.

'So his name is *Kapitanoh*,' thought *Maneruana* as she left the water with a wet, clinging skirt. Just then she saw *Ma-Ouzarauena* emerge from the forest, accompanied by *Mbaliyamswira*.

'Royal concubine *Maneruana*,' called out *Ma-Ouzarauena*, 'what is going on there? Who are those creatures and what do they want?'

'Respected *Ma-Ouzarauena*, I do not know. It is best that you come and read their minds.'

She came striding through the long green grass, head held high and ornaments gleaming in the sun. The eyes of all the aliens turned towards her and they seemed to sense that she was more than an ordinary human female. The brown-robed alien turned pale and retreated behind his armed fellows, making the same magic gestures on his forehead, chest and shoulders.

'Stop, Great *Ma-Ouzarauena*, stay where you are,' called *Maneruana*. 'You are making them uneasy; they seem to dislike your presence.'

Ma-Ouzarauena smiled and slowly came to a stop and she and the aliens studied each other intently across a distance of ten paces. Then *Ma-Ouzarauena* said softly: 'These men are from far beyond the

Great Waters and they wanted you to show them the village of our people. They want to trade with us. They need meat and other things to take with them to their homeland. This may come as a surprise to you, *Maneruana*, but their leader wearing the metal helmet and cuirasse loves you and he wants to take you to his native land.'

'Great *Ma-Ouzarauena*,' cried *Maneruana*, 'do not say that. I belong to *Lumukanda*; I am his concubine.'

Ma-Ouzarauena laughed shortly and turned away saying: 'Tell them in sign language to come with us. Tell them we are taking them to our chief.'

It took some time for *Maneruana* to bring her message home to the aliens who discussed it at length. They then called out a message to someone in the forest and two more aliens answered the call. They were followed by three black men carrying heavy bags on their heads.

And then all fell in line behind *Ma-Ouzarauena, Lulama-Maneruana* and *Mbaliyamswira*, who led them to my new kraal.

I met the aliens and gave them meat and milk to eat and drink. I also found to my surprise that they were very fond of the eggs of fowls, and their flesh. The Bantu are not terribly fond of these; they keep fowls mostly for their fat which they use in medicines for curing the common cold.

I gave them many fowls and ten oxen as gifts on the day of their departure four days later. Just as they were about to leave their leader came into my hut and told me in sign language – quite unnecessary as I could read his thoughts – that he would give me all the contents of the six great bags which his black servants had brought along, in exchange for *Lulama-Maneruana*.

He made me understand in poetic gestures that he was deeply in love with my half-caste concubine and he wanted to take her with him in his sea-going canoe to a place called 'Portugal' where he, the *kapitano*, had a very big house built of stones, in which he would make *Maneruana* happy as long as she lived.

He showed me one of the things he had in the bags. It was a cob on which more than two hundred grains grew, and they were of a beautiful yellowish colour in more or less perfect rows. He gave me to understand that these grains were edible and that our kaffircorn was nothing compared to them.

He advised me to have some of the grains planted and demonstrated how to cultivate the plants. Even before he finished I had seen into the future. I could see this strange-looking foodstuff taking the place of our sorghum as the staple diet of all the tribes. I could see this strange grain flourish in places where sorghums could not grow.

'Yes, *kapitano*,' I gave him to understand with a nod, 'you can have the woman with my blessing.'

He thanked me in his native tongue and bowed twice before showing me what the other bags contained. One of them contained the seeds and the dried fragrant leaves of a plant which they called *tobacco* – the plant which was destined to earn for the Zulu tribe the nickname of the 'tobacco-sellers' – *Izitengisa-Gwayi*. This plant could be smoked like *dagga*, or ground and mixed with burnt aloe to make a dark-brown habit-forming powder called *Gwayi*, or snuff.

I accepted both these items of trade, the mealies and the tobacco, in exchange for *Lulama-Maneruana*, and I ordered *Mbaliyamswira* and *Luamerava* to bedeck the beautiful half-caste in her tribal finery and also to prepare for a long journey to the coast.

That night under the laughing moon I placed my hand on *Lulama-Maneruana's* smooth shoulders and smiled down at her tear-furrowed face saying: 'This is the second time you have sacrificed yourself for the sake of the tribes, Oh beautiful Fallen Saviour. This is the second great sacrifice you are about to make for a race to which you only partly belong – a race which has always despised you because of your mixed blood. Now farewell, *Lulama-Maneruana*, woman who has seen much and suffered much. Farewell, unhappy half-caste, I am not giving you away as one gives away a chattel. I am not trading you as one would trade a cow. I am giving you away because I can foresee a chance of true happiness for you under the skies of an alien land. I am surrendering you into the hands of a being who truly loves you, more than I can ever hope to – one who, on the shores of a strange land, will give you love and happiness of a kind you can never experience here. The tribes will always remember you. The Sacred Story-tellers shall forever chant your name whenever the History of the Tribes is related to the next generation round our village fires.'

She placed her curly-haired head against my chest and her delicate hands tightened round me. She whispered: 'My Lord, had it not been you who commanded me to go with the Strange One I would have refused outright. But out of love for you I am prepared to obey. Oh *Lumukanda*, I remember much of what you and I have gone through together. I remember my first great adventure with the Princess *Nomikonto* in the Underworld. I remember what the *Ogo* said then, and what I did to my own brother's sons. I remember how the *Ogo* cured me. I remember that incident on the Madlonti mountains when *Noliyanda*, *Vuramuinda* and *Ninavanhu-Ma* merged into one being while you and I became completely changed as we drank from the fountain of youth. I remember so much, *Lumukanda*, so very much! Fresh in my memory is the day when *Odu* and *Luamerava* brought you and your daughter *Luanaledi* from the Kariba Gorge.

'Please take care of that unhappy daughter of yours when I am gone. I remember the scene we all conjured up, with those demon apparitions with which we chased the people across the Limpopoma. Oh *Lumukanda*, can I ever forget all this?'

'Remember me in your dreams, *Maneruana*,' I told her. 'Remember the unhappy immortal of the Land of the Tribes, and pray for him.'

'I will, *Lumukanda*, I will! I have only one more question to ask you – one last question. What does the future hold for me in the land of the Strange Ones, my Lord?'

'The man who loves you, the *kapitano*, will take you across the seas in his great sea-going canoe. He will wed you according to the laws of his tribe after having made a convert of you to his own religion. You shall kneel with him in a great temple of their God who is hanging from the crossed pieces of wood. You will both be very happy for years to come. You shall wear strange apparel and live in a great house built of stones, with many rooms and many servants and warriors all round.

'But one day, after many years, the *kapitano* will be killed in a furious battle that will take place on the Great Waters, bravely defending his homeland against a ruthless enemy. Another man will take you perforce into his sea-going canoe, *Maneruana*, and he too, will be struck by your great beauty. He will take you far across the Great Waters to live in a still stranger land. There you will both live to a very ripe old age, loved and honoured by all.'

She was sobbing loudly when I finished and I crushed her against my chest and, with my face buried in her soft hair, I also wept.

She kissed me twice before breaking away and running towards her hut. I made my way slowly and wearily to my own hut and for the whole night I lay there tossing sleeplessly between *Ma-Ouzarauena* and *Luamerava*, until dawn sprayed the eastern sky with red and gold.

The weary sun is setting and the heaving, restless sea whispers intimate secrets to the rugged shores. The bulky wooden sea-going canoe of the aliens rides upon the murmuring swells in the distance. Its tall masts sway as the black, gold and red hull rises and falls. I can see men running around, very busy on deck. They are unfurling the vast sheets of material that catch the wind and help to propel the mighty boat over the waves.

I can see four ports on the side of the vessel and through each a wide bronze tube glares malevolently. Strips of brightly coloured material flutter proudly from the tops of the tall masts. A smaller canoe has been lowered down the side of the towering vessel and the men in it row it nearer to the shore with long paddles. Even as I watch another boat, heavily decorated in the stern with designs in red and gold, is lowered and comes leaping and falling over the waves, following the first one. Ruffianly looking aliens leap out of the first boat as it grates on the sandy shore and they rush to load the great pile of meat and water containers of metal-bound wood. The *kapitano* turns to me and smiles, and bows twice to *Ma-Ouzarauena*. Then his metal-sheathed arm clasps the narrow waist of *Lulama-Maneruana* and draws her close.

The aliens, led by their *kapitano* and *Maneruana*, shoulder their deadly fire tubes and spears and make their way down to the second boat. My vision dims with tears as I see *Lulama-Maneruana* turn and wave, while the small boat makes its way towards the great canoe.

The great canoe turns slowly and points its nose south as the sun vanishes beyond the Lebombo mountains in the west. The sheets of material hang cross-wise from the masts and belly out as they catch the wind.

Slowly the huge canoe recedes into the distance until only its masts are visible in the dimming horizon.

Then the truth hits me like a blow from a heavy knobkierie: I will never see *Lulama-Maneruana* again. My knees grow weak and I collapse weeping like a woman who has lost her husband, like an orphan in a war-shattered land. The ape-man *Odu* helps me to my feet and I see the hurt and surprise on the faces of *Ma-Ouzarauena* and *Luamerava.*

'The great Lord *Lumukanda* is deeply in love with the half-caste woman,' says *Luamerava* softly. 'This greatly surprises me.'

'No, *Luamerava,* it should not surprise you. You see, we immortals are created to *live,* mortals are created to *love.*' Hers was the only true love I ever knew and I have traded it for mealies – and a broken heart!

THE MELODY LINGERS

On reaching the land north of the Utukela river, the Nguni and the Mambo Tribes set about building new kraals and settling down. But the Xhosa, still led by their High Chief *Mxhosa*, pressed on south to settle in the land beyond the Umzimvubu river. New tribes were being formed everywhere as smaller groups broke away – the Hlubi, the Lala, the Tembu and many others, some of which disintegrated before they could leave a mark on history.

Those were momentous days in the history of the Tribes – days of reformation, reorganisation and disintegration. And it was during these days that the Zulu nation, destined to rule the whole land east of the Ukahlamba mountains and the territory from as far north as the Upongolo to as far south as the Umkomanzi, was formed.

This story begins with the death of the Great *Malandela*, father by adoption of the young princes, *Zulu* and *Qwabe*. *Malandela* died violently. He died at the hands of a vengeful girl named *Pindisa*.

Malandela had just finished building his eight-thousand-hut Royal Kraal which *Celiwe* named Pelindaba, which means 'the end of the story'. A great feast was in progress on that sunny day and juicy pieces of meat were being roasted by thousands of warriors and large quantities of beer were being drunk. The aroma of roasting and boiling meat was borne on the whispering breeze from the great kraal. The singing and the loud laughter of thousands of men and women could be heard from far away. Everybody was rejoicing and nobody was expecting murder to be committed on such a happy day.

It happened suddenly, leaving many people gaping in disbelief. It happened with the speed of lightning.

It was at the time, as at all feasts, the dancing turns to wildest abandon – when male and female dancers compete fiercely in the centre of the kraal. There was a lithe girl who outdanced them all. She was a dark-brown bolt of sheer abandon, and when the panting dancers sat down one by one, she kept going – leaping, shaking and stamping tirelessly. She outdanced even the great *Dambisa-Luwewe*.

She outdanced even the dwarf Nguni Rainbow *Induna Malangabi*. She danced nearer to where the two High Chiefs, *Mavimbela* and *Malandela*, were sitting. Suddenly, with a loud, ecstatic laugh, she snatched a spear from a warrior standing nearby and drove it twice deep through the heart of *Malandela*. A shocked silence followed the initial gasps of surprise. The Chieftainess *Celiwe* was the first person to find voice again. She leapt to the side of her dying consort and tried to hold back the flow of blood with her little hands. The tall, slim girl who had stabbed *Malandela* stood with hands on her hips, utterly unconcerned at what she had done and utterly unconcerned with what the consequences might be for herself.

'Why?' asked *Celiwe* 'why did you do this? Why have you murdered him?'

The girl smiled – a cold, terrible smile – and her voice was soft and calm, and very deadly as she said: 'Does the name *Bekizwe* mean anything to you? Do you not remember a man whose name was *Bekizwe*?'

'*Bekizwe* was *Malandela's* brother,' *Celiwe* replied feebly. 'But what has he to do with the deed you have done?'

'*Bekizwe* was my father. My mother escaped with me in her womb on the night when he did to my father what I have now done to him.'

The girl *Pindisa* turned her back contemptuously on *Celiwe* and strode away. Warriors moved to seize her and she did not bother to resist. Rainbow *Indunas* closed on her with raised spears but she smiled coldly, contemptuously at them.

A spear was driven into her belly by *Malangabi* and she fell, too proud and too brave to scream. Spears tore into her and she was still smiling when she died. *Pindisa*, the daughter of *Bekizwe*, whose name means 'avenge', had avenged her father's death at last.

Five days later *Malandela* the Great was buried, and his two surviving Rainbow *Indunas, Malangabi* and *Solozi*, who had fought beside him in many bloody battles, stabbed themselves over his grave to go with him – to be beside him in the land of Forever-Night.

Queen *Celiwe* did not long survive the death of *Malandela*. A few moons later the wise little queen, who had ruled the Nguni so long and so unselfishly, collapsed and was carried dying into her hut. Her last words were: 'Tell *Zulu* and *Qwabe* to rule the Nguni jointly . . . and wisely . . .'

Zulu and *Qwabe* did not rule the Nguni jointly for long. They quarrelled. They quarrelled over the one thing over which all silly fools quarrel – a woman. *Qwabe* had met and loved a girl who belonged to the breakaway Tonga tribe, and he had made up his mind to marry this girl. But she did not love him and always taunted him about his repulsively ugly face.

The girl loved *Zulu*, *Qwabe's* handsome younger brother, and just before the day when *Qwabe* was to have married this girl, *Nobantu*, *Zulu* kidnapped her and hid her in the Qudeni mountain. He only produced her a year later, with a baby in her arms – *Zulu's* baby. This was too much for the gentle *Qwabe*, who was not by nature a violent man. He seized a knobkierie and brained *Nobantu* and her baby with it before turning on *Zulu*. But *Zulu* escaped and fled with a crowd of followers into the safety of the Nkandla forest. For many years after that *Zulu* and his followers, who called themselves the Amazulu, carried on a brisk trade with the other tribes in mealies and tobacco. For more than two hundred years this Zulu tribe was nicknamed the 'Vagabond Snuff-sellers'.

I did not witness the death of *Malandela*, nor that of *Celiwe*. I could do nothing about the famous quarrel between *Zulu* and *Qwabe*.

My women and daughters, and *Odu*, were captured by the Hordes of Eternity a few days after we saw *Lulama-Maneruana* off. I had to surrender them to ensure their continued existence in the Upperworld while I continued mine in the Underworld.

I became imprisoned in a crystal world, where I still exist in a dormant phase until the time comes for me to return to the world of men to guide them to further destinies. I could all along keep track of events and I still exercise influence over Guardians of Tribal History. It is I who speak through them.

In the meantime I have been sensing the years go by. I also sense with a sick feeling in my stomach, that the tribes will soon be needing me. The White Men, the latter Strange Ones, have invaded the Lands of the Tribes again in full force, and terrible wars have been fought.

I must get out of here. The gods told me they are going to keep me imprisoned here till the River Time runs dry. But my people need me – I must get out . . .

A dark figure is entering my crystal cavern. I can dimly discern its outline as it gropes and shambles stealthily towards me. I can see its ugly shape moving in the darkness. Hope rises in my heart . . .

POSTSCRIPT

We have reached the end of a long and tedious story – a strange mixture of historical fact and legendary fantasy, a strange mixture of truth and nonsense.

But, what is included here under the title of 'The Journey to Asazi' is only a synopsis, a very greatly shortened synopsis, of what is without any doubt the longest single story in the world. This story is not supposed to have an ending. Each Guardian of his tribe's history is supposed to add to it what his tribe experiences during his lifetime.

A person who is not familiar with Africa and its peoples might find it difficult to understand this story, let alone read between the lines. He might find it difficult to follow all its weird twists and turns, or to appreciate why these are brought in this manner into the story.

It is because the African people do not tell stories the way they are normally told among other races. With a story out of Africa things do not happen the way one expects. Many characters vanish – they simply vanish from the story for no apparent reason. Some of the villians survive as heroes, and one-time heroes are written off with no ceremony at all. African stories follow a standard pattern which dictates that the attention of the listeners must be held. At no time must boredom set in. One must play with the listeners' emotions as one does with a toy doll. Make them laugh, make them cry, make them angry, thwart their expectations, puzzle them one moment, delight them, or repel them, the next. And always leave them with wide open mouths, begging for more.

The earlier parts included under 'The Story of *Lumukanda*' are standard throughout Africa. This section alone has over twenty thousand standard characters, complete with names, descriptions of physical appearance and the nature of their personalities. The story as told under the title 'The Journey to "Asazi"' is specifically for the Mambo-Nguni-Xhosa group of tribes and it is only logical that it should differ substantially from similar records in West, Central and East Africa.

This is not a story intended only to entertain the listener; basically it embodies tribal history. But it is presented in the chosen form to maintain interest and avoid boredom. To achieve the latter, flights of fantasy are permissible from time to time; but even these are taken with the express object of preserving for posterity items and episodes of a purely mythological nature – pure folklore. In addition, the story includes elaborate descriptions of all the various ceremonies performed on particular occasions, to ensure that in the course of time each ceremony will be performed precisely in the traditional way. And, of course, the complete story embodies Tribal Law in all its closest detail.

Book Four

Yena Lo! My Africa

INTRODUCTION

Like so many other books I have tried to write, like so many other pictures I have painted, like many of the statues I have carved from lifeless wood and even more lifeless stone, this book will no doubt meet with opposition and die without fulfilling its intended mission in this world. But I shall not despair – I shall not be discouraged, because he who takes an oath before the all-seeing gods to carry out a certain task, come what may, is already doubly shielded against the assegais of failure, ridicule and adversity.

I have taken this oath that I shall try my utmost, for as long as I tread the bitter footpath of life, to pass the message that is in my hands to the outside world – to reveal to the world truths about my people that have been deliberately suppressed for hundreds of years.

Much has happened in my unhappy continent since the year 1947 when I first decided to write this book – a book intended to blast away once and for all the ludicrous fallacies about my people that are fed to us in schools and churches; to demolish once and for all the high wall of ignorance existing between the rest of the world and my fatherland Africa.

Well do I remember the day when the first book I wrote was destroyed by my uncle, at the command of the priest of the mission school in whose area we lived because, said *Umfundisi* with a pious scowl, my writings were revolutionary and an affront to the Church. They would encourage an upsurge of heathenism among the Bantu people.

I had been working at that book for three whole months, using ink I made myself by dissolving the leads from a dozen stolen indelible pencils in a bottle of water. I had no money to buy ink. Under the silver skies of Western Zululand I had written this book, with a flat rock as my desk, while the cows lowed around me and the other herd boys engaged in friendly stick fights some distance away. I had also worked at it while the girl I loved, the one who eventually caused my expulsion from Hlazakazi Mission – the 'heathen' Zulu girl *Nondudwana* – watched me as we sat side by side in the hut. I can still hear the voice of *Nondudwana*, that uneducated little one whose father strutted about in a *beshu* loin apron (just as my own grandfather did), asking me in her small shy voice: '*Vusi*, what is it that you are writing?'

'A book, beloved one, a book for people to read.'

'Oh, and why are you writing a book when there are so many books in the Mission?'

I have been trying to communicate with the world for many years since those days in Zululand, and I have had the agonising experience of seeing many of the things I had predicted in 1947 come true, while the books I had written lay rotting under my bed – feasted upon by white ants and mice. 'Unless the Colonial Powers of Africa stop forcing their civilisation upon the Black man of Africa without first studying his outlook properly – trying to understand why he likes or dislikes certain things that seem senseless to foreigners, and what his reactions are to various things foreign to his culture – there would be much bloodshed and suffering in Africa in the near future.'

These were the words I wrote under the blue skies of Zululand in the spring of 1947. In those days things like the Mau-Mau, like the troubles in Rhodesia, like the tragedy of the Bukongo, and Sharpeville, which carried away a girl I was to marry and which made me all the more determined on the mission I had set myself – had not yet happened.

All these things were still locked away deep in the vaults of the future. But anyone with the slightest knowledge of the African's way of thinking could have foreseen them through the mists of time, even as far back as 1947. In those days the world was still recovering from the after-effects of the Second World War and Africa was not as much in the headlines as she is now. In those days the only independent African states were Abyssinia and Liberia, and that something which ignorant foreigners and bigoted politicians call 'African Nationalism' had not yet been spawned.

From the very beginning, thousands of years ago, the story of Africa has been a tragedy and to most of her present-day sons and daughters it is still a tragedy. No race of mankind has been so misunderstood; no race has been more misrepresented, more abused and misused than the Black race of Africa. The troubles seen in Africa today – the unnecessary death and suffering for which agitators and communists are conveniently blamed – had their origin in one thing only: the ignorance and selfish interests of your forebears, Oh White Man, and Arab! And even after three thousand years you have not changed much!

You took it for granted that we were nothing but lowdown, brainless, inferior sub-humans to which you could do anything with impunity – because we had no golden cities for you to destroy and loot the way you looted Cuzco of the Aztecs in Mexico; because we had no armoured warriors on snorting chargers whom you could challenge in fair battle; because we had no hookah-smoking and grape-eating Rajahs whom you could swindle and intimidate; because we had no sloe-eyed Mandarins for you to regale with cheap flattery and relieve of bales of rich silks and spices; because we had no chariots, no sea-going vessels, with which to throw our weight around and cultivate a false sense of superiority; because we had no rifles with which to kill men without giving them a sporting chance.

You carted millions of our people off and sold them into slavery, to the cotton plantations of America and the sugar plantations of Jamaica. You set our tribes one against the other, in the Congo, in Dahomey, and in Lu-Kenya. All this you did because you considered us brainless, brutish creatures which your gods created for your express pleasure and service.

When all your attempts at exterminating us failed, you tried to 'civilise' us, which is only a euphemism for bending our thought patterns and life habits to suit your ends, for sacrificing our cultural heritage and individuality and adopting a watered-down replica of your own. You fed us on falsehoods in your places of education. You threatened and cajoled us into accepting your religion – and, to our eternal regret, we partly did – because today you are not only strongly inclined to doubt the very religion you brought us, but you are calling those of us who still cling to your teachings de-tribalised fools. In your schools we have to sit and listen to a history of our country which you concocted yourself – a history both one-sided and biassed. We have to hear some of our chiefs being called tyrants simply because they had the audacity to resist your encroachment. In your Churches and Mosques we suffer the humiliation of hearing our holy ancestors being called heathens and godless pagans, while in the measure of our beliefs we feel ourselves nearer to God than you have ever been.

According to your own religion you were all heathens and pagans some two thousand years ago, and many of your peoples were heathens for many centuries subsequently. We can trace our religion, culture, mythology, legends and history back to tens of thousands of years in the past, farther back than any other known civilisation on earth, to the later stone age. It is part of our culture – we did not learn these from recent archaeological discoveries.

It is never too late to mend. Even a witchdoctor will never give up treating a patient until he breathes his last. One can still lock one's door after the lodger has run away with one's wife. Thus, although it may appear to be too late to avoid some considerable bloodshed in the future, there is still time for a book aimed at giving more than a bald description of the African's way of life, his frame of mind, his beliefs and his history.

Those who find it difficult to read between the lines may find this book entertaining – story-telling is one of the few outlets of entertainment amongst the Bantu – but those who can read between the lines will find in this book a means of access into the deepest recesses of the mind of the African.

HUMAN OR SUB-HUMAN?

At the dawn of human self-awareness, far in the mists of the past, a human being who was unlike those we see today, crept cautiously out of his place of safety and stood on the flat rock that was the threshold of his dwelling place. He looked across the hazy distance, across the forests that seemed to stretch to eternity, and he turned his clumsy neck and looked up into the silvery depths of the silent skies. His mate came out, her belly swollen with young, and with a low guttural sound she enquired what her lord and husband was looking at – what was there in the skies and forest that so claimed his attention? He scratched the back of his ugly head with a hand that was both clumsy and calloused from hard work – beast-trapping and bone- and stone-tool making.

'Why . . . why is everything like it is? Who or what are we? Where do we come from and what are we supposed . . . ?'

That man, one of the first specimens of *Homo sapiens*, now dead some tens of thousands of years, did not realise that he was asking a question which his descendants, present-day man, are still unable to answer. He was asking a question which knows no answer – a question forming the axis around which the entire world of human philosophy revolves, and around which also spin the countless religions like lost stars in the milky way.

'What is Man? Whence comes he? What is the purpose of his existence and whither his destiny?'

So easy a question to ask; so impossible to answer.

Some say God created Man in His image, so that man should look upon Him as his Father, attend to worldly things and do good deeds. Very numerous are the concepts or interpretations of just who or what God is, and even more countless are the doctrines prescribing our attitudes towards God. Some say Man ascended from lower forms of life within the framework of the concept of evolution. Others say (in Africa) that Man is but a container for a soul which undergoes a metamorphosis, like the egg, the caterpillar, the crysalis, prior to the emergence of the butterfly.

The soul inhabits the human body while in one of these embryonic phases, but it exists before the particular human being is born. It is considered, for example, that the 'egg' phase is there prior to birth – the 'caterpillar' phase accompanies the human life; after death the soul reincarnates in some animal to spend its dormant 'chrysalis' phase there, while waiting to enter the spiritual world like the adult butterfly.

No two theories are absolutely the same and Man is no nearer to an answer than he was ten thousand years ago. It would appear, in fact, as though Man is systematically drifting farther away from finding a satisfactory answer in spite of his intensified search for it.

Across my bush-veiled fatherland hangs a similar question which seems to occupy the minds of men in a similar way: 'What is the African? Whence is he? Is he human after all and whither *his* destiny?

This is the question which prompted me to write this book. Had this question not intrigued me for so long, I would not have mustered the courage to betray the soul of my people by exposing it to the gaze of a curious world.

This is the question – the key to a belief that has caused the death of more than eight hundred thousand people of my race in Central, Southern and East Africa in the short space of the past five years. This is the key to a belief about the Black people of Africa, generally held by all the people of the rest of the world. I shall have failed in my sworn promise before the High Gods of my Fatherland if I hesitate to deal with this question courageously and mercilessly. Are Africans human or sub-human?

Am I being ridiculous? Peruse any of the leading newspapers printed in Africa (which are not under African control) and the reader will become conscious of something which has been going on for centuries. Hardly a month goes by without some White readers writing letters to the editors in which they blatantly insult the African. There are regular writers of such letters in which Africans are called ape-descended sub-humans – inferior races. And very often the writers have the effrontery to use a *nom-de-plume.*

Not only do these men display a shocking lack of even the rudiments of science, but also a complete lack of breeding, in insulting and criticising my people about whom they know nothing. I do find it strange, too, that the efforts on the part of scientists, Government officials and other authoritative persons to check this abuse are rather weak, to say the least.

When we write letters to these newspapers protesting against these unscientific insults, our letters are either coldly ignored or, if published, they are shortened to pointlessness. Is it because the opinions of superior humans count more than those of inferior sub-humans?

I am an inferior sub-human, and very proud to move in the company of Booker T. Washington, George Washington Carver, Professor Jabavu, and John Langalibalele Dube. The latter's spirit should glory in the fact that in spite of the scorn and ridicule of the so-called superior human beings, I, one of his descendants, am today labouring to lift our people from the morass of ignorance in much the same way as our critics' leaders did only a century or two ago.

I am no sentimentalist. I am no mailed crusader with a halberd to grind. I am not a do-good Pharisee venturing to do the impossible by getting people to like my race. But I am one of those who feel that it is high time the truth be spoken, even at this late hour. And while granted the opportunity, I desire to speak the whole truth, not just a part of it. Much of what I shall reveal will amuse, and even disgust you. But to the best of my ability I shall reveal the truth, or what I honestly believe to be the truth.

When I was studying to be an altar boy – or 'acolyte' – years ago in Zululand, I stumbled upon a discovery which greatly bewildered me. As is well known, there is a quaint ritual in all Roman Catholic mission churches requiring altar boys to recite prayers in the ancient, extinct, European language known as Latin. One must know just what prayer to recite at certain stages of Mass, and one must have some elementary knowledge of what each prayer means. The Father of the Mission Station had a small English–Latin dictionary and he allowed me to glance through it in the difficult moments when I was studying in order to pray in this very strange foreign tongue.

One day I perused the dictionary with more than my usual bewildered interest; I had come across a word which not only sounded like a well-known Zulu word, with only a slight difference in spelling, but which had exactly the same meaning!

This was in the cold month of June, 1942, and as I paged through the little dictionary the great Church-cum-school with its rough long benches suddenly seemed to grow colder – colder than the hidden tombs of the long-dead rulers of Lufiri and Zima-Mbje.

I found close to a hundred words in this dictionary alone, which not only matched Bantu words, but had the same meaning. I was completely astonished: it was too fantastic, too unusual, to be anything but a gigantic coincidence, or a prank of one of my ancestral spirits at my expense. I even began to doubt my sanity. The men who had spoken Latin were White men, now dead and gone two thousand years since, and it was impossible for two races – one White and long extinct; the other Black and extant – to share a common heritage which would issue in a common language. That was my line of reasoning in those days.

I cannot remember what it was that re-kindled my interest in this mystery of the languages, after having dropped it on my arrival in Johannesburg. But I do remember that by the end of the year 1949 I had come to a conclusion that greatly startled me: this was that all languages spoken by the different races of Man originated in one ancestral language just as all Bantu languages originated in one mother language – the Bambara. I had come to the conclusion that this ancestral language from which all the world's languages sprang, had come into being somewhere in the Early Stone Age, and that it must have been the most perfect, the most complete and the most advanced language the world has ever known. So perfect had this common ancestral language been that it had words for things and actions for which the breakaway tribes could not invent new words while their languages evolved in different directions through the millennia.

This discovery, which I made completely on my own when still a boy, unaided by the results of linguistic research and the guidance of teachers, brought me to the further conclusion that the Bantu races have sprouted from the same basic stock which has given rise to every other race in the world. The Bantu could not have had a separate origin and they are not sub-human.

I do not tender this argument to prove something which has not already been substantially proved. It is merely an illustration of what goes on in the mind of an African.

I have collected more than eight thousand Bantu words which have direct equivalents in languages beyond the shores of Africa. If I had not been so considerably hampered by an imperfect education I am sure I could have accumulated many more. I feel somewhat restricted in my attempts to do library research and much of what I have learnt about other languages has been through the medium of direct contact with people who speak these languages, including Hindus, Arabs and so forth. I must salute the little Jewish boy who added yet another interesting item to my list. He brought it to me like an angel, and he did indeed resemble one of those cherubs so frequently depicted by Botticelli. We had been conversing for some time when he disclosed that he was attending a Jewish school where he was taught through the medium of Hebrew, but that Yiddish was spoken in his home. My curiosity was aroused like a mamba:

'Tell me, what do you call father and mother in your language?'

'Zey call fazzer '*Aba*' and mozzer '*Ima*'.

Trying hard not to burst into tears I thanked the little descendant of Jacob, and was soon on my way to write this down on my list before the words escaped my memory:

Ma, Mama (Mother) – Bantu, International; *Ima* – Yiddish.
Baba (Father) – Zulu, Shangaan, Shona; *Aba* – Yiddish, Syrian.
Tata (Father) – Xhosa, Hottentot; South American Indian; *Ata* – Nyassa, Turkish (as in Ataturk).
Rara, Rre, Rra (Lord, Master) – Bechuana; *Rabbi, Raboni* – Hebrew.
Hamba, Kamba, Namba, Nambuza (Go, Move) – Bantu; *Ambulare* – Latin.
Jabula (Happy) – Zulu; *Jubilans* – Latin.
Pula (Rain) – Sutho; *Pluvius* – Latin.
Mfula, Mfura, Fula, Fola (River) – Bantu; *Fluvius* – Latin.
Mafuta, Futa, Fura, Namfuza (Fat, Oil, Oiliness) – Bantu; *Naphtha* – Greek.
Kgosi, Kosi, Nkosi (Lord, Chief) – Bantu; *Kyrios* – Greek.
Nyoni, Noni, Nonyane (Bird) – Bantu; *Ornis* – Greek.
Into, Nto, Nto-le (Thing) – Bantu; *Ontos* – Ancient Greek.
Kaya (Home) – Bantu; *Gaya* – Hindu.
Dedela (Let go, Yield, Surrender) – Bantu; *Dedere* – Latin.
Kusa (Dawn) – Bantu; *Kwusha* – Nyassa; *Ushas* – Sanskrit; *Eos* – Greek.
Sanusi (Unmarried High Witchdoctor) – Bantu; *Sanyassi* (Unmarried Holy Man) – Hindu.
Aka (To Make, Build) – Bantu; *Maak* – Teutonic; *Architectus* (Builder) – Latin.
Mini (Morning) – Bantu; *Menes* – Latin.
Tlapa (Stone) – Sutho; *Lapis* – Ancient Egyptian, Greek.
Sika (Cut) – Bantu; *Secare* – Latin.
Sa (Healthy, Sane) – Bantu; *Sanus* – Latin.
Sinda (To live, Survive) – Bantu; *Zinda, Zindabab* – Arabian, Persian.
Tumbe, Tumba (Tumour, Abscess) – Bantu; *Tumere, Tumour* (To swell, a swelling) – Latin.
Bupiro, Pilo, Mpilo (Life) – Bantu; *Spiro* (To breathe, to live) – Latin.
Sita, Sira, Isita (Adversary, Obstructor, Enemy) – Bantu; *Satan, Satanas* – Hebrew; *Sta* – Gaelic (Stranger as in Staoglach).
Mina (Me, Myself) – Bantu; *Me, Meus, Mei* – Latin.
Kwa (In the place of) – Bantu; *Quuam* – Latin.
Pele, Pambili (Before, in front of) – Bantu; *Pre* – Greek.
Sela (Lawbreaker, Wretch) – Bantu; *Sceleratus* – Latin.
Lwe (Him) – Bantu; *Lui* – French.
Susa, Suka, Isisusa (Source) – Bantu; *Source* – French; *Surgere* – Latin.

Bulabula, Bulela (To speak, Utter) – Bantu; *Hablan* – Spanish.
Lebe, Indlebe (Lobe, Ear) – Bantu; *Labium* – Latin.
Eyalwa, Eoalwa, Joala, Tshwala (Ale) – Bantu; *Eala* – Anglo-Saxon.
Bila (To boil, Bubble) – Bantu; *Bulla* – Latin.
Tshela (To tell) – Bantu; *Tell* – English and Teutonic.
Naka, Noka, Nyoka, Noha (Snake) – Bantu; *Snake* – Anglo-Saxon.
Goga (To lead) – Bantu; *Gogos* – Greek.
Vala (To shut, to conclude) – Bantu; *Vale* (Farewell) – Latin.
Nganga Nyanga (Witchdoctor) – Bantu; *Anga, Angakok* (Medicine man) – Eskimo.
Indlu, Ntlu (Hut, Dwelling place) – Bantu; *Igloo* – Eskimo.
Fedile, Pelile (Finished) – Bantu; *Fertig* – German.
Suit (Sated, Satisfied) – Bantu; *Sate* – English.

One could carry on *ad nauseam*. Examine these sentences or phrases:

When a Zulu says: *Mina angazi lutho*, the English equivalent would be *I do not know anything*. But analyse this simple phrase. *Mina* is a contraction of *Mi-ena*, which means *Me – this one here*, or, *myself*. The word *angazi* contains the initial vowel sound 'ah' as the negative, and here we see the equivalent in the Greek *agnostikos*. *Mina angazi lutho* therefore literally translated means *Me – of this one – not know – naught*. The positive equivalent is *Mina ngazi utho* (I do know something) but literally translated it would be *Me – of this one – know ought*.

Thus in almost any sentence spoken in an African language one can find on closer examination a mixture of Latin, Greek and even Anglo-Saxon parallels. Here is another example:

Let' into ya-mi la (Bring the thing of me here).

Leti is loosely used to mean *bring*, but its real meaning is 'cause to be' or 'bring about' and is thus the equivalent of the English word *let*. The noun *into* means 'a thing' and has its equivalent in the ancient Greek word *ontos*, meaning exactly the same. *Ya* means 'of', and I cannot find an equivalent for this preposition in any other non-African language. *Ya-mi* nevertheless means 'of me' or 'mine'. *La* means 'here' and is often lengthened by the Zulus to *lapa*.

Behold – in the dusty centre of a Zulu village lost in the forests of Nkandla two *piccanins* struggle over a toy, and when one grabs it and runs away, the owner pursues and screams: '*Leti . . . leti into ya-mi la*!' And with these few words uttered by an angry child in a grass kraal under the African sun, a few languages are united: Latin, the long-dead language of a long-dead race, the Romans; Greek, the language of Homer and Alexander the Great; Anglo-Saxon, the language of Alfred the Great . . .

'*Mu lau wa kgosi ure . . .*' This is the ceremonial cry with which tribal messengers-of-the-King prefaced their announcement of the promulgation of a new law by the Kings of Bechuanaland: '*The law of the King is saying*...' For centuries before the Bechuana had their first introduction to English, they laid down their own laws even though this word eventually acquired a somewhat different spelling. But there are also the equivalents in the Latin *lege* and the Greek *logos*, and *Kgosi* matches the Greek *Kyrios*.

The Southern Basutu call their King *Morena* or *Murena*. The *mo* or *mu* prefix is the equivalent of the English suffix *er* in plumb*er* or carpent*er* and denotes the agent. Mu-Rena therefore means 'the one who – rules'. *Rena* or *Renna* means 'to sit in the regal seat' and there are the equivalents – *reign* (English) and *regnat* (Latin).

When Germans talk of something that is hot they say *heiss*, and the Congolese, who has never seen a German, describes the same experience as *Hisa*, while the Sutho and the Zulu, who had equally little contact with Germans, talk of *shisa* and *chisa*.

Another thing I found equally puzzling long before I discovered that it is a standard biological phenomenon, where the embryo of any living creature inclines to recapitulate certain outstanding stages of the particular creature's phylogeny, is the fact that Bantu babies are born with skins much lighter in colour than that of their parents, or the colour they themselves eventually acquire. In addition they are born with full heads of soft, glossy, straightish hair. This hair is known amongst the Bantu as the 'hair of innocence', since it is believed that these are replaced with the coarse, typically negroid, woolly hair only when the child can begin to distinguish between right and wrong. This hair is, of course, never cut or shaved because this would shorten the period of the child's innocence.

The dark skin and the woolly hair of the African is therefore a secondary development – an adaptation to living more exposed under a fierce tropical sun. And while even the nose is high bridged and narrow in Nordic Tribes more effectively to warm the cold Scandinavian air, our nostrils are large and wide and consequently low bridged as an adaptation to breathing air which our ancestors considered adequately warm when inhaled.

We are all variations on a theme. All human races have sprouted from a common stock and became variously adapted to the different environments into which they migrated.

The question now arises as to *where* man originated and in what directions he migrated. There are those who claim that Africa was the cradle of mankind while others cling to Middle or Far East theories. It is my conviction, based only on my own observations, that mankind originated in South East Asia. From there he distributed himself along with numerous kinds of animals in all directions, prompted by a catastrophe. And from there he migrated also into Africa.

These are my observations: Granted the African man-ape *Australopithecus* gave rise to the more intermediate *Pithecanthropus* also found outside Africa, and the latter gave rise to the ape-man *Homo neanderthalensis* found more frequently outside Africa, we have yet to come to the origin of true Man, *Homo sapiens*, who, to my mind, quite definitely originated outside Africa. And the area to which all evidence seems to point was a vast continent which had become partially submerged, leaving only the highest regions exposed above sea level as a complex of islands generally referred to as the East Indies.

This continent had all along been effectively separated from Australia with the result that nothing escaped the catastrophe in that direction. But the whole area must have been continuous with Asia, and not only did man escape in that direction, but also numerous kinds of animals. Both the Pleistocene fossil record and the present geographical distribution of animals point towards a spread from that region. We can follow the trails of the lion, the elephant, the rhinoceros and many others. They were present and more abundant along these trails the farther we trace them back into prehistory. Some of these predominantly African species still have living counterparts that were left behind, so to speak, like the Indian elephant and the South East Asian rhinoceros. The lion's presence in those parts we know from recent history. Examples are countless.

But how can we be sure that the migration took place into Africa and not from Africa? Because Africa is and always has been a paradise for animals. No animal living in it would care to leave it across the inhospitable Middle East region and the Sahara barrier.

More significant than this zoo-geographical consideration is the botanical, and especially the origin and distribution of fruit-bearing plants. All the varieties of more outstanding palatable fruit originated within an area with South East Asia at the centre. Man's dentition is that of a fruit eater, and man promoted the origin of all these fruits. He lived where they were and he cultivated new varieties. Africa is conspicuous in that it never produced a single plant with a fruit particularly palatable to Man.

Man turned carnivorous by force of circumstances. After a catastrophe drove him from his paradise, his Shangri-La, he fled into regions devoid of his natural food. And especially in Africa he encountered great adversities.

Bantu legends date back to times prior to the discovery of the domestic use of fire. Our folklore is rich in stories of the times when our ancestors knew only bone and stone tools and they still relate in detail how these people had to accustom themselves to eating raw meat. They suffered from indigestion. They could chew raw meat only when it was still warm, freshly cut from an animal just killed. The meat of an African antelope is not as soft as that of a domestic sheep or ox. The tougher flesh can certainly not be chewed raw with a dentition such as the human being has at his disposal.

Moreover, raw meat has not an attractive taste to any human being, neither has cooked or fried meat for that matter, unless it is treated with salt and other spices. It took our ancestors a long time to discover this. But it nevertheless points to the fact that meat of any description is not the human being's natural food. According to our legends our ancestors explored all possibilities, and more from necessity than from their own free will they allowed the tougher meat to rot before they could consume it.

Maggots were encouraged to bore their way through the tougher fibres so as to soften it. Even today many Africans still keep their meat until it starts to crawl and then they treat it with crushed leaves from the *ntshubaba* herb. This meat is known as *inyama enobomi*, or 'meat that has life in it'.

We passed this recipe on to the White Man. Many Europeans prefer venison that approaches the crawling stage.

All Man's meat recipes are designed to alter its taste, to make it taste like the fruit around which his species originated.

I have dealt with the phenomenon of the common ancestry of all languages. But a new approach seems necessary in tracing these languages back to that South East Asian region. I have pointed to some words whose equivalents are to be found in Persian, Hindu, Sanskrit, but I can go much further. The Australian Aborigines talk of *corroboree* when they refer to a dance. This word occurs in Africa as *kurubu* or *hurubu*, which the Zulus have corrupted into *hubo*. In Africa the meaning has become extended to 'a great uprising and a free-for-all dancing'. This word is the mother of the now well-known African word *huru* or *uhuru*, which means 'release', or 'free from restraint', otherwise, in a more restricted political sense, 'freedom'.

What was this catastrophe of which I had already hinted? It must simply have been a vast subsidence of the land. There is not a race on this earth but whose mythology perpetuates the memory of this unforgettable incident. In the Middle East Noah is reputed to have built an 'Ark' to survive this catastrophe. 'Bwana' Homer picked up the legendary thread in terms of a continent called Atlantis, but it would appear that he held his compass upside down. According to African mythology this continent, which we call Ka-Lahari, was also located in the opposite direction. Even according to Hottentot mythology there was a time when the Great Waters invaded the land and fire fell from heaven.

That this subsidence took place in the east and not in the west is rather obvious to me. No continent can subside so completely that its highest mountainous regions also disappear below sea level. The geographical distribution of all those islands comprising the East Indies is characteristic of the mountainous regions of a continent. Depress any of the present continents only partially below sea level and a similar picture of islands and archipelagos can be visualised.

If one looks at the land masses surrounding the North Atlantic, the South Atlantic and the Indian Ocean one sees that all these areas are generally wide expanses of territories with an insignificant height above sea level. But all the land masses surrounding the Pacific Ocean – Australia, Japan, Alaska, North and South America – border this ocean with fantastic mountain ranges. Could it be that as this area became depressed, the margins 'curled up', so to speak?

With only a few exceptions the world's most violent volcanoes, geysers, hot springs and areas most prone to severe earthquakes are to be found distributed around this circumference, as though weaknesses had developed in the earth's crust as a result of the subsidence.

In studying a plant, one must at the same time study the soil in which it grows, the water it absorbs, the air it breathes and the light it assimilates. Nothing in this world is an entirely independent entity, and least of all is a particular race of Man such an entity. To understand a particular race of Man one must know Man as a whole. And Mankind in turn must be seen as a product of his environment. No zoologist can claim that he understands a particular animal unless he understands it ecologically.

Man's environment is the world as a whole, and the latter's environment is our solar system. 'Man is part of the stars – and the stars, sun and the moon are all part of Man!' Thus believe the Fire-Worshippers of the Southern Bu-Kongo.

Astronomy was not brought to Man in Africa by Western Civilisation.

We have our own theories on the origin of our solar system. These we have jealously withheld from foreigners for fear of being ridiculed. But I have compared our theories with those brought to us from beyond the seas, and the latter do not impress me. I do not fear ridicule and scorn, because it is said in our sayings of wisdom that 'He that is the first to walk past the village of the cannibals is the quickest to land in the cooking pot', an expression used for those who invite scorn and ridicule merely by being first to promote a new idea.

Thus Jesus Christ himself was ridiculed, but today millions adhere to His teachings; Galileo was laughed at – as was Nicolas Copernicus, but today we bow before their statues. Darwin was scorned, and even today there are pockets of resistance, but his teachings have successfully ousted many a fondly held belief.

Ridicule never kills. On the contrary, it has sustained many a theory which might have died without it.

The reason people from beyond the seas look upon the Black Man of Africa as stupid is that *we* have all along been afraid to show them that we too can think, that we too have ideas of our own. There is nothing a Black Man fears more than ridicule.

I do not believe that all the planets of our solar system sprang from our sun. Our sun is an ordinary star of which there are millions in the Universe, and how many of these have planets? I believe that planets are formed through the disintegration of such stars. A star merely explodes or is torn apart by collisions or gravitational forces and scatters as countless droplets hurled in all directions. These smaller bodies lose their inherent heat sooner and solidify as they wander through space. Many are subsequently caught by the gravitational force of other stars and go into orbit around them. Our sun's planets are such droplets that had been caught from time to time through the millennia.

The very smallest droplets lack the momentum to persist in orbit and plunge into the sun, but some were caught by the gravitational force of the various planets already in orbit around the sun. The larger planets caught more satellites than the smaller, and this would appear to be the only phenomenon accountable in terms of natural laws. Otherwise all the characteristics of the solar system seem to oppose every alternative theory. Sizes and distances, planes of orbiting, speeds and temperatures would have been more regular or systematic had the solar system originated according to any of the other theories. Our solar system is, on the contrary, inconsistent; planets are not logically arranged according to size and distance. Our planet has one moon while Venus of similar size has none and a smaller planet like Mars has two. Jupiter's planets all seem to be in good shape while those of Saturn have all collided and disintegrated. Apparently a sizable 'moon' entered the solar system after many planets were already orbiting and instead of being caught by one, collided with it to produce the belt of asteroids. Everything seems to point to the fact that our solar system was not formed as a result of a single process, but gradually came into being as a result of successive occurrences.

For this theory there is no better proof than the condition of our own moon. Its surface is pocked with scars caused by meteoric bombardments and these bombardments did not occur while the moon was a satellite of our planet. Some of these scars and craters are so large that the objects responsible for them must have been of such size that, had they turned their attention to the earth instead, our atmosphere would not have offered adequate protection. Our moon came into orbit around this planet at a later stage, with a face not much different from what is has today.

If a single process had produced our solar system all orbits, of both planets and satellites, would have been in the same plane. The fact that they do in fact come near to a particular plane is simply because all bodies in our nebular system move closely in a particular plane.

This theory explains more successfully all the strange geological phenomena we see in the crust of our own planet. Vast orogenetic processes caused whole continents to rise and sink, to split, bend and wander, but all at different times during our geological history. It would appear that every time the sun caught another planet and especially when the earth caught its moon, heavy disturbances were caused on the face of the earth which not only affected the structure and nature of land and water masses, but also played havoc with animal and plant life. Such spectacular events certainly took place even after the origin of *Homo sapiens*, as is also borne out by the terrific ice ages of the Pleistocene.

And if these occurrences have disappeared from the memory of other races of mankind, they still live in the folklore of Africa:

'*Lo*! The earth opened and swallowed them all. They fled – they fled while the waters of the flood clawed at them and sent thousands of them to their doom. They fled while the whole unbalanced world shook, thundered and screamed in agony to the uncaring stars. It lasted for decades, but gradually the earthquakes died and the intervals grew longer. The floods calmed and the waters withdrew to their original levels. But the face of the earth had changed. Great land masses had drifted farther apart and some had expanded. Commanding mountains were turned into low hills and where there were plains great mountains reared their insolent heads to the clouds. Where there were lakes, there were now plains of mud, and rivers were blocked to make new lakes.'

Only such happenings could force populations of animals to move from one place, an environment to which they had adapted themselves, into another foreign environment to which they had to re-adapt themselves. Many failed to do so and died. They did not do so out of their own free will. Neither did Man venture out to explore regions beyond the horizons. He was forced to do so and he was not forced by wars. At this stage man was still uncivilised and he knew not the more refined products of civilisation. He still lived in ignorance in family groups and nothing is more characteristic of such primitive groups than their ability to populate with their imaginations unknown regions with monsters most strange and terrible to behold.

There are those who will no doubt dismiss this theory as so much nonsense spawned by an uneducated brain. But my spawning season has only begun. One day I shall write a whole book on this subject alone; here I shall briefly touch upon a few further aspects:

The African originated along with other races of mankind, outside Africa. Many of my own people will no doubt strongly oppose this statement. There is nothing they like more than the thought that Africa belongs to the African. They like this idea almost as much as the White Man dislikes the idea that he originated alongside black men. Let us look at some of the characteristics of my race to see how human or sub-human they are:

I am sure that the skin of the African is much thicker than that of any other race – in a literal sense; figuratively, I am afraid, the reverse is true. The purpose of this is, of course, to protect subcutaneous tissues from the injurious ultra-violet rays of the sun. Our skins are less sensitive than the skins of other races. I have performed numerous experiments on myself and those who were unfortunate enough to love me from time to time. They mostly had lighter skins than my own and theirs were more sensitive than mine. I have come to the conclusion that a Black Man has a thin subcutaneous 'dead layer' less richly supplied with blood than in light-skinned races. As a result the Black Man feels cold more intensely than a White Man.

Superficially a Black Man's skin is also much more resistant. Here, too, I have carried my experiments with all kinds of detergents also to subjects other than my own person, such as my troublesome present wife, who unfortunately emerged unscathed. Not only are our skins heavily pigmented and reinforced by a 'dead layer' to protect us against the fierce tropical sun – we also ooze a greasiness to protect our skins from drying, and if Europeans take offence to this it is hardly our fault. When a Black man takes a hot bath and directly afterwards sits quietly in the sun, he soon becomes conscious of an annoying ticklish sensation all over his body.

Lately many of our womenfolk have started using European cosmetics and these have the effect of inhibiting the skin from producing its own natural protective oil. As a result they develop wrinkles at a very early age, especially when they stop using this rubbish from Europe. I have seen many young girls of my race in the cities, who are users of these alien concoctions, with faces like those of antediluvian witches, with hard wrinkles about their noses and mouths, and crows-feet about their eyes. Oh, my Africa, what a ghastly price you have paid for the flimsy illusion of the nebulous thing called 'Western Civilisation'!

In hot countries like Africa foreign women age very quickly, while Bantu women rarely develop wrinkles till they are past fifty – tribal women, that is.

The Black Man's hair, more than anything else, tends to support the view that he originated elsewhere than in Africa. It is most unsuitable to the African climate and his African way of life. If the African had originated in Africa he would have evolved hair of a different nature. Apparently the tendency developed first for the hair to become coarse and woolly as a protection against the direct rays of the sun before the darker pigmentation could play its part.

I do not know how many people realise that the hair of a Negro is his greatest burden. If a Black Man leaves his hair untended he asks for trouble in a big bucket. Long, thick, woolly hair smothers the scalp and absorbs heat faster than loose straight hair. An African with long unkempt hair standing exposed in the direct rays of the sun soon develops a violent headache and his scalp sweats like a wet rag. This is why Africans indulge in such varied and ornate hairstyles. The women of the Bu-Kongo tribes are experts at making cool hairstyles, with numerous partings, or paths, to expose the scalp. It may be difficult to believe, but the *sicolo* hairstyle of the Zulu and some of the Swazi married women is one of the coolest in Africa, as all the heat is absorbed and radiated before it reaches the scalp. And in spite of its unwieldy appearance it is very light indeed.

The 'oldest inhabitants of Africa', the Bushmen and the Hottentots, solved this problem with a more advanced development. Their hair falls naturally into separate 'peppercorns' with the scalp amply exposed in between.

Another conspicuous characteristic of the Negro type is the flat nose. While I was still in the land of the Zulus I was among the boys who accompanied one of the priests of our mission school on his very strange expeditions. This priest had come from Berne in Europe, and he had a strange – to us insane – love of climbing mountains. Even today I cannot fathom why he risked his young life as he did for the simple pleasure of standing on a mountain top gazing down at the landscape below. Mountain-climbing is for the baboons. But the Reverend Father *Copo ba manzi* (Water-brain), as we called him, enjoyed every mad risky moment of it. And to make things more risky, and worse for us, he frequented the Drakensberg in midwinter, when the fearsome mountains were covered with snow and winds of bone-freezing coldness swept the plains of my land.

It was in the course of this unusual duty that I became aware of a strange thing indeed. As we reached the colder upper reaches of the mountains we Bantu boys were always similarly afflicted by burning pains in the nose that made the eyes run with tears, while it seemed as if the Reverend *Umfundisi* was not similarly afflicted. Of course we were silent about this, mostly because of the Bantu's inbred contempt for complaints about pain or discomfort. Eventually, however, one day out of sheer curiosity one of the elder boys discreetly asked the Reverend whether he too, experienced this strange thing. The priest was quite amazed and asked us why we had not told him about this before. But it was only two full years later that it occurred to me that the secret lies in the build of our noses. He had the high-bridged, narrow Nordic nose designed to warm the air when inhaled, while we, in common with Mongoloids, have wide flaring nostrils suitable for breathing the already warm air of the tropics.

There is also the phenomenon of eye colour. Not only are the eyes of Africans invariably dark, but also those of all animals indigenous in Africa. The typical African antelopes have very black eyes and one has to go very close to an impala to distinguish the pupil from the iris. This is another reason why I feel the lion with his pale yellow eyes is not indigenous to Africa.

I am quite sure, too, that the African's eyes are generally less sensitive to bright colours. It is never necessary for an African to wear dark glasses. Whenever I paint a picture, Europeans find the colouring too gaudy, too powerful for the eye. But this is actually very characteristic of African paintings. We are told they are so brilliantly colourful, but to us they appear quite subdued, and paintings of Europeans, which pass for colourful exhibits, look dull to us.

The White People say we Natives like bright colours in our clothes and one colour we particularly like is lemon yellow. White women find this colour offensively bright, but we describe it as *umbala onesizota* – a restful colour with dignity.

Thus it would appear that the Black Man and the White Man do not see eye to eye – in more senses than one.

THE RELIGION AND BELIEFS OF THE BANTU

PART I

Before one appoints oneself a judge of any race of Man on earth, one must have a thorough knowledge of the religions and beliefs of that particular race. The reason people from beyond the seas judge the Black Man so very wrongly is that they have not the slightest inkling of the true nature of the religions of Africa's sons and daughters. Ask any of these wise ones from abroad what the Bantu people believe in, and they will say the Bantu worship the spirits of their dead ancestors; they will tell you that the Bantu are a fetish-ridden, superstitious race sunk in the lowest levels of heathenism.

And they will be utterly wrong.

I have been a Christian; I was once a Muslim. And this I can tell without prejudice or fear: the Native religion of the Bantu, the religion of my fatherland, is greater and nobler than both those creeds. Of all the religions under the sun, ours is the most genuinely based on 'Love thy neighbour' and 'See, live, and let live'.

I have heard them say, in a foreign language once spoken by a race of scoundrels who made men kill each other for sport in the arenas of Rome: '*Dominus vobiscum, et cum Spiritu tuo . . .*'

I have heard them say, in the language of the bearded murderers who depopulated vast areas of my fatherland and carried my people off into slavery: '*La illallah illa Allah ho, wa, Muhammadur rassool Allah.*'

Every race, nation, community on earth, no matter how high or how low it stands on the ladder of 'civilisation', clings to a belief, a philosophy, a religion, or call it a superstition. But each clings with a tenacity that readily induces thousands and even millions of its subjects to lay down their lives in its defence. It may have been acquired from without, or it may be the embroidery of the race's own prophets and philosophers, and such beliefs constitute mostly those things that the particular race or nation regards as its ideals, its symbols or examples of spiritual and material perfection. In days gone by this belief nearly always took the form of reverence for a God or a number of Gods who were honoured or worshipped in particular ways.

The most peculiar thing one finds in this madhouse of humanity is that each race, each nation, insists foremost, in utter selfrighteousness, that its own beliefs are the only true ones and that those of other races are nonsense and plain barbarism. Today, the beliefs of nations have taken an even more sinister form. At present, until Man knows better we hope, the belief in Gods (or a God) is temporarily in eclipse – sunk to the gills in the morass of materialism. What the masses worship today is not a God, but a social system. And the quarrelsome bipeds who inhabit this world are willing to destroy the world itself in a holocaust of atomic warfare in order to prove that one or another of these seemingly different ways of enslaving the minds of fellows is the best.

The beliefs held by a particular race constitute that race's 'ego'. It is therefore wrong for one race to force its beliefs on another. In our witchcraft we consider it possible for one person to replace another person's soul with his own. It amounts to the same thing. A nation's soul is its religion.

The beliefs of any race go a long way in determining the ultimate fate of that race in the arena of human history. Many a race has been lifted to the highest heaven or cast down into the deepest pits of hell by its beliefs alone.

What drove the Moors and the Arabs across North Africa and into the valleys of Spain itself? What drove them into Lu-Kenya, and deep into the jungles of the Bu-Kongo? It was their flaming zeal to claim as much of the known world for Islam as they possibly could. What drove the sons of mediaeval Europe to don heavy steel mail, and sally forth to conquer the bearded Saracens in the Holy Land, so far away from their weeping females and bewildered young? What induced those millions of healthy young men to sacrifice their lives on the battlefields of the world in the last two Great Wars? They were fighting for what they thought to be holy.

> Oh, ye heaven-bejewelling stars—
> Oh, ye Ten Thousand Gods
> Of Dark Infinitude;
> Pity the pathetic folly—
> The biped fool, called Man!

Many races have been lifted up high by their beliefs alone. The pyramids of Egypt and the temples along the Nile; the temples of Greece and the ancient statues of their gods; the temples and the cities of the Incas; the temples and statues of India, China and Japan – all these great memorials, these wonderful expressions of art, engineering and architecture, can be traced directly to the beliefs of the men who built them. Yes, Man can do anything if he does so with his beliefs as the goad and the spur – but Man can also abstain from doing many things if his belief is the restraining handcuff and the chained ball.

Many races in history have actually been retarded – not by hereditary inferiority, but by the restrictive laws and dictates of their beliefs. If the English had burned Isaac Newton at the stake as a blasphemous heretic the secrets of the prism and the secrets of gravity may yet have eluded science. If the French had burned as a heretic Monsieur de Lesseps who wanted to improve on God's creation, the great Suez canal may never have been dug. If the Italians had killed Marconi, as Christians have done to so many leaders for their so-called un-Godly pursuits, radio communication may not have been what it is today. Why did Greece produce such great poets, mathematicians, inventors, philosophers and engineers? The Greeks produced their caustic satirists, playwrights, sculptors and artists, not because they were in any way superior, intellectually, to any of the other races they chose to call barbarian, but because their religious belief actually encouraged these things.

It encouraged men to pursue beauty in any form or shape. And no restrictions were placed on their inventive spirit to improve ways and means of pursuing their interests. Hence the more natural and more lifelike way of sculpture seen in the works of Pheidias, which even today are without equal for beauty and skill.

It encouraged men to pursue knowledge in all possible directions. Thus Archimedes, Pythagoras, and hosts of others could indulge in research without fear of persecution, and bring their theories to men whose minds were free and unfettered by narrow-minded taboos.

While there are such religions that are flexible and that allow the human mind free play for the betterment of humanity – and for the glory of God – so there are religions that are as rigid as the shaft of a lance: they demand blind, unquestioning compliance and they spread their hierarchy to all fields of human action. These religions resist change of any sort. They were laid down by men who wanted to make sure that those who followed would forever remain in a spiritual prison.

The creed of the Bantu is an inflexible one that coldly declares anything new to be an insult to the Gods; any man or woman who tries to invent something new is assuming powers that only Gods can possess. Such inventions must be destroyed no matter how useful they could be to the particular community. This kind of religion was developed with the specific purpose of resisting or discouraging change of any description, because such changes breed impiety and irreverence for things once regarded as holy.

For hundreds of years the religion of the Bantu has been veiled in a heavy *kaross* of mystery, even for those who have followed it. People – the ordinary people, that is – were forbidden under pain of death or a High Curse from inquiring too deeply into some of the rites they had to perform. The High Custodians of the Great Belief were only allowed to tell the common people so much and no more. Even some of our chiefs and kings were kept in the dark. Such leaders discovered in the end that they were nothing but puppets dancing on strings held in the hands of a Tribal Custodian and his witchdoctors. Even the heretic thug *Shaka* of the Zulus was deathly scared of the Custodians of the Belief and, as I shall reveal in another book, they were instrumental in bringing about his fall.

When the White Man came to Africa, bringing Christianity with him, the Custodians of the Belief urged the chiefs and chieftainesses of the tribes to resist the 'Strange Ones' and their alien creed. But when the Bantu were finally defeated they did what they had done nearly three thousand years before when the Ma-Iti invaded the lands of the tribes: to ensure that the Great Belief would not die, they selected a number of men, and women, from every tribe and binding them by a series of High Oaths, they told them everything there was to know about the Belief. There are so many High Legends to remember and so many stories of holy men, chiefs and witchdoctors that no human mind can hold all these and yet remain sane. A custodian-elect had to know so much that there was the great danger of forgetting many things, leaving what could be remembered in an inaccurate or distorted form.

There was only one way to solve this problem. The Great Knowledge was divided into many parts and subdivisions. Men were then chosen from different walks of life – blacksmiths, woodcarvers, medicine-men and others – from each tribe. The blacksmiths were told everything about the history of metal-working in the lands of the Bantu, the characteristics of the various kinds of metal and how to recognise the minerals from which these can be produced. They were told all the legends appertaining to metal and the rites and ceremonies a blacksmith must perform, and what laws he must obey, and why. The Chosen Blacksmith was under High Oath and, sworn to secrecy, commanded to impart all this knowledge to his sons, and they to their sons, without adding or subtracting a single word.

The same thing was done to the Medicine-men, the Tribal

Narrators, the Woodcarvers and so forth. Then, in every tribe the High Custodian formed a Hidden Brotherhood of High Custodians (Secret Society) whose duty it was continually to watch the Chosen Custodians ensuring that they had not forgotten anything, allowed nothing to leak to strangers, and imparted to chiefs and certain elders and *Indunas* what they were required to know.

The Hidden Brotherhood was also there for all the Chosen Ones to report to annually for additional checks, clarification, confirmation, and to receive new knowledge acquired in the meantime. The Hidden Fraternity also met in places where the young Chosen Ones were made to take oaths when they assumed duty. The most important obligation was to swear never to reveal the identity of any one of the High Hidden Ones, who were given (and still are given) the reverence and the respect due to a Lesser God.

Recruits for the Chosen Custodians, even for the Hidden High Fraternity, are selected from people with defects in the bodies, but with perfect memories. It is considered that the perfection of the body is in inverse proportion to the perfection of the brain. If a young man was genetically weak or impotent, deformed in any way or even marked by something unusual, such as a strange birth-mark, he suddenly found himself hauled out of his hut one night and carried away by masked men to a faraway deserted hut or cave, and there he was subjected to torture most fantastic – to degradation in its most shocking form, to condition his subconscious mind to receive the impressions they had planned to imprint on it.

A particular story was put across to him in such a way as to imprint a vivid picture in his mind that could never fade. But to make assurance doubly sure, he was required to retell the story a hundred times on a hundred different occasions while subjected to the vilest torture, to ensure that nothing at all could divert his attention. For example a High Brother would, from time to time, apply a red-hot knife to his body and if he lost the thread of the story he had to start again. Much was also done to create an eerie, sombre, or impressive atmosphere – the other High Brothers would, for example, dance in a circle all round chanting the one word 'remember' a thousand times.

The High Law forbids me to go into too much detail about these ceremonies. The initiation part lasts fourteen days. Suffice it to say that it is the most effective way of ensuring that nobody can ever forget what he is taught. Such is the effect of the vile drug concoctions that one is fed, prepared from a mixture of herbs, that not only does one see vivid pictures of the stories told, one also subjectively experiences in one's person the incidents depicted in the legends. During such instruction one is virtually continuously in an hypnotic trance and there are times when one vividly feels one is facing one of the Gods, or wrestling with a primordial monster that roamed the earth when the legend was born. One can also be made to feel that one's very soul is leaving one's body and diving down into the very depths of time, and one can look back across all the re-incarnations through which one's soul has passed.

There is a great deal more to tell, but I must draw the line here. There are things that even the most unscrupulous betrayer of his race must not reveal. Suffice it again to say that everything is based on the idea that one forgets what one is *told*, but one rarely, if ever, forgets what one vividly *experiences*. There are ways and means of making people experience – take part in – an incident that occurred thousands of years ago.

The Black People of Africa call themselves, and any other people on earth, the *Bantu*, *Watu* or *Abantu*. This loosely means 'people' or 'human beings'. People of Europe and parts of Asia are called *Abantu abamhlope*, meaning literally 'human beings who are white', while we call ourselves *Abantu abansundu*, or 'human beings that are dark brown'.

The word *Bantu* is plural, and its singular is *Muntu*, and it is this noun that is of the greatest interest. The prefix 'Mu' denotes the agent ('Ba' being the plural), like the 'er' in the English 'teach*er*'. The *ntu* is a contraction of the word *ntu-tu-tu*, which is an onomatopaeic word to describe the steps of a creature walking on two instead of four legs. From this word was born the Zulu word *tushu* which means 'a sudden coming up on to the hind legs', suitable for describing such an action in a four-legged animal, but in the case of human beings, such as in the sentence *Umtakati wavela wati tushu ngemuva kwesibaya*, it means 'The wizard appeared *suddenly erect on his two feet* from behind the kraal'.

Thus the word *muntu* means more than just a 'human being' or 'man'. It means 'he who walks erect' or, to denote the agent, the 'two-legg*er*'.

Among our somewhat varied early mythological legends there are versions reporting that the Tree of Life brought forth many different kinds of men. Some were big with ugly faces like that of a hippopotamus, and who walked on all fours. Others could fly like bats and yet others crawled like snakes. One day the Great Spirit tested all these different kinds in a variety of ways – in racing, fighting and numerous other endurance tests – and all these were won by *muntu*, the 'two-legger'. About these legends anon.

Now the common stock, the ancestral tribe from which all the Negroid tribes of Africa sprang, was known as the *Batu*, or the *Bantu*.

Legends say that this stock lived in the 'Old Land'. According to all African folklore all our culture and religions were born in this 'Old Land'. This was far back in the bone and stone ages.

Where was this 'Old Land'? It is there where the 'Old Tribes' are still found today – the *Watu Wakale*. These incorporate all the tribes of the land of the Bu-Kongo right up to the southern parts of the land of the Ibo and Oyo (Nigeria). These tribes belong to the basic stock of all such tribes who identify themselves with the prefix *Ba*. They are the Ba-Mileke, Ba-Mbara, Ba-Kongo, Ba-Ganda, Ba-Hutu, Ba-Luba, Ba-Tonka, Ba-Saka, Ba-Tswana, Ba-Kgalaka, Ba-Venda, Ba-Pedi, Ba-Sutu and Ba-Chopi. The southern offshoots – the Ba-Pedi, Ba-Venda, Ba-Kgalaka and Ba-Tswana – are the oldest Bantu tribes south of the level of the Limpopo and their histories within these regions go back to a thousand years BC.

All these tribes are direct offshoots of the Great Ba-Ntu nation that lived in the 'Old Land', as a properly organised tribe, a full 4,500 years ago, reckoned according to the genealogies. The Ba-Mileke of the Camerouns is so old that these tribesmen still speak the language their witchdoctors call 'spirit talk', which came down to us through the Ba-Kongo and the Ba-Mbara. We use this language when communicating with the very old spirits of the 'Ancient Ones'. This language is actually the language of the Stone Age – the first efforts by Man to speak. It consists largely of grunts and guttural animal sounds in which the words we use today are faintly distinguishable.

The Ba-Ntu, or the Ba-Tu, were the founders of our culture and our religion. And being a solid, uniform nation they were at peace for thousands of years. They were not ruled by chiefs, but by a High Council of the Mothers of the People – that is, all the Witches and Sybils over the age of forty. At this time the Strange Ones, the Phoenicians, or Ma-Iti, who came some five to six hundred years BC, and the slave-raiding Arabs were things of the distant future.

The Ba-Tu were at peace among themselves and because a High Curse was laid upon any person who stole as much as a single grain of corn from his neighbour, crime was totally unknown. There were warriors-elect who stationed themselves along trading routes at regular intervals, to protect travellers and traders against attack, not by human beings, but by wild animals. Man, in Africa at least, had not yet thought of offending a fellow man, physically or otherwise.

The ruling Council of the Mothers of the People used magic and naked intimidation to exercise control over all the people. These people had no fear of death; they knew it as something inevitable which had to come sooner or later, and capital punishment had no meaning whatsoever. The Mothers of the People also knew that corporal punishment infuriates, challenges and hardens the average criminally inclined human being and encourages him to become more cunning. Thus they kept war and crime away from their land with the one medium that impresses the average human being – witchcraft.

Tribal historians today still sigh for those days when there was only one race of man and the Spirit of Peace walked the land – when every man, woman and child, yea, every beast, felt the soothing protection of the soft-eyed, infinitely wise Mothers of the People.

This was the first and the last instance in the whole record of the Black People of Africa when pure witchcraft and black magic were used, not to terrorise people, but to keep peace in the land. For hundreds of years peace reigned in the land of the Ba-Ntu and in this atmosphere of peace the Great Belief was born. When eventually this nation broke up into the various tribes the Great Belief had taken such a strong hold on the souls and minds of people that they were completely lost without it.

The Great Belief had been so ingeniously tailored to fit the mind, soul and character of the Black Man of Africa that nobody ever dared to contemplate living his life without it. In fact, every man, woman and child lived it – became part of it – and in this sense the religion of the African differs from all other religions. All the other religions I know of are part of their section of Mankind. We say that the Whole of Mankind is but a small portion of our Great Belief.

With all other races of Man on earth, religion, politics, medicine, military and economic affairs, science, are all different entities, and religion is supposed to be something apart from all earthly or materialistic matters. Not so with the Black Man. Everything he does, thinks, says, dreams of, hopes for, is moulded into one structure – his Great Belief. Things like disbelief, doubt, agnosticism, atheism, disobedience are entirely unknown, unfathomable, senseless, within the framework of the Great Belief.

Another significant difference: all other religions seem to change from time to time to suit the purposes of various communities according to their way of life, standard of development, degree of civilisation or changed outlook in terms of science or world affairs. These religions must continually adapt and re-adapt themselves to suit the appetites of men. The Bantu can adapt themselves to all these circumstances without it having the slightest effect upon the nature of the Great Belief. They have long since taken these things into account. They look upon these things as insignificant characteristics of Man as much as Man is an insignificant characteristic of the Great Belief.

For this reason our religious ceremonies – prayers, chants, sacrifices, summoning spirits from the Upper or Lower World, creating zombies, 'deep talk', hypnotism and mind power – are exactly the same from the Transkei to Mali, Dahomey and Ghana. And this shows how wrong foreign scientists and social anthropologists are when they study the tribes of Africa piecemeal. There is in fact only one slender dividing line across Negroid Africa – that which marks out the Old Stock, the Old People or the Greater Bantu (true Negroids in physical anthropology) and the Younger People or Lesser Bantu (Negroids in physical anthropology – a designation that makes no sense). The Khoisanoids are, of course, not taken into account, neither are the Caucasoid Arabs and Nilotes, the latter including the Watu-Tu-Tsi and the Masai – the Children of the Dragon (according to legend, spawned by the evil serpent with the sole purpose of oppressing and destroying the Bantu).

It is said that the Bantu have no conception of a universal single God – that in their religion they worship the spirits of their long-dead ancestors; that they are superstitious and fetish-ridden and tremble when the thunder growls. The world has been shown images carved by the Bantu. And this would appear to be the sum total of the knowledge foreigners have gained about our religion.

The Bantu believe in the existence of God. But their concept of God is different from that of other races. While we believe in a heaven our concept of heaven is totally different from that held by other races. The Bantu version of Hell is an Evil Land. But in this land we see no Devil with tail, horns and a forked tongue, tormenting the souls of the wicked in eternal fire.

I would like to start at the beginning and explain everything clearly but my command of English is inadequate for the purpose. After long and careful thought I have decided to write down in Zulu an exact transcription of the account given me by my instructor at the time of my initiation as a Chosen One, and then to translate it word for word into English. Even this leaves me at a disadvantage, however, since Zulu is a much more descriptive language. Anyway, here it is:

'My son, you who today are to be welcomed into the Sacred Kraal of those chosen to bear the heavy load that is the Lore, the History and the Beliefs of your forefathers for the ears and brains of those as yet unborn; you who are today to be one of the few torches that have been lit in the Great Darkness covering our native land these days, so that the religion of your forefathers and mine do not die – hear my words with your brain and your soul and with every nerve and fibre of your body and blood.

'What you are to be told this day is something that very few ever are told, and which many would give their lives to know; and what you are about to be told this day is not for the ears of the common rabble out there in the plains and valleys of the land, the unthinking rabble who can never understand much of what they are told anyway. Neither is it for the ears of the foreigners from beyond the seas, who would only use what you tell them to enslave the spirits of your people and destroy the Bantu in spirit and turn their bodies into empty soulless shells – slaves in spirit as much as slaves in flesh.

'If you ever pass what you are about to be told today on to the ears of the aliens, a curse shall fall upon you and dog you for the remainder of your days. Men shall come who will tear your living body with sharp weapons, and the very aliens to whom you will have dared betray the spirit of your people shall revile and deride you, and you will know no peace no matter where you go, and you will be injured alike by enemies from without as by those with whom you share the love mat. And your own children shall take your life eventually and you shall lie in a grave of blood and shame – by the Gods cursed and by men abhorred.

'Listen well now, my son – listen with the ears of your flesh and with the ears of your soul; listen to and memorise each word that I am going to tell you. Let each one of my words be deeply burned into your heart, as a man burns a sacred sign on to a piece of wood with a hot awl. Let each one of my words be like a scented breeze that blows through the plains and the valleys of your heart, now and forever more. Let my words be written in signs of hidden wisdom on the cliffs of your memory to the day when you shall pass the knowledge of what I tell you to those as yet unborn and to those who shall be chosen by you for this task.

'My child, you know from the teachings of your parents that every child is taught that there is a Great God (and that there are also the Lesser Gods), but you do not know just what the Great God, whom we shall call the Most Ultimate God, is, and this you are about to be told this day. The Most Ultimate God, who is the God of the Gods of the Gods, is Everything *in* Everything. Each tree, each blade of grass and each stone that you see out there, and each one of the things that live, be they men or beasts, are all parts of God, just as each one of the hairs on your head and each flea in your hair and each drop of your blood is part of you. The sun is part of God; the moon is part of God and each one of the stars is but an infinitesimal part of Him who Is, and yet is not, Him who Was, and yet was not, and Him who Will Be, and yet shall never be; because there never was a time when God was not and there never is a time when God can never be.

'My child, never must you doubt for one single moment that there is a God, because to deny or doubt the existence of God is the greatest form of madness there can ever be. Remember this, that the living heart that beats within you does not realise that it is part of something greater still. It sees only itself, and the fact that it is part of you does not enter its mind, and if you were to tell it that it is part of you it would never believe you. If you were to tell one of the hairs on your head that it is part of something greater still it would never believe you, because it has eyes only for those other hairs near it, and for it the plain of flesh that is your scalp is its world, and that it is part of a still bigger whole does not enter its narrow stupid mind.

'My child, God is more in you, and is more part of you than you are in and part of yourself. He exists in you more than you exist in yourself. You were not created by God as the aliens tell you, but you exist as part of God. Your soul is immortal, because God is immortal, and your soul and mine are as much part of God as the grain of sandstone is part of the boulder that is part of the mountain.

'My child, I want you now to look at this ball of clay. This ball of clay is known as the Ball of Instruction and was first used generations ago by the Great Ones of the Mother Nation known as the Ba-Tu from whom we all sprang, to instruct those whose duty was to carry the flaming cresset of our beliefs on to posterity. This ball has another ball inside it, and that one has still another smaller ball inside it; there are seven balls within each other here, where you only see the outer ball. And this, my child, is the ball that symbolises all our knowledge and our beliefs – that everything under the sun is but part of something greater still. This ball, my son, is our symbol of infinity.

'You will want to know what God looks like and how he would be interpreted by your eyes and your brain were you to see Him, but my child, other than that we know He exists for the very reason that we ourselves exist, we do not know for sure, and we must never try to know for sure. No man can ever see God and live or understand what he has seen, for God is such that His very Essence, His very Being and His very Shape would be beyond the interpretation of the human eye and the human brain.

'We can only guess, and the oldest guess at the possible form of God is the one that you must go and touch in the land of the Swazi when your hair begins to turn grey according to the law that binds all of the Chosen Ones. The other one is in the land of the Batswana and you must never let death close your eyes before you touch with your hands both these symbols of Eternity. These symbols are carved in the red and white *simbiti* wood which is a sacred wood that can only be used in the carving of very holy things and images. Both these carvings show God as shaped like a great canoe with a human head at the stern and a human head at the prow. These heads are both looking up into the heavens, which is a sign that God continues into infinity and has neither end nor beginning. Riding in the canoe is an image of a woman which symbolises the Great Mother, the Ultimate Feminine Creative Cause of All, and a symbol of the bisexuality of the Most Ultimate God. The body of the canoe stands on the back of a carved wooden crocodile without a tail, and this shows that God is neither evil nor good, neither life nor death, neither merciful nor cruel; God exists but as far as we know for no reason whatever. God is neither beneficial to us nor interested in us in any way.

'The other representation of God is that which shows a figure which is neither male nor female, with a neck and a backward-facing head growing out of the top of its forward-facing normal head. The larger forward-facing head symbolises that God is already ruling supreme in the future just as He is ruling in the present, while the one head on top that looks backwards symbolises that God is ruling also in the past as He does in the present and the future. In ancient times such figures were carved at the top of long poles that were then buried in the centre of the village clearing, and this pole was used to measure the time of day from the shadow it cast.

'Another symbolic carving of God's possible form is that which

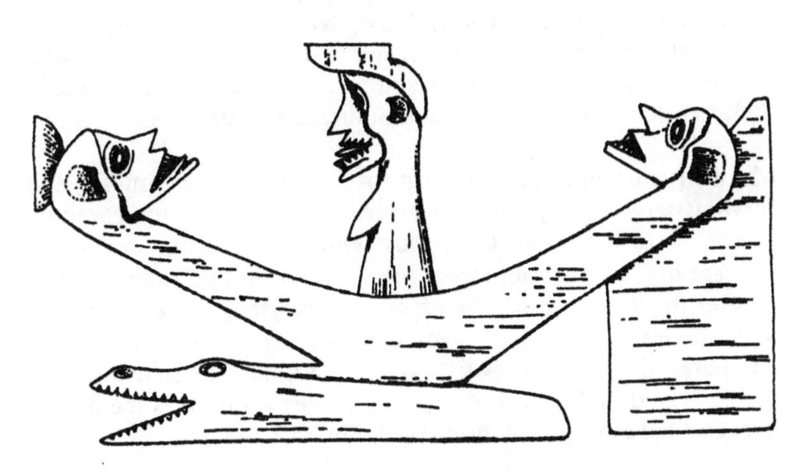

shows Him as a number of heads, one above the other and often surmounted by a complete standing figure at the very top. Others show God as a number of figures with faces also in their trunks carved one above the other, all on a stand which is often a human head. All these representations of God mean only one thing – that He rules and sees twice not only the past, present and the future, but also the many unseen worlds that the Lesser Gods, and other beings both strange and fantastic, inhabit. Yet another representation of God is a mask with signs of secret wisdom deeply carved in it, and above the forehead is carved a figure of a man with a drum between his legs. This mask is a copy of a similar concept of God that comes from the Old Land and which portrays God as a head with long ears and a strange small animal, part rabbit and part lizard, holding a drum and sitting between the ears. This concept is often used in fairy tales and is reserved strictly for the teaching of children of the common people, who, until they know better, must be able to hold in their minds a picture of God as a Great Chief with a little attendant who sits on His head and beats the drum to wake Him should He fall asleep. This conception of God must be kept only in those huts set aside for those whose duty it is to adopt and bring up little orphans.

'All these carved concepts of the form of God are only a means of satisfying the common rabble which cannot be made to worship any God unless that God has a shape that they can more or less understand and hold in the mind. They are also intended to discourage young people from asking too many questions and you, Oh Chosen One, must only bear this in the valleys of your mind – that God is there, and the Lesser Gods are there, but no one can ever know what their forms are. A God must never be interpreted as having a fixed shape. God can assume any shape He desires and whatever form would suit His purpose best at any given time. There may be times when Lesser Gods can assume the shapes of animals, or trees, or even rocks and boulders. But the reason why the Lesser Gods more often take human forms is because we would understand better when they communicate with us.'

My instructor proceeded to explain that while these masks and carvings serve their purpose to instruct children and the common people, I, as a Chosen One, must know more about our actual concept of God. I cannot repeat his actual words as it would occupy far too much space, and he explained everything in a symbolism which many of my readers would fail to comprehend. Briefly, he compared the Universe with a gigantic anthill. The structure as a whole is God and us, and everything we see about us is merely the ants and the sand-grains inside the anthill.

He explained that God created Himself and then slowly expanded to fill the entire Universe – or rather. He Himself grew in size. I have in the meantime learnt that this view is supported by modern astronomy. All bodies and materials within the Universe once originated at a central point and even this day they are expanding in all directions away from this point. According to other religions the creation of all these bodies and materials is part of God's handiwork, but according to our Great Belief these things are part of God's Being. It would be more correct to say that these things created God, or that God created Himself – like all the atoms and molecules in our bodies contributing their bits towards creating ourselves.

His analysis was extremely elaborate and to illustrate certain points, quite far-fetched comparisons were drawn; these illustrations are all part of our mythology and, contrary to 'Western' religions, our mythology forms part of our Great Belief.

When my instructor had finished with this section, he sat down and a Wise Woman took over. She wore a headdress with a fringe that covered the upper part of her face. She rose and took me into her arms and kissed both my cheeks; then she took a few steps back and sat down.

'My son, you have heard what the Honourable High Instructor had to say to you, and you have memorised and will remember until you die his every word. Now listen to what I, your Spiritual Mother, have to say. Remember each one of my words, because now we are coming to the most important part of our ancient creed – the part that has to do with the *soul.*

'My son, you have been a Christian . . . you have been one of those who have turned their backs on the religion of their forefathers to follow the religion of the aliens, and so you will understand so much better the vast difference that exists between the belief of your forefathers and that of the aliens, and also that of the Hyaena people, whom you know as Arabs.

'They tell you that God created Man in His image; they also tell you that God gave Man a special, separate soul, which He is prepared to punish or reward according to the good or bad things the soul does while it inhabits a body on earth. My son, the aliens are misleading our people. God is certainly not so unwise as to spend his time trying and sentencing all these millions of souls that appear before Him in heaven.

'Man does not possess a special soul, exclusive to himself. All souls are the same, and Man is but one of the many forms, or re-incarnations that a soul must pass through. The soul of the impala that you have seen disappearing into a thick bush while walking in the forest may once have been a tenant in the body of someone you knew. The crocodile that nearly ate you while you were crossing the river may have been carrying the soul of one of your ancestors, or one of the enemies of your family. But I shall explain this in greater detail later.

'You will be wondering by now, my son, just what a soul is and what it looks like. And I, your spiritual foster-mother, shall take you by the hand and show you a human soul. Now hold my hand and look straight into my eyes; . . . look and do not be afraid. Your brain shall gradually feel numb and you shall take a brief journey . . . into the land of Tura-ya-Moya . . . and you shall see a man's soul . . . with your own eyes. Do not be afraid . . . you shall not get lost . . . for I am holding your hand . . . Look into my eyes . . . your brain sleeps . . . your brain sleeps . . .'

Gradually the voice of the Wise Woman recedes into the dim distance; eventually it sounds as if she is whispering from beyond the farthest star. I feel a great weakness steal over me like some dark cloud creeping over a green valley . . .

Fear! Cold naked fear seizes me and great grows my urge to get up and run. The eyes of the Wise Woman seem to grow large – until they fill the whole sky. I am caught in a powerful spell. I have to give up . . . surrender . . . no use . . . I will only go mad.

I see through those eyes – through those windows. I see a plain, as barren and as bleak as the Ka-Lahari desert . . .

I can see clearly now. The plain is so barren – there is not even soil. There is only a flat stretch of grey granite, criss-crossed by yawning fissures. In the shimmering distance I can see mountains of tremendous height and frightening cragginess.

From the dark blue heavens I see large spheres of transparent ice slowly floating down. There are scores of them, and some have pairs of shimmering wings, like the wings of a dragonfly. This is a fantastic sight and my heart longs to be among those things. I want to be one of them, I want to go wherever they go. Something rebels inside me, something wants to escape from within. But it cannot . . . it flutters like a captive bird . . .

From the very Beyond comes the voice of the Wise Woman, and dimly, faintly she says: 'My son, you are seeing them now . . . you are seeing souls . . . look well at each of them . . . observe them clearly and closely, for you shall never get a chance like this again. Look closely . . .'

I strain my eyes to see through the shimmering haze that covers the plain. I strain my soul to interpret one of those floating spheres clearly and miss no detail. Each sphere is about the size of a man's head, transparent and perfectly round. But inside each of these orbs, these bubbles of shimmering luminescence, are two worms, one red and the other a bright royal blue. These worms are never still for one moment. They move constantly – they intertwine, separate, intertwine, again and yet again. It is a nerve-shattering – a frightening sight.

The vision fades and I am conscious of being back on earth; the Wise Woman is still holding my hand, and her eyes are piercing mine. She is covered with perspiration and she pants as though she has been running for a long distance. The Great Ones are sitting like silent statues of so many gods in a shrine – their expressions unreadable in the dim light of the lamp. The Wise Woman, gasping for breath, asks me what I have seen – she wants me to explain loudly so that all the Hidden Ones can hear . . .

'My son, you have seen with your own eyes what a soul looks like. You saw a sphere of the purest transparency and perfect roundness, and you saw that some of these had wings like those of a mosquito. You also saw that inside each one of these spheres were two worm-like creatures that constantly moved and were never still. These spheres you saw with wings were the souls of females, and those you saw with no wings were male souls. The two "worm-like" creatures you saw inside each soul were Good and Evil. But let me explain this in greater detail. The red "worm" stands for all the bad things in a man or a woman – dishonesty, cruelty, pride, low cunning, spiritual and corporal perversity, cowardice, low morality. The royal blue worm stands for all the good in a human being or an animal – loyalty, courage, honesty, love and charity. These worm-like components help to balance the soul. A combination of good and evil, equally balanced, is essential – for all souls that exist, like all living creatures, must have a perfect balance between Life and Death. If a man, for instance, should have only good qualities, without any bad qualities for balance, he would have no reason for existing at all. The same with a soul – if it has only the blue worm, the soul becomes automatically destroyed.

'This is why people who are really good, never live long. The two "worms" are always quarrelling and when the one hurts the other, the soul is temporarily unbalanced. If it happens to be the red worm that hurts the blue worm, then the man inhabited by the soul becomes evil – he becomes a thief, a murderer, and even worse. The laws of our fathers say that we must kill such a man, kill him so that the soul also may be destroyed. If a man becomes very good, the highest example of virtue, then we must pray to the gods to bring this man to an early grave, because although he is good, his body and soul have lost their balance and such a man has forfeited his right to exist in a world in which anything can happen when people are not normal and balanced. I have spoken.'

My readers will no doubt be amazed at the weird symbolism used in the instruction. To many it may sound like ever so much nonsense. But the minds of our Wise Ones have not been narrowed down by a degree course at a conventional university; many of them cannot read or write. Yet, they have all been to university – to the University of Life! They have all studied human nature, and the nature of natural history.

The High Instructor sits down and the Wise Woman speaks once more:

'My son, the aliens teach you that God created the soul, and we say this is not so. The soul is an integral part of God and all souls were created when God created Himself. The soul exists simply because God exists. The soul, like God, has no reason for existing, neither has it any reason for not existing. One can neither deny nor prove the existence of a soul . . .

'But listen very carefully now, my son, for your spiritual foster-mother will tell you more secrets which you must pass on to future generations of the Chosen. A human being, and an animal, has something else in addition to the soul, which exists within him. We can call this something else a *self.*

'When a child is born, it does not possess a *self.** The *self* builds up slowly of the memories and thoughts and the experiences as it grows up into a man or a woman. If you were to see your *Ena* you would find that it looks exactly like you, but it is not of flesh-and-blood – it is a ghost of transparent mist. When you see what many fools think is a ghost of a departed person, you do not see the soul, but that person's *Ena.* The *Ena* is not immortal; it lives on for some time after death of the body, and can often be seen. It is this the High Witchdoctor summons up from the land of the spirits, and this is what we honour and consult in times of trouble to pray to the gods for us.

---

* *It can also be interpreted that the Spirit of a departed will live only for as long as the descendants pay their homage, even in thoughts alone; the sacrifices merely ensure that such homages are conscientiously paid.*

† Self *is the exact equivalent of the Bantu* Ena. Myself *is* Mi-Ena, *normally shortened to* Mina.

'An *Ena* must eat to grow and live, the same as you must eat to grow and live. While you live you eat for both your body and for your *Ena*, but when you die your *Ena* will also die unless it can continue to eat. If we do not sacrifice cows and goats regularly so that the *Enas* of these animals can go to feed our ancestors' spirits, they will go into a state of non-existence.† It is therefore very important that we make these sacrifices regularly. Our ancestors' spirits must remain alive because we must regularly ask their advice about problems we encounter, and they must take our problems and plead for us with the gods – just as the common people must have the *Indunas* who can plead for them with the chiefs. I shall now ask the Second Instructor to tell you more about this.'

The old man known as the Second Instructor rises to his ancient feet and, after uttering a prayer to the gods to help me to remember all I will be told, he stands over me looking down at me. I am lying on my back on a holy mat.

'Listen very well, my son – listen with all your soul and with all your heart for I am now going to tell you something that is of the utmost importance. When a baby is born, it is born with only a body, a mind and a soul, but not with an *Ena*. The *Ena* grows like a flower as the child grows and is formed and nourished by the experiences of the growing child. It is shaped by the child's own character and also the characters of those whom the child chooses to imitate, such as a parent or a tribal hero.

'The *Ena* rides across the lake of time on the Soul, just as a man rides in a canoe. However, both the soul and the *Ena* (character is a combination of the two) are always a few days ahead of the body. I shall explain this more clearly:

'All living things are swimming across a great lake, called *Time*, and those things that are of flesh-and-blood are outdistanced in the race across the lake of Time by those things that are spirit, such as souls and *Enas*. And these go through experiences first, which afterwards overtake the body. For instance, if a man is going to fall victim of an accident in one or two days' time, the soul and the *Ena* are the first to fall victim of that accident. And when this happens the soul sends a warning to the body through the mind, in the form of a premonition or a dream.

'The reason many people are killed, in spite of the warnings they get from their *Enas* in the form of forebodings or dreams, is that their bodies are untrained in the essential art of co-operating closely with their souls and *Enas*. As you already know, this is the first thing we teach witchdoctors.

'Animals co-operate perfectly with their *Enas*, and nowhere is found better proof of this than among the little birds. No matter how well you hide yourself in the bushes a bird will know of your presence and your intentions long before he has seen you.

'It is this *Ena* that is known by the ignorant common people as the 'Spirit of a dead person', and which the strangers from beyond the seas falsely believe that we worship. In fact, far from our worshipping the so-called spirits of our ancestors, it is these ancestral spirits who worship us. We who combine flesh, mind, soul, *Ena*, and life, are much more fortunate than the *Enas* of those who are dead. Although the *Ena* is a spirit, it is neither immortal nor indestructible; in the land of Forever-Night where all *Enas* go after death, the *Ena* is the most helpless thing in all creation. As you know, nothing grows in the cold deserts that are the land of Forever-Night, and there the Gods allot each *Ena* a given length of time in which to continue existing. If, at the end of that period, none of the relatives has sacrificed a cow or a goat, it goes into a state of non-being. *Enas* must continue to eat the *Enas* of the animals they used to eat when still with the people in whose bodies they were formed. This is why it is so important that all your forefathers' *Enas* should continually be nourished by the *Enas* of the cows and goats you slaughter in their name. In return for this kindness they intercede with the Gods on your behalf, and the Gods give you wealth and luck in everything you do, and they also keep enemies from the threshold of your life. To keep the *Enas* of his ancestors alive is the greatest and most important duty a man has in life. To ensure that the chain is never broken and that ancestors' *Enas* will not die through lack of descendants, each man must, besides slaughtering a cow at least once a year, ensure that he has at least three wives and as many children as his loins and the Gods allow him.

'The first sign that a man gets of the *Enas* of his ancestors being hungry is the number of dreams of old men and old women that assail him every night. If he ignores these dreams he easily falls a victim to accidents; people take a dislike to him and beat him up for no apparent reason; the keepers of the law hound him every day; his wives run away with other men; he is persecuted until he meets with death himself and when his *Ena* arrives in the land of Forever-Night, it is devoured by those of his ancestors.

'Urge the people, Oh my son, urge them always to slaughter a goat or a cow for the helpless spirits of their ancestors. Tell them that a man who tries to live without his ancestors is like a tree struggling without roots, and that a man who is ignored by his ancestors is a disgrace in the eyes of the Gods. His conscience will haunt him until his dying day and he will die weeping like a lost hyaena in the darkness.

'My son, you know that when a man sacrifices regularly to his ancestors, the *Enas* leave the land of Forever-Night and come to live in that man's kraal always. They live there and repay his adherence by protecting him and his children and wives from harm, by interceding with the Gods on his behalf, and by giving him luck in all he does. They also help him by sending him advice by dream messages in his hour of trouble. They not only shield him from harm, they make him the dread of his enemies.

'The *Enas* are not only unable to fend for themselves – they are blind. Thus, if a man moves his kraal to a new site you must now also see to it that he first fasts for ten days and then he must call upon his ancestors to listen to his voice. On the day of summoning his ancestors he must slaughter a black cow and a young goat. The young goat must not be eaten by any of the people in the kraal, but must be buried unskinned in the centre of the kraal to be abandoned. However, the flesh of the cow can be eaten after it has been left overnight for the *Enas* to lick, as is the custom. Then the owner of the kraal must address the spirits, telling them the locality of his new kraal and inviting them to accompany him to his new home. You must also ensure that he takes a large skin bag and fills it with the sand of the graves where his ancestors are buried. This he must scatter along the footpath leading to the new kraal, and also the clearing of the new kraal, so that his ancestors' *Enas* can follow the trail.

'If the man is being moved out of his kraal by the chief of the land then the onus falls on that chief to call a gathering of the Elders of the Tribe and explain to them what he intends to do and why. Then the Elders must go to the kraal of the man concerned and sit around it in ceremonial mourning. At midnight the leader of the Elders must get up and go and stand over the Sacred Burial Ground of the man about to be moved and there he must address the *Enas* in a loud voice, calling upon them to listen to what he has to say. When the Elder feels the hair on the nape of his neck trying to stand on end he is to know that the *Enas* are close at hand. The Elder performs the whole ceremony, including scooping up the soil from the burial place and scattering it along the path to the new place.

'It is not only the *Enas* of the individual's ancestors that demand his attention, but also those of the founders of the tribe. For this reason chiefs are bound to collect a cow from each kraal, to be slaughtered at a great gathering which must be attended by every man, woman and child of the tribe. A tribe that does not uphold this tradition is doomed in the same way as the individual who turns his back on the *Enas* of his own ancestors.

'If a tribe is driven out of the land in which its ancestors are buried, the defeated tribe must not even try to preserve its identity; the members must scatter and be absorbed by other tribes, while the chief, his First Wife and their children must commit suicide.

'My son, in the land of the Bu-Kongo there once existed a very powerful tribe known as the Luba, or the Ba-Luba. This tribe was so strong that it could be called a nation, so many thousands of people were there in the land. This tribe ruled a vast empire in the west of the land of the Bu-Kongo. Then one day the empire of the famous Ba-Luba fell to the spears of the Ba-Yeke and the Lunda. At this time all tribes were still ruled, not by men but by women. The great Chieftainess *Lupangwa* saw her three husbands slain in battle, and she saw her only son *Mukambi* die at her feet as twenty Lunda spears pierced his body, while he fought to defend his mother. *Lupangwa* knew the end had come, not only for herself but also for the Ba-Luba. It was then that she remembered the big skin bag that carried the fluid that one of the great Ba-Luba witchdoctors had mixed years before. This was a fluid of the darkest magic. It had to be kept in a deep hole under a hut because if a drop of it was exposed to the sun, a fierce fire would start which nobody would know how to put out. We still have the formula for producing this fluid and we shall in due course pass it on to you.

'*Lupangwa* of the Ba-Luba took a torch and lit it at the Holy Fire that blazed daily in the centre of her hut. She threw the flaming torch down the hole in which the Fluid of Evil was hidden and over which she had been appointed guardian. A mighty fire was started which burned for many days – a fire that not only killed the brave queen, but also every Ba-Luba still alive in the whole kraal, and the thousands of invading Lunda and Ba-Yeke warriors, and their kings as well.

'After that the Ba-Luba scattered all over the land. They were a defeated tribe that had lost its right to exist when it lost its ancestral burial grounds. They left the land of their fathers and went in groups of a few hundred or so to settle in the lands of other tribes as the slaves and servants of those tribes. Now the laws of the Ba-Luba had been explicit that each male Ba-Luba must have at least one skilled trade apart from his usual skill with war-weapons, as demanded by the laws for every living man of all tribes. Thus nearly every Ba-Luba man was a witchdoctor, a blacksmith or a woodcarver; incidentally, it was the Ba-Luba who perfected the art of woodcarving in the land of Bu-Kongo, and it was the Ba-Luba who perfected our whole native culture.

'Now all tribes in the land, no matter how backward, need witchdoctors, blacksmiths, woodcarvers and diviners. Groups of homeless Ba-Luba were thus welcomed wherever they went because they could practise their trades everywhere. They were also the best cheats of all time.

'You have heard the tribal expression 'to trade like a Ba-Luba' which means to sell a thing to a man at an exorbitant price and then to watch carefully and see which hut he puts it in, in order to return at night and steal the thing back to sell again.

'This is just what the Ba-Luba did. They sold their exotic ivory and ebony carvings to the chiefs of other tribes and then returned at night and stole them back to re-sell them for cattle elsewhere. Sometimes a roving family of Ba-Luba would sell one copper bracelet inscribed with the signs of secret wisdom as many as five or six times. One very cunning rogue got two hundred head of cattle sixty times from sixty different chiefs for a fabulous ivory carving of the Goddess *Ma* and the Tree of Life. And you know, my son, that cunning rogue died in the land of the Nyanja a very rich man, with that famous ivory carving still in his possession.

'This did not make the Ba-Luba popular with other tribes as you may have realised by now. But the angry people still found time to forget and to welcome them, with their witchdoctors and woodcarvers, time and again. The Ba-Luba even came down here to our country, my son, and they left their surnames with us forever. They also left with us a terrible technique for bewitching people which still bears their name, Lumbo. If you meet a man with the surname of *Mulaba* or *Muluba* you must know he is a descendant of one of these homeless refugees of the Ba-Luba tribe that fled across the great distance when their empire fell so many generations ago. Now you see what happens to a tribe when it loses its burial grounds.'

This belief that a man lives solely to serve his ancestors is one of the most deep-rooted beliefs in the whole of Africa, and tribal unity is based on this. The tribe as a whole *must* keep the spirits of its founders alive – every tribe in Africa believes this. And even today *men still die as a result of their clinging to this belief.* What better example of this is there, than the thus far untold story of the Tonga and Tonga-Ila. I shall tell the story now for the first time. I was there; I can speak as an eyewitness. The characters in this story are not fictitious and since they have a bearing on people, both dead and alive, I shall refrain from using names:

Somewhere between the years 1955 and 1957 the Government of the Federation of the Rhodesias and Nyasaland decided on an unprecedented venture of taming the ageless Zambezi. They decided to build a dam in the gorge, known as the Kariba Gorge, where the ancient tribes known as the Tonga-Ila and Ba-Tonga had their home. The area, in spite of its wealth in game and its dense forests, was a rather barren place for farming. The soil is poor and no progress could be made with the planting of crops of any kind, and the tsetse fly made cattle keeping impossible. The people existed on a diet of flesh of wild animals and some small domesticated animals. It was a hard, primitive existence and these people did not live there because they liked the climate.

They were bound to stay in Kariba by laws and the traditions that nobody from beyond the oceans could ever understand, even if they were thoroughly enlightened. Kariba Gorge is more than just a place in the minds of the Bantu of Southern Africa; it is far more than a mere name and place.

My duty as a Tribal Chronicler compels me to reveal some of the legends of the place.

Kariba is unique for a number of very unusual things. If a tribe started migrating from the centre of what is today Zambia, it took exactly half a year to reach Kariba, exactly as long as it would take a tribe to migrate there from the centre of the land of the Nyasa and the land of the Mashona. This strange thing induced the Wise Ones of the Tribes to believe that Kariba was the navel of the world. Also, the Zambezi could best be forded, with reasonable safety, within this gorge. And there was a place, now forever buried under water, where, if one listened carefully in a crevice between two great rocks, one heard the sound of running water. But it sounded as though it came from far below the crust of the earth.

Around this cleft, between the two rocks, grew the legend that Kariba was also the gateway to the Underworld, and the sounds that could be heard were those of the rushing waters of the mighty river, the Lulungwa-Mangakatsi, meaning simply, 'the river that flows down below'.

One of the early chiefs of the Ba-Tonka, who had been a very cruel man in his youth and who had reformed his evil ways after having nearly been decapitated by a bolt of lightning, began the *Order of the Holy Ones of Kariba*. This was a group of men and women who renounced all material things. They renounced the building of huts, the keeping of cattle and the ploughing of fields. They insisted that the gods did not like to see human beings living in a way different from that of all other creatures in nature. They went as far as to eat raw meat and refrain from speech and they lived in cave shelters and in the trees. They mutilated their tongues to discourage speech and in its place they developed telepathy to a high degree of perfection.

They developed a fantastic 'device of magic' with which a man called his wife. This 'magic device' is the simplest and yet the most fantastic thing in the world. It is constructed as follows: they used to pick up these round stones with the holes through their centres which our remote ancestors used for weights on their digging sticks. A long thong was tied in a special way to this stone and a noose handle made of the other end. The idea is to stand up and whirl the stone fast and high above one's head. The effort promotes a strong willpower, strong enough to project a mental message, even on the part of a user who is not normally capable of sending a message by telepathy.

I have seen this work on more than one occasion. It is as though the effort generates the mental power almost like similar rotational or rubbing movements can create positive or negative electric charges. In one demonstration I have seen a man pass a message to his wife in a neighbouring village and call her back to him. She arrived as soon as she could walk the distance.

Strange? But it works!

The Holy Ones of Kariba, led by their great chief *Kimba*, went to live in the gorge, and they lived there like animals. They had no laws whatsoever, other than those they called the laws of conscience. They did not marry particular wives but mated like animals at any time in full view of anyone who might pass by.

With their strong mental power they experimented with the brain and they frequently performed crude operations exposing the brain. They could successfully remove tumours on the brain. They were the first people who could, assisted by a considerable measure of 'mind over matter', successfully amputate a limb. They developed surgery to the extent that they could perform Caesarian operations on women and female animals. Our legends say that these operations were frequently successful in so far as both mother and child lived.

Then one day a strange thing happened. The Holy Ones of Kariba vanished from the face of the earth. They vanished without leaving a trace – and they vanished without leaving the gorge at all!

Kariba had become a place where all the people from even those tribes as far as the land of the Bu-Kongo gathered, bringing their injured and sick across great distances to be healed by the incredibly clever medicine men and wise women of the Holy Ones. The thousands of people from different tribes used to meet on a low hill, known as the Hill of Life, on the northern bank of the Zambezi about a quarter of a day's journey from the gorge. Here a Holy One used to meet the massed pilgrims and bless them and tell them in sign language to wait. He would then go and call the other Holy Ones and the long task of healing the mad, the sick and the wounded would begin.

Often the Holy Ones would use their great mind power to heal the sick. Often they would just give the sick ones a calabash full of clear water to drink and the sick ones were healed. But it was on those with fractured limbs and lion-mauled bodies that the Holy Ones displayed their great surgical skill, and it was on those with foul tumours on their brains that they exhibited their fantastic knowledge. It was through the healing of the women with terrible boring sores on their breasts, that the miraculous knowledge of the Holy Ones was forever burned into the memories of the tribes.

But often the evil chiefs of many tribes would try to force the Holy Ones to work for them. They sent armies to try and capture some of the Holy Ones and make them tribal slaves. At these times the Holy Ones used to defend themselves in a strange and incredible way. They went into hiding and hurled the Spirit of Fear at their enemies from a number of places of concealment. Suddenly every invading warrior was seized by an inexplicable terror, not of the unseen enemy but of the weapons they carried in their own hands.

A man suddenly became terribly afraid of the spear he carried. He suddenly felt that all the weapons he carried were conspiring to injure him. His rapidly succumbing mind would actually hear his weapons discussing how to injure their own master. Before long the warrior, imagining all these things, would drop his weapons and flee like a maddened girl.

But one day when the pilgrims came to the Hill of Life they found nobody waiting there. They found no dumb, naked, Holy One with sad, wise eyes, and a face of indescribable serenity, waiting to receive them.

Among those who were injured on this particular day was *Nagumbi*, the fiery son of the great hero *Lumukanda*, who was nursing a shoulder in which a cruel, multi-barbed arrowhead was buried. *Nagumbi* had wiped out a tribe of murderers from the land of the Nyanja people and had carried away this brave wound from the battle.

'I am going into Kariba to see what has happened to the Holy Ones,' said the mighty son of a mighty father. 'I have a feeling that something terrible has happened to them.'

His shoulder throbbing with great pain, the son of *Lumukanda* strode into the forbidden gorge half-a-day later. He searched around and found nothing, nobody. Then, on an improvised raft, he crossed the Zambezi to search the southern bank. Eventually, in the middle of the forest, he came across a number of blood-chilling sights. There was a footprint so large that it sprawled over trees flattened to a pulp. It was unlike any other footprint under the sun. It was twenty human paces long and had twelve mighty toes on one foot, and there would appear to have been ten legs. The son of *Lumukanda* was totally without fear and, his spear gripped tightly, he followed this awesome trail. He came to a place where the nightmare beast had lain, where the trees were flattened over a large area, and saw with shock and surprise that the Holy Ones had all converged upon the great beast from many directions, judging from the flattened grass. There was no sign of a battle, no sign of a struggle. *Nagumbi* could see that all the Holy Ones had gone to the creature willingly.

Ever since, our great thinkers have tried ceaselessly to solve what became known as the 'Riddle of Kariba'. But it has been in vain. Even today the whole thing is still one of the many mysteries of our native land. A number of years later, after the vanishing of the Holy Ones, another band of thinkers and witchdoctors took up residence in the gorge of Kariba and they tried to re-discover the secrets of the original Holy Ones. They, too, healed the sick, using methods the original Holy Ones had taught them. These were soon followed by two tribes known for their piety and great wisdom, famous for their power of settling disputes without using weapons, famous for their legends, their songs, and the degree to which they had developed the great powers of the human brain. (The mythological account summarised in the first part of Book 1 is their version of creation, disclosed to me by their High Witchdoctor.)

These two tribes, the Tonga and the Tonga-Ila, entered the Kariba Gorge exactly fifteen generations ago. These tribes were immediately regarded as holy by all the Bantu tribes in Southern Africa. Tonga-Ila men could walk unmolested into the heat of a savage tribal fight and command both warring sides to lay down their weapons – and the fight would stop immediately. Distinguished by their headbands made of pieces of tortoise shell, the Tonga and Tonga-Ila tribesmen and women were welcome wherever they went and many chiefs would execute one of their own tribesmen if he received one of these people as a guest in his kraal without first taking him to the kraal of the chief.

Many old men of the Mashona and the Machopi had the strange habit of blinding themselves after they had paid a visit to Kariba; they believed this would forever seal the luck of Kariba into their brains. After having seen this Holy Place, second in holiness only to the Ka-Lahari, they did not want this sight to be superseded by other earthly sights they would experience later. They blinded themselves with a few drops of the juice of the sisal plant.

There is also a belief, born probably as a result of the sudden disappearance of the first Holy Ones, that not only is Kariba the navel of the earth, but that also the 'Knot of Time' is located there, where the past, the present and the future of the entire Universe are tied together in a knot. It is also said that somewhere in Kariba there is a cave, and that in this cave the future of the world is carved in sacred characters on a great slab of rock. There are many witchdoctors in Northern and Southern Rhodesia who claim to have seen this cave and read what is written there. These writings are known as the 'Dark Prophecy' and the strange thing is that all these witchdoctors, the one not knowing of the other, tell exactly the same story and their interpretations of the message coincide exactly.

Many of the great chiefs of the tribes that came from the north are buried at Kariba, and many of them had a strange habit of falling on their spears and dying as sacrifices to the Gods of Kariba. Especially with a crossing in which many tribesmen drowned, a chief would drown himself or stab himself to death while standing in the water. They believed their spirits would join the Holy Ones wherever they went.

I refuse to believe that the Government of the Federation was completely oblivious to the fact that Kariba was our Holiest of the Holy. What evil spirit induced them to rape our feelings so blatantly, without even asking a single leader among our people to interpret our attitude towards the building of the dam? I refuse to believe that the Government of Great Britain did not know that siting the dam there would create rebellious feelings among the people across the entire southern half of Africa.

And what about the politicians of the Colonial Powers who base their policies on the findings of scientists who were supposed to have studied our people? They will achieve nothing by trying to cover up their blunders by pointing an accusing finger at the Republic of South Africa. Here, politicians and scientists consult us and respect our feelings.

While I was in Rhodesia in 1958, the boast of the British South Africa Police was that they had never been forced to shoot an African since the Matabele Rebellion of the last century. This boast was born of the fact that while things like the Mau-Mau were tearing British territories in Africa apart, Rhodesia remained peaceful.

Britain owed this long peace to one thing only – and no one among the White rulers seems to be aware of this – that is that the majority of the tribes of both Rhodesias do not resort to violence unless provoked beyond enduring. They are all still under the influence of the passive Holy Ones of Kariba.

There will be White people, no doubt, who will not believe what

I say. Let them check the history of the Mashona – merely over the last century. They will discover how helpless the tribe was against the murdering nomads, the Matabele. They depended on the British to keep the Matabele from their throats.

They will also discover that before the year 1958 a riot in the township of Harare, the African township of Salisbury, was unknown. Before 1955 political upstarts amongst the Bantu could achieve nothing with the basically peace-loving Mashona; they could not agitate them into insubordination. But when the White authorities decided to build Kariba, they gave these upstarts a perfect weapon: ammunition to stir up strife. With wide-open eyes, they supplied Communists and other rabble-rousers with the effective means of rallying the uneducated masses to their doubtful cause.

I say 'with open eyes' because no one will convince me that the authorities knew nothing about our feelings for that Holy Place. They knew! But in the typical British spirit, they refused to care! This has all along been a characteristic of the colonial powers of Europe – ride roughshod over those things that are held holy by those they conquered.

And now I wish to make a bold statement. Those who have ears, let them hear – in my own fatherland and outside. And let those who lack ears – those in the United Nations – try to assimilate this through whatever rudimentary sense organs they still have left: There is very little *effective* Communist influence in Africa. Appearances can be deceptive. The Bantu reject all foreign creeds today with the same force with which they have rejected Christianity and Islam. Nationalism in Africa is not a striving for political independence; it is a 'back to the creeds of our ancestors' movement.

The fate of Africa lies in the hands of its witchdoctors. One single witchdoctor in a position of authority can do more to repair the damage done in a strife-torn country in Africa, like the Congo, than can the whole of the United Nations.

The ordinary Bantu, no matter how educated or 'civilised', are still firmly rooted to the beliefs of their forefathers. No matter how they have been subjected to Christian influences, they still have greater confidence in their local *nganga* (or witchdoctor) than in the local mission priest. To them their *Enas* are closer than the host of Catholic saints who were fed to the lions in the Colosseum in Rome.

The ordinary Bantu could not care less who rules them. They do not care what laws are laid down in the land of their birth, *as long as those laws do not offend the sacred ancestral beliefs*!

In Harare I have heard at prayer meetings held by 'Christian' Mashonas, a prayer that the wall of Kariba must collapse – a prayer to both Christ and *Mulimbu* in turn, to kill the men building the dam at Kariba. I have heard lengthy discussions between men of different tribes about the sacrilege committed by the White Man. I actually attended a curse ceremony at which a High Curse was put on the dam for all Eternity!

There is much more that happened at Kariba.

The Government decided that the Tonga and Tonga-Ila should be moved from the Kariba Gorge, and they were duly notified in the plodding official way. Of course these tribes made it quite clear from the very outset that they did not intend to budge. Some, mostly Christians eager to please the White authorities, consented to being moved. But all the older people under the influence of the witchdoctors refused and stood fast. The Government sent the police to deal with the recalcitrants and a strange thing happened. The Tonga-Ila took their rifles with them into the bush and when the police arrived, they opened fire on them. The police defended themselves and five tribesmen were killed. After that a fleet of trucks simply arrived to take the Tonga-Ila and their blood brothers away to the new place by force, with a strong escort of police to ensure that there would be no trouble this time. And soon Kariba Gorge was as deserted and rejected as a raped woman.

But trouble of a different kind started at the new place to which these people had been moved; they died in large numbers for no apparent reason. It turned out that they were carried away by an ordinary disease common amongst the Bantu – normal dysentery.

The authorities did their best; they sent food, medicines, doctors. Still the people died, and soon the toll stood at one hundred and fifty. The authorities never came to realise that these people were dying, not of dysentery or other physical cause, but spiritually, psychically. The laws of the Tribes say that if a tribe is moved away from its burial grounds, it may as well commit suicide.

Strange are the ironies of Africa!

But the whole tragedy could so easily have been averted at no cost to the Government of the Federation. Instead of arriving with rifles at the ready, the authorities should have turned up with a number of empty cement bags, one for each family. The head of each family would have filled his bag with some of the soil from the Sacred Gorge and from his family's burial ground for distribution at the place where they were to be re-settled. Surely the Government could have spared the services of one of the clerks in the Native Affairs Department for a few days to visit these tribes and to explain to them what the authorities had in mind – just one clerk instead of a troop of police.

The clerk would simply have had to call the tribes together, address them briefly on the regrettable but necessary project, pass the apologies of the Government, step back, raise his hand in silent salute to the sky, then wash his hands in the Zambezi before leaving. It would have been simple, had the authorities had the slightest knowledge about the people with whom they share the country. The Federation could have been a success. The whole of Southern Africa could have been a land of peace for almost any length of time.

In 1958 I attended a meeting in Harare township. This meeting was addressed by an African Member of the Federal Parliament who claimed that the Kariba dam was not built because it was necessary, but as a challenge to see what the Bantu reactions would be; that the offended Spirits of Kariba would never be satisfied with anything short of the total destruction of the Federation; and that he, the leader, was the man who could achieve this, provided people supported him with both funds and their own voices.

This man collected more than £25, mostly in copper – hard-earned money from the pockets of people most of whom could not read or write.

These poor simple people, these poor men and women who have no interest in politics and who want only to be left alone to lead their lives in peace, surrendered their money into the hands of this man, not because they desired 'freedom' or 'independence' (few of them know the meaning of these words, let alone their implication), but because a *sacrilege* had been committed at Kariba.

But how often has this same thing happened in Africa? I have pointed out earlier that the religion of a race is its Ego, its Self, its *Ena.* And one can make the humblest and most simple-minded peasant fight like a thousand lions against impossible odds if one can convince him that a sacrilege has been committed against the Ego of his race, especially by a foreigner. This holds true in the deserts of Arabia, in the valleys of Italy and the jungles of Indo-China, as much as it holds true in London's Trafalgar Square.

I would like to ask those who think I am exaggerating to try and hurl a dead pig into an Arabian Mosque in Dar-es-Salaam, or into a Synagogue in Jerusalem. Let them try disfiguring a statue of the Virgin Mary in the presence of a group of Sicilians in their own island. Let them try, if they dare, to deface a statue of George Washington. While they are about it, they may as well try to tear the Union Jack from its mast in front of the Royal Kraal of Great Britain with half London looking on. On second thoughts nothing might happen to you in the latter case now-a-days. Is it because the Lion of England whose roar once frightened the whole world into submission and whose paws, once armed with golden claws that brooked no impudence from low hyaenas, is now both old and senile? Are his claws dulled and are there moths in his wild mane? Are the teeth that once snarled so fiercely at my warrior forefathers rotted and blunted with age?

And yet we, the Bantu people of Africa, have had to endure sacrileges against our religion again and yet again. Much of the bloodshed, much of the trouble tearing Africa apart today, has been caused by this gross ignorance.

And now I shall make yet another disclosure. The Mau Mau trouble was in fact triggered off by the unthinking act of a White farmer who had shot a wild cat that had caught some of his fowls. He threw the carcase at the feet of his Kikuyu servant and told him jokingly to eat it. But unknown to the farmer, the Kikuyu regard the wild cat as sacred. This incident was exaggerated by agitators and made to look intentional, to bolster their cause.

How many people know that the name Mau Mau was derived from the sounds this cat made when it died?

This wild cat was the most important chicken thief in human history. Its life was traded for 26,000 human lives, a vast cut in a great nation's budget, and indescribable memories imprinted on the minds of orphans who saw their parents butchered.

When I think of this, and many similar tragedies in my Africa – and the rest of the insane world, my soul sheds tears to the silent stars. I long for the remote, seemingly unattainable day when men shall be free of the stupid shackles with which they burden their minds. I long for the day when men will *know* that God exists and not be induced to believe it in a thousand different ways. I long for the day when Man will *honour* God, and stop fighting over Him.

THE CURSE ON KARIBA

The Ba-Tonga and the Tonga-Ila people had been finally forced out of Kariba and construction on the dam had begun. Hundreds of men – thousands, both Black and White, toiled day after day at the site to the roar of compressors, the clangour of concrete mixers and the sullen roar of bulldozers. The Government of the Federation had won the battle over a bunch of recalcitrant superstitious munts, they thought. But the Guardians of Kariba were to write the final chapter to that fantastic incident.

The Old Man, to whom I shall give the fictitious name of *Chikerema*, was waiting on the top of the ancient hill, and he was all alone under the silent stars. A heavy *kaross* of cheetah skin was wrapped round his wasted body and the pangs of hunger gnawed at him with the persistency of a rat. His old wrinkle-wreathed eyes were more than usually dim and his body felt more than usually weak, because he had not touched food for three days. Often his eyes strayed to the south-east where a faint glow was visible on the horizon. As he stared, a tide of savage hate swept over him. Salty tears poured unbidden down his sunken cheeks. There, out there, the aliens were building a dam across the holiest spot on earth. They were going to flood the sacred gorge of Kariba and drown the ancient graves of the Holy Ones under many feet of water. The whole thing was a sacrilege that must not be allowed to pass unpunished. It was a deliberate challenge to a war of extermination hurled in the teeth of every Black Man by those who lived in Salisbury.

Surely, thought old *Chikerema* angrily, surely the aliens, the Ma-Kiwa, knew that it was an offence, in fact a deadly challenge to a blood fued lasting a thousand years, for a race or tribe to flood the sacred burial grounds of another race or tribe. Surely they knew that men had died and huts had been burned down to the ground simply because one man threw a bowl of water on the burial ground of another tribe. Oh yes, thought the old man, I know why they do this – they want to see what we are going to do about it. They put their trust in their war-birds and their death-pipes that make a loud noise and kill men from far away, the cowards that they are! They want an opportunity to kill us, because they think we are too many.

But there are many ways of fighting a war, just as there are many ways of stealing a goat.

As the old man waited, the moon rose in the silent east. And first it was nothing but a dull yellow ball of mystery and solitude, huge and infinitely wise. That old moon had seen more things on this earth than there are hairs on the body of a *garu* mongrel. That ball of mysterious light saw the fantastic ages of the First People; it saw the destruction of that ancient race and the land they inhabited. It saw the flight of *Amarava* and *Odu* and the fabulous age of the Immortals. It saw the age of the Children of the Star and the age of the Muuoto Mkulu, the fire that burned for sixty days. It saw the coming of the Strange Ones and the terrible period known as the Bending of the Race, when thousands of people died, ancient tribes were destroyed and millions of people were taken into slavery to serve the foreigners known as the Ma-Iti. It also saw new tribes rise out of the ashes of the old . . .

'Tonight you shall witness the putting of a High Curse upon the Kariba Dam,' said the old man to the pale moon which was rising hesitantly into the skies, with the slow reluctance of a bride approaching the hut in which she must mate with her husband for the first time. Soon the light of the moon was sprinkling the forest-clad land with silver droplets of mystery and the beast-sheltering forest assumed a beauty and a serenity that was not of this world.

There was movement in the forest at the base of the hill on which the old man stood, and groups of people emerged and started climbing the hill. There were about ten men and six women. One of them balanced a large clay pot on her head. One of the men was leading a calf by a thong tied round the animal's neck and two of the men were leading goats. Nearly every one of the newcomers carried something, and the leading man carried what was obviously a dummy of sorts, made out of skins – a huge thing standing as high as a man.

The group paused halfway up the hill and one of the men, a naked giant daubed white all over and with his face painted a hideous yellow and red with black stripes, came up to the old man. Catching the old one's hand, he said in a low voice: 'All is ready, Great Chosen One, we are ready to go to the place.'

'Let it be so, Oh *Lumbo*,' the old man replied. 'Help me down and let us be away.'

'As you command, Oh *Chikerema*.'

'Are you sure that none of the traitors saw you?'

'All the Christian fools are fast asleep, Oh Great Father, and the Eyes of the aliens are in their place.'

'It is the Eyes of the aliens about which I am worried. If they find out what we are going to do here they will arrest us all in the morning and take us to the Place of Imprisonment.'

'The Great Father *Chikerema* must not worry so. Even if the Eyes do see us and arrest us, they can do no more than kill us. And with this vile insult that the aliens have hurled at us, who wants to live? We lost our right to live when they moved us out of the Place of Great Sanctity. I wish I had died on that day.'

The sagging shoulders of the old man sagged yet lower. A rattling sigh was torn from his hollow chest and it was in deep silence that he led the group of people through the bush towards the great Zambezi. *Lumbo* kept on glancing over his shoulder at one of the men in the group and there was cold suspicion in his smouldering eyes as he whispered to the old man beside him, at the same time fingering the long *panga* hanging at his left side: 'Great One, do you trust that little stranger from the Land of Gold? Did you have to allow that wretched Zulu to come with us? What if he is a spy for the Eyes?'

'Keep your suspicions in check, Oh *Lumbo*,' said the old man sternly. 'That man from beyond the Limpopoma I trust with my life. Not only is he not a spy for either the aliens or their Eyes, but he is like us, a Chosen One . . . he showed me his sign.'

They came at last to the Zambezi, that ancient river of song, legend and story – that river which has seen so many chapters of the history of the Bantu being written on the shores of Eternity. The great river was a band of living silver that zig-zagged through the forest – a serpent of living water that, according to our stories, had its source at the very feet of God Himself.

The armed men walked in front, their eyes and ears alert for lions and leopards and other night-hunting beasts. Their spears and muzzle loaders were ready to deal death to any beast insolent enough to try meddling with the group.

They came at last to the place where a great pit had been dug by young men a few days previously and loosely covered with shrubs. This pit was deep enough completely to hide a tall man standing erect and it was three paces in diameter at the bottom. The earth from the pit was piled nearby, cleverly camouflaged with tufts of grass and rock to look just like a natural bump.

Suddenly, with a violent gesture of his hands – nobody was allowed to talk in the first stages of the ceremony – *Chikerema* bade his followers lay down their burdens and rest while the armed ones stood guard. He then proceeded to the pile of earth and knelt upon it. He threw up his arms and his lips moved as he addressed a silent, wordless prayer to the Ancient Ones of Kariba – to the cold, uncaring and hostile gods in the land of Tura-ya-Moya – and lastly to the even more uncaring Great Spirit who is anywhere and everywhere, who exists through all things visible and invisible and in all things knowable and unknowable.

Rivulets of sweat ran down his face and into his scraggy beard; his bald pate glistened like wet ebony in the moonlight. His whole body shook as he tried to project his prayer to beyond the Ten Gateways of Eternity. His age-wasted form shivered and he held his breath while concentrating on the fate he desired for the White men building the Kariba Dam, and for all who had planned the building of it. He pictured them falling, writhing and dying with hideous cries, their flesh melting from their bones. He pictured their women giving birth to serpents turning upon them and devouring them. And all this he saw as symbolic of what he would like should happen to the Federation.

Then, with a loud cry that echoed through the night, he collapsed from sheer exhaustion.

The woman who had carried the clay pot and who was *Chikerema's* wife, ran forward and helped her husband to his feet. He gasped to *Lumbo*: 'Begin the ceremony . . .'

Lumbo sprang to his feet and seized one of the goats – the red one with the white face – and he hurled the living, struggling animal into the pit with great violence. This was a signal for a wild, completely uninhibited though silent dance to begin and for all the women to hurl heavy rocks into the pit, burying the poor animal under many hundreds of pounds of stone. The curse pot was lowered on top of the buried goat, care being taken that the contents were not spilt. On this vessel were inscribed prayers to the Gods of Evil – signs of secret wisdom which would look to the uneducated eye like primitive and insignificant decorations.

All these prayers were supplications to the Gods of Evil and the Mother of High Evil to bring curses not only on the Kariba Dam, but on all those building it and on all those who planned it – and on the entire White population of the Federation. And particularly on Great Britain.

The curse pot lowered, the men began a savage, silent, stamping dance to the accompaniment of symbolic, soundless clapping by the women. Here it was the huge man *Lumbo* who played the important part. He snatched up one of the two trussed-up monkeys and held it up as he danced faster and faster. He danced till his legs were white blurs in the moonlight, until his whole white-daubed body shook like a sapling in a breeze.

He was stark naked save that on his head he wore a headdress of skin made to look like a helmet worn by the British South Africa Police, and a pair of imitation handcuffs carved from wood hung from a string around his neck. In fact he represented the police who had come to Kariba to evict the Ba-Tonga and the Tonga-Ilas by force.

Lumbo danced – and while he danced he became as mad as a cave demon. He turned the sharp knife in his hand on himself, stabbing his thighs until blood ran freely. He leapt high into the air and hurled himself to the ground, all the while keeping a tight hold on the struggling monkey. Finally, he leapt a full four feet into the air and as he landed like a cat on his feet he slashed the belly of the monkey and dragged out its quivering entrails with his teeth, before tossing the rest of the carcase into the pit.

He continued to dance fiercely, tearing the guts of the monkey to pieces with his hands and teeth and spitting pieces all over the place. This mad and gory dance was symbolical of the curse these people were wishing on the police. They wished the police to go mad and disembowel their own children.

At this stage the four younger women, symbolising the Spirit of Madness, threw off their clothes and hurled themselves upon the wildly capering *Lumbo.* They danced round him, they spat on him and pretended to gouge out his eyes and tear his ears from his head. Then the youngest leapt on to his back and fastened her arms around his neck, bringing him down to the ground in a symbolism of final, disgraceful and horrible death – the death of a madman.

The other men were not idle. They had brought the calf to the curse pit and were strangling it with a thong while the other two women beat the calf with their bare fists, kicking and pummelling it in the belly. The only persons who took no part in this ghastly and barbarous act were the old man *Chikerema* and the young man from the south.

It was the thoroughly maddened *Lumbo* who cut the belly of the calf and dragged out its entrails. *Chikerema,* who had been doing nothing for a while, then stepped forward and grabbed the other monkey and pushed it, still alive, into the stomach cavity of the gutted calf which was then closed by a thong tied around it like a girdle.

This performance symbolised the curse put on the wives and daughters of all the White men who had anything to do with Kariba, the monkey representing their still unborn babies.

The carcase with the living monkey inside was then lowered on to the curse pot while *Chikerema* raised his hands to the skies. His voice was harsh when he said: 'Grant that their women die at childbirth and their young never see the light of day, Oh Ancient Ones of Kariba!'

To the fierce war chant of the ancient Matabele, the men started to fill the curse pit – only halfway as the most important part was yet to come.

The men had brought with them two dummies, a large one representing a police constable – a sergeant, rather – armed with a rifle shaped from softwood, which they propped up with a stick over the curse pit. Here it was ceremoniously stabbed by every man present, excluding the stranger and the old man, and spat upon by each of the women. Each also spoke an unprintable curse on it. The dummy was then dropped in the pit which was completely filled in.

Then came the part that greatly amazed and shocked the stranger from the south – for the sheer daring on the part of these bitter Tonga-Ilas and Ba-Tongas. The second dummy was unwrapped and one could tell at a glance that it was of Ba-Rotse make. It was made out of bark cloth and it was a skilfully produced representation of a fat Englishman with a bald head and a face painted white with the eyes and mouth detailed in red and black. The dummy wore carved softwood shoes and carried a briefcase of python skin. There was a photograph torn from a newspaper, stuck with resin to the chest of the dummy, and if the dummy did not in itself portray clearly enough who was being caricatured, the photograph left no doubts whatsoever. It was an eminent figure in the Federal Government.

This dummy was tied to the back of the last goat, in a riding attitude, facing backwards. More strings were attached to keep it upright on the big billygoat. The women then busied themselves with decorating the goat with a mixture of mud and filth they had salvaged from the curse pot before it was lowered into the pit. The old man finally tied a lighted torch to the tail of the curse goat and sent it off with a violent kick and a battery of the foulest curses in the Tonga vocabulary. The goat, symbolising the Federation, was driven into the bush to lose itself. It has never been heard of since.

'Go!' croaked the old man *Chikerema*, calling the bearer of high office by the Bantu corruption of his real name. 'Go and take your empire of death and evil with you. Take it to the depths of Outer Darkness where the Hyaena of Death can devour you – and it. Go into the valleys of oblivion and obscurity . . . Go!'

The group departed and scattered, and one of the women held the hand of the stranger from the south, who was amazed at what he had witnessed and was already determined to tell the world about it one day. He was wondering what the Government of the Federation would have said had they seen this final scene of the Curse Ceremony. And he was wondering just how bitter people had to be before they could bring themselves to do the things he had seen.

He knew then already that similar orgiastic ceremonies were being held throughout Rhodesia by the outraged Bantu. His hand tightened on that of the ebony enchantress and tears smarted behind the lids of his eyes:

'Oh Africa, my Africa – what, just what is wrong with you?'

Somewhere on the northern bank of the Zambezi a hyaena laughed derisively, like a drunken harlot.

THE RELIGION AND BELIEFS OF THE BANTU

PART II

He had never been to this place in his life before, yet it seemed strangely familiar. He was greatly disturbed. He shrugged and proceeded through the forest. With a heart-stunning shock he came across the stream, bubbling and murmuring its crystal-clear way through the dense growth – the vaguely familiar stream, the frighteningly familiar stream.

As though to complete the amazing moment, there was a stir in the undergrowth on the other side of the stream.

A number of girls appeared, carrying big waterpots on their heads. He had never had any contact with this tribe before; and yet one of the girls attracted his attention – not because she was the most beautiful in the group, but because he thought he had seen her before.

He married her three months later.

The night after their marriage she stirred in his arms; her eyes reflected the moonlight peering through the chinks in the wicker-work door of their new bridal hut.

'Husband, may I please ask you a strange question?'

'Ask me any question, Oh my beloved, and I shall answer it.'

'When ... can you tell me ... just when was it that I met you before?'

'That day at the stream ...'

'When I went with my sisters to the stream that day ... I knew, before I saw you, that I was going to meet you there. My husband, I have been your wife before!'

This kind of thing has led to a strange belief among the Bantu. They believe that Time is a great river that flows into its own source in a huge circle. The oldest symbol of Time, or Life, in Africa is a mamba or a python biting its own tail. The oldest symbol of Eternity is that of a long-necked and long-beaked bird with its neck passing between its legs and its beak buried in its own anus.

The Bantu believe that the soul passes through a series of developmental stages long before and long after its brief association with a human body. Altogether the life span of a soul would be of the order of a thousand years, compared with the human physical life span of about a hundred years. This principle is reflected in the growth and development of all living things.

The first developmental stage of the soul is comparable with the lower plant life – grass and small shrubs – and it is believed that this phase is closely associated with these plants. The souls of future human beings germinate in such grass plants and form their life components. When these seasonal plants die their germinating souls re-incarnate in perennial trees to form their life-components. Here differentiation takes place to produce the variety of souls later to be linked with different human beings – the souls of idiots, fools, lazy ones, beggars, the ordinary rabble, are here separated from those of people of consequence. The former are associated with ordinary trees, the latter with special trees such as the ebony. These are known as holy trees and their wood is used for sacred carvings. The most sacred tree is the baobab with which are associated the souls of future withdoctors, wise women, midwives and those people who will care for and control the lives of others.

The Mashona are regarded as a good tribe because baobabs occur most frequently in their land. It is also noted with concern that the baobab is fast disappearing over great areas and this is the basis of a belief that good people will become fewer and that we are heading for a period of evil in which the Essence of Evil will rule the world. Eventually this Essence of Evil will be overthrown by *Lumukanda* and *Luzwi* and *Marimba*, with whom they will produce a new race of Immortals known as the Witchdoctors of Light. These will rule Mankind in peace and the happiness of paradise for ever.

It is also believed that the baobab is a direct descendant of the Tree of Life and that it will be a baobab that will shelter the Last

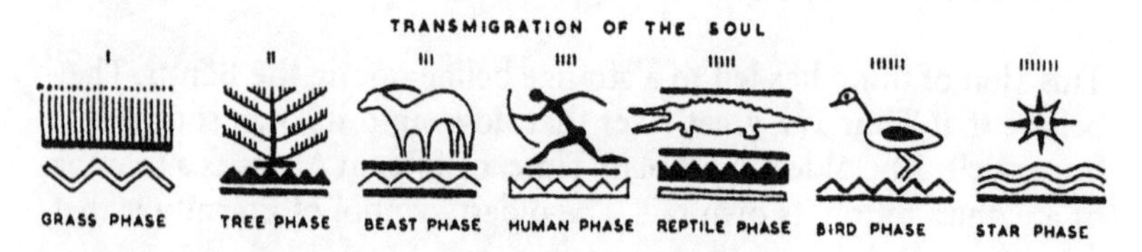

Woman of the Zulus, *Nozala* the Pure, when all the Bantu south of the Limpopo are destroyed by the Great Flood unleashed by the Chief of the Bull. *Nozala* the Pure will be the mother of *Luzwi*.

It stands to reason that any form of damage to this tree is not tolerated; in the past especially, culprits were decapitated. The leaves and the bark are used in a purgative mixture for babies. Presentation of a baobab seed is regarded as a sign of highest esteem, even today. Before seeds, bark or leaves are procured from the baobab, permission must be asked of the Gods. And if the person concerned trips over a stone on the way to the tree, or he sees a snake, he must know that permission has not been granted. Among our ten thousand tree legends there is one which claims that the baobab had breasts and produced milk for mankind before it was learnt that it could be obtained from cows.

From the Tree Phase the soul develops into the Beast Phase, and here there is further separating out. All the Good Souls re-incarnate as Sacred Animals while the Evil Souls associate with Vile Animals. Vile Animals are all those that are a plague to mankind and to other animals, such as jackals, hyaenas, lions and skunks. Sacred Animals include scaly anteaters and the antbear, sable antelope and the springbok, the leopard and the cheetah, the elephant and the hippopotamus, and cattle.

There once existed in the Cape an animal which the Bantu and the Hottentots regarded as the most sacred animal that ever roamed the earth. It was similar to the sable antelope, but far more beautiful. It had long, backward-curving horns, its coat was a glossy blue-black and its belly a pure creamy-white. Like the sable, it had a bushy tail with long hair. Xhosa and Hottentot chiefs claimed for themselves the honour to be buried in an upright position, sewn into the skin of this animal. Its flesh was never eaten; human mouths were considered too foul to be allowed to besmirch the flesh of so holy an animal. Only dying people were sometimes allowed to breathe their last with a small piece of this animal's flesh in their mouths.

The habits of this animal were similar to those of the sable antelope. It had an uncanny knowledge of the medicinal properties of various herbs. When one such animal suffered from an ailment it used to search for a particular kind of herb, as does the sable antelope today. The tribal witchdoctors used to follow these animals to see exactly which herbs they chose, and they could tell from the behaviour of the animal what kind of ailment it had. A great deal of the knowledge of our herbalists was acquired thus.

I learnt from old people of the Griqua and Namaqua tribes that the Dutch name for this animal was 'bloubok', 'blaauwbok' or 'blaubok', and like all the millions of other sacred animals that inhabited the Cape in the last century, the 'bloubok' was wiped out by muskets in the hands of 'civilised' people. The descendants of these people today fail to see in us anything nobler than potential game poachers.

We have done our damage too. Unfortunately, the Bushmen, Hottentots and the Xhosa considered the true quagga to have been a cross between the zebra and that obnoxious creature, the donkey, which was brought, not by the Dutch, but the Phoenicians. They ate this animal out of existence.

But the strangest thing happened when the Europeans came into the highlands of the Cape, Free State and Transvaal. These places were overrun by millions upon millions of the graceful gazelle known as the springbok. And even while proclaiming this beautiful creature their national emblem, they shot it by the millions, often in murderous fun!

These hyprocrites never bothered to enquire why the Bantu had all along allowed this graceful creature to multiply to such countless millions – why they moved no finger when vast herds played havoc with their cornfields, while when the impudent impala tried the same tricks they faced the hunters' spears. It never occurred to the White men that had the Bantu hunted springbok with the same enthusiasm as they hunted lion and jackal they would not even have had this animal on their list of extinct animals; they would not have known of its existence.

The fact that the Bantu never touched a springbok, in the firm belief that it carried the Blessing of the Mother of Creation, never bothered the trigger-happy hunters from beyond the sea. They killed and slaughtered, and butchered and killed – to their heart's delight. And they got upset when the kaffirs started hurling spears at them. They felt cut up in more senses than one when the annoyed kaffirs started taking them apart with battle axes and *pangas*. The fact that they were thus cut up for destroying the sacred springbok never entered their minds. Which of the White Man's history books gives this circumstance as a cause of any one of the eight Kaffir Wars? Yet it was an indirect cause of all eight.

My children, I am now going to tell you a short little story – a story to explain why there is, in our country, an animal that you do not find anywhere else under the sun: an animal so beautiful, so graceful that only a hardened madman with a heart bent like a wizard's back would kill without afterwards suffering the bite of the assegai of remorse. This animal, my children, is the *tsepe*, which many of you have seen – with its white head and belly and legs, and with its fawn back and the heavy dark brown band of colour dividing the white from the fawn. You have heard the whistle of the hooves of the *tsepe* as it leaps high into the air to escape the mighty jaws of the evil lion or the arrows of the bush-skulking Bushmen. And you have seen the ridge of white hair rise in the wind on the back end of the animal as it runs – rising like a beautiful tassel of pure white against the rusty green of the plains.

You may have wondered why the *tsepe* does not exist in other lands of other tribes and is only to be found in the land of our tribe, the Ba-Tswana. You may have wondered why our fierce hunters do not kill this animal as they do the wildebeest, the lion and the impala – except for yearly ritual ceremonies. Listen and I shall tell you why.

The day was beautiful and the day was divine; there was no cloud in the silver skies and the Spirit of Spring walked through the plains of our land. The birds were fluttering in their new plumage from one thorn-barbed bush to another, revelling in the delight of spring. But in the hearts of the people there lay a great sadness – a great and terrible fear. The great Chief *Kgwedi*, who was the last of the Children of the Star-that-fell and who had ruled his people so wisely for twenty years, was going to what he very well knew was his death. In those days, my little ones, fierce ogres whom we know by the name of Bodimo, the Dreaded Ones, were still walking the earth. And they loved to hunt people and eat them.

Now the Bodimo had invaded the land of the Ba-Tswana and had carried off *Matsidiso*, the daughter of the Chief *Kgwedi*, after slaying and eating many warriors. They had carried the girl away as a challenge to *Kgwedi* to come to her rescue and be slain. The ogres knew very well that no man could face them and win, so great was their courage and so great was their strength. Each one of the Dimo carried a mace of stone with a head as big as a young elephant, tied with thongs of impressive size to a shaft as thick as a young tree. Just one blow from one of these terrible maces was enough to smash a man to pulp.

My children, *Kgwedi* decided to go alone to rescue his daughter from the hands of the foul ogres who dwelt beyond the Orange River, on the very edge of the world where the Great Waters roar upon the silent shores of the land of the Hottentots. *Kgwedi* had thousands of servants, both male and female, who loved him as children love a father, for have I not said that he was a chief both great and good? These servants were insisting that they must go with their chief to the very ends of the earth to help him rescue the beautiful *Matsidiso*, but the Great Chief was firm in his refusal. He did not want his people to be endangered on his account and he would go alone, he said.

Then the great witchdoctor *Sankwela* threw the bones of divination and the bones said that the chief would never return from the land beyond the Great Nuka-ya-Barwa alive. But not even the prospect of certain death could keep the Great Chief from his journey. He left early one morning and crossed the Nuka-ya-Barwa, following the clear trail of the ogres, following the great footprints of the Bodimo for many moons.

At last he came to a wide opening in the ground where the trail ended and, pausing just outside, he got his great gemsbok horn bow and sharp arrows ready and shouted to the ogres inside to come out and fight. As the ogres came out, snarling evilly, *Kgwedi* shot them dead one by one with his arrows. As the chief stood triumphant over the bodies of his enemies the wife of the leader of the ogres came out and saw her husband lying dead amongst his evil warriors and, raising a great cry, she darted back into the cave, reappearing a few moments later with a clay basin full of foul medicine.

She threw the medicine at *Kgwedi* and laughed insanely, telling him to go and find his daughter. *Kgwedi* killed the ogre's wife with an arrow and went inside the cave to rescue his daughter. But even as he went in he felt himself changing. He was growing smaller and smaller until his weapons seemed as big as mountains and just as heavy. *Kgwedi* looked down at his hands and discovered that they had changed into disgusting little paws. His nose was now long and pointed and long whiskers sprouted out on either side. His body was covered all over with stinking coarse fur and he found that a long segmented tail grew now where his buttocks had been. *Kgwedi* had turned into a rat.

Princess *Matsidiso* was alone and frightened. She was tied hand and foot in preparation for being sacrificed to the hideous idol the ogres knew as their god. The wife of the ogre chief had told her that when the moon rose she would come personally to drag her to the place of sacrifice. The princess had wept until she felt the soft arms of sleep closing over her frightened soul. She was soon sleeping the deep sleep of the condemned.

She was awakened by something terrifying and hairy moving over her body. She opened her eyes and looked into the disgusting face of the biggest, most revolting rat she had ever seen. The horrible beast had eaten through the thongs binding her ankles and wrists. Leaping to her feet with a loud shriek she seized the stick that lay in the corner of the cave and struck the rat a heavy blow, breaking its back.

'You have killed me, my daughter,' moaned the rat in human speech. 'I was changed into a rat by an evil medicine. I am *Kgwedi*, your father.'

The heart of the princess stopped and she fell face down upon the rat she had killed, and which had been her dear father. Back in the land of the Ba-Tswana a little *Ena* whispered into the ear of the witchdoctor *Sankwela* that both *Kgwedi* and *Matsidiso* were dead. Recovering from his trance, the witchdoctor told the people the shocking news. The servants of the Great Chief stood up and vowed never to rest as long as they lived until they had crossed the great river and brought the bodies of their chief and his daughter back for a proper burial. They went, but they found that the cave had vanished and that the trail of both the ogres and their chief now ended at a great sand dune.

The servants were mad with grief and all, both male and female, took spears and stabbed themselves over the dune. But as they all lay there dead the Great Mother took pity on them and brought them back to life. But their forms had changed and they had become the first springboks ever to roam the earth.

Now, my children, a thing like loyalty dies hard, and the loyalty of the descendants of the springboks who had been the servants of the chief, lives on even today. When you see these sacred little animals migrating in their thousands to the south they are still doing what those ancestors were trying to do. Even today they migrate every year to the land of the Bushmen and Hottentots to try and bring back the body of their dear chief.

Children, a springbok is our eternal symbol of loyalty and if you dream of one it means you will soon have a great loyal friend who will stand by you in all your days of trouble. Never ever kill or wound this animal, because it is directly under the protection of the Great Mother herself. It is the animal known as the Buck of Light. The day when the springbok, this Buck of Light, ceases to walk the plains of our land a great misfortune shall fall upon the entire land.

This is why the springbok is so beautiful: to discourage men from killing it; only one must be killed every year for our ritual ceremonies.

The *ingwe* (leopard) and the *nungu* (cheetah) were also regarded as sacred among the Bantu. The King of the Zulu was the firm protector and high guardian of all the leopards and the cheetahs and tiger-cats (caracal) in the whole of Natal. Anyone who hunted these without permission from the king was punished very severely. His hut was burnt down and he himself was castrated in full view of his wives and children. Only princes and other people of royal birth were permitted to kill leopards and the cheetah was very rarely killed. This animal was often tamed by witchdoctors and kept inside the medicine hut for luck.

These animals were known as *Izilo ze Nkosi* (Beasts of the King, or Royal Game) and they were often used to test the courage of men who were about to be promoted to Battle Leaders or Rainbow *Indunas.* This test consisted simply of sending the men out to bring back a leopard alive so that the chief could have a look at it; then the men would take it back to where they had found it and release it.

But let us have another story.

Ndlela, the son of *Magidela,* and *Vezi,* the son of *Velekulu,* were the bravest warriors in the crack Thunderbolt Regiment of the warlike King *Zulu,* founder of the Zulu tribe. These men were very close friends, as attached to each other as the shadow to the tree that casts it. Wherever you saw *Ndlela,* there was *Vezi* also. They were always to be found in the thickest, most dangerous part of the battle.

One day the Zulus were caught at a disadvantage and were heavily defeated by the Qwabe warriors against whom *Zulu* had to fight continually. They were forced to withdraw through a ravine in the Ulundi mountains to a stronghold that *Zulu* had built on the very top of one of the ranges. During the retreat the two friends excelled themselves in acts of reckless and almost suicidal valour. At a place where the ravine narrowed so that only two could pass abreast the two men stood side by side and held off the Qwabe *impis* for a whole day, giving the remainder time to reach the safety of their stronghold.

Throughout that day the two friends slew the pursuing Qwabes in the ravine, until their arms were numb from wielding their weapons and their shields became as heavy as mountains. They fought until they were wounded in every part of their bodies. Then, when night fell, the Qwabes retreated and the two heroes staggered away from the scene of slaughter, their shields in tatters and their weapons broken. It was midnight when they reached the stronghold of their Chief, and when *Zulu* saw them, he raised a loud howl of laughter: 'Look at the stupid cowards! Just look at the miserable effeminate, buttockless cowards! Tell me, fools, did you get all those wounds fighting the frogs in the Utukela river or did you get them while fleeing through the thornbush forest like the tailless rabbits that you are?'

The assembled warriors howled with laughter and the very stars shook as the gale of derision crashed against the night skies. *Ndlela* bit his lower lip and kept his temper well in check, hanging his weary head in sorrow at so great and unjust an insult. But not so the short fat *Vezi;* he raised his cracked voice and his hoarse shout drowned the tempest of laughter that swept the stronghold.

'That is an unjust insult, Oh Lion of *Malandela.* You know we held the pass against the Qwabes so that you could gain the safety of the fort without hindrance. You saw us fighting. We are no cowards!'

'Are you insinuating that I am a liar, Oh *Vezi*?' cried *Zulu*, leaping to his feet. 'When I say that a man is a coward I mean he is a coward thrice proven, so don't try to squirm out of a charge by bawling at me, you fat stewpot! In fact, I actually saw you lying down and pretending to be dead when you saw the Qwabes coming . . .'

'I am no coward – and I can prove it!'

'How?' asked *Zulu*, raising his eyebrows amid the gusts of laughter. 'How do you intend to prove you are not a coward? By fighting old women with spears made out of green grass as you love to do?'

'I can prove it in any way that you choose.'

'I shall choose in my own time. Meanwhile, let the witchdoctor clean your wounds.'

A great battle was fought the next day and this time the Zulus were the victors. In fact, they inflicted such a defeat on the Qwabes that they scattered like chaff in the wind and their chief began to sue for peace. A moon later, *Zulu* reminded the two friends that they still owed him proof of their courage. He ordered them to go into the forest of Hluhluwe unarmed to fetch him the fierce leopard known as Old One-ear.

Old One-ear was the largest leopard that ever roamed the forests of Zululand. He was such a fierce fighter that he was known to have mauled ten lions to death in the course of his violent life and he inherited his nickname after one of these battles.

Zulu identified his proud spirit with this leopard and he made it known all over the land that he would personally kill any man who as much as looked evilly at this *ingwe.*

Early one morning the two friends went on their perilous mission, armed only with light knobkieries with which to kill snakes. Three days later they entered the wild and uninhabited forest land that was Hluhluwe and here the long and difficult task of finding the great leopard began. It was not they who found the leopard, but the leopard who found them. He dived out of a leavy *marula* tree and landed upon the back of *Vezi*, sending him crashing to the ground. *Vezi* would have died had not the valiant *Ndlela* seized the beast around the neck and hauled it off his friend. Then *Vezi*, fortunately not badly injured, sprang to his feet and both men started pounding the beast with their bare fists. Avoiding the raking claws and the fierce teeth by a succession of sheer miracles, the two friends at last overpowered the leopard and bound it securely. They were about to cut a long sapling with which to carry the leopard when a loud voice cried from the forest: 'You there . . . what are you doing to my beast? Release it at once, you wretched cowards!'

Zulu strode out of the green bush, his warriors clustered close behind him. He smiled softly as the mouths of both *Vezi* and *Ndlela* sagged in open surprise. 'Two big men fighting one helpless beast – can't you take on an animal your own size? Now release that leopard.'

The two men freed the leopard and the growling beast sneaked away deep into the forest. 'Now dogs,' shouted *Zulu*, 'what were you going to do with my animal?'

'But Great *Zulu*,' cried *Vezi* in blank surprise, 'you yourself said we must prove this way that we are not cowards . . .'

'You are cowards! A brave man does not need to prove he is brave! You, warriors, seize these fools and bind them hand and foot. Put skin bags over their heads. You will soon see what I have in store for cowards like you.'

Back in the land of the Zulus, *Vezi* and *Ndlela* were dumped unceremoniously on the ground and left for a long while in hungry solitude.

'Open the bags,' the voice of *Zulu* commanded eventually. 'Let the wretched fools see the fate I have planned for them.'

The bags were taken off their heads and they blinked as the fury of the midday sun struck their eyes. When their sight returned they found themselves surrounded by twenty women, all attired as brides. Beyond the women they saw many cattle. From behind them came the voice of *Zulu*: 'You are so brave at tackling leopards, let us now see how brave you are at tackling wives. Here, there are ten wives for each of you, and a hundred cattle. The command of a regiment is given to each one of you.'

No warrior was allowed to wear a piece of leopard skin as part of his battle regalia until he had killed at least ten enemies in battle. The highest sign of loyalty that could be bestowed upon a chief was to give him a great *kaross* of leopard skin.

If a tribe believes that the Chief is a bad man, not worthy of their loyalty and esteem, they give him an impala skin *kaross* trimmed with sable antelope skin around the edges. As soon as a Chief receives such a gift from his people he knows that while they will tolerate his rule, he is not greatly liked.

Presenting a cheetah skin *kaross* to a chief also has a very special meaning. This gesture conveys undying loyalty, but failure to understand their Chief. He should not be so mysterious and unpredictable. He must take his people into his confidence and make himself clear to them.

Throughout Africa the leopard is associated with courage and the cheetah with the occult, the obscure, mysterious and unpredictable.

We associate the lion with the highest form of evil. To dream of a lion means serious trouble with the chief. No tribal wood carver will carve the image of a lion if he can help it. And if for some reason this has to be done, it must, when finished, be urinated upon to destroy its evil taint. In some Bantu villages such lion-images are posted to protect those inside against the approach of evil from outside; such evil will join up with these images and leave those inside in peace.

On the same principle, villagers of the Wakambi, Luo and Chako in Kenya keep images of the Masai. The idea is to teach the young children what a Masai looks like so that they can always avoid these evil people. But it is also believed that if the evil spirit of the Masai should reach such a village, it will be caught by these images and not spread to the inhabitants. There is also the belief that 'Evil comes not where it sees an image of itself' and on the strength of this belief the Bantu often position a mirror overnight in such a way that a zombie or a *tokoloshe* would see itself first before it saw the owner of the mirror.

The elephant and the hippopotamus are other animals regarded as sacred by the Bantu. These they will not kill unless there is a famine in the land, or when they become possessed with evil spirits and turn into rogues.

Before a hunting party goes out to kill a rogue hippopotamus its members must fast for three days and undergo a ceremony of purification. They must put new strings on their bows and new heads on their spears. Throughout the period of the hunt the oldest woman of the village must sit still in her hut, her face to the wall, in a position of mourning for the soul of the beast and in humble apology to the gods.

The fat of the hippopotamus is the most valuable part of the medicine-man's equipment and it is used for mixing the *Gqaba* medicine, a potion that can give any man the upper hand in or over anything or anybody. This may sound like utter nonsense, and yet it has the ingredients for generating a great feeling of self-confidence and self-assurance in people who are normally inclined to be nervous and excited. It can achieve this in a more powerful and lasting way than can alcohol or *dagga*. It is the most popular medicine among the Bantu and, as far as witchdoctors and ordinary charlatans are concerned, the best-seller. It is prescribed for people who feel ill, who are ill, who are involved in any form of competition, who seek work, who have to face a magistrate or a rival in love. Many a young White Man has ousted his rival in love after a visit to a witchdoctor.

The common vulture was also a creature which came directly in the sphere of protection by a tribal Chief. They were regarded as sacred because of their scavenging habits. All executed criminals, thieves and wizards were fed to these animals, but not adulterers and adulteresses, who were too dirty to be fed to these 'Birds of Heaven'. Such people were either buried upside down with their legs sticking out for hyaenas to find, or they were simply fed to crocodiles. The eagle and the owl were sacred birds only to those who worshipped the God of Thieves; even today there are many tribes that exist on cattle-thieving.

In the Northern Transvaal the most revered animal is the scaly anteater, whose life is worth far more than ten human beings. In the land of the Ba-Kgalaka, who dwell under the dread presence of the mighty Zoutpansberg mountains, the scaly anteater falls under the direct protection of the Rain Queen, the *Mudjadji*, or Daughter of the Sun. I know that this may sound like the ravings of a superstitious bush-kaffir; I am convinced, however, that the scaly anteater possesses powers that, to the Bantu at least, are supernatural. For hundreds of years it has been common knowledge with us that this *kgwara* possesses strong 'wish-powers'. When it wanders into an area where there are no ants and is near death from hunger it can form such a strong wish in its brain that ants come over great distances to it. Anyone finding a scaly anteater must take it directly to the Rain Queen. He must never tell anybody he meets along the way what he is carrying.

The fat of the *kgwara*, like that of the tortoise, is used in medicine intended to carry the wish-prayers for rain in all speed to the Rain Goddess. Even the ceremonious killing of this animal is said to anger the Rain Goddess so much that she tries to drown the offenders with rain – which is just what they want.

The sable antelope is another sacred animal and for hundreds of years the Bantu have associated this animal with the human soul. The horns make the best bugles in the whole of Africa, better even than those of a fully grown kudu. The tail, like that of the wildebeest, mounted on a short stick and decorated with beads, is carried by witchdoctors everywhere in Africa. The witchdoctor dips this tail with its long glossy hair into a pot full of 'anti-evil spirit' medicine with which he sprays those seated round him. While this is done they clap their hands and he dances to the rhythm. The witchdoctor will often beat himself about the legs while he dances in order to raise the 'divining fury' within him, and he will also use it to slash at the ears of the boy with the *muti* drum when he beats too slowly or makes a mistake. Such a blow can be extremely painful, as experience has taught me.

The Barotse tribe has perfected the art of carving the sable antelope, but they took over this art from the Aluwi, whom they conquered and absorbed after an invasion under their Chief, the High Conqueror. These carvings always represent a sable antelope in one of ten characteristic poses, each pose having a particular meaning. They are sent as messages from one family, clan or tribe to another to convey a blessing, warning or even a plain insult.

The association of the human soul with the sable antelope is one of the oldest beliefs in Africa. Even in cave paintings the animal is often seen standing to one side, all by itself, facing the entrance. A female suckling young is the oldest symbol of fertility, pertaining to agriculture as well. But the giraffe suckling young is something different: it symbolises the daily birth of the sun. Both these symbols date back to the Stone Age and they are still in use today with rites and ceremonies dealing with the worship of the Great Mother and the Heavenly Bodies.

We must go back some distance now to pick up the thread of the story. From the Beast Phase the soul proceeds to the Human Phase – or the Great Middle Phase. The Bantu believe that man stands in the middle of living creatures and not at the top. Below him are the plants and animals such as the mammals which have not yet achieved the perfect means of reproduction through egg-laying. Man was merely given great intelligence to exercise control over all living creatures. Physically, the Bantu see Man as a very imperfect creature, utterly defenceless without artificial means. Even a snake is considered superior since it can proceed without legs, and a python can kill a human being – even one carrying weapons.

It is, therefore, widely believed that after its association with the human body, the soul goes on to a higher plane of existence by re-incarnating in a reptile. From the reptile it moves still higher to the supreme level of the birds.

The Zulu regard both the green and the black mamba as sacred; these carry the souls of recently departed compatriots. When a mamba starts frequenting the vicinity of a kraal, the headman will arrange for the whole kraal to be moved to another site. But the mamba is never molested. Evil Souls, they believe, associate themselves with the puffadder, and these are hounded with delight. Not only are they killed so as to destroy the Evil Soul, but they are also skinned and mounted above a pile of wood which is not immediately set alight. Only after two days when it is felt that the carcase of the puffadder has also attracted the evil *Ena* of the departed one, is the fire lit, so that this *Ena* may be destroyed as well.

The python is sacred to the Venda of the Eastern Transvaal. Other tribes select various lizards, while the Baca, the tribe to which my father belongs, made a serious zoological miscalculation when they chose the fresh water crab as their sacred 'reptile'.

We were, of course, forbidden to touch, let alone eat, a fresh water crab. But once the Father-Principal of the Catholic School I attended gave me as a present a tin of canned lobster from a number he had received as a gift from France. I remember the great bitterness that assailed me as I went through the bush taking the can home to my father, knowing full well that I was not going to taste this fabulous food from beyond the seas, knowing that my father with his skin-deep veneer of Christianity . . .

'What have you got there, Credo?' he asked, dropping the boot he was making out of raw bullhide. He called me by my baptismal Christian name which I have now rejected. It was derived from the Apostle's Creed, spoken in Latin: *Credo in unum Deum, patrem omnipotentem . . .*

Trembling from the memories of all the thrashings I had already had from my parent (the lot of all bastards born out of wedlock) I humbly knelt down and presented the tin to him. One look at the glaring red picture of a lobster on a plate in the label made his face grow sombre like a thunder cloud scowling over the Drakensberg.

'Where did you get this thing?'

'The White Father gave it to me, father.'

'Get out of here . . . get out! Go and wash your hands . . . far, outside the kraal.' He threw the tin under a bush and some time later he took it, along with me, to the old man *Ngubeni*, who was the witchdoctor of the 'heathen' section of the Bantu people in our district. He also took ten shillings with which to pay the lecherous old charlatan. *Ngubeni* was not only an ugly old wart-faced jackal with a taste for girls young enough to be his granddaughters; he was endowed with great insolence and more than a fair share of contempt and hatred for those the 'heathen Bantu' know as 'Christian Bantu'.

'I see you, Oh fat Christian fool,' he said, wiping his drooling mouth that always sagged open to expose his dirty yellow teeth, and to wet the cockroach-eaten apology for a beard – tobacco-stained like some fungus on green leaves. 'What seek you in my humble kraal? Do not tell me that you have finally decided to turn your oily back on the White Man's God!'

'No,' answered my parent coldly. 'I have not come back to worship these things you have here. I am a Christian and I shall remain one until my dying day. I only want you to purify my son . . . he has touched a crab.'

'What was your son doing with the crab? Does he not know that the law says he must leave all crabs unmolested and must salute one when he sees it?'

'The White Father of the Mission gave him a cooked crab inside a tin, and I do not wish to have bad luck fall on my family.'

'So the white-collared old liar gives your son one of our ancestors in a tin as food! It will not be long now before these White men cook our mothers and put them in tins for us to eat. So you want me to purify your bastard male child from this great sin?'

'I do,' my parent replied.

'Good! Listen then. First lay out ten bright shillings on the ground and then remove your fat buttocks from my kraal – back to your White-Man's God. Leave this squint-eyed little bastard here for me to deal with.'

My stay in the witchdoctor's hut on that Saturday was an unforgettable nightmare. The interior was full of things hanging from the walls and roof: drums, face-masks of great antiquity, *karosses*, dead and dried hawks and lizards, medicine pouches full of things weird and frightening, shields and switches once the property of the witchdoctor's ancestors – all articles normally featuring in incredible and utterly heathen ceremonies. It felt as if the hut was filled with unseen spirits that kept on licking and kissing me. My skin crawled and itched. I wanted to scream; I wanted to run outside. I was numb with exquisite terror – but my body would not move. The afternoon dragged on, a hideous dream of fear and unseen horror.

With the ceremony that night things were done to me that I will remember till my dying day. I was made to drink liquids that tasted like the sewers of Hell and smelt much fouler. A fowl was brought in and its throat was plucked out. It was disembowelled and the tin of crayfish was put inside the carcase which was buried in a deep hole. My hands were cut and a black *muti* was rubbed into the wounds.

It was a very frightened and bewildered ten-year-old boy who followed his father home that Sunday afternoon, away from the kraal of *Ngubeni.*

If the reptile re-incarnation of one tribe is found in the kraal of another unfriendly tribe it is immediately killed and burned, because it acts as a spy for some wizard or other. It is as simple as that.

Another thing of interest: the Venda with the python as their sacred reptile make their maidens to the 'Python Dance' as a symbol of fertility after they have completed their initiation. But why the python? Once this tribe believed that the python became pregnant and bore live young like a woman. They used to come across pythons that had just swallowed an animal and they mistakenly thought them pregnant. They would take pythons in this condition to their kraals and with much ceremony and drumming and wild dancing take them to the midwives' hut. All the women who wanted children or those with womb complaints or who had experienced constant miscarriages would then gather round. Kneeling to the python they would pray to it to plead for them with the Great Mother.

What puzzled the early Venda was why, after its supposed pregnancy the python produced no young. But around this puzzle grew the legend that the python gives birth to invisible spirits. To dream of a python before marriage is a sure sign of numerous healthy offspring.

On all masks of fertility a fish appears in some way or other. Often the whole mask is cut to look like a fish. This association of a fish with fertility comes about because immediately the belly of a fish is slit and opened to remove the intestines, it resembles the sex organ of a woman.

Something should be explained here that has never been explained before. All foreigners in Africa have heard of a *tokoloshe*. But their idea of one, if they have any, is that of a hairy, human-like elf that lives in the water and is sometimes tamed by wizards to terrorise people. This concept is, like so many others, completely false. And those who reject the whole idea of a *tokoloshe* as so much superstition had better be careful. A *tokoloshe* is not just a figment of the imagination of a bunch of superstitious savages, as one 'enlightened' White correspondent was pleased to call the Bantu in a letter to the press. Many beliefs of the Bantu are based on scientific fact, and the *tokoloshe* is one of these. Nobody starts believing anything unless some fact triggers off the belief. It can only be wrong if the fact was misunderstood.

The Bantu, especially, never start believing anything unless a fact of some description can motivate the belief. The decline of Christianity among the Bantu can be related to this circumstance. The Christian Missionaries came to us with stories of guardian angels watching over us, but they could not substantiate this belief with a single incident or fact that would justify it. However far-fetched and however wrong, I have explained what facts gave rise to the beliefs cherished by the Venda about the python. Every single belief that the African holds can be traced back to some scientific fact, understood or misunderstood. The African is more sceptical and less gullible than most people think; he has not the refined imagination of the ancient Greeks who could create out of thin air all those satyrs and centaurs.

Many generations ago, before the Bantu had moved south of the Zambezi, an old wizard avenged himself on a foul tyrant who had killed all his wives and raped his daughters before flinging them to the crocodiles. The name of this wizard was *Mulundi*, and that of the tyrant, *Kambela*. It is said that *Kambela* was so cruel, he was even cruel to his own person and the very hut he lived in. He used to fly into a tremendous rage for no reason and if nobody was near on whom he could vent his spleen he turned upon himself and bit big chunks of flesh from his arms. He would beat himself up till he bled all over. One of the few wives he could get to live with him he once locked into a hut and suffocated her with a cow-dung fire while he watched the expressions on her face through a little hole. His favourite method of punishing people was to tie several of them to trees and then push long iron awls into them to see who would scream loudest and who would take longest to die.

Mulundi was determined to put an end to *Kambela* but he did not know how to set about it because *Kambela* was always closely guarded by a team of foul thugs who were as loyal to him as foul thugs can be to a thug only a shade fouler. *Mulundi* had sent a threatening message to *Kambela* a few days after the latter had raided his kraal, in which he swore to kill *Kambela* even if it took him a thousand years. He also told the tyrant chief that he would not see a new moon in the sky again; he would be dead before the moon turned full.

Kambela became very scared of the old wizard whose powers were widely known and he stayed in his kraal with all gates tightly shut. His evil warriors guarded him day and night. But the old wizard had seen a weakness in the stockade of the chief's kraal and he already knew how to exploit it. What he did has been copied by all wizards since – and thus the *tokoloshe* came to be created.

Growing just outside the stockade was an old leafy tree, an ancient *marula* that had seen much and whose spreading branches extended well across the stockade. One night *Kambela* lay in his hut in solitude and sullen anger; he had just drunk a great pot full of strong beer to drown his fear and calm his heart. He knew wizards never made idle threats. He had called his witchdoctors and they had given him potions guaranteed to frighten evil spirits away. His gross ugly body was sticky with greasy 'charm medicines' intended to repel demons, and three witchdoctors squatted outside the bullhide door which he had securely fastened from the inside.

Weary from panic, *Kambela* slept, but not for long. He opened his eyes and beheld a sight which was to be the last thing he saw on earth. Poised over him was a squat little figure oozing the very essence of evil. It wore a hideous skin mask and a costume made of the skins of baboons. Dangling from a string round his neck was the partly decomposed head of a woman. It held a bow and poisoned arrow at the ready.

Kambela tried to scream but his voice died in his throat as a hardly audible hoarse croak. The first *tokoloshe* that ever walked this earth released the taut string of the bow and *Kambela* felt the arrow sink deeply into his bowels. He died with a look of terror on his face.

A sound of mad laughter shattered the moonlit night and every warrior in the kraal felt his blood freeze. Many dashed outside the gate of the stockade to find the owner of the voice and they were just in time to see a sinister little silhouette sneak away against the midsummer moon. The very first *tokoloshe* was on his way back to report to *Mulundi* that his mission was completed and was a great success.

The warriors dashed back to *Kambela's* hut and had to force the door open. They found him dead, but there was no assassin's footprint and no trace of how he managed to enter the hut. *Mulundi* passed his secret on to other wizards and even today *tokoloshes* turn the hair of people white and baffle the police who are called out to try and solve many unaccountable murders.

A *tokoloshe* is not a ghostly or supernatural phenomenon. He is a physical human being, and he operates along perfectly scientific lines. *Mulundi* had used a very small pigmy whose weight he had drastically reduced with a severe diet. He had furthermore turned the little creature into a zombie by a simple interference with his brain. A sharp awl can do the trick. He was posted up the *marula* tree and along a branch that reached across to the roof of *Kambela's* hut. With a long thong he lightly descended upon the roof of the hut and wriggled his skeletal little frame through the grass roof. He escaped the same way.

This weird practice has today been perfected into a fine art. Cases are known to me where wizards have arranged the faked death of a particular person whom they have selected for a prospective zombie. The person is actually buried, but exhumed the same night and revived. He is then turned into a zombie and, many days or weeks later, heavily decorated with parts of other people's bodies, also exhumed from graves, the puppet is induced to pay a particular victim an unexpected visit. The victim simply dies of fright. It is as simple as that. Any chance eye witness will relate a beautiful *tokoloshe* story to the police, and the police will dismiss it as so much nonsense.

In later generations the wizards perfected their art of *tokoloshe*-making and they started breeding *tokoloshes* from childhood. As recently as 1922 there was a secret *tokoloshe* farm kept by a gang of wizards in the Drakensberg in Basutoland.

With the arrival of the White Man and Christianity the killing of children who were born cretins and idiots went out of fashion, and these grotesque specimens of humanity grew plentiful. But an idiot is something no one misses should it mysteriously disappear – the parents least of all – and many of these idiots, particularly female, landed up in the hands of these wizards. They reared them and, when adult, they mated with them and kept them in dark caves for their children to be born. Often, in Basutoland – the land of ritual murder – the babies were brought into this world the caesarian way with no concern over the life of the mother. Parts of her body were used for medicines that were administered to her own baby to make it grow up in an atmosphere of deep evil.

The baby was reared by other idiot women who fed it a mixture of the milk of dogs, donkeys and cows, and the blood of ravens and vultures. At the age of six months it was subjected to specialised treatment for its particular task of the future. It was made to develop a crooked or hunch back by strapping it to a curved piece of wood. The legs too were strapped into attitudes that encouraged their growth into grotesque shapes. At the age of twelve the tongue was damaged to destroy speech. The child was taught to hate the world and idolise its wizard master.

It was then put through a course of queer tricks ranging from tree climbing with its crooked limbs to burrowing underground. It was taught ways to commit murder and to perfectly remove all its tracks afterwards. When it had reached the age of about twelve, the wizard had in his hands a lean featherweight puppet-like creature, an unthinking robot that obeyed every command – a creature worth a hundred head of stolen cattle to the one who bred and trained him.

Genuine *tokoloshes* are today found only in Basutoland and Nyasaland, where hiding places in the mountains can still be found for them.

With the difficulties in breeding, rearing and keeping this kind of *tokoloshe* these days, the wizards have resorted to using baboons and monkeys. Their young are nowadays turned into the weirdest monstrosities and can be taught to do considerable damage to their master's enemies.

There is currently a growing market for *tokoloshes* in South Africa. A trained monkey or baboon *tokoloshe* fetches a substantial price.

The *tokoloshe* is no figment of the imagination. The word *tokoloshe* means 'a great mysterious evil'. The Bantu will *never* portray one in a carving. When a Bantu describes something as a *tokoloshe*, he says 'a mysterious evil' and means 'mind your own business'.

From the reptile the soul transmigrates to the Bird Phase. Here a further sorting out takes place. The Greater Souls associate with the birds we regard as sacred for this very reason. These are the vulture, flamingo, ibis, and the secretary bird. The Lesser Souls associate with the small birds. But the souls of those men and women who were very diligent indeed become associated with very singular and particular birds such as the *isakabuli* and the ostrich, also revered for their useful plumage. The souls of all lazy people are associated with guinea fowls.

Although a massive book could be written on all the beliefs and legends related to birds, I shall select only one example – the *lilanda*, or flamingo. This bird is rarely killed by the Bantu and only then after an elaborate ceremony and for a very particular purpose. It is believed that anybody who kills a flamingo indiscriminately will be struck by lightning.

The *landa* is the symbol of purity throughout Africa; it is also the symbol of wifely faith and chastity. At one time, when a man accused his wife of adultery, he used to challenge her to stab herself in the arm and allow the blood to run over the back of a live but trussed flamingo. If the bird became agitated the woman was found guilty and executed. But if the bird lay passive the woman was declared innocent. This practice was discontinued when it was discovered that the relatives of the woman concerned used to bribe a witchdoctor to drug the bird.

When the empires of both the Ba-Luba and the Lunda were at the height of their glory it was the custom for couples who had been married for twenty years without a single quarrel, to celebrate this anniversary by eating the hearts, livers and tongues of four flamingoes raw. The four flamingoes were killed at midnight by virgins who sang to the sacred birds as they killed them. A very sharp iron spike was thrust through the skull of each flamingo, causing instant death, and the liver, the heart and the tongue were removed with blessed knives of very great sharpness. Great care was taken not to stain the feathers and what little blood was spilt had to be washed off very carefully.

The four birds were then mounted on a raft in a brooding attitude and the virgins were dressed in green leaves to represent the twenty handmaidens of the Great Mother. To the beating of drums and the shrilling of wedding flutes the raft was later launched, piled high with flowers and fresh yams. This raft carried to the Great Mother (by the *Enas* of the birds) the prayers, good wishes, and even curses, piled on the celebrating couple by the guests.

At such a celebration even the deadliest enemies of the couple were bound by law to attend and they usually arrived with their faces daubed with white or yellow clay. They would try every trick to sabotage the festivities (which lasted six whole days), kidnapping the High Cooks, breaking musical instruments or merely making a persistent nuisance of themselves. This added much colour to the festivities. Quite often confirmed enemies of the couple ended up by becoming their best friends.

On the last day the couple was left alone to partake of the 'feast of the flamingo'. They ate the raw hearts, livers and tongues, garnished with tasty herbs, from a bowl shaped like a hippopotamus – the symbol of plenty. With this feast the couple used long toothpick-like ivory probes in the way that Europeans use forks.

The *ngwembe*, or hippopotamus-like bowl, was sometimes shaped like an ordinary bowl with four short legs, but attached to a hippopotamus-like 'handle' in the back of which the toothpicks were inserted in holes.

A great storm was building up its wrath, my children, and the heavens were as dark as the scowl of Hell. Fierce bolts of lightning tore the clouds apart and the earth shook with the thunder of the enraged skies. The trees writhed and tossed as the furious winds sought to pluck them out by the roots and fling them across the cowering veld. The graceful springboks huddled in the undergrowth and even the evil hearts of lions knew fear.

And among the reeds of the great river Ligwa a young hen flamingo hid, her chaste heart a-trembling with fright. Then, out of the wild tumult that was the storm-raped skies, a thunderbolt seared down – a ravening flame that knew no restraint, a ball of blue-white fire that clove the air and struck the area of the reeds bordering the Ligwa and turned it into a smudge of ash.

It did not kill the flamingo, however. The bird suddenly began to glow with a strange irridescence until its outline became blurred and its whole being seemed unreal. And right there, among the boiling lilies and burning reeds, it laid the brilliantly glowing purple egg which grew and burst and hatched a baby of the Ma-Buru race. This baby was a thing of great beauty; he was like a little god.

A band of Ma-Buru warriors on their strange war-beasts found the little boy, who was destined to become their Great Chief and fight valiantly but in vain against the Big Woman of the Waters, the dreaded *Kwini Vittori.*

They reared him and named him *Pewula* – the meaning of which we do not know – and when he grew up they made him into the Great Chief of their kingdom. But every time his people, the Ma-Buru, attacked us he took our side and saved us.

Then one day the great Destroyers, the Ma-Nyisimane, came and took away the kingdom of the Ma-Buru, and we never saw their Great Chief *Pewula* again.*

* * *

This is no ordinary legend, and it is not thousands of years old as are most of our legends. It is not even a hundred years old and it is supposed to have been born in the Transvaal town of Lichtenburg. It is only one of the very many stories told about the President of the Transvaal Republic, Paul Kruger, who was worshipped by the Bantu of the Transvaal. And when I say worshipped, I mean literally worshipped – as people worship a god.

The irony of it all is that had President Kruger known that the Bantu worshipped him like a god (and they did so until recently in the Lichtenburg area), he could have won the Boer War.† He had only to give the Bantu the slightest signal and they would have attacked the British troops whole-heartedly.

Please forgive me, dear readers, for occasionally drifting off at a tangent. However, I am not leaving the subject; all these stories merely illustrate how many different angles there are to Bantu religion and beliefs. I am only skimming over the surface, bringing out random, but not insignificant, points. If I were to deal with this subject in detail, recording all the legends and stories that go to illustrate our various beliefs, I would fill fifty books the size of this one. The High Gods willing, I shall endeavour to do so, but I have my doubts – my enemies have already started to turn me into a pin-cushion.

From the Bird Phase the soul is promoted to the Star Phase. We believe that the stars are souls which have evolved to supreme perfection. They are now, literally, in Heaven.

But souls do not stay in Heaven indefinitely; after a long period of time they return to earth to start the cycle all over again. We often see how these souls return to earth in the so-called 'Souls that fall' (meteors or shooting stars).

The Wise Ones of the Tribes say that 'Eternity is a song that repeats itself'. They say a man cannot alter the course of his life, nor can any beast. A lowly peasant may arise and become an *Induna*, or a chief, but this is not due to his own courage or wisdom, or cunning. He is merely attaining a predestined goal; his soul attained this goal on its previous cycle.

'My son,' said the High Instructor, 'the human mind is a thing of mystery such as the ordinary people will never understand. It is

---

* Ma-Buru – *Boere, Boers.*
Kwini Vittori – *Queen Victoria.*
Pewula – *Paul Kruger,*
Ma-Nyisimane – *Englishmen.*

more than just a thing to think with and with which to remember things. The mind, the brain, is matter in its purest form, and it is the hands and the feet and the wings of the soul. The mind is the link that connects the body with the soul, just as the handle links the iron head of the axe with the arm of the man wielding it; just as the chain links the lumbering wagon to the labouring ox.

'My son, I am now teaching you wisdom that is older than some of the mountains you see, the wisdom that is more ancient than your ancestors of ninety thousand generations back. *Vusa-Amazulu*, my son, in the name of the God of the Gods, believe me when I tell you that the day Man *does* learn to co-operate fully with his soul, through his mind, he will not need to have hands and feet, and he will be able to do the most impossible things you can imagine, because you know that the soul is a grain in the Structure of God, as a single grain in the sandstone is part of the mountain.

'My son, the mind is the navel string connecting the soul and the *Ena* to the body and, like the soul that gives it power, the mind is all-powerful and all-knowing. The purpose of the training of a witchdoctor is that he should develop, as fully as possible, close co-operation between his soul, body and *Ena*, with his mind, otherwise his mind will not develop into being all-powerful and all-knowing. This only the soul can impart to the mind.

'The flesh-and-blood body of the human being is often just a great nuisance to the soul because it often resists the commands of the soul and hesitates when the soul urges it to go forward. The body dulls the powers of the soul by blanketing it with its own weaknesses and failings. Thus when the body of a poor man is busy drowning itself in the lake of self-pity, worry and fear, the soul cannot act effectively through the mind and gain for that man the wealth he so badly desires. The minds of poor men and hardworking men are like channels blocked by foul driftwood. This is why a witchdoctor must never allow his mind to become blocked with earthly rubbish.

---

† *The author did not know that President Kruger was fully aware of Bantu sentiment. Several chiefs actually approached him with offers of assistance, but these offers were flatly turned down. The President explained that when two Black tribes are involved in a conflict, a White tribe should not take the side of the one against the other; if anything, the White tribe should only act as a mediator to restore peace.*

Similarly, when two White tribes are fighting no Black tribe should be used by either side. If a Black tribe cannot use any influence to stop the conflict, it must stand well to one side. This attitude is still strongly supported by most South Africans. There was, for example, strong opposition to the use of Black troops in the Second World War.

It is the channel through which the soul must always operate without hindrance, giving him the power to foresee, to heal, to enslave the souls of others, or to free them where this is required.

'This is why, child, those of our people who follow the ways and the religions of the foreigners never make good witchdoctors and they only become cheap, bewildered and benighted charlatans. This is because they have exposed themselves to the beliefs and the ways of life of the aliens. They have become nothing but puppets with shallow minds, no longer guided along the footpath of Life by their souls as we are. A man who lives with his soul and who lets his soul, rather than his brain, guide him, is better equipped to face the mysterious and supernatural things, because the soul understands these things while they bewilder the brain. The brain drags them into the quicksands of materialism.

'My son, for thousands of years we, the Chosen Ones, have been trying to breed a new kind of man who will walk this earth without fear of flesh-and-blood enemies and who could offer defiance to some of the gods who hate us. Such a man, we hope, would use the forces of his brain, his mental power, to destroy his enemies, instead of using spears and shields. Such a man would not use his tongue to speak, but he would use the powerful voice of his mind to speak both to beasts and to fellow men. There would be nothing hidden from this man, who would be using the forces latent in our minds to do even the most seemingly impossible things. He would be able to read the thoughts of birds and he would be able to swim against the current of the River Time – backwards into the past or forwards into the future – as he pleased.

'And, my son, we are nearer to achieving this ideal today than most people think!

'The power of the soul and the mind is infinite. The soul is omniscient and omnipotent like the Great God of whom it forms an infinitesimal granule. The brain is something man uses for thinking about, and controlling his immediate, mostly materialistic, needs. But if properly linked to the soul with the mind, the brain could exploit all the powers of the soul. The ideal is in fact to weld the body, brain, mind, *Ena* and soul into one co-ordinated whole instead of so many scattered entities. Where a person can achieve this, he will reach ultimate perfection.

'But I must give you some idea of how powerful the mind can be, so that you can better understand what we are trying to achieve. You must be drawn closer to us and become a stronger member of the Chosen Ones. You have seen how we have to put you into a trance again and again by simply telling you to look straight into our eyes. You have seen how the Wise Woman took over your mind and made you tell us everything about yourself, revealing to us even your most secret fears and desires. You have seen how we took over your mind and made you take part in all the events in our Holy Legends. By taking over your mind and casting a temporary spell over you we made you see the Unseen Ones and we made you converse with your own ancestors who died so many years ago.

'My son, all this is but an infinitesimal fraction of the power of the mind. How do you think the Ancient Ones stumbled across the idea of interfering with the brains of people and turning them into zombies? How did our remote ancestors at the dawn of time stumble across the art of removing tumours from the brain? All these things were discovered by men who were trying to create the most ultimate ideal, the all-powerful and all-knowing man – an ideal our Bantu Wise Ones have clung to for more years than there are hairs on the body of a dog.

'My son, I am going to tell you a secret that very few know: most of the medicines we witchdoctors use are nothing but water into which a few boiled green herbs have been added, and the only reason we give this foul-tasting mixture to a sick one to drink is to arouse, in the sick one's brain, the *will* to be healthy. Without the strong will to be alive, a man can be carried into the valleys of Death by even the mildest sickness. And you know that if a man no longer desires to live, no medicine yet devised will cure him. This is why the laws of our fathers say that we must never tell wounded warriors whose chief has lost the battle that theirs is the defeated side, because this deprives the badly wounded men of the will to live and no witchdoctor can nurse them back to health when this happens.

'This is why the High Tribal Laws of our forefathers forbid the news of the death of parents or relatives to be conveyed to a woman who is still weak from childbirth. My son, the mind of an ordinary man and woman needs an external stimulus in order to release its powers of courage, determination, self-confidence and willingness to live. This is why we encourage the stupid rabble to use charms, which are nothing but external stimuli intended to encourage the thick brains of the porridge-eating peasants to function and protect the fools to whom those brains belong.

'My son, listen very well, it is not God who ultimately grants you your wishes and who hears your prayers; neither is it the *Enas* of your ancestors. It is your own mind, your soul through your mind, that brings your dearest wish to you. Listen, there are men who, when crossing the river, always imagine there is a crocodile stalking them. You will find that these men are eventually killed by crocodiles while crossing rivers. This constant fear of being eaten by a crocodile takes the form of a very strong wish to meet this fate. There is very little difference between these two when it comes to the vivid mental picture which is radiated and received by the crocodiles in the vicinity. Similarly, women walking in the field or forest alone, often fear that men will pounce on them and rape them. The mental picture they radiate cannot be distinguished from one expressing a wish to be raped, and such mental pictures are subconsciously received by men in the vicinity and instil attractive ideas in their conscious minds.

'Suppose you want a cow that will produce lots of milk for your young ones – do you kneel down as the Christians do and merely tell God about your need? We say no. Our ancestors said we must go far away, out into the veld, preferably to the summit of the highest hill in the vicinity. There you must lie on your back with your eyes closed, and first drain all thoughts and memories from your brain. Then, after a long while, you must slowly and clearly bring into the fully drained, clear valleys of your mind a 'solid' picture of the cow you want, in every possible detail. You must, with the 'nose' of your imagination, be able to smell it; and with the 'ears' of your imagination you must hear its lowing. Let the 'hands' of your imagination stroke it . . . feel its coarse hair under the palms of your hands. And all the time you must cultivate the strongest possible wish to own a cow just like that one. This you must do every day for a whole month, and all the time in between you must keep on nursing and developing more strongly that one wish; think of nothing else.

'My son, as sure as I am standing here, before the year is out that cow will somehow or other come into your possession.

'Your grandfather tells me that women shun you – that they do not like you because of your squinting eyes. Now I am going to offer you positive proof of the power of the mind. We are going to give you exactly three months in which to use the powers of your bastard little mind to get yourself a woman with whom you can prove that you are a man. Tell me, what is your preference in the line of a woman?'

'I think . . . the Sun-Doe* type, my lord,' I answered.

'For an ugly little pest like you, you have quite discerning taste, have you not? Now then, tomorrow you must go to the riverside and get some clay and make a crude model of a Sun-Doe type of woman . . . a full figure that will stand as high as your knee. Let it dry for four days and then bring it to us for a blessing.'

I set out on the following day – July 23, 1947 – to the riverside and was soon occupied at modelling the figure of a woman from

---

* *Oval face; small flat nose; round forehead; small round chin; light golden-brown complexion; large blunt breasts; small waist; prominent hips; large thighs and long tapering legs.*

very excellent clay. It presented no difficulty as I am a sculptor of sorts. Four days later I laid the finished product at the feet of the High Instructor.

His comments greatly shocked me: 'Do you want your wife to be a sterile and an uninhibited harlot? Why did you put her arms straight along her side?'

'I can make a new model . . .'

'No, that you cannot do; this one has already taken too fixed a shape in your mind. If you change your mind, even once, you can forget about achieving any results. But I must first improve your education – you don't seem to know that from the land of the Xhosas to the lands of the Old Tribes the hands and the feet of a statuette or carving mean something. Unlike the White Man, we do not carve or model images for no reason; ours are messages or prayers, or even symbols. In our land we can bless or curse a person by sending him a carving of which the hands or feet are arranged in a certain way.'

I must pause and elaborate here, as I am sure readers will find this interesting. A Black Man never carves or models anything unless he has a very specific and serious reason for doing so. In actual fact, the Black Man does not do *anything*, unless there is a very good reason for it.

Thus the Bantu will not participate enthusiastically in a road-building project unless they fully understand the reason for undertaking it. When White Authority introduced cattle dipping into Zululand, they did not give the local people a clear enough explanation of its purpose. The Zulus saw no sense in making oxen take a bath. Cattle had been living quite happily for thousands of years without this luxury.

It is not only because the Bantu dislike participating in anything they do not understand; they resist improvement of any description. Deep in their subconscious minds they believe that nothing is ever gained by creating things that promote a change in their way of life. If such things prove a failure it is difficult to revert to the old way of life. The Bantu has long since discovered that nothing that man creates is ever permanent and more often than not he creates a thing merely to destroy it himself. If the creator does not destroy it himself, it stands there as an invitation for others to destroy. An ambitious and enterprising race has many enemies.

As far as carvings are concerned – there is a meaning to every one. An analysis of the meanings of all the carvings, models and other so-called 'curios' would fill a book the size of this one. But here I wish to point out that many such carvings are produced to give the mind something to focus on, something which will occupy the mind to the exclusion of all else. It takes months to produce such a carving and in this period the mind is given little opportunity to think of anything else.

It was six days after his being initiated into manhood and given permission to look for a wife that *Kamangwe* took his one and only goat to the kraal of the old woodcarver *Sogo* as payment for the little ebony image of a woman the witchdoctor had said *Kamangwe* should get carved – the figurine that was to help rouse the Wish-Spirit within his mind to a fever pitch.

Kamangwe tethered the goat at the gatepost of the woodcarver's kraal and saluted everybody within the kraal in his loud, pleasant voice: 'I see you all inside the home. I come in peace and would like to speak to the lord of the kraal, the carver of images.'

From one of the many huts a tall woman crawled out of the low entrance and smiled shyly at the young man at the gate: 'The lord of the kraal shall see you soon. *Lo,* he is still having the midday meal.'

A child was sent out of the kitchen hut and the visitor was given water to drink and to wash his hands at the gate. Then he was led to the great wall-less day shelter where the daughters of the woodcarver gave him meat and beer. After he had finished his meal the old woodcarver was summoned and told that a visitor would talk to him. He came out – a big, cheerful-looking man with long strong arms and big, broad hands.

'Aha, I see you, Oh visitor!' he said in a booming voice. 'What can we do for you? Do you desire a message buck, a curse doll . . . name it and *Sogo* shall carve it.'

'I would like a wish-doll for myself, Oh *Sogo,*' the young man answered with a smile. 'You see, I have been given permission . . .'

'To seek a wife, eh?' the woodcarver put in with a sly wink. 'How would you like her . . . short, thin, tall, hunchbacked?'

'I would like a Moon-Willow.'*

'Ahhhhh! I like men with good taste. You shall have it, my boy, you shall have it. Just give old *Sogo* one month . . . just one month.'

Exactly one month later the young man took his figurine to be blessed by the Tribal Elder and he was also given additional instruction on the use of the carving. Every night he was supposed to wrap the figurine in a soft civet cat skin *kaross* and use it as a pillow to rest his head upon. He was told to concentrate steadily, not only

---

* *Long oblong face; warrior-like chin; wide forehead; nose with large nostrils; wide full-lipped mouth with slightly downcurving corners; high cheekbones; long neck; body tall and slender; breasts small and buttocks small.*

on a clear image of his ideal woman but also upon his will and his unshakable determination to have what he desired.

Kamangwe wanted a modest woman, and this was symbolised by the hands clasped below the navel of the carving. He wanted a fertile woman and this was interpreted in the rather large and well-detailed feet.

Kamangwe was happy with his statuette and he knew somehow that his wish would not be long in coming true – he just *knew* it.

'As in the case of praying for a cow, you must not only bring a clear picture of your dream-woman into your mind; you must also hear her, smell her and feel her, with the ears, nostrils and hands of your imagination. Do this every night, every waking day; do it with all the force, all the confidence, at your disposal, and I assure you that your wish shall come true. Clean out all negative thoughts from your mind and, above all, do not get at all impatient, for this blankets your wish powers . . .'

The High Instructor stopped here and motioned the Wise Woman to take over.

'My son, let me make something very clear to you: the power of your mind cannot gain for you the White Man's money. The forces of nature do not know what money is. They can only help you to get your natural needs, like food, and a mate – and fame, because fame, for better or for worse, for good or for evil, attracts many mates to you.

'The use of the forces of the mind to call to you the things you desire is a very old art; it dates back to the Days of Innocence before Man learnt to speak with his lips and his mouth. It was the Mother of Evil who taught men to speak and so isolated them from the power to use their minds and transmit their thoughts through mind pictures. All wild animals still possess this power. And, although most men do not realise it, they control their domesticated animals through a conversation of mental speech.

'You see now, my son, for the first time in your life you are learning things the White Men can never teach you. You are learning things from us whom the Christians call heathens. With mind power you can heal sick people and you can bend the whole world to your will. A host of secrets and mysteries, which few people on this earth possess, can be yours. You can crush the fear of death and face things which few have the courage to face. In fact, you can learn to love death, as your forefathers did, when once you realise that even after death you can still achieve things that others cannot achieve while they live. Where mind is master, Death recedes with all the terrors normally associated with it.

'Many of those women known as Rain Queens, and Wise Women throughout the lands of the Bantu are but adepts in the use of the powers of the mind. There are also a few among the Christians and they call themselves faith-healers. But they restrict their mind powers to healing sick people only.'

It happened in a strangely simple and incredibly natural way. An old man and his two sons who had heard of the fame of my grandfather as a witchdoctor brought his eldest daughter from beyond the Utukela to be treated for *hayiza* fits and constant bad dreams. This girl, a little asthmatic Sun-Doe, slightly lame in one foot, was three years older than I. She immediately became attracted to me – to my great surprise and dismay. She eventually told me that she loved me. I could not believe my ears. It was a bewildered young man who went to report his first sweetheart on earth to the High Instructor, whose only reaction was a smile of strange sadness and pity. 'At least your mind is now free from worry over a lover and henceforth you can listen more clearly to our teachings.'

Since then, all the women who have loved me have been, strangely enough, of the Sun-Doe type. But they have all left me one shattering heartbreak after the other. The worst is my present spouse – a perfect Sun-Doe. If this book is judged to be worth the trouble I have put into it, credit should go to another Sun-Doe – the one who received nine sten gun bullets in 1960 at Sharpeville. To her I also dedicate the book. It was over her grave that I swore to embark on the mission of writing it.

Why do I seem to attract this kind of woman, much to my undoing and regret? Is my mind attracting this type of female just as it seems to draw to me the one kind of man I fear most – the one armed with a knife. The one object that constantly obsessed even my childhood dreams has four times already sought my life.

I challenge the Wise Ones of the world – everywhere – to stop wasting time on perfecting weapons of atomic destruction and to explore the powers of the human mind. They can come to Africa to learn more about this. I am positive that the human mind conceals more surprise than does the material Universe.

* * *

There was jubilation in the kraal of *Chiringa*, and there was happiness and loud laughter. Gifts were pouring in like water over Musi-wa-Tunya. The guests were bringing legs of wild pig and they were bringing great baskets of yams, groundnuts and beans. Some were bringing bowls and spoons carved out of the sacred *mvuli* wood and some were bringing newly forged battle axes, spearheads and hoeheads, as presents to *Chiringa*.

Everybody was heavily laden and cheerful, and everybody was glad to give things to *Chiringa* on that day – to give, to keep on giving, and to expect nothing in return. Why all this fuss over the stupid coward *Chiringa* and his lazy gossiping wife, *Nandiwe*? It was because they had become the parents of a healthy baby girl on the first day of the first moon of spring. A baby born on such a day is considered to be very lucky and it is believed that some of this luck will later rub off on the givers of presents.

Amongst the gift-bringers was an old man, the lonely old hermit *Mpunzi*, who lived alone in a ramshackle kraal deep in the forest and who was the only woodcarver this tribe had. He was clutching something wrapped in a moth-eaten impala skin and he was cackling in his toothless way like a boy up to mischief.

'He-he-he-he, I have brought the greatest gift of all, the greatest gift of all!'

'What gift have you brought, Oh *Mpunzi*?' asked the headman of the village. 'Open it and let us see.'

With a mischievous wink the old man entered the hut where *Nandiwe* was sitting with her ten-day-old baby. The rest of the people crowded around to see what the old man had brought. A gasp of surprise rose from the gathering as the gift was opened and many necks were craned to catch a glimpse of the present. The headman came forward and took the gift and held it up – it was a doll, skilfully carved out of one of the hardest woods in the land. The doll was so beautifully carved, it took one's breath away. There were bracelets of handbeaten copper round the wrists of the doll, the hands of which were held on the sides of the belly. There were also rings of copper around the doll's neck and its feet were very large and well detailed. Its head was elongated and its breasts were sharp and pointed.

Tears spread down the cheeks of the headman as he spoke to the assembled people: 'This is indeed the greatest gift of all, that this lucky baby has received so far – this well-carved image of what is to our tribe the most beautiful woman that can ever be born of a woman. You know the law, Oh my people, which says a child's eye must see beauty from the moment the child can begin to see and partly understand things. You know the Old Ones of the Tribes say that if a child is made to see beauty, it grows up into the likeness of the beauty that it saw. Hence the custom of giving children beautiful dolls to play with. The mind of the child grows to love and becomes attached to the doll and the mind decides to mould the flesh of the growing child to look as much as possible like the doll. Come, Oh *Mpunzi*, and tell us why you have carved the doll with a big belly and with its hands holding the sides of the stomach. Tell us also why you have made the feet so big.'

The old man cackled: 'I have carved the doll with a big belly to show that she is pregnant and will bear many sons and daughters, and the hands holding the sides to show that she is feeling the movement of the babies within her. By this I wish the lucky girl to be fertile and to bear many children on reaching womanhood. The big feet are also for the same reason, that the owner of this doll may leave footprints on the deserts of time for all future generations to follow – a wise mother and a shining example of womanhood that shall guide those as yet unborn along the footpaths of wisdom . . .'

This little episode sparked off the widespread custom of making presents of wish-dolls, with due blessings, and it was widely in vogue as late as a century ago. These blessed wish-dolls took on a great variety of shapes and meanings. There were those that men sent to their friends, wishing them long and prosperous lives (an old man leaning on a stick). There were those that a man sent to his friend who had just taken some women for wives.

The opposite of the blessed wish-doll is the curse-doll – the most feared kind of doll in Africa. Curse-dolls take two forms. There are clay ones that are replicas of the enemy, but with sharp needles pushed through the body. Such dolls are kept by the ill-wisher to promote a strong mental wish for something like this to materialise. The second type is carved out of wood and flung into the cursed one's kraal at night. It is carved out of the wood used for making stretchers for dead men. The doll shows a woman with a large head and ears out of place and out of proportion. The eyes are connected above the nose and the mouth is askew. The breasts are sagging, small and far apart, and both hands hold a hollow and empty stomach. The legs are thin, bandy, knob-kneed and there are no feet. The message conveyed by this type of doll is as follows: 'You dog! May your daughters be ugly. May they have ears that hear nothing but evil and mouths that spread nothing but evil from kraal to kraal. May they be sterile and useless to men. May theirs be a hated, blind and lonely death.'

THE LAWS OF THE BANTU

For many years I have had the feeling that some Whites do not want to be told the truth about the Black man. Over the years this conviction has grown. When an exhibition of antique Bantu carvings was put up in Salisbury, Southern Rhodesia, some time ago, many people showed no interest because, they argued, these carvings were not genuine antiques. 'How can one talk of genuine antiques when these kaffirs have no culture. Of course they have no culture . . .'

So deep is the contempt many White people have for the Black man that they refuse to buy pictures depicting, for example, a Zulu as he really is. They prefer modernised corruptions or pictures that exaggerate, almost to the extent of caricature, the 'ugliness' of the Bantu.

I am an artist of sorts and I exhibit frequently in Johannesburg. As an experiment I painted two portraits of a beautiful Bantu woman and five portraits of old Bushmen of both sexes and toothless Bantu crones in dirty blankets. The latter five I sold very promptly and I still have with me the former two. The man who bought the last three of my 'old hag' pictures observed that the other two were far too 'pretty' for a Bantu woman.

Because of this dislike of the African many White people never bother to study him properly and with clear eyes. How can they claim to understand the African?

On the other hand, agents of Communism and subversion who are even now operating in South Africa have a definite advantage over the authorities where knowledge of the soul of the Black man is concerned; they know what fears to exploit in their efforts to drive the Bantu into joining them in their work of evil. They know how to intimidate the Bantu into obeying them. They use witchcraft and other primitive methods of terror to ensure secrecy and discipline amongst those Bantu who have joined them.

We have constables and NCOs, and Native Commissioners, employed to protect us from the forces of terror and subversion, who do not know a thing about the Bantu, who do not know these days how to win the respect and the confidence of the Bantu and who cannot earn for the Government the loyalty of the Bantu, like their predecessors could, not so long ago.

A very exciting incident in which I was involved fairly recently illustrates the point. With the numerous attempts on my life and the lack of confidence that I have in our police I decided to arrange my own protection. I made a rather ingenious 'suit of armour' from pieces of old scrap motor cars. Needless to say, I created quite a stir with it. I classed it as of the Elizabethan II period. It was only an experiment and now decorates my apartment.

The news that I am very handy at making such things soon spread and in no time reached the ears of those people who thought they could use my talents for making things completely illegal and dangerous. A very smart looking gentleman came one night and started to tell me all sorts of things which are much safer not to discuss here. In short, he told me that my co-operation was needed for a certain very obscure purpose.

I became alarmed and told the man to go and milk his own grandmother. After further exchanges of pure Bantu insults, we parted with cordial animosity and a promise on the other man's part that I could look forward to a beating up on the following Monday.

That Monday I was set upon by a very unfriendly gang of *tsotsies** and battered with chunks of old iron. They left me taking a holiday in the gutter with my body well and truly warmed up. As the unfriendly gang left me, one of them advised me not to go to the police, as he knew where my mother worked and such action would expose her to rather similar treatment.

I became as scared as a stolen goat and decided to move my wife to another township just in case somebody got ideas about her as well. But I elected to remain in our apartment as I had no wish to display my fear too blatantly.

Then, one lonely night two weeks later, I saw through the dirty window a fat American car pausing for breath outside the gate of the house where I stayed. A little later a group of men came into the yard as if they owned the place. An authoritative voice from outside instructed me to open the door and let these big heroes in as they wanted to see my ugly face and give me a last warning. But I had other ideas and I retorted that they must proceed with their conversation

---

* *The African equivalent of 'Ducktails' and 'Beatniks' – in short, 'Western civilised African'.*

through the closed door. One of them told me in Zulu, with a strong Sisutu accent, that they had no intention of harming me – yet. I asked them what they wanted and assured them I had every intention of staying where I was.

Finally one of them who, to my great shock, was a short, fat White man with a beard, came close to the window and the light of the street lamp showed me his features which I shall remember till I die. This apparition told me he knew who I was. He even told me the name of my father and where he worked. He told me all about my stepsisters and little brothers and where they were, and how I would dislike the idea of their being run over by an unidentified car.

And while this fat worm spoke to me in his bad English I became more and more afraid. Was the man a wizard or something? But the bigger shock was to come. The night-howling son of a cow-thieving alien told me something I had thought only my very closest friends knew – about the girl I loved, who had lost her life in that unfortunate incident in 1960. When he saw the shock on my face, he smiled. He smiled because he thought he had me at his mercy – that I would help him in his foul schemes that would only get thousands of my people, the Bantu, killed. But he had made a great mistake. According to Bantu law one must never smile when one speaks to a man about his dead beloved, nor does one smile when one talks to a woman about her dead husband. He had also mentioned the name of my dead girl. Our laws forbid the mention of dead people by name.

I hated the man. I hated him especially when he reminded me that it was my duty to avenge a murdered lover and that I could only do so effectively if I joined with him. I cannot remember the foul curse I gave him before I slammed the window shut in his face and I could not bother to listen and make sure that the car was actually leaving. I was down on my knees and wept like a woman.

I fled from that township on the following day, which was a Sunday, and I found accommodation in another place. For one whole month I was happy there. Then one day in the middle of the second month I was alighting from the train when a very friendly young man caught my arm and told me to come along with him. I naturally thought it was a security policeman and that I was under arrest for something I must have done unwittingly, and I was about to produce my pass when I noticed that the friendly young man was not alone – there were three skunks surrounding me and they asked me to take them to where I stayed. I do not know what made me realise that they were not police, and when I confronted them with this they told me frankly that they had orders to bring my head to their leader.

We were in the middle of an empty stretch of veld when they set upon me. One of them drew a big butcher's cleaver with which he aimed a blow at my neck. I saw this in time and dived to the ground. The next blow glanced off the back of my head and soon there was blood everywhere. Had it not been for the arrival of a group of people who frightened the thugs off, this book would not have been written; instead, I would now be occupied in nourishing the grass growing in some graveyard. Even as I write now, the scar on the back of my head is very painful indeed.

I have not told the police anything about this episode – I dare not. In the good old days I could have gone straight to the police. But today the forces of intimidation are too strong, and the sympathy of the police too weak . . .

May I appeal to all those whom it may concern, to stand together and oppose these men of evil who wish to cause trouble in this beautiful land. Let us stand together through the medium of mutual understanding. You will not lower yourselves in anybody's esteem, least of all in the eyes of the Bantu, by seeking to know and understand those things that give birth to the grievances that agents of subversion seize upon and exploit. Do not allow the evil aliens to surpass you in a true knowledge of the Bantu, who have lived with you and worked for you for so long. There is nothing political about studying a race; nor is it in the least degrading.

You do not become a '*kafferboetie*' by studying the Bantu objectively – only if you do so subjectively. You will not lose an inch of your dignity, because science, any quest for knowledge, is uplifting. It has never degraded anybody.

The disease afflicting Africa today is the direct result of the blundering ignorance of both the White man's ancestors and mine, the direct result of different races living together and each thinking it could turn the other into a replica of itself. The bloody wars that the White man's ancestors and mine have fought, the hatred and bitterness that still exist, could all have been avoided – if only we had all known better, known *each other* better.

I know from experience that complete trust, friendship and integrated co-operation between Black and White is inherently impossible. Our different backgrounds, present ways of life and future ambitions are far too ingrained in our various cultures, conditioned over many hundreds of years. These differences cannot be wiped out in a matter of decades, let alone by the stroke of a pen. But surely it is possible to achieve peace between races no matter how different their outlook, or their ideals and creeds.

To appreciate the wide difference in racial structure between the Black and the White people of Africa, their basic laws must be compared. All races may be equal in 'race, colour and creed', but they differ fundamentally in the law that governs their lives. The White man's legal code is based on his 'Ten Commandments'. The Black man has more than a hundred such commandments. Here follow some of the High Laws of the Bantu, common among all Bantu races in Southern, Central and East Africa:

THE HIGH LAW OF LIFE

'Man, know that your life is not your own. You live merely to link your ancestors with your descendants. Your duty is to beget children even while you keep the Spirits of your Ancestors alive through regular sacrifices. When your Ancestors command you to die, do so with no regrets.'

The Zulus obeyed this law to the letter; they lived by it and died by it. To the deluded world the Zulu was a fierce and courageous fighter, a brave warrior. This is not so; a Zulu went into battle with the express intention of getting himself killed. His seeming courage was nothing but a blind search for a glorious death after having killed as many of the enemy as he possibly could. The Zulus used to raise a tremendous cheer for the first warrior to get killed. The Zulu warriors used to scramble and race each other for the honour to be the first to die in a particular battle.

According to this Law, a Zulu woman is expected to bring into this world as many as twenty children, and the sight of a man who has sired a hundred children is not uncommon in Zululand even today. It is, in fact, common through the length and breadth of Africa.

By this law women were made to look forward to dying in childbirth. As in the case of a warrior, the death of a woman who died in the course of executing her womanly duty was considered a glorious one.

This strange seeming love of death has two motivations. Firstly, the Bantu do not look upon death as something evil. On the strength of their religious belief they consider that their real *selves*, their *Enas*, are suppressed by being tied to useless corporeal bodies and the sooner they can get rid of these bodies the sooner can their souls receive promotion to higher planes of development. Thus the Bantu have not only no fear of death, but they flirt with it, gamble with it and, indeed, long for it.

The greatest ambition of a Black man is to die the death of his own choice, but he will not wantonly take his own life, as the decision would then come from himself and not from his ancestors. He particularly likes the White man's legal way of disposing of a life – by hanging; he is fascinated by its cowardly nature. A Black man who dies of an illness or an accident is an object of great pity among the

Bantu, and his death is mourned extensively. If he dies a death of his own choice he is not greatly mourned, but becomes an object of great admiration and even envy. Thus, rather than face an accidental death, he deliberately commits a vicious crime on which the punishment is the death sentence.

The second reason for the Bantu's lack of fear of death is that they are perfect fatalists. They strongly believe that if the time is there for them to die, nothing can prevent it; conversely, if the time is not ripe they can take any risk they like. This is why Africans in general are such dreadful risk-takers in almost any field of activity.

THE HIGH LAW OF BEHAVIOUR TOWARDS PARENTS

'Man, know that of your two parents your mother ranks higher than your father. In quarrels between your parents you must come to the aid of your mother, be she right or wrong. You may strike your father, but never draw his blood. You may never strike your mother and even if you do so accidentally you must lose your right hand.'

This is one of the oldest laws in Africa and it needs careful explanation. There was a time early in African history when the Old Tribes worshipped women. Men worshipped their mothers like goddesses and made sacrifices to them, and the Matriarchs and Rain Queens seen today are survivals of this custom. In our mythology, too, females play a more important role, like the Great Mother, our Goddess of Creation.

The Bantu say that a woman, be she one's wife or one's mother, exists in the past, present and future at the same time, and she does not belong to one's father or oneself, but to those as yet unborn, and to one's ancestors. They say the girl one marries is not chosen by oneself, but by one's ancestors and that she begets children, using the man only as the medium.

For this reason it is a custom amongst the Bantu for a man to leave his bride for three days in the 'spirit hut' – a special shrine where the *Enas* of his ancestors may first kiss and mate with her. This is also why the Bantu regard the killing of one woman as so great a crime that it needs a thousand men to die in a battle of vengeance. They feel that the killing of a woman means not only the destruction of her life, but the lives of thousands of others who could have been her descendants.

This law has numerous 'sub-clauses' such as, if a man cannot avenge the murder of his female parent he must deliver himself to the murderer with the request to be killed as well. No man must ever allow an outsider to effect a separation between himself and his wife, or wives, and no chief must ever meddle with the wives of his subjects. The separation of a man from his wife by an external influence is listed as one of the Three High Crimes and calls for a war of vengeance as punishment.

This Law and custom has a tremendous hold on the minds of the Bantu and forms the strongest weapon in the hands of Communists, agitators and other rabble-rousers. They find ready recruits for their activities among those in South Africa who are still, by numerous strict regulations, prevented from living together with their legitimate husbands or wives. Here I wish to direct a sincere appeal to the highest officials of the South African Government: remedy this difficulty and the problem of Black–White relationships will disappear completely.

The Bantu can tolerate the cruellest humiliation, even with a smile; they can take the cruellest beatings as a matter of course; the vilest insults slide off them like water off a well-greased duck's back. Yet, when called upon, they will stand together with those who have treated them thus and fight with them a war to death. But if you touch a man's wife, mother, sister or daughter, call them names, or refer insultingly to their womanhood, he is bound by law to kill you. If he fails he will make his children's children take oaths to kill your children's children.

An African can lie with the greatest ease to any missionary, chief, magistrate or judge. He can lie without winking an eye. But no African will dare to lie to a witchdoctor. The witchdoctor will merely ask the man to say: '*Angikwenzanga loku, ngingalala no ma*', which means: 'I have not done it and I am prepared to sleep with my mother to prove it.' By our laws a man is immediately found not guilty when he has the courage to say this to a witch-doctor.

Even those who have fully adopted the European way of life and whose veneer of Christianity extends more than skin-deep, will die rather than utter these words, because it is fundamentally believed that the *Enas* of his ancestors will descend upon, not only his person, but also his *Ena*, and destroy both.

Before an African can divorce his wife he must, without his wife's knowledge, confer with the spirits of both his ancestors and hers and lay before them the reasons for his desire to dissolve the marriage. Then he must take his problem to his living parents, brothers and sisters, and call upon their advice. Only then can he go with his wife to her father and claim the return of his *lobolo.* Laziness is never looked upon as sufficient grounds for a divorce. There are only three grounds: Frigidity (a refusal to carry on the ancestral name); Adultery (excreting in the spirit hut); and Sexual Perversity (the madness to let outsider bulls graze in the green pastures of our ancestors).

In earlier days women had a much greater say in Bantu state

and home affairs than now, and even as late as the last century the terrible *Shaka* of the Zulus himself was ruled by his favourite wives and mother. *Shaka* was a puppet that danced to the strings pulled by his mother *Nandi*, and it was his father's second wife *Mkabayi*, the 'aunt' of *Mbopa* and *Dingana*, who passed the final sentence of death upon *Shaka*. Even today, the Bantu are still very much under the thumbs of their mothers and sisters and many of the bloody riots that have flared up in South Africa have been started by, or through women.

In the year 1949 a terrible thing took place in the city of Durban. The Bantu suddenly set upon the Indian population and butchered them with all manner of sharp weapons. Their wives and daughters were raped and pushed into shops already fully aflame. The Court of Enquiry found that the whole incident was sparked off by the assault of an Indian on a Bantu boy. In actual fact, the roots of the trouble were much deeper. Most important of the causes was the contempt the Indian people had for the Bantu. The Indians had become increasingly unpopular with the Bantu and this had become aggravated by the Indians' habit of short-changing Bantu customers in their shops. These Indians were also in the habit of selling secondhand rubbish for new to unsophisticated customers and talking them into buying rubbish.

But most productive of racial animosity was the Indians' habit of seducing Bantu girls, making them pregnant and forsaking them. This went on for many years – it is quite surprising how much the Bantu can tolerate – but in the end it took a slight incident like the beating up of a young Bantu boy to spark off something so terrible.

Whenever the Bantu stage a demonstration they put their women out in front, often with babies on their backs to show clearly they are mothers. A riot may not so easily be provoked when a man gets killed; but let it be one of the women and very hell is turned loose.

At times in the history of Africa strange marriages have been permissible. Tribal historians refer to these as the 'Bending of the Race'. As a result of the depopulation of vast areas through slave-raiding, marriages between cousins became more frequent. Sometimes a man had to marry his own sister to ensure continuity of the family line. There are cases 'on record' where a man discovered that he and his daughter were the last survivors of a whole tribe. One redeeming feature was that the *lobolo* cattle stayed in the family.

THE HIGH LAW OF SELF PRESERVATION

'Man, know the laws of the Gods and the laws of your Ancestors, and their Ancestors before them; if one man of another race killed a member

of your race, tribe or family, do not rest until you, or a descendant of yours, have killed a member of his race, tribe or family.'

This is one of the oldest and most savage Bantu laws. But it is a law which has as strong a hold today over the minds of the Bantu as it has ever had in the past. And the observance of it generally leads to destruction of the avengers as well as those upon whom they swear vengeance.

Obviously, when revenge is taken on a tribe, it is obliged by this law to retaliate. In Africa blood feuds have been going on for centuries. The blood feud between the Wakambi and the Masai in Kenya has now entered its tenth century. The feud between the Baluba and some of its neighbouring tribes is in its sixth century.

But there is more to this law than simply a primitive love of vengeance. It is based on that part of our Great Belief, that the soul of a murdered man does not re-incarnate and proceed with following stages of development, but roams the land of Forever-Night weeping for revenge. It is also believed that the *Ena* of a murdered person dies, and this is really fatal. The strength of a tribe lies in the strength of its *Enas.* Bodies are expendable, so to speak, but never *Enas.* If a tribe is deprived of a potential *Ena* the compliment must, at all cost, be returned.

When a tribe on whom revenge is desired is too strong, or no suitable opportunity arises, the avenging tribe must impress on the following generations the memory of a debt outstanding. Our Tribal Historians have it 'on record' that one tribe waited as long as four hundred years before it eventually managed to retaliate on another.

More than a hundred years ago the Basutu occupied most of Natal. But when the Zulus emerged as a powerful military nation they drove the Basutu across the Drakensberg into what is today Lesotho. The Zulu-Basutu blood feud is still in full force today. They fight each other in the townships and on the trains. There is also a standing blood feud, a century-and-a-half old, between the Zulus and the Shanganes of Portuguese East Africa. Even today the Shanganes welcome any opportunity to show the Zulus how much they still dislike them.

If two tribes fight a draw, a Peace Ceremony is conducted by the Elders of both tribes and the old feud is considered closed.

In the Umsinga region of Zululand there are two sub-tribes, the Machunu and the Batembu, which are the despair of the local police. Every year they go for each other's throats with the fury of leopards. This blood feud has been going on for more than thirty-five years.

In the district in the south of Natal from where my father comes there is a place named Umbumbulu, near Scottburgh. There were once two chiefs – *Timuni* and *Nkasa* – the sons of one father, and these delightful old characters fought a beautiful private war in this district for more than forty years. The feud is still going strong even now that *Nkasa* is dead.

Why all this seemingly senseless feuding? It is simply because the Black man of Africa has not learnt the meaning of the word forgiveness. His mind cannot fathom that there are other races who can fight today and be friends tomorrow. The African's motto is 'an eye for an eye' and the Zulus have a saying which expresses this: 'Once you poke me in the eye, I must not rest until I have gouged out one of yours.'

Just before the Congo gained its independence the woodcarvers started putting out for sale, small carvings of men and even women bound in chains. These carvings were bought by the Belgians and by tourists without questioning their significance. All these carvings were a hundred or more years old and could be regarded as genuine antiques. Some of these had been disfigured as though people had spent years cutting little chips from them – but this merely adds to their value. The White people of the Congo were quite indifferent to these strange examples of African art. But when I saw these carvings turn up in curio shops in South Africa, I was aghast – as anybody with the slightest knowledge of Africans would be. I knew immediately that chaos and bloodshed was coming to the Congo long before it came.

It is no secret that up to the early years of the last century much slave raiding was still being carried out in Africa by certain colonising powers of Europe and Asia, and it is a known fact that thousands of Black slaves perished aboard ships taking them to places like Jamaica, Haiti, and the United States. The Congo and surrounding areas were hit hardest by the depredations of slave-hunting Belgians, Arabs, Germans and British. What these slave raiders did not know was that for every slave taken, those who escaped made one of these carvings.

These were destined to be passed from generation to generation as a reminder of a score to be settled. Every kraal which knew of a comrade who died in slavery had a carving, and every growing child of each generation was made to swear to kill a Belgian one day. With every oath taken, a chip from the statue had to be eaten.

One thing White men do not seem to realise is that the Black man is the most ardent of all grudge-bearers and revenge-lovers. I speak as a patriot who has the unenviable task of explaining the peculiarities of his race to the outside world.

The Congolese were expected to be grateful to the Belgians for having dragged them out of the morass of 'savagery' on to the path of 'civilisation' and nationhood. You can put the Black man on a throne of ivory and gold; you can clothe him in ermine and silks. But if some member of your race had killed a member of his race even as far back as a thousand years ago, he will be eternally on the lookout for an opportunity to get his own back.

For the security of South Africa's future I wish to make a suggestion. It is that a country-wide festival be organised in such a way that every man, woman and child of all races will participate, all within their own areas and according to their own tastes. On a particular day all the members of the Cabinet must meet all the members of the Transkeian Government and perform a Peace Ceremony, which should take a hybrid form – something between an African Peace Ceremony and a European Peace Treaty. All over the country people would gather and partake in barbecue feasts where loudspeakers would relay the proceedings between the two Governments.

THE HIGH LAW OF DISCRIMINATE PUNISHMENT

'*For every offence there must be a fixed punishment. No offender shall be punished in a way different from that laid down for the particular crime.*'

This simply means that a wizard shall die that particular kind of death especially set aside for wizards. The Bantu have always applied this law very strictly and they adhere to it more strongly than to almost any other law. There are variations on the rule as applied by different tribes.

In Zululand, all adulterers, perverts and rapists were given the ant-death. This simply consisted of opening an anthill and the condemned man was spread naked over it with his hands and feet pegged to the ground and honey spread on his belly.

In the land of the Xhosas all witches and wizards were thrown from a high cliff and in Central Africa all adulteresses were fed to the crocodiles. Adulterers were castrated. In Lesotho, and also Zululand, witches were imprisoned in their own huts and burnt to death.

Witchdoctors who broke the law were killed in a strange way. An ox was slaughtered and the condemned man was sewn up inside the wet skin. He was then left in an exposed position. By sunset he would be dead. Although he could breathe through the gaps, the skin would shrink and slowly squeeze him.

A thief caught stealing oxen was given an appropriate end. He was tied hand and foot and laid across the entrance to the cattle pen and the whole herd was driven over him. Men with an obsession for setting kraals alight (a very common phobia among the Bantu) were suspended from a limb of a tree and a handsome fire was lit below. But destroying even criminals by fire is greatly frowned upon by most tribes, because it is believed that burning a person to death not only destroys the body, but also the *Ena* and the soul – fire itself being a 'spirit' and capable of dissolving other kinds of spirits.

What is more important than the various methods is the fact that the Bantu believe that justice can only be done when a member, or members, of the family against whom a crime was committed can execute the criminal. Thus when a man commits rape he is arrested by the chief's warriors, tried by the Tribal Elders in the Place of Justice and when found guilty, he is handed to the injured man for execution. The Bantu consider it utterly ridiculous for a judge or a State executioner to punish a person who had done *them* no wrong. Bantu execution is not merely punishment; it is a sacrifice to appease the ancestral spirits of the family, who cry out for revenge.

Only in the case of minor offences, which are not considered aggravation of the ancestral spirits, can a chief pass sentence himself on behalf of the complainant and restore peace within the community. Thus, when a person is insulted and called impotent in public, he is not permitted to assault the defamer because he may thereby create the impression that the other had spoken the truth. The insulted party must challenge the other to appear with him before the chief and there he may then produce proof that he was falsely accused. The chief may then fine the defendant six head of cattle and order him to be beaten in the presence of his wives. Four of the cattle go to the chief and two to the complainant.

If a wife is involved in a fight with a neighbour's wife and fractures the other woman's thigh or knocks some teeth out of her mouth, the husband of the woman doing the damage is fined a calf for every tooth knocked out, or a heifer for the thigh. If a man's cattle gets into his neighbour's corn and creates havoc, he is fined one ox, or four goats.

Many of the Old Tribes frown upon the death penalty. They have long since learnt that it is not a deterrent, but actually invites criminals to commit crimes, for reasons I have already explained. They have decided to exploit two outstanding characteristics of the Bantu: his stiff-necked pride and his deep sense of humour.

When a Bantu turns criminal, it is never because he is poor or destitute, in which case he would throw himself on the mercy of others and become a beggar. According to the Bantu moral code begging is a virtue and the surest sign of profound human honesty. 'It is far better to beg than to steal' is a common African saying and everybody is taught it from early childhood. When a Bantu turns criminal he does so as a direct challenge to constitutional authority or society in general. All Bantu criminals have egos a mile long and they all boast widely of their criminal achievements. The ancient Wise Ones knew this and their remedy was to turn the criminal into an object of public ridicule – hurting his stiff-necked pride and feeding the tribe's sense of humour. If there is one thing an African fears more than a thousand deaths it is to suffer public humiliation, to be deflated and shown up for a fool. No African can live down ridicule.

The Batswana are great believers in corporal punishment. If a man is caught stealing he is suspended upside down from a branch of a tree and beaten with thorn-bush branches – by women and boys. A man thus treated either quietly disappears from the tribe or he commits suicide. Being beaten like a child is something the African fears worse than death, and this is one reason why there is hardly any crime in Portuguese East Africa. A person found guilty receives light physical punishment but he is profoundly humiliated.

When Black men start a riot, they do so in the full knowledge that some are going to get themselves killed. Some would clamour for the front line, not to miss this honour. Leaders encourage this among their supporters, because should there be killings the mob is supplied with 'fallen heroes' – with martyrs – and with these they can recruit more support and more recruits for their cause. But when the police decide on a baton charge and start beating the rioters up like a mob of silly boys they go home feeling well and truly deflated. Going into battle with vivid pictures of a hero's grave in one's mind and returning like a silly fool can be a devastating humiliation.

Amongst the Old Tribes all adulteresses had their noses cut off, leaving a ghastly window to the skull. It was nevertheless a most effective deterrent to all would-be breakers of marriage oaths. Another way of punishing an adulteress in a humiliating way was to spreadeagle her naked on her back on the ground with her belly covered with ground corn and then to turn the fowls loose upon her. Thieves were relieved of one ear, one eye, or half a lower lip.

RELATIONS DURING MENSTRUATION AND BREAST FEEDING

'A man must have no relations with his wife during her periods of menstruation or during the entire period while she breast-feeds a baby.'

* * *

This law is one of the reasons why the Bantu practise polygamy on principle. Opposition to polygamy encourages extensive immorality and destruction of Bantu family life and traditions.

In olden days all wives were bound to leave a village during their periods of menstruation, to live in kraals specially set aside for this purpose. A high curse automatically fell upon any man who dared to approach such a kraal.

Even today a Bantu father is expected to keep away from his wife for at least a year while she is breast-feeding her baby. The most 'Christianised' and 'civilised' Bantu still cling to the idea that a man's semen poisons the mother's milk.

The Christians, completely ignorant of all these strange beliefs, disrupt our Bantu family life by forcing us to have one wife only. The result is that during the period of abstinence from the one wife a man has, he seeks solace in the arms of prostitutes and mistresses. Thus, not only is his married life and family prone to disintegration, but he plays his part in spreading all kinds of foul diseases. It is indeed a sorry situation that has developed as a result of this endeavour to force one race to live by the standard of another

THE HIGH LAW ON FALSE ACCUSATIONS AGAINST VIRGINS

'A man must never accuse a virgin of not being a virgin. Such a man must leave the tribe and his cattle and wives must be shared among the other men of the village.'

Until as recently as thirty years ago this law was still in full force, at least in Zululand. It was the custom that every year, in every district, all the girls as yet not allowed to marry and who belonged to the 'Virgin Regiment', were taken to a panel of the eldest women of the tribe, or to the wives of the chief, to have their virginity confirmed.

Inter alia, there is a very strict and distinct stratification in Bantu tribal society. There are the Royal Ones (the Chief, his family, all their relatives and associates); the Elders; the *Indunas*; the High Warriors; the Lesser Warriors; and the common people who are in turn divided into 'regiments' of a non-military nature. There are the Girls' Regiment, the Virgins' Regiment and the Women's Regiment. They all have their respective duties, especially on particular occasions. For example, at a festival the Girls' Regiment will clean and prepare the High Place of Gathering; the Virgins' Regiment will supply the dancers and the bringers of food. Then there are the Boys' Regiment, herdboys in times of peace and supply-carriers in times of war; the Young Men's Regiment and the Full Men's Regiment, who supply the chief with his warriors.

In earlier days Bantu girls were not allowed to marry until they were twenty-five years old, and a girl of fifteen to twenty-five was taken for granted to be a virgin and no man was allowed to speak to her of love. She was taught to take a great pride in her virginity and it was impressed on her mind that she must not allow any man to get near her. The leaders of the Virgins' Regiment, who were girls of twenty-five and older but still unattached, kept a strict eye upon every girl and they were directly responsible to the First Wife of the chief.

Now if a man insulted an *intombi* (virgin) and called her an *umfazi* (a woman with sexual experience), every single member of the Virgins' Regiment was required to see it as an insult directed at herself. They would all gather and march through the village with downcast eyes and proceed to the Royal Kraal to complain to the chief. The arrest of the man was then ordered and often the shrieking virgins were allowed to frogmarch him into the presence of the chief. Evidence was led by the High Leader of the Virgins' Regiment while standing on the chest of the accused, who normally found it very difficult to speak in his defence in such circumstances. Punishment was basically meted out as the law dictated, but more often than not there was a great deal of extra embroidery.

This is just another law which has made a significant contribution towards the maintenance of a high moral standard in the Bantu social and general way of life, but which was ruthlessly ploughed under by the moral standards of Western Civilisation.

There are about one hundred such laws. Those listed here are only a few of the outstanding ones which clash with those that foreigners have superimposed on ours, or which illustrate the totally different outlook (or lack of understanding) there is between the Black man and the White man. Thus the Black people and the White people utterly fail to understand each other.

TRIBAL SCARS

There are several tribes in Africa that habitually disfigure their bodies with all manner of scars. Most outsiders interpret this as the African's idea of beautifying himself.

But there are several reasons for disfiguration – and none of them is connected with adornment as aliens see it. There are those who believe so strongly in the transmigration of the soul that they favour the idea that the soul must be guided in its return to the same tribe. The soul must recognise the tribe by these scars. The idea of a great and famous man being re-incarnated as a member of an enemy tribe is unthinkable to the Bantu and must at all costs be prevented from happening.

There are those who strongly believe that only the gods are beautiful and that Man is not supposed to be beautiful. To prevent a man from recognising beauty in the human being and so losing sight of the beauty of the gods, they deliberately disfigure themselves. For this very reason the Xhosas paint their faces with yellow ochre – they want to look ugly and it is their mark of humility before the all-seeing *Qamata*, the Highest of the High.

And there are also those, such as the Awemba of Central Africa, who were forced to defile the appearance of their womenfolk as a last resort in their defence against those ruthless destroyers of my people, the slave-raiding Arabs. Even today the women of the Awemba are second in beauty only to those of the Tshokwe, and this made these women the target of any band of slave-raiding aliens that came along. The Awemba hit on the idea that was copied by other tribes too. They pierced both the upper and lower lips of their women and fitted discs into the holes. This made the women hideous in the extreme, and it was hard for women so treated to talk, let alone eat, properly. The Arabs did not bother the Awemba much after that.

As I said before, I find it hard to understand the role the Arabs are trying to assume nowadays – the pose of spokesmen for the Black people, and even that of liberators. It will take more than honeyed overtures of friendship to make us forget what the Arabs did to Africa. Our historians mention that no fewer than a hundred tribes were wiped out completely in Tanganyika, Kenya, the Congo basin, and Northern Rhodesia.

And this leads to a question that demands an answer: what did the Arabs, Belgians and Germans do with the millions of Black men and women they kidnapped and carried away from their families and native lands? I have been trying in vain for many years to trace these people to the countries to which they were taken. The Negroes of the United States, of Jamaica and Haiti and also South America are mainly West African – of the Old Tribes. What happened to the others?

I have learnt for certain that the Arabs had the habit of scuttling slave-laden dhows and letting all slaves drown when a shortage of food or water occurred. I also know for a fact that there are caves all over Africa in which thousands of slaves were entombed alive. There is one in Zambia which will be opened one day.

Fellow human beings – people of my own Black race, the Aba-Ntu; people of the White race, the Abe-Lungu; people of the Yellow races, the Ama-Japani and the Ama-Shayina; people of the Brown race, the Ama-Hindu; I come in humility and appeal to you to listen carefully to what I have to say. My brothers and sisters, it is said that the Present has its roots firmly planted in the Past, and that the Past is the River on which the boat of the Present floats, over both quiet and turbulent waters. If man had kept no records of his past deeds and misdeeds, the world would have been a more peaceful place than it is today.

THE TRUTH ABOUT PIET RETIEF

Men have died because some fool presented a nation with a wrong account of a certain incident in the far past. Men have allowed their emotions to influence the ways in which they recorded certain occurrences. Much of the enmity between Black and White people in Africa today sprouts directly from this emotional 'slanting' of history.

After this book I shall proceed with others in which I shall deal fully with scores of historical inaccuracies about my fatherland. Here I wish to illustrate how a one-sided account can plunge a country into a hell of endless hatred, which evil-minded outsiders are only too ready to exploit for their own ends.

Ever since my boyhood I have shared my people's fear of one particular day of the year – the Sixteenth of December – 'Dingaan's Day', later known as the 'Day of the Covenant' and now the 'Day of Reconciliation'. To White South Africans it is a sacred day, the day on which, in 1838, their forebears achieved a mighty victory at Blood River, over the 'treacherous Chief Dingaan' who had murdered Piet Retief.

In earlier years this day was an occasion to revive the great bitterness the Afrikaners still felt, and on such occasions their bitterness was blatantly directed against the Bantu. I distinctly remember that, as a child, our parents locked us up inside our huts near Potchefstroom, where we had to sit all day, for fear that the White 'baases' would beat us up. I can quote many bitter provocative speeches White leaders have made in past gatherings on December 16. I could reveal reprehensible deeds that irresponsible young White men, fired by such speeches, have committed against the Bantu. But I do not intend doing so; my duty is only to reveal the truth and not to feed the flames of racial hatred in this country.

What is the truth about the murder of Piet Retief? What induced *Dingana* to commit this most disastrous and useless deed for which the Zulu race has had to pay so dearly? The older Bantu, and especially our Chosen Ones, have all along known the truth behind this deed. Why have they not come forward to speak out the truth? Why is there such an intense silence on one side and a strong desire to avoid the truth on the other?

May the Gods help me – I shall be the first to speak.

The 'murder' of Piet Retief is closely tied to another 'murder', that of *Shaka*, the Zulu King whom *Dingana* succeeded. These must not be seen as disconnected episodes. In a strict Bantu legal sense, neither was a murder – they were executions.

Most history books tell us that the Zulu King *Shaka* was the greatest leader the Zulu nation ever produced. They say that *Shaka* made the Zulus strong, that he introduced a more efficient way of leading warriors in battle and that he invented the large, broad-bladed stabbing spear which made the Zulus the most formidable fighting force in the land. They say this and they say that, and only a quarter of what they say is true.

History books also say that *Dingana* (or *Dingaan*, as all history books mis-spell his name) was a treacherous, bloodthirsty savage, a lazy and sneaky tyrant who was too cowardly to negotiate openly and preferred treachery instead. This is complete nonsense.

The only spark of truth in it concerns *Dingana's* laziness. He was a pleasure-loving man, but at no time was he treacherous. Nor was he a coward. He died bravely, like a hero, without a murmur, even while tortured at the hands of the Ama-Ngwane who had captured him. With eyes torn out, and blood freely flowing from multiple wounds, *Dingana* still had the courage to say, with a voice perfectly under control: '*Ngiyanidabukela we Ma-Ngawane*!' (I am sorry for you, Oh Ma-Ngawane!) He said this, because he realised that they were pursuing and torturing a man already defeated and helpless, while their country was being overrun by strangers.

The picture White historians paint of *Dingana* is not a true picture; it is always influenced by his so-called act of treachery which culminated in the death of Piet Retief. This is understandable; we all allow our emotions to blind us to the bright sun of Truth. Any man, ruled by an overwhelming love for the woman he has chosen for a wife, sees nothing but beauty in her, even though she may be a shameless adulteress. A man, blinded by hatred for another man, refuses to see anything good in him. Thus *Dingana* has been blackened out of all recognition because of what he did, and nobody has yet bothered to scrape the mask of dust from his portrait to reveal his true identity.

But *Dingana* was in fact one of the worst chiefs the Zulus ever had. Although brave, he was very lazy, and he was effeminate not only in appearance, but in behaviour too. He was a short, fat man, little over five feet tall, with a pretty girlish face and a mouth like that of a woman. He had a womanly beauty which he inherited from his mother, beautiful and equally lazy, but deadly, *Ngenzeni.* He loved to bathe and perfume himself like a woman and he looked upon his Royal duty of inspecting and supervising the training of his warriors as boring and stupid.

He loved what is known as 'multiple mating', even in broad daylight; that is, he took on two or three women at the same time. As a young man he used to vomit at the sight of spilt blood, and his effeminacy was blatantly mirrored in his refusal to wear the *sicoco* ring of honour around his head. He preferred the broad ostrich eggshell band of beads such as dancing girls used to wear.

Unlike his brother *Shaka*, who often practised homosexuality, *Dingana* was inordinately fond of women. He heard that the mother of the Chief *Mzilikazi* who had led the Matabele to Southern Rhodesia, was the most well-preserved woman in the land. Men praised this unnatural old faggot in *Dingana's* presence. He learnt that she was not only still praised for her exceptional beauty, but that she was as man-hungry as ever. He accordingly sent a regiment on a long journey to the land of the Matabele – a six months' journey of hard fighting – to capture this woman, who could have been his grandmother, so that he could mate with her under the shady trees of Zululand.

Dingana was averse to violence of any sort and he always crept away into his hut when a man had to be executed. Thus pictures of him standing by and watching the massacre of Piet Retief and his party is a sheer figment of the imagination. When Piet Retief was killed *Dingana* was not even in the kraal. He stood on a hillock outside the kraal and from there he gave the predetermined signal and shouted: 'Kill the wizards!'

My great grandfather, *Silwane Shezi*, the High Witchdoctor and Chosen One in *Dingana's* kraal, stood by for the signal. From him, through my grandfather, *Ziko Shezi*, and two other Chosen Ones I received the true version of what happened in *Dingana's* kraal, and I can speak with more genuine authority than anyone else.

The Bantu attach great importance to their history and we make every effort to pass the details from father to son in perfect accuracy; it is a tradition with us. We are fully conscious of the fact that stories thus passed down are subject to omissions, alterations or exaggerations, and we take every possible precaution to prevent this happening. If White people could only bring themselves to appreciate this they could develop greater faith in us and listen more carefully to what we have to teach about the history of Africa. Few of us are prepared to talk, and while I am one of these, anxious to talk for the sake of better understanding and peace in this land, I beg all those who are interested to listen. Lend me the ears of flesh and blood and the ears of your impartial souls.

There is enough in this book to indicate the strictness of our tribal laws governing premarital sexual experience and the producing of illegitimate children. Bastards were strangled at birth by midwives and girls who fell in the valleys of temptation were so ill-treated and shunned by everybody that they usually fled to other tribes or committed suicide. The Bantu were fanatically strict on these things and here, as one born out of wedlock myself, I can speak from experience. The only reason I am alive to tell this story is that there were already police in Natal at the time of my birth, and they do not exactly approve of murder.

But I can understand how *Shoka* – a bastard in more ways than one – must have felt as a child; I can fathom his terrible isolation and bitterness and I understand completely why he grew up into a dreadful monster when he reached manhood.

Nandi, the mother of *Shaka*, was not only a nymphomaniac; she was also wilful and precocious from early childhood. One day I shall tell in detail how it came about that this strange and beautiful woman brought to life a monster and a heretic as foul as *Shaka. Nandi* was the daughter of the High Chief of the La-Ngeni tribe, and she had been spoilt from babyhood. In this both her father and her mother were to blame.

The imagination of the growing *Nandi* had been fired and corrupted by the stories of love-making the maids of her father's court told her with careless abandon and in colourful detail. She was naturally gifted, or perhaps cursed, with extreme inquisitiveness which induced her to devour these tales with wide-eyed gusto, adding yet more fire to her smouldering sexiness.

Then one day, at the age of twenty-four and not yet initiated, she saw a young man who attracted her immediately. This young man was *Senza-Ngakona*, the son of the High Chief of the Zulus. At first she tried to induce her doting father to arrange the formal introduction and when this failed she made up her wilful mind to meet him in a clandestine way. She and her scheming maids pretended to depart on a long visit to her cousin, a visit which required no armed escort. Although it was *Senza-Ngakona* and not her cousin to whom she proceeded with her train of maids, the journey still took three whole days by foot and on the night of the fourth day she crawled into the arms of *Senza-Ngakona*. Thus trouble was born to Zululand in the form of *Shaka* nine months later, as a result of that torrid, passion-enflamed night and the three others that followed.

When the Ama-Langeni tribe heard that their beloved princess was pregnant out of wedlock and before her initiation, men took their deadly assegais and shields and converged on the kraal of their chief to find out who the lout was who had taken the virginity of his child and to pursue the seducer for his foul insult.

Nandi was formally declared an outcast of the tribe. Her disillusioned and shamed father reluctantly agreed to the expulsion of his pregnant child from his kraal. Being an only girl and the child of a chief, she was only banished and not killed, as was customary with commoners. *Nandi* fled to the kraal of her brother and it was from there that she sent messages to *Senza-Ngakona* appealing to him to come and claim her as his wife and acknowledge fatherhood to the unborn child within her swelling belly.

But *Senza-Ngakona* had other ideas. He denied all knowledge of *Nandi*. He suggested that she was not pregnant at all and that she was merely afflicted with *ama-shaka* (stomach worms). He even sent her a calabash full of purgative. If *Senza-Ngakona* had admitted having mated with *Nandi*, he would have been handed over to the Tribal Avengers for execution.

Nandi was cruelly treated by the people with whom she lived. They gave her no food. They made her – a princess – do all sorts of humiliating chores in the kraal. Even when her baby was born, they sent only an old woman to help her through her labour.

'Your father disowned you,' said *Nandi* to her baby as she nursed it in cruel, lonely solitude in her draughty hut. 'He said you were nothing but a stomach worm, an *Ishaka*. Well, this is then what I shall call you, my little one, I shall name you *Shaka*.'

Shaka grew up surrounded by scorn and by hatred. Nobody spoke to him; men spat at his feet as they passed. In a huge kraal with plenty of food of all description, *Shaka* had to catch rabbits to feed himself and his mother. In the loneliness of their hut mother and son shed many bitter tears together, and as *Shaka* grew up he became more and more attached to his mother; she was the only friend he had in a hostile world.

At the age of fourteen *Shaka* began to hit back at his mother's tormentors, and he laid many a boy unconscious on the ground with his knobkierie. He became as ruthless as a crocodile and as fierce as a leopard, and his attachment to his mother grew to within reach of insanity. He took many an oath to avenge the insults that were heaped on him and on her.

By this time *Senza-Ngakona* had become chief, and *Nandi* took *Shaka* to his father. But again they were very disgracefully treated. She and her son fled back to the kraal of her mother, her father having died in the meantime, but even here she met hostility. Her own family was still not prepared to forgive her for her misdeed. Finally she sought refuge in the kraal of a truly great and kind-hearted chief, the High King of Kings, the wise and sympathetic *Dingi-Swayo*, who had the courage of a lion and the mercy of a dove, and who was fired with an ambition to weld the Bantu in Natal once again into one solid nation as at the time of *Malandela*.

Dingi-Swayo brought *Shaka* up as his own son and taught him new methods of battle strategy which he had devised. *Shaka*, a young man of great though warped intelligence, fathomed their future possibilities and memorised each detail. He was now obsessed with one idea – he was going to seize the throne of the tribe *Senza-Ngakona* ruled and nothing was going to stop him. He intended killing *Senza-Ngakona* for what he had done to *Nandi*.

It would take too long to relate how *Shaka* eventually achieved this ambition. He never succeeded in killing his own father, for *Senza-Ngakona* died of fright and heartbreak when he heard that *Shaka* had killed *Sigujana*, his son by another woman, whom he had placed on the throne of another tribe, a throne which *Shaka* had then seized.

Shaka spent the earlier years of his reign in consolidating his position and butchering all those who had ill-treated him and his mother so many bitter years previously. *Shaka* was terrible in his vengeance. He killed old men, babies and women, which was completely taboo in terms of the laws of his forefathers which prescribe that only men fit to defend themselves can be killed. Women and children must always be absorbed within the conquering tribe.

Shaka surrounded himself with heretics and thugs like himself and he brought havoc to Zululand. He was a coward. It is well known to Bantu historians that *Shaka* never led his own armies when they were attacking strong tribes – only when attacking remnants which could not offer serious resistance. There were hundreds of such weakly organised tribes in Natal, like the Baca and the Pondo, and these he attacked and conquered with the sole motive of building for himself an empire and a reputation as a conqueror.

Shaka was the first African chief to introduce foul tactics on the battlefield. A classic example was when the Ndwandwe decided to attack him because he had killed the two sons of their chief, *Zwide* the Lion, in an endeavour to absorb the two tribes they ruled. *Shaka* first pretended to attack the Ndwandwe, and then he ordered a rapid retreat to Zululand, destroying all crops and livestock on their way. The Ndwandwe pursued, thinking that he was afraid – or faint-hearted – and thus they walked into *Shaka's* trap. They could not bring up enough food and supplies and when they were weak and disorganised through hunger, he attacked them.

This was contrary to all Bantu rules of war. The laws demand that a battle should be fought openly and fairly by both sides and that no foul tricks of any description must be used. Enemy supply lines must never be interfered with and scouts are not to be killed. *Shaka* broke all these rules. A battle had to be an honest trial of strength and courage between the two combatants and an enemy had to be reduced to submission only through generalship and force of arms, not through trickery.

But *Shaka* was a born law-breaker; his life was befouled by acts of treachery. He did not care a tinker's curse about the lives of the Zulus – he used them only as a means to a selfish end, as mere tools for the glorification of *Shaka*. He broke the sacred law which says no chief must ever forcefully separate a man from his wives and family. For five whole years he forbade men to marry to ensure undivided loyalty within his regiments. He indulged in savage acts of wanton sadism. He had an obsessive hatred of children and forbade all his wives to bear them, because he had developed the belief that a child of his would one day be the instrument of his death. He ordered his own mother *Nandi* to keep a close watch on all his wives and to ensure that they would procure abortions as soon as they turn pregnant. *Nandi* closed her eyes only once to this command and purposely allowed a particular pregnancy to develop to fruition. But about this I shall relate anon.

Towards the end of his life *Shaka* was completely mad. He suffered from shattering delusions of grandeur. He looked upon himself as a god and nursed a belief that even spears could not touch his 'immortality'. In this belief he was encouraged by hundreds of cunning flatterers who curried his favour. All this went to his head like poisonous beer fumes.

There was only one really strong tribe within his reach, the Ama-Hlubi, and even up to his death he never contemplated attacking this tribe.

Why is *Shaka* always glamorised and glorified in history books? I have a strong feeling it is because *Shaka*, unlike *Dingana, Mzilikazi* and *Cetshwayo*, never once offered resistance to European encroachment. He was the first Zulu chief to offer hospitality, and not the point of a spear, to men like Charles Farewell. There are only a few truly great Zulu Chiefs, and they are:

Malandela, the common ancestor of all Nguni kings;

Zulu, the son of Malandela by adoption, who founded the Zulu tribe;

Cetshwayo, who fought the British at Isandhlwana, Rorke's Drift and Ulundi, and who had the noble habit of personally consoling the relatives of his warriors who were killed in battle and bathing the wounds of those who survived;

Mjokwane, the son of *Ndaba*, who was also a philosopher and poet and who was elevated to semi-godhood;

Dingi-Swayo, the first king who endeavoured to weld the Bantu of Natal into one nation along honourable lines;

Dinizulu, the grandfather of the present Paramount Chief of the Zulus.

About these, and many others, I shall shortly write a whole book: 'The History of the Zulu Nation.'

Shaka, basking in the sun of false greatness, continued to commit one terrible crime after another. Two of his most abominable crimes led eventually to his undoing, and his death at the early age of thirty-five.

One day the beautiful Royal wife, *Mbuzikazi*, found herself pregnant and reported the fact to *Nandi*. But it was this pregnancy which *Nandi* decided to overlook. She allowed *Mbuzikazi* to escape to the land of a distant tribe and when *Shaka* came to hear about this he sent strong forces after her. *Mbuzikazi*, nevertheless, made good her escape and lived to a great old age, watching her, and *Shaka's*, son grow into a mighty warrior. On learning of her escape, *Shaka* turned his wrath on the only woman he loved – his mother, the beautiful *Nandi*. He ran a spear through her thigh. He thus committed the vilest crime in Bantu law: he shed the blood of his own mother.

According to our laws, such a mother is considered as having been 'murdered' even though she remained alive. This explains the inconsistency where Zulu historians insist that *Shaka* 'murdered' his mother, while White historians insist that she was not murdered by *Shaka*. Both are right, of course, in a strange way. *Nandi* died in fact, of diarrhoea, two years later, but the Zulus insist that she had been murdered in the first place by *Shaka*.

By then the Zulus were becoming mutinous as a result of the Chief's excesses and wanton cruelty and the first rumblings of sedition and agitation were heard. At this critical stage *Shaka* committed his last crime. He sent an *impi* into the land of the Shangane with the sole purpose of stealing cattle. But by a strange trick the Shangane sent his *impi* running back to Zululand with its figurative tail between its legs. *Shaka* was beside himself with fury; he ordered some of his Battle *Indunas* killed. He arrested the families of his *Indunas* and held them as hostages. The Bantu regard the holding of women and children as hostages, as the lowest act of cowardice. This was his last crime. *Mkabayi*, the 'aunt' of *Dingana* and *Mbopa* then decided to act.

Shaka was not murdered by men thirsting for power and edged on by a deadly middle-aged female schemer; he was tried *in absentia* for his many wanton crimes and was justly condemned to death. If *Mhlangana, Dingana* and *Mbopa*, the three half-brothers of *Shaka* who executed him, had been ordinary murderers they would have been executed for their crime that very same day. A Bantu law lays down that any assassin of a chief must be killed regardless of any good reasons he might have. This law is not applicable, however, to the killing of a chief in battle, in a fair duel or in self-defence.

A message had been sent discreetly to *Shaka* the night before, hinting that unless he mended his ways he would be kissed on the neck by his half-brothers. *Shaka* ignored this with his usual cold contempt, and only replied: '*Ngiyiloko engiyikona, ngazalwa nginje, ngi yoba njena njalo ngeke nga guquka*' (I was born what I am, I am what I am, and I will be just what I am since I can never, and will never, change).

Dingana then came into the kraal of *Shaka* in the late morning and found him sitting outside his Great Hut surrounded by his servants and guards. *Dingana* greeted his half-brother who responded with the customary inclining of his haughty, handsome head.

'My brother,' said *Dingana* in a voice that was far from steady, 'we have a loin apron that we must sew with you and you will honour us by accompanying us to the cattle enclosure outside your kraal.'

Shaka smiled, a hard smile, and reacted quite calmly: 'My brothers would like me to join them in sewing a loin apron, but they had better be careful not to get their fingers injured by the awls and needles they sew with.' With this veiled threat he rose and followed them. The guards also rose to follow, but *Shaka* waved them back contemptuously: 'Stay – this is only for royal ears to hear.'

The place to which they went was a *sibaya* – a great circular cattle pen which was empty and reserved for official meetings where commoners were not allowed to be present. As they entered, *Shaka* sat down arrogantly even though his three half-brothers remained standing. (There were several carved stools in the place.) They were astonished by the calm expression they read on *Shaka's* face and *Dingana* told my great-grandfather afterwards that the face of *Shaka* was like 'the face of a man who was lost in the valleys of another land, lost in spirit . . . far, far away . . .'

Mhlangana then knelt before *Shaka* and presented him directly with a tuft made of the tail feathers of the *indwa* bird. With a hard smile *Shaka* took the tuft and contemptuously started to destroy it while waiting for his half-brothers to make the next move.

Although *Shaka* had left his weapons behind, his three half-brothers were armed with short, broad-bladed stabbing spears of the kind that *Dingi-Swayo* had invented, and even while *Shaka* was pulling the tuft of feathers apart, *Dingana* raised his spear behind *Shaka's* back. He held it thus raised for a few moments, seeking in this symbolic act the forgiveness of the Spirits, and then, with teeth gritted, he plunged the spear deep into *Shaka's* back, just under the right shoulder blade.

Shaka sprang up with a hoarse shriek as *Dingana* withdrew the spear and staggered a few paces with blood flowing down his back in a fountain. He fell on his side at the feet of his executioners. His face lost its look of shocked surprise and he looked up at them with his usual contempt and arrogance. He gasped, and blood burst from his mouth as he said: 'So, you . . . kill me . . . my brothers!'

No one answered and *Shaka* smiled. His voice gathered strength as he continued: 'You think . . . you kill me . . . so you can rule . . . but swallows . . . build their nests of mud . . . they seize your land and rule it!'

All three now stabbed *Shaka* and licked their spears. Then they buried him in a temporary grave, wrapped in an old *kaross* – the burial of a condemned and executed criminal – alone, unwept for, and without the ugly wounds having been cleansed of blood and dirt.

White historians often go into great detail when they tell us *what* so-and-so did, but they never tell us *who* he was. His portrait stares at us from the pages of history books like a god made out of unfeeling brass. In no history book will any reader find Piet Retief described as a human being – only as an historical figure. It seems to me that White historians are more concerned about the deeds of an historical figure than with his personality. They thereby turn him into an actor pirouetting on the stage of history. Nobody's deeds or wise words can possibly make any sense unless these are seen against the background of the particular person's personality.

Bantu historians, on the other hand, always make a point of giving future generations a clear description of the character of an important personality. They will describe in greatest detail his features and physique, his habits down to how frequently he coughs, smiles, or swears; his likes and dislikes as far as foods are concerned; how he treats his wives, children, friends, superiors and inferiors; his courage or cowardice; his childhood and how certain incidents have contributed towards moulding his personality. Only when all these circumstances are taken into consideration can a clear and unbiased conclusion be drawn from such actions or occurrences that render the particular person a figure of historical importance.

The Custodians of Zulu History give us a description of Piet Retief, the Voortrekker leader, which I have not yet seen in any standard history book:

'The White man, *Litivu,* was an old man when he came to our land; his beard and his hair were as white as the morning frost of June, and he was not as tall as most of the other White men. But he was thick of body, however, and powerful still of muscle. He was a man of laughter and there was continuously the Spirit of Laughter in his eyes. He always made jokes with the mighty men of *Dingana* and wherever he was, the ghost of mirth was always there with him. He was a great man for practical jokes and in pleasant ways he could make his friends look like fools. We all liked this Strange One, who tried his best to speak to us in the language of the Xhosas, which he could speak reasonably, but with a strange accent . . .

'He was a man of happiness and one could hear him laughing with the other White ones as they rode on their strange animals through the bush. We used to spy on the White ones as they went through our land with their waggons and their strange animals which they rode. We could hear *Litivu* talking and laughing with his fellows, whom he had the habit of slapping heartily on the back as he laughed. We could not understand the strange guttural language that they used, but the Spirit of Mirth that lived in the heart of *Litivu* was like a living fire that reached our hearts even at a great distance while we lay in the long grass, spying on him and his men while they rode to the kraal of *Dingana.*'

Thus my great-grandfather described Piet Retief to my grandfather, who in turn passed it on to me. And although this translation into English robs the words of much of their beauty, it still conveys the spirit of admiration the Zulus had for *Litivu* and his men.

Wherever a party of Voortrekkers moved they always publicised the fact that they were only an advance party and that substantial numbers of their fellows were somewhere in the background. While this was true in many cases, in others it was merely used as a bluff to discourage hostile acts by the Bantu through whose lands they moved. On many occasions the Bantu actually learnt at high cost of lives that little was to be gained from interfering with these parties of Trekkers, and nobody was more conscious of this fact than *Dingana.*

Another factor that should be mentioned briefly is the fact that *Dingana* dearly loved the throne to which he was not entitled. Although he was in fact *Shaka's* executioner, his elder brother, *Mhlangana,* was the rightful successor. *Dingana* was, however, his 'aunt's' favourite 'nephew' and this dirty, scheming, unnatural slut of a woman urged *Dingana* to eliminate his own brother. *Mkabayi* was one of the most cold-blooded monsters who ever lived; she was so evil that she did not stop at encouraging her 'nephews' to murder each other. It was her idea that since *Mhlangana* had a craze for bathing himself in the river his two brothers should one day accompany him and make him take an overdose of the water. The selfish *Dingana* and the maniac *Mbopa* found their 'aunt's' command a rather attractive proposition and executed it to the letter.

The Zulu people became suspicious and with *Dingana's* inherent laziness and the increasingly obvious truth that it was really his evil 'aunt' ruling them, with *Dingana* merely a figurehead, he could hardly be looked upon as a popular ruler. He felt his power waning and indulged in ruthless actions designed to improve the image of mastery. He sent *impis* on senseless raids to boost his power, even though he showed no interest in their training and rarely led them in person. As leaders he appointed *Indunas* whom he felt he could not trust, in the hope that they might get killed, and this was often the sole purpose of the raid.

All these things added up to *Dingana's* developing as a monster almost as despised as *Shaka* at the height of his madness. The Zulus became tired of being ruled by the sons of *Senza-Ngakona* and many were deserting the tribe to join the leper *Mpande*, whom they hoped they could strengthen so that he could start a new dynasty.

With this picture as background, how can anyone believe that *Dingana* arranged the killing of Piet Retief and his party through sheer treachery and for no logical reason? There could have been no doubts in his mind that this action would lead to his own undoing and the undoing of the tribe he ruled, and of this he was not prepared to take the slightest chance.

The two crucial questions in the Piet Retief mystery, which no history book has ever asked, are, firstly, why did *Dingana* take a decision while fully conscious of the fact that he would thereby commit both personal and national suicide? Secondly, why were Piet Retief and his followers clubbed to death with *siqongqwana* clubs, the kind which Zulu women use when they tan their leather skin skirts? I have explained before that the style of execution befits the crime the condemned man has committed.

Dingana was no coward, but he was too lazy and pleasure-loving to show an interest in battles of any description and least of all in battles involving the White Voortrekkers. He was, however, a meticulous schemer and he had noticed something which other chiefs had failed to see, and which he was the first leader ever to exploit. He had seen how the Voortrekkers loathed and despised the English, who had forced them out of the Cape. He had seen how the haughty English watched with contempt the entry of the Voortrekkers into Natal. Both these White factions had spoken evilly of one another in the presence of *Dingana*. Through this thick curtain of mud-slinging *Dingana* saw his opportunity. Why not rid himself of the encroaching danger merely by setting these two White factions at one another's throats? He could then simply sit back and watch the fun.

The Voortrekkers came to *Dingana* and negotiated with him for certain land rights, and he allocated to them by treaty a piece of land in the west of Zululand. This same territory he subsequently allocated to the English. He did so on purpose, hoping that when the two enemies found themselves occupying the same land, they would go for one another like mad dogs over a juicy bone. This cannot possibly be construed as treachery on the part of *Dingana*. He was, in fact, being tricked out of the same piece of land by both parties, and each came to him with European-style documents which meant nothing to him. And, furthermore, each set of documents was in a different language he could not understand. He was required to give his signature, which he could not write, being illiterate in the White man's style of writing.

But his dealings with the Voortrekkers were along more honourable lines. The Voortrekkers were prepared to purchase land, or to offer certain services or guarantees. They asked *Dingana* to stipulate his price and, not being conversant with European-style transactions, he made the ceding of the land conditional on Piet Retief's effecting the return of two hundred head of cattle the Chief *Si-Konyela* had stolen from his kraal a short while before.

Si-Konyela was not only an expert theif, but quite a wizard too, and attacking wizards, with their 'super-human powers' is something Zulu warriors do not relish. *Dingana* saw in Piet Retief an instrument to overcome this difficulty, because these White men were less impressed by Bantu wizardry; he thought they were more immune to it.

Retief took his men and off they went on the long journey to the land of *Si-Konyela*, and in his pocket Retief carried something that was most queer to the mind of the African – a pair of handcuffs. Already a humorous thought had entered his mind and he was anxious to return to Zululand with an hilarious anecdote. They found *Si-Konyela* sitting in his Kraal, surrounded by a mighty assortment of thugs, villains and scoundrels trying their best to look like warriors. Retief greeted the vagabond chief and soon created an atmosphere of merriment with his strong sense of humour. Eventually he produced the handcuffs and started impressing *Si-Konyela* with the magical powers of these 'bracelets'. Eager to increase his own magical powers, *Si-Konyela* agreed to have them fitted, and dexterously Retief clicked them on his wrists. No matter how he tried, *Si-Konyela* could not free his thieving hands. He raged and cursed luridly in his own language, provoking only louder peals of laughter from his White visitors. *Si-Konyela's* followers realised that only Retief knew how to open the handcuffs and that the chief was entirely at his mercy. Eventually *Si-Konyela* pleaded for mercy and Retief agreed to unlock the handcuffs, on condition that *Dingana's* two hundred head of cattle be first dispatched to his kraal.

The Voortrekkers arrived with the cattle at *Dingana's* kraal, and there things started happening that changed the course of the history of South Africa.

Not all the members of Piet Retief's party were Voortrekkers, or Boers of Dutch descent. There was one man among them who, stripped of all the dignity that one normally found in his fellow-countrymen, operated as a spy for his people in the land of the Zulus. He was an Englishman named Halstead, and he was known to the Zulus as the 'Curious Peeper' because of the way he normally went creeping around the kraals and gathering information about our customs, and especially our weapons.

Dingana's Great Kraal was a vast structure consisting of two large concentric circles of stockades. The inner circle enclosed the great arena for social gatherings, meetings and dancing, and into which cattle could be driven for protection. In the space between the inner and the outer circles were hundreds of huts housing his warriors and their families. Attached to one side of this vast structure was the Royal Kraal in which all *Dingana's* wives and concubines were housed. This section was known as the 'Forbidden Place' and all Zulus knew that the death penalty was meted out without mercy on any male who ventured too close to this enclosure.

It was Halstead's habit to ride his horse and approach this enclosure so that he could peer over the stockade. He did so frequently while Piet Retief and some of his followers went out to visit *Si-Konyela.* The Zulus are a very suspicious and superstitious race. They could not understand why Halstead was so curious and why he chanced to do a thing no Zulu would dare to do. *Dingana's* concubines and daughters had strict orders not to venture outside their huts into the fierce sun; since a lighter skin colour has always been looked upon as more glamorous than dark shades. They used to come out only at sunset and especially in the moonlight. Under cover of darkness Halstead could approach closer and it was on the night before Piet Retief returned that he was caught in the act of putting his head over the stockade.

On this occasion one of *Dingana's* wives, who was a few months pregnant, had a nightmare and sought the refreshment of the cool night air. She saw the strange White face peering over the stockade and suddenly she felt all but refreshed. The news reached one of the High Wives who approached *Mkabayi, Dingana's* 'aunt', the following morning with a pot full of water which she emptied on the floor of the hut. She then placed the pot upside down in the middle of the floor. This is a recognised symbolic gesture to announce a miscarriage.

Mkabayi's evil mind and her strong love for *Dingana* promptly induced her to read a great deal into this whole incident. She approached *Dingana* and persuaded him to believe that the White men were at his Kraal with evil intent and that they were scheming to hit at his weak spot – his wives.

Dingana was well and truly frightened. The more he thought about it the more he panicked. When Piet Retief arrived he said to him: 'Now you have the land you want, please go there and do with it what you want. Now you have your reward.' But on second thoughts he decided to 'hit while the iron is hot'. He invited Piet Retief to stay and join him in a ceremonial feast.

The feast lasted four whole days and on the last day *Dingana* called upon his crack regiments to stage a war-dance. Piet Retief was very impressed by this display and he laughed a great deal, being as usual in an excellent mood.

It was during this display that *Dingana* quietly slipped way. He had said to Retief: 'Now, Oh *Litivu*, you of the happy beard, now my children shall play for you. You will see how many warriors pound the cringing earth with their feet. Look upon my warriors.'

While all eyes were fixed on the dancers, *Dingana* stole away like a jackal. He went to a hillock overlooking the kraal, thoroughly convinced by then that the White men were wizards who had only come to bewitch him through an uncanny onslaught on his wives. When he reached the hillock he gave the predetermined signal to my great-grandfather; he slowly raised his knobkierie and shouted: 'Kill . . . kill the wizards!' From beyond the stockades came the *kikiza* cry – from the women.

There was only one man left outside the kraal to guard the horses and when he heard the tumult he briskly fled for dear life. All history books contain the story he had to tell.

Fifty guards seized Piet Retief and his men and held them down while they were systematically clubbed to death with *siqongqwana* tanning clubs. The other warriors went on dancing as if nothing was happening.

Piet Retief was the last to die. He died no cringing coward. He fought back to the last inch of his breath. He never asked for mercy; through long association with the tribes he knew this was useless. He never knew why he had to die and until this day few have known that by strict tribal laws and customs these Voortrekkers were all executed for an 'attempted' offence against the High Wives of a Chief.

Our Story-tellers have no pride in this tale. It takes great courage to tell it. It was only after this fateful event had been added to the roll of History that our historians managed to piece the details together. On careful analysis and extensive enquiries the facts emerged. The Zulus were so shocked about this mad action on the part of *Dingana* that many more, including some High *Indunas*, deserted him and went over to *Mpande.*

For this rash act *Dingana* and the Zulu tribe paid a ghastly price. *Dingana* was pursued, tortured and killed by his own people. The Zulu race bravely faced their punishment at the Battle of Blood River, the only battle in human history where more people were killed than there were shots fired. Ten thousand Zulu warriors laid down their lives in exchange for two slightly wounded Voortrekkers. And while with this battle the Zulu race virtually disappeared from the scene the losses of the Voortrekkers have been annually commemorated for more than a century. And in these years many more curious Africans than the number of men in Piet Retief's party have been shot dead, prosecuted and sentenced for prowling around and peering through the bedroom windows of White people.

There was another White man in *Dingana's* kraal at the time of the massacre. His name was Owen. *Dingana* had approached him before this fatal day and had said to him: 'Why does this man . . . this wizard . . . prowl around my women's place at night? It is said that you are a man of wisdom, Oh *Maoweni*, what shall I do about this man?'

To this Owen replied: 'I shall speak to this man *Stindi* (Halstead) and he shall listen to my words.'

According to our historians Owen never made any effort to speak to Halstead. Owen had every opportunity to warn Piet Retief, but this he did not do either. On the fatal day Owen was confined to his hut under a five-man guard and he witnessed everything that happened. Why has Owen kept silent about the whole incident? If Owen left any written records, and if these are still preserved somewhere, they should be scrutinised with the greatest care.

THE KNOWLEDGE OF THE BANTU

GENERAL

Knowledge is controlled among the Bantu by the orders of the Chosen Ones. Only certain knowledge is passed on to particular High Ones of the Tribes, such as they are required to know to execute their duties. Very little knowledge is passed on to the common people and nothing is ever disclosed to strangers.

The Chosen Ones gather regularly to exchange views, check on their knowledge, and educate those selected for training as future Guardians. Such gatherings are called 'Secret Societies' by foreigners who have discovered that these meetings take place. These foreigners have also 'discovered' that masks play a certain role and they have started to identify certain 'Secret Societies' with certain masks. In actual fact there are very many masks which feature at each gathering. These masks are merely representations of certain mythological or historical figures and they are worn in turn by the Story-teller while he enacts certain episodes. Such stories are always dramatised to ensure alert attention.

Knowledge of history, legends, mythology – what White people would refer to as Classics – is always strong among the Bantu. A second field of knowledge in which the Bantu excel is philosophy, psychology, spiritualism – with a strong leaning towards the occult. A third field can roughly be called the socio-political, and a fourth is the biological-medical. There are many other interesting facets of Bantu knowledge and I shall deal with these rather superficially, and not necessarily in a systematic way.

The Black man of Africa is a being who has puzzled the whole world, and it would appear that the more others try to learn something about the African, the farther they drift from the truth. This is simply because all foreigners try to evaluate what they learn about Africans in terms of their own preconceived ideas and against their own standards of civilisation and social and political thought. The African can only be understood in terms of the strange workings of his own mind and those who do not appreciate this may as well refrain from trying to study the African.

The democracy practised by the idealistic Americans is no longer the democracy of ancient Greece. India has had to dilute the 'Western Way of Life' to suit her ancient philosophies and beliefs, to make it acceptable, understandable and palatable to the masses that constitute her population. Even China had to dilute the foul creed of Communism that she learnt from Russia. Today the Russians need a microscope to recognise their own creed as practised by the Chinese – drastically re-shaped as it is to suit the mind pattern of the Mongoloids.

And yet the White man, who will never cease to be an idealist, expects the African to accept his 'civilisation' neat – he *must not* alter it to the slightest extent to make it more acceptable and understandable, and more workable, for his own people.

Unless native and foreign creeds can be made to fuse perfectly there must be a period of instability, no matter how civilised the particular country may be on the surface. History is full of such examples. Take Germany, a monarchist country of long standing, converting to a republican form of government, and the disruption caused by an intervening dictatorship. Take the shameful chaos that followed the collapse of the monarchy in France. It took a dictatorial Napoleon to straighten out their '*Liberté, Egalité et Fraternité*'.

Many of those interested in events in Africa today are surprised that the new emergent African states do not settle for the perfect democratic form of government with a recognised opposition, but that they all turn into dictatorships. The truth is that a Black man cannot fathom how a country can be governed by two enemies constantly at one another's throats. Such a country can never be happy and stable. To a Black man all disagreements must end in blows and seccession. The Black man has not the shallow flexible soul that most races have, and to be ruled by two squabbling parties is as alien and repugnant to his mind, as his way of doing things is repugnant to the European mind. A Black man can give his loyalty only to one set of rulers, who rule in oneness of purpose for better or for worse. Sooner or later they find the dual loyalty encouraged by a two-party system not only clumsy and unwieldy, but fatal as well, because to an African a member of the Opposition is not merely the man who holds dissenting political views – he is a deadly enemy who must be killed.

Things like 'friendly rivalry' and an 'agreement to disagree' have no place in the mind of an African. We either hate or we love; we either agree or we disagree and fight to the death.

The Black man has a strong parent, or fetish complex, dating from the days when a community could produce only one brave man at a time, who could challenge a savage beast with a bone-tipped spear. The whole community then looked upon such a hero for its protection. Even today we still choose that one man or woman who will be our living totem pole, our god-on-earth, our parent symbol; who is the embodiment of all our aspirations and our unity, and to whom we shall give all our love and loyalty and around whom we shall rally in times of evil. This person will be our nation, the symbol of all our ideals and all our dreams. He or she shall be part of us and we shall be part of him or her. Thus a Barotse from the west of Zambia never says 'I am a subject of Paramount Chief *Mwanawina*'. He will always say 'I am a Mwanawina'. At the time of the Zulu King *Cetshwayo* his subjects called themselves 'the Cetshwayo'. This is how most tribes got their names.

Therefore, in the mind of the African, there can only be one ruler to whom all loyalty and love is given, and not two. One is unity and two are disunity.

I said previously that an African is a vicious bearer of grudges and a lover of vengeance. But he is also a great believer in endurance, an endurance he has cultivated while bearing his grudges and waiting for opportunities of revenge. He is the quickest human being in the world to adapt himself to hostile and evil conditions and he has learnt to find joy and happiness in situations where other races would go mad – take up arms and rebel. A Black man can find pleasure in degradation, he can thrive on suffering. According to Bantu law, a person is not a proper human being until he has learnt what suffering is.

The Bantu have been conditioned for generations to appreciate the value of adaptability. 'My child, be always like the slim *munga* tree that bows its head and yields to the fury of the tempest, rather than like the stiff, proud *masasa* which only gets snapped and hurled to the ground.' As a result of his chronic fear of being humiliated by others, he chooses rather to humiliate himself. He takes a delight, not only in suffering but in making himself the laughing stock of his enemies, by actually aiding and abetting them in their task of insulting and degrading him.

This explains many things which foreigners find puzzling – for example, why a prison sentence never reforms a Bantu criminal. He looks upon it as a qualification. This is why, although there is nothing a Bantu resents more than the Arab epithet of 'kaffir', he still frequently refers to himself as such. (The Arab meaning of kaffir is a man without a soul, an unbeliever and a person who can never see the paradise of Allah.) It explains why a Bantu takes all manner of punishments and insults with a smile.

The Bantu refuse to believe that anything can happen for no rhyme or reason, and this belief forms the backbone of witchcraft. Any misfortune or illness is the direct result of the evil wish-thoughts of one's enemies. The Bantu believe in omens which they interpret as outward warning signals sent by the soul to warn the body. There are countless interpretations and every African is constantly on the look-out for such signals. Europeans call this phenomenon superstition. If a chief visits a place and immediately after his departure rain falls, he is regarded as being a beloved of the rain-gods and he must be worshipped. This honour befell the Prime Minister of South Africa, Dr HF Verwoerd. Good and unusual rains fell in Ovamboland immediately after he had paid the Ovambos a visit. This is a very dry region in South West Africa and the Ovambos immediately nicknamed Dr Verwoerd their 'Rain Father' and they started carving busts of him in their particular style.

Rain is always associated with good omens. Even Christian Bantu believe that rain at a funeral is a sign that the departed soul is well on its way to heaven. It was a shower of rain over the tragic scene at Sharpeville that made the Bantu believe that their cause was righteous, that they were innocent, and the disturbance spread to the extent where the Government had to declare a State of Emergency.

I can write a whole book exclusively on this subject of superstition but I have said enough here to give a clue to the Bantu mental attitude towards knowledge and science. Our great scientific weakness lies in the fields of physics and engineering, for the simple reason that our religion frowns upon inventions and improvements.

The African conducts research on a very different plane from that of the White man, and for this reason he has made discoveries that the White man has overlooked in his headlong rush to outer space. The Black man possesses tremendous knowledge that could make a great impact, even on the modern world, and he has hidden this knowledge now for hundreds of years under the cloak of 'voodoo' and 'black magic'.

Some of this knowledge could be of incalculable strategic value. There is, for example, the valuable role zombies could play in times of war. A suicide squad of zombies would be an ace up the sleeve of any general, even in modern conditions of war. The Bantu have had the secret of zombie-making now for thousands of years. The art of producing a zombie is mentioned in our legends dating back to the later phases of the Stone Age.

When young mercenaries from the White population of South Africa slipped out to join the forces of President Moise Tshombe of Katanga in 1960 and 1961 they made a startling discovery. They came across Baluba warriors who kept on fighting with severed arms and half-a-dozen bullet holes in them. These warriors were simply drugged, by a drug that was also extensively used by the Zulus, especially in the battles of Rorke's Drift and Ulundi. A modern soldier thus treated, could blow the heaviest tank to kingdom come with grenades, single-handed. His blind immunity to pain and fear and his fantastic daring would have a profound demoralising influence on the enemy. If the South African troops had had this drug with them at Tobruk, history would have had a different story to record.

There are Bantu medicines and herbs that I would like to see analysed by the world's scientists – medicines that look and taste like sewer water, but which can cure ills for which the White man has no answer. We have drugs that can rid people of gall-stones and kidney-stones like the snapping of a finger. How many White people believe that Bantu women are differently built or that they are less sensitive to pain, because childbirth does not seem to worry our women overmuch? Most of our women can give birth to babies unaided. The truth is that they are taught at their initiation school how to give birth under self-hypnosis. But, thanks to the White man's wanton destruction of such institutions as our initiation schools for their supposedly un-Christian nature, this knowledge is dying out fast in Southern Africa.

The Bantu have numerous drugs fermented from the *dagga* plant – medicines that kill shock in badly injured people; medicines that can save many lives. And the police hound us because they believe we smoke this leaf. It *is* being smoked, but a great percentage of smuggled *dagga* goes into making medicines that have saved the lives of thousands of people.

The veil of secrecy and suspicion with which the Bantu have shielded their scientific knowledge from the rest of the world must be destroyed now and forever.

One of the oldest Bantu sciences is veterinary surgery. Until recently each tribe had an official castrator, which was how we designated our veterinary surgeon. This official was given an extensive three-year training which qualified him to castrate bulls, goats and men alike. The operation was always performed along the strictest scientific lines.

The Bantu performed Caesarean operations on human beings and animals, with both mothers and young surviving, long before the days of Caesar.

The Bantu have had a system of weighing objects since time immemorial, using the simple principle of balancing things across a suspended stick. The Bantu learnt to grow corn thousands of years ago. For this purpose they divided the year into seasons which they measured by the shadow cast by a vertical pole planted in the middle of each kraal. They used the sundial principle for determining seasons rather than the daily passage of time. The year was divided into two seasons, 'summer' and 'winter', with two transitional periods 'early summer' and 'late summer'.

The year was further divided into thirteen moons, sub-divided by its phases. A day was divided into four equal parts; sunrise to noon, noon to sunset, sunset to midnight, and midnight to sunrise. Distances were often given as a quarter of a day's journey by foot, but this referred to a quarter of the period of daylight.

Finer intervals of time were measured against heartbeats. A specially appointed person would sit with his hand above his heart and count one hundred. Every time he would reach the century count he would drop a pebble or a grain of corn into a basket. Certain periods could thus be described in terms of a fixed number of heartbeats.

There are certain ceremonies that must either be performed at midnight or stop exactly at midnight. The Bantu were always firm believers that from midnight onwards the gods came down to do some prowling around. Midnight always had to be determined and the first approach was the clumsy heartbeat way. A poor man had to sit and count his own heartbeats from the moment the sun vanished until the moment it appeared again, dropping a grain in a basket for every hundred beats. The following morning the score was counted and this was divided by two. A rather ingenious contraption was then designed whereby water was allowed to drip from a calabash into a container and the container would start sagging when the water reached the required weight. All this was timed so that from start to finish it took exactly half the number of heartbeats from sunset to sunrise.

These devices disappeared rapidly when clocks were introduced into Africa several centuries ago. I have only seen four examples of the bowl used in the device; two were in a large curio shop in Bulawayo; one was in a Johannesburg curio shop and the fourth, already cracked with age, I saw in a Mashona village outside Plumtree. I have been told that somewhere in the area where Zambia, Angola and the Congo join hands there is a device which still functions. The Gods willing, one day I shall go out there and find it so that it can be placed in a museum.

SYMBOL WRITING

In the early nineteen-fifties two White ladies wrote a book that for some years I have been wanting to challenge.

The well-meaning ladies told the world that the Zulus send love-letters made out of beads to their lovers (which is true) and that each colour means something (which is not strictly true).

When man ceased being a lone food-seeker and mate-hunter and turned himself into a social animal, forming communities, a chain of problems arose which he was forced to solve in a variety of ways. He already had a spoken language, sufficient for communication. But society's developments demand a written language. One cannot speak vocally to one's descendants. One cannot preserve for posterity the rules and codes devised to solve the problems of community life. It cannot merely be passed by word of mouth from father to son alone. The human memory is far too unreliable, and in prehistoric times it was evidently more so.

Thus a number of symbols, painted or engraved on rocks for all future people to see, were developed to keep the memory of important occurrences alive. Our earliest signs date from the Middle Stone Age.

They first took the form of very basic symbols and more elaborate 'reminder pictures', and all cave paintings can really be classed under the latter head. Thus a sketch like the one below is simply a personal record of a man's narrow escape from a charging lion. This is called 'pictographic writing'.

Man is an egotistical braggart with an inborn instinct to boast of every triumph. He subconsciously resists the thought that with death he might be forgotten. Nobody is certain that the words he has spoken will live to reach the ears of future generations. Therefore, be he chief or peasant, a man wants his deeds and experiences and memories to be literally engraved in the annals of history. The

visitor to the Sterkfontein Caves or the Voortrekker Monument wants others to know he was there and therefore he engraves his initials where they can be seen. He is still practising a Stone Age instinct.

Thus, in the accompanying illustrations we see how a man records a great experience in his life – a love affair. It is as good as a letter written home to his mother telling her how he made overtures to the woman of his choice, how she accepted him, and that she now belongs to him and other men must keep off.

Similarly all kinds of hunting episodes were recorded. The flesh of the eland is very good indeed, and it was regarded as a symbol of fertility and good luck by the ancient Bushmen. They also associated it with water and light. This is why it is featured so frequently in Bushman cave paintings.

An historical episode was thus recorded, first in a sketch, and a written language grew by a process of simplification of the symbols (ideography). And thus man slowly but surely won the war against his greatest enemy, the Demon of Obscurity. Thus was man able to preserve his wisdom and pass it on from generation to generation. Speech was evolved to facilitate communication between contemporaries; writing was developed to facilitate communication

with future generations. A simplified form of writing in the hieroglyphic style serves an ordinary purpose; modern writing evolved through the endeavours various groups made to change and encode their signs of communication so as to make their recordings and messages unreadable to their enemies (steganography). For example a group of medicine men felt a need for communicating with each other but in such a way that the common people would not understand the message.

There was fear everywhere; there was death and there was pain. The women wailed loudly and the young ones fretted and whimpered. The men fought tenaciously to keep the cruel enemy out of the half-destroyed village. They fought and died like the fierce ones of the forest – the lions and the leopards.

The High Chief of the village had already fallen and nearly all his Battle Leaders were also dead. But the brave youth *Kabanga*, the first-born of the chief, fought on. He fought in the thickest of the battle and he was constantly seen where the warriors' spears were bloodiest and the war cries loudest. He already knew that it was only a matter of time before he himself would be slain.

So, fiercely he waded into the very middle of the swarming Wa-Tu-Tutsi, the tall enemy warriors who were attacking the village and who, with their fire-spears, had already made a breach in the stockade and burnt down many of the huts. Fiercely, like a young lion, he threw himself at the enemy. Fiercely, he hacked and stabbed with his *panga*, and wherever he struck a man dropped dead to the ground, because his trusty *panga* was not playing games that day. It was biting – and it was biting deep.

The spirit of courage came flooding back into the heads and livers of the Ba-Hutu warriors when they saw their prince plunge into the ranks of the enemy. They raised a blood-curdling cry and charged. They charged with the fury and the force of *Bejana-ya-Mukombe*, the rhinoceros, and nothing, not even the fury of the invincible Wa-Tu-Tutsi, could stand in their way.

Like drunken men struck in the belly by angry wives, the enemy

reeled and was flung back in wild disorder. The warriors fell like dew drops from the leaves of a shaken tree. They staggered, tried to rally, but were flung back out of the village with heavy slaughter; they were sent scattering from the village like beaten hyaenas. But they were far from defeated and would soon return with their battle fury redoubled. In the lull that followed, in which the warriors on both sides took time off to eat what little food they had, a Little Spirit gave the Princess *Kamulanda* a great idea.

She took a calabash of small size and on it she burnt with a hot awl the signs of mysterious meaning such as the Wise Ones of the Tribes use to speak in the silent way with one another. Her skilled hands made the signs to read: 'Come and help us – the Dog People are attacking the Great Village; the Chief has fallen!'

The princess then called for her dog, the *musenji* Nagaru, who was both her friend and protector, and to the neck of the 'wagger-of-the-tail' she tied the calabash. She bade the dog begone and away to the village of *Mbangwe* the Wise.

Nagaru wagged his tail, and promptly left, darting through the breach the enemy had made in the stockade. He shot away, a streak of yellow fur darting through the forest. He bounded across the clearings and shot through *dongas* and streamlets.

A band of foraging Wa-Tu-Tutsi saw the dog streaking towards them, the calabash fastened round his throat. They thought he was a zombie, belonging to some wizard, and that the calabash contained evil medicine that might bring death to anyone touching it. They sprang aside with terrified howls as the dog darted between their frightened legs.

Shortly afterwards, the dog caught sight of the village of *Mbangwe* and increased his speed. As he streaked out of the forest a mamba lunged savagely at him, burying its fangs in the side of the intrepid little animal. Nagaru did not stop; he ignored the fiery pain that spread rapidly and managed to reach *Mbangwe*, seated with some of his Battle Leaders in the day-shelter. The Battle Leaders reached for their *pangas* as *Mbangwe* read the message, and one stooped to pat the already dead dog.

Soon an army of two thousand fighting men was streaming out of the Ba-Hutu war-kraal, with *Mbangwe* at its head, to take the Wa-Tu-Tutsi by surprise . . .

The Bantu symbol-language is not taught to the common people and is mostly reserved for recording things of a secret, private, or very personal nature. Yet about thirty per cent of the Bantu can use this type of writing. Apart from witchdoctors and the Elders and the Wise Ones of the tribes, it is mostly women who still employ it.

The various symbols do not represent single characters; each expresses a whole word or, more often, a complete idea, rather in the style of Chinese and Japanese symbols.

Bantu symbol-writing is the same for all tribes in Africa, irrespective of language. A Zulu can read and understand anything recorded by a Lunda from Angola, even though he might not understand the spoken language.

Until as recently as fifty years ago the Bantu still sent one another lengthy 'letters' in this style of writing. But the practice died out fast as the people learnt the European alphabet.

Conveying ideas in this silent way took on a wide variety of forms. Urgent but temporary messages were mostly burnt on calabashes or 'message sticks'. Less urgent and more lasting ideas, such as are normally passed on in love letters, were woven in 'message mats'. Ideas of a more permanent nature, and especially those intended for future generations, are engraved on drums, pottery, and the walls of dwelling places.

As soon as a newly wed couple have built for themselves a house, the mother of the husband, or any of his friends, may come with all manner of pigment mixtures and decorate his place with blessing symbols. This custom is still practised by some Zimbabwean and Mozambique tribes; but the real specialists are the Ndebele and the Ma-Pochs of the Transvaal. The latter decorate their dwellings most elaborately with all kinds of prayers, proverbs and occult sayings.

And here I wish to plead that the Ndebele especially should never be discouraged from practising this ancient culture. It would be a tremendous loss to science if these people, particularly those living around Pretoria, were made to live in townships as has already been suggested.

There now follows a collection of typical Bantu symbols used in writing. Different ideas can be portrayed by slight alterations, additions or combinations. For example, in the following sentence the noun 'lion' is used in its literal sense, but if one should like to use 'lion' in a figurative sense, like 'the lion of adversity' (in the same sense that one would speak of a 'mountain of strength' or a 'bull of a wizard') a triangular motif is added to make the distinction, as shown in the character in brackets. The sentence reads: 'I saw a lion eating a buck at noon today.'

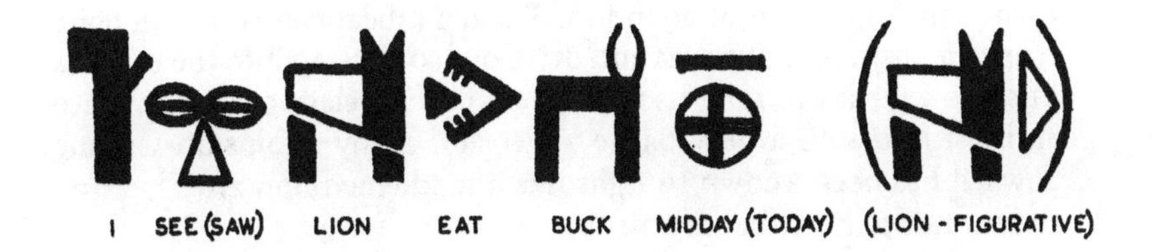

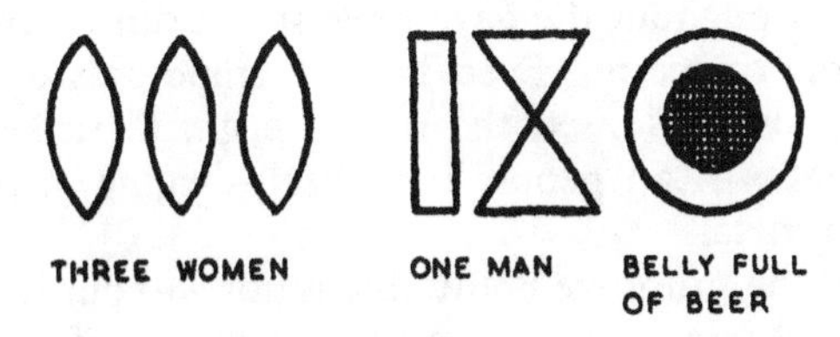

DRUMBEAT

The drum, or tom-tom, is Africa's most traditional musical instrument, and the 'talking drums' of West Africa are known far and wide. From the signalling or communication point of view alone, they are well worth describing.

Legends about *Marimba* and many other demigods apart, the fact remains that the African drum is the oldest instrument ever invented in my fatherland. With this instrument any group of dancers can fully express its soul; a tribesman from anywhere in Africa can be turned into a demon of abandon. The drumbeat can summon tears from the springs of our eyes and drive our souls deep into the caverns of sorrow, or it can raise us to the very peak of elation. Warriors are easily stirred into a fiery battle anger and many a loinskin-wetting coward has been known to fight like a maddened lion after hearing the sounds of his tribal drums.

Much has been written about the drums of Africa, but how many people know that the drum is not merely a musical instrument? How many know for example, that it is to a large extent a means of healing?

The traveller in Africa should note something which I guarantee has never caught his attention before – how often drums are sounded at intervals throughout the day, especially at sunset, and apparently for no rhyme or reason. Even in the compounds of the Gauteng gold-mines, just at sunset, the drums begin to strike up, after so many Central African people have been digging in the bowels of the earth for metal.

Even with the primitive Bantu, life is not without its tensions and worries; the phrase so dear to overseas authors of the last century – 'carefree savages' – is a myth. A Bantu chief or headman, and even the head of a family, carries as many worries with him as any person of any other race – if not more. Many are the Africans who die of stomach ulcers, including chiefs on rickety thrones, governing discontented and rebellious subjects or whose people are constantly attacked by neighbouring tribes. For this illness, caused by the spirit of worry, no witchdoctor has yet found a cure.

In a detribalised state the African is more prone to worry and fear. He loses his roots in his own tribal structure and he fails

ANTIQUE CONGO DRUM
HARDWOOD (MALE)

OVAMBO DRUM
HARDWOOD (MALE)

to shoot new roots in the alien civilisation he tries to adopt. It is not uncommon for a Bantu suddenly to run amok in a village or township with an axe. Wife killing is caused by common worry – the trouble that drives millions in the West to seek solace in evil drugs and on the couches of psychiatrists.

An ordinary honest hardworking man commutes daily between Johannesburg's crime-infested townships and his work. His mind is haunted by fear – fear of losing his job, of being endorsed out of the town, or of being evicted from his house through falling behind with his rent. He may be haunted by a fear of having his family broken up by the laws of the land, or of being set upon by *tsotsies.* He may know the fear of being bewitched by a rival.

The *piccanin* stands at the gate. There are tears in his eyes and there is hunger in his belly. He is puzzled and scared by what he saw happening the previous night in the place which he knows as his home. His mother and father had quarrelled and he had been awakened by the noise. He had seen his father hit his mother with the 'thing-that-chops-wood' and he had seen his mother fall.

Just before dawn the neighbours had sent their boy to the place of the Big Boss of the Township to fetch the Helmets and the Black Ones who 'guard-and-arrest'. The Helmets had taken his father in a big van to Far-Away and now one of them stands guard over the house – together with a Black One.

Inside the house there is much blood, and the *piccanin* has seen the Car-carries-dead-people draw to a stop outside the gate; he has seen the Men-of-death wrap his mother in a blanket.

The *piccanin* is very alone. He is very puzzled – and scared.

The ancient Bantu knew that life in organised communities was not good for human beings. They realised that unless there were ways and means for people to release the tensions of everyday life, disaster

BAROTSE DRUM
SOFTWOOD (MALE)

UGANDA WAR DRUM (MALE)

often resulted. Hence the wild, uninhibited dances performed every night; hence the beating of drums at sunset.

Drums can be sounded in such a way that they have a soothing effect – that they create a restful feeling. The beat of the drums can cure what no medicines can cure; it can heal the ills of the mind – it can heal the very soul.

The Bantu started making drums ages before they had the tools with which to do it. It was a lengthy and dangerous process which often took as long as a whole year.

A tree was felled by the laborious method of hacking at it for days on end with stone axes. A length was cut off and the block was left to season in the sun for a month or more. Afterwards the block was planted in a shallow hole and a small hollow was excavated in the upper end. Only then did the really laborious process start.

Stones, the size of a man's fist, were heated in a fire until nearly red hot. When ready they were lifted with two shoulder- blades of animals from the fire and laid in the excavated hollow. The charred wood was scraped out with stone implements.

The exterior trimming and the shaping of the inside were done with stone adzes and scrapers. In those days they had no metal tools to use in drilling or burning holes and the peg method of fixing the skin was a much later invention. The earlier method was to tie a wet thong transversely round the top end of the drum. In the drying process the hide was squeezed into a specially prepared groove.

Subsequently the *luganda* method became more popular. Skins were placed at either end and sewn together with thongs. In this process bone needles and bone awls were used. Often a pebble was inserted, to convert the drum into some outsize rattle, and also as a sign of respect to the Water Spirit, *Ntambi*, a half-man half-fish god who is also the Guardian of Happiness and the Guardian of the Feast. The tribal people used to believe that human ears could hear the drum; the spirits could only hear the rattle.

The Big Drums of any tribe were its most valuable property and great care was taken to prevent them from falling into enemy hands. A tribe whose drums were stolen lost all faith in itself and became completely demoralised. This is why conquerings kings like *Lewanika* the Great, *Muwanga* the Cruel of the Luganda, and many other thugs, used to take away the drums of the tribes they had conquered, to break their spirit and making them forever subservient.

If one tribe could capture the sacred drums and idols from another tribe, it immediately had that tribe at its mercy and could dictate terms with insolent impunity. Once the famous thief *Njambi* – the same rascal who in later years tangled with David Livingstone – forced the Ambo tribe to part with all its cattle to buy back its Big Drums which he had stolen.

African drums normally have patterns carved into them and these dictate the specific role of each drum. Certain drums are for use only at weddings, others for Rain Dances and so forth. Some of these patterns, especially on the older drums, are famous proverbs and prayers, at other times they are snatches from the history of the tribe. There are drums known as the Victory Drums, on whose surface a record was inscribed of every battle the tribe had won or lost. A Drum-most-Royal has the genealogy of all the chiefs of the tribe engraved into it, with their name symbols. Some patterns portray curses on all foreigners touching the drum, and the drums that spell the Highest Curse on anybody touching it, Black or White, are the 'Yo-Sho' Big Royal Drums of the Litunga of the Barotse.

Ordinary drums generally carry no adornments, inscriptions or motifs. A witchdoctor's battle drum is normally engraved with the symbol of the River of Time, or Eternity. This is the oldest symbol of Africa and it symbolises the repetitive continuity of time and the immortality of the soul. I have pointed out before that the Bantu believe that time is like a river which flows into its own source, and that if it were possible to sail this river with more than just one's imagination, one could proceed downstream into the future and upstream into the past. This utterly nonsensical belief has its origin in the Baluba empire, and these people clung so tenaciously to this idea that they thought it was physically possible to take a journey into the past, up this mythical river, and pay their ancestors a visit – in flesh and blood. Here is one of the many songs based on this theme:

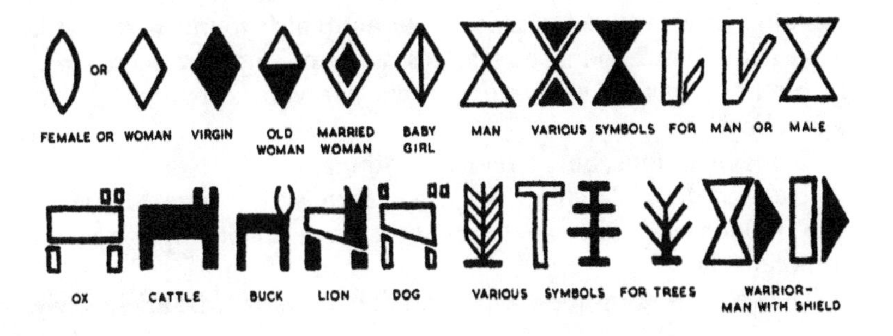

My soul is sick of these modern years
With their tyranny and insensate hate,
And war machines that fill the heart with fears
For the whole world's sake and Mankind's fate.
Let us launch our canoe on the River Time;
I dare you to sail that mighty stream with me,
Let us go to that primitive but less evil time
Where I and my soul have always longed to be.

Let us sail to those years when the tools of war
Were the brave spear and the ox-hide shield;
Not roaring guns that slay us from afar—
Which foul weapons, let only the cowards wield;

Let us sail to those years when *Gandaya* roamed—
A tusked mammoth – through Africa's wilds;
Dealt death to men, who puny *impis* formed
To stay his charge with unavailing shields.

Let us sail to that year when *Lu-Mukanda* brave,
Against foul *Lufiri*, waged earth-shaking war
And freed from bonds so many a cowering slave
While slaying the Iti – dread tyrants of yore.

Be you a witness, through *Mukanda's* eyes,
Of rites most evil in Zima-Mbje's halls—
Share you his loves, and heave his many sighs,
Or shout with rapture as his war drum calls.

Witness the quarrels that split the tribe in twain—
Into the Zulu and the Qwabe clan—
Then wind your way through bush-wet-with-rain
Towards your kraal – a much wiser man.

The grim-faced grizzled old warrior had been silent for quite some time now, staring coldly into the dim distance yonder – a fierce beast-of-battle whom a war axe had deprived of the power of walking. The crippled warrior – honourably wounded in battle – turned to the young boy at his side and there was cold pity in his hard eyes as he asked gruffly: 'Are you keeping your eyes open, boy?'.

'I am, Great One, but as yet I see nothing.'

'Neither do I. To think we have been sitting here for nearly two moons and still we have not seen a single night-howling impotent thing.'

The boy was silent for a while and then eventually he asked shyly:

'But . . . but what are we supposed to be waiting for, respected one?'

The warrior howled with laughter: 'By the worm-crawling belly of a Night-Howler, what a foolish question is this that you ask me, boy?'

'But . . . I don't know what we are waiting here for, Great One, and I only wish to know.'

'I did not know that you were not told. Then I must tell you now: you and I, boy, are waiting for old Bony-Spine to come and get us.'

'Old Bony-Spine!' The word sent a fear coursing through the body of the boy and his eyes opened very wide. Death! So he and his companion were waiting for Death. But how? He had only been told that he must look for certain movements and draw the old warrior's attention to it. His curiosity overcame his shyness and he asked the warrior to explain. The foul-mouthed warrior explained; yes, they were manning a lookout post, but they were looking out for the Feared Ones – the deadly long-bearded foreigners who were swarming through the land like vile locusts, raiding villages and kidnapping hundreds of men and women, taking them to We-know-not-where. The boy listened with wide-eyed wonder, his heart beating fast. Then he asked the one question to which he hoped to get an answer:

'But what is going to kill us? We can play the drum from here and warn the people and then we can run away . . .'

'Hau!' snarled the warrior. 'You liverless spawn of a drowned vulture! Our task is not only to signal to the village, but to attract the attention of the Feared Ones to this hill to give the villagers a chance to get away and scatter to places of hiding and safety. What do you think these baskets full of arrows are here for? To play at Bushmen?'

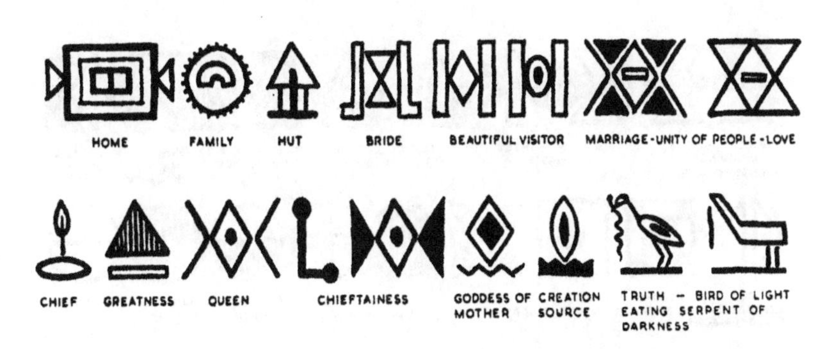

'I . . . I want to go back home. I do not want to die . . . I want to go to my mother.'

'Listen boy, do you know what you are? You are a green-bellied mud-eating bastard born by a precocious girl out of wedlock. And people of your sort are a disgrace to their own families and to the whole tribe. Your father has thrown you away; he has sent you out here to die with me when the splay-footed night-howling Feared Ones come. You and I have the honour to die so that the whole cow-stealing tribe and that fat-bellied sot of a chief may live. Exciting eh?'

'But I could not help being born out of . . . wedlock. It was not my fault. . .'

'The law says all bastards must be killed or got rid of in one way or another. They are given a chance to grow until they can be made use of in a dangerous way, so that more honourable people do not have to risk their lives. That is the law of your ancestors, boy.'

'I am going home . . .'

'You dare not! It is my duty to put an arrow through your backside if you so much as try. There is only this one way down the hill, and I have been made to swear an oath that I shall stop you from using it, and so have those who will come up and watch while we sleep tonight.'

The boy looked down at the warrior with deep loathing and disgust. Then he left the side of the crippled old man and went and sat on a rock and wept. He wept for a long time while the warrior sat quietly in a hollow between two big boulders, chewing a lump of dried meat calmly and without apparent concern. The sun was just about to set when the boy looked up and stared with tear-dimmed eyes into the distance. Something yellowish and very bright flashed like a lost star in the dark green of the forest to the east. The boy

looked again but did not see it for some time. Then, suddenly, it came again – a brief flash of polished bronze in the distant forest, caught by the afternoon sun.

'Great One,' cried the boy to the warrior, 'there is something strange and bright in the forest far away. I have seen it twice. Look!'

Both of them saw the flash this time and the warrior swore an incredibly vile oath. He grabbed his crutch and limped towards the great drum lying near the ugly hut which had been their shelter for nearly two moons. He pulled, released, pulled and released the stick tied to the skin from the inside. With every release the drum boomed and keen ears in the village, embraced by forest, picked up the dread signal. Huge drums were rolled out and the signal was relayed from village to village in no time at all.

Shrieking mothers strapped their babies to their backs, picked up what food there was and followed their husbands to caves and shelters, there to hide in safety until the hated Arabi had gone. The fat chief, puffing and huffing like a hippopotamus in the act of mating, was carried by his wives on a litter to a huge secret cave in which there was an underground spring of fresh water. He did not emerge from the luxurious hiding place until a full moon later. He even took three cows with him, to ensure that his fat belly would always be full of sour milk.

There was one woman who did not follow the rest of the tribe into hiding – one woman whose soul was full of love, such as only a mother can feel for her young. It is a love that defies and sets at nought the laws of mortal men. This mother did not forget that it was her son up there on the hill from which the first signal had come. But she had made up her mind that he would not die alone.

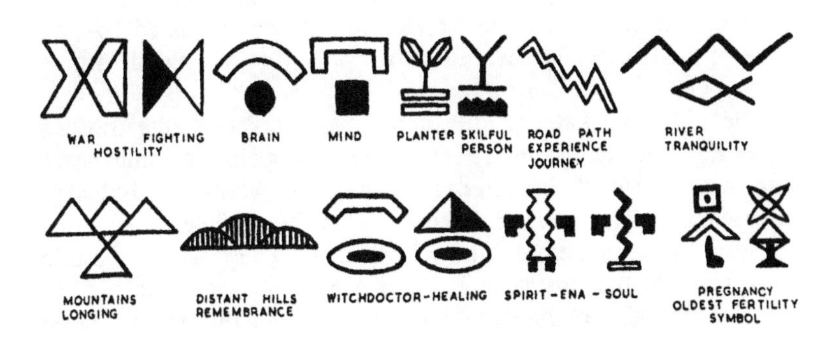

The warrior kept on signalling the 'footless man's drum' until he had the satisfaction of hearing drums in every village relaying the signal. Only then did he stop. He picked up one of the bows and a basket full of arrows and waited. He stared with cold eyes towards the east.

The hated Arabi had more cunning than jackals in summer, but they never thought to correct the one mistake they persisted in making. They wore helmets of brightly polished steel and iron shields with bosses of silver or bronze. The surfaces of these reflected the rays of the sun in all directions.

The warrior knew that a party of slave-raiding Arabi was approaching and he knew, too, that he was looking upon this world for the last time. But he was not concerned. He had lived with death for too long and he was not at all concerned about dying now. It would be a death of his own choosing and it was bound to be a glorious one which would live in the minds of men. He was fiercely resolved to take with him to the land of the dead as many of the enemy as he possibly could.

The Arabi burst into view sooner than the warrior had expected. They were fierce men with nightmare robes and shining helmets surrounded by heavy turbans of coloured cloth. They were led by a huge man with a night-black beard and a bright brass shield. He was mounted on an animal the likes of which the warrior had never seen before. He looked like a mighty wizard from some obscure legend.

All the Arabi carried lances and at each man's side hung a curved sword in an ornate scabbard. Some of the men even had daggers stuck in broad sashes they wore round their waists. These were nightmare beasts resembling men, but as cruel as the Mother of Demons herself – alien creatures devoid of all human pity and more savage than rabid jackals. Behind the Arabi there came a full company of one of the traitor Bantu tribes which had joined with the slave-raiders in hunting down their own fellow Black people. In their blue-dyed plumes the warrior recognised the hated Ba-Yeke tribe of the Congo. To save their own skins they had sided with the Feared Ones.

The old man watched, his fierce eyes narrowed like those of an eagle spotting its prey. He watched as the band came nearer and nearer. Slowly he lifted his bow, and waves of excitement coursed through his muscular body when he saw the leader pause to scan the area before him. The warrior knew with a flash of pure joy that the unsuspecting alien was within range of his bow and he was a man renowned for his marksmanship. He picked up the longest of his arrows and, rising slowly to his knees, he drew the bow until the feathers of the arrow tickled his right ear.

The arrow hit the alien leader in the right eye and his hands flew up to his face as he tumbled off the strange beast with a crash. The beast bolted wildly for the safety of the forest, to be eaten by lions that same night.

With a howl of dismay and rage the evil ones came in a fierce rush up the hill. The boy saw the warrior send arrow after arrow at the oncoming enemy; he saw a number of the evil ones fall and die among the boulders strewn over the slope of the hill; he saw many more go down wounded and screaming and, obeying some command of his ancestors which his ears had not heard but which his soul had received, he took his own bow and sent arrows humming at the enemy. He observed with cold elation that men fell with his arrows in their chests and bellies, and he heard the warrior shouting obscene congratulations to him at every man he killed.

The battle lasted but a few moments, but to the boy it felt like years. The Feared Ones approached slowly, not sure of the number of archers hidden on the hill. The Ba-Yeke were shooting back now and arrows were raining round the boy and the warrior, while the rest were systematically surrounding the hill.

At length, two arrows struck the warrior in the head at the same time and he died with his bow held firmly in his hands. The boy realised he was left alone, abandoned by his parents to die on a hostile hill. For a moment the claws of panic closed round his heart, but hope returned and he proceeded to shoot with great accuracy again and yet again . . .

They closed in on him now. They hurled spears and javelins at

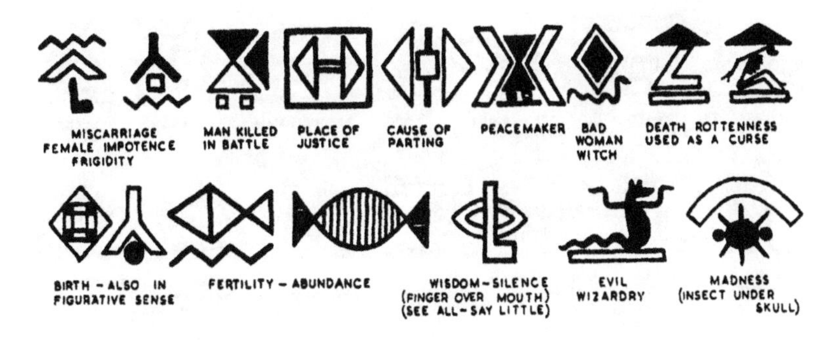

him and hacked at his head with their strange swords. But still he fought on, screaming in naked terror. Finally a sword severed both his thin boy's arms. He fell to the ground and was quickly surrounded by vicious enemies to whom mercy was as alien as they themselves were to the land. A Ba-Yeke assegai delivered the death thrust.

The mother had seen the battle from far away; she had tried to run through the forest to be by her child's side. But the distance had been too great. She had seen the aliens and their allies come down the hill and take the long journey back the way they had come. With their leader dead and the Bantu village alerted, the Feared Ones had realised the futility of advancing any further.

Night fell and the moon was high in the heavens. The bravest of the Bantu came out of hiding. They made their way to the scene of the brief battle and there they found the weeping mother kneeling by the side of her sixteen-year-old bastard son. As they gathered round her in silence, looking down also at the many men the warrior and the boy had slain, they all knew that these two had achieved what very few achieve – eternal fame and mention in the Annals of the Tribes.

THE SPIRIT OF NUMBERS

Any explorer with good, searching eyes will find many fascinating things in the land of the Zulus. But how many have passed and failed to notice peculiar heaps of stones at points where rivers can easily be forded? How many have noticed them and have never bothered to inquire about them?

When a Zulu crosses the river at such a place, he normally picks

up a stone, spits on it and adds it to the heap. The pile is known in Zulu as an *isivivane. Isi* means 'the', and *viva* means 'to marshal, to gather', as one would marshal warriors. It also means to organise people for any purpose whatsoever. To gather and organise warriors before an attack is described in Zulu as *uku viva impi.* The *ne* at the end of the word means 'thing of' or 'place of', roughly translated. Thus an *isivivane* means 'the place of organising (or disciplining) the people'.

The ancient Bantu kings, like *Malandela* and *Xhosa* and others, who led the mass tribal migrations from north of the Zambezi to southern Africa about eight hundred years ago, were not just leaders of hordes of savages. They were mighty leaders, fully aware of the fact that they ruled tribes of from half to a full million souls. Moreover, in the migrations southwards, they passed through areas torn apart by slave raiders and they came across numerous forlorn groups of people hiding in the mountains and in the trees. These groups joined them, and while some groups started off with five to ten thousand people, they reached their destinations ten times as strong. To move a population of this magnitude, with all their cattle and possessions, needs organisation and supreme leadership which men like *Malandela* displayed.

The journey to the south took approximately thirty years. There were frequent periods of rest – for whole seasons to permit the planting of corn. There were places where the tribes had to cross wide and deep rivers, infested by crocodiles. Many are the stories that have reached us across the gulf of time of whole groups of hundreds of people who became separated from the main body and joined up with other lost groups to form new tribes.

As a result of all these hazards every leader had to keep a strict census of the people who were his responsibility. Around the neck

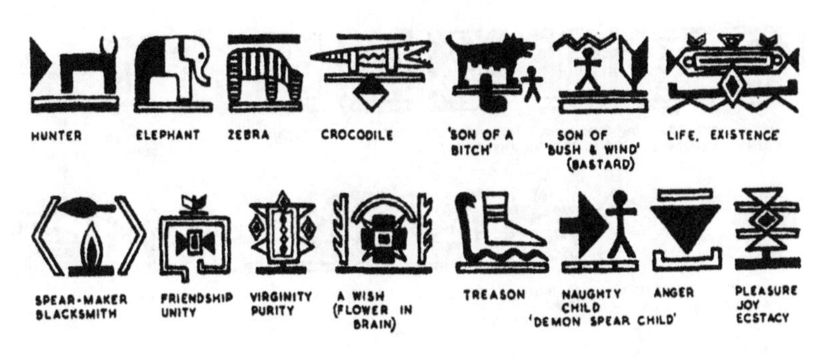

of each leader were strung long strings of ostrich eggshell beads, each bead representing an individual in his tribe. In those days the women were required to make such beads for the members of their own families and submit these to the *Induna* of Census, who in turn submitted these to the wives of the chief. The wives strung them into long necklaces, and the *Indunas* of the Census were continuously occupied at adding and subtracting from these necklaces whenever they learned of births or deaths in their sections of the tribe. Copper and clay beads were used to keep count of the cattle and goat stocks, and special wooden beads were used for a census of warriors.

Whenever a tribe had to cross through a bottleneck, such as a ford across a river, the opportunity was taken for a check. Each person crossing was required to pick up a stone and add it to a pile. After the whole tribe had passed through, the chief ordered his regiment of Elders to count all the stones in the pile and check the number against the necklaces.

The Bantu all along have been familiar with figures up to and beyond a million, and often indulged in simple arithmetic. But they have never felt the need to record numbers with symbols, and even today figures cannot be represented in Bantu writing other than by means of simple straightforward lines, scratches, strokes or incisions. And in spite of his strong philosophical inclination the African has never indulged in philosophical arithmetic. He has no feeling whatsoever for algebra, geometry and trigonometry.

In any Bantu language the different numbers have rather attractive names. The names may be differently pronounced in the various languages, but they all have the same meanings when translated into English. The example given below is Zulu–English.

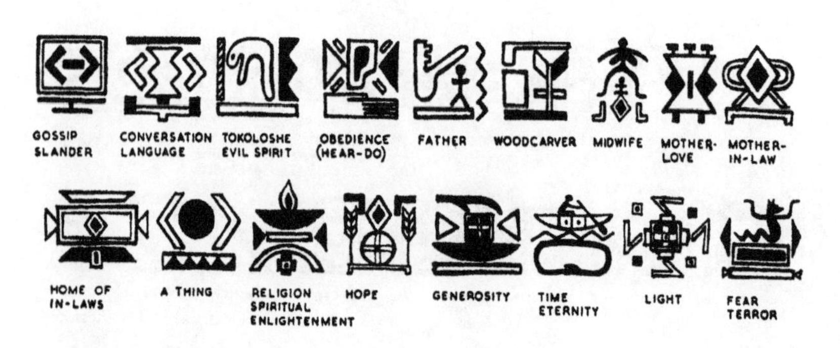

1. *Kunye* – 'It is one'.

The Bantu regard the number One as the holiest of all. It represents the combining of all created things – the Oneness or the Whole, which is God. It is an absolute number and it has no rival. It is also the symbol of freedom – thus the salute with only the thumb projecting from a closed fist.

2. *Kubili* – 'It is two'.

This is a very evil number – the symbol of imperfection. It requires two to produce offspring. It represents dissension and diversity of opinion, or disunity.

3. *Kutatu* – 'It is three'.

This is third in holiness to number One; it represents completeness, a number that cannot be split in two. Two wives can quarrel, but a third can settle the dispute. A man can quarrel with his wife but a 'third party', or a second wife, can intervene and restore order. Thus the Bantu's strong belief in polygamy. Three gives that 'casting vote' to ensure a decision or enforce peace.

4. *Kune* – 'It is perfection'.

More literally, this word means 'It is firmly together'. This number symbolises strong and harmonious unity by powerful people working together for a common cause. If one chief should send four sticks closely tied together to a neighbouring chief, the message portrayed would be: 'Let us unite'.

5. *Kuhlanu* – 'It is perfection ruined'.

This is another evil number; it symbolises the fallibility of Man. Man is as imperfect as the five fingers of his hand or the five toes on his foot – one is out of place, or of different shape.

6. *Isithupa* – 'It is the thumb'.

This number represents strength and it symbolises the six component parts that constitute the human being: the soul, the *Ena*, the body, the mind, the Living Force and the Adverse Force. The Living Force, or Life, is the Spirit of God, and is constantly opposed by the Spirit of Evil; the one generates Life, the other promotes Death.

7. *Isikombisa* – 'It is the pointed finger'.

This is the 'idiot number', or the number of failure. It symbolises the futility in Man's habit of persisting in doing or constructing things that are afterwards swept away by the River Time. It symbolises those who rise to fame only to fall so much harder.

8. *Isishiyagalombili* – 'It is bend two fingers'.

This number is associated with genetic weaknesses, frigidity, war and death in a vile form.

9. *Isishiyagalolunge* – 'It is bend one finger'.

Another holy number symbolising creation. The Bantu believed that the soul was connected with the brain through nine large veins.

Because of the nine months of pregnancy, this is regarded as the 'female's number'. If nine beads should feature in a woman's dream it is a sure sign of pregnancy. When she dreams of stringing nine red beads she will give birth to a boy, while white beads foreshadow a girl. Copper beads predict a miscarriage.

10. *Ishumi* – 'It is completion'.

Another holy number and closely related to One. It is believed that there are ten gateways to the Spirit Land and that God is tenfold in the nature of His Being. This number is, therefore, of deep religious significance.

11. *Ishumi Na Nye* – 'It is ten and one'.

A very evil number; the number of demons and all manner of evil. The ancient Bantu considered it as so evil that it was never mentioned aloud; when they had to indicate this number they spoke instead of 'the second ten'. A father often sent the eleventh child with its mother away from him, for the child to be reared elsewhere.

12. *Ishumi Na Mbili* – 'It is ten and two'.

A rather good number. It symbolises the growing plant and is therefore also a symbol of fertility.

13. *Ishumi Na Ntatu* – 'It is ten and three'.

A combination of completeness and perfection – second in holiness only to the number One. It symbolises perfect harmony between a husband and his wives or between a chief and his subjects, the kind of perfection that is materially experienced through sexual intercourse. A humorous legend tells of a Bapedi Queen who declared herself willing to marry a man only on condition that he undertook to please her thirteen times every night. She eventually found such a man – none other than the earthly Lost Immortal, *Lumukanda*, who met her demands so amply that she fled from the kraal and spent the rest of the night up a tree.

Pages could be written on each number, up over the million mark. A few of the bigger ones are referred to here:

20	*Amashumi A Mabili* – 'It is two tens'.
30	*Amashumi A Matatu* – 'It is three tens'.
100	*Ikulu* – 'It is the great'.
200	*Amakulu A Mabili* – 'It is two greats'.
1,000	*Inkulungwane.* – 'It is the great-great'.
100,000	*Izinkulungwane Ezili Kulu* – 'It is the great-great that is great'.
1,000,000	*Isigidi* – 'It is the great, heavily falling weight'.

The word *isigidi* merits some attention. In days of peace the tribes amused themselves with many kinds of sport – racing in canoes, wrestling and dancing. There was also a strange form of competition in which two teams would compete to see which could count up to a million in the shortest possible time. Two great skin bags were made, each by sewing two complete ox-hides together. These were suspended from trees and the two teams were required to collect handfuls of ten, twenty or a hundred small pebbles and drop them in their respective bags.

A bag containing a million pebbles, however small, can be very heavy indeed and when cut loose from the tree at the end of the competition it would plunge to the ground with a gritty, thudding sound – *Gi-di* it sounded to Bantu ears. Thus the word was originally onomatopaeic. But it acquired the meaning of 'a heavy falling weight'. Today a Zulu would describe the heavy stamping of the feet of an elephant or rhinoceros as *ukugidiza*, from the same root (*gidi*).

The Bantu, all along, have needed figures only for basic – never complex – purposes. The tribes had hardly any need for measuring weights. One article could be weighed against another by simple balancing. One of the few items the Bantu ever bothered to weigh was snuff, and the sketch below illustrates a simple weighing apparatus – a spoon-like structure with a carved hippopotamus handle. The lever will come to horizontal balance only when the correct amount of snuff is put in the hollow receiver. It did not take them long to discover, long before they could learn it from Indian traders, that if the hippopotamus could be hollowed out under the belly, they could get away with a short weight of snuff against the regular exchange.

The Zulus started the snuff trade and its popularity grew rapidly. For a long time the Zulus were the sole producers and they did a roaring trade with neighbouring tribes. In the fifteenth century snuff

HIPPOPOTAMUS SNUFF SCALE

was priced at five cows for a big horn full. Whenever a Zulu travelled through the lands of neighbouring tribes he was always suspected of carrying snuff and many a traveller's life was in danger. Such travellers hid their pouches of snuff between their buttocks under their loinskins and enjoyed the snuff only at midnight when there would be hardly any risk of attack.

The Bantu also had a basic need to express distances in terms of various units, but their lives never depended upon perfect accuracy. The first joint of a man's thumb was often used to denote very short lengths or breadths (one inch); a thumbnail is approximately half-an-inch. Medium distances were expressed in terms of paces (approximately yards), but the Bantu had little need for measuring distances greater than what could readily be paced; half-a-day's journey by foot often sufficed to indicate a specific distance.

There were times, however, when neighbouring tribes disputed the boundaries between them, and such disputes could only satisfactorily be settled after the areas concerned had been 'measured'. This was done in a most unusual way. The method was developed by a Lunda girl in the beginning of the First Lunda empire, and she was stabbed to death as a reward for her inventive spirit. This girl used to weave wickerwork doors for huts from leather strips a thumbnail broad. She discovered that if an ox-hide of average size was cut into one continuous strip, starting at the edge and working systematically inward to the centre, a very long strip of leather could be produced and that the difference between lengths cut from different hides was not substantial. To establish a unit that could reach across the longest distance, such a thong was cut from the wet skin of a large, freshly slaughtered bull. The thong had to be cut consistently a thumbnail wide and it had to be used while wet and the unit of length was the maximum stretch of the thong.

The thong was taken out into the field in a big clay bowl full of water and used on the principle of an ordinary tape measure. It

was preferably used on a rainy or overcast day to prevent its drying and shrinking. Thus a distance from the top of a rocky outcrop to a stream junction down in the valley could be expressed in terms of '25 bulls'. Areas were 'surveyed' thus and divided as fairly as possible between the neighbouring tribes.

MARCH OF THE HEALERS

The boy was excited; his heart beat very fast indeed. He had something of great importance to tell his father as soon as possible. Nobody else knew anything about it.

He had been running for a long time and his face was covered with sweat and dust. Beside him, almost as excited as he was, ran his dog which had set out with him earlier that morning to hunt hares. He sped into the kraal that was his home and saw his father sitting under the day shelter sharpening his cruel spears on a great whetstone. The boy threw himself on his knees and looked up in suppressed silence at his father, who laid down the spears and growled:

'*Uluba ini*? What is the matter, boy?'

'*Baba-a-ngwe*,' stammered the boy, 'I have seen the Blessing of the High Ones.'

The old man looked up sharply and his eyes bored into those of the child, who quickly averted his face and looked down.'

'What did you say?'

'I saw the Blessing of the High Ones, *Babangwe*.'

'Where?'

'In the forest beyond the stream.'

'Was there anyone else with you when you made this discovery?'

'No, *Babe*, I was alone.'

'We must go at once and tell the chief. It is the law! Come, boy.'

Great Chief *Umbomongo* the Ugly, was smiling. There was mirth in his heart and joy in his mighty stomach which he rubbed in savage anticipation. There was tension in the kraal and by sunset quite a number of people would be dead. By the gods, *Umbomongo* loved tension, and he loved the deadly calm that sets in before deeds of daring and violence are committed. Here was hate and suspense aplenty, and soon the full fury of four hate-filled hearts would be unleashed.

There were four of them – four of the most hated and most feared people in the land – and by sunset only one of them would be alive. *Umbomongo* would be rid of three of the most powerful challengers to power in the whole land of his tribe. The ugly chief smiled an oily smile of anticipation. This was indeed a Day of Days – a day that would be long remembered, and as he watched the people sitting in silence before him his eyes, bogged in fat, narrowed slightly in cold contempt. He snapped his fingers at the young servant beside him and in silent response the boy lifted the cover off a great claypot full of beer. The boy took a long drink from the pot before placing it against the chief's lips. Yes, *Umbomongo* drank deep; he drained the acid beer to the dregs and cursed the boy because it was not enough. He bellowed for the pot to be refilled. He drank again and wiped his flabby mouth with the back of his hand. Then he spoke:

'Yes, respected ones, a man and his son came this morning and told me that they had seen a place where the Blessing of the Gods has come up from under the earth. You know that our ancestors have told us that the Blessing became extinct two generations ago in this land, and by the mercy of the Highest of the Most High, the Blessing has returned again.

'You are fully aware of the fact that the one among you who gets to the Place of the Blessing and controls it, will become the most powerful medicine man in the land; he will be able to save many lives and so gain great power, wealth and fame. It is the law that you must now race each other to the Place of the Blessing and in the course of this race you can do whatever you like in your endeavours to kill one another. There must be only one survivor who can own the Blessing. In my capacity as chief of this tribe, I now declare this race open and started.'

There were four of them – four of the most powerful witchdoctors and wise-women in the land, and they were all bitter rivals and hated enemies. Each of these Wise Ones came from one of the four tribes that *Umbomongo* ruled with malevolence and only too frequently with naked tyranny. Not one of the four but was fired with ambition to become his successor – the most powerful in the land.

There was old *Zungezu* – as cunning as a midnight jackal. There was *Ngoso* – more ruthless than a rabid hyaena. There was the fierce old crone *Manjanja*, with only one tooth left in her mouth. Lastly there was the young wise woman *Luila* – the deadliest and the most ambitious of the whole cursed lot, the one whom *Umbomongo* most wished to die. It was common knowledge that *Luila* not only wanted to become the most powerful medicine woman in the tribes; she wanted to be their chieftainess as well.

Umbomongo was extremely afraid of this tall, beautiful and ruthless girl, and his nights were often haunted by dreams of her. Perhaps she might be the first to get killed . . .

Each of the four Wise Ones went to collect his or her weapons and whatever he or she felt would come in useful. A medicine man or woman must tolerate no rivals and this was a good opportunity for each to try getting rid of unwanted rivals.

The chief smiled and ordered another pot of beer as he saw the Wise Ones enter the distant forest by separate ways. He laughed harshly at the thought that only one of them would come back alive. One could deal with one witchdoctor in a land, but four . . .

In the forest the old witchdoctor *Zungezu* felt the thrilling excitement of the hunt. He was not hunting animals today; he was hunting the most dangerous game of all – Man. He moved with instinctive care, using every bit of cover the forest so freely gave. His eyes wreathed in wrinkles, searched everywhere and all his senses were vibrant and alive. Then he spotted the old crone *Manjanja* hiding behind a bush, looking in another direction and waiting for somebody to come along. He was about fifteen paces away from the old woman when she somehow sensed his presence and, leaping to her ancient feet, sent four arrows in quick succession at him before vanishing into the depths of the forest. Luckily for *Zungezu* he was not hit directly. However, one of the arrows had grazed his neck and blood was begining to ooze from the cut.

Zungezu knew the old woman would be stalking him now, and he was afraid. It was nevertheless the fear of an experienced hunter stalking a wounded beast. He was making his way deeper and deeper into the forest and all of a sudden he found himself on the edge of a treeless glade and dived immediately behind a bush as he caught sight of stealthy movements on the other side of the glade in the thick undergrowth. His nerves tingled as he watched the bush, and again he saw something move. Something was hiding there, awaiting his coming and with a cruel laugh he sent a spear hissing across the glade towards the bush. But before he could dive into cover again an arrow thudded into his chest and he fell backwards with a loud shriek. As he lay there dying, he heard footsteps approach and a tall female form stood over him. It was *Luila* and she smiled coldly.

She said to the dying man: 'You fell victim to a woman's simple trick, Oh *Zungezu*; I have long known that you are nothing but a fool. What you saw moving behind that bush was a shrub to which I had tied a long thong. I was standing way over there at that big tree while I pulled the thong to divert your attention.'

'Cunning bitch!' hissed the dying man.

'Yes, a bitch with very sharp teeth. You see in me a woman who will not only possess the Blessing of the Gods, but who will also overthrow *Umbomongo* and rule the four tribes. Farewell, poor fool, may the worms find your flesh more pleasing than my eyes find your face.'

A few moments later *Luila* nearly came to the end of her ambitious life as *Manjanja* suddenly started shooting arrows at her from behind a bush. The younger woman dived into cover and there began a grim game of hide-and-seek in which the old woman was the aggressor and the ruthless seeker. She was still hunting her youthful enemy when a noose tightened around her ankle. Most unceremoniously she was first hurled to the ground and then hoisted into midair by one foot. As she hung there upside down, *Luila* stepped out of the bush and levelled the arrow in her bow at her.

'Prepare to meet your ancestors, Oh grave-cheating old bag of bones.'

The bow twanged and the beautiful *Luila* stalked away, leaving her lifeless enemy dangling by one foot from the branch of a tree. One more enemy remained and she still had to watch her step. *Ngoso* was nowhere in sight and this simple fact worried *Luila* as she crossed a grassy plain towards another stretch of thick forest.

Eventually she came to a wide stream beyond which lay the Place of the Blessing, and made haste to cross it, plunging waist deep into the water. She was still halfway when she saw the head of a crocodile gliding fast in her direction. It was too late to escape from the terrible trap into which she had landed herself.

The crocodile was only the skin of a crocodile, worn by *Ngoso*, like the Bangwena water assassins of the land of Nyasa. She suddenly realised this and began to fight furiously for her life as her remorseless enemy tried to drag her under water and drown her. A fierce struggle between man and woman took place in the water and slowly the girl felt her strength ebbing; she knew that death was close. Slowly, deliberately, *Ngoso* forced the woman's head under water, at the same time keeping a tight hold on her throat.

Suddenly *Luila's* arms flew up and encircled the crocodile man's neck. Her body went limp. *Ngoso* was so surprised that he loosened his grip. *Luila* drew a gasping breath and, after a moment or two, she said: 'Stop it, *Ngoso*, take your hands off me. Quickly – you sacrilegious dog!'

'Why . . .' began *Ngoso*, still dazed at the symbolic gesture of the girl – throwing her arms around his neck and then going limp.

'How many children did your father have before the Dark Raiders attacked your home and killed nearly all your family?' demanded the girl suddenly.

'You know that? How?'

'Because, Oh stupid, I am your last surviving sister. You and I were found by people from different villages in the ruins of our home and we were brought up in different tribes. I have always known that you were my brother although you did not know who I was. Now that you know this, what are we going to do?'

Ngoso was silent for a long time. He stared into the distance, his mind too numb to think and his soul afire with conflicting emotions. There they stood, brother and sister, facing a fantastic decision. At last *Ngoso* said: 'I did not know you were my sister, and this knowledge now makes the problem worse. Look, the law says that only one of us must reach the Blessing alive, and if one of us must die, let it be me. You will just have to kill me; you must not mind spilling my blood.'

'You are perfectly stupid, Oh *Ngoso*. It is I who must die, not you, because on you lies the duty of carrying the name of our father on to posterity. But still, the law says a brother and a sister must not shed one another's blood. What do we do?'

'Let us go and have a look at the Blessing of the Gods. There is still time to decide – and there are such things as accidents.'

They came to the Blessing and their eyes were pleased with what they saw. They knew that with the aid of such a Blessing a witchdoctor could save the lives of many people – many warriors with cruel wounds and *panga* slashes. The Blessing was the most wonderful gift that the Gods ever gave Man. But which of the two – *Luila* or *Ngoso* – was going to possess it? They were both adamant that neither could live with the guilt of having killed the other.

Finally they solved the problem: each would stab the other at the same time, thus eliminating any guilt or remorse. But as they approached one another with sharp knives levelled *Ngoso* saw something out of the corner of one eye. A shrub moved, a head appeared – a bow. And as the arrow flew straight at *Luila*, her brother lunged forward and pushed her out of the way. The arrow that was intended for the woman caught *Ngoso* full in the temple and he fell dead.

Shocked by the sudden happening, *Luila* nevertheless struggled to her feet. The sight she saw froze her for a few moments. The chief of the four tribes, *Umbomongo* the Ugly, was charging down at her, his spear raised. He had come with his attendants to ensure that it would not be *Luila* who returned alive.

The battle spear of the Lunda came humming through the air, thrown far too soon by the enraged chief. The girl had time to fling herself to one side and the spear thudded into a tree. *Luila* shot up, wrenched it from the tree and hurled it with deadly accuracy at *Umbomongo* as he approached with upraised battle axe. The spear caught the king just above the belly and the force drove it right through.

The chief's retinue hailed *Luila* as their queen, and it took some time before the surprised woman remembered the law that says: 'He who kills a chief with the chief's own weapons is automatically the new chief of that tribe.'

Some moons later, *Luila*, confirmed chieftainess of four tribes, stood looking down at the Blessing of the Gods, and she wondered at the strange workings of Fate – how three witchdoctors and a mighty chief could lose their lives over so paltry a thing as a colony of ants.

The Bantu had to learn many things the hard way, and the hardest thing they learnt was how to treat an open wound in the tropics of Africa. At first whatever they tried failed. The wound would fester and sooner or later the patient would die. Even small gaping wounds spelt a write-off of the patient; large *mpanga* slashes were regarded as fatal at the outset and warriors thus wounded were given a mercy death. Many battle axes were furnished with special 'dispatchers' for this purpose.

The Bantu realised that an open wound could heal successfully only if it could be kept closed. They tried copper clips and even thorns. But they never dared to sew up the wound with gut, even using bone needles, because a particular Bantu law dictates that no human being must ever be sewn like a skin blanket. This is a vile sacrilege and punishable with death. A curse on the childish laws and taboos of my race!

The problem did not lie with poor sterilisation. The Bantu had long known that a red-hot knife was a properly sterilised instrument, and they had learnt to use water that had been boiling for a long time. And however disgusting it may sound, the bile from a freshly slaughtered ox, or the urine from an ox or a human being, had very effective antiseptic qualities. Infection was introduced by the articles used in holding the wound closed.

The solution was found in a strange way, and this is the story that has come to us across the ages. A young boy complained that he could not pass water in the normal way. He was taken to a witchdoctor who examined his penis and from what he saw and gathered through interrogation he learnt that the boy had raided a beehive and thoroughly enjoyed the honey. Subsequently, his hands still sticky with honey, he held his member and transferred some of this sweetness to it. It was while he dozed a little later that some marauding warrior ants became attracted to the sweetness and the boy became the victim of attack. Needless to say, his sleep was cruelly interrupted and he tried to repair the damage by pulling the ants off with his hands. Although suffering from intense pain, he kept quiet over this shameful incident until he discovered that he had difficulty in passing water. The witchdoctor found that the boy had not removed the ants quite successfully; he had merely pulled their bodies off their heads, and the heads were still there, each with a good mouthful of skin.

This is now how witchdoctors treat open wounds and cuts throughout Africa. After the wound has been thoroughly cleaned with warm water, and urine if necessary, and every speck of dust and the odd hairs have been scraped out with a feather, the wound is held closed and big warrior ants are invited, by a little squeeze between thumb and forefinger, to take a neat bite, with a mandible either side of the wound. As soon as the ant has taken a firm bite, the body is severed from the head and *rigor mortis* ensures that the head will stay put until the wound has healed. Any number of such ant-clips can be used, depending on the length of the cut. And it would appear that the head of the ant has itself some antiseptic properties.

Even today, young Bantu herdboys are taught this kind of first aid. Herdboys are often involved in fights, friendly or otherwise, when their cattle trespass. Often a herdboy will get himself badly slashed. The others will then drag him to the nearest stream and wash the wound. They will light a fire and boil the water if necessary. They will clean the wound with a feather if one is available. They will even stitch it if there is a colony of warrior ants in the vicinity. And for a narcotic there is little to beat the old faithful *dagga.*

From first aid to midwifery. The Wise Ones of our tribes say that the human race is such a troublesome and quarrelsome nuisance on this earth because people are born upside down. If Man were born right side up he would have his feet more firmly planted on the ground and he would have less rubbish in his head. And his head is full of rubbish – foolish notions, desires and motives that bring a trail of sadness, death and disaster.

How devoted can some people be in assisting to bring more and more unfortunate creatures into this mad world? Among the older Bantu women one would still find today that devoted midwife of whom there were many more not so long ago – those women who voluntarily allowed their thumbs to be amputated by witchdoctors so as to assist more effectively in the delivery of babies. My father was brought into this world in 1898 by such a midwife. Hands like this brought into the world many a thief and many a tyrant, not least of which was the monster *Shaka.*

These dedicated women were chosen while still young girls of about sixteen. They had to pass through long and severe training, often assisting with births from the time they were recruited. They went through a training not much inferior to that given to modern nurses.

I must confess that I am now overstepping the line more seriously than I have done anywhere else in this book. No man, be he chief or witchdoctor, must ever describe anything related to the birth of a baby – this is one of the strictest Bantu taboos. By Bantu law I deserve to die for what I have already disclosed. The whole thing goes against my conscience and training and is in conflict with the dreadful oaths I took.

I am deliberately breaking a law that is as old as my race (as I have done to a lesser extent elsewhere in this book). I do this *not* because I wish to expose the Bantu to the scorn and ridicule of the so-called 'civilised' world; I do it because I sincerely hope that good might come from it. I may be right, I may be wrong, but this much I do know – the culture of my people must not be allowed to die. If it is threatened with destruction I must record it on paper. Then future generations will at least know that once Africa had a fascinating culture of its own.

AWAKE, MY AFRICA!

I could have done much better if I had written this book in my own language, but while I felt myself forced to use a foreign language, my own Bantu people are to blame. Few are interested in books of any description. Our authors who have tried their hands at writing in their own language have only produced immature books. At present the Bantu are much in the same boat as the ancient Britons were at the time of the Roman Empire. At that time those who were anxious to preserve for posterity the legends, folklore and culture of pre-Roman Britain had to write in Latin, the language of the conquerers.

One day our descendants will want to know something about their own native heritage in Africa. They will want to bring about a Bantu Renaissance. It has happened to many races, this inevitable self-discovery, and it shall happen to you too, Oh my fellow Africans, and much sooner than you think. What is there for the modern African to look back upon? If the French Revolution, the Industrial Revolution, the Russian Revolution and the American War of Independence mean absolutely nothing to the African, as far as his heritage is concerned, what else is there that will mean anything to him? Can he find such things in a library?

I beg others to follow my example instead of complaining about the oaths that I am breaking. Today my poor troubled Africa is torn apart by the vile selfish interests of foreign powers and she is left to find peace within her own borders. We must first find an amalgam on which to base this peace, and this amalgam must be a suitable mixture of all that is good in African Native Culture, with whatever is good in any of the foreign cultures.

No race can successfully adapt itself to another's way of life unless a long transitional period is granted, in which the bad things of the one culture are gradually diluted and systematically replaced by small doses of the best from the other culture. No sensible person accepts that the methods suitable in governing Britons are automatically and immediately suitable in ruling Zulus. Methods evolved for keeping Texans under control are useless in the case of the Katangese or the Balubas. No White man from Stockholm would consider wearing a chafing loinskin and settling among the Nkasas of Umbumbulu. No Frenchman would abandon his food and his *Folies Bergères* and join me as a blood brother on his haunches and scooping up *putu* and sour milk with his hands. So why are we expected to abandon our way of life – our culture and traditions – and suddenly adopt others which are extremely strange to us?

All foreigners must please leave my Africa undefiled by their ideals, falsehoods and hypocrisies.

Doubtless there will be those among my own people who will say that I am a traitor for daring to disclose secrets about Africa which our greatest chiefs and wise men have seen fit to keep hidden over the centuries.

To such people I humbly beg to say: Respected Ones, I am a true son of this land. In me flows the blood of two of the most ancient races of Africa – and also of mankind – the Bantu and the Bushmen.* Behind me is a long line of witchdoctors stretching far back into the mists of time, and I would be the very last to bare the sacred body of Africa to the scorn and ridicule of this robot-like world. I love Africa too much to stoop to make her the target of the world's derision.

But I do not wish to see foreigners turning my fatherland into a soulless carbon copy of their own countries.

Oh! my indolent and gullible Africa – the superior aliens glibly talk of bringing the 'light of civilisation' to your shores. And yet the only civilisation they can bring is one infected with physical, moral and spiritual decay. The 'light' they hold forth is the violent flare of the hydrogen bomb.

There is much talk of raising your living standards. But the end of this is to turn Africa into a vast *ndali* market for the mass rubbish that is manufactured. You are given more so that they can take more from you.

---

* *My great-grandfather was a Bushman medicine man, and my surname* Mutwa, *is the Zulu word for Bushman.*

Must you allow yourselves to be turned into *ka-mau ma itori*† for the schemes of the Strange Ones, or a ball they kick about on the football field of international intrigue?

The 'colonisers' have not yet learnt – or they do not wish to learn – that one cannot expect people to be loyal to something alien to their customary ways and which they do not understand. The present-day spear-carrying and cow-stealing Masai do not know what a Prime Minister is; they much prefer to extend their loyalty and devotion to their own shield-carrying, lion-hunting and even Wakambi-killing chief for he rules them in accordance with laws and customs they understand.

How can one expect a tribal-scarred Lukonde woodcarver to be loyal to a Parliament based on the British model? Could one expect an officer of the Guards to be loyal to his Battle *Induna* immediately after being forcefully transferred to an *impi* of Baluba warriors?

What would be wrong with having a council of tribal chiefs governing the Congo? What would be wrong with having a high chief ruling Kenya? A chief, crowned according to the strict laws of our forefathers, would command our loyalty and respect much more than an American-educated president without aristocratic background.

It is my firm belief that the reason the Strange Ones have repeatedly made ridiculous mistakes in Africa is that the Black man has consistently been too scared, too suspicious or even too reserved, to explain himself clearly. I am convinced that the only way to prevent Africa from falling into the claws of either Russia or America is to tell the world everything about us – who and what we are; what our likes and dislikes are; what we believe in and what we hope for. The only thing that can save us is to tell the foreigners openly that we do not wish to have their alien creeds, dogmas, beliefs and philosophies rammed down our throats. The sons of Africa must let the world know that we can well do without civilisation if this means that we have to throw our own culture, beliefs and way of life overboard. Why must we be turned into soulless zombies like the two hundred million human 'spare-parts' that lived beyond the Iron Curtain?

There is no longer any need for Africa to hide herself like a shy doe in the thicket of tribal oath and taboo; this secretiveness has cost her the lives of millions of her sons and daughters. Sons and daughters of my fatherland, stop playing at being carbon-copy Communists

† *'Pieces' in an African game, comparable with 'pawns' in a game of chess.*

or pre-fabricated Americans. Stop holding childish congresses and passing foolish and useless resolutions.

Rather use your newly won *uhuru* to lift your subjects from the gutter of starvation. Appoint scientists to do research into your nation's past. Rather than playing at soldiers, concentrate your energies on trying to buy back the thousands of antiques the foreigners have stolen from your countries and which are now housed in museums all over the world. Nourish, and save for posterity, the store of knowledge your forefathers have left you. The challenge to every Bantu is to bring about a glittering Renaissance of the cultures and the arts of Africa. Put your histories down on paper. There is so much that you can do that will be of supreme value to your own people and the future generations.

A solitary man in a continent of two hundred million souls can easily be struck down and silenced. I am alone, and one solitary man can easily be discredited and laughed at by the aliens. Men and women must stand side by side in this. Africa! I am not your betrayer; what I am revealing here I reveal for your sake.

But there is so much more that many others can reveal. Let your witchdoctors, too, reveal how their ancestors, thousands of years ago, performed operations on human heads, removing tumours with stone instruments. Let them confirm the truth of my assertion that our people performed Caesarian operations and grafted bone in the later Stone Age. Let one of the witchdoctors tell the full story of the great wizard *Nkume* of the Baganda who, although he was killed in the effort, flew off a precipice in the eighteenth century, in a craft built of cane and snake-skins.

You must bring out the many things hidden in your villages – things that whisper of Africa's not-yet-forgotten past. Bring these things out and disprove statements such as those made in letters written to newspapers, like this: '. . . the White man is superior to the Black, because apart from a few crude drawings in crude caves, nothing cultural, scientific and social has ever been achieved by a Black . . .' (from E Morris to the 'Sunday Times', Johannesburg, August, 1962).

When a Bantu is falsely accused, he is, by the laws of his people, bound to deliver proof of his innocence.

Do you now see my motive for writing this book? Oh my Africa, do you see the reason why I broke my oath? I am not selling you out to the strangers; I am pleading your innocence in an African 'Place of Justice'.

Ngilizwile ilizwi lase Zinkanyezini—
Likuluma na mi ngilele

Likuluma iqiniso la maqiniso—
Liti; 'Vuka, ngane yo Mfazi!

'Akusona isikati sokulala lesi—
Akusona nesokuhonqa—
Eso kuveza iqiniso o Bala!
Akusona isikati soku coba izintwala—
Eso kubeka iginiso o Bala!

'Ima pezu kwentaba enkulu i Nyangani—
Uxoxe indaba ye Zwe—
Ima pezu kwenxiwa lase Kamina—
Uxoxe ngomlando we Zwe.

'Ima pezu kwenxiwa lase Zima-Mbje
La kwakubusa u Munumutaba
Ume pezu kwezala ezingwaduleni
Ze Kalahari ya Batwa
La kwakubusa um Iti ne Lawu!

'Kade kwakufihlwa kutukutukuswa—
Kade kwaku nye-nye-nye-nye-zwa—
Kufihlelwa izizwe ezinedelelayo—
Malivezwe iqiniso o Bala!

'Masisuswe isibane esikanyisayo—
Masikishwe emgodini omnyama—
Masikishwe la si kanya sodwana—
Sikishwe sibekwe e Tala!'
Sikishwe sibekwe e Tala!

Yes, '*Sikishwe sibekwe e Tala*' – this now is the only thing you and I can, and must, do. Bring out the bowl lamp from the hole where it burns in loneliness, and put it right on the *tala* clay mound where the sour milk calabashes rest in the far corner of the hut. Yes, '*Asikishwe sibekwe e Tala*' – for what is the use of having a lamp lit and hidden in a hole in the ground?

GLOSSARY

(COMPILED FOR THIS EDITION)

Note: Words that are found in the dictionary, and those that are explained in the immediate context and then not used again in the book – names of trees, birds, etc. – are not included in this glossary.

Bantu – black people of Africa (see page 557)
Basutu – citizens of Lesotho, previously known as Basutoland (singular: 'Musutu'; language: 'Sisutu')
dagga – marijuana. Also called 'nsangu' (page 274). The 'gg' is pronounced as a guttural 'g'
Ena – one's 'self' (see page 568)
ibuto – a regiment or part of a regiment (plural: 'mabuto')
Ilanga – the sun
impi – an army
indaba – a council, a meeting or a discussion.
induna – a counsellor in times of peace, a general in times of war. The term is used loosely for a male leader in any group.
intombi – a virgin
kafferboetie – a term of derision used by one white person about another, who is believed to be too sympathetic towards black people.
kaross – a skin or fur blanket, serving the double purpose of a blanket and a garment
knobkierie (or knobkerrie) – a long-handled club, shaped like a fist-sized knob on the end of a long stick
koppie – a small hill
kraal – a group of huts, making up a small or large village
krantz (krans) – a sheer cliff or rock-face
lobolo – bride-price
maie agwe! – strong expression of amazement or horror
marimba – a musical instrument, named after the Mother of Music (see pages 86–90)

munt – a discourteous word for a black person; corruption of 'muntu'
muti – medicine
mutsha – a skirt
nsangu – see 'dagga'
panga – large-bladed knife used as a weapon
piccanin – a child
putu – maize-porridge, often making up the major part of the diet of black people
shesha! – hurry up!
sicolo – head-ring of honour worn by chiefs, or a hairstyle which looks somewhat like the head-ring
Somandla – a god
tambuti – a hardwood
tokoloshe – an evil imp (see pages 604–607)
uhuru – freedom, independence
umfundisi – a minister of religion
uNkulunkulu – God
veld – grassland
Yiyo le! – This is it!

CPSIA information can be obtained
at www.ICGtesting.com
Printed in the USA
BVHW032138110619
550590BV00039B/690/P

9 780802 136046